The yellowbacks... classics of popular fiction

The yellowjackets or yellowbacks were a great series of bestselling adventure and crime thrillers that had its origins in the mid to late 19th century following on from the 'penny dreadfuls'. They virtually began the mass market revolution of the early 20th century with a clear standard format and imprint/series livery (what would today be called branding). Hodder & Stoughton published the yellowjackets in two main series with series run dates of: 1923-1939 and later 1949-1957.

As the tagline ('where thrillers really began') on the back cover implies, the imprint and series focused on thrillers that were the bestsellers of their time. This current reissue or retro revival if you will, brings back many of these masterpieces, now classics in their own way and extends it further by including key titles from that period that were either great crime or thriller or even general commercial fiction (including sub-genres of noir, horror, gothic, romance, westerns, etc.) influences of their time. There are some perennial favourites and many rarities either lost or not easily available being revived in the current series. Writers and characters ranged from adventure heroes like Bulldog Drummond, Allan Quatermain, Richard Hannay or the Saint through thriller grandmasters Edgar Wallace and E. Phillips Oppenheim, crime and mystery maestros like Patricia Wentworth, GK Chesterton, Agatha Christie and the Detection club, to western and swashbucklers like Zane Grey, Max Brand, Captain Blood and even romance or general fiction classics like Hermina Black, Denise Robins, Marie Corelli or Stella Morton. These were books that had storytelling at their heart and always entertained.

The yellowbacks had both hardback (with varying design elements) and paperback (which built the series look) versions with the latter still carrying the imprint 'yellowjacket'. The current reissues pay tribute to both and use an amalgam of elements from both editions while retaining the complete yellow (or 'mustard-plaster') livery with the author's name in blue beveled type with a 'simulated emboss' effect and a white outer 'outline', and the book title in black. These reissues retain the distinctive size of the original mass market paperback and follow the three main category variations—the thrillers (crime, westerns, mystery, adventure) had blue lettering for the author's name, while Romance and softer general fiction had red; and other categories like humour had green.

For more detail and a full list of titles visit https://www.hachetteindia.com/home/yellowbacks

THE COMPLETE CHARLIE CHAN

VOLUME I

THE COMPLETE CHARLIE CHAN

Earl Derr Biggers was born in Warren, Ohio on August 24, 1884. Years later, while attending Harvard University, Biggers showed little passion for the classics, preferring instead writers such as Rudyard Kipling and Richard Harding Davis. Following his graduation from Harvard in 1907, he worked briefly for the Cleveland Plain Dealer and at Bobbs-Merrill publishers. By 1908, Biggers was hired at the Boston Traveler to write a daily humor column. Soon, however, he became that paper's drama critic. It was at this time that he met Elanor Ladd, who would later become his wife and who would have a marked influence in his writing. He is best know as the creator of Charlie Chan

THE COMPLETE CHARLIE CHAN

Earl Derr Biggers

VOLUME I

The House without a Key
The Chinese Parrot
Behind That Curtain

The Complete Charlie Chan
The House without a Key in 1925; *The Chinese parrot* first published in 1926 by Curtis; *Behind That Curtain* first published in 1928 by Bobbs-Merrill

1

The texts in these editions in most cases have been reprinted as is, with minimal editorial changes and by and large no bowdlerizing for political correctness; though in some editions, a few words and phrases considered archaic, or those considered offensive now, along with archaic punctuation may have been modified in places to make the text more accessible to today's readers. The narratives, language, beliefs, social mores and/or cultural depictions, in these volumes are a reflection of their times and must be viewed as such. They may also contain certain cultural, racial and gender prejudices and stereotypes that may be outdated or clearly wrong then and wrong today; but their removal would be tantamount to claiming these prejudices never existed. The Publisher does not endorse or support those depictions or stereotypes; and these books have been made available for a discerning audience that will read it for entertainment value and a chronicle/record of popular fiction of past times.

Cover design by Priya Singh adapted from the original classic yellowjacket by Hodder & Stoughton.

Cover illustration by Ishan Trivedi.

Series note: Some of the books in the series (unless otherwise credited) may have cover or inside illustrations from the original yellowbacks or early editions, and while full restoration has been attempted, some images may be grainy or faded due to the condition of the original material. The end notes or bonus material or blurb details may have been sourced from the public domain or free use publications such as Wikipedia and attribution is hereby made also allowing similar free use reproduction from here. Sources requiring further specific attribution may write in and further detailing and/or corrections shall be made in subsequent printings/editions.

Reprint specifications may be subject to change including but not limited to finishes, paper, colour sections.

ISBN: 978-93-5731-069-7

Hachette Book Publishing India Pvt. Ltd.
4th & 5th Floors, Corporate Centre,
Plot No. 94, Sector 44, Gurugram - 122 003, India

Typeset in Electra LT STD 10/12.5 pt by Manipal Technologies Limited, Manipal

Printed and bound in India by Manipal Technologies Limited, Manipal

CONTENTS

The House without a Key

To MY MOTHER AND FATHER

CONTENTS

I

KONA WEATHER

Miss Minerva Winterslip was a Bostonian of good standing, and long past the romantic age. Yet beauty thrilled her still, even the semi-barbaric beauty of a Pacific island. As she walked slowly along the beach she felt the little catch in her throat that sometimes she had known in Symphony Hall, Boston, when her favorite orchestra rose to some new and unexpected height of loveliness.

It was the hour at which she liked Waikiki best, the hour just preceding dinner and the quick tropic darkness. The shadows cast by the tall coconut palms lengthened and deepened, the light of the falling sun flamed on Diamond Head and tinted with gold the rollers sweeping in from the coral reef. A few late swimmers, reluctant to depart, dotted those waters whose touch is like the caress of a lover. On the springboard of the nearest float a slim brown girl poised for one delectable instant. What a figure! Miss Minerva, well over fifty herself, felt a mild twinge of envy—youth, youth like an arrow, straight and sure and flying. Like an arrow the slender figure rose, then fell; the perfect dive, silent and clean.

Miss Minerva glanced at the face of the man who walked beside her. But Amos Winterslip was oblivious to beauty, he had made that the first rule of his life. Born in the Islands, he had never known the mainland beyond San Francisco. Yet there could be no doubt about it, he was the New England conscience personified—the New England conscience in a white duck suit.

"Better turn back, Amos," suggested Miss Minerva. "Your dinner's waiting. Thank you so much."

"I'll walk as far as the fence," he said. "When you get tired of Dan and his carryings-on, come to us again. We'll be glad to have you."

"That's kind of you," she answered, in her sharp crisp way. "But I really must go home. Grace is worried about me. Of course, she can't understand. And my conduct *is* scandalous, I admit. I came over to Honolulu for six weeks, and I've been wandering about these islands for ten months."

"As long as that?"

She nodded. "I can't explain it. Every day I make a solemn vow I'll start packing my trunks—tomorrow."

"And tomorrow never comes," said Amos. "You've been taken in by the tropics. Some people are."

"Weak people, I presume you mean," snapped Miss Minerva. "Well, I've never been weak. Ask anybody on Beacon Street."

He smiled wanly. "It's a strain in the Winterslips," he said. "Supposed to be Puritans, but always sort of yearning toward the lazy latitudes."

"I know," answered Miss Minerva, her eyes on that exotic shore line. "It's what sent so many of them adventuring out of Salem harbor. Those who stayed behind felt that the travelers were seeing things no Winterslip should look at. But they envied them just the same—or maybe for that very reason." She nodded. "A sort of gypsy strain. It's what sent your father over here to set up as a whaler, and got you born so far from home. You know you don't belong here, Amos. You should be living in Milton or Roxbury, carrying a little green bag and popping into a Boston office every morning."

"I've often thought it," he admitted. "And who knows—I might have made something of my life—"

They had come to a barbed-wire fence, an unaccustomed barrier on that friendly shore. It extended well down on to the beach; a wave rushed up and lapped the final post, then receded.

Miss Minerva smiled. "Well, this is where Amos leaves off and Dan begins," she said. "I'll watch my chance and run around the end. Lucky you couldn't build it so it moved with the tide."

"You'll find your luggage in your room at Dan's, I guess," Amos told her. "Remember what I said about—" He broke off suddenly. A stocky, white-clad man had appeared in the garden beyond the barrier, and was moving rapidly toward them. Amos Winterslip stood rigid for a moment, an angry light flaming in his usually dull eyes. "Goodbye," he said, and turned.

"Amos!" cried Miss Minerva sharply. He moved on, and she followed. "Amos, what nonsense! How long has it been since you spoke to Dan?"

He paused under an algaroba tree. "Thirty-one years," he said. "Thirty-one years the tenth of last August."

"That's long enough," she told him. "Now, come around that foolish fence of yours, and hold out your hand to him."

"Not me," said Amos. "I guess you don't know Dan, Minerva, and the sort of life he's led. Time and again he's dishonored us all—"

"Why, Dan's regarded as a big man," she protested. "He's respected—"

"And rich," added Amos bitterly. "And I'm poor. Yes, that's the way it often goes in this world. But there's a world to come, and over there I reckon Dan's going to get his."

Hardy soul though she was, Miss Minerva was somewhat frightened by the look of hate on his thin face. She saw the uselessness of further argument. "Goodbye, Amos," she said.

"I wish I might persuade you to come East some day—" He gave no sign of hearing, but hurried along the white stretch of sand.

When Miss Minerva turned, Dan Winterslip was smiling at her from beyond the fence. "Hello, there," he cried. "Come this side of the wire and enjoy life again. You're mighty welcome."

"How are you, Dan?" She watched her chance with the waves and joined him. He took both her hands in his.

"Glad to see you," he said, and his eyes backed him up. Yes, he did have a way with women. "It's a bit lonely at the old homestead these days. Need a young girl about to brighten things up."

Miss Minerva sniffed. "I've tramped Boston in galoshes too many winters," she reminded him, "to lose my head over talk like that."

"Forget Boston," he urged. "We're all young in Hawaii. Look at me."

She did look at him, wonderingly. He was sixty-three, she knew, but only the mass of wavy white hair overhanging his temples betrayed his age. His face, burned to the deepest bronze by long years of wandering under the Polynesian sun, was without a line or wrinkle. Deep-chested and muscular, he could have passed on the mainland for a man of forty.

"I see my precious brother brought you as far as the deadline," he remarked as they moved on through the garden. "Sent me his love, I presume?"

"I tried to get him to come round and shake hands," Miss Minerva said.

Dan Winterslip laughed. "Don't deprive poor Amos of his hate for me," he urged. "It's about all he lives for now. Comes over every night and stands under that algaroba tree of his, smoking cigarettes and staring at my house. Know what he's waiting for? He's waiting for the Lord to strike me down for my sins. Well, he's a patient waiter, I'll say that for him."

Miss Minerva did not reply. Dan's great rambling house of many rooms was set in beauty almost too poignant to be borne. She stood, drinking it all in again, the poinciana trees like big crimson umbrellas, the stately golden glow, the gigantic banyans casting purple shadows, her favorite hau tree, seemingly old as time itself, covered with a profusion of yellow blossoms. Loveliest of all were the flowering vines, the bougainvillea burying everything it touched in brick-red splendor. Miss Minerva wondered what her friends who every spring went into sedate ecstasies over the Boston Public Gardens would say if they could see what she saw now. They would be a bit shocked, perhaps, for this was too lurid to be quite respectable. A scarlet background—and a fitting one, no doubt, for Cousin Dan.

They reached the door at the side of the house that led directly into the living-room. Glancing to her right, Miss Minerva caught through the lush foliage glimpses of the iron fence and tall gates that fronted on Kalia Road. Dan opened the door for her, and she stepped inside. Like most apartments of its sort in the Islands, the living-room was walled on but three sides, the fourth was a vast expanse of wire screening. They crossed the polished floor and entered the big hall beyond. Near the front door a Hawaiian woman of uncertain age rose slowly from her chair. She was a huge, high-breasted, dignified specimen of that vanishing race.

"Well, Kamaikui, I'm back," Miss Minerva smiled.

"I make you welcome," the woman said. She was only a servant, but she spoke with the gracious manner of a hostess.

"Same room you had when you first came over, Minerva," Dan Winterslip announced. "Your luggage is there—and a bit of mail that came in on the boat this morning. I didn't trouble to send it up to Amos's. We dine when you're ready."

"I'll not keep you long," she answered, and hurried up the stairs.

Dan Winterslip strolled back to his living-room. He sat down in a rattan chair that had been made especially for him in Hong Kong, and glanced complacently about at the many evidences of his prosperity. His butler entered, bearing a tray with cocktails.

"Two, Haku?" smiled Winterslip. "The lady is from Boston."

"Yes-s," hissed Haku, and retired soundlessly.

In a moment Miss Minerva came again into the room. She carried a letter in her hand, and she was laughing.

"Dan, this is too absurd," she said.

"What is?"

"I may have told you that they were getting worried about me at home. Because I haven't been able to tear myself away from Honolulu, I mean. Well, they're sending a policeman for me."

"A policeman?" He lifted his bushy eyebrows.

"Yes, it amounts to that. It's not being done openly, of course. Grace writes that John Quincy has six weeks' vacation from the banking house, and has decided to make the trip out here. 'It will give you someone to come home with, my dear,' says Grace. Isn't she subtle?"

"John Quincy Winterslip? That would be Grace's son."

Miss Minerva nodded. "You never met him, did you, Dan? Well, you will, shortly. And he certainly won't approve of you."

"Why not?" Dan Winterslip bristled.

"Because he's proper. He's a dear boy, but oh, so proper. This journey is going to be a great cross for him. He'll start disapproving as he passes Albany, and think of the long weary miles of disapproval he'll have to endure after that."

"Oh, I don't know. He's a Winterslip, isn't he?"

"He is. But the gypsy strain missed him completely. He's all Puritan."

"Poor boy." Dan Winterslip moved toward the tray on which stood the amber-colored drinks. "I suppose he'll stop with Roger in San Francisco. Write him there and tell him I want him to make this house his home while he's in Honolulu."

"That's kind of you, Dan."

"Not at all. I like youth around me—even the Puritan brand. Now that you're going to be apprehended and taken back to civilization, you'd better have one of these cocktails."

"Well," said his guest, "I'm about to exhibit what my brother used to call true Harvard indifference."

"What do you mean?" asked Winterslip.

"I don't mind if I do," twinkled Miss Minerva, lifting a cocktail glass.

Dan Winterslip beamed upon her. "You're a good sport, Minerva," he remarked, as he escorted her across the hall.

"When in Rome," she answered, "I make it a point not to do as the Bostonians do. I fear it would prove a rather thorny path to popularity."

"Precisely."

"Besides, I shall be back in Boston soon. Tramping about to art exhibits and Lowell Lectures, and gradually congealing into senility."

But she was not in Boston now, she reflected, as she sat down at the gleaming table in the dining-room. Before her, properly iced, was a generous slice of papaya, golden yellow and inviting. Somewhere beyond the foliage outside the screens, the ocean murmured restlessly. The dinner would be perfect, she knew, the Island beef dry and stringy, perhaps, but the fruits and the salad more than atoning.

"Do you expect Barbara soon?" she inquired presently.

Dan Winterslip's face lighted like the beach at sunrise. "Yes, Barbara has graduated. She'll be along any day now. Nice if she and your perfect nephew should hit on the same boat."

"Nice for John Quincy, at any rate," Miss Minerva replied. "We thought Barbara a lively charming girl when she visited us in the East."

"She's all of that," he agreed proudly. His daughter was his dearest possession. "I tell you, I've missed her. I've been mighty lonesome."

Miss Minerva gave him a shrewd look. "Yes, I've heard rumors," she remarked, "about how lonesome you've been."

He flushed under his tan. "Amos, I suppose?"

"Oh, not only Amos. A great deal of talk, Dan. Really, at your age—"

"What do you mean, my age? I told you we're all young out here." He ate in silence for a moment. "You're a good sport—I said it and I meant it. You must understand that here in the Islands a man may behave a—a bit differently than he would in the Back Bay."

"At that," she smiled, "all men in the Back Bay are not to be trusted. I'm not presuming to rebuke you, Dan. But—for Barbara's sake—why not select as the object of your devotion a woman you could marry?"

"I could marry this one—if we're talking about the same woman."

"The one I refer to," Miss Minerva replied, "is known, rather widely, as the Widow of Waikiki."

"This place is a hotbed of gossip. Arlene Compton is perfectly respectable."

"A former chorus girl, I believe."

"Not precisely. An actress—small parts—before she married Lieutenant Compton."

"And a self-made widow."

"Just what do you mean by that?" he flared. His gray eyes glittered.

"I understand that when her husband's aeroplane crashed on Diamond Head, it was because he preferred it that way. She had driven him to it."

"Lies, all lies!" Dan Winterslip cried. "Pardon me, Minerva, but you mustn't believe all you hear on the beach." He was silent for a moment. "What would you say if I told you I proposed to marry this woman?"

"I'm afraid I'd become rather bromidic," she answered gently, "and remind you that there's no fool like an old fool." He did not speak. "Forgive me, Dan. I'm your first cousin, but a distant relative for all that. It's really none of my business. I wouldn't care—but I like you. And I'm thinking of Barbara—"

He bowed his head. "I know," he said, "Barbara. Well, there's no need to get excited. I haven't said anything to Arlene about marriage. Not yet."

Miss Minerva smiled. "You know, as I get on in years," she remarked, "so many wise old saws begin to strike me as utter nonsense. Particularly that one I just quoted." He looked at her, his eyes friendly again. "This is the best avocado I ever tasted," she added. "But tell me, Dan, are you sure the mango is a food? Seems more like a spring tonic to me."

By the time they finished dinner the topic of Arlene Compton was forgotten and Dan had completely regained his good nature. They had coffee on his veranda—or, in Island parlance, lanai—which opened off one end of the living-room. This was of generous size, screened on three sides and stretching far down on to the white beach. Outside the brief tropic dusk dimmed the bright colors of Waikiki.

"No breeze stirring," said Miss Minerva.

"The trades have died," Dan answered. He referred to the beneficent winds which—save at rare, uncomfortable intervals—blow across the Islands out of the cool northeast. "I'm afraid we're in for a stretch of Kona weather."

"I hope not," Miss Minerva said.

"It saps the life right out of me nowadays," he told her, and sank into a chair. "That about being young, Minerva—it's a little bluff I'm fond of."

She smiled gently. "Even youth finds the Kona hard to endure," she comforted. "I remember when I was here before—in the eighties. I was only nineteen, but the memory of the sick wind lingers still."

"I missed you then, Minerva."

"Yes. You were off somewhere in the South Seas."

"But I heard about you when I came back. That you were tall and blonde and lovely, and nowhere near so prim as they feared you were going to be. A wonderful figure, they said—but you've got that yet."

She flushed, but smiled still. "Hush, Dan. We don't talk that way where I come from."

"The eighties," he sighed. "Hawaii was Hawaii then. Unspoiled, a land of opera bouffe, with old Kalakaua sitting on his golden throne."

"I remember him," Miss Minerva said. "Grand parties at the palace. And the afternoons when he sat with his disreputable friends on the royal lanai, and the Royal Hawaiian Band played at his feet, and he haughtily tossed them royal pennies. It was such a colorful, naive spot then, Dan."

"It's been ruined," he complained sadly. "Too much aping of the mainland. Too much of your damned mechanical civilization—automobiles, phonographs, radios—bah! And yet—and yet, Minerva—away down underneath there are deep dark waters flowing still."

She nodded, and they sat for a moment busy with their memories. Presently Dan Winterslip snapped on a small reading light at his side. "I'll just glance at the evening paper, if you don't mind."

"Oh, do," urged Miss Minerva.

She was glad of a moment without talk. For this, after all, was the time she loved Waikiki best. So brief, this tropic dusk, so quick the coming of the soft alluring night. The carpet of the waters, apple-green by day, crimson and gold at sunset, was a deep purple now. On top of that extinct volcano called Diamond Head a yellow eye was winking, as though to hint there might still be fire beneath. Three miles down, the harbor lights began to twinkle, and out toward the reef the lanterns of

Japanese sampans glowed intermittently. Beyond, in the roadstead, loomed the battered hulk of an old brig slowly moving toward the channel entrance. Always, out there, a ship or two, in from the East with a cargo of spice or tea or ivory, or eastward bound with a load of tractor salesmen. Ships of all sorts, the spic and span liner and the rakish tramp, ships from Melbourne and Seattle, New York and Yokohama, Tahiti and Rio, any port on the seven seas. For this was Honolulu, the Crossroads of the Pacific—the glamourous crossroads where, they said, in time all paths crossed again. Miss Minerva sighed.

She was conscious of a quick movement on Dan's part. She turned and looked at him. He had laid the paper on his knee, and was staring straight ahead. That bluff about being young—no good now. For his face was old, old.

"Why, Dan—" she said.

"I—I'm wondering, Minerva," he began slowly. "Tell me again about that nephew of yours."

She was surprised, but hid it. "John Quincy?" she said. "He's just the usual thing, for Boston. Conventional. His whole life has been planned for him, from the cradle to the grave. So far he's walked the line. The inevitable preparatory school, Harvard, the proper clubs, the family banking house—even gone and got himself engaged to the very girl his mother would have picked for him. There have been times when I hoped he might kick over—the war—but no, he came back and got meekly into the old rut."

"Then he's reliable—steady?"

Miss Minerva smiled. "Dan, compared with that boy, Gibraltar wabbles occasionally."

"Discreet, I take it?"

"He invented discretion. That's what I'm telling you. I love him—but a little bit of recklessness now and then—However, I'm afraid it's too late now. John Quincy is nearly thirty."

Dan Winterslip was on his feet, his manner that of a man who had made an important decision. Beyond the bamboo curtain that hung in the door leading to the living-room a light appeared. "Haku!" Winterslip called. The Japanese came swiftly.

"Haku, tell the chauffeur—quick—the big car! I must get to the dock before the *President Tyler* sails for San Francisco. Wikiwiki!"

The servant disappeared into the living-room, and Winterslip followed. Somewhat puzzled, Miss Minerva sat for a moment, then rose and pushed aside the curtain. "Are you sailing, Dan?" she asked.

He was seated at his desk, writing hurriedly. "No, no—just a note—I must get it off on that boat—"

There was an air of suppressed excitement about him. Miss Minerva stepped over the threshold into the living-room. In another moment Haku appeared with an announcement that was unnecessary, for the engine of an automobile was humming in the drive. Dan Winterslip took his hat from the Japanese. "Make yourself at home, Minerva—I'll be back shortly," he cried, and rushed out.

Some business matter, no doubt. Miss Minerva strolled aimlessly about the big airy room, pausing finally before the portrait of Jedediah Winterslip, the father of Dan and Amos, and her uncle. Dan had had it painted from a photograph after the old man's death; it was the work of an artist whose forte was reputed to be landscapes—oh, it must assuredly have been landscapes. Miss Minerva thought. But even so there was no mistaking the power and personality of this New Englander who had set up in Honolulu as a whaler. The only time she had seen him, in the eighties, he had been broken and old, mourning his lost fortune, which had gone with his ships in an Arctic disaster a short time before.

Well, Dan had brought the family back, Miss Minerva reflected. Won again that lost fortune and much more. There were queer rumors about his methods—but so there were about the methods of Bostonians who had never strayed from home. A charming fellow, whatever his past. Miss Minerva sat down at the grand piano and played a few old familiar bars—*The Beautiful Blue Danube*. Her thoughts went back to the eighties.

Dan Winterslip was thinking of the eighties too as his car sped townward along Kalakaua Avenue. But it was the present that concerned him when they reached the dock and he ran, panting a little, through a dim pier shed toward the gangplank of the *President Tyler*. He had no time to spare, the ship was on the point of sailing. Since it was a through boat from the Orient it left without the ceremonies that attend the departure of a liner plying only between Honolulu and the mainland. Even so, there were cries of "Aloha," some hearty and some tremulous, most of the travelers were bedecked with leis, and a confused little crowd milled about the foot of the plank.

Dan Winterslip pushed his way forward and ran up the sharp incline. As he reached the deck he encountered an old acquaintance, Hepworth, the second officer.

"You're the man I'm looking for," he cried.

"How are you, sir," Hepworth said. "I didn't see your name on the list."

"No, I'm not sailing. I'm here to ask a favor."

"Glad to oblige, Mr Winterslip."

Winterslip thrust a letter into his hand. "You know my cousin Roger in 'Frisco. Please give him that—him and no one else—as soon after you land as you possibly can. I'm too late for the mail—and I prefer this way anyhow. I'll be mighty grateful."

"Don't mention it—you've been very kind to me and I'll be only too happy—I'm afraid you'll have to go ashore, sir. Just a minute, there—" He took Winterslip's arm and gently urged him back on to the plank. The instant Dan's feet touched the dock, the plank was drawn up behind him.

For a moment he stood, held by the fascination an Islander always feels at sight of a ship outward bound. Then he turned and walked slowly through the pier-shed. Ahead of him he caught a glimpse of a slender lithe figure which he recognized at once as that of Dick Kaohla, the grandson of Kamaikui. He quickened his pace and joined the boy.

"Hello, Dick," he said.

"Hello." The brown face was sullen, unfriendly.

"You haven't been to see me for a long time," Dan Winterslip said. "Everything all right?"

"Sure," replied Kaohla. "Sure it's all right." They reached the street, and the boy turned quickly away "Goodnight," he muttered.

Dan Winterslip stood for a moment, thoughtfully looking after him. Then he got into the car. "No hurry now," he remarked to the chauffeur.

When he reappeared in his living-room, Miss Minerva glanced up from the book she was reading. "Were you in time, Dan?" she asked.

"Just made it," he told her.

"Good," she said, rising. "I'll take my book and go upstairs. Pleasant dreams."

He waited until she reached the door before he spoke. "Ah—Minerva—don't trouble to write your nephew about stopping here."

"No, Dan?" she said, puzzled again.

"No. I've attended to the invitation myself. Goodnight."

"Oh—goodnight," she answered, and left him.

Alone in the great room, he paced restlessly back and forth over the polished floor. In a moment he went out on to the lanai, and found the newspaper he had been reading earlier in the evening. He brought it back to the living-room and tried to finish it, but something seemed to trouble him. His eyes kept straying—straying—with a sharp exclamation he tore one corner from the shipping page, savagely ripped the fragment to bits.

Again he got up and wandered about. He had intended paying a call down the beach, but that quiet presence in the room above—Boston in its more tolerant guise but Boston still—gave him pause.

He returned to the lanai. There, under a mosquito netting, was the cot where he preferred to sleep; his dressing-room was near at hand. However, it was too early for bed. He stepped through the door on to the beach. Unmistakable, the soft treacherous breath of the Kona fanned his cheek—the "sick wind" that would pile the breakers high along the coast and temporarily blight this Island paradise. There was no moon, the stars that usually seemed so friendly and so close were now obscured. The black water rolled in like a threat. He stood staring out into the dark—out there to the crossroads where paths always crossed again. If you gave them time—if you only gave them time—

As he turned back, his eyes went to the algaroba tree beyond the wire, and he saw the yellow flare of a match. His brother Amos. He had a sudden friendly feeling for Amos, he wanted to go over and talk to him, talk of the far days when they played together on this beach. No use, he knew. He sighed, and the screen door of the lanai banged behind him—the screen door without a lock in a land where locks are few.

Tired, he sat in the dark to think. His face was turned toward the curtain of bamboo between him and the living-room. On that curtain a shadow appeared, was motionless a second, then vanished. He caught his breath—again the shadow. "Who's there?" he called.

A huge brown arm was thrust through the bamboo. A friendly brown face was framed there.

"Your fruit I put on the table," said Kamaikui. "I go bed now."

"Of course. Go ahead. Goodnight."

The woman withdrew. Dan Winterslip was furious with himself. What was the matter with him, anyhow? He who had fought his way through unspeakable terrors in the early days—nervous—on edge—

"Getting old," he muttered. "No, by heaven—it's the Kona. That's it. The Kona. I'll be all right when the trades blow again."

When the trades blew again! He wondered. Here at the crossroads one could not be sure.

II

THE HIGH HAT

John Quincy Winterslip walked aboard the ferry at Oakland feeling rather limp and weary. For more than six days he had been marooned on sleepers—his pause at Chicago had been but a flitting from one train to another—and he was fed up. Seeing America first—that was what he had been doing. And what an appalling lot of it there was! He felt that for an eternity he had been staring at endless plains, dotted here and there by unesthetic houses the inmates of which had unquestionably never heard a symphony concert.

Ahead of him ambled a porter, bearing his two suitcases, his golf clubs and his hat-box. One of the man's hands was gone—chewed off, no doubt, in some amiable frontier scuffle. In its place he wore a steel hook. Well, no one could question the value of a steel hook to a man in the porter's profession. But how quaint—and western!

The boy indicated a spot by the rail on the forward deck, and the porter began to unload. Carefully selecting the man's good hand, John Quincy dropped into it a tip so generous as to result in a touching of hook to cap in a weird salute. The object of this attention sank down amid his elaborate trappings, removed the straw hat from his perspiring head, and tried to figure out just what had happened to him.

Three thousand miles from Beacon Street, and two thousand miles still to go! Why, he inquired sourly of his usually pleasant self, had he ever agreed to make this absurd expedition into heathen country? Here it was late June, Boston was at its best. Tennis at Longwood, long mild evenings in a single shell on the Charles, weekends and golf with Agatha Parker at Magnolia. And if one must travel, there was Paris. He hadn't seen Paris in two years and had been rather planning a quick run over, when his mother had put this preposterous notion into his head.

Preposterous—it was all of that. Traveling five thousand miles just as a gentle hint to Aunt Minerva to return to her calm, well-ordered life behind purple window-panes on Beacon Street. And was there any chance that his strong-minded relative would take the hint? Not one in a thousand. Aunt Minerva was accustomed to do as she pleased—he had an uncomfortable, shocked recollection of one occasion when she had said she would do as she damn well pleased.

John Quincy wished he was back. He wished he was crossing Boston Common to his office on State Street, there to put out a new issue of bonds. He was not yet a member of the firm—that was an honor accorded only to Winterslips who were bald and a little stooped—but his heart was in his work. He put out a bond issue with loving apprehension, waiting for the verdict as a playwright waits behind the scenes on a first night. Would those First Mortgage Sixes go over big, or would they flop at his feet?

The hoarse boom of a ferry whistle recalled John Quincy to his present unbelievable location on the map. The boat began to move. He was dimly conscious of a young person of feminine gender who came and sat at his side. Away from the slip and out into the harbor the ferry carried John Quincy, and he suddenly sat up and took notice, for he was never blind to beauty, no matter where he encountered it.

And he was encountering beauty now. The morning air was keen and dry and bright. Spread out before him was that harbor which is like a tired navigator's dream come true. They passed Goat Island, and he heard the faint echo of a bugle, he saw Tamalpias lifting its proud head toward the sparkling sky, he turned, and there was San Francisco scattered blithely over its many hills.

The ferry plowed on, and John Quincy sat very still. A forest of masts and steam funnels—here was the water front that had supplied the atmosphere for those romantic tales that held him spellbound when he was a boy at school—a quiet young Winterslip whom the gypsy strain had missed. Now he could distinguish a bark from Antwerp, a great liner from the Orient, a five-masted schooner that was reminiscent of those supposedly forgotten stories. Ships from the Treaty Ports, ships from coconut islands in southern seas. A picture as intriguing and colorful as a back drop in a theater—but far more real.

Suddenly John Quincy stood up. A puzzled look had come into his calm gray eyes. "I—I don't understand," he murmured.

He was startled by the sound of his own voice. He hadn't intended to speak aloud. In order not to appear too utterly silly, he looked around for someone to whom he might pretend he had addressed that remark. There was no one about—except the young person who was obviously feminine and therefore not to be informally accosted.

John Quincy looked down at her. Spanish or something like that, blue-black hair, dark eyes that were alight now with the amusement she was striving to hide, a delicate oval face tanned a deep brown. He looked again at the harbor—beauty all about the boat, and beauty on it, Much better than traveling on trains!

The girl looked up at John Quincy. She saw a big, broad-shouldered young man with a face as innocent as a child's. A bit of friendliness, she decided instantly, would not be misunderstood.

"I beg your pardon," she said.

"Oh—I—I'm sorry," he stammered. "I didn't mean—I spoke without intending—I said I didn't understand—"

"You didn't understand what?"

"A most amazing thing has happened," he continued. He sat down, and waved his hand toward the harbor. "I've been here before."

She looked perplexed. "Lots of people have," she admitted.

"But—you see—I mean—I've never been here before."

She moved away from him. "Lots of people haven't." She admitted that, too.

John Quincy took a deep breath. What was this discussion he had got into, anyhow? He had a quick impulse to lift his hat gallantly and walk away, letting the whole matter drop. But no, he came of a race that sees things through.

"I'm from Boston," he said.

"Oh," said the girl. That explained everything.

"And what I'm trying to make clear—although of course there's no reason why I should have dragged you into it—"

"None whatever," she smiled. "But go on."

"Until a few days ago I was never west of New York, never in my whole life, you understand. Been about New England a bit, and abroad a few times, but the West—"

"I know. It didn't interest you."

"I wouldn't say that," protested John Quincy with careful politeness. "But there was such a lot of it—exploring it seemed a hopeless undertaking. And then—the family thought I ought to go, you see—so I rode and rode on trains and was—you'll pardon me—a bit bored. Now—I come into this harbor, I look around me, and I get the oddest feeling. I feel that I've been here before."

The girl's face was sympathetic. "Other people have had that experience," she told him. "Choice souls, they are. You've been a long time coming, but you're home at last." She held out a slim brown hand. "Welcome to your city," she said.

John Quincy solemnly shook hands. "Oh, no," he corrected gently. "Boston's my city. I belong there, naturally. But this—this is familiar." He glanced northward at the low hills sheltering the Valley of the Moon, then back at San Francisco. "Yes, I seem to have known my way about here once. Astonishing, isn't it?"

"Perhaps—some of your ancestors—"

"That's true. My grandfather came out here when he was a young man. He went home again—but his brothers stayed. It's the son of one of them I'm going to visit in Honolulu."

"Oh—you're going on to Honolulu?"

"Tomorrow morning. Have you ever been there?"

"Ye—es." Her dark eyes were serious. "See—there are the docks—that's where the East begins. The real East. And Telegraph Hill—" she pointed; no one in Boston ever points, but she was so lovely John Quincy overlooked it— "and Russian Hill, and the Fairmont on Nob Hill."

"Life must be full of ups and downs," he ventured lightly. "Tell me about Honolulu. Sort of a wild place, I imagine?"

She laughed. "I'll let you discover for yourself how wild it is," she told him. "Practically all the leading families came originally from your beloved New England. 'Puritans with a touch of sun,' my father calls them. He's clever, my father," she added, in an odd childish tone that was wistful and at the same time challenging.

"I'm sure of it," said John Quincy heartily. They were approaching the Ferry Building and other passengers crowded about them. "I'd help you with that suitcase of yours, but I've got all this truck. If we could find a porter—"

"Don't bother," she answered. "I can manage very well." She was staring down at John Quincy's hat box. "I—I suppose there's a silk hat in there?" she inquired.

"Naturally," replied John Quincy.

She laughed—a rich, deep-throated laugh. John Quincy stiffened slightly. "Oh, forgive me," she cried. "But—a silk hat in Hawaii!"

John Quincy stood erect. The girl had laughed at a Winterslip. He filled his lungs with the air sweeping in from the open spaces, the broad open spaces where men are men. A weird reckless feeling came over him. He stooped, picked up the hat box, and tossed it calmly over the rail. It bobbed indignantly away. The crowd closed in, not wishing to miss any further exhibition of madness.

"That's that," said John Quincy quietly.

"Oh," gasped the girl, "you shouldn't have done it."

And indeed, he shouldn't. The box was an expensive one, the gift of his admiring mother at Christmas. And the topper inside, worn in the gloaming along the water side of Beacon Street, had been known to add a touch of distinction even to that distinguished scene.

"Why not?" asked John Quincy. "The confounded thing's been a nuisance ever since I left home. And besides—we do look ridiculous at times, don't we? We easterners? A silk hat in the tropics! I might have been mistaken for a missionary." He began to gather up his luggage. "Shan't need a porter any more," he announced gaily. "I say—it was awfully kind of you—letting me talk to you like that."

"It was fun," she told him. "I hope you're going to like us out here. We're so eager to be liked, you know. It's almost pathetic."

"Well," smiled John Quincy, "I've met only one Californian to date. But—"

"Yes?"

"So far, so good!"

"Oh, thank you." She moved away.

"Please—just a moment," called John Quincy. "I hope—I mean, I wish—"

But the crowd surged between them. He saw her dark eyes smiling at him and then, irrevocably as the hat, she drifted from his sight.

III

MIDNIGHT ON RUSSIAN HILL

A few moments later John Quincy stepped ashore in San Francisco. He had taken not more than three steps across the floor of the Ferry Building when a dapper Japanese chauffeur pushed through the crowd and singling out the easterner with what seemed uncanny perspicacity, took complete charge of him.

Roger Winterslip, the Japanese announced, was too busy to meet ferries, but had sent word that the boy was to go up to the house and after establishing himself comfortably there, join his host for lunch downtown. Gratified to feel solid ground once more beneath his feet, John Quincy followed the chauffeur to the street. San Francisco glittered under the morning sun.

"I always thought this was a foggy town," John Quincy said.

The Japanese grinned. "Maybe fog come, maybe it do not. Just now one time maybe it do not. Please." He held open the car door.

Through bright streets where life appeared to flow with a pleasant rhythm, they bowled along. Beside the curbs stood the colorful carts of the flower venders, unnecessarily painting the lily of existence. Weary traveler though he was, John Quincy took in with every breath a fresh supply of energy. New ambitions stirred within him, bigger, better bond issues than ever before seemed ridiculously easy of attainment.

Roger Winterslip had not been among those lured to suburban life down the peninsula; he resided in bachelor solitude on Nob Hill. It was an ancient, battered house viewed from without, but within, John Quincy found, were all known comforts. A bent old Chinaman showed him his room and his heart leaped up when he beheld, at last, a veritable bath.

At one o'clock he sought out the office where his relative carried on, with conspicuous success, his business as an engineer and builder. Roger proved a short florid man in his late fifties.

"Hello, son," he cried cordially. "How's Boston?"

"Everyone is quite well," said John Quincy. "You're being extremely kind—"

"Nonsense. It's a pleasure to see you. Come along."

He took John Quincy to a famous club for lunch. In the grill he pointed out several well-known writers. The boy was not unduly impressed, for Longfellow, Whittier and Lowell were not among them. Nevertheless it was a pleasant place, the service perfect, the food of an excellence rare on the codfish coast.

"And what," asked Roger presently, "do you think of San Francisco?"

"I like it," John Quincy said simply.

"No? Do you really mean that?" Roger beamed. "Well, it's the sort of place that ought to appeal to a New Englander. It's had a history, brief, but believe me, my boy, one crowded hour of glorious life. It's sophisticated, knowing, subtle. Contrast it with other cities—for instance, take Los Angeles—"

He was off on a favorite topic and he talked well.

"Writers," he said at last, "are for ever comparing cities to women. San Francisco is the woman you don't tell the folks at home an awful lot about. Not that she wasn't perfectly proper—

I don't mean that—but her stockings were just a little thinner and her laugh a little gayer—people might misunderstand. Besides, the memory is too precious to talk about. Hello."

A tall, lean, handsome Englishman was crossing the grill on his way out. "Cope! Cope, my dear fellow!" Roger sped after him and dragged him back. "I knew you at once," he was saying, "though it must be more than forty years since I last saw you."

The Britisher dropped into a chair. He smiled a wry smile. "My dear old chap," he said. "Not so literal, if you don't mind."

"Rot!" protested Roger. "What do years matter? This is a young cousin of mine, John Quincy Winterslip, of Boston. Ah—er—just what is your title now?"

"Captain. I'm in the Admiralty."

"Really? Captain Arthur Temple Cope, John Quincy." Roger turned to the Englishman. "You were a midshipman, I believe, when we met in Honolulu. I was talking to Dan about you not a year ago—"

An expression of intense dislike crossed the captain's face. "Ah, yes, Dan. Alive and prospering, I presume?"

"Oh, yes," answered Roger.

"Isn't it damnable," remarked Cope, "how the wicked thrive?"

An uncomfortable silence fell. John Quincy was familiar with the frankness of Englishmen, but he was none the less annoyed by this open display of hostility toward his prospective host. After all, Dan's last name was Winterslip.

"Ah—er—have a cigarette," suggested Roger.

"Thank you—have one of mine," said Cope, taking out a silver case. "Virginia tobacco, though they are put up in Piccadilly. No? And you, sir—" He held the case before John Quincy, who refused a bit stiffly.

The captain nonchalantly lighted up. "I beg your pardon—what I said about your cousin," he began. "But really, you know—"

"No matter," said Roger cordially. "Tell me what you're doing here."

"On my way to Hawaii," explained the captain. "Sailing at three today on the Australian boat. A bit of a job for the Admiralty. From Honolulu I drop down to the Fanning Group—a little flock of islands that belongs to us," he added with a fine paternal air.

"A possible coaling station," smiled Roger.

"My dear fellow—the precise nature of my mission is, of course, a secret." Captain Cope looked suddenly at John Quincy. "By the way, I once knew a very charming girl from Boston. A relative of yours, no doubt."

"A—a girl," repeated John Quincy, puzzled.

"Minerva Winterslip."

"Why," said John Quincy, amazed, "you mean my Aunt Minerva."

The captain smiled. "She was no one's aunt in those days," he said. "Nothing auntish about her. But that was in Honolulu in the eighties—we'd put in there on the old wooden *Reliance*—the poor unlucky ship was limping home crippled from Samoa. Your aunt was visiting at that port—there were dances at the palace, swimming parties—ah, me, to be young again."

"Minerva's in Honolulu now," Roger told him.

"No—really?"

"Yes. She's stopping with Dan."

"With Dan." The captain was silent for a moment "Her husband—"

"Minerva never married," Roger explained.

"Amazing," said the captain. He blew a ring of smoke toward the paneled ceiling. "The more shame to the men of Boston. My time is hardly my own, but I shall hope to look in on her." He rose. "This was a bit of luck—meeting you again, old chap. I'm due aboard the boat very shortly—you understand, of course." He bowed to them both, and departed.

"Fine fellow," Roger said, staring after him. "Frank and British, but a splendid chap."

"I wasn't especially pleased," John Quincy admitted, "by the way he spoke of Cousin Dan."

Roger laughed. "Better get used to it," he advised. "Dan is not passionately beloved. He's climbed high, you know, and he's trampled down a few on his way up. By the way, he wants you to do an errand for him here in San Francisco."

"Me!" cried John Quincy. "An errand?"

"Yes. You ought to feel flattered. Dan doesn't trust everybody. However, it's something that must wait until dark."

"Until dark," repeated the puzzled young man from Boston.

"Precisely. In the meantime I propose to show you about town."

"But—you're busy. I couldn't think of taking you away—"

Roger laid his hand on John Quincy's shoulder. "My boy, no westerner is ever too busy to show a man from the East about his city. I've been looking forward to this chance for weeks. And since you insist on sailing tomorrow at ten, we must make the most of our time."

Roger proved an adept at making the most of one's time in San Francisco. After an exhilarating afternoon of motoring over the town and the surrounding country, he brought John Quincy back to the house at six, urging him to dress quickly for a dinner of which he apparently had great hopes.

The boy's trunk was in his room, and as he put on a dinner coat he looked forward with lively anticipation to a bit of San Francisco night life in Roger's company. When he came downstairs his host was waiting, a distinguished figure in his dinner clothes, and they set out blithely through the gathering dusk.

"Little place I want you to try." Roger explained as they sat down at a table in a restaurant that was outwardly of no special note. "Afterward we'll look in on that musical show at the Columbia."

The restaurant more than justified Roger's hopes of it. John Quincy began to glow with a warm friendly feeling for all the world, particularly this city by the western gate. He did not think of himself as a stranger here. He wasn't a stranger, anyhow. The sensation he had first experienced in the harbor returned to him. He had been here before, he was treading old familiar ground. In far, forgotten, happy times he had known the life of this city's streets. Strange, but true. He spoke to Roger about it.

Roger smiled. "A Winterslip, after all," he said. "And they told me you were just a sort of—of Puritan survival. My father used to know that sensation you speak of, only he felt it whenever he entered a new town. Might be something in reincarnation, after all."

"Nonsense," said John Quincy.

"Probably. Just the blood of the roaming Winterslips in your veins." He leaned across the table. "How would you like to come to San Francisco to live?"

"Wha-what?" asked John Quincy, startled.

"I'm getting along in years, and I'm all alone. Lots of financial details in my office—take you in there and let you look after them. Make it worth your while."

"No, no, thank you," said John Quincy firmly. "I belong back east. Besides, I could never persuade Agatha to come out here."

"Agatha who?"

"Agatha Parker—the girl I'm engaged to—in a way. Been sort of understood between us for several years. No," he added, "I guess I'd better stay where I belong."

Roger Winterslip looked his disappointment. "Probably had," he admitted. "I fancy no girl with that name would follow you here. Though a girl worth having will follow her man anywhere—but no matter." He studied John Quincy keenly for a moment. "I must have been wrong about you, anyhow."

John Quincy felt a sudden resentment. "Just what do you mean by that?" he inquired.

"In the old days," Roger said, "Winterslips were the stuff of which pioneers are made. They didn't cling to the apron-strings of civilization. They got up some fine morning and nonchalantly strolled off beyond the horizon. They lived—but there, you're of another generation. You can't understand."

"Why can't I?" demanded John Quincy.

"Because the same old rut has evidently been good enough for you. You've never known a thrill. Or have you? Have you ever forgot to go to bed because of some utterly silly reason—because, for example, you were young and the moon was shining on a beach lapped by southern seas? Have you ever lied like a gentleman to protect a woman not worth the trouble? Ever made love to the wrong girl?"

"Of course not," said John Quincy stiffly.

"Ever run for your life through crooked streets in the rowdy quarter of a strange town? Ever fought with a ship's officer—the old-fashioned kind with fists like flying hams? Ever gone out on a man hunt and when you got your quarry cornered, leaped upon him with no weapon but your bare hands? Have you ever— "

"The type of person you describe," John Quincy cut in, "is hardly admirable."

"Probably not," Roger agreed. "And yet—those are incidents from my own past, my boy." He regarded John Quincy sadly. "Yes, I must have been wrong about you. A Puritan survival, after all."

John Quincy deigned no reply. There was an odd light in the older man's eyes—was Roger secretly laughing at him? He appeared to be, and the boy resented it.

But he forgot to be resentful at the revue, which proved to be witty and gay, and Roger and he emerged from the theater at eleven the best of friends again. As they stepped into Roger's car, the older man gave the chauffeur an address on Russian Hill.

"Dan's San Francisco house," he explained, as he climbed in after John Quincy. "He comes over about two months each year, and keeps a place here. Got more money than I have."

Dan's San Francisco house? "Oh," said John Quincy, "the errand you mentioned?"

Roger nodded. "Yes." He snapped on a light in the top of the limousine, and took an envelope from his pocket. "Read this letter. It was delivered to me two days ago by the Second Officer of the *President Tyler*."

John Quincy removed a sheet of note paper from the envelope. The message appeared to be rather hastily scrawled.

"DEAR ROGER," he read. "You can do me a great service—you and that discreet lad from Boston who is to stop over with you on his way out here. First of all, give John Quincy my regards and tell him that he must make my house his home while he is in the Islands. I'll be delighted to have him.

"About the errand. You have a key to my house on Russian Hill. Go up there—better go at night when the caretaker's not likely to be around. The lights are off, but you'll find candles in the pantry. In the store room on the top floor is an old brown trunk. Locked, probably—smash the lock if it is. In the lower section you'll find a battered strong box made of ohia wood and bound with copper. Initials on it—T. M. B.

"Wrap it up and take it away. It's rather an armful, but you can manage it. Have John Quincy conceal it in his luggage and some dark night when the ship's about half-way over, I want him to take it on deck and quietly drop it overboard. Tell him to be sure nobody sees him. That's all. But send me a guarded cable when you get the box, and tell him to send me a radio when the Pacific has it at last. I'll sleep better then.

"Not a word, Roger. Not a word to anyone. You'll understand. Sometimes the dead past needs a bit of help in burying its dead.

"YOUR COUSIN DAN."

Solemnly John Quincy handed the letter back into Roger's keeping. The older man thoughtfully tore it to bits and tossed them through the car window open beside him. "Well," said John Quincy. "Well—" A fitting comment eluded him.

"Simple enough," smiled Roger. "If we can help poor old Dan to sleep better as easily as that, we must do it, eh?"

"I—I suppose so," John Quincy agreed.

They had climbed Russian Hill, and were speeding along a deserted avenue lined by imposing mansions. Roger leaned forward. "Go on to the corner," he said to the chauffeur. "We can walk back," he explained to John Quincy. "Best not to leave the car before the house. Might excite suspicion."

Still John Quincy had no comment to make. They alighted at the corner and walked slowly back along the avenue. In front of a big stone house, Roger paused. He looked carefully in all directions, then ran with surprising speed up the steps. "Come on," he called softly.

John Quincy came. Roger unlocked the door and they stepped into a dark vestibule. Beyond that, darker still, was a huge hall, the dim suggestion of a grand staircase. Here and there an article of furniture, shrouded in white, stood like a ghost, marooned but patient. Roger took out a box of matches.

"Meant to bring a flashlight," he said, "but I clean forgot. Wait here—I'll hunt those candles in the pantry."

He went off into the dark. John Quincy took a few cautious steps. He was about to sit down on a chair—but it was like sitting on the lap of a ghost. He changed his mind, stood in the middle of the floor, waited. Quiet, deathly quiet. The black had swallowed Roger, with not so much as a gurgle.

After what seemed an age, Roger returned, bearing two lighted candles. One each, he explained. John Quincy took his, held it high. The flickering yellow flame accentuated the shadows, was really of small help.

Roger led the way up the grand staircase, then up narrower flight. At the foot of still another flight, in a stuffy passage on the third floor, he halted.

“Here we are,” he said. “This leads to the storage room under the roof. By gad, I’m getting too old for this sort of thing. I meant to bring a chisel to use on that lock. I know where the tools are—I’ll be gone only a minute. You go on up and locate the trunk.”

“All—all right,” answered John Quincy.

Again Roger left him. John Quincy hesitated. Something about a deserted house at midnight to dismay the stoutest heart—but nonsense! He was a grown man. He smiled, and started up the narrow stair. High above his head the yellow light of the candle flickered on the brown rafters of the unfinished store room.

He reached the top of the stairs, and paused. Gloom, gloom everywhere. Odd how floor boards will creak even when no one is moving over them. One was creaking back of him now.

He was about to turn when a hand reached from behind him and knocked the candle out of his grasp. It rolled on the floor, extinguished.

This was downright rude! “See here,” cried John Quincy, “wh—who are you?”

A bit of moonlight struggled in through a far window, and suddenly between John Quincy and that distant light there loomed the determined figure of a man. Something told the boy he had better get ready, but where he came from one had a moment or two for preparation. He had none here. A fist shot out and found his face, and John Quincy Winterslip of Boston went down amid the rubbish of a San Francisco attic. He heard, for a second, the crash of planets in collision, and then the clatter of large feet on the stairs. After that, he was alone with the debris.

He got up, thoroughly angry, and began brushing off the dinner coat that had been his tailor's pride. Roger arrived. "Who was that?" he demanded breathlessly. "Somebody went down the back stairs to the kitchen. Who was it?"

"How should I know?" inquired John Quincy with pardonable peevishness. "He didn't introduce himself to me." His cheek was stinging; he put his handkerchief to it and noted in the light of Roger's candle that it was red when it came away. "He wore a ring," added John Quincy. "Damned bad taste!"

"Hit you, eh?" inquired Roger.

"I'll say he did."

"Look!" Roger cried. He pointed. "The trunk-lock smashed." He went over to investigate. "And the box is gone. Poor old Dan!"

John Quincy continued to brush himself off. Poor old Dan's plight gave him a vast pain, a pain which had nothing to do with his throbbing jaw. A fine nerve poor old Dan had to ask a complete stranger to offer his face for punishment in a dusty attic at midnight. What was it all about, anyhow?

Roger continued his search. "No use," he announced. "The box is gone, that's plain. Come on, we'll go downstairs and look about. There's your candle on the floor."

John Quincy picked up the candle and relighted it from Roger's flame. Silently they went below. The outer door of the kitchen stood open. "Left that way," said Roger. "And, see"—he pointed to a window with a broken pane— "that's where he came in."

"How about the police?" suggested John Quincy.

Roger stared at him. "The police? I should say not! Where's your discretion, my boy? This is not a police matter. I'll have a new glass put in that window tomorrow. Come on—we might as well go home. We've failed."

The note of reproof in his voice angered John Quincy anew. They left the extinguished candles on a table in the hall, and returned to the street.

"Well, I'll have to cable Dan," Roger said, as they walked toward the corner. "I'm afraid he'll be terribly upset by this. It won't tend to endear you to him, either."

"I can struggle along," said John Quincy, "without his affection."

"If you could only have held that fellow till I came—"

"Look here," said John Quincy, "I was taken unawares. How could I know that I was going up against the heavyweight champion in that attic? He came at me out of the dark—and I'm not in condition—"

"No offense, my boy," Roger put in.

"I see my mistake," went on John Quincy. "I should have trained for this trip out here. A stiff course in a gymnasium. But don't worry. The next lad that makes a pass at me will find a different target. I'll do a daily three dozen and I'll take boxing lessons. From now on until I get home, I'll be expecting the worst."

Roger laughed. "That's a nasty cut on your cheek," he remarked. "We'd better stop at this drug store and have it dressed."

A solicitous drug clerk ministered to John Quincy with iodine, cotton and court plaster, and he reentered the limousine bearing honorably the scar of battle. The drive to Nob Hill was devoid of light chatter.

Just inside the door of Roger's house, a whirlwind in a gay gown descended upon them. "Barbara!" Roger said. "Where did you come from?"

"Hello, old dear," she cried, kissing him. "I motored up from Burlingame. Spending the night with you—I'm sailing on the *President Tyler* in the morning. Is this John Quincy?"

"Cousin John," smiled Roger. "He deserves a kiss too. He's had a bad evening."

The girl moved swiftly toward the defenseless John Quincy. Again he was unprepared, and this time it was his other cheek that suffered, though not unpleasantly. "Just by way of welcome," Barbara laughed. She was blonde and slender. John Quincy thought he had never seen so much energy imprisoned in so slight a form, "I hear you're bound for the Islands?" she said.

"Tomorrow," John Quincy answered. "On your boat."

"Splendid!" she cried. "When did you get in?"

"John Quincy came this morning," Roger told her.

"And he's had a bad evening?" the girl said. "How lucky I came along. Where are you taking us, Roger?"

John Quincy stared. Taking them? At this hour?

"I'll be getting along upstairs," he ventured.

"Why, it's just after twelve," said Barbara. "Lots of places open. You dance, don't you? Let me show you San Francisco. Roger's a dear old thing—we'll let him pay the checks."

"Well—I—I—" stammered John Quincy. His cheek was throbbing and he thought longingly of that bed in the room upstairs. What a place, this West!

"Come along!" The girl was humming a gay little tune. All vivacity, all life. Rather pleasant sort at that. John Quincy took up his hat.

Roger's chauffeur had lingered a moment before the house to inspect his engine. When he saw them coming down the steps, he looked as though he rather wished he hadn't. But escape was impossible; he climbed to his place behind the wheel.

"Where to, Barbara?" Roger asked. "Tait's?"

"Not Tait's," she answered. "I've just come from there."

"What! I thought you motored in from Burlingame?"

"So I did—at five. I've traveled a bit since then. How about some chop-suey for this Boston boy?"

Good lord, John Quincy thought. Was there anything in the world he wanted less? No matter. Barbara took him among the Chinese.

He didn't give a hang about the Chinese. Nor the Mexicans, whose restaurants interested the girl next. At the moment, he was unsympathetic toward Italy. And even toward France. But he struggled on the international round, affronting his digestion with queer dishes, and dancing thousands of miles with the slim Barbara in his arms. After scrambled eggs at a place called Pete's Fashion, she consented to call it an evening.

As John Quincy staggered into Roger's house, the great clock in the hall was striking three. The girl was still alert and sparkling. John Quincy hastily concealed a yawn.

"All wrong to come home so early," she cried. "But we'll have a dance or two on the boat. By the way, I've been wanting to ask. What does it mean? The injured cheek?"

"Why—er—I—" John Quincy remarked. Over the girl's shoulder he saw Roger violently shaking his head. "Oh, that," said John Quincy, lightly touching the wound. "That's where the West begins. Goodnight. I've had a bully time." And at last he got upstairs.

He stood for a moment at his bedroom window, gazing down at the torchlight procession of the streets through this amazing city. He was a little dazed. That soft warm presence close by his side in the car—pleasant, very pleasant. Remarkable girls out here. Different!

Beyond shone the harbor lights. That other girl—wonderful eyes she had. Just because she had laughed at him his treasured hat box floated now forlorn on those dark waters. He yawned again. Better be careful. Mustn't be so easily influenced. No telling where it would end.

IV

A FRIEND OF TIM'S

It was another of those mornings on which the fog maybe did not come. Roger and his guests were in the limousine again; it seemed to John Quincy that they had left it only a few minutes before. So it must have seemed to the chauffeur too as, sleepy-eyed, he hurried them toward the waterfront.

"By the way, John Quincy," Roger said, "you'll want to change your money before you go aboard."

John Quincy gathered his wandering thoughts. "Oh, yes, of course," he answered.

Roger smiled. "Just what sort of money would you like to change it for?" he inquired.

"Why—" began John Quincy. He stopped. "Why, I always thought—"

"Don't pay any attention to Roger," Barbara laughed. "He's spoofing you." She was fresh and blooming, a little matter like three a.m. made no difference to her. "Only about one person out of a thousand in this country knows that Hawaii is a part of the United States, and the fact annoys us deeply over in the Islands. Dear old Roger was trying to get you in wrong with me by enrolling you among the nine hundred and ninety-nine."

"Almost did it, too," chuckled Roger.

"Nonsense," said Barbara. "John Quincy is too intelligent. He's not like that congressman who wrote a letter to 'the American Consul at Honolulu.'"

"Did one of them do that?" smiled John Quincy.

"He certainly did. We almost gave up the struggle after that. Then there was the senator who came out on a junket, and began a speech with: 'When I get home to my country—' Someone in the audience shouted: 'You're there now, you big stiff!' It wasn't elegant, of course, but it expressed our feeling perfectly. Oh, we're touchy, John Quincy."

"Don't blame you a bit," he told her. "I'll be very careful what I say."

They had reached the Embarcadero, and the car halted before one of the piers. The chauffeur descended and began to gather up the baggage. Roger and John Quincy took a share of it, and they traversed the pier-shed to the gangplank.

"Get along to your office, Roger," Barbara said.

"No hurry," he answered. "I'll go aboard with you, of course."

Amid the confusion of the deck, a party of girls swept down on Barbara, pretty lively girls of the California brand. John Quincy learned with some regret that they were there only to see Barbara off. A big broad-shouldered man in white pushed his way through the crowd.

"Hello there!" he called to Barbara.

"Hello, Harry," she answered. "You, know Roger, don't you? John Quincy, this is an old friend of mine, Harry Jennison."

Mr Jennison was extremely goodlooking, his face was deeply tanned by the Island sun, his hair blond and wavy, his gray eyes amused and cynical. Altogether, he was the type of man women look at twice and never forget; John Quincy felt himself at once supplanted in the eyes of Barbara's friends.

Jennison seized the boy's hand in a firm grip. "Sailing too, Mr Winterslip?" he inquired. "That's good. Between us we ought to be able to keep this young woman entertained."

The shore call sounded, and the confusion increased. Along the deck came a little old lady, followed by a Chinese woman servant. They walked briskly, and the crowd gave way before them.

"Hello—this is luck," cried Roger. "Madame Maynard—just a moment. I want you to meet a cousin of mine from Boston." He introduced John Quincy. "I give him into your charge. Couldn't find a better guide, philosopher and friend for him if I combed the Islands."

The old lady glanced at John Quincy. Her black eyes snapped. "Another Winterslip, eh?" she said. "Hawaii's all cluttered up with 'em now. Well, the more the merrier. I know your aunt."

"Stick close to her, John Quincy," Roger admonished.

She shook her head. "I'm a million years old," she protested. "The boys don't stick so close any more. They like 'em younger. However, I'll keep my eye on him. My good eye. Well, Roger, run over some time." And she moved away.

"A grand soul," said Roger, smiling after her. "You'll like her. Old missionary family, and her word's law over there."

"Who's this Jennison?" asked John Quincy.

"Him?" Roger glanced over to where Mr Jennison stood, the center of an admiring feminine group. "Oh, he's Dan's lawyer. One of the leading citizens of Honolulu, I believe. John J. Adonis himself, isn't he?" An officer appeared, herding the reluctant throng toward the gangplank. "I'll have to leave you, John Quincy. A pleasant journey. When you come through on your way home, give me a few more days to try to convince you on my San Francisco offer."

John Quincy laughed. "You've been mighty kind."

"Not at all." Roger shook his hand warmly. "Take care of yourself over there. Hawaii's a little too much like Heaven to be altogether safe. So long, my boy, so long."

He moved away. John Quincy saw him kiss Barbara affectionately and with her friends join the slow procession ashore.

The young man from Boston stepped to the rail. Several hundred voices were calling admonitions, promises, farewells. With that holiday spirit so alien to John Quincy's experience, those ashore were throwing confetti. The streamers grew in number, making a tangle of color, a last frail bond with the land. The gangplank was taken up, clumsily the *President Tyler* began to draw away from the pier. On the topmost deck a band was playing—*Aloha-oe*, the sweetest, most melancholy song of goodbye ever written. John Quincy was amazed to feel a lump rising in his throat.

The frail, gay-colored bond was breaking now. A thin veined hand at John Quincy's side waved a handkerchief. He turned to find Mrs Maynard. There were tears on her cheeks.

"Silly old woman," she said. "Sailed away from this town a hundred and twenty-eight times. Actual count—I keep a diary. Cried every time. What about? I don't know."

The ship was well out in the harbor now. Barbara came along, Jennison trailing her. The girl's eyes were wet.

"An emotional lot, we Islanders," said the old lady. She put her arm about the girl's slim waist. "Here's another one of 'em. Living way off the way we do, any goodbye at all—it saddens us." She and Barbara moved on down the deck.

Jennison stopped. His eyes were quite dry. "First trip out?" he inquired.

"Oh, yes," replied John Quincy.

"Hope you'll like us," Jennison said. "Not Massachusetts, of course, but we'll do our best to make you feel at home. It's a way we have with strangers."

"I'm sure I shall have a bully time," John Quincy remarked. But he felt somewhat depressed. Three thousand miles from Beacon Street—and moving on! He waved to someone he fancied might be Roger on the dock, and went to find his stateroom.

He learned that he was to share his cabin with two missionaries. One was a tall, gloomy old man with a lemon-colored face—an honored veteran of the foreign field named Upton. The other was a ruddy-cheeked boy whose martyrdom was still before him. John Quincy suggested drawing lots for a choice of berths, but even this mild form of gambling appeared distasteful to these emissaries of the church.

"You boys take the berths," said Upton. "Leave me the couch. I don't sleep well anyhow." His tone was that of one who prefers to suffer.

John Quincy politely objected. After further discussion it was settled that he was to have the upper berth, the old man the lower, and the boy the couch. The Reverend Mr Upton seemed disappointed. He had played the role of martyr so long he resented seeing anyone else in the part.

The Pacific was behaving in a most unfriendly manner, tossing the great ship about as though it were a piece of driftwood. John Quincy decided to dispense with lunch, and spent the afternoon reading in his berth. By evening he felt better, and under the watchful and somewhat disapproving eyes of the missionaries, arrayed himself carefully for dinner.

His name being Winterslip, he had been invited to sit at the captain's table. He found Madame Maynard, serene and twinkling, at the captain's right, Barbara at his left, and Jennison at Barbara's side. It appeared that oddly enough there was an aristocracy of the Islands, and John Quincy, while he thought it quaint there should be such distinctions in an outpost like Hawaii, took his proper place as a matter of course.

Mrs Maynard chatted brightly of her many trips over this route. Suddenly she turned to Barbara. "How does it happen, my dear," she asked, "that you're not on the college boat?"

"All booked up," Barbara explained.

"Nonsense," said the frank old lady. "*You* could have got on. But then"—she looked meaningly toward Jennison—"I presume this ship was not without its attraction."

The girl flushed slightly and made no reply.

"What," John Quincy inquired, "is the college boat?"

"So many children from Hawaii at school on the mainland," the old lady explained, "that every June around this time they practically fill a ship. We call it the college boat. This year it's the *Matsonia*. She left San Francisco today at noon."

"I've got a lot of friends aboard her," Barbara said. "I do wish we could beat her in. Captain, what are the chances?"

"Well, that depends," replied the captain cautiously.

"She isn't due until Tuesday morning," Barbara persisted. "Wouldn't it be a lark if you could land us the night before? As a favor to me, Captain."

"When you look at me like that," smiled the officer, "I can only say that I'll make a supreme effort. I'm just as eager as you to make port on Monday—it would mean I could get off to the Orient that much sooner."

"Then it's settled," Barbara beamed.

"It's settled that we'll try," he said. "Of course, if I speed up there's always the chance I may arrive off Honolulu after sundown, and be compelled to lay by until morning. That would be torture for you."

"I'll risk it," Barbara smiled. "Wouldn't dear old dad be pleased if I should burst upon his vision Monday evening?"

"My dear girl," the captain said gallantly, "any man would be pleased to have you burst upon his vision any time."

There was, John Quincy reflected, much in what the captain said. Up to that moment there had been little of the romantic in his relations with girls; he was accustomed to look upon them merely as tennis or golf opponents or a fourth at bridge. Barbara would demand a different classification. There was an enticing gleam in her blue eyes, a hint of the eternal feminine in everything she did or said, and John Quincy was no wooden man. He was glad that when he left the dinner table, she accompanied him.

They went on deck and stood by the rail. Night had fallen, there was no moon, and it seemed to John Quincy that the Pacific was the blackest, angriest ocean he had ever seen. He stood gazing at it gloomily.

"Homesick, John Quincy?" Barbara asked. One of his hands was resting on the rail. She laid her own upon it.

He nodded. "It's a funny thing. I've been abroad a lot, but I never felt like this. When the ship left port this morning, I nearly wept."

"It's not so very funny," she said gently. "This is an alien world you're entering now. Not Boston, John Quincy, nor any other old, civilized place. Not the kind of place where the mind rules. Out here it's the heart that charts our course. People you're fond of do the wildest, most unreasonable things, simply because their minds are sleeping and their hearts are beating fast. Just—just remember, please, John Quincy."

There was an odd note of wistfulness in her voice. Suddenly at their side appeared the white-clad figure of Harry Jennison.

"Coming for a stroll, Barbara?" he inquired.

For a moment she did not reply. Then she nodded. "Yes," she said. And called over her shoulder as she went: "Cheer up, John Quincy."

He watched her go, reluctantly. She might have stayed to assuage his loneliness. But there she walked along the dim deck, close to Jennison's side.

After a time, he sought the smoking-room. It was deserted, but on one of the tables lay a copy of the *Boston Transcript*. Delighted, John Quincy pounced upon it, as Robinson Crusoe might have pounced on news from home.

The issue was ten days old, but no matter. He turned at once to the financial pages. There it was, like the face of a well-beloved friend, the record of one day's trading on the Stock Exchange. And up in one corner, the advertisement of his own banking house, offering an issue of preferred stock in a Berkshire cotton mill. He read eagerly, but with an odd detached feeling. He was gone, gone from that world, away out here on a black ocean bound for picture-book islands. Islands where, not so long ago, brown tribes had battled, brown kings ruled. There seemed no link with that world back home, those gay-colored streamers of confetti breaking so readily had been a symbol. He was adrift. What sort of port would claim him in the end?

He threw the paper down. The Reverend Mr Upton entered the smoking-room.

"I left my newspaper here," he explained. "Ah—did you care to look at it?"

"Thank you, I have," John Quincy told him.

The old man picked it up in a great bony hand. "I always buy a *Transcript* when I get the chance," he said. "It carries me back. You know, I was born in Salem, over seventy years ago."

John Quincy stared at him. "You've been a long time out here?" he asked.

"More than fifty years in the foreign field," answered the old man. "I was one of the first to go to the South Seas. One of the first to carry the torch down there—and a dim torch it was, I'm afraid. Afterward I was transferred to China." John Quincy regarded him with a new interest. "By the way, sir," the missionary continued, "I once met another gentleman named Winterslip. Mr Daniel Winterslip."

"Really?" said John Quincy. "He's a cousin of mine. I'm to visit him in Honolulu."

"Yes? I heard he had returned to Hawaii, and prospered. I met him just once—in the eighties, it was, on a lonely island in the Gilbert group. It was—rather a turning point in his life, and I have never forgotten." John Quincy waited to hear more, but the old missionary moved away. "I'll go and enjoy my

Transcript," he smiled. "The church news is very competently handled."

John Quincy rose and went aimlessly outside. A dreary scene, the swish of turbulent waters, dim figures aimless as himself, an occasional ship's officer hurrying by. His stateroom opened directly on the deck, and he sank into a steamer chair just outside the door.

In the distance he saw his room steward, weaving his way in and out of the cabins under his care. The man was busy with his last duties for the night, refilling water carafes, laying out towels, putting things generally to rights.

"Evening, sir," he said as he entered John Quincy's room. Presently he came and stood in the door, the cabin light at his back. He was a small man with gold-rimmed eye-glasses and a fierce gray pompadour.

"Everything O.K., Mr Winterslip?" he inquired.

"Yes, Bowker," smiled John Quincy. "Everything's fine."

"That's good," said Bowker. He switched off the cabin light and stepped out on to the deck. "I aim to take particular care of you, sir. Saw your home town on the sailing list. I'm an old Boston man myself."

"Is that so?" said John Quincy cordially. Evidently the Pacific was a Boston suburb.

"Not born there, I don't mean," the man went on. "But a newspaper man there for ten years. It was just after I left the University."

John Quincy stared through the dark. "Harvard?" he asked.

"Dublin," said the steward. "Yes, sir—" He laughed an embarrassed little laugh. "You might not think it now, but the University of Dublin, Class of 1901. And after that, for ten years, working in Boston on the *Gazette*—reporting, copy desk, managing editor for a time. Maybe I bumped into you there—at the Adams House bar, say, on a night before a football game."

"Quite possible," admitted John Quincy. "One bumped into so many people on such occasions."

"Don't I know it?" Mr Bowker leaned on the rail, in reminiscent mood. "Great times, sir. Those were the good old days when a newspaper man who wasn't tanked up was a reproach to a grand profession. The *Gazette* was edited mostly from a place called the Arch Inn. We'd bring our copy to the city editor there—he had a regular table—a bit sloppy on top, but his desk. If we had a good story, maybe he'd stand us a cocktail."

John Quincy laughed.

"Happy days," continued the Dublin graduate, with a sigh. "I knew every bartender in Boston well enough to borrow money. Were you ever in that place in the alley back of the Tremont Theater—?"

"Tim's place," suggested John Quincy, recalling an incident of college days.

"Yeah, bo. Now you're talking. I wonder what became of Tim. Say, and there was that place on Boylston—but they're all gone now, of course. An old pal I met in 'Frisco was telling me it would break your heart to see the cobwebs on the mirrors back in Beantown. Gone to the devil, just like my profession. The newspapers go on consolidating, doubling up, combining the best features of both, and an army of good men go on the town. Good men and true, moaning about the vanished days and maybe landing in jobs like this one of mine." He was silent for a moment. "Well, sir, anything I can do for you—as a mutual friend of Tim's—"

"As a friend of Tim's," smiled John Quincy, "I'll not hesitate to mention it."

Sadly Bowker went on down the deck. John Quincy sat lonely again. A couple passed, walking close, talking in low tones. He recognized Jennison and his cousin. "Between us we ought to be able to keep this young woman entertained," Jennison had said. Well, John Quincy reflected, his portion of the entertainment promised to be small.

V

THE BLOOD OF THE WINTERSLIPS

The days that followed proved that he was right. He seldom had a moment alone with Barbara; when he did, Jennison seemed always to be hovering near by, and he did not long delay making the group a threesome. At first John Quincy resented this, but gradually he began to feel that it didn't matter.

Nothing appeared to matter any more. A great calm had settled over the waters and over John Quincy's soul. The Pacific was one vast sheet of glass, growing a deeper blue with every passing hour. They seemed to be floating in space in a world where nothing ever happened, nothing could happen. Quiet restful days gave way to long brilliant nights. A little walk, a little talk, and that was life.

Sometimes John Quincy chatted with Madame Maynard on the deck. She who had known the Islands so many years had fascinating tales to tell, tales of the monarchy and the missionaries. The boy liked her immensely, she was a New Englander at heart despite her glamourous lifetime in Hawaii.

Bowker, too, he found excellent company. The steward was that rarity even among college graduates, an educated man; there was no topic upon which he could not discourse at length and brilliantly. In John Quincy's steamer trunk were a number of huge imposing volumes—books he had been meaning to tackle long ago, but it was Bowker who read them, not John Quincy.

As the days slipped by, the blue of the water deepened to ultramarine, the air grew heavier and warmer. Under-foot throbbed the engines that were doing their best for Barbara and an early landing. The captain was optimistic, he predicted they would make port late Monday afternoon. But Sunday night a fierce sudden storm swept down upon them, and lashed the ship with a wet fury until dawn. When the captain appeared at luncheon Monday noon, worn by a night on the bridge, he shook his head.

"We've lost our bet, Miss Barbara," he said. "I can't possibly arrive off Hololulu before midnight."

Barbara frowned. "But ships sail at any hour," she reminded him. "I don't see why—if we sent radios ahead—"

"No use," he told her. "The Quarantine people keep early hours. No, I'll have to lay by near the channel entrance until official sunrise—about six. We'll get in ahead of the *Matsonia* in the morning. That's the best I can offer you."

"You're a dear, anyhow," Barbara smiled. "That old storm wasn't your fault. We'll drown our sorrow tonight with one last glorious dance—a costume party." She turned to Jennison. "I've got the loveliest fancy dress—Marie Antoinette—I wore it at college. What do you say, Harry?"

"Fine!" Jennison answered. "We can all dig up some sort of costume. Let's go."

Barbara hurried off to spread the news. After dinner that evening she appeared, a blonde vision straight from the French Court, avid for dancing. Jennison had rigged up an impromptu pirate dress, and was a striking figure. Most of the other passengers had donned weird outfits; on the Pacific boats a fancy dress party is warmly welcomed and amusingly carried out.

John Quincy took small part in the gaiety, for he still suffered from New England inhibitions. At a little past eleven he drifted into the main saloon and found Madame Maynard seated there alone.

"Hello," she said. "Come to keep me company? I've sworn not to go to bed until I see the light on Diamond Head."

"I'm with you," John Quincy smiled.

"But you ought to be dancing, boy. And you're not in costume."

"No," admitted John Quincy. He paused, seeking an explanation. "A—a fellow can't make a fool of himself in front of a lot of strangers."

"I understand," nodded the old lady. "It's a fine delicacy, too. But rather rare, particularly out this way."

Barbara entered, flushed and vibrant. "Harry's gone to get me a drink," she panted. She sat down beside Mrs Maynard. "I've been looking for you, my dear. You know, you haven't read my palm since I was a child. She's simply wonderful—" this to John Quincy. "Can tell you the most amazing things."

Mrs Maynard vehemently shook her head. "I don't read 'em any more," she said. "Gave it up. As I've grown older, I've come to understand how foolish it is to peer into the future. Today—that's enough for me. That's all I care to think about."

"Oh, please," the girl pouted.

The old woman took Barbara's slim hand in hers, and studied the palm for a moment. John Quincy thought he saw a shadow cross her face. Again she shook her head.

"*Carpe diem*," she said. "Which my nephew once translated as 'grab the day.' Dance and be happy tonight, and let's not try to look behind the curtain. It doesn't pay, my dear. Take an old woman's word for that."

Harry Jennison appeared in the door. "Oh, here you are," he said. "I've got your drink waiting in the smoking-room."

"I'm coming," the girl said, and went. The old woman stared after her.

"Poor Barbara," she murmured. "Her mother's life was none too happy, either—"

"You saw something in her hand—" John Quincy suggested.

"No matter," the old lady snapped. "There's trouble waiting for us all, if we look far enough ahead. Now, let's go on deck. It's getting on toward midnight."

She led him out to the starboard rail. A solitary light, like a star, gleamed in the distance. Land, land at last. "Diamond Head?" John Quincy asked.

"No," she said. "That's the beacon on Makapuu Point. We shall have to round Koko Head before we sight Honolulu." She stood for a moment by the rail, one frail hand resting upon it. "But that's Oahu," she said gently. "That's home. A sweet land, boy. Too sweet, I often think. I hope you'll like it."

"I'm sure I shall," replied John Quincy gallantly.

"Let's sit down here." They found deck chairs. "Yes, a dear land," she went on. "But we're all sorts, in Hawaii—just as it is the whole world over—honest folks and rascals. From the four corners of the globe men come to us—often because they were no longer welcome at home. We offer them a paradise, and some repay us by becoming good citizens, while others rot away. I often think it will take a lot of stamina to make good in Heaven—and Hawaii is the same."

The tall emaciated figure of the Reverend Mr Upton appeared before them. He bowed. "Good evening, Madame. You're nearly home."

"Yes," she said. "Glad of it, too."

He turned to John Quincy. "You'll be seeing Dan Winterslip in the morning, young man."

"I expect I shall," John Quincy replied.

"Just ask him if he recalls that day on Apiang Island in the eighties. The Reverend Frank Upton."

"Of course," replied John Quincy. "But you haven't told me much about it, you know."

"No, I haven't." The missionary dropped into a chair. "I don't like to reveal any secrets about a man's past," he said. "However, I understand that the story of Dan Winterslip's early life has always been known in Honolulu." He glanced toward Madame Maynard.

"Dan was no saint," she remarked. "We all know that."

He crossed his thin legs. "As a matter of fact, I'm very proud of my meeting with Dan Winterslip," he went on. "I feel that in my humble way I persuaded him to change his course—for the better."

"Humph," said the old lady. She was dubious, evidently.

John Quincy was not altogether pleased at the turn the conversation had taken. He did not care to have the name of a Winterslip thus bandied about. But to his annoyance, the Reverend Mr Upton was continuing.

"It was in the eighties, as I told you," said the missionary. "I had a lonely station on Apiang, in the Gilbert group. One morning a brig anchored just beyond the reef, and a boat came ashore. Of course, I joined the procession of natives down to the beach to meet it. I saw few enough men of my own race.

"There was a ruffianly crew aboard, in charge of a dapper, rather handsome young white man. And I saw, even before they beached her, midway in the boat, a long pine box.

"The white man introduced himself. He said he was First Officer Winterslip, of the brig *Maid of Shiloh*. And when he mentioned the name of the ship, of course I knew at once. Knew her unsavory trade and history. He hurried on to say that their captain had died the day before, and they had brought him ashore to bury him on land. It had been the man's last wish.

"Well." The Reverend Mr Upton stared at the distant shore line of Oahu. "I looked over at that rough pine box—four

Malay sailors were carrying it ashore. 'So Tom Brade's in there,' I said. Young Winterslip nodded. 'He's in there, right enough,' he answered. And I knew I was looking on at the final scene in the career of a famous character of the South Seas, a callous brute who knew no law, a pirate and adventurer, the master of the notorious *Maid of Shiloh*. Tom Brade, the blackbirder."

"Blackbirder?" queried John Quincy.

The missionary smiled. "Ah, yes—you come from Boston. A blackbirder, my boy, is a shipping-master who furnishes contract labor to the plantations at so much a head. It's pretty well wiped out now, but in the eighties! A horrible business—the curse of God was on it. Sometimes the laborers came willingly. Sometimes. But mostly they came at the point of a knife or the muzzle of a gun. A bloody, brutal business.

"Winterslip and his men went up the beach and began to dig a grave under a coconut palm. I followed. I offered to say a prayer. Winterslip laughed—not much use, he said. But there on that bright morning under the palm I consigned to God the soul of a man who had so much to answer for. Winterslip agreed to come to my house for lunch. He told me that save for a recruiting agent who had remained aboard the brig, he was now the only white man on the ship.

"During lunch, I talked to him. He was so young—I discovered this was his first trip. 'It's no trade for you,' I told him. And after a time, he agreed with me. He said he had two hundred blacks under the hatches that he must deliver to a plantation over in the Kings-mill group, and that after he'd done that, he was through. 'I'll take the *Maid* back to Sydney, Dominie,' he promised, 'and turn her over. Then I'm pau. I'm going home to Honolulu.'"

The Reverend Mr Upton rose slowly. "I learned later that he kept his word," he finished. "Yes, Dan Winterslip went home, and the South Seas saw him no more. I've always been a little proud of my part in that decision. I've had few rewards. It's not everywhere that the missionaries have prospered in a worldly way—as they did in Hawaii." He glanced at Madame Maynard. "But I've had satisfactions. And one of them arose from that meeting on the shore at Apiang. It's long past my bed hour—I must say goodnight."

He moved away. John Quincy sat turning this horror over and over in his mind. A Winterslip in the blackbirding business! That was pretty. He wished he was back on Beacon Street.

"Sweet little dig for me," the old lady was muttering indignantly. "That about the missionaries in Hawaii. And he needn't be so cocky. If Dan Winterslip dropped blackbirding, it was only because he'd found something more profitable, I fancy." She stood up suddenly. "At last," she said.

John Quincy rose and stood beside her. Far away a faint yellow eye was winking. For a moment the old lady did not speak.

"Well, that's that," she said finally, in a low voice. "I've seen Diamond Head again. Goodnight, my boy."

"Goodnight," John Quincy answered.

He stood alone by the rail. The pace of the *President Tyler* was slowing perceptibly. The moon came from behind a cloud, crept back again. A sort of unholy calm was settling over the hot, airless, deep blue world. The boy felt a strange restlessness in his heart.

He ascended to the boat deck, seeking a breath of air. There, in a secluded spot, he came upon Barbara and Jennison—and stopped, shocked. His cousin was in the man's arms, and their bizarre costumes added a weird touch to the scene. They did not see John Quincy, for in their world at that moment there were only two. Their lips were crushed together, fiercely—

John Quincy fled. Good lord! He had kissed a girl or two himself, but it had been nothing like that.

He went to the rail outside his stateroom. Well, what of it? Barbara was nothing to him, a cousin, yes, but one who seemed to belong to an alien race. He had sensed that she was in love with Jennison; this was no surprise. Why did he feel that frustrated pang deep in his heart? He was engaged to Agatha Parker.

He gripped the rail, and sought to see again Agatha's aristocratic face. But it was blurred, indistinct. All Boston was blurred in his memory. The blood of the roaming Winterslips, the blood that led on to blackbirding and hot breathless kisses in the tropic night—was it flowing in his veins too? Oh, lord—he should have stayed at home where he belonged.

Bowker, the steward, came along. "Well, here we are," he said. "We'll anchor in twelve fathoms and wait for the pilot and the doctor in the morning. I heard they'd been having Kona weather out this way, but I imagine this is the tail end of it. There'll be a moon shortly, and by dawn the old trades will be on the job again, God bless them."

John Quincy did not speak. "I've returned all your books, sir," the steward went on, "except that one by Adams on *Revolutionary New England*. It's a mighty interesting work. I intend to finish it tonight, so I can give it to you before you go ashore."

"Oh, that's all right," John Quincy said. He pointed to dim harbor lights in the distance. "Honolulu's over there, I take it."

"Yeah—several miles away. A dead town, sir. They roll up the sidewalks at nine. And let me give you a tip. Keep away from the okolehau."

"The what?" asked John Quincy.

"The okolehau. A drink they sell out here."

"What's it made of?"

"There," said Bowker, "you have the plot for a big mystery story. What *is* it made of? Judging by the smell, of nothing very lovely. A few gulps, and you hit the ceiling of eternity. But oh, boy—when you drop! Keep off it, sir. I'm speaking as one who knows."

"I'll keep off it," John Quincy promised.

Bowker disappeared. John Quincy remained by the rail, that restless feeling growing momentarily. The moon was hidden still, the ship crept along through the muggy darkness. He peered across the black waters toward the strange land that awaited him.

Somewhere over there, Dan Winterslip waited for him too. Dan Winterslip, blood relative of the Boston Winterslips, and ex-blackbirder. For the first time, the boy wished he had struck first in that dark attic in San Francisco, wished he had got that strong box and cast it overboard in the night. Who could say what new scandal, what fresh blot on the honored name of Winterslip, might have been averted had he been quicker with his fists?

As John Quincy turned and entered his cabin, he made a firm resolution. He would linger but briefly at this, his journey's end. A few days to get his breath, perhaps, and then he would set out again for Boston. And Aunt Minerva would go with him, whether she wanted to or not.

VI

BEYOND THE BAMBOO CURTAIN

Had John Quincy been able to see his Aunt Minerva at that moment, he would not have been so sure that he could persuade her to fall in with his plans. He would, indeed, have been profoundly shocked at the picture presented by his supposedly staid and dignified relative.

For Miss Minerva was sitting on a grass mat in a fragrant garden in the Hawaiian quarter of Honolulu. Pale golden Chinese lanterns, inscribed with scarlet letters, hung above her head. Her neck was garlanded with ropes of buff ginger blossoms twined with maile. The sleepy, sensuous music of ukulele and steel guitar rose on the midnight air and before her, in a cleared space under the date palms, Hawaiian boys and girls were performing a dance she would not be able to describe in great detail when she got back to Beacon Street.

Miss Minerva was, in her quiet way, very happy. One of the ambitions of her life had been realized, and she was present at a luau, or native Hawaiian feast. Few white people are privileged to attend this intimate ceremony, but Honolulu friends had been invited on this occasion, and had asked her to go with them. At first she had thought she must refuse, for Dan was expecting Barbara and John Quincy on Monday afternoon. When on Monday evening he had informed her that the

President Tyler would not land its passengers until the next day, she had hastened to the telephone and asked to reconsider her refusal.

And she was glad she had. Before her, on another mat, lay the remnants of a dinner unique in her experience. Dan had called her a good sport, and she had this evening proved him to be correct. Without a qualm she had faced the queer food wrapped in brown bundles, she had tasted everything, poi served in individual calabashes, chicken stewed in coconut milk, squid and shrimps, limu, or sea-weed, even raw fish. She would dream tonight!

Now the feasting had given way to the dance. The moonlight was tracing lacy patterns on the lawn, the plaintive wail of the music rose ever louder, the Hawaiian young people, bashful at first in the presence of strangers, were bashful no longer. Miss Minerva closed her eyes and leaned back against the trunk of a tall palm. Even in Hawaiian love songs there is a note of hopeless melancholy, it touched her emotions as no symphony ever could. A curtain was lifted and she was looking into the past, the primitive, barbaric past of these Islands in the days before the white men came.

A long, heart-breaking crescendo, and the music stopped, the swaying bodies of the dancers were momentarily still. It seemed to Miss Minerva's friends an opportune moment to depart. They entered the house and in the stuffy little parlor, took leave of their brown, smiling host and hostess. The baby whose arrival in the world was the inspiration for the luau awoke for a second and smiled at them too. Outside in the narrow street their car was waiting.

Through silent, deserted Honolulu they motored toward Waikiki. As they passed the Judiciary Building on King Street the clock in the tower struck the hour of one. She had not been out so late, Miss Minerva reflected, since that night when a visiting company sang *Parsifal* at the Boston Opera House.

The iron gates that guarded the drive at Dan's house were closed. Leaving the car at the curb, Miss Minerva bade her friends goodnight and started up the walk toward the front door. The evening had thrilled her, and she moved with the long confident stride of youth. Dan's scarlet garden was shrouded in darkness, for the moon, which had been playing an in-and-out game with the fast-moving clouds all evening, was again obscured. Exotic odors assailed her nostrils, she heard all about her the soft intriguing noises of the tropic night. She really should get to bed, she knew, but with a happy truant feeling she turned from the front walk and went to the side of the house for a last look at the breakers.

She stood there under a poinciana tree near the door leading into Dan's living-room. For nearly two weeks the Kona wind had prevailed, but now on her cheek, she thought she felt the first kindly breath of the trades. Very wide awake, she stared out at the dim foaming lines of surf between the shore and the coral reef. Her mind strayed back to the Honolulu she had known in Kalakaua's day, to that era when the Islands were so naive, so colorful—unspoiled. Ruined now, Dan had said, ruined by a damned mechanical civilization. "But away down underneath, Minerva, there are deep dark waters flowing still."

The moon came out, touching with silver the waters at the crossroads, then was lost again under fleecy clouds. With a little sigh that was perhaps for her lost youth and the eighties, Miss Minerva pushed open the unlocked door leading into the great living-room, and closed it gently so as not to waken Dan.

An intense darkness engulfed her. But she knew her way across the polished floor and set out confidently, walking on tiptoe. She had gone half-way to the hall door when she stopped, her heart in her mouth. For not five feet away she saw the luminous dial of a watch, and as she stared at it with frightened eyes, it moved.

Not for nothing had Miss Minerva studied restraint through more than fifty years. Many women would have screamed and fainted, Miss Minerva's heart pounded madly, but that was all. Standing very still, she studied that phosphorescent dial. Its movement had been slight, it was now at rest again. A watch worn on someone's wrist. Someone who had been on the point of action, but had now assumed an attitude of cautious waiting.

Well, Miss Minerva grimly asked herself, what was she going to do about it? Should she cry out a sharp: "Who's there?" She was a brave woman, but the fool-hardiness of such a course was apparent. She had a vision of that dial flashing nearer, a blow, perhaps strong hands at her throat.

She took a tentative step, and then another. Now, surely, the dial would stir again. But it remained motionless, steady, as though the arm that wore it were rigid at the intruder's side.

Suddenly Miss Minerva realized the situation. The wearer of the watch had forgotten the tell-tale numerals on his wrist, he thought himself hidden in the dark. He was waiting for her to go on through the room. If she made no sound, gave no sign of alarm, she might be safe. Once beyond that bamboo curtain leading into the hall, she could rouse the household.

She was a woman of great will power, but it took all she had to move serenely on her way. She shut her lips tightly and accomplished it, veering a bit from that circle of light that menaced her, looking back at it over her shoulder as she went. After what seemed an eternity the bamboo curtain received her, she was through it, she was on the stairs. But it seemed to her that never again would she be able to look at a watch or a clock and find that the hour was anything save twenty minutes past one!

When she was half-way up the stairs, she recalled that it had been her intention to snap on the lights in the lower hall. She did not turn back, nor did she search for the switch at the head of the stairs. Instead, she went hastily on into her room, and just as though she had been an ordinary woman she closed her door and dropped down, trembling a little, on a chair.

But she was no ordinary woman, and in two seconds she was up and had reopened her door. Her sudden terror was evaporating; she felt her heart beat in a strong regular rhythm again. Action was what was required of her now, calm confident action; she was a Winterslip and she was ready.

The servants' quarters were in a wing over the kitchen, she went there at once and knocked on the first door she came to. She knocked once, then again, and finally the head of a very sleepy Japanese appeared.

"Haku," said Miss Minerva, "there is someone in the living-room. You must go down and investigate at once."

He stared at her, seeming unable to comprehend.

"We must go down," amended Miss Minerva.

"Wikiwiki!"

He disappeared, and Miss Minerva waited impatiently. Where was her nerve, she wondered, why hadn't she seen this through alone? At home, no doubt, she could have managed it, but here there was something strange and terrifying in the very air. The moonlight poured in through a small window beside her, forming a bright square at her feet. Haku reappeared, wearing a gaudy kimono that he often sported on the beach.

Another door opened suddenly, and Miss Minerva started. Bah! What ailed her, anyhow, she wondered. It was only Kamaikui, standing there a massive figure in the dim doorway, a bronze statue clad in a holoku.

"Someone in the living-room," Miss Minerva explained again. "I saw him as I came through."

Kamaikui made no reply, but joined the odd little procession. In the upper hall Haku switched on the lights, both upstairs and down. At the head of the stairs there was a brief pause—then Miss Minerva took her rightful place at the head of the line. She descended with a firm step, courageous and competent,

Boston at its best. After her followed a stolid little Japanese in a kimono gay with passionate poppies, and a Polynesian woman who wore the fearful Mother Hubbard of the missionaries as though it were a robe of state.

In the lower hall Miss Minerva did not hesitate. She pushed on through the bamboo curtain and her hand—it trembled ever so slightly—found the electric switch and flooded the living-room with light. She heard the crackle of bamboo behind her as her strange companions followed where she led. She stood looking curiously about her.

There was no one in sight, no sign of any disturbance, and it suddenly occurred to Miss Minerva that perhaps she was behaving in a rather silly fashion. After all, she had neither seen nor heard a living thing. The illuminated dial of a watch that moved a little—might it not have been a figment of her imagination? She had experienced a stirring evening. Then, too, she remembered, there had been that small glass of okolehau. A potent concoction!

Kamaikui and Haku were looking at her with the inquiring eyes of little children. Had she roused them for a fool's errand? Her cheeks flushed slightly. Certainly in this big brilliant room, furnished with magnificent native woods and green with many potted ferns, everything seemed proper and in order.

"I—I may have been mistaken," she said in a low voice. "I was quite sure—but there's no sign of anything wrong. Mr Winterslip has not been resting well of late. If he should be asleep we won't waken him."

She went to the door leading on to the lanai and pushed aside the curtain. Bright moonlight outside revealed most of the veranda's furnishings, and here, too, all seemed well. "Dan," Miss Minerva called softly. "Dan. Are you awake?"

No answer. Miss Minerva was certain now that she was making a mountain out of a molehill. She was about to turn back into the living-room when her eyes, grown more accustomed to the semi-darkness, noted a rather startling fact.

Day and night, over Dan's cot in one corner of the lanai, hung a white mosquito netting. It was not there now.

"Come, Haku," Miss Minerva said. "Turn on the light out here."

Haku came, and the green-shaded lamp glowed under his touch. The little lamp by which Dan had been reading his evening paper that night when he had seemed suddenly so disturbed, and rushed off to send a letter to Roger in San Francisco. Miss Minerva stood recalling that incident, she recalled others, because she was very reluctant to turn toward that cot in the corner. She was conscious of Kamaikui brushing by her, and then she heard a low, half-savage moan of fear and sorrow.

Miss Minerva stepped to the cot. The mosquito netting had been torn down as though in some terrific struggle and there, entangled in the meshes of it, she saw Dan Winterslip. He was lying on his left side, and as she stared down at him, one of the harmless little Island lizards ran up his chest and over his shoulder—and left a crimson trail on his white pajamas.

VII

ENTER CHARLIE CHAN

Miss Minerva leaned far over, her keen eyes seeking Dan's face. It was turned toward the wall, half buried in the pillow. "Dan," she said brokenly. She put her hand on his cheek. The night air was warm and muggy, but she shivered a little as she drew the hand quickly away. Steady! She must be steady now.

She hurried through the living-room to the hall; the telephone was in a closet under the front stairs. Her fingers were trembling again as she fumbled with the numerals on the dial. She got her number, heard finally an answering voice.

"Amos? Is that you, Amos? This is Minerva. Come over here to Dan's as quickly as you can."

The voice muttered in protest. Miss Minerva cut in on it sharply.

"For God's sake, Amos, forget your silly feud. Your brother is dead."

"Dead?" he repeated dully.

"Murdered, Amos. Will you come now?"

A long silence. What thoughts, Miss Minerva wondered, were passing through the mind of that stern unbending Puritan?

"I'll come," a strange voice said at last. And then, a voice more like that of the Amos she knew: "The police! I'll notify them, and then I'll come right over."

Returning to the hall, Miss Minerva saw that the big front door was closed. Amos would enter that way, she knew, so she went over and opened it. There was, she noted, an imposing lock, but the key had long since been lost and forgotten. Indeed, in all Dan's great house, she could not recall ever having seen a key. In these friendly trusting islands, locked doors were obsolete.

She reentered the living-room. Should she summon a doctor? But no, it was too late, she knew that only too well. And the police—didn't they bring some sort of doctor with them? Suddenly she began to wonder about the police. During all her time in Honolulu she had never given them a thought before. Away off here at the end of the world—did they have policemen? She couldn't remember ever having seen one. Oh, yes—there was that handsome, brown-skinned Hawaiian who stood on a box at the corner of Fort and King Streets, directing traffic with an air that would have become Kamehameha himself. She heard the scrape of a chair being moved on the lanai, and went to the door.

"Nothing is to be touched out here," she said. "Leave it just as it was. You'd better go upstairs and dress, both of you."

The two frightened servants came into the living-room, and stood there regarding her. They seemed to feel that this terrible affair called for discussion. But what was there to be said? Even in the event of murder, a Winterslip must maintain a certain well-bred aloofness in dealing with servants. Miss Minerva's feeling for them was kindly. She sympathized with their evident grief, but there was, she felt, nothing to discuss.

"After you've dressed," she ordered, "stay within reach. You'll both be wanted."

They went out, Haku in his absurd costume, Kamaikui moaning and muttering in a way that sent shivers up and down Miss Minerva's spine. They left her there alone—with Dan—and she who had always thought herself equal to anything still hesitated about going out on the lanai.

She sat down in a huge chair in the living-room and gazed about her at the trappings of wealth and position that Dan had left for ever now. Poor Dan. Despite all the whispering against him, she had liked him immensely. It is said of many—usually with small reason—that their lives would make an interesting book. It had been said of Dan, and in his case it was true. What a book his life would have made—and how promptly it would have been barred for all time from the shelves of the Boston Public Library! For Dan had lived life to the full, made his own laws, fought his battles without mercy, prospered and had his way. Dallied often along forbidden paths, they said, but his smile had been so friendly and his voice so full of cheer—always until these last two weeks.

Ever since that night he sent the letter to Roger, he had seemed a different man. There were lines for the first time in his face, a weary apprehensive look in his gray eyes. And how furious he had been when, last Wednesday, he received a cable from Roger. What was in that message, Miss Minerva wondered; what were those few typewritten words that had caused him to fly into such a rage and set him to pacing the floor with tigerish step?

She thought of him as she had seen him last—he had seemed rather pathetic to her then. When the news came that the *President Tyler* could not dock until morning, and that Barbara—

Miss Minerva stopped. For the first time she thought of Barbara. She thought of a sprightly, vivacious girl as yet untouched by sorrow—and of the morning's home-coming. Tears came into her eyes, and it was through a mist she saw the bamboo curtain that led into the hall pushed aside, and the thin white face of Amos framed there.

Amos entered, walking gingerly, for he was treading ground he had sworn his feet should never touch. He paused before Miss Minerva.

"What's this?" he said. "What's all this?"

She nodded toward the lanai, and he went out there. After what seemed a long time, he reappeared. His shoulders drooped wearily and his watery eyes were staring.

"Stabbed through the heart," he muttered. He stood for a moment regarding his father's picture on the wall. "The wages of sin is death," he added, as though to old Jedediah Winterslip.

"Yes, Amos," said Miss Minerva sharply. "I expected we should hear that from you. And there's another one you may have heard—judge not that ye be not judged. Further than that, we'll waste no time moralizing. Dan is dead, and I for one am sorry."

"Sorry!" repeated Amos drearily. "How about me? My brother—my young brother—I taught him to walk on this very beach—"

"Yes." Miss Minerva looked at him keenly. "I wonder. Well, Dan's gone. Someone has killed him. He was one of us—a Winterslip. What are we going to do about it?"

"I've notified the police," said Amos.

"Then why aren't they here? In Boston by this time—but then, I know this isn't Boston. Stabbed, you say. Was there any sign of a weapon?"

"None whatever, that I could see."

"How about that Malay kris on the table out there? The one Dan used as a paper cutter?"

"I didn't notice," Amos replied. "This is a strange house to me, Minerva."

"So it is." Miss Minerva rose and started for the lanai. She was her old competent self again. At that moment a loud knock sounded on the screen door at the front of the house. Presently there were voices in the hall, and Haku ushered three men into the living-room. Though evidently police, they were all in plain clothes. One of them, a tall, angular Yankee with the look of a sailing master about him, stepped forward.

"I'm Hallet," he said. "Captain of Detectives. You're Mr Amos Winterslip, I believe?"

"I am," Amos answered. He introduced Miss Minerva. Captain Hallet gave her a casual nod; this was man's business and he disliked having a woman involved.

"Dan Winterslip, you said," he remarked, turning back to Amos. "That's a great pity. Where is he?"

Amos indicated the lanai. "Come, Doctor," Hallet said, and went through the curtain, followed by the smaller of the two men.

As they went out, the third man stepped farther into the room, and Miss Minerva gave a little gasp of astonishment as she looked at him. In those warm islands thin men were the rule, but here was a striking exception. He was very fat indeed, yet he walked with the light dainty step of a woman. His cheeks were as chubby as a baby's, his skin ivory tinted, his black hair close-cropped, his amber eyes slanting. As he passed Miss Minerva he bowed with a courtesy encountered all too rarely in a work-a-day world, then moved on after Hallet.

"Amos!" cried Miss Minerva. "That man—why he—"

"Charlie Chan," Amos explained. "I'm glad they brought him. He's the best detective on the force."

"But—he's a Chinaman!"

"Of course."

Miss Minerva sank into a chair. Ah, yes, they had policemen out here, after all.

In a few moments Hallet came briskly back into the living-room. "Look here," he said. "The doctor tells me Mr Winterslip has been dead a very short while. I don't want your evidence just yet—but if either of you can give me some idea as to the hour when this thing happened—"

"I can give you a rather definite idea," said Miss Minerva calmly. "It happened just previous to twenty minutes past one. Say about one fifteen."

Hallet stared at her. "You're sure of that?"

"I ought to be. I got the time from the wrist watch of the person who committed the murder."

"What! You saw him!"

"I didn't say that. I said I saw his wrist watch."

Hallet frowned. "I'll get that straight later," he said. "Just now I propose to comb this part of town. Where's the telephone?"

Miss Minerva pointed it out to him, and heard him in earnest conversation with a man at headquarters named Tom. Tom's job, it seemed, was to muster all available men and search Honolulu, particularly the Waikiki district, rounding up any suspicious characters. He was also to have on hand, awaiting his chief's return, the passenger lists of all ships that had made port at Honolulu during the past week.

Hallet returned to the living-room. He took a stand directly in front of Miss Minerva. "Now," he began, "you didn't see the murderer, but you saw his wrist watch. I'm a great believer in taking things in an orderly fashion. You're a stranger here. From Boston, I believe?"

"I am," snapped Miss Minerva.

"Stopping in this house?"

"Precisely."

"Anybody here besides you and Mr Winterslip?"

Miss Minerva's eyes flashed. "The servants," she said. "And I would like to call your attention to the fact that I am Dan Winterslip's first cousin."

"Oh, sure—no offense. He has a daughter, hasn't he?"

"Miss Barbara is on her way home from college. Her ship will dock in the morning."

"I see. Just you and Winterslip. You're going to be an important witness."

"It will be a novel experience, at any rate," she remarked.

"I dare say. Now, go back—" Miss Minerva glared at him—it was a glare that had frightened guards on the Cambridge subway. He brushed it aside. "You understand that I haven't time for please, Miss Winterslip. Go back and describe last evening in this house."

"I was here only until eight-thirty," she told him, "when I went to a luau with some friends. Previous to that, Mr Winterslip dined at his usual hour and we chatted for a time on the lanai."

"Did he seem to have anything on his mind?"

"Well, he has appeared a bit upset—"

"Wait a minute!" The captain took out a note-book. "Want to put down some of this. Been upset, has he? For how long?"

"For the past two weeks. Let me think—just two weeks ago tonight—or rather, last night—he and I were sitting on the lanai, and he was reading the evening paper. Something in it seemed to disturb him. He got up, wrote a note to his cousin Roger in San Francisco, and took it down for a friend aboard the *President Tyler* to deliver. From that moment he appeared restless and unhappy."

"Go on. This may be important."

"Last Wednesday morning he received a cable from Roger that infuriated him."

"A cable. What was in it?"

"It was not addressed to me," said Miss Minerva haughtily.

"Well, that's all right. We'll dig it up. Now, about last night. Did he act more upset than ever?"

"He did. But that may have been due to the fact he had hoped his daughter's ship would dock yesterday afternoon, and had learned it could not land its passengers until this morning."

"I see. You said you was only here until eight-thirty?"

"I did not," replied Miss Minerva coldly. "I said I was here only until eight-thirty."

"Same thing."

"Well, hardly."

"I'm not here to talk grammar," Hallet said sharply. "Did anything occur—anything out of the ordinary—before you left?"

"No. Wait a moment. Someone called Mr Winterslip on the telephone while he was at dinner. I couldn't help overhearing the conversation."

"Good for you!" She glared at him again. "Repeat it."

"I heard Mr Winterslip say: 'Hello, Egan. What—you're not coming over? Oh, yes you are. I want to see you. I insist on it. Come about eleven. I want to see you.' That was, at least, the import of his remarks."

"Did he seem excited?"

"He raised his voice above the ordinary tone."

"Ah, yes." The captain stared at his note-book. "Must have been Jim Egan, who runs this God-forsaken Reef and Palm Hotel down the beach." He turned to Amos. "Was Egan a friend of your brother?"

"I don't know," said Amos.

"You see, Amos was not a friend of his brother, either," explained Miss Minerva. "There was an old feud between them. Speaking for myself, I never heard Dan mention Egan, and he certainly never came to the house while I was here."

Hallet nodded. "Well, you left at eight-thirty. Now tell us where you went and when you got back. And all about the wrist watch."

Miss Minerva rapidly sketched her evening at the luau. She described her return to Dan's living-room, her adventure in the dark—the luminous dial that waited for her to pass.

"I wish you'd seen more," Hallet complained. "Too many people wear wrist watches."

"Probably not many," said Miss Minerva, "wear a wrist watch like that one."

"Oh. It had some distinguishing mark?"

"It certainly did. The numerals were illuminated, and stood out clearly—with an exception. The figure 2 was very dim—practically obliterated."

He looked at her admiringly. “Well, you certainly had your wits about you.”

“That’s a habit I formed early in life,” replied Miss Minerva. “And old habits are hard to break.”

He smiled, and asked her to continue. She told of rousing the two servants and, finally, of the gruesome discovery on the lanai.

“But it was Mr Amos,” Hallet said, “who called the station.”

“Yes. I telephoned him at once, and he offered to attend to that.”

Hallet turned to Amos. “How long did it take you to reach here, Mr Winterslip?” he inquired.

“Not more than ten minutes,” said Amos.

“You could dress and get here in that time?”

Amos hesitated. “I—I did not need to dress,” he explained. “I hadn’t gone to bed.”

Hallet regarded him with a new interest. “Half past one—and you were still up?”

“I—I don’t sleep very well,” said Amos. “I’m up till all hours.”

“I see. You weren’t on friendly terms with your brother? An old quarrel between you?”

“No particular quarrel. I didn’t approve of his manner of living, and we went separate ways.”

“And stopped speaking to each other, eh?”

“Yes. That was the situation,” Amos admitted.

“Humph.” For a moment the captain stared at Amos, and Miss Minerva stared at him too. Amos! It flashed through her mind that Amos had been a long time alone out there on the lanai before the arrival of the police.

“Those two servants who came downstairs with you, Miss Winterslip,” Hallet said. “I’ll see them now. The others can go over until morning.”

Haku and Kamaikui appeared, frightened and wide-eyed. The Japanese had nothing to tell, he had been sleeping soundly from nine until the moment Miss Minerva knocked on his door. He swore it. But Kamaikui had something to contribute.

"I come here with fruit." She pointed to a basket on the table. "On lanai out there are talking—Mr Dan, a man, a woman. Oh, very much angry."

"What time was that?" Hallet asked.

"Ten o'clock I think."

"Did you recognize any voice except your master's?"

Miss Minerva thought the woman hesitated a second. "No. I do not."

"Anything else?"

"Yes. Maybe eleven o'clock. I am sitting close to window upstairs. More talking on lanai. Mr Dan and other man. Not so much angry this time."

"At eleven, eh? Do you know Mr Jim Egan?"

"I have seen him."

"Could you say if it was his voice?"

"I could not say."

"All right. You two can go now." He turned to Miss Minerva and Amos. "We'll see what Charlie has dug up out here," he said, and led the way to the lanai.

The huge Chinaman knelt, a grotesque figure, by a table. He rose laboriously as they entered.

"Find the knife, Charlie?" the captain asked.

Chan shook his head. "No knife are present in neighborhood of crime," he announced.

"On that table," Miss Minerva began, "there was a Malay kris, used as a paper cutter—"

The Chinaman nodded, and lifted the kris from the desk. "Same remains here still," he said, "untouched, unsullied. Person who killed carried individual weapon."

"How about fingerprints?" asked Hallet.

"Considering from recent discovery," Chan replied, "search for fingerprints are hopeless one." He held out a pudgy hand, in the palm of which lay a small pearl button. "Torn from kid's glove," he elucidated. "Aged trick of criminal mind. No fingerprints."

"Is that all you've got?" asked his chief.

"Most sincere endeavors," said Chan, "have revealed not much. However, I might mention this." He took up a leather bound book from the table. "Here are written names of visitors who have enjoyed hospitality of the house. A guest book is, I believe, the term. You will find that one of the earlier pages has been ruthlessly torn out. When I make discovery the volume are lying open at that locality."

Captain Hallet took the book in his thin hand. "All right, Charlie," he said. "This is your case."

The slant eyes blinked with pleasure. "Most interesting," murmured Chan.

Hallet tapped the note-book in his pocket. "I've got a few facts here for you—we'll run over them later." He stood for a moment, staring about the lanai. "I must say we seem a little shy on clues. A button torn from a glove, a page ripped from a guest book. And a wrist watch with an illuminated dial on which the figure 2 was damaged." Chan's little eyes widened at mention of that. "Not much, Charlie, so far."

"Maybe more to come," suggested the Chinaman. "Who knows it?"

"We'll go along now," Hallet continued. He turned to Miss Minerva and Amos. "I guess you folks would like a little rest. We'll have to trouble you again tomorrow."

Miss Minerva faced the Chinaman. "The person who did this must be apprehended," she said firmly.

He looked at her sleepily. "What is to be, will be," he replied in a high, sing-song voice.

"I know—that's your Confucius," she snapped. "But it's a do-nothing doctrine, and I don't approve of it."

A faint smile flickered over the Chinaman's face. "Do not fear," he said. "The fates are busy, and man may do much to assist. I promise you there will be no do-nothing here." He came closer. "Humbly asking pardon to mention it, I detect in your eyes slight flame of hostility. Quench it, if you will be so kind. Friendly cooperation are essential between us." Despite his girth, he managed a deep bow. "Wishing you goodmorning," he added, and followed Hallet.

Miss Minerva turned weakly to Amos. "Well, of all things—"

"Don't you worry about Charlie," Amos said. "He has a reputation for getting his man. Now you go to bed. I'll stay here and notify the—the proper people."

"Well, I will lie down for a little while," Miss Minerva said. "I shall have to go early to the dock. Poor Barbara! And there's John Quincy coming too." A grim smile crossed her face. "I'm afraid John Quincy won't approve of this."

She saw from her bedroom window that the night was breaking, the rakish coconut palms and the hau tree were wrapped in a gray mist. Changing her dress for a kimono, she lay down under the mosquito netting on the bed. She slept but briefly, however, and presently was at her window again. Day had come, the mist had lifted, and it was a rose and emerald world that sparkled before her tired eyes.

The freshness of that scene revivified her. The trades were blowing now—poor Dan, he had so longed for their return. The night, she saw, had worked its magic on the blossoms of the hau tree, transformed them from yellow to a rich mahogany, through the morning they would drop one by one upon the sand. In a distant algaroba a flock of myna birds screamed at the new day. A party of swimmers appeared from a neighboring cottage and plunged gaily into the surf.

A gentle knock sounded on the door, and Kamaikui entered. She placed a small object in Miss Minerva's hand.

Miss Minerva looked down. She saw a quaint old piece of jewelry, a brooch. Against a background of onyx stood the outline of a tree, with emeralds forming the leaves, rubies the fruit, and a frost of diamonds over all.

"What is this, Kamaikui?" she asked.

"Many, many years Mr Dan have that. One month ago he gives it to a woman down the beach."

Miss Minerva's eyes narrowed. "To the woman they call the Widow of Waikiki?"

"To her, yes."

"How do you happen to have it, Kamaikui?"

"I pick it up from floor of lanai. Before policemen come."

"Very good." Miss Minerva nodded. "Say nothing of this, Kamaikui. I will attend to the matter."

"Yes. Of course." The woman went out.

Miss Minerva sat very still, staring down at that odd bit of jewelry in her hand. It must date back to the eighties, at least.

Close above the house sounded the loud whir of an aeroplane. Miss Minerva turned again to the window. A young lieutenant in the air service, in love with a sweet girl on the beach, was accustomed to serenade her thus every morning at dawn. His thoughtfulness was not appreciated by many innocent bystanders, but Miss Minerva's eyes were sympathetic as she watched him sweep exultantly out, far out, over the harbor.

Youth and love, the beginning of life. And on that cot down on the lanai, Dan—and the end.

VIII

STEAMER DAY

Out in the harbor, by the channel entrance, the *President Tyler* stood motionless as Diamond Head, and from his post near the rail outside his stateroom, John Quincy Winterslip took his first look at Honolulu. He had no feeling of having been here before; this was an alien land. Several miles away he saw the line of piers and unlovely warehouses that marked the waterfront; beyond that lay a vast expanse of brilliant green pierced here and there by the top of a modest skyscraper. Back of the city a range of mountains stood on guard, peaks of crystal blue against the azure sky.

A trim little launch from Quarantine chugged importantly up to the big liner's side, and a doctor in a khaki uniform ran briskly up the accommodation ladder to the deck not far from where the boy stood. John Quincy wondered at the man's vitality. He felt like a spent force himself. The air was moist and heavy, the breeze the ship had stirred in moving gone for ever. The flood of energy that had swept over him in San Francisco was but a happy memory now. He leaned wearily on the rail, staring at the bright tropical landscape before him—and not seeing it at all.

He saw instead a quiet, well-furnished Boston office where at this very moment the typewriters were clicking amiably and the stock ticker was busily writing the story of another day. In a few hours—there was a considerable difference of time—the market would close and the men he knew would be piling into automobiles and heading for the nearest country club. A round of golf, then a calm, perfectly served dinner, and after that a quiet evening with a book. Life running along as it was meant to go, without rude interruption or disturbing incident; life devoid of ohia wood boxes, attic encounters, unwillingly witnessed love scenes, cousins with blackbirding pasts. Suddenly John Quincy remembered, this was the morning when he must look Dan Winterslip in the eye and tell him he had been a bit dilatory with his fists. Oh, well—he straightened resolutely—the sooner that was done, the better.

Harry Jennison came along the deck, smiling and vigorous, clad in spotless white from head to foot. "Here we are," he cried. "On the threshold of paradise!"

"Think so?" said John Quincy.

"Know it," Jennison answered. "Only place in the world, these islands. You remember what Mark Twain said—"

"Ever visited Boston?" John Quincy cut in.

"Once," replied Jennison briefly. "That's Punch Bowl Hill back of the town—and Tantalus beyond. Take you up to the summit some day—wonderful view. See that tallest building? The Van Patten Trust Company—my office is on the top floor. Only drawback about getting home—I'll have to go to work again."

"I don't see how anyone can work in this climate," John Quincy said.

"Oh, well, we take it easy. Can't manage the pace of you mainland people. Every now and then some go-getter from the States comes out here and tries to hustle us." He laughed. "He dies of disgust and we bury him in a leisurely way. Been down to breakfast?"

John Quincy accompanied him to the dining saloon. Madame Maynard and Barbara were at the table. The old lady's cheeks were flushed and her eyes sparkled; Barbara, too, was in her gayest mood. The excitement of coming home had made her very happy—or was her happiness all due to that? John Quincy noted her smile of greeting for Jennison, and rather wished he knew less than he did.

"Prepare for a thrill, John Quincy," the girl said. "Landing in Hawaii is like landing nowhere else on the globe. Of course, this is a through boat, and it isn't welcomed as the Matson liners are. But there'll be a crowd waiting for the *Matsonia* this morning, and we'll steal a little of her aloha."

"A little of her what?" inquired John Quincy.

"Aloha—meaning loving welcome. You shall have all my leis, John Quincy. Just to show you how glad Honolulu is you've come at last."

The boy turned to Madame Maynard. "I suppose this is an old story to you?"

"Bless you, my boy," she said. "It's always new. A hundred and twenty-eight times—yet I'm as thrilled as though I were coming home from college." She sighed. "A hundred and twenty-eight times. So many of those who once hung leis about my neck are gone for ever now. They'll not be waiting for me—not on this dock."

"None of that," Barbara chided. "Only happy thoughts this morning. It's steamer day."

Nobody seemed hungry, and breakfast was a sketchy affair. John Quincy returned to his cabin to find Bowker strapping up his luggage.

"I guess you're all ready, sir," said the steward. "I finished that book last night, and you'll find it in your suitcase. We'll be moving on to the dock shortly. All good luck to you—and don't forget about the okolehau."

"It's graven on my memory," smiled John Quincy. "Here—this is for you."

Bowker glanced at the bank-note and pocketed it. "You're mighty kind, sir," he remarked feelingly. "That will sort of balance up the dollar each I'll get from those two missionaries when we reach China—if I'm lucky. Of course, it's rather distasteful to me to accept anything. From a friend of Tim's, you know."

"Oh, that's for value received," said John Quincy, and followed Bowker on deck.

"There she is," announced Bowker, pausing by the rail. "Honolulu. The South Seas with a collar on, driving a Ford car. Polynesia with a private still and all the other benefits of the white man's civilization. We'll go out at eight tonight, thank heaven."

"Paradise doesn't appeal to you," suggested John Quincy.

"No. Nor any other of these bright-colored lands my poor old feet must tread. I'm getting fed up, sir." He came closer. "I want to hang my hat somewhere and leave it there. I want to buy a little newspaper in some country town and starve to death on the proceeds of running it. What a happy finish! Well, maybe I can manage it, before long."

"I hope so," said John Quincy.

"I hope so, too," said Bowker. "Here's wishing you a happy time in Honolulu. And one other word of warning—don't linger there."

"I don't intend to," John Quincy assured him.

"That's the talk. It's one of those places—you know—dangerous. Lotus on the menu every day. The first thing you know, you've forgot where you put your trunk. So long, sir."

With a wave of the hand, Tim's friend disappeared down the deck. Amid much confusion, John Quincy took his place in line for the doctor's inspection, passed the careful scrutiny of an immigration official who finally admitted that maybe

Boston was in the Union, and was then left to his own devices and his long, long thoughts.

The *President Tyler* was moving slowly toward the shore. Excited figures scurried about her decks, pausing now and then to stare through lifted glasses at the land. John Quincy perceived that early though the hour was, the pier toward which they were heading was alive with people. Barbara came and stood by his side.

"Poor old dad," she said, "he's been struggling along without me for nine months. This will be a big morning in his life. You'll like dad, John Quincy."

"I'm sure I shall," he answered heartily.

"Dad's one of the finest—" Jennison joined them. "Harry, I meant to tell the steward to take my luggage ashore when we land."

"I told him," Jennison said. "I tipped him, too."

"Thanks," the girl replied. "I was so excited, I forgot."

She leaned eagerly over the rail, peering at the dock. Her eyes were shining. "I don't see him yet," she said. They were near enough now to hear the voices of those ashore, gay voices calling flippant greetings. The big ship edged gingerly closer.

"There's Aunt Minerva," cried John Quincy suddenly. That little touch of home in the throng was very pleasant. "Is that your father with her?" He indicated a tall anemic man at Minerva's side.

"I don't see—where—" Barbara began. "Oh—that—why, that's Uncle Amos!"

"Oh, is that Amos?" remarked John Quincy, without interest. But Barbara had gripped his arm, and as he turned he saw a wild alarm in her eyes.

"What do you suppose that means?" she cried. "I don't see dad. I don't see him anywhere."

"Oh, he's in that crowd somewhere—"

"No, no—you don't understand! Uncle Amos! I'm—I'm frightened."

John Quincy didn't gather what it was all about, and there was no time to find out. Jennison was pushing ahead through the crowd, making a path for Barbara, and the boy meekly brought up the rear. They were among the first down the plank. Miss Minerva and Amos were waiting at the foot.

"My dear." Miss Minerva put her arms about the girl and kissed her gently. She turned to John Quincy. "Well, here you are—"

There was something lacking in this welcome. John Quincy sensed it at once.

"Where's dad?" Barbara cried.

"I'll explain in the car—" Miss Minerva began.

"No, now! Now! I must know now!"

The crowd was surging about them, calling happy greetings, the Royal Hawaiian Band was playing a gay tune, carnival was in the air.

"Your father is dead, my dear," said Miss Minerva.

John Quincy saw the girl's slim figure sway gently, but it was Harry Jennison's strong arm that caught her.

For a moment she stood, with Jennison's arm about her. "All right," she said. "I'm ready to go home." And walked like a true Winterslip toward the street.

Amos melted away into the crowd, but Jennison accompanied them to the car. "I'll go out with you," he said to Barbara. She did not seem to hear. The four of them entered the limousine, and in another moment the happy clamor of steamer day was left behind.

No one spoke. The curtains of the car were drawn but a warm streak of sunlight fell across John Quincy's knees. He was a little dazed. Shocking, this news about Cousin Dan. Must have died suddenly—but no doubt that was how things always happened out this way. He glanced at the white stricken face of the girl beside him, and because of her his heart was heavy.

She laid her cold hand on his. "It's not the welcome I promised you, John Quincy," she said softly.

"Why, my dear girl, I don't matter now."

No other word was spoken on the journey, and when they reached Dan's house, Barbara and Miss Minerva went immediately upstairs. Jennison disappeared through a doorway at the left; evidently he knew his way about. Haku volunteered to show John Quincy his quarters, so he followed the Japanese to the second floor.

When his bags were unpacked, John Quincy went downstairs again. Miss Minerva was waiting for him in the living-room. From beyond the bamboo curtain leading to the lanai came the sound of men's voices, mumbling and indistinct.

"Well," said John Quincy, "how have you been?"

"Never better," his aunt assured him.

"Mother's been rather worried about you. She'd begun to think you were never coming home."

"I've begun to think it myself," Miss Minerva replied.

He stared at her. "Some of those bonds you left with me have matured. I haven't known just what you wanted me to do about them."

"What," inquired Miss Minerva, "is a bond?"

That sort of wild reckless talk never did make a hit with John Quincy. "It's about time somebody came out here and brought you to your senses," he remarked.

"Think so?" said his aunt.

A sound upstairs recalled John Quincy to the situation. "This was rather sudden—Cousin Dan's death?" he inquired.

"Amazingly so."

"Well, it seems to me that it would be rather an intrusion—our staying on here now. We ought to go home in a few days. I'd better see about reservations—"

"You needn't trouble," snapped Miss Minerva. "I'll not stir from here until I see the person who did this brought to justice."

"The person who did what?" asked John Quincy.

"The person who murdered Cousin Dan," said Miss Minerva.

John Quincy's jaw dropped. His face registered a wide variety of emotions. "Good lord!" he gasped.

"Oh, you needn't be so shocked," said his aunt. "The Winterslip family will still go on."

"Well, I'm not surprised," remarked John Quincy, "when I stop to think. The things I've learned about Cousin Dan. It's a wonder to me—"

"That will do," said Miss Minerva. "You're talking like Amos, and that's no compliment. You didn't know Dan. I did—and I liked him. I'm going to stay here and do all I can to help run down the murderer. And so are you."

"Pardon me. I am not."

"Don't contradict. I intend you shall take an active part in the investigation. The police are rather informal in a small place like this. They'll welcome your help."

"My help! I'm no detective. What's happened to you, anyhow? Why should you want me to go round hobnobbing with policemen—"

"For the simple reason that if we're not careful some rather unpleasant scandal may come out of this. If you're on the ground you may be able to avert needless publicity. For Barbara's sake."

"No, thank you," said John Quincy. "I'm leaving for Boston in three days, and so are you. Pack your trunks."

Miss Minerva laughed. "I've heard your father talk like that," she told him. "But I never knew him to gain anything by it in the end. Come out on the lanai and I'll introduce you to a few policemen."

John Quincy received this invitation with the contemptuous silence he thought it deserved. But while he was lavishing on it his best contempt, the bamboo curtain parted and the policemen came to him. Jennison was with them.

"Goodmorning, Captain Hallet," said Miss Minerva brightly. "May I present my nephew, Mr John Quincy Winterslip, of Boston."

"I'm very anxious to meet Mr John Quincy Winterslip," the captain replied.

"How do you do," said John Quincy. His heart sank. They'd drag him into this affair if they could.

"And this, John Quincy," went on Miss Minerva, "is Mr Charles Chan, of the Honolulu detective force."

John Quincy had thought himself prepared for anything, but— "Mr—Mr Chan," he gasped.

"Mere words," said Chan, "cannot express my unlimitable delight in meeting a representative of the ancient civilization of Boston."

Harry Jennison spoke. "This is an appalling business, Miss Winterslip," he said. "As perhaps you know, I was your cousin's lawyer. I was also his friend. Therefore I hope you won't think I am intruding if I show a keen interest in what is going forward here."

"Not at all," Miss Minerva assured him. "We shall need all the help we can get."

Captain Hallet had taken a paper from his pocket. He faced John Quincy.

"Young man," he began, "I said I wanted to meet you. Last night Miss Winterslip told me of a cablegram received by the dead man about a week ago, which she said angered him greatly. I happen to have a copy of that message, turned over to me by the cable people. I'll read it to you:

"John Quincy sailing on *President Tyler* stop owing to unfortunate accident he leaves here with empty hands. Signed, Roger Winterslip."

"Yes?" said John Quincy haughtily.

"Explain that, if you will."

John Quincy stiffened. "The matter was strictly private," he said. "A family affair."

Captain Hallet glared at him. "You're mistaken," he replied. "Nothing that concerns Mr Dan Winterslip is private now. Tell me what that cable meant, and be quick about it. I'm busy this morning."

John Quincy glared back. The man didn't seem to realize to whom he was talking. "I've already said—" he began.

"John Quincy," snapped Miss Minerva. "Do as you're told!"

Oh, well, if she wanted family secrets aired in public! Reluctantly John Quincy explained about Dan Winterslip's letter, and the misadventure in the attic of Dan's San Francisco house.

"An ohia wood box bound with copper," repeated the captain. "Initials on it, T. M. B. Got that, Charlie?"

"It is written in the book," said Chan.

"Any idea what was in that box?" asked Hallet.

"Not the slightest," John Quincy told him.

Hallet turned to Miss Minerva. "You knew nothing about this?" She assured him she did not. "Well," he continued, "one thing more and we'll go along. We've been making a thorough search of the premises by daylight—without much success, I'm sorry to say. However, by the cement walk just outside that door"—he pointed to the screen door leading from the living-room into the garden— "Charlie made a discovery."

Chan stepped forward, holding a small white object in the palm of his hand.

"One-half cigarette, incompletely consumed," he announced. "Very recent, not weather stained. It are of the brand denominated Corsican, assembled in London and smoked habitually by Englishmen."

Hallet again addressed Miss Minerva. "Did Dan Winterslip smoke cigarettes?"

"He did not," she replied. "Cigars and a pipe, but never cigarettes."

"You were the only other person living here."

"I haven't acquired the cigarette habit," snapped Miss Minerva. "Though undoubtedly it's not too late yet."

"The servants, perhaps?" went on Hallet.

"Some of the servants may smoke cigarettes, but hardly of this quality. I take it these are not on sale in Honolulu?"

"They're not," said the captain. "But Charlie tells me they're put up in air-tight tins and shipped to Englishmen the world over. Well, stow that away, Charlie." The Chinaman tenderly placed the half cigarette, incompletely consumed, in his pocketbook. "I'm going on down the beach now to have a little talk with Mr Jim Egan," the captain added.

"I'll go with you," Jennison offered. "I may be able to supply a link or two there."

"Sure, come along," Hallet replied cordially.

"Captain Hallet," put in Miss Minerva, "it is my wish that some member of the family keep in touch with what you are doing, in order that we may give you all the aid we can. My nephew would like to accompany you—"

"Pardon me," said John Quincy coldly, "you're quite wrong. I have no intention of joining the police force."

"Well, just as you say," remarked Hallet. He turned to Miss Minerva. "I'm relying on you, at any rate. You've got a good mind. Anybody can see that."

"Thank you," she said.

"As good as a man's," he added.

"Oh, now you've spoiled it. Goodmorning."

The three men went through the screen door into the bright sunshine of the garden. John Quincy was aware that he was not in high favor with his aunt.

"I'll go up and change," he said uncomfortably "We'll talk things over later—"

He went into the hall. At the foot of the stairs he paused.

From above came a low, heart-breaking moan of anguish. Barbara. Poor Barbara, who had been so happy less than an hour ago.

John Quincy felt his head go hot, the blood pound in his temples. How dare anyone strike down a Winterslip! How dare anyone inflict this grief on his Cousin Barbara! He clenched his fists and stood for a moment, feeling that he, too, could kill.

Action—he must have action! He rushed through the living-room, past the astonished Miss Minerva. In the drive stood a car, the three men were already in it.

"Wait a minute," called John Quincy. "I'm going with you."

"Hop in," said Captain Hallet.

The car rolled down the drive and out on to the hot asphalt of Kalia Road. John Quincy sat erect, his eyes flashing, by the side of a huge grinning Chinaman.

IX

AT THE REEF AND PALM

They reached Kalakaua Avenue and, swerving sharply to the right, Captain Hallet stepped on the gas. Since the car was without a top, John Quincy was getting an unrestricted view of this land that lay at his journey's end. As a small boy squirming about on the hard pew in the First Unitarian Church, he had heard much of Heaven, and his youthful imagination had pictured it as something like this. A warm, rather languid country, freshly painted in the gaudiest colors available.

Creamy white clouds wrapped the tops of the distant mountains, and their slopes were bright with tropical foliage. John Quincy heard near at hand the low monotone of breakers lapping the shore. Occasionally he caught a glimpse of apple-green water and a dazzling white stretch of sand. "Oh, Waikiki! Oh, scene of peace—" What was the rest of that poem his Aunt Minerva had quoted in her last letter—the one in which she had announced that she was staying on indefinitely. "And looking down from tum-tum skies, the angels smile on Waikiki." Sentimental, but sentiment was one of Hawaii's chief exports. One had only to look at the place to understand and forgive.

John Quincy had not delayed for a hat, and the sun was beating down fiercely on his brown head. Charlie Chan glanced at him.

"Humbly begging pardon," remarked the Chinaman, "would say it is unadvisable to venture forth without headgear. Especially since you are a malihini."

"A what?"

"The term carries no offense. Malihini—stranger, newcomer."

"Oh." John Quincy looked at him curiously. "Are you a malihini?"

"Not in the least," grinned Chan. "I am kamaaina—old-timer. Pursuing the truth further, I have been twenty-five years in the Islands."

They passed a huge hotel, and presently John Quincy saw Diamond Head standing an impressive guardian at the far end of that lovely curving beach. A little farther along the captain drew up to the curb and the four men alighted. On the other side of a dilapidated fence was a garden that might have been Eden at its best.

Entering past a gate that hung sorrowfully on one hinge they walked up a dirt path and in a moment a ramshackle old building came into view. They were approaching it on an angle, and John Quincy saw that the greater part of it extended out over the water. The tottering structure was of two stories, with double-decked balconies on both sides and the rear. It had rather an air about it; once, no doubt, it had been worthy to stand in this setting. Flowering vines clambered over it in a friendly endeavor to hide its imperfections from the world.

"Some day," announced Charlie Chan solemnly, "those rafters underneath will disintegrate and the Reef and Palm Hotel will descend into the sea with a most horrid gurgle."

As they drew nearer, it seemed to John Quincy that the Chinaman's prophecy might come true at any moment. They paused at the foot of a crumbling stair that led to the front door, and as they did so a man emerged hurriedly from the Reef and Palm. His once white clothes were yellowed, his face lined, his eyes tired and disillusioned. But about him, as about the hotel, hung the suggestion of a distinguished past.

"Mr Egan," said Captain Hallet promptly.

"Oh—how are you?" the man replied, with an accent that recalled to John Quincy's mind his meeting with Captain Arthur Temple Cope.

"We want to talk to you," announced Hallet brusquely.

A shadow crossed Egan's face. "I'm frightfully sorry," he said, "but I have a most important engagement, and I'm late as it is. Some other time—"

"Now!" cut in Hallet. The word shot through the morning like a rocket. He started up the steps.

"Impossible," said Egan. He did not raise his voice. "Nothing on earth could keep me from the dock this morning—"

The captain of detectives seized his arm. "Come inside!" he ordered.

Egan's face flushed. "Take your hand off me, damn you! By what right—"

"You watch your step, Egan," advised Hallet angrily. "You know why I'm here."

"I do not."

Hallet stared into the man's face. "Dan Winterslip was murdered last night," he said.

Jim Egan removed his hat, and looked helplessly out toward Kalakaua Avenue. "So I read in the morning paper," he replied. "What has his death to do with me?"

"You were the last person to see him alive," Hallet answered. "Now quit bluffing and come inside."

Egan cast one final baffled glance at the street, where a trolley bound for the city three miles away was rattling swiftly by. Then he bowed his head and led the way into the hotel.

They entered a huge, poorly furnished public room, deserted save for a woman tourist writing post-cards at a table, and a shabby Japanese clerk lolling behind the desk. "This way,"

Egan said, and they followed him past the desk and into a small private office. Here all was confusion, dusty piles of magazines and newspapers were everywhere, battered old ledgers lay upon the floor. On the wall hung a portrait of Queen Victoria; many pictures cut from the London illustrated weeklies were tacked up haphazardly. Jennison spread a newspaper carefully over the window-sill and sat down there. Egan cleared chairs for Hallet, Chan and John Quincy, and himself took his place before an ancient roll-top desk.

"If you will be brief, Captain," he suggested, "I might still have time—" He glanced at a clock above the desk.

"Forget that," advised Hallet sharply. His manner was considerably different from that he employed in the house of a leading citizen like Dan Winterslip. "Let's get to business." He turned to Chan. "Got your book, Charlie?"

"Preparations are complete," replied Chan, his pencil poised.

"All right." Hallet drew his chair closer to the desk. "Now Egan, you come through and come clean. I know that last night about seven-thirty you called up Dan Winterslip and tried to slide out of an appointment you had made with him. I know that he refused to let you off, and insisted on seeing you at eleven. About that time you went to his house. You and he had a rather excited talk. At one-twenty-five Winterslip was found dead. Murdered, Egan! Now give me your end of it."

Jim Egan ran his fingers through his curly, close-cropped hair—straw-colored once, but now mostly gray. "That's all quite true," he said. "Do—do you mind if I smoke?" He took out a silver case and removed a cigarette. His hand trembled slightly as he applied the match. "I did make an appointment with Winterslip for last night," he continued. "During the course of the day I—changed my mind. When I called up to tell him so, he insisted on seeing me. He urged me to come at eleven, and I went."

"Who let you in?" Hallet asked.

"Winterslip was waiting in the garden when I came. We went inside—"

Hallet glanced at the cigarette in Egan's hand. "By the door leading directly into the living-room?" he asked.

"No," said Egan. "By the big door at the front of the house. Winterslip took me out on his lanai, and we had a bit of a chat regarding the—the business that had brought me. About half an hour later, I came away. When I left Winterslip was alive and well—in good spirits, too. Smiling, as a matter of fact."

"By what door did you leave?"

"The front door—the one I'd entered by."

"I see." Hallet looked at him thoughtfully for a moment. "You went back later, perhaps."

"I did not," said Egan promptly. "I came directly here and went to bed."

"Who saw you?"

"No one. My clerk goes off duty at eleven. The hotel is open, but there is no one in charge. My patronage is—not large."

"You came here at eleven-thirty and went to bed," Hallet said. "But no one saw you. Tell me, were you well acquainted with Dan Winterslip?"

Egan shook his head. "In the twenty-three years I've been in Honolulu, I had never spoken to him until I called him on the telephone yesterday morning."

"Humph." Hallet leaned back in his chair and spoke in a more amiable tone. "As a younger man, I believe you traveled a lot?"

"I drifted about a bit," Egan admitted. "I was just eighteen when I left England—"

"At your family's suggestion," smiled the captain.

"What's that to you?" Egan flared.

"Where did you go?"

"Australia. I ranched it for a time—and later I worked in Melbourne."

"What doing?" persisted Hallet.

"In—in a bank."

"A bank, eh? And then—"

"The South Seas. Just—wandering about—I was restless—"

"Beach-combing, eh?"

Egan flushed. "I may have been on my uppers at times, but damn it—"

"Wait a minute," Hallet cut in. "What I want to know is—those years you were drifting about—did you by any chance run into Dan Winterslip?"

"I—I might have."

"What sort of an answer is that! Yes or no?"

"Well, as a matter of fact, I did," Egan admitted. "Just once—in Melbourne. But it was a quite unimportant meeting. So unimportant Winterslip had completely forgotten it."

"But you hadn't. And yesterday morning, after twenty-three years' silence between you, you called him on the telephone. On rather sudden business."

"I did."

Hallet came closer. "All right, Egan. We've reached the important part of your story. What was that business?"

A tense silence fell in the little office as they awaited Egan's answer. The Englishman looked Hallet calmly in the eye. "I can't tell you that," he said.

Hallet's face reddened. "Oh, yes, you can. And you're going to."

"Never," answered Egan, without raising his voice.

The captain glared at him. "You don't seem to realize your position."

"I realize it perfectly."

"If you and I were alone—"

"I won't tell you under any circumstances, Hallet."

"Maybe you'll tell the prosecutor—"

"Look here," cried Egan wearily. "Why must I say it over and over? I'll tell nobody my business with Winterslip. Nobody, understand!" He crushed the half-smoked cigarette savagely down on to a tray at his side.

John Quincy saw Hallet nod to Chan. He saw the Chinaman's pudgy little hand go out and seize the remnant of cigarette. A happy grin spread over the Oriental's fat face. He handed the stub to his chief.

"Corsican brand!" he cried triumphantly.

"Ah, yes," said Hallet. "This your usual smoke?"

A startled look crossed Egan's tired face. "No, it's not," he said.

"It's a make that's not on sale in the Islands, I believe?"

"No, I fancy it isn't."

Captain Hallet held out his hand. "Give me your cigarette case, Egan." The Englishman passed it over, and Hallet opened it. "Humph," he said. "You've managed to get hold of a few, haven't you?"

"Yes. They were—given me."

"Is that so? Who gave them to you?"

Egan considered. "I'm afraid I can't tell you that, either," he said.

Hallet's eyes glittered angrily. "Let me give you a few facts," he began. "You called on Dan Winterslip last night, you entered and left by the front door, and you didn't go back. Yet just outside the door leading directly into the living-room, we have found a partly smoked cigarette of this unusual brand. Now will you tell me who gave you these Corsicans?"

"No," said Egan, "I won't."

Hallet slipped the silver cigarette case into his pocket, and stood up. "Very well," he remarked. "I've wasted all the time I intend to here. The district court prosecutor will want to talk to you—"

"Of course," agreed Egan, "I'll come and see him—this afternoon—"

Hallet glared at him. "Quit kidding yourself and get your hat!"

Egan rose too. "Look here," he cried, "I don't like your manner. It's true there are certain matters in connection with Winterslip I can't discuss, and that's unfortunate. But surely you don't think I killed the man. What motive would I have—"

Jennison rose quickly from his seat on the window-ledge and stepped forward. "Hallet," he said, "there's something I ought to tell you. Two or three years ago Dan Winterslip and I were walking along King Street, and we passed Mr Egan here. Winterslip nodded toward him. 'I'm afraid of that man, Harry,' he said. I waited to hear more, but he didn't go on, and he wasn't the sort of client one would prompt. 'I'm afraid of that man, Harry.' Just that, and nothing further."

"It's enough," remarked Hallet grimly. "Egan, you're going with me."

Egan's eyes flashed. "Of course," he cried bitterly. "Of course I'm going with you. You're all against me, the whole town is against me, I've been sneered at and belittled for twenty years. Because I was poor. An out-cast, my daughter humiliated, not good enough to associate with these New England blue-bloods—these thin-lipped Puritans with a touch of sun—"

At sound of that familiar phrase, John Quincy sat up. Where, where—oh, yes, on the Oakland ferry—

"Never mind that," Hallet was saying. "I'll give you one last chance. Will you tell me what I want to know?"

"I will not," cried Egan.

"All right. Then come along."

"Am I under arrest?" asked Egan.

"I didn't say that," replied Hallet, suddenly cautious. "The investigation is young yet. You are withholding much needed information, and I believe that after you've spent a few hours at the station, you'll change your mind and talk. In fact, I'm sure of it. I haven't any warrant, but your position will be a lot more dignified if you come willingly without one."

Egan considered a moment. "I fancy you're right," he said. "I have certain orders to give the servants, if you don't mind—"

Hallet nodded. "Make it snappy. Charlie will go with you."

Egan and the Chinaman disappeared. The captain, John Quincy and Jennison went out and sat down in the public room. Five minutes passed, ten, fifteen—

Jennison glanced at his watch. "See here, Hallet," he said. "The man's making a monkey of you—"

Hallet reddened, and stood up. At that instant Egan and Chan came down the big open stairway at one side of the room. Hallet went up to the Englishman.

"Say, Egan—what are you doing? Playing for time?"

Egan smiled. "That's precisely what I'm doing," he replied. "My daughter's coming in this morning on the *Matsonia*—the boat ought to be at the dock now. She's been at school on the mainland, and I haven't seen her for nine months. You've done me out of the pleasure of meeting her, but in a few minutes—"

"Nothing doing," cried Hallet. "Now you get your hat. I'm pau."

Egan hesitated a moment, then slowly took his battered old straw hat from the desk. The five men walked through the blooming garden toward Hallet's car. As they emerged into the street, a taxi drew up to the curb. Egan ran forward, and the girl John Quincy had last seen at the gateway to San Francisco leaped out into the Englishman's arms.

"Dad—where were you?" she cried.

"Cary, darling," he said. "I was so frightfully sorry—I meant to be at the dock but I was detained. How are you, my dear?"

"I'm fine, dad—but—where are you going?" She looked at Hallet; John Quincy remained discreetly in the background.

"I've—I've a little business in the city, my dear," Egan said. "I'll be home presently, I fancy. If—if I shouldn't be, I leave you in charge."

"Why, dad—"

"Don't worry," he added pleadingly. "That's all I can say now, Cary. Don't worry, my dear." He turned to Hallet. "Shall we go. Captain?"

The two policemen, Jennison and Egan entered the car. John Quincy stepped forward. The girl's big perplexed eyes met his.

"You?" she cried.

"Coming, Mr Winterslip?" inquired Hallet.

John Quincy smiled at the girl. "You were quite right," he said. "I haven't needed that hat."

She looked up at him. "But you're not wearing any at all. That's hardly wise—"

"Mr Winterslip!" barked Hallet.

John Quincy turned. "Oh, pardon me, Captain," he said. "I forgot to mention it, but I'm leaving you here. Goodbye."

Hallet grunted and started his car. While the girl paid for her taxi out of a tiny purse, John Quincy picked up her suitcase.

"This time," he said, "I insist on carrying it." They stepped through the gateway into the garden that might have been Eden on one of its better days. "You didn't tell me we might meet in Honolulu," the boy remarked.

"I wasn't sure we would." She glanced at the shabby old hotel. "You see, I'm not exactly a social favorite out here." John Quincy could think of no reply, and they mounted the crumbling steps. The public room was quite deserted. "And why *have* we met?" the girl continued. "I'm fearfully puzzled. What was dad's business with those men? One of them was Captain Hallet—a policeman—"

John Quincy frowned. "I'm not so sure your father wants you to know."

"But I've got to know, that's obvious. Please tell me."

John Quincy relinquished the suitcase, and brought forward a chair. The girl sat down.

"It's this way," he began. "My Cousin Dan was murdered in the night."

Her eyes were tragic. "Oh—poor Barbara!" she cried. That's right, he mustn't forget Barbara. "But dad—oh, go on please—"

"Your father visited Cousin Dan last night at eleven, and he refuses to say why. There are other things he refuses to tell."

She looked up at him, her eyes filled with sudden tears. "I was so happy on the boat," she said. "I knew it couldn't last."

He sat down. "Nonsense. Everything will come out all right. Your father is probably shielding someone—"

She nodded. "Of course. But if he's made up his mind not to talk, he just simply won't talk. He's odd that way. They may keep him down there, and I shall be all alone—"

"Not quite alone," John Quincy told her.

"No, no," she said. "I've warned you. We're not the sort the best people care to know—"

"The more fools they," cut in the boy. "I'm John Quincy Winterslip, of Boston. And you—"

"Carlota Maria Egan," she answered. "You see, my mother was half Portuguese. The other half was Scotch-Irish—my father's English. This is the melting pot out here, you know." She was silent for a moment. "My mother was very beautiful," she added wistfully. "So they tell me—I never knew."

John Quincy was touched. "I thought how beautiful she must have been," he said gently. "That day I met you on the ferry."

The girl dabbed at her eyes with an absurd little handkerchief, and stood up. "Well," she remarked, "this is just another thing that has to be faced. Another call for courage—I must meet it." She smiled. "The lady manager of the Reef and Palm. Can I show you a room?"

"I say, it'll be a rather stiff job, won't it?" John Quincy rose too.

"Oh, I shan't mind. I've helped dad before. Only one thing troubles me—bills and all that. I've no head for arithmetic."

"That's all right—I have," replied John Quincy. He stopped. Wasn't he getting in a little deep?

"How wonderful," the girl said.

"Why, not at all," John Quincy protested. "It's my line, at home." Home! Yes, he had a home, he recalled. "Bonds and interest and all that sort of thing. I'll drop in later in the day to see how you're getting on." He moved away in a mild panic. "I'd better be going now," he added.

"Of course." She followed him to the door. "You're altogether too kind. Shall you be in Honolulu long?"

"That depends," John Quincy said. "I've made up my mind to one thing. I shan't stir from here until this mystery about Cousin Dan is solved. And I'm going to do everything in my power to help in solving it."

"I'm sure you're very clever, too," she told him.

He shook his head. "I wouldn't say that. But I intend to make the effort of my life. I've got a lot of incentives for seeing this affair through." Something else trembled on his tongue. Better not say it. Oh, lord, he was saying it. "You're one of them," he added, and clattered down the stairs.

"Do be careful," called the girl. "Those steps are even worse than they were when I left. Just another thing to be repaired—some day—when our ship comes in."

He left her smiling wistfully in the doorway and hurrying through the garden, stepped out on Kalakaua Avenue. The blazing sun beat down on his defenseless head. Gorgeous trees flaunted scarlet banners along his path, tall coconut palms swayed above him at the touch of the friendly trades, not far away rainbow-tinted waters lapped a snowy beach. A sweet land—all of that.

Did he wish that Agatha Parker were there to see it with him? Pursuing the truth further, as Charlie Chan would put it, he did not.

X

A NEWSPAPER RIPPED IN ANGER

When John Quincy got back to the living-room he found Miss Minerva pacing up and down with the light of battle in her eyes. He selected a large, comfortable-looking chair and sank into it.

"Anything the matter?" he inquired. "You seem disturbed."

"I've just been having a lot of pilikia," she announced.

"What's that—another native drink?" he said with interest. "Could I have some too?"

"Pilikia means trouble," she translated. "Several reporters have been here, and you'd hardly credit the questions they asked."

"About Cousin Dan, eh?" John Quincy nodded. "I can imagine."

"However, they got nothing out of me. I took good care of that."

"Go easy," advised John Quincy. "A fellow back home who had a divorce case in his family was telling me that if you're not polite to the newspaper boys they just plain break your heart."

"Don't worry," said Miss Minerva. "I was diplomatic, of course. I think I handled them rather well, under the circumstances. They were the first reporters I'd ever met—though I've had the pleasure of talking with gentlemen from the *Transcript*. What happened at the Reef and Palm Hotel?"

John Quincy told her—in part.

"Well, I shouldn't be surprised if Egan turned out to be guilty," she commented. "I've made a few inquiries about him this morning, and he doesn't appear to amount to much. A sort of glorified beach-comber."

"Nonsense," objected John Quincy. "Egan's a gentleman. Just because he doesn't happen to have prospered is no reason for condemning him without a hearing."

"He's had a hearing," snapped Miss Minerva. "And it seems he's been mixed up in something he's not precisely proud of. There, I've gone and ended a sentence with a preposition. Probably all this has upset me more than I realize."

John Quincy smiled. "Cousin Dan," he reminded her, "was also mixed up in a few affairs he could hardly have looked back on with pride. No, Aunt Minerva, I feel Hallet is on the wrong trail there. It's just as Egan's daughter said—"

She glanced at him quickly. "Oh—so Egan has a daughter?"

"Yes, and a mighty attractive girl. It's a confounded shame to put this thing on her."

"Humph," said Miss Minerva.

John Quincy glanced at his watch. "Good lord—it's only ten o'clock!" A great calm had settled over the house, there was no sound save the soft lapping of waves on the beach outside. "What, in heaven's name, do you do out here?"

"Oh, you'll become accustomed to it shortly," Miss Minerva answered. "At first, you just sit and think. After a time, you just sit."

"Sounds fascinating," said John Quincy sarcastically.

"That's the odd part of it," his aunt replied, "it is. One of the things you think about, at first, is going home. When you stop thinking, that naturally slips your mind."

"We gathered that," John Quincy told her.

"You'll meet a man on the beach," said Miss Minerva, "who stopped over between boats to have his laundry done. That was twenty years ago, and he's still here."

"Probably they haven't finished his laundry," suggested John Quincy, yawning openly. "Ho, hum. I'm going up to my room to change, and after that I believe I'll write a few letters." He rose with an effort and went to the door. "How's Barbara?" he asked.

Miss Minerva shook her head. "Dan was all the poor child had," she said. "She's taken it rather hard. You won't see her for some time, and when you do—the least said about all this, the better."

"Why, naturally," agreed John Quincy, and went upstairs.

After he had bathed and put on his whitest, thinnest clothes, he explored the desk that stood near his bed and found it well supplied with note paper. Languidly laying out a sheet, he began to write.

"DEAR AGATHA: Here I am in Honolulu and outside my window I can hear the lazy swish of waters lapping the famous beach of—"

Lazy, indeed. John Quincy had a feeling for words. He stopped and stared at an agile little cloud flitting swiftly through the sky—got up from his chair to watch it disappear over Diamond Head. On his way back to the desk he had to pass the bed. What inviting beds they had out here! He lifted the mosquito netting and dropped down for a moment—

Haku hammered on the door at one o'clock, and that was how John Quincy happened to be present at lunch. His aunt was already at the table when he staggered in.

"Cheer up," she smiled. "You'll become acclimated soon. Of course, even then you'll want your nap just after lunch every day."

"I will not," he answered, but there was no conviction in his tone.

"Barbara asked me to tell you how sorry she is not to be with you. She's a sweet girl, John Quincy."

"She's all of that. Give her my love, won't you?"

"Your love?" His aunt looked at him. "Do you mean that? Barbara's only a second cousin—"

He laughed. "Don't waste your time match-making, Aunt Minerva. Someone has already spoken for Barbara."

"Really? Who?"

"Jennison. He seems like a fine fellow, too."

"Handsome, at any rate," Miss Minerva admitted. They ate in silence for a time. "The coroner and his friends were here this morning," said Miss Minerva presently.

"That so?" replied John Quincy. "Any verdict?"

"Not yet. I believe they're to settle on that later. By the way, I'm going downtown immediately after lunch to do some shopping for Barbara. Care to come along?"

"No, thanks," John Quincy said. "I must go upstairs and finish my letters."

But when he left the luncheon table, he decided the letters could wait. He took a heavy volume with a South Sea title from Dan's library, and went out on to the lanai. Presently Miss Minerva appeared, smartly dressed in white linen.

"I'll return as soon as I'm pau," she announced.

"What is this pau?" John Quincy inquired.

"Pau means finished—through."

"Good lord," John Quincy said. "Aren't there enough words in the English language for you?"

"Oh, I don't know," she answered, "a little Hawaiian sprinkled in makes a pleasant change. And when one reaches my age, John Quincy, one is eager for a change. Goodbye."

She left him to his book and the somnolent atmosphere of Dan's lanai. Sometimes he read, colorful tales of other islands farther south. Sometimes he sat and thought. Sometimes he just sat. The blazing afternoon wore on; presently the beach beyond Dan's garden was gay with bathers, sunburned men and girls, pretty girls in brief and alluring costumes. Their cries as they dared the surf were exultant, happy. John Quincy was keen to try these notable waters, but it didn't seem quite the thing—not just yet, with Dan Winterslip lying in that room upstairs.

Miss Minerva reappeared about five, flushed and—though she well knew it was not the thing for one of her standing in the Back Bay—perspiring. She carried an evening paper in her hand.

"Any news?" inquired John Quincy.

She sat down. "Nothing but the coroner's verdict. The usual thing—person or persons unknown. But as I was reading the paper in the car, I had a sudden inspiration."

"Good for you. What was it?"

Haku appeared at the door leading to the living-room. "You ring, miss?" he said.

"I did. Haku, what becomes of the old newspapers in this house?"

"Take and put in a closet beside kitchen," the man told her.

"See if you can find me—no, never mind. I'll look myself."

She followed Haku into the living-room. In a few minutes she returned alone, a newspaper in her hand.

"I have it," she announced triumphantly. "The evening paper of Monday, June sixteenth—the one Dan was reading the night he wrote that letter to Roger. And look, John Quincy—one corner has been torn from the shipping page!"

"Might have been accidental," suggested John Quincy languidly.

"Nonsense!" she said sharply. "It's a clue, that's what it is. The item that disturbed Dan was on that missing corner of the page."

"Might have been, at that," he admitted. "What are you going to do—"

"You're the one that's going to do it," she cut in. "Pull yourself together and go into town. It's two hours until dinner. Give this paper to Captain Hallet—or better still, to Charlie Chan. I am impressed by Mr Chan's intelligence."

John Quincy laughed. "Damned clever, these Chinese!" he quoted. "You don't mean to say you've fallen for that bunk. They seem clever because they're so different."

"We'll see about that. The chauffeur's gone on an errand for Barbara, but there's a roadster in the garage—"

"Trolley's good enough for me," said John Quincy. "Here, give me the paper."

She explained to him how he was to reach the city, and he got his hat and went. Presently he was on a trolley-car surrounded by representatives of a dozen different races. The melting pot of the Pacific, Carlota Egan had called Honolulu, and the appellation seemed to be correct. John Quincy began to feel a fresh energy, a new interest in life.

The trolley swept over the low swampy land between Waikiki and Honolulu, past rice fields where quaint figures toiled patiently in water to their knees, past taro patches, and finally turned on to King Street. Every few moments it paused to take aboard new immigration problems, Japs, Chinamen, Hawaiians, Portuguese, Philippinos, Koreans, all colors and all creeds. On it went. John Quincy saw great houses set in blooming groves, a Japanese theater flaunting weird posters not far from a Ford service station, then a huge building he recognized as the palace of the monarchy. Finally it entered a district of modern office buildings.

Mr Kipling was wrong, the boy reflected, East and West could meet. They had.

This impression was confirmed when he left the car at Fort Street and for a moment walked about, a stranger in a strange land. A dusky policeman was directing traffic on the corner, officers of the United States army and navy in spotless duck strolled by, and on the shady side of the street Chinese girls, slim and immaculate in freshly laundered trousers and jackets, were window shopping in the cool of the evening.

"I'm looking for the police station," John Quincy informed a big American with a friendly face.

"Get back on to King Street," the man said. "Go to your right until you come to Bethel, then turn makai—"

"Turn what?"

The man smiled. "A malihini, I take it. Makai means toward the sea. The other direction is mauka—toward the mountains. The police station is at the foot of Bethel, in Kalakaua Hale."

John Quincy thanked him and went on his way. He passed the post-office and was amazed to see that all the lock boxes opened on the street. After a time, he reached the station. A sergeant lounging behind the desk told him that Charlie Chan was at dinner. He suggested the Alexander Young Hotel or possibly the All American Restaurant on King Street.

The hotel sounded easiest, so John Quincy went there first. In the dim lobby a Chinese house boy wandered aimlessly about with broom and dust pan, a few guests were writing the inevitable post-cards, a Chinese clerk was on duty at the desk. But there was no sign of Chan, either in the lobby or in the dining-room at the left. As John Quincy turned from an inspection of the latter, the elevator door opened and a Britisher in mufti came hurriedly forth. He was followed by a Cockney servant carrying luggage.

"Captain Cope," called John Quincy.

The captain paused. "Hello," he said. "Oh—Mr Winterslip—how are you?" He turned to the servant. "Buy me an evening paper and an armful of the less offensive-looking magazines." The man hurried off, and Cope again addressed John Quincy. "Delighted to see you, but I'm in a frightful rush. Off to the Fanning Islands in twenty minutes."

"When did you get in?" inquired John Quincy. Not that he really cared.

"Yesterday at noon," said Captain Cope. "Been on the wing ever since. I trust you are enjoying your stop here—but I was forgetting. Fearful news about Dan Winterslip."

"Yes," said John Quincy coolly. Judging by the conversation in that San Francisco club, the blow had not been a severe one for Captain Cope. The servant returned.

"Sorry to run," continued the captain. "But I must be off. The service is a stern taskmaster. My regards to your aunt. Best of luck, my boy."

He disappeared through the wide door, followed by his man. John Quincy reached the street in time to see him rolling off in a big car toward the docks.

Noting the cable office near by, the boy entered and sent two messages, one to his mother and the other to Agatha Parker. He addressed them to Boston, Mass. U. S. A., and was accorded a withering look by the young woman in charge as she crossed out the last three letters. There were only two words in each message, but he returned to the street with the comfortable feeling that his correspondence was now attended to for some time to come.

A few moments later he encountered the All American Restaurant and going inside, found himself the only American in the place. Charlie Chan was seated alone at a table, and as John Quincy approached, he rose and bowed.

"A very great honor," said the Chinaman. "Is it possible that I can prevail upon you to accept some of this terrible provision?"

"No, thanks," answered John Quincy. "I'm to dine later at the house. I'll sit down for a moment, if I may."

"Quite overwhelmed," bobbed Charlie. He resumed his seat and scowled at something on the plate before him. "Waiter," he said. "Be kind enough to summon the proprietor of this establishment."

The proprietor, a suave little Japanese, came gliding. He bowed from the waist.

"Is it that you serve here insanitary food?" inquired Chan.

"Please deign to state your complaint," said the Japanese.

"This piece of pie are covered with finger-marks," rebuked Chan. "The sight are most disgusting. Kindly remove it and bring me a more hygienic sector."

The Japanese picked up the offending pastry and carried it away.

"Japanese," remarked Chan, spreading his hands in an eloquent gesture. "Is it proper for me to infer that you come on business connected with the homicide?"

John Quincy smiled. "I do," he said. He took the newspaper from his pocket, pointed out the date and the missing corner. "My aunt felt it might be important," he explained.

"The woman has a brain," said Chan. "I will procure an unmutilated specimen of this issue and compare. The import may be vast."

"You know," remarked John Quincy, "I'd like to work with you on this case, if you'll let me."

"I have only delight," Chan answered. "You arrive from Boston, a city most cultivated, where much more English words are put to employment than are accustomed here. I thrill when you speak. Greatest privilege for me, I would say."

"Have you formed any theory about the crime?" John Quincy asked.

Chan shook his head. "Too early now."

"You have no fingerprints to go on, you said."

Chan shrugged his shoulders. "Does not matter. Fingerprints and other mechanics good in books, in real life not so much so. My experience tell me to think deep about human people. Human passions. Back of murder what, always? Hate, revenge, need to make silent the slain one. Greed for money, maybe. Study human people at all times."

"Sounds reasonable," admitted John Quincy.

"Mostly so," Chan averred. "Enumerate with me the clues we must consider. A guest book devoid of one page. A glove button. A message on the cable. Story of Egan, partly told. Fragment of Corsican cigarette. This newspaper ripped maybe in anger. Watch on living wrist, numeral 2 undistinct."

"Quite a little collection," commented John Quincy.

"Most interesting," admitted the Chinaman. "One by one, we explore. Some cause us to arrive at nowhere. One, maybe two, will not be so unkind. I am believer in Scotland Yard method—follow only essential clue. But it are not the method here. I must follow all, entire."

"The essential clue," repeated John Quincy.

"Sure." Chan scowled at the waiter, for his more hygienic sector had not appeared. "Too early to say here. But I have fondness for the guest book with page omitted. Watch also claims my attention. Odd enough, when we enumerate clues this morning, we pass over watch. Foolish. Very goodlooking clue. One large fault, we do not possess it. However, my eyes are sharp to apprehend it."

"I understand," John Quincy said, "that you've been rather successful as a detective."

Chan grinned broadly. "You are educated, maybe you know," he said. "Chinese most psychic people in the world. Sensitives, like film in camera. A look, a laugh, a gesture perhaps. Something go click."

John Quincy was aware of a sudden disturbance at the door of the All American Restaurant. Bowker, the steward, gloriously drunk, was making a noisy entrance. He plunged into the room, followed by a dark, anxious-looking youth.

Embarrassed, John Quincy turned away his face, but to no avail. Bowker was bearing down upon him, waving his arms.

"Well, well, well, well!" he bellowed. "My o' college chum. See you through the window." He leaned heavily on the table. "How you been, o' fellow?"

"I'm all right, thanks," John Quincy said.

The dark young man came up. He was, from his dress, a shore acquaintance of Bowker's. "Look here, Ted," he said. "You've got to be getting along—"

"Jush a minute," cried Bowker. "I want y' to meet Mr Quincy from Boston. One best fellows God ever made. Mushual friend o' Tim's—you've heard me speak of Tim—"

"Yes—come along," urged the dark young man.

"Not yet. Gotta buy thish boy a lil' drink. What you having, Quincy, o' man?"

"Not a thing," smiled John Quincy. "You warned me against these Island drinks yourself."

"Who—me?" Bowker was hurt. "You're wrong that time, o' man. Don' like to conter—conterdict, but it mush have been somebody else. Not me. Never said a word—"

The young man took his arm. "Come on—you're due on the ship—"

Bowker wrenched away. "Don' paw me," he cried. "Keep your hands off. I'm my own mashter, ain't I? I can speak to an o' friend, can't I? Now, Quincy, o' man—what's yours?"

"I'm sorry," said John Quincy. "Some other time."

Bowker's companion took his arm in a firmer grasp. "You can't buy anything here," he said. "This is a restaurant. You come with me—I know a place—"

"Awright," agreed Bowker. "Now you're talking. Quincy, o' man, you come along—"

"Some other time," John Quincy repeated.

Bowker assumed a look of offended dignity. "Jush as you say," he replied. "Some other time. In Boston, hey? At Tim's place. Only Tim's place is gone." A great grief assailed him. "Tim's gone—dropped out—as though the earth swallowed him up—"

"Yes, yes," said the young man soothingly. "That's too bad. But you come with me."

Submitting at last, Bowker permitted his companion to pilot him to the street. John Quincy looked across at Chan.

"My steward on the *President Tyler*," he explained. "The worse for wear, isn't he?"

The waiter set a fresh piece of pie before the Chinaman.

"Ah," remarked Chan, "this has a more perfect appearance." He tasted it. "Appearance," he added with a grimace, "are a hellish liar. If you are quite ready to depart—"

In the street Chan halted. "Excuse abrupt departure," he said. "Most honored to work with you. The results will be fascinating, I am sure. For now, good evening."

John Quincy was alone again in that strange town. A sudden homesickness engulfed him. Walking along, he came to a news-cart that was as well supplied with literature as his club reading room. A brisk young man in a cap was in charge.

"Have you the latest *Atlantic*?" inquired John Quincy.

The young man put a dark brown periodical into his hand. "No," said John Quincy. "This is the June issue. I've seen it."

"July ain't in. I'll save you one, if you say so."

"I wish you would," John Quincy replied. "The name is Winterslip."

He went on to the corner, regretting that July wasn't in. A copy of the *Atlantic* would have been a sort of link with home, a reminder that Boston still stood. And he felt the need of a link, a reminder.

A trolley-car marked "Waikiki" was approaching. John Quincy hailed it and hopped aboard. Three giggling Japanese girls in bright kimonos drew in their tiny sandaled feet and he slipped past them to a seat.

XI

THE TREE OF JEWELS

Two hours later, John Quincy rose from the table where he and his aunt had dined together.

"Just to show you how quick I am to learn a new language," he remarked, "I'm quite pau. Now I'm going makai to sit on the lanai, there to forget the pilikia of the day."

Miss Minerva smiled and rose too. "I expect Amos shortly," she said as they crossed the hall. "A family conference seemed advisable, so I've asked him to come over."

"Strange you had to send for him," said John Quincy, lighting a cigarette.

"Not at all," she answered. She explained about the long feud between the brothers.

"Didn't think old Amos had that much fire in him," commented John Quincy, as they found chairs on the lanai. "A rather anemic specimen, judging by the look I had at him this morning. But then, the Winterslips always were good haters."

For a moment they sat in silence. Outside the darkness was deepening rapidly, the tropic darkness that had brought tragedy the night before. John Quincy pointed to a small lizard on the screen.

"Pleasant little beast," he said.

"Oh, they're quite harmless," Miss Minerva told him. "And they eat the mosquitos."

"They do, eh?" The boy slapped his ankle savagely. "Well, there's no accounting for tastes."

Amos arrived presently, looking unusually pale in the half-light. "You asked me to come over, Minerva," he said, as he sat down gingerly on one of Dan Winterslip's Hong Kong chairs.

"I did. Smoke if you like." Amos lighted a cigarette, which seemed oddly out of place between his thin lips. "I'm sure," Miss Minerva continued, "that we are all determined to bring to justice the person who did this ghastly thing."

"Naturally," said Amos.

"The only drawback," she went on, "is that in the course of the investigation some rather unpleasant facts about Dan's past are likely to be revealed."

"They're bound to be," remarked Amos coldly.

"For Barbara's sake," Miss Minerva said. "I'm intent on seeing that nothing is revealed that is not absolutely essential to the discovery of the murderer. For that reason, I haven't taken the police completely into my confidence."

"What!" cried Amos.

John Quincy stood up. "Now look here, Aunt Minerva—"

"Sit down," snapped his aunt. "Amos, to go back to a talk we had at your house when I was there, Dan was somewhat involved with this woman down the beach. Arlene Compton, I believe she calls herself."

Amos nodded. "Yes, and a worthless lot she is. But Dan wouldn't see it, though I understand his friends pointed it out to him. He talked of marrying her."

"You knew a good deal about Dan, even if you never spoke to him," Miss Minerva went on. "Just what was his status with this woman at the time of his murder—only last night, but it seems ages ago."

"I can't quite tell you that," Amos replied. "I do know that for the past month a malihini named Leatherbee—the black sheep of a good family in Philadelphia, they tell me—has been hanging around the Compton woman, and that Dan resented his presence."

"Humph." Miss Minerva handed to Amos an odd old brooch, a tree of jewels against an onyx background. "Ever see that before, Amos?"

He took it, and nodded. "It's part of a little collection of jewelry Dan brought back from the South Seas in the eighties. There were ear-rings and a bracelet, too. He acted rather queerly about those trinkets—never let Barbara's mother or anyone else wear them. But he must have got over that idea recently. For I saw this only a few weeks ago."

"Where?" asked Miss Minerva.

"Our office has the renting of the cottage down the beach occupied at present by the Compton woman. She came in not long ago to pay her rent, and she was wearing this brooch." He looked suddenly at Miss Minerva. "Where did you get it?" he demanded.

"Kamaikui gave it to me early this morning," Miss Minerva explained. "She picked it up from the floor of the lanai before the police came."

John Quincy leaped to his feet. "You're all wrong, Aunt Minerva," he cried. "You can't do this sort of thing. You ask the help of the police, and you aren't on the level with them. I'm ashamed of you—"

"Please wait a moment," said his aunt.

"Wait nothing!" he answered. "Give me that brooch. I'm going to turn it over to Chan at once. I couldn't look him in the eye if I didn't."

"We'll turn it over to Chan," said Miss Minerva calmly, "if it seems important. But there is no reason in the world why we should not investigate a bit ourselves before we do so. The woman may have a perfectly logical explanation—"

"Rot!" interrupted John Quincy. "The trouble with you is, you think you're Sherlock Holmes."

"What is your opinion, Amos?" inquired Miss Minerva.

"I'm inclined to agree with John Quincy," Amos said. "You are hardly fair to Captain Hallet. And as for keeping anything dark on account of Barbara—or on anybody's account—that won't be possible, I'm afraid. No getting round it, Minerva, Dan's indiscretions are going to be dragged into the open at last."

She caught the note of satisfaction in his tone, and was nettled by it. "Perhaps. At the same time, it isn't going to do any harm for some member of the family to have a talk with this woman before we consult the police. If she should have a perfectly sincere and genuine explanation—"

"Oh, yes," cut in John Quincy. "She wouldn't have any other kind."

"It won't be so much what she says," persisted Miss Minerva. "It will be the manner in which she says it. Any intelligent person can see through deceit and falsehood. The only question is, which of us is the intelligent person best fitted to examine her."

"Count me out," said Amos promptly.

"John Quincy?"

The boy considered. He had asked for the privilege of working with Chan, and here, perhaps, was an opportunity to win the Chinaman's respect. But this sounded rather like a woman who would be too much for him.

"No, thanks," he said.

"Very good," replied Miss Minerva, rising. "I'll go myself."

"Oh, no," cried John Quincy, shocked.

"Why not? If none of the men in the family are up to it. As a matter of fact, I welcome the opportunity—"

Amos shook his head. "She'll twist you round her little finger," he predicted.

Miss Minerva smiled grimly. "I should like to see her do it. Will you wait here?"

John Quincy went over and took the brooch from Amos's hand. "Sit down, Aunt Minerva," he said. "I'll see this woman. But I warn you that immediately afterward I shall send for Chan."

"That," his aunt told him, "will be decided at another conference. I'm not so sure, John Quincy, that you are the proper person to go. After all, what experience have you had with women of this type?"

John Quincy was offended. He was a man, and he felt that he could meet and outwit a woman of any type. He said as much.

Amos described the woman's house as a small cottage several hundred yards down the beach, and directed the boy how to get there. John Quincy set out.

Night had fallen over the island when he reached Kalia Road, a bright silvery night, for the Kona weather was over and the moon traveled a cloudless sky. The scent of plumaria and ginger stole out to him through hedges of flaming hibiscus; the trade winds, blowing across a thousand miles of warm water, still managed a cool touch on his cheek. As he approached what he judged must be the neighborhood of the woman's house, a flock of Indian myna birds in a spreading algaroba screamed loudly, their harsh voices the only note of discord in that peaceful scene.

He had some difficulty locating the cottage, which was almost completely hidden under masses of flowering alamander, its blossoms pale yellow in the moonlight. Before the door, a dark fragrant spot under a heavily laden trellis, he paused uncertainly. A rather delicate errand, this was. But he summoned his courage and knocked.

Only the myna birds replied. John Quincy stood there, growing momentarily more hostile to the Widow of Waikiki. Some huge coarse creature, no doubt, a man's woman, a good fellow at a party—that kind. Then the door opened and the boy got a shock. For the figure outlined against the light was young and slender, and the face, dimly seen, suggested fragile loveliness.

"Is this Mrs Compton?" he inquired.

"Yeah—I'm Mrs Compton. What do you want?" John Quincy was sorry she had spoken. For she was, obviously, one of those beauties so prevalent nowadays, the sort whom speech betrays. Her voice recalled the myna birds.

"My name is John Quincy Winterslip." He saw her start. "May I speak with you for a moment?"

"Sure you can. Come in." She led the way along a low narrow passage into a tiny living-room. A pasty-faced young man with stooped shoulders stood by a table, fondling a cocktail shaker.

"Steve," said the woman, "this is Mr Winterslip. Mr Leatherbee."

Mr Leatherbee grunted. "Just in time for a little snifter," he remarked.

"No, thanks," John Quincy said. He saw Mrs Compton take a smoking cigarette from an ash tray, start to convey it to her lips, then, evidently thinking better of it, crush it on the tray.

"Well," said Mr Leatherbee, "your poison's ready, Arlene." He proffered a glass.

She shook her head, slightly annoyed. "No."

"No?" Mr Leatherbee grinned. "The more for little Stevie." He lifted a glass. "Here's looking at you, Mr Winterslip."

"Say, I guess you're Dan's cousin from Boston," Mrs Compton remarked. "He was telling me about you." She lowered her voice. "I've been meaning to get over to your place all day. But it was such a shock—it knocked me flat."

"I understand," John Quincy replied. He glanced at Mr Leatherbee, who seemed not to have heard of prohibition. "My business with you, Mrs Compton, is private."

Leatherbee stiffened belligerently. But the woman said: "That's all right. Steve was just going."

Steve hesitated a moment, then went. His hostess accompanied him. John Quincy heard the low monotone of their voices in the distance. There was a combined odor of gin and cheap perfume in the air; the boy wondered what his mother would say if she could see him now. A door slammed, and the woman returned.

"Well?" she said. John Quincy perceived that her eyes were hard and knowing, like her voice. He waited for her to sit down, then took a chair facing her.

"You knew my Cousin Dan rather intimately," he suggested.

"I was engaged to him," she answered. John Quincy glanced at her left hand. "He hadn't come across—I mean, he hadn't given me a ring, but it was—you know—understood between us."

"Then his death is a good deal of a blow to you?"

She managed a baby stare, full of pathos. "I'll say it is. Mr Winterslip was kind to me—he believed in me and trusted me. A lone woman way out here don't get any too much char—kindness."

"When did you see Mr Winterslip last?"

"Three or four days ago—last Friday evening, I guess it was."

John Quincy frowned. "Wasn't that rather a long stretch?"

She nodded. "I'll tell you the truth. We had a little—misunderstanding. Just a lover's quarrel, you know. Dan sort of objected to Steve hanging around. Not that he'd any reason to—Steve's nothing to me—just a weak kid I used to know when I was trouping. I was on the stage—maybe you heard that."

"Yes," said John Quincy. "You hadn't seen Mr Winterslip since last Friday. You didn't go to his house last evening?"

"I should say not. I got my reputation to think of—you've no idea how people talk in a place like this—"

John Quincy laid the brooch down upon the table. It sparkled in the lamplight—a reading lamp, though the atmosphere was not in the least literary. The baby stare was startled now. "You recognize that, don't you?" he asked.

"Why—yes—it's—I—"

"Just stick to the truth," said John Quincy, not unkindly. "It's an old piece of jewelry that Mr Winterslip gave you, I believe."

"Well—"

"You've been seen wearing it, you know."

"Yes, he did give it to me," she admitted. "The only present I ever got from him. I guess from the look of it Mrs Noah wore it on the Ark. Kinda pretty, though."

"You didn't visit Mr Winterslip last night," persisted John Quincy. "Yet, strangely enough, this brooch was found on the floor not far from his dead body."

She drew in her breath sharply. "Say—what are you? A cop?" she asked.

"Hardly," John Quincy smiled. "I am here simply to save you, if possible, from the hands of the—er—the cops. If you have any real explanation of this matter, it may not be necessary to call it to the attention of the police."

"Oh!" She smiled. "Say, that's decent of you. Now I will tell you the truth. That about not seeing Dan Winterslip since Friday was bunk. I saw him last night."

"Ah—you did? Where?"

"Right here. Mr Winterslip gave me that thing about a month ago. Two weeks ago he came to me in a sort of excited way and said he must have it back. It was the only thing he ever give me and I liked it and those emeralds are valuable—so—well, I stalled a while. I said I was having a new clasp put on it.

He kept asking for it, and last night he showed up here and said he just had to have it. Said he'd buy me anything in the stores in place of it. I must say he was pretty het up. So I finally turned it over to him and he took it and went away."

"What time was that?"

"About nine-thirty. He was happy and pleasant and he said I could go to a jewelry store this morning and take my pick of the stock." She looked pleadingly at John Quincy. "That's the last I ever saw of him. It's the truth, so help me."

"I wonder," mused John Quincy.

She moved nearer. "Say, you're a nice kid," she said. "The kind I used to meet in Boston when we played there. The kind that's got some consideration for a woman. You ain't going to drag me into this. Think what it would mean—to me."

John Quincy did not speak. He saw there were tears in her eyes. "You've probably heard things about me," she went on, "but they ain't true. You don't know what I been up against out here. An unprotected woman don't have much chance anywhere, but on this beach, where men come drifting in from all over the world—I been friendly, that's my only trouble. I was homesick—oh, God, wasn't I homesick! I was having a good time back there, and then I fell for Bill Compton and came out here with him, and sometimes in the night I'd wake up and remember Broadway was five thousand miles away, and I'd cry so hard I'd wake him. And that made him sore—"

She paused. John Quincy was impressed by the note of true nostalgia in her voice. He was, suddenly, rather sorry for her.

"Then Bill's plane crashed on Diamond Head," she continued, "and I was all alone. And these black sheep along the beach, they knew I was alone—and broke. And I was homesick for Forty-second Street, for the old boarding-house and the old gang and the Automat and the chewing-gum sign, and try-outs at New Haven. So I gave a few parties just to forget, and people began to talk."

"You might have gone back," John Quincy suggested.

"I know—why didn't I? I been intending to, right along, but every day out here is just like any other day, and somehow you don't get round to picking one out—I been drifting—but honest to God if you keep me out of this I'll go home on the first boat. I'll get me a job, and—and—If you'll only keep me out of it. You got a chance now to wreck my life—it's all up to you—but I know you ain't going to—"

She seized John Quincy's hand in both of hers, and gazed at him pleadingly through her tears. It was the most uncomfortable moment of his life. He looked wildly about the little room, so different from any in the house on Beacon Street. He pulled his hand away.

"I'll—I'll see," he said, rising hastily. "I'll think it over."

"But I can't sleep tonight if I don't know," she told him.

"I'll have to think it over," he repeated. He turned toward the table in time to see the woman's slim hand reach out and seize the bit of jewelry. "I'll take the brooch," he added.

She looked up at him. Suddenly John Quincy knew that she had been acting, that his emotions had been falsely played upon, and he felt again that hot rush of blood to the head, that quick surge of anger, he had experienced in Dan Winterslip's hall. Aunt Minerva had predicted he couldn't handle a woman of this type. Well, he'd show her—he'd show the world. "Give me that brooch," he said coldly.

"It's mine," answered the woman stubbornly.

John Quincy wasted no words; he seized the woman's wrist. She screamed. A door opened behind them.

"What's going on here?" inquired Mr Leatherbee.

"Oh, I thought you'd left us," said John Quincy.

"Steve! Don't let him have it," cried the woman. Steve moved militantly nearer, but there was a trace of caution in his attitude.

John Quincy laughed. "You stay where you are, Steve," he advised. "Or I'll smash that sallow face of yours." Strange talk for a Winterslip. "Your friend here is trying to hang on to an important bit of evidence in the murder up the beach, and with the utmost reluctance I am forced to use strong-arm methods." The brooch dropped to the floor, he stooped and picked it up. "Well, I guess that's about all," he added. "I'm sorry if you've been homesick, Mrs Compton, but speaking as a Bostonian, I don't believe Broadway is as glamourous as you picture it. Distance has lent enchantment. Good night."

He let himself out, and found his way to Kalakaua Avenue. He had settled one thing to his own satisfaction; Chan must know about the brooch, and at once. Mrs Compton's story might be true or not, it certainly needed further investigation by some responsible person.

John Quincy had approached the cottage by way of Kalia Road, he was planning to return to Dan's house along the better lighted avenue. Having reached that broad expanse of asphalt, however, he realized that the Reef and Palm Hotel was near at hand. There was his promise to Carlota Egan—he had said he would look in on her again today. As for Chan, he could telephone the Chinaman from the hotel. He turned in the direction of the Reef and Palm.

Stumbling through the dark garden, he saw finally the gaunt old hulk of the hotel. Lights of low candle power burned at infrequent intervals on the double-decked veranda. In the huge lobby a few rather shabby-looking guests took their ease. Behind the desk stood—nobody but the Japanese clerk.

John Quincy was directed to a telephone booth, and his keen Bostonian mind required Nipponese aid in mastering the dial system favored by the Honolulu telephone company. At length he got the police station. Chan was out, but the answering voice promised that he would be told to get in touch with Mr Winterslip immediately on his return.

"How much do I owe you?" inquired John Quincy of the clerk.

"Not a penny," said a voice, and he turned to find Carlota Egan at his elbow. He smiled. This was more like it.

"But I say—you know—I've used your telephone—"

"It's free," she said. "Too many things are free out here. That's why we don't get rich. It was so kind of you to come again."

"Not at all," he protested. He looked about the room. "Your father—"

She glanced at the clerk, and led the way out to the lanai at the side. They went to the far end of it, where they could see the light on Diamond Head, and the silvery waters of the Pacific sweeping in to disappear at last beneath the old Reef and Palm.

"I'm afraid poor dad's having a bad time of it," she said, and her voice broke slightly. "I haven't been able to see him. They're holding him down there—as a witness, I believe. There was some talk of bail, but I didn't listen. We haven't any money—at least, I didn't think we had."

"You didn't think—" he began, puzzled.

She produced a small bit of paper, and put it in his hand. "I want to ask your advice. I've been cleaning up dad's office, and just before you came I ran across that in his desk."

John Quincy stared down at the little pink slip she had given him. By the light of one of the small lamps he saw that it was a check for five thousand dollars, made out to "Bearer" and signed by Dan Winterslip. The date was that of the day before.

"I say, that looks important, doesn't it?" John Quincy said. He handed it back to her, and thought a moment. "By gad—it is important. It seems to me it's pretty conclusive evidence of your father's innocence. If he had that, his business with Cousin Dan must have come to a successful end, and it isn't likely he would—er—do away with the man who signed it and complicate the cashing of it."

The girl's eyes shone. "Just the way I reasoned. But I don't know what to do with it."

"Your father has engaged a lawyer, of course."

"Yes, but a rather poor one. The only kind we can afford. Should I turn this over to him?"

"No—wait a minute. Any chance of seeing your father soon?"

"Yes. It's been arranged I'm to visit him in the morning."

John Quincy nodded. "Better talk with him before you do anything," he advised. He had a sudden recollection of Egan's face when he refused to explain his business with Dan Winterslip. "Take this check with you and ask your father what he wants done with it. Point out to him that it's vital evidence in his favor."

"Yes, I guess that's the best plan," the girl agreed. "Will—will you sit down a moment?"

"Well." John Quincy recalled Miss Minerva waiting impatiently for news. "Just a moment. I want to know how you're getting on. Any big arithmetical problems come up yet?"

She shook her head. "Not yet. It really isn't so bad, the work. We haven't many guests, you know. I could be quite happy—if it weren't for poor dad." She sighed. "Ever since I can remember," she added, "my happiness has had an if in it."

He led her on to speak about herself, there in the calm night by that romantic beach. Through her talk flashed little pictures of her motherless childhood on this exotic shore, of a wearing fight against poverty and her father's bitter struggle to send her to school on the mainland, to give her what he considered her proper place in the world. Here was a girl far different from any he had met on Beacon Street, and John Quincy found pleasure in her talk.

Finally he forced himself to leave. As they walked along the balcony they encountered one of the guests, a meek little man with stooped shoulders. Even at that late hour he wore a bathing suit.

"Any luck, Mr Saladine?" the girl inquired.

"Luck ith againth me," he lisped, and passed hastily on.

Carlota Egan laughed softly. "Oh, I really shouldn't," she repented at once. "The poor man."

"What's his trouble?" asked John Quincy.

"He's a tourist—a business man," she said. "Des Moines, or some place like that. And he's had the most appalling accident. He's lost his teeth."

"His teeth!" repeated John Quincy.

"Yes. Like so many things in this world, they were false. He got into a battle with a roller out by the second raft, and they disappeared. Since then he spends all his time out there, peering down into the water by day, and diving down and feeling about by night. One of the tragic figures of history," she added.

John Quincy laughed.

"That's the most tragic part of it," the girl continued. "He's the joke of the beach. But he goes on hunting, so serious. Of course, it is serious for him."

They passed through the public room to the front door. Mr Saladine's tragedy slipped at once from John Quincy's mind.

"Goodnight," he said. "Don't forget about the check, when you see your father tomorrow. I'll look in on you during the day."

"It was so good of you to come," she said. Her hand was in his. "It has helped me along—tremendously."

"Don't you worry. Happy days are not far off. Happy days without an if. Hold the thought!"

"I'll hold it," she promised.

"We'll both hold it." It came to him that he was also holding her hand. He dropped it hastily. "Goodnight," he repeated, and fled through the garden.

In the living-room of Dan's house he was surprised to find Miss Minerva and Charlie Chan sitting together, solemnly staring at each other. Chan rose hurriedly at his entrance.

"Hello," said John Quincy. "I see you have a caller."

"Where in the world have you been?" snapped Miss Minerva. Evidently entertaining a Chinaman had got a bit on her nerves.

"Well—I—" John Quincy hesitated.

"Speak out," said Miss Minerva. "Mr Chan knows everything."

"Most flattering," grinned Chan. "Some things are not entirely well known to me. But about your call on Widow of Waikiki I learn soon after door receives you."

"The devil you did," said John Quincy.

"Simple enough," Chan went on. "Study human people, as I relate to you. Compton lady was friend to Mr Dan Winterslip. Mr Leatherbee rival friend. Enter jealous feelings. Since morning both of these people are under watchful regard of Honolulu police. Into the scene, you walk. I am notified and fly to beach."

"Ah—does he also know—" began John Quincy.

"About the brooch?" finished Miss Minerva. "Yes—I've confessed everything. And he's been kind enough to forgive me."

"But not nice thing to do," added Chan. "Humbly begging pardon to mention it. All cards should repose on table when police are called upon."

"Yes," said Miss Minerva, "he forgave me, but I have been gently chided. I have been made to feel, as he puts it, most naughty."

"So sorry," bowed Chan.

"Well, as a matter of fact," said John Quincy, "I was going to tell Mr Chan the whole story at once." He turned to the Chinaman. "I've already tried to reach you by telephone at the station. When I left the woman's cottage—"

"Police affairs forbid utmost courtesy," interrupted Chan. "I cut in to remark from the beginning, if you will please do so."

"Oh, yes," smiled John Quincy. "Well, the woman herself let me in, and showed me into her little living-room. When I got there this fellow Leatherbee was mixing cocktails by the table—"

Haku appeared at the door. "Mr Charlie Chan wanted by telephone," he announced.

Chan apologized and hastened out.

"I intend to tell everything," John Quincy warned his aunt.

"I shan't interfere," she answered. "That slant-eyed Chinaman has been sitting here looking at me more in sorrow than in anger for the better part of an hour, and I've made up my mind to one thing. I shall have no more secrets from the police."

Chan reentered the room. "As I was saying," John Quincy began, "this fellow Leatherbee was standing by the table, and—"

"Most sorry," said Chan, "but the remainder of that interesting recital is to be told at the station-house."

"At the station-house!" cried John Quincy.

"Precisely the fact. I am presuming you do me the great honor to come with me to that spot. The man Leatherbee is apprehended aboard boat *Niagara* on verge of sailing to Australia. Woman are also apprehended in act of tearful farewell. Both now relax at police station."

"I thought so," said John Quincy.

"One more amazing fact comes into light," added Chan. "In pocket of Leatherbee are the page ruthlessly extracted from guest book. Kindly procure your hat. Outside I have waiting for me one Ford automobile."

XII

TOM BRADE THE BLACKBIRDER

In Hallet's room at headquarters they found the Captain of Detectives seated grimly behind his desk staring at two reluctant visitors. One of the visitors, Mr Stephen Leatherbee, stared back with a look of sullen defiance. Mrs Arlene Compton, late of Broadway and the Automat, was dabbing at her eyes with a tiny handkerchief. John Quincy perceived that she had carelessly allowed tears to play havoc with her make-up.

"Hello, Charlie," said Hallet. "Mr Winterslip, I'm glad you came along. As you may have heard, we've just pulled this young man off the *Niagara*. He seemed inclined to leave us. We found this in his pocket."

He put into the Chinaman's hand a time-yellowed page obviously from Dan Winterslip's guest book. John Quincy and Chan bent over it together. The inscription was written in an old-fashioned hand, and the ink was fading fast. It ran:

"In Hawaii all things are perfect, none more so than the hospitality I have enjoyed in this house.—Joseph E. Gleason, 124 Little Bourke Street, Melbourne, Victoria."

John Quincy turned away, shocked. No wonder that page had been ripped out! Evidently Mr Gleason had not enjoyed the privilege of studying A. S. Hill's book on the principles of rhetoric. How could one thing be more perfect than another?

"Before I take a statement from these people," Hallet was saying, "what's all this about a brooch?"

John Quincy laid the piece of jewelry on the captain's desk. He explained that it had been given Mrs Compton by Dan Winterslip, and told of its being discovered on the floor of the lanai.

"When was it found?" demanded the captain, glaring his disapproval.

"Most regrettable misunderstanding," put in Chan hastily. "Now completely wiped out. The littlest said, sooner repairs are made. Mr Winterslip has already tonight examined this woman—"

"Oh, he has, has he!" Hallet turned angrily on John Quincy. "Just who is conducting this case?"

"Well," began John Quincy uncomfortably, "it seemed best to the family—"

"Damn the family!" Hallet exploded. "This affair is in my hands—"

"Please," broke in Chan soothingly. "Waste of time to winnow that out. Already I have boldness to offer suitable rebukes."

"Well, you talked with the woman, then," said Hallet. "What did you get out of her?"

"Say, listen," put in Mrs Compton. "I want to take back anything I told this bright-eyed boy."

"Lied to him, eh?" said Hallet.

"Why not? What right did he have to question me?" Her voice became wheedling. "I wouldn't lie to a cop," she added.

"You bet your life you wouldn't," Hallet remarked. "Not if you know what's good for you. However, I want to hear what you told this amateur detective. Sometimes lies are significant. Go on, Winterslip."

John Quincy was deeply annoyed. What was this mix-up he had let himself in for, anyhow? He had a notion to rise, and with a cold bow, leave the room. Something told him, however, that he couldn't get away with it.

Very much on his dignity, he repeated the woman's story to him. Winterslip had come to her cottage the night before to make a final appeal for the brooch. On his promise to replace it with something else, she had given it up. He had taken it and left her at nine-thirty.

"That was the last she saw of him," finished John Quincy.

Hallet smiled grimly. "So she told you, at any rate. But she admits she was lying. If you'd had the sense to leave this sort of thing to the proper people—" He wheeled on the woman. "You were lying, weren't you?"

She nodded nonchalantly. "In a way. Dan did leave my cottage at nine-thirty—or a little later. But I went with him—to his house. Oh, it was perfectly proper. Steve went along."

"Oh, yes—Steve." Hallet glanced at Mr Leatherbee, who did not appear quite the ideal chaperon. "Now, young woman, go back to the beginning. Nothing but the truth."

"So help me," said Mrs Compton. She attempted a devastating smile. "I wouldn't lie to you, Captain—you know I wouldn't. I realize you're a big man out here, and—"

"Give me your story," cut in Hallet coldly.

"Sure. Dan dropped into my place for a chat last night about nine, and he found Mr Leatherbee there. He was jealous as sin, Dan was—honest to God, I don't know why. Me and Steve are just pals—eh, Steve?"

"Pals, that's all," said Steve.

"But anyhow, Dan flew off the handle, and we had one grand blow-up. I tried to explain Steve was just stopping over on his way to Australia, and Dan wants to know what's detaining him. So Steve tells about how he lost all his money at bridge on the boat coming out here. 'Will you move on,' says Dan, 'if I pay your passage?' And Steve answers he will, like a shot. Am I getting this straight, Steve?"

"Absolutely," approved Mr Leatherbee. "It's just as she says, Captain. Winterslip offered to give—loan me passage money. It was only a loan. And I agreed to sail on the *Niagara* tonight. He said he had a little cash in his safe at the house, and invited Arlene and me to go back with him—"

"Which we did," said Arlene. "Dan opened the safe and took out a roll of bills. He peeled off three hundred dollars. You didn't often see him in that frame of mind—but as I was saying, he give the money to Steve. Then Steve begins to beef a little—yes, you did, Steve—and wants to know what he's going to do in Australia. Says he don't know a soul down there and he'll just plain starve. Dan was sore at first, then he laughs a nasty little laugh and goes over and tears that there page out of the guest book and gives it to Steve. 'Look him up and tell him you're a friend of mine,' he says. 'Maybe he'll give you a job. The name is Gleason. I've disliked him for twenty years, though he don't know that!'"

"A dirty dig at me," Leatherbee explained. "I took the loan and this Gleason's address and we started to go. Winterslip said he wanted to talk to Arlene, so I came away alone. That was about ten o'clock."

"Where did you go?" Hallet asked.

"I went back to my hotel downtown. I had to pack."

"Back to your hotel, eh? Can you prove it?"

Leatherbee considered. "I don't know. The boy at the desk may remember when I came in, though I didn't stop there for my key—I had it with me. Anyhow, I didn't see Winterslip after that. I just went ahead with my preparations to sail on the *Niagara*, and I must say you've got your nerve—"

"Never mind that!" Hallet turned to the woman. "And after Leatherbee left—what happened then?"

"Well, Dan started in on that brooch again," she said. "It made me sore, too—I never did like a tight-wad. Besides, my nerves was all on edge, I'm funny that way, rows get me all upset. I like everybody pleasant around me. He went on arguing, so finally I ripped off the brooch and threw it at him, and it rolled away under the table somewhere. Then he said he was sorry, and that was when he offered to replace it with something more up-to-date. The best money could buy—that was what he promised. Pretty soon we was friends again—just as good friends as ever when I came away, about ten-fifteen. His last words was that we'd look round the jewelry stores this morning. I ask you, Captain, is it reasonable to think I'd have anything to do with murdering a man who was in a buying mood like that?"

Hallet laughed. "So you left him at ten-fifteen—and went home alone?"

"I did. And when I saw him last he was alive and well—I'll swear to that on a stack of Bibles as high as the Times Building. Gee, don't I wish I was safe on Broadway tonight!"

Hallet thought for a moment. "Well, we'll look into all this. You can both go—I'm not going to hold you at present. But I expect you both to remain in Honolulu until this affair is cleared up, and I advise you not to try any funny business. You've seen tonight what chance you've got to get away."

"Oh, that's all right." The woman stood, looking her relief. "We've got no reason to beat it, have we, Steve?"

"None in the world," agreed Steve. His facetious manner returned. "Speaking for myself," he added, "innocent is my middle name."

"Goodnight, all," said Mrs Compton, and they went out.

Hallet sat staring at the brooch. "A pretty straight story," he remarked, looking at Chan.

"Nice and neat," grinned the Chinaman.

"If true." Hallet shrugged his shoulders. "Well, for the present, I'm willing to believe it." He turned to John Quincy. "Now, Mr Winterslip," he said severely, "I want it understood that any other evidence your family digs up—"

"Oh, that's all right," interrupted the boy. "We'll turn it over at once. I've already given to Chan the newspaper my cousin was reading that night he wrote the letter to Roger Winterslip."

Chan took the paper from his pocket. "Such a busy evening," he explained, "the journal was obscure in my mind. Thanks for the recollection." He called to his chief's attention the mutilated corner.

"Look into that," said Hallet.

"Before sleeping," promised Chan. "Mr Winterslip, we pursue similar paths. The honor of your company in my humble vehicle would pleasure me deeply." Once in the car on the deserted street, the Chinaman spoke again. "The page ripped from guest book, the brooch lying silent on floor. Both are now followed into presence of immovable stone wall. We sway about, looking for other path."

"Then you think those two were telling the truth?" John Quincy asked.

"As to that, I do not venture to remark," Chan replied.

"How about those psychic powers?" inquired John Quincy.

Chan smiled. "Psychic powers somewhat drowsy just now," he admitted. "Need prodding into wakefulness."

"Look here," said John Quincy, "there's no need for you to take me out to Waikiki. Just drop me on King Street, and I'll get a trolley."

"Making humble suggestion," Chan replied, "is it not possible you will accompany me to newspaper rooms, where we set out on different path?"

John Quincy looked at his watch; it was ten minutes past eleven. "I'll be glad to, Charlie," he said.

Chan beamed with pleasure. "Greatly honored by your friendly manner," he remarked. He turned into a side street. "Newspaper of this nature burst out at evening, very quiet now. Somebody may loiter in rooms, if we have happy luck."

They had just that, for the building of the evening journal was open, and in the city room an elderly man with a green shade over his eyes hammered on a typewriter.

"Hello, Charlie," he said cordially.

"Hello, Pete. Mr Winterslip of Boston, I have all the honor to present this Pete Mayberry. For many years he explore waterfront ferreting for whatever news are hiding there."

The elderly man rose and removed his eye-shade, revealing a pleasant twinkle. He was evidently interested to meet a Winterslip.

"We pursue," continued Chan, "one copy of paper marked June sixteen, present year. If you have no inclination for objecting."

Mayberry laughed. "Go to it, Charlie. You know where the files are."

Chan bowed and disappeared. "Your first appearance out here, Mr Winterslip?" inquired the newspaper man.

John Quincy nodded. "I've only just got here," he said, "but I can see it's a rather intriguing place."

"You've said it," smiled Mayberry. "Forty-six years ago I came out from Portsmouth, New Hampshire, to visit relatives. I've been in the newspaper game here ever since—most of the time on the waterfront. There's a life-work for you!"

"You must have seen some changes," remarked John Quincy inanely.

Mayberry nodded. "For the worse. I knew Honolulu in the glamourous days of its isolation, and I've watched it fade into an eighth carbon copy of Babbittville, U.S.A. The waterfront's just a waterfront now—but once, my boy! Once it oozed romance at every pore."

Chan returned, carrying a paper. "Much to be thankful for," he said to Mayberry. "Your kindness are quite overwhelming—"

"Anything doing?" asked Mayberry eagerly.

Chan shook his head. "Presently speaking, no. Our motions just now must be blackly clouded in secrecy."

"Well," said the reporter, "when it comes time to roll them clouds away, don't forget me."

"Impossibility," protested Chan. "Goodnight."

They left Mayberry bending over his typewriter, and at Chan's suggestion went to the All American Restaurant, where the Chinaman ordered two cups of "your inspeakable coffee." While they waited to be served, he spread out on the table his complete copy of the newspaper, and laying the torn page on its counterpart, carefully removed the upper right-hand corner.

"The missing fragment," he explained. For a time he studied it thoughtfully, and finally shook his head. "I apprehend nothing to startle," he admitted. He handed it across the table. "If you will condescend greatly—"

John Quincy took the bit of newspaper. On one side was the advertisement of a Japanese dealer in shirtings who wrote his own publicity. Anyone might carry off, he said, six yards for the price of five. And in case the buyer cried loudly in amaze, how can do, it was a matter he was happy to explain. John Quincy laughed aloud.

"Ah," said Chan, "you are by rights mirthful. Kiku-chi, purveyor of shirting cloth, seize on grand English language and make it into idiotic jumble. On that side are nothing to detain us. But humbly hinting you reverse the fragment—"

John Quincy reversed it. The other side was a part of the shipping page. He read it carefully, news of sailings and arrivals, there would be places for five passengers to the Orient on the *Shinyo Maru*, leaving Wednesday, the *Wilhelmina* was six hundred and forty miles east of Makupuu Point, the brig *Mary Jane* from the Treaty Ports——

John Quincy started, and caught his breath. A small item in tiny print had met his eye.

"Among the passengers who will arrive here on the *Sonoma* from Australia a week from Saturday are: Mr and Mrs Thomas Macan Brade, of Calcutta—"

John Quincy sat staring at the unwashed window of the All American Restaurant. His mind went back to the deck of the *President Tyler*, to a lean old missionary telling a tale of a bright morning on Apiang, a grave under a palm tree. "Mr and Mrs Thomas Macan Brade, of Calcutta." He heard again the missionary's high-pitched voice. "A callous brute, a pirate and adventurer. Tom Brade, the blackbirder."

But Brade had been buried in a long pine box on Apiang. Even at the Crossroads of the Pacific, his path and that of Dan Winterslip could hardly have crossed again.

The waiter brought the coffee. Chan said nothing, watching John Quincy closely. Finally the Chinaman spoke: "You have much to tell me."

John Quincy looked around quickly, he had forgotten Chan's presence.

His dilemma was acute. Must he here in this soiled restaurant in a far town reveal to a Chinaman that ancient blot on the Winterslip name? What would Aunt Minerva say? Well, only a short time ago she had remarked that she was resolved to have no more secrets from the police. However, there was family pride—

John Quincy's eye fell on the Japanese waiter. What were those lines from *The Mikado*? "But family pride must be denied and mortified and set aside."

The boy smiled. "Yes, Charlie," he admitted, "I have much to tell you." And over the inspeakable coffee of the All American Restaurant he repeated to the detective the story the Reverend Frank Upton had told on the *President Tyler*.

Chan beamed. "Now," he cried, "we arrive in the neighborhood of something! Brade the blackbirder, master *Maid of Shiloh* boat, on which Mr Dan Winterslip are first officer—"

"But Brade was buried on Apiang," protested John Quincy.

"Yes, indeed. And who saw him, pardon me? Was it then an unsealed box? Oh, no!" Chan's eyes were dancing. "Please recollect something more. The strong box of ohia wood. Initials on it are T.M.B. Mysteries yet, but we move, we advance!"

"I guess we do," admitted John Quincy.

"This much we grasp," Chan continued. "Dan Winterslip repose for quiet hour on lanai, in peaceful reading. This news assault his eye. He now leaps up, paces about, flees to dock to send letter requesting, please the ohia wood box must be buried deep in Pacific. Why?" Fumbling in his pocket, Chan took out a sheaf of papers, evidently lists of steamer arrivals. "On Saturday just gone by, the *Sonoma* make this port. Among passengers—yes—yes—Thomas Macan Brade and honorable wife, Calcutta. It is here inscribed they arrive to stay, not being present when *Sonoma* persist on journey. On the night of Monday, Mr Dan Winterslip are foully slain."

"Which makes Mr Brade an important person to locate," said John Quincy.

"How very true. But the hurry are not intense. No boats sailing now. Before sleeping, I will investigate downtown hotels, Waikiki tomorrow. Where are you, Mr Brade?" Chan seized the check. "No—pardon me—the honor of paying for this poison-tasting beverage must be mine."

Out in the street, he indicated an approaching trolley. "It bears imprint of your destination," he pointed out. "You will require sleep. We meet tomorrow. Congratulations on most fruitful evening."

Once more John Quincy was on a Waikiki car. Weary but thrilled, he took out his pipe and filling it, lighted up. What a day! He seemed to have lived a lifetime since he landed that very morning. He perceived that his smoke was blowing in the face of a tired little Japanese woman beside him. "Pardon me," he remarked, and knocking the pipe against the side rail, put it in his pocket. The woman stared at him in meek startled wonder; no one had ever asked her pardon before.

On the seat behind John Quincy a group of Hawaiian boys with yellow leis about their necks twanged on steel guitars and sang a plaintive love song. The trolley rattled on through the fragrant night; above the clatter of the wheels the music rose with a sweet intensity. John Quincy leaned back and closed his eyes.

A clock struck the hour of midnight. Another day—Wednesday—it flashed through his mind that today his firm in Boston would offer that preferred stock for the shoe people in Lynn. Would the issue be over-subscribed? No matter.

Here he was, out in the middle of the Pacific on a trolley-car. Behind him brown-skinned boys were singing a melancholy love song of long ago, and the moon was shining on crimson poinciana trees. And somewhere on this tiny island a man named Thomas Macan Brade slept under a mosquito netting. Or lay awake, perhaps, thinking of Dan Winterslip.

XIII

THE LUGGAGE IN ROOM NINETEEN

John Quincy emerged from sleep the next morning with a great effort, and dragged his watch from under the pillow. Eight-thirty! Good lord, he was due at the office at nine! A quick bath and shave, a brief pause at the breakfast table, a run past the Public Gardens and the Common and down to School Street—

He sat up in bed. Why was he imprisoned under mosquito netting? What was the meaning of the little lizard that sported idly outside the cloth? Oh, yes—Honolulu. He was in Hawaii, and he'd never reach his office by nine. It was five thousand miles away.

The low murmur of breakers on the beach confirmed him in this discovery and stepping to his window, he gazed out at the calm sparkling morning. Yes, he was in Honolulu entangled in a murder mystery, consorting with Chinese detectives and Waikiki Widows, following clues. The new day held interesting promise. He must hurry to find what it would bring forth.

Haku informed him that his aunt and Barbara had already breakfasted, and set before him a reddish sort of cantaloupe which was, he explained in answer to the boy's question, a papaya. When he had eaten, John Quincy went out on the lanai. Barbara stood there, staring at the beach. A new Barbara, with the old vivacity, the old joy of living, submerged; a pale girl with sorrow in her eyes. John Quincy put his arm about her shoulder; she was a Winterslip and the family was the family. Again he felt in his heart that flare of anger against the "person or persons unknown" who had brought this grief upon her. The guilty must pay—Egan or whoever, Brade or Leatherbee or the chorus girl. Pay and pay dearly—he was resolved on that.

"My dear girl," he began. "What can I say to you—"

"You've said it all, without speaking," she answered. "See, John Quincy, this is my beach. When I was only five I swam alone to that first float. He—he was so proud of me."

"It's a lovely spot, Barbara," he told her.

"I knew you'd think so. One of these days we'll swim together out to the reef, and I'll teach you to ride a surf-board. I want your visit to be a happy one."

He shook his head. "It can't be that," he said, "because of you. But because of you, I'm mighty glad I came."

She pressed his hand. "I'm going out to sit by the water. Will you come?"

The bamboo curtain parted, and Miss Minerva joined them. "Well, John Quincy," she said sharply, "this is a pretty hour for you to appear. If you're going to rescue me from lotus land, you'll have to be immune yourself."

He smiled. "Just getting acclimated," he explained. "I'll follow you in a moment, Barbara," he added, and held open the door for her.

"I waited up," Miss Minerva began, when the girl had gone, "until eleven-thirty. But I'd had very little sleep the night before, and that was my limit. I make no secret of it—I'm very curious to know what happened at the police station."

He repeated to her the story told by Mrs Compton and Leatherbee. "I wish I'd been present," she said. "A pretty woman can fool all the men in Christendom. Lies, probably."

"Maybe," admitted John Quincy. "But wait a minute. Later on, Chan and I followed up your newspaper clue. And it led us to a startling discovery."

"Of course it did," she beamed. "What was it?"

"Well," he said, "first of all, I met a missionary on the boat." He told her the Reverend Frank Upton's tale of that morning on Apiang, and added the news that a man named Thomas Macan Brade was now in Honolulu.

She was silent for a time. "So Dan was a blackbirder," she remarked at last. "How charming! Such a pleasant man, too. But then, I learned that lesson early in life—the brighter the smile, the darker the past. All this will make delightful reading in the Boston papers, John Quincy."

"Oh, they'll never get it," her nephew said.

"Don't deceive yourself. Newspapers will go to the ends of the earth for a good murder. I once wrote letters to all the editors in Boston urging them to print no more details about homicides. It hadn't the slightest effect—though I did get an acknowledgment of my favor from the *Herald*."

John Quincy glanced at his watch. "Perhaps I should go down to the station. Anything in the morning paper?"

"A very hazy interview with Captain Hallet. The police have unearthed important clues, and promise early results. You know—the sort of thing they always give out just after a murder."

The boy looked at her keenly. "Ah," he said, "then you read newspaper accounts of the kind you tried to suppress?"

"Certainly I do," snapped his aunt. "There's little enough excitement in my life. But I gladly gave up my port wine because I felt intoxicants were bad for the lower classes, and—"

Haku interrupted with the news that John Quincy was wanted on the telephone. When the boy returned to the lanai, there was a brisk air of business about him.

"That was Charlie," he announced. "The day's work is about to get under way. They've located Mr and Mrs Brade at the Reef and Palm Hotel, and I'm to meet Charlie there in fifteen minutes."

"The Reef and Palm," repeated Miss Minerva. "You see, it keeps coming back to Egan. I'd wager a set of Browning against a modern novel that he's the man who did it."

"You'd lose your Browning, and then where would you be when the lecture season started?" laughed John Quincy. "I never knew you to be so stupid before." His face became serious. "By the way, will you explain to Barbara that I can't join her, after all?"

Miss Minerva nodded. "Go along," she said. "I envy you all this. First time in my life I ever wished I were a man."

John Quincy approached the Reef and Palm by way of the beach. The scene was one of bright serenity. A few languid tourists lolled upon the sand; others, more ambitious, were making picture post-card history out where the surf began. A great white steamer puffed blackly into port. Standing in water up to their necks, a group of Hawaiian women paused in their search for luncheon delicacies to enjoy a moment's gossip.

John Quincy passed Arlene Compton's cottage and entered the grounds of the Reef and Palm. On the beach not far from the hotel, an elderly Englishwoman sat on a camp stool with an easel and canvas before her. She was seeking to capture something of that exotic scene—vainly seeking, for John Quincy, glancing over her shoulder, perceived that her work was terrible. She turned and looked at him, a weary look of protest against his intrusion, and he was sorry she had caught him in the act of smiling at her inept canvas.

Chan had not yet arrived at the hotel, and the clerk informed John Quincy that Miss Carlota had gone to the city. For that interview with her father, no doubt. He hoped that the evidence of the check would bring about Egan's release. It seemed to him that the man was being held on a rather flimsy pretext, anyhow.

He sat down on the lanai at the side, where he could see both the path that led in from the street and the restless waters of the Pacific. On the beach near by a man in a purple bathing suit reclined dejectedly, and John Quincy smiled in recollection. Mr Saladine, alone with his tragedy, peering out at the waters that had robbed him—waiting, no doubt, for the tide to yield up its loot.

Some fifteen or twenty minutes passed, and then John Quincy heard voices in the garden. He saw that Hallet and Chan were coming up the walk and went to meet them at the front door.

"Splendid morning," said Chan. "Nice day to set out on new path leading unevitably to important discovery."

John Quincy accompanied them to the desk. The Japanese clerk regarded them with sullen unfriendliness; he had not forgotten the events of the day before. Information had to be dragged from him bit by bit. Yes, there was a Mr and Mrs Brade stopping there. They arrived last Saturday, on the steamship *Sonoma*. Mr Brade was not about at the moment. Mrs Brade was on the beach painting pretty pictures.

"Good," said Hallet, "I'll have a look around their room before I question them. Take us there."

The Japanese hesitated. "Boy!" he called. It was only a bluff; the Reef and Palm had no bell-boys. Finally, with an air of injured dignity, he led the way down a long corridor on the same floor as the office and unlocked the door of nineteen, the last room on the right. Hallet strode in and went to the window.

"Here—wait a minute," he called to the clerk. He pointed to the elderly woman painting on the beach. "That Mrs Brade?"

"Yes-s," hissed the Japanese.

"All right—go along." The clerk went out. "Mr Winterslip, I'll ask you to sit here in the window and keep an eye on the lady. If she starts to come in, let me know." He stared eagerly about the poorly furnished bedroom. "Now, Mr Brade, I wonder what you've got?"

John Quincy took the post assigned him, feeling decidedly uncomfortable. This didn't seem quite honorable to him. However, he probably wouldn't be called upon to do any searching himself, and if policemen were forced to do disagreeable things—well, they should have thought of that before they became policemen. Not that either Hallet or Chan appeared to be embarrassed by the task before them.

There was a great deal of luggage in the room—English luggage, which is usually large and impressive. John Quincy noted a trunk, two enormous bags, and a smaller case. All were plastered with labels of the *Sonoma*, and beneath were the worn fragments of earlier labels, telling a broken story of other ships and far hotels.

Hallet and Chan were old hands at this game; they went through Brade's trunk rapidly and thoroughly, but without finding anything of note. The captain turned his attention to the small traveling case. With every evidence of delight he drew forth a packet of letters, and sat down with them at a table. John Quincy was shocked. Reading other people's mail was, in his eyes, something that simply wasn't done.

It was done by Hallet, however. In a moment the captain spoke. "Seems to have been in the British civil service in Calcutta, but he's resigned," he announced to Chan. "Here's a letter from his superior in London referring to Brade's thirty-six years on the job, and saying he's sorry to lose him." Hallet took up another letter, his face brightened as he read. "Say—this is more like it!" He handed the typewritten page to Chan. The Chinaman looked at it, and his eyes sparkled. "Most interesting," he cried, and turned it over to John Quincy.

The boy hesitated. The standards of a lifetime are not easily abandoned. But the others had read it first, so he put aside his scruples. The letter was several months old, and was addressed to Brade in Calcutta.

"Dear Sir: In reply to your inquiry of the sixth instant, would say that Mr Daniel Winterslip is alive and is a resident of this city. His address is 3947 Kalia Road, Waikiki, Honolulu, T.H."

The signature was that of the British consul at Honolulu. John Quincy returned the epistle to Hallet, who put it in his pocket. At that instant Chan, who had been exploring one of the larger bags, emitted a little grunt of satisfaction.

"What is it, Charlie?" Hallet asked.

The Chinaman set out on the table before his chief a small tin box, and removed the lid. It was filled with cigarettes. "Corsican brand," he announced cheerfully.

"Good," said Hallet. "It begins to look as though Mr Thomas Macan Brade would have a lot to explain."

They continued their researches, while John Quincy sat silent by the window. Presently Carlota Egan appeared outside. She walked slowly to a chair on the lanai, and sat down. For a moment she stared at the breakers, then she began to weep.

John Quincy turned uncomfortably away. It came to him that here in this so-called paradise sorrow was altogether too rampant. The only girls he knew were given to frequent tears, and not without reason.

"If you'll excuse me—" he said. Hallet and Chan, searching avidly, made no reply, and climbing over the sill, he stepped on to the lanai. The girl looked up as he approached.

"Oh," she said, "I thought I was alone."

"You'd like to be, perhaps," he answered. "But it might help if you told me what has happened. Did you speak to your father about that check?"

She nodded. "Yes, I showed it to him. And what do you think he did? He snatched it out of my hand and tore it into a hundred pieces. He gave me the pieces to—to throw away. And he said I was never to mention it to a soul."

"I don't understand that," frowned John Quincy.

"Neither do I. He was simply furious—not like himself at all. And when I told him you knew about it, he lost his temper again."

"But you can rely on me. I shan't tell anyone."

"I know that. But of course father wasn't so sure of you as—as I am. Poor dad—he's having a horrible time of it. They don't give him a moment's rest—keep after him constantly—trying to make him tell. But all the policemen in the world couldn't—Oh, poor old dad!"

She was weeping again, and John Quincy felt toward her as he had felt toward Barbara. He wanted to put his arm about her, just by way of comfort and cheer. But alas, Carlota Maria Egan was not a Winterslip.

"Now, now," he said, "that won't do a bit of good."

She looked at him through her tears. "Won't it? I—I don't know. It seems to help a little. But"—she dried her eyes—"I really haven't time for it now. I must go in and see about lunch."

She rose, and John Quincy walked with her along the balcony. "I wouldn't worry if I were you," he said. "The police are on an entirely new trail this morning."

"Really?" she answered eagerly.

"Yes. There's a man named Brade stopping at your hotel. You know him, I suppose?"

She shook her head. "No, I don't."

"What! Why, he's a guest here."

"He was. But he isn't here now."

"Wait a minute!" John Quincy laid his hand on her arm, and they stopped. "This is interesting. Brade's gone, you say?"

"Yes. I understand from the clerk that Mr and Mrs Brade arrived here last Saturday. But early Tuesday morning, before my boat got in, Mr Brade disappeared and he hasn't been seen since."

"Mr Brade gets better all the time," John Quincy said. "Hallet and Chan are in his room now, and they've unearthed some rather intriguing facts. You'd better go in and tell Hallet what you've just told me."

They entered the lobby by a side door. As they did so, a slim young Hawaiian boy was coming in through the big door at the front. Something in his manner caught the attention of John Quincy, and he stopped. At that instant a purple bathing suit slipped by him, and Mr Saladine also approached the desk. Carlota Egan went on down the corridor toward room nineteen, but John Quincy remained in the lobby.

The Hawaiian boy moved rather diffidently toward the clerk. "Excuse me, please," he said. "I come to see Mr Brade. Mr Thomas Brade."

"Mr Brade not here," replied the Japanese.

"Then I will wait till he comes."

The clerk frowned. "No good. Mr Brade not in Honolulu now."

"Not in Honolulu!" The Hawaiian seemed startled by the news.

"Mrs Brade outside on the beach," continued the Japanese.

"Oh, then Mr Brade returns," said the boy with evident relief. "I call again."

He turned away, moving rapidly now. The clerk addressed Mr Saladine, who was hovering near the cigar case. "Yes, sir, please?"

"Thigarettes," said the bereft Mr Saladine.

The Japanese evidently knew the brand desired, and handed over a box.

"Juth put it on my bill," said Saladine. He stood for a moment staring after the Hawaiian, who was disappearing through the front door. As he swung round his eyes encountered those of John Quincy. He looked quickly away and hurried out.

The two policemen and the girl entered from the corridor. "Well, Mr Winterslip," said Hallet, "the bird has flown."

"So I understand," John Quincy answered.

"But we'll find him," continued Hallet. "I'll go over these islands with a drag-net. First of all, I want a talk with his wife." He turned to Carlota Egan. "Get her in here," he ordered. The girl looked at him. "Please," he added.

She motioned to the clerk, who went out the door.

"By the way," remarked John Quincy, "someone was just here asking for Brade."

"What's that!" Hallet was interested.

"A young Hawaiian, about twenty, I should say. Tall and slim. If you go to the door, you may catch a glimpse of him."

Hallet hurried over and glanced out into the garden. In a second he returned. "Humph," he said. "I know him. Did he say he'd come again?"

"He did."

Hallet considered. "I've changed my mind," he announced. "I won't question Mrs Brade, after all. For the present, I don't want her to know we're looking for her husband. I'll trust you to fix that up with your clerk," he added to the girl. She nodded. "Lucky we left things as we found them in nineteen," he went on. "Unless she misses that letter and the cigarettes, which isn't likely, we're all right. Now, Miss Egan, we three will go into your father's office there behind the desk, and leave the door open. When Mrs Brade comes in, I want you to question her about her husband's absence. Get all you can out of her. I'll be listening."

"I understand," the girl said.

Hallet, Chan and John Quincy went into Jim Egan's sanctum. "You found nothing else in the room?" the latter inquired of the Chinaman.

Chan shook his head. "Even so, fates are in smiling mood. What we have now are plentiful."

"Sh!" warned Hallet.

"Mrs Brade, a young man was just here inquiring, for your husband." It was Carlota Egan's voice.

"Really?" The accent was unmistakably British.

"He wanted to know where he could find him. We couldn't say."

"No—of course not."

"Your husband has left town, Mrs Brade?"

"Yes. I fancy he has."

"You know when he will return, perhaps?"

"I really couldn't say. Is the mail in?"

"Not yet. We expect it about one."

"Thank you so much."

"Go to the door," Hallet directed John Quincy.

"She's gone to her room," announced the boy.

The three of them emerged from Egan's office.

"Oh, Captain," said the girl, "I'm afraid I wasn't very successful."

"That's all right," replied Hallet. "I didn't think you would be." The clerk was again at his post behind the desk. Hallet turned to him. "Look here," he said. "I understand someone was here a minute ago asking for Brade. It was Dick Kaohla, wasn't it?"

"Yes-s," answered the Japanese.

"Had he been here before to see Brade?"

"Yes-s. Sunday night. Mr Brade and him have long talk on the beach."

Hallet nodded grimly. "Come on, Charlie," he said. "We've got our work cut out for us. Wherever Brade is, we must find him."

John Quincy stepped forward. "Pardon me, Captain," he remarked. "But if you don't mind—just who is Dick Kaohla?"

Hallet hesitated. "Kaohla's father—he's dead now—was a sort of confidential servant to Dan Winterslip. The boy's just plain no good. And oh, yes—he's the grandson of that woman who's over at your place now. Kamaikui—is that her name?"

XIV

WHAT KAOHLA CARRIED

Several days slipped by so rapidly John Quincy scarcely noted their passing. Dan Winterslip was sleeping now under the royal palms of the lovely island where he had been born. Sun and moon shone brightly in turn on his last dwelling place, but those who sought the person he had encountered that Monday night on his lanai were still groping in the dark.

Hallet had kept his word, he was combing the Islands for Brade. But Brade was nowhere. Ships paused at the crossroads and sailed again; the name of Thomas Macan Brade was on no sailing list. Through far settlements that were called villages but were nothing save clusters of Japanese huts, in lonely coves where the surf moaned dismally, over pineapple and sugar plantations, the emissaries of Hallet pursued their quest. Their efforts came to nothing.

John Quincy drifted idly with the days. He knew now the glamour of Waikiki waters; he had felt their warm embrace. Every afternoon he experimented with a board in the malihini surf, and he was eager for the moment when he could dare the big rollers farther out. Boston seemed like a tale that is told, State Street and Beacon memories of another more active existence now abandoned. No longer was he at a loss to understand his aunt's reluctance to depart these friendly shores.

Early Friday afternoon Miss Minerva found him reading a book on the lanai. Something in the nonchalance of his manner irritated her. She had always been for action, and the urge was on her even in Hawaii.

"Have you seen Mr Chan lately?" she inquired.

"Talked with him this morning. They're doing their best to find Brade."

"Humph," sniffed Miss Minerva. "Their best is none too good. I'd like to have a few Boston detectives on this case."

"Oh, give them time," yawned John Quincy.

"They've had three days," she snapped. "Time enough. Brade never left this island of Oahu, that's certain. And when you consider that you can drive across it in a motor in two hours, and around it in about six, Mr Hallet's brilliance does not impress. I'll have to end by solving this thing myself."

John Quincy laughed. "Yes, maybe you will."

"Well, I've given them the two best clues they have. If they'd keep their eyes open the way I do—"

"Charlie's eyes are open," protested John Quincy.

"Think so? They look pretty sleepy to me."

Barbara appeared on the lanai, dressed for a drive. Her eyes were somewhat happier; a bit of color had come back to her cheeks. "What are you reading, John Quincy?" she asked.

He held up the book. "*The City by the Golden Gate*," he told her.

"Oh, really? If you're interested, I believe dad had quite a library on San Francisco. I remember there was a history of the stock exchange—he wanted me to read it, but I couldn't."

"You missed a good one," John Quincy informed her. "I finished it this morning. I've read five other books on San Francisco since I came."

His aunt stared at him. "What for?" she asked.

"Well—" He hesitated. "I've taken sort of a fancy to the town. I don't know—sometimes I think I'd rather like to live there."

Miss Minerva smiled grimly. "And they sent you out to take me back to Boston," she remarked.

"Boston's all right," said her nephew hastily. "It's Winterslip headquarters—but its hold has never been strong enough to prevent an occasional Winterslip from hitting the trail. You know, when I came into San Francisco harbor, I had the oddest feeling." He told them about it. "And the more I saw of the city, the better I liked it. There's a snap and sparkle in the air, and the people seem to know how to get the most out of life."

Barbara smiled on him approvingly. "Follow that impulse, John Quincy," she advised.

"Maybe I will. All this reminds me—I must write a letter." He rose and left the lanai.

"Does he really intend to desert Boston?" Barbara asked.

Miss Minerva shook her head. "Just a moment's madness," she explained. "I'm glad he's going through it—he'll be more human in the future. But as for leaving Boston! John Quincy! As well expect Bunker Hill Monument to emigrate to England."

In his room upstairs, however, John Quincy's madness was persisting. He had never completed that letter to Agatha Parker, but he now plunged into his task with enthusiasm. San Francisco was his topic, and he wrote well. He pictured the city in words that glowed with life, and he wondered—just a suggestion—how she'd like to live there.

Agatha was now, he recalled, on a ranch in Wyoming—her first encounter with the West—and that was providential. She had felt for herself the lure of the wide open spaces. Well, the farther you went the wider and opener they got. In California life was all color and light. Just a suggestion, of course.

As he sealed the flap of the envelope, he seemed to glimpse Agatha's thin patrician face, and his heart sank. Her gray eyes were cool, so different from Barbara's, so very different from those of Carlota Maria Egan.

On Saturday afternoon John Quincy had an engagement to play golf with Harry Jennison. He drove up Nuuanu Valley in Barbara's roadster—for Dan Winterslip's will had been read and everything he possessed was Barbara's now. In that sheltered spot a brisk rain was falling, as is usually the case, though the sun was shining brightly. John Quincy had grown accustomed to this phenomenon; "liquid sunshine" the people of Hawaii call such rain, and pay no attention to it. Half a dozen different rainbows added to the beauty of the Country Club links.

Jennison was waiting on the veranda, a striking figure in white. He appeared genuinely glad to see his guest, and they set out on a round of golf that John Quincy would long remember. Never before had he played amid such beauty. The low hills stood on guard, their slopes bright with tropical colors—the yellow of kukui trees, the gray of ferns, the emerald of ohia and banana trees, here and there a splotch of brick-red earth. The course was a green velvet carpet beneath their feet, the showers came and went. Jennison was a proficient driver, but the boy was his superior on approaches, and at the end of the match John Quincy was four up. They putted through a rainbow and returned to the locker room.

In the roadster going home, Jennison brought up the subject of Dan Winterslip's murder. John Quincy was interested to get the reaction of a lawyer to the evidence.

"I've kept more or less in touch with the case," Jennison said. "Egan is still my choice."

Somehow, John Quincy resented this. A picture of Carlota Egan's lovely but unhappy face flashed through his mind. "How about Leatherbee and the Compton woman?" he asked.

"Well, of course, I wasn't present when they told their story," Jennison replied. "But Hallet claims it sounded perfectly plausible. And it doesn't seem likely that if he'd had anything to do with the murder, Leatherbee would have been fool enough to keep that page from the guest book."

"There's Brade, too," John Quincy suggested.

"Yes—Brade complicates things. But when they run him down—if they do—I imagine the result will be nil."

"You know that Kamaikui's grandson is mixed up somehow with Brade?"

"So I understand. It's a matter that wants looking into. But mark my words, when all these trails are followed to the end, everything will come back to Jim Egan."

"What have you against Egan?" inquired John Quincy, swerving to avoid another car.

"I have nothing against Egan," Jennison replied. "But I can't forget the look on Dan Winterslip's face that day he told me he was afraid of the man. Then there is the stub of the Corsican cigarette. Most important of all, Egan's silence regarding his business with Winterslip. Men who are facing a charge of murder, my boy, talk, and talk fast. Unless it so happens that what they have to say would further incriminate them."

They drove on in silence into the heart of the city. "Hallet tells me you're doing a little detective work yourself," smiled Jennison.

"I've tried, but I'm a duffer," John Quincy admitted. "Just at present my efforts consist of a still hunt for that watch Aunt Minerva saw on the murderer's wrist. Whenever I see a wrist watch I get as close to it as I can, and stare. But as most of my sleuthing is done in the day time, it isn't so easy to determine whether the numeral two is bright or dim."

"Persistence," urged Jennison. "That's the secret of a good detective. Stick to the job and you may succeed yet."

The lawyer was to dine with the family at Waikiki. John Quincy set him down at his office, where he had a few letters to sign, and then drove him out to the beach. Barbara was gowned in white; she was slim and wistful and beautiful, and considering the events of the immediate past, the dinner was a cheerful one.

They had coffee on the lanai. Presently Jennison rose and stood by Barbara's chair. "We've something to tell you," he announced. He looked down at the girl. "Is that right, my dear?"

Barbara nodded.

"Your cousin and I"—the lawyer turned to the two from Boston— "have been fond of each other for a long time. We shall be married very quietly in a week or so—"

"Oh, Harry—not a week," said Barbara.

"Well, as you wish. But very soon."

"Yes, very soon," she repeated.

"And leave Honolulu for a time," Jennison continued. "Naturally, Barbara feels she cannot stay here for the present—so many memories—you both understand. She has authorized me to put this house up for sale—"

"But, Harry," Barbara protested, "you make me sound so inhospitable. Telling my guests that the house is for sale and I am leaving—"

"Nonsense, my dear," said Aunt Minerva. "John Quincy and I understand, quite. I sympathize with your desire to get away." She rose.

"I'm sorry," said Jennison. "I did sound a little abrupt. But I'm naturally eager to take care of her now."

"Of course," John Quincy agreed.

Miss Minerva bent over and kissed the girl. "If your mother were here, dear child," she said, "she couldn't wish for your happiness any more keenly than I do." Barbara reached up impulsively and put her arms about the older woman.

John Quincy shook Jennison's hand. "You're mighty lucky."

"I think so," Jennison answered.

The boy went over to Barbara, "All—all good wishes," he said. She nodded, but did not reply. He saw there were tears in her eyes.

Presently Miss Minerva withdrew to the living-room, and John Quincy, feeling like a fifth wheel, made haste to leave the two together. He went out on the beach. The pale moon rode high amid the golden stars, romance whispered through the coconut palms. He thought of the scene he had witnessed that breathless night on the *President Tyler*—only two in the world, love quick and overwhelming—well, this was the setting for it. Here on this beach they had walked two and two since the beginning of time, whispering the same vows, making the same promises, whatever their color and creed. Suddenly the boy felt lonely.

Barbara was a Winterslip, and not for him. Why then did he feel again that frustrated pang in his heart? She had chosen and her choice was fitting, what affair was it of his?

He found himself moving slowly toward the Reef and Palm Hotel. For a chat with Carlota Egan? But why should he want to talk with this girl, whose outlook was so different from that of the world he knew? The girls at home were on a level with the men in brains—often, indeed, they were superior, seemed to be looking down from a great height. They discussed that article in the latest *Atlantic*, Shaw's grim philosophy, the new Sargent at the Art Gallery. Wasn't that the sort of talk he should be seeking here? Or was it? Under these palms on this romantic beach, with the moon riding high over Diamond Head?

Carlota Egan was seated behind the desk in the deserted lobby of the Reef and Palm, a worried frown on her face.

"You've come at the psychological moment," she cried, and smiled. "I'm having the most awful struggle."

"Arithmetic?" John Quincy inquired.

"Compound fractions, it seems to me. I'm making out the Brades' bill."

He came round the desk and stood at her side. "Let me help you."

"It's so fearfully involved." She looked up at him, and he wished they could do their sums on the beach. "Mr Brade has been away since Tuesday morning, and we don't charge for any absence of more than three days. So that comes out of it. Maybe you can figure it—I can't."

"Charge him anyhow," suggested John Quincy.

"I'd like to—that would simplify everything. But it's not dad's way."

John Quincy took up a pencil. "What rate are they paying?" he inquired. She told him, and he began to figure. It wasn't a simple matter, even for a bond expert. John Quincy frowned too.

Someone entered the front door of the Reef and Palm. Looking up, John Quincy beheld the Hawaiian boy, Dick Kaohla. He carried a bulky object, wrapped in newspapers.

"Mr Brade here now?" he asked.

Carlota Egan shook her head. "No, he hasn't returned."

"I will wait," said the boy.

"But we don't know where he is, or when he will come back," the girl protested.

"He will be here soon," the Hawaiian replied. "I wait on the lanai." He went out the side door, still carrying his clumsy burden. John Quincy and the girl stared at each other.

"'We move, we advance!'" John Quincy quoted in a low voice. "Brade will be here soon! Would you mind going out on the lanai and telling me where Kaohla is now?"

Quickly the girl complied. She returned in a few seconds. "He's taken a chair at the far end."

"Out of earshot?"

"Quite. You want the telephone—"

But John Quincy was already in the booth. Charlie Chan's voice came back over the wire.

"Most warm congratulations. You are number one detective yourself. Should my self-starter not indulge in stubborn spasm, I will make immediate connection with you."

John Quincy returned to the desk, smiling. "Charlie's flying to us in his Ford. Begins to look as though we were getting somewhere now. But about this bill. Mrs Brade's board and room I make sixteen dollars. The charge against Mr Brade—one week's board and room minus four days' board—totals nine dollars and sixty-two cents."

"How can I ever thank you?" said the girl.

"By telling me again about your childhood on this beach." A shadow crossed her face. "Oh, I'm sorry I've made you unhappy."

"Oh, no—you couldn't." She shook her head. "I've never been—so very happy. Always an 'if' in it, as I told you before. That morning on the ferry I think I was nearest to real happiness. I seemed to have escaped from life for a moment."

"I remember how you laughed at my hat."

"Oh—I hope you've forgiven me."

"Nonsense. I'm mighty glad I was able to make you laugh like that." Her great eyes stared into the future, and John Quincy pitied her. He had known others like her, others who loved their fathers, built high hopes for them, then saw them drift into a baffled old age. One of the girl's slender, tanned hands lay on the desk, John Quincy put his own upon it. "Don't be unhappy," he urged. "It's such a wonderful night. The moon—you're a what-you-may-call-it—a kamaaina, I know, but I'll bet you never saw the moon looking so well before. It's like a thousand-dollar gold piece, pale but negotiable. Shall we go out and spend it?"

Gently she drew her hand away. "There were seven bottles of charged water sent to the room. Thirty-five cents each—"

"What? Oh, the Brades' bill. Yes, that means two forty-five more. I'd like to mention the stars too. Isn't it odd how close the stars seem in the tropics—"

She smiled. "We mustn't forget the trunks and bags. Three dollars for bringing them up from the dock."

"Say—that's rather steep. Well, it goes down on the record. Have I ever told you that all this natural beauty out here has left its imprint on your face? In the midst of so much loveliness, one couldn't be anything but—"

"Mrs Brade had three trays to the room. That's seventy-five cents more."

"Extravagant lady! Brade will be sorry he came back, for more reasons than one. Well, I've got that. Anything else?"

"Just the laundry. Ninety-seven cents."

"Fair enough. Adding it all up, I get thirty-two dollars and sixty-nine cents. Let's call it an even thirty-three."

She laughed. "Oh, no. We can't do that."

Mrs Brade came slowly into the lobby from the lanai. She paused at the desk. "Has there been a message?" she inquired.

"No, Mrs Brade," the girl answered. She handed over the slip of paper. "Your bill."

"Ah, yes. Mr Brade will attend to this the moment he returns."

"You expect him soon?"

"I really can't say." The Englishwoman moved on into the corridor leading to nineteen.

"Full of information, as usual," smiled John Quincy. "Why, here's Charlie now."

Chan came briskly to the desk, followed by another policeman, also in plain clothes.

"Automobile act noble," he announced, "having fondly feeling for night air." He nodded toward his companion. "Introducing Mr Spencer. Now, what are the situation? Humbly hinting you speak fast."

John Quincy told him Kaohla was waiting on the lanai, and mentioned the unwieldy package carried by the boy. Chan nodded.

"Events are turning over rapidly," he said. He addressed the girl. "Please kindly relate to this Kaohla that Brade has arrived and would wish to encounter him here." She hesitated. "No, no," added Chan hastily, "I forget nice heathen delicacy. It is not pretty I should ask a lady to scatter false lies from ruby lips. I humbly demand forgiveness. Content yourself with a veiled pretext bringing him here."

The girl smiled and went out. "Mr Spencer," said Chan, "I make bold to suggest you interrogate this Hawaiian. My reckless wanderings among words of unlimitable English language often fail to penetrate sort of skulls plentiful round here."

Spencer nodded and went to the side door, standing where he would not be seen by anyone entering there. In a moment Kaohla appeared, followed by the girl. The Hawaiian came in quickly but seeing Chan, stopped, and a frightened look crossed his face. Spencer startled him further by seizing his arm.

"Come over here," said the detective. "We want to talk to you." He led the boy to a far corner of the room, Chan and John Quincy followed. "Sit down—here, I'll take that." He removed the heavy package from under the boy's arm. For a moment the Hawaiian seemed about to protest, but evidently he thought better of it. Spencer placed the package on a table and stood over Kaohla.

"Want to see Brade, eh?" he began in a threatening tone.

"Yes."

"What for?"

"Business is private."

"Well, I'm telling you to come across. You're in bad. Better change your mind and talk."

"No."

"All right. We'll see about that. What have you got in that package?" The boy's eyes went to the table, but he made no answer.

Chan took out a pocket knife. "Simple matter to discover," he said. He cut the rough twine, unwound several layers of newspapers. John Quincy pressed close, he felt that something important was about to be divulged.

The last layer of paper came off. “Hot dog!” cried Chan. He turned quickly to John Quincy. “Oh, I am so sorry—I pick up atrocious phrase like that from my cousin Mr Willie Chan, Captain of All Chinese baseball team—”

But John Quincy did not hear, his eyes were glued to the object that lay on the table. An ohia wood box, bound with copper—the initials T.M.B.

“We will unlatch it,” said Chan. He made an examination. “No, locked most strongly. We will crash into it at police station, where you and I and this silent Hawaiian will now hasten. Mr Spencer, you will remain on spot here. Should Brade appear, you know your duty.”

“I do,” said Spencer.

“Mr Kaohla, do me the honor to accompany,” continued Chan. “At police headquarters much talk will be extracted out of you.”

They turned toward the door. As they did so, Carlota Egan came up. “May I speak to you a moment?” she said to John Quincy.

“Surely.” He walked with her to the desk.

“I went to the lanai just now,” she whispered breathlessly. “Someone was crouching outside the window near where you were talking. I went closer and it was—Mr Saladine!”

“Aha,” said John Quincy. “Mr Saladine had better drop that sort of thing, or he’ll get himself in trouble.”

“Should we tell Chan?”

“Not yet. You and I will do a little investigating ourselves first. Chan has other things to think about. And we don’t want any of our guests to leave unless it’s absolutely necessary.”

“We certainly don’t,” she smiled. “I’m glad you’ve got the interests of the house at heart.”

“That’s just where I’ve got them—” John Quincy began, but Chan cut in.

"Humbly begging pardon," he said, "we must speed. Captain Hallet will have high delight to encounter this Kaohla, to say nothing of ohia wood box."

In the doorway, Kaohla crowded close to John Quincy, and the latter was startled by the look of hate he saw in the boy's stormy eyes. "You did this," muttered the Hawaiian. "I don't forget."

XV

THE MAN FROM INDIA

They clattered along Kalakaua Avenue in Chan's car.

John Quincy sat alone on the rear seat; at the detective's request he held the ohia wood box on his knees.

He rested his hands upon it. Once it had eluded him, but he had it now. His mind went back to that night in the attic two thousand miles away, the shadow against the moonlit window, the sting of a jewel cutting across his cheek. Roger's heartfelt cry of "Poor old Dan!" Did they hold at last, in this ohia wood box, the answer to the mystery of Dan's death?

Hallet was waiting in his room. With him was a keen-eyed, efficient looking man evidently in his late thirties.

"Hello, boys," said the captain. "Mr Winterslip, meet Mr Greene, our district court prosecutor."

Greene shook hands cordially. "I've been wanting to meet you, sir," he said. "I know your city rather well. Spent three years at your Harvard Law School."

"Really?" replied John Quincy with enthusiasm.

"Yes. I went there after I got through at New Haven. I'm a Yale man, you know."

"Oh," remarked John Quincy, without any enthusiasm at all. But Greene seemed a pleasant fellow, despite his choice of college.

Chan had set the box on the table before Hallet, and was explaining how they had come upon it. The captain's thin face had brightened perceptibly. He inspected the treasure. "Locked, eh?" he remarked. "You got the key, Kaohla?"

The Hawaiian shook his head sullenly. "No."

"Watch your step, boy," warned Hallet. "Go over him, Charlie."

Chan went over him, rapidly and thoroughly. He found a key ring, but none of the keys fitted the lock on the box. He also brought to light a fat roll of bills.

"Where'd you get all that money, Dick?" Hallet inquired.

"I got it," glowered the boy.

But Hallet was more interested in the box. He tapped it lovingly. "This is important, Mr Greene. We may find the solution of our puzzle in here." He took a small chisel from his desk, and after a brief struggle, pried open the lid.

John Quincy, Chan and the prosecutor pressed close, their eyes staring eagerly as the captain lifted the lid. The box was empty.

"Filled with nothing," murmured Chan. "Another dream go smash against stone wall."

The disappointment angered Hallet. He turned on Kaohla. "Now, my lad," he said. "I want to hear from you. You've been in touch with Brade, you talked with him last Sunday night, you've heard he's returning tonight. You've got some deal on with him. Come across and be quick about it."

"Nothing to tell," said the Hawaiian stubbornly.

Hallet leaped to his feet. "Oh, yes you have. And by heaven, you're going to tell it. I'm not any too patient tonight and I warn you if you don't talk and talk quick I'm likely to get rough." He stopped suddenly and turned to Chan. "Charlie, that Inter-Island boat is due from Maui about now. Get down to the dock and watch for Brade. You've got his description?"

"Sure," answered Chan. "Thin pale face, one shoulder descended below other, gray mustaches that droop in saddened mood."

"That's right. Keep a sharp lookout. And leave this lad to us. He won't have any secrets when we get through with him, eh, Mr Greene?"

The prosecutor, more discreet, merely smiled.

"Mr Winterslip," said Chan. "The night is delicious. A little stroll to moonly dock—"

"I'm with you," John Quincy replied. He looked back over his shoulder as he went, and reflected that he wouldn't care to be in Kaohla's shoes.

The pier-shed was dimly lighted and a small but diversified group awaited the incoming boat. Chan and John Quincy walked to the far end and there, seated on a packing-case, they found the waterfront reporter of the evening paper.

"Hello, Charlie," cried Mr Mayberry. "What you doing here?"

"Maybe friend arrive on boat," grinned Chan.

"Is that so?" responded Mayberry. "You boys over at the station have certainly become pretty mysterious all of a sudden. What's doing, Charlie?"

"All pronouncements come from captain," advised Chan.

"Yeah, we've heard his pronouncements," sneered Mayberry. "The police have unearthed clues and are working on them. Nothing to report at present. It's sickening. Well, sit down, Charlie. Oh—Mr Winterslip—good evening. I didn't recognize you at first."

"How are you," said John Quincy. He and Chan also found packing-cases. There was a penetrating odor of sugar in the air. Through a wide opening in the pier-shed they gazed along the waterfront and out upon the moonlit harbor. A rather exotic and intriguing scene, John Quincy reflected, and he said as much.

"Think so?" answered Mayberry. "Well, I don't. To me it's just like Seattle or Galveston or any of those stereotyped ports. But you see—I knew it when—"

"I think you mentioned that before," John Quincy smiled.

"I'm likely to mention it at any moment. As far as I'm concerned, the harbor of Honolulu has lost its romance. Once this was the most picturesque waterfront in the world, my boy. And now look at the damned thing!" The reporter relighted his pipe. "Charlie can tell you—he remembers. The old ramshackle, low-lying wharves. Old Naval Row with its sailing ships. The wooden-hulled steamers with a mast or two—not too proud to use God's good winds occasionally. The bright little row-boats, the *Aloha*, the *Manu*, the *Emma*. Eh, Chan?"

"All extinct," agreed Chan.

"You wouldn't see a Rotary Club gang like this on a pier in those days," Mayberry continued. "Just Hawaiian stevedores with leis on their hats and ukuleles in their hands. Fishermen with their nets, and maybe a breezy old-time purser—a glad-hander and not a mere machine." He puffed a moment in sad silence. "Those were the days, Mr Winterslip, the days of Hawaii's isolation, and her charm. The cable and the radio hadn't linked us up with the so-called civilization of the mainland. Every boat that came in we'd scamper over it, hunting a newspaper with the very latest news of the outside world. Remember those steamer days, Charlie, when everybody went down to the wharf in the good old hacks of yesteryear, when the women wore holokus and lauhala hats, and Berger was there with his band, and maybe a prince or two—"

"And the nights," suggested Charlie.

"Yeah, old-timer, I was coming to the nights. The soft nights when the serenaders drifted about the harbor in row-boats, and the lanterns speared long paths on the water—"

He seemed about to weep. John Quincy's mind went back to books he had read in his boyhood.

"And occasionally," he said, "I presume somebody went aboard a ship against his will?"

"I'll say he did," replied Mr Mayberry, brightening at the thought. "Why, it was only in the nineties I was sitting one night on a dock a few yards down, when I saw a scuffle near the landing, and one of my best friends shouted to me: 'Goodbye, Pete!' I was up and off in a minute, and I got him away from them—I was younger in those days. He was a good fellow, a sailorman, and he wasn't intending to take the journey that bunch had planned for him. They'd got him into a saloon and drugged him, but he pulled out of it just in time—oh, well, those days are gone for ever now. Just like Galveston or Seattle. Yes, sir, this harbor of Honolulu has lost its romance."

The little Inter-Island boat was drawing up to the pier, and they watched it come. As the gangplank went down, Chan rose.

"Who you expecting, Charlie?" asked Mayberry.

"We grope about," said Chan. "Maybe on this boat are Mr Brade."

"Brade!" Mayberry leaped to his feet.

"Not so sure," warned Chan. "Only a matter we suppose. If correct, humbly suggest you follow to the station. You might capture news."

John Quincy and Chan moved up to the gangplank as the passengers descended. There were not many aboard. A few Island business men, a scattering of tourists, a party of Japanese in western clothes, ceremoniously received by friends ashore—a quaint little group all bowing from the waist. John Quincy was watching them with interest when Chan touched his arm.

A tall stooped Englishman was coming down the plank. Thomas Macan Brade would have been easily spotted in any crowd. His mustache was patterned after that of the Earl of Pawtucket, and to make identification even simpler, he wore a white pith helmet. Pith helmets are not necessary under the kindly skies of Hawaii; this was evidently a relic of Indian days.

Chan stepped forward. "Mr Brade?"

The man had a tired look in his eyes. He started nervously. "Y—yes," he hesitated.

"I am Detective-Sergeant Chan, Honolulu police. You will do me the great honor to accompany me to the station, if you please."

Brade stared at him, then shook his head. "It's quite impossible," he said.

"Pardon me, please," answered Chan. "It are unevitable."

"I—I have just returned from a journey," protested the man. "My wife may be worried regarding me. I must have a talk with her, and after that—"

"Regret," purred Chan, "are scorching me. But duty remains duty. Chief's words are law. Humbly suggest we squander valuable time."

"Am I to understand that I'm under arrest?" flared Brade.

"The idea is preposterous," Chan assured him. "But the captain waits eager for statement from you. You will walk this way, I am sure. A moment's pardon. I introduce my fine friend, Mr John Quincy Winterslip, of Boston."

At mention of the name, Brade turned and regarded John Quincy with deep interest. "Very good," he said. "I'll go with you."

They went out to the street, Brade carrying a small hand-bag. The flurry of arrival was dying fast. Honolulu would shortly return to its accustomed evening calm.

When they reached the police station, Hallet and the prosecutor seemed in high good humor. Kaohla sat in a corner, hopeless and defeated; John Quincy saw at a glance that the boy's secret was his no longer.

"Introducing Mr Brade," said Chan.

"Ah," cried Hallet, "we're glad to see you, Mr Brade. We'd been getting pretty worried about you."

"Really, sir," said Brade, "I am completely at a loss—"

"Sit down," ordered Hallet. The man sank into a chair. He too had a hopeless, defeated air. No one can appear more humble and beaten than a British civil servant, and this man had known thirty-six years of baking under the Indian sun, looked down on by the military, respected by none. Not only his mustache but his whole figure drooped "in saddened mood." Yet now and then, John Quincy noted, he flashed into life, a moment of self-assertion and defiance.

"Where have you been, Mr Brade?" Hallet inquired.

"I have visited one of the other islands. Maui."

"You went last Tuesday morning?"

"Yes. On the same steamer that brought me back."

"Your name was not on the sailing list," Hallet said.

"No. I went under another name. I had—reasons."

"Indeed?"

The flash of life. "Just why am I here, sir?" He turned to the prosecutor. "Perhaps you will tell me that?"

Greene nodded toward the detective. "Captain Hallet will enlighten you," he said.

"You bet I will," Hallet announced. "As perhaps you know, Mr Brade, Mr Dan Winterslip has been murdered."

Brade's washed-out eyes turned to John Quincy. "Yes," he said. "I read about it in a Hilo newspaper."

"You didn't know it when you left last Tuesday morning?" Hallet asked.

"I did not. I sailed without seeing a paper here."

"Ah, yes. When did you see Mr Dan Winterslip last?"

"I never saw him."

"What! Be careful, sir."

"I never saw Dan Winterslip in my life."

"All right. Where were you last Tuesday morning at twenty minutes past one?"

"I was asleep in my room at the Reef and Palm Hotel. I'd retired at nine-thirty, as I had to rise early in order to board my boat. My wife can verify that."

"A wife's testimony, Mr Brade, is not of great value—"

Brade leaped to his feet. "Look here, sir! Do you mean to insinuate—"

"Take it easy," said Hallet smoothly. "I have a few matters to call to your attention, Mr Brade. Mr Dan Winterslip was murdered at one-twenty or thereabouts last Tuesday morning. We happen to know that in his youth he served as first officer aboard the *Maid of Shiloh*, a blackbirder. The master of that vessel had the same name as yourself. An investigation of your room at the Reef and Palm—"

"How dare you!" cried Brade. "By what right—"

"I am hunting the murderer of Dan Winterslip," broke in Hallet coolly. "And I follow the trail wherever it leads. In your room I found a letter from the British Consul here addressed to you, and informing you that Winterslip was alive and in Honolulu. I also found this tin of Corsican cigarettes. Just outside the living-room door of Winterslip's house, we picked up the stub of a Corsican cigarette. It's a brand not on sale in Honolulu."

Brade had dropped back into his chair, and was staring in a dazed way at the tin box in Hallet's hand. Hallet indicated the Hawaiian boy in the corner. "Ever see this lad before, Mr Brade?" Brade nodded.

"You had a talk with him last Sunday night on the beach?"

"Yes."

"The boy's told us all about it. He read in the paper that you were coming to Honolulu. His father was a confidential servant in Dan Winterslip's employ and he himself was brought up in the Winterslip household. He could make a pretty good guess at your business with Winterslip, and he figured you'd be pleased to lay hands on this ohia wood box. In his boyhood he'd seen it in a trunk in the attic of Winterslip's San Francisco house. He went down to the *President Tyler* and arranged with a friend aboard that boat, the quartermaster, to break into the house and steal the box. When he saw you last Sunday night he told you he'd have the box as soon as the *President Tyler* got in, and he arranged to sell it to you for a good sum. Am I right so far, Mr Brade?"

"You are quite right," said Brade.

"The initials on the box are T.M.B." Hallet persisted. "They are your initials, are they not?"

"They happen to be," said Brade. "But they were also the initials of my father. My father died aboard ship in the South Seas many years ago, and that box was stolen from his cabin after his death. It was stolen by the first officer of the *Maid of Shiloh*—by Mr Dan Winterslip."

For a moment no one spoke. A cold shiver ran down the spine of John Quincy Winterslip and a hot flush suffused his cheek. Why, oh, why, had he strayed so far from home? In Boston he traveled in a rut, perhaps, but ruts were safe, secure. There no one had ever brought a charge such as this against a Winterslip, no whisper of scandal had ever sullied the name. But here Winterslips had run amuck, and there was no telling what would next be dragged into the light.

"I think, Mr Brade," said the prosecutor slowly, "you had better make a full statement."

Brade nodded. "I intend to do so. My case against Winterslip is not complete and I should have preferred to remain silent for a time. But under the circumstances, of course I must speak out. I'll smoke, if you don't mind." He took a cigarette from his case and lighted it. "I'm a bit puzzled just how to begin. My father disappeared from England in the seventies, leaving my mother and me to shift for ourselves. For a time we heard nothing of him, then letters began to arrive from various points in Australia and the South Seas. Letters with money in them, money we badly needed. I have since learned that he had gone into the blackbirding trade; it is nothing to be proud of, God knows, but I like to recall in his favor that he did not entirely abandon his wife and boy.

"In the eighties we got word of his death. He died aboard the *Maid of Shiloh* and was buried on the island of Apiang in the Gilbert Group—buried by Dan Winterslip, his first officer. We accepted the fact of his death, the fact of no more letters with remittances, and took up our struggle again. Six months later we received, from a friend of my father in Sydney, a brother captain, a most amazing letter.

"This letter said that, to the writer's certain knowledge, my father had carried a great deal of money in his cabin on the *Maid of Shiloh*. He had done no business with banks, instead he had had this strong box made of ohia wood. The man who wrote us said that he had seen the inside of it, and that it contained jewelry and a large quantity of gold. My father had also shown him several bags of green hide, containing gold coins from many countries. He estimated that there must have been close to twenty thousand pounds, in all. Dan Winterslip, the letter said, had brought the *Maid of Shiloh* back to Sydney and turned over to the proper authorities my father's clothing and personal effects, and a scant ten pounds in money. He had made no mention of anything further. He and the only other white man aboard the *Maid*, an Irishman named Hagin, had left at once for Hawaii. My father's friend suggested that we start an immediate investigation.

"Well, gentlemen"—Brade looked about the circle of interested faces—"what could we do? We were in pitiful circumstances, my mother and I. We had no money to employ lawyers, to fight a case thousands of miles away. We did make a few inquiries through a relative in Sydney, but nothing came of them. There was talk for a time, but the talk died out, and the matter was dropped. But I—I have never forgotten.

"Dan Winterslip returned here, and prospered. He built on the foundation of the money he found in my father's cabin a fortune that inspired the admiration of Honolulu. And while he prospered, we were close to starvation. My mother died, but I carried on. For years it has been my dream to make him pay. I have not been particularly successful, but I have saved, scrimped. I have the money now to fight this case.

"Four months ago I resigned my post in India and set out for Honolulu. I stopped over in Sydney—my father's friend is dead, but I have his letter. I have the depositions of others who knew about that money—about the ohia wood box. I came on here, ready to face Dan Winterslip at last. But I never faced him. As you know, gentlemen"—Brade's hand trembled slightly as he put down his cigarette— "someone robbed me of that privilege. Some unknown hand removed from my path the man I have hated for more than forty years."

"You arrived last Saturday—a week ago," said Hallet, after a pause. "On Sunday evening Kaohla here called on you. He offered you the strong box?"

"He did," Brade replied. "He'd had a cable from his friend, and expected to have the box by Tuesday. I promised him five thousand dollars for it—a sum I intended Winterslip should pay. Kaohla also told me that Hagin was living on a ranch in a remote part of the Island of Maui. That explains my journey there—I took another name, as I didn't want Winterslip to follow my movements. I had no doubt he was watching me."

"You didn't tell Kaohla you were going, either?"

"No, I didn't think it advisable to take him completely into my confidence. I found Hagin, but could get nothing out of him. Evidently Winterslip had bought his silence long ago. I realized the box was of great importance to me, and I cabled Kaohla to bring it to me immediately on my return. It was then that the news of Winterslip's death came through. It was a deep disappointment, but it will not deter me." He turned to John Quincy. "Winterslip's heirs must pay. I am determined they shall make my old age secure."

John Quincy's face flushed again. A spirit of rebellion, of family pride outraged, stirred within him. "We'll see about that,

Mr Brade," he said. "You have unearthed the box, but so far as any proof about valuables—money—"

"One moment," cut in Greene, the prosecutor. "Mr Brade, have you a description of any article of value taken from your father?"

Brade nodded. "Yes. In my father's last letter to us—I was looking through it only the other day—he spoke of a brooch he had picked up in Sydney. A tree of emeralds, rubies and diamonds against an onyx background. He said he was sending it to my mother—but it never came."

The prosecutor looked at John Quincy. John Quincy looked away. "I'm not one of Dan Winterslip's heirs, Mr Brade," he explained. "As a matter of fact, he was a rather distant relative of mine. I can't presume to speak for his daughter, but I'm reasonably sure that when she knows your story, this matter can be settled out of court. You'll wait, of course?"

"I'll wait," agreed Brade. "And now, Captain—"

Hallet raised his hand. "Just a minute. You didn't call on Winterslip? You didn't go near his house?"

"I did not," said Brade.

"Yet just outside the door of his living-room we found, as I told you, the stub of a Corsican cigarette. It's a matter still to be cleared up."

Brade considered briefly. "I don't want to get anyone into trouble," he said. "But the man is nothing to me, and I must clear my own name. In the course of a chat with the proprietor of the Reef and Palm Hotel, I offered him a cigarette. He was delighted when he recognized the brand—said it had been years since he'd seen one. So I gave him a handful, and he filled his case."

"You're speaking of Jim Egan," suggested Hallet delightedly.

"Of Mr James Egan, yes," Brade replied.

"That's all I want to know," said Hallet. "Well, Mr Greene—"

The prosecutor addressed Brade. "For the present, we can't permit you to leave Honolulu," he said. "But you are free to go to your hotel. This box will remain here until we can settle its final disposition."

"Naturally." Brade rose.

John Quincy faced him. "I'll call on you very soon," he promised.

"What? Oh, yes—yes, of course." The man stared nervously about him. "If you'll pardon me, gentlemen, I must run—I really must—"

He went out. The prosecutor looked at his watch. "Well, that's that. I'll have a conference with you in the morning, Hallet. My wife's waiting for me at the Country Club. Goodnight, Mr Winterslip." He saw the look on John Quincy's face, and smiled. "Don't take those revelations about your cousin too seriously. The eighties are ancient history, you know."

As Greene disappeared, Hallet turned to John Quincy. "What about this Kaohla?" he inquired. "It will be a pretty complicated job to prosecute him and his house-breaking friend on the *President Tyler*, but it can be done—"

A uniformed policeman appeared at the door, summoning Chan outside.

"Oh, no," said John Quincy. "Let the boy go. We don't want any publicity about this. I'll ask you, Captain, to keep Brade's story out of the papers."

"I'll try," Hallet replied. He turned to the Hawaiian. "Come here!" The boy rose. "You heard what this gentleman said. You ought to be sent up for this, but we've got more important things to attend to now. Run along—beat it—"

Chan came in just in time to hear the last. At his heels followed a sly little Japanese and a young Chinese boy. The latter was attired in the extreme of college-cut clothes; he was an American and he emphasized the fact.

"Only one moment," Chan cried. "New and interesting fact emerge into light. Gentlemen, my Cousin Willie Chan, captain All Chinese baseball team and demon back-stopper of the Pacific!"

"Pleased to meetchu," said Willie Chan.

"Also Okamoto, who have auto stand on Kalakaua Avenue, not far from Winterslip household— "

"I know Okamoto," said Hallet. "He sells okolehau on the side."

"No, indeed," protested the Japanese. "Auto stand, that is what."

"Willie do small investigating to help out crowded hours," went on Chan. "He have dug up strange event out of this Okamoto here. On early morning of Tuesday, July first, Okamoto is roused from slumber by fierce knocks on door of room. He go to door— "

"Let him tell it," suggested Hallet. "What time was this?"

"Two of the morning," said the Japanese. "Knocks were as described. I rouse and look at watch, run to door. Mr Dick Kaohla here is waiting. Demand I drive him to home over in Iwilei district. I done so."

"All right," said Hallet. "Anything else? No? Charlie—take them out and thank them—that's your specialty." He waited until the Orientals had left the room, then turned fiercely on Kaohla. "Well, here you are back in the limelight," he cried. "Now, come across. What were you doing out near Winterslip's house the night of the murder?"

"Nothing," said the Hawaiian.

"Nothing! A little late to be up doing nothing, wasn't it? Look here, my boy, I'm beginning to get you. For years Dan Winterslip gave you money, supported you, until he finally decided you were no good. So he stopped the funds and you and he had a big row. Now, didn't you?"

"Yes," admitted Dick Kaohla.

"On Sunday night Brade offered you five thousand for the box. You thought it wasn't enough. The idea struck you that maybe Dan Winterslip would pay more. You were a little afraid of him, but you screwed up your courage and went to his house—"

"No, no," the boy cried. "I did not go there."

"I say you did. You'd made up your mind to double-cross Brade. You and Dan Winterslip had another big scrap, you drew a knife—"

"Lies, all lies," the boy shouted, terrified.

"Don't tell me I lie! You killed Winterslip and I'll get it out of you! I got the other and I'll get this." Hallet rose threateningly from his chair.

Chan suddenly reentered the room, and handed Hallet a note. "Arrive this moment by special messenger," he explained.

Hallet ripped open the envelope and read. His expression altered. He turned disgustedly to Kaohla. "Beat it!" he scowled.

The boy fled gratefully. John Quincy and Chan looked wonderingly at the captain. Hallet sat down at his desk. "It all comes back to Egan," he said. "I've known it from the first."

"Wait a minute," cried John Quincy. "What about that boy?"

Hallet crumpled the letter in his hand. "Kaohla? Oh, he's out of it now."

"Why?"

"That's all I can tell you. He's out of it."

"That's not enough," John Quincy said. "I demand to know—"

Hallet glared at him. "You know all you're going to," he answered angrily. "I say Kaohla's out, and that settles it. Egan killed Winterslip, and before I get through with him—"

"Permit me to say," interrupted John Quincy, "that you have the most trusting nature I ever met. Everybody's story goes with you. The Compton woman and that rat Leatherbee come in here and spin a yarn, and you bow them out. And Brade! What about Brade! In bed at one-twenty last Tuesday morning, eh? Who says so? He does. Who can prove it? His wife can. What was to prevent his stepping out on the balcony of the Reef and Palm and walking along the beach to my cousin's house? Answer me that!"

Hallet shook his head. "It's Egan. That cigarette—"

"Yes—that cigarette. Has it occurred to you that Brade may have given him those cigarettes purposely—"

"Egan did it," cut in Hallet stubbornly. "All I need now is his story; I'll get it. I have ways and means—"

"I congratulate you on your magnificent stupidity," cried John Quincy. "Goodnight, sir."

He walked along Bethel Street, Chan at his side.

"You are partly consumed by anger," said the Chinaman. "Humbly suggest you cool. Calm heads needed."

"But what was in that note? Why wouldn't he tell us?"

"In good time, we know. Captain honest man. Be patient."

"But we're all at sea again," protested John Quincy. "Who killed Cousin Dan? We get nowhere."

"So very true," agreed Chan. "More clues lead us into presence of immovable stone wall. We sway about, seeking still other path."

"I'll say we do," answered John Quincy. "There comes my car. Goodnight!"

Not until the trolley was half-way to Waikiki did he remember Mr Saladine. Saladine crouching outside that window at the Reef and Palm. What did that mean? But Saladine was a comic figure, a lisping searcher after bridge-work in the limpid waters of Waikiki. Even so, perhaps his humble activities should be investigated.

XVI

THE RETURN OF CAPTAIN COPE

After breakfast on Sunday morning, John Quincy followed Miss Minerva to the lanai. It was a neat world that lay outside the screen, for Dan Winterslip's yard boy had been busy until a late hour the night before, sweeping the lawn with the same loving thoroughness a housewife might display on a precious Oriental rug.

Barbara had not come down to breakfast, and John Quincy had seized the opportunity to tell his aunt of Brade's return, and repeat the man's story of Dan Winterslip's theft on board the *Maid of Shiloh*. Now he lighted a cigarette and sat staring seriously out at the distant water.

"Cheer up," said Miss Minerva. "You look like a judge. I presume you're thinking of poor Dan."

"I am."

"Forgive and forget. None of us ever suspected Dan of being a saint."

"A saint! Far from it! He was just a plain—"

"Never mind," put in his aunt sharply. "Remember, John Quincy, man is a creature of environment. And the temptation must have been great. Picture Dan on that ship in these easy-going latitudes, wealth at his feet and not a soul in sight to claim it. Ill-gotten wealth, at that. Even you—"

"Even I," said John Quincy sternly, "would have recalled I am a Winterslip. I never dreamed I'd live to hear you offering apologies for that sort of conduct."

She laughed. "You know what they say about white women who go to the tropics. They lose first their complexion, then their teeth, and finally their moral sense." She hesitated. "I've had to visit the dentist a good deal of late," she added.

John Quincy was shocked "My advice to you is to hurry home," he said.

"When are you going?"

"Oh, soon—soon."

"That's what we all say. Returning to Boston, I suppose?"

"Of course."

"How about San Francisco?"

"Oh, that's off. I did suggest it to Agatha, but I'm certain she won't hear of it. And I'm beginning to think she'd be quite right." His aunt rose. "You'd better go to church," said John Quincy severely.

"That's just where I am going," she smiled. "By the way, Amos is coming to dinner tonight, and he'd best hear the Brade story from us, rather than in some garbled form. Barbara must hear it too. If it proves to be true, the family ought to do something for Mr Brade."

"Oh, the family will do something for him, all right," John Quincy remarked. "Whether it wants to or not."

"Well, I'll let you tell Barbara about him," Miss Minerva promised.

"Thank you so much," replied her nephew sarcastically.

"Not at all. Are you coming to church?"

"No," he said. "I don't need it the way you do."

She left him there to face a lazy uneventful day. By five in the afternoon Waikiki was alive with its usual Sunday crowd—not the unsavory holiday throng seen on a mainland beach, but a scattering of good-looking people whose tanned straight bodies would have delighted the heart of a physical culture enthusiast. John Quincy summoned sufficient energy to don a bathing suit and plunge in.

There was something soothing in the warm touch of the water, and he was becoming more at home there every day. With long powerful strokes he drew away from the malihini breakers to dare the great rollers beyond. Surf-board riders flashed by him; now and then he had to alter his course to avoid an outrigger canoe.

On the farthest float of all he saw Carlota Egan. She sat there, a slender lovely figure vibrant with life, and awaited his coming. As he climbed up beside her and looked into her eyes he was—perhaps from his exertion in the water—a little breathless.

"I rather hoped I'd find you," he panted.

"Did you?" She smiled faintly. "I hoped it too. You see, I need a lot of cheering up."

"On a perfect day like this!"

"I'd pinned such hopes on Mr Brade," she explained. "Perhaps you know he's back—and from what I can gather, his return hasn't meant a thing so far as dad's concerned. Not a thing."

"Well, I'm afraid it hasn't," John Quincy admitted. "But we mustn't get discouraged. As Chan puts it, we sway about, seeking a new path. You and I have a bit of swaying to do. How about Mr Saladine?"

"I've been thinking about Mr Saladine. But I can't get excited about him, somehow. He's so ridiculous."

"We mustn't pass him up on that account," admonished John Quincy. "I caught a glimpse of his purple bathing suit on the first float. Come on—we'll just casually drop in on him. I'll race you there."

She smiled again, and leaped to her feet. For a second she stood poised, then dived in a way that John Quincy could never hope to emulate. He slipped off in pursuit, and though he put forth every effort, she reached Saladine's side five seconds before he did.

"Hello, Mr Saladine," she said. "This is Mr Winterslip, of Boston."

"Ah, yeth," responded Mr Saladine, gloomily. "Mr Winterthlip." He regarded the young man with interest.

"Any luck, sir?" inquired John Quincy sympathetically.

"Oh—you heard about my accthident?"

"I did, sir, and I'm sorry."

"I am, too," said Mr Saladine feelingly. "Not a thrath of them tho far. And I muth go home in a few dath."

"I believe Miss Egan said you lived in Des Moines?"

"Yeth. Deth—Deth—I can't thay it."

"In business there?" inquired John Quincy nonchalantly.

"Yeth. Wholethale grothery buthineth," answered Mr Saladine, slowly but not very successfully.

John Quincy turned away to hide a smile. "Shall we go along?" he said to the girl. "Good luck to you, sir." He dove off, and as they swam toward the shore, he reflected that they were on a false trail there—a trail as spurious as the teeth. That little business man was too conventional a figure to have any connection with the murder of Dan Winterslip. He kept these thoughts to himself, however.

Half-way to the beach, they encountered an enormous figure floating languidly on the water. Just beyond the great stomach John Quincy perceived the serene face of Charlie Chan.

"Hello, Charlie," he cried. "It's a small ocean, after all! Got your Ford with you?"

Chan righted himself and grinned. "Little pleasant recreation," he explained. "Forget detective worries out here floating idle like leaf on stream."

"Please float ashore," suggested John Quincy. "I have something to tell you."

"Only too happy," agreed Chan.

He followed them in and they sat, an odd trio, on the white sand. John Quincy told the detective about Saladine's activities outside the window the night before, and repeated the conversation he had just had with the middle westerner. "Of course, the man seems almost too foolish to mean anything," he added.

Chan shook his head. "Begging most humble pardon," he said, "that are wrong attitude completely. Detective business made up of unsignificant trifles. One after other our clues go burst in our countenance. Wise to pursue matter of Mr Saladine."

"What do you suggest?" John Quincy asked.

"Tonight I visit city for night work to drive off my piled tasks," Chan replied. "After evening meal, suggest you join with me at cable office. We despatch message to postmaster of this Des Moines, inquiring what are present locality of Mr Saladine, expert in wholeselling provisions. Your name will be signed to message, much better than police meddling."

"All right," John Quincy agreed, "I'll meet you there at eight-thirty."

Carlota Egan rose. "I must get back to the Reef and Palm. You've no idea all I have to do—"

John Quincy stood beside her. "If I can help, you know—"

"I know," she smiled. "I'm thinking of making you assistant manager. They'd be so proud of you—in Boston."

She moved off toward the water for her homeward swim, and John Quincy dropped down beside Chan. The Chinaman's little amber eyes followed the girl. "Endeavoring to make English language my slave," he said, "I pursue poetry. Who were the great poet who said—'She walks in beauty like the night?'"

"Why, that was—er—who was it?" remarked John Quincy helpfully.

"Name is slippery," went on Chan. "But no matter. Lines pop into brain whenever I see this Miss Egan. Beauty like the night, Hawaiian night maybe, lovely as purest jade. Most especially on this beach. Spot of heart-breaking charm, this beach."

"Surely is," agreed John Quincy, amused at Chan's obviously sentimental mood.

"Here on gleaming sand I first regard my future wife," continued Chan. "Slender as the bamboo is slender, beautiful as blossom of the plum—"

"Your wife," repeated John Quincy. The idea was a new one.

"Yes, indeed." Chan rose. "Recalls I must hasten home where she attends the children who are now, by actual count, nine in number." He looked down at John Quincy thoughtfully. "Are you well-fitted with the armor of preparation?" he said. "Consider. Some night the moon has splendor in this neighborhood, the cocoa-palms bow lowly and turn away their heads so they do not see. And the white man kisses without intending to do so."

"Oh, don't worry about me," John Quincy laughed; "I'm from Boston, and immune."

"Immune," repeated Chan. "Ah, yes, I grasp meaning. In my home I have idol brought from China with insides of solid stone. He would think he is—immune. But even so I would not entrust him on this beach. As my cousin Willie Chan say with vulgarity, see you later."

John Quincy sat for a time on the sand, then rose and strolled toward home. His path lay close to the lanai of Arlene Compton's cottage, and he was surprised to hear his name called from behind the screen. He stepped to the door and looked in. The woman was sitting there alone.

"Come in a minute, Mr Winterslip," she said.

John Quincy hesitated. He did not care to make any social calls on this lady, but he did not have it in him to be rude. He went inside and sat down gingerly, poised for flight. "Got to hurry back for dinner," he explained.

"Dinner? You'll want a cocktail."

"No, thanks. I'm—I'm on the wagon."

"You'll find it hard to stick out here," she said a little bitterly. "I won't keep you long. I just want to know—are those boneheads down at the station getting anywhere, or ain't they?"

"The police," smiled John Quincy. "They seem to be making progress. But it's slow. It's very slow."

"I'll tell the world it's slow. And I got to stick here till they pin it on somebody. Pleasant outlook, ain't it?"

"Is Mr Leatherbee still with you?" inquired John Quincy.

"What do you mean is he still with me?" she flared.

"Pardon me. Is he still in town?"

"Of course he's in town. They won't let him go, either. But I ain't worrying about him. I got troubles of my own. I want to go home." She nodded toward a newspaper on the table. "I just got hold of an old *Variety* and seen about a show opening in Atlantic City. A lot of the gang is in it, working like dogs, rehearsing night and day, worrying themselves sick over how long the thing will last. Gee, don't I envy them. I was near to bawling when you came along."

"You'll get back all right," comforted John Quincy.

"Say—if I ever do! I'll stop everybody I meet on Broadway and promise never to leave 'em again." John Quincy rose. "You tell that guy Hallet to get a move on," she urged.

"I'll tell him," he agreed.

"And drop in to see me now and then," she added wistfully. "Us easterners ought to stick together out here."

"That's right, we should," John Quincy answered. "Goodbye."

As he walked along the beach, he thought of her with pity. The story she and Leatherbee had told might be entirely false; even so, she was a human and appealing figure and her homesickness touched his heart.

Later that evening when John Quincy came downstairs faultlessly attired for dinner, he encountered Amos Winterslip in the living-room. Cousin Amos's lean face was whiter than ever; his manner listless. He had been robbed of his hate; his evenings beneath the algaroba tree had lost their savor; life was devoid of spice.

Dinner was not a particularly jolly affair. Barbara seemed intent on knowing now the details of the search the police were conducting, and it fell to John Quincy to enlighten her. Reluctantly he came at last to the story of Brade. She listened in silence. After dinner she and John Quincy went out into the garden and sat on a bench under the hau tree, facing the water.

"I'm terribly sorry I had to tell you that about Brade," John Quincy said gently. "But it seemed necessary."

"Of course," she agreed. "Poor dad! He was weak—weak—"

"Forgive and forget," John Quincy suggested. "Man is a creature of environment." He wondered dimly where he had heard that before. "Your father was not entirely to blame—"

"You're terribly kind, John Quincy," she told him.

"No—but I mean it," he protested. "Just picture the scene to yourself. That lonely ocean, wealth at his feet for the taking, no one to see or know."

She shook her head. "Oh, but it was wrong, wrong. Poor Mr Brade. I must make things right with him as nearly as I can. I shall ask Harry to talk with him tomorrow—"

"Just a suggestion," interposed John Quincy. "Whatever you agree to do for Brade must not be done until the man who killed your father is found."

She stared at him. "What! You don't think that Brade—"

"I don't know. Nobody knows. Brade is unable to prove where he was early last Tuesday morning."

They sat silent for a moment; then the girl suddenly collapsed and buried her face in her hands. Her slim shoulders trembled convulsively and John Quincy, deeply sympathetic, moved closer. He put his arm about her. The moonlight shone on her bright hair, the trades whispered in the hau tree, the breakers murmured on the beach. She lifted her face, and he kissed her. A cousinly kiss he had meant it to be, but somehow it wasn't—it was a kiss he would never have been up to on Beacon Street.

"Miss Minerva said I'd find you here," remarked a voice behind them.

John Quincy leaped to his feet and found himself staring into the cynical eyes of Harry Jennison. Even though you are the girl's cousin, it is a bit embarrassing to have a man find you kissing his fiancée. Particularly if the kiss wasn't at all cousinly—John Quincy wondered if Jennison had noticed that.

"Come in—I mean, sit down," stammered John Quincy. "I was just going."

"Goodbye," said Jennison coldly.

John Quincy went hastily through the living-room, where Miss Minerva sat with Amos. "Got an appointment downtown," he explained, and picking up his hat in the hall, fled into the night.

He had intended taking the roadster, but to reach the garage he would have to pass that bench under the hau tree. Oh, well, the colorful atmosphere of a trolley was more interesting, anyhow.

In the cable office on the ground floor of the Alexander Young Hotel, Chan was waiting, and they sent off their inquiry to the postmaster at Des Moines, signing John Quincy's name and address. That attended to, they returned to the street. In the park across the way an unseen group of young men strummed steel guitars and sang in soft haunting voices; it was the only sign of life in Honolulu.

"Kindly deign to enter hotel lobby with me," suggested Chan. "It is my custom to regard names in register from time to time."

At the cigar stand just inside the door, the boy paused to light his pipe, while Chan went on to the desk. As John Quincy turned he saw a man seated alone in the lobby, a handsome, distinguished man who wore immaculate evening clothes that bore the stamp of Bond Street. An old acquaintance, Captain Arthur Temple Cope.

At sight of John Quincy, Cope leaped to his feet and came forward. "Hello, I'm glad to see you," he cried, with a cordiality that had not been evident at former meetings. "Come over and sit down."

John Quincy followed him. "Aren't you back rather soon?" he inquired.

"Sooner than I expected," Cope rejoined. "Not sorry, either."

"Then you didn't care for your little flock of islands?"

"My boy, you should visit there. Thirty-five white men, two hundred and fifty natives, and a cable station. Jolly place of an evening, what?"

Chan came up, and John Quincy presented him. Captain Cope was the perfect host. "Sit down, both of you," he urged. "Have a cigarette." He extended a silver case.

"Thanks, I'll stick to the pipe," John Quincy said. Chan gravely accepted a cigarette and lighted it.

"Tell me, my boy," Cope said when they were seated, "is there anything new on the Winterslip murder? Haven't run down the guilty man, by any chance."

"No, not yet," John Quincy replied.

"That's a great pity. I—er—understand the police are holding a chap named Egan?"

"Yes—Jim Egan, of the Reef and Palm Hotel."

"Just what evidence have they against Egan, Mr Winterslip?"

John Quincy was suddenly aware of Chan looking at him in a peculiar way. "Oh, they've dug up several things," he answered vaguely.

"Mr Chan, you are a member of the police force," Captain Cope went on. "Perhaps you can tell me?"

Chan's little eyes narrowed. "Such matters are not yet presented to public," he replied.

"Ah, yes, naturally." Captain Cope's tone suggested disappointment.

"You have interest in this murder, I think?" Chan said.

"Why, yes—everyone out this way is puzzling about it, I fancy. The thing has so many angles."

"Is it possible that you were an acquaintance with Mr Dan Winterslip?" the detective persisted.

"I—I knew him slightly. But that was many years ago."

Chan stood. "Humbly begging pardon to be so abrupt," he said. He turned to John Quincy. "The moment of our appointment is eminent—"

"Of course," agreed John Quincy. "See you again, Captain." Perplexed, he followed Chan to the street. "What appointment—" he began, and stopped. Chan was carefully extinguishing the light of the cigarette against the stone facade of the hotel. That done, he dropped the stub into his pocket.

"You will see," he promised. "First we visit police station. As we journey, kindly relate all known facts concerning this Captain Cope."

John Quincy told of his first meeting with Cope in the San Francisco club, and repeated the conversation as he recalled it.

"Evidence of warm dislike for Dan Winterslip were not to be concealed?" inquired Chan.

"Oh, quite plain, Charlie. He certainly had no love for Cousin Dan. But what—"

"Immediately he was leaving for Hawaii—pardon the interrupt. Does it happily chance you know his date of arrival here?"

"I do. I saw him in the Alexander Young Hotel last Tuesday evening when I was looking for you. He was rushing off to the

Fanning Islands, and he told me he had got in the previous day at noon—"

"Monday noon to put it lucidly."

"Yes—Monday noon. But Charlie—what are you trying to get at?"

"Groping about," Chan smiled. "Seeking to seize truth in my hot hands."

They walked on in silence to the station, where Chan led the way into the deserted room of Captain Hallet. He went directly to the safe and opened it. From a drawer he removed several small objects, which he carried over to the captain's table.

"Property Mr Jim Egan," he announced, and laid a case of tarnished silver before John Quincy. "Open it—what do you find now? Corsican cigarettes." He set down another exhibit. "Tin box found in room of Mr Brade. Open that, also. You find more Corsican cigarettes."

He removed an envelope from his pocket and taking out a charred stub, laid that too on the table. "Fragment found by walk outside door of Dan Winterslip's mansion," he elucidated. "Also Corsican brand."

Frowning deeply, he removed a second charred stub from his pocket and laid it some distance from the other exhibits. "Cigarette offered just now with winning air of hospitality by Captain Arthur Temple Cope. Lean close and perceive. More Corsican brand!"

"Good lord!" John Quincy cried.

"Can it be you are familiar with these Corsicans?" inquired Chan.

"Not at all."

"I am more happily located. This afternoon before the swim I pause at public library for listless reading. In Australian newspaper I encounter advertising talk of Corsican cigarette. It are assembled in two distinct fashions, one, labeled on tin 222, holds Turkish tobacco. Note 222 on tin of Brade. Other labeled

444 made up from Virginia weeds. Is it that you are clever to know difference between Turkish and Virginia tobacco?"

"Well, I think so—" began John Quincy.

"Same with me, but thinking are not enough now. The moment are serious. We will interrogate expert opinion. Honor me by a journey to smoking emporium."

He took a cigarette from Brack's tin, put it in an envelope and wrote something on the outside, then did the same with one from Egan's case. The two stubs were similarly classified.

They went in silence to the street. John Quincy, amazed by this new turn of events, told himself the idea was absurd. But Chan's face was grave, his eyes awake and eager.

John Quincy was vastly more amazed when they emerged from the tobacco shop after a brisk interview with the young man in charge. Chan was jubilant now.

"Again we advance! You hear what he tells us. Cigarette from Brade's tin and little brother from Egan's case are of identical contents, both being of Turkish tobacco. Stub found near walk are of Virginia stuff. So also are remnant received by me from the cordial hand of Captain Arthur Temple Cope!"

"It's beyond me," replied John Quincy. "By gad—that lets Egan out. Great news for Carlota. I'll hurry to the Reef and Palm and tell her—"

"Oh, no, no," protested Chan. "Please to let that happy moment wait. For the present, indulge only in silence. Before asking Captain Cope for statement we spy over his every move. Much may be revealed by the unsuspecting. I go to station to make arrangements—"

"But the man's a gentleman," John Quincy cried. "A captain in the British Admiralty. What you suggest is impossible."

Chan shook his head. "Impossible in Rear Bay at Boston," he said, "but here at moorly crossroads of Pacific, not so much so. Twenty-five years of my life are consumed in Hawaii, and I have many times been witness when the impossible roused itself and occurred."

XVII

NIGHT LIFE IN HONOLULU

Monday brought no new developments, and John Quincy spent a restless day. Several times he called Chan at the police station, but the detective was always out.

Honolulu, according to the evening paper, was agog. This was not, as John Quincy learned to his surprise, a reference to the Winterslip case. An American fleet had just left the harbor of San Pedro bound for Hawaii. This was the annual cruise of the graduating class at Annapolis; the war-ships were overflowing with future captains and admirals. They would linger at the port of Honolulu for several days and a gay round of social events impended—dinners, dances, moonlight swimming parties.

John Quincy had not seen Barbara all day; the girl had not appeared at breakfast and had lunched with a friend down the beach. They met at dinner, however, and it seemed to him that she looked more tired and wan than ever. She spoke about the coming of the war-ships.

"It's always such a happy time," she said wistfully. "The town simply blooms with handsome boys in uniform. I don't like to have you miss all the parties, John Quincy. You're not seeing Honolulu at its best."

"Why—that's all right," John Quincy assured her.

She shook her head. "Not with me. You know, we're not such slaves to convention out here. If I should get you a few invitations—what do you think, Cousin Minerva?"

"I'm an old woman," said Miss Minerva. "According to the standards of your generation, I suppose it would be quite the thing. But it's not the sort of conduct I can view approvingly. Now, in my day—"

"Don't you worry, Barbara," John Quincy broke in. "Parties mean nothing to me. Speaking of old women, I'm an old man myself—thirty my next birthday. Just my pipe and slippers by the fire—or the electric fan—that's all I ask of life now."

She smiled and dropped the matter. After dinner, she followed John Quincy to the lanai. "I want you to do something for me," she began.

"Anything you say."

"Have a talk with Mr Brade, and tell me what he wants."

"Why, I thought that Jennison—" said John Quincy.

"No, I didn't ask him to do it," she replied. For a long moment she was silent. "I ought to tell you—I'm not going to marry Mr Jennison, after all."

A shiver of apprehension ran down John Quincy's spine. Good lord—that kiss! Had she misunderstood? And he hadn't meant a thing by it. Just a cousinly salute—at least, that was what it had started out to be. Barbara was a sweet girl, yes, but a relative, a Winterslip, and relatives shouldn't marry, no matter how distant the connection. Then, too, there was Agatha. He was bound to Agatha by all the ties of honor. What had he got himself into, anyhow?

"I'm awfully sorry to hear that," he said. "I'm afraid I'm to blame—"

"Oh, no," she protested.

"But surely Mr Jennison understood. He knows we're related, and that what he saw last night meant—nothing." He was rather proud of himself. Pretty neat the way he'd got that over.

"If you don't mind," Barbara said, "I'd rather not talk about it any more. Harry and I will not be married—not at present, at any rate. And if you'll see Mr Brade for me—"

"I certainly will," John Quincy promised. "I'll see him at once." He was glad to get away, for the moon was rising on that "spot of heart-breaking charm."

A fellow ought to be more careful, he reflected as he walked along the beach. Fit upon himself the armor of preparation, as Chan had said. Strange impulses came to one here in this far tropic land; to yield to them was weak. Complications would follow, as the night the day. Here was one now, Barbara and Jennison estranged, and the cause was clear. Well, he was certainly going to watch his step hereafter.

On the far end of the Reef and Palm's first floor balcony, Brade and his wife sat together in the dusk. John Quincy went up to them.

"May I speak with you, Mr Brade?" he said.

The man looked up out of a deep reverie. "Ah, yes—of course—"

"I'm John Quincy Winterslip. We've met before."

"Oh, surely, surely sir." Brade rose and shook hands. "My dear—" he turned to his wife, but with one burning glance at John Quincy, the woman had fled. The boy tingled—in Boston a Winterslip was never snubbed. Well, Dan Winterslip had arranged it otherwise in Hawaii.

"Sit down, sir," said Brade, somewhat embarrassed by his wife's action. "I've been expecting someone of your name."

"Naturally. Will you have a cigarette, sir." John Quincy proffered his case, and when the cigarettes were lighted, seated himself at the man's side. "I'm here, of course, in regard to that story you told Saturday night."

"Story?" flashed Brade.

John Quincy smiled. "Don't misunderstand me. I'm not questioning the truth of it. But I do want to say this, Mr Brade—

you must be aware that you will have considerable difficulty establishing your claim in a court of law. The eighties are a long time back."

"What you say may be true," Brade agreed. "I'm relying more on the fact that a trial would result in some rather unpleasant publicity for the Winterslip family."

"Precisely," nodded John Quincy. "I am here at the request of Miss Barbara Winterslip, who is Dan Winterslip's sole heir. She's a very fine girl, sir—"

"I don't question that," cut in Brade impatiently.

"And if your demands are not unreasonable—" John Quincy paused, and leaned closer. "Just what do you want, Mr Brade?"

Brade stroked those gray mustaches that drooped "in saddened mood." "No money," he said, "can make good the wrong Dan Winterslip did. But I'm an old man, and it would be something to feel financially secure for the rest of my life. I'm not inclined to be grasping—particularly since Dan Winterslip has passed beyond my reach. There were twenty thousand pounds involved. I'll say nothing about interest for more than forty years. A settlement of one hundred thousand dollars would be acceptable."

John Quincy considered. "I can't speak definitely for my cousin," he said, "but to me that sounds fair enough. I have no doubt Barbara will agree to give you that sum"—he saw the man's tired old eyes brighten in the semi-darkness— "the moment the murderer of Dan Winterslip is found," he added quickly.

"What's that you say?" Brade leaped to his feet.

"I say she'll very likely pay you when this mystery is cleared up. Surely you don't expect her to do so before that time?" John Quincy rose too.

"I certainly do!" Brade cried. "Why, look here, this thing may drag on indefinitely. I want England again—the Strand, Piccadilly—it's twenty-five years since I saw London. Wait!

Damn it, why should I wait! What's this murder to me—by gad, sir—" He came close, erect, flaming, the son of Tom Brade, the blackbirder, now. "Do you mean to insinuate that I—"

John Quincy faced him calmly. "I know you can't prove where you were early last Tuesday morning," he said evenly. "I don't say that incriminates you, but I shall certainly advise my cousin to wait. I'd not care to see her in the position of having rewarded the man who killed her father."

"I'll fight," cried Brade. "I'll take it to the courts—"

"Go ahead," John Quincy said. "But it will cost you every penny you've saved, and you may lose in the end. Good night, sir."

"Goodnight!" Brade answered, standing as his father might have stood on the *Maid of Shiloh's* deck.

John Quincy had gone half-way down the balcony when he heard quick footsteps behind him. He turned. It was Brade, Brade the civil servant, the man who had labored thirty-six years in the oven of India, a beaten, helpless figure.

"You've got me," he said, laying a hand on John Quincy's arm. "I can't fight. I'm too tired, too old—I've worked too hard. I'll take whatever your cousin wants to give me—when she's ready to give it."

"That's a wise decision, sir," John Quincy answered. A sudden feeling of pity gripped his heart. He felt toward Brade as he had felt toward that other exile, Arlene Compton. "I hope you see London very soon," he added, and held out his hand.

Brade took it. "Thank you, my boy. You're a gentleman, even if your name is Winterslip."

Which, John Quincy reflected as he entered the lobby of the Reef and Palm, was a compliment not without its flaw.

He didn't worry over that long, however, for Carlota Egan was behind the desk. She looked up and smiled, and it occurred to John Quincy that her eyes were happier than he had seen them since that day on the Oakland ferry.

"Hello," he said. "Got a job for a good book-keeper?"

She shook her head. "Not with business the way it is now. I was just figuring my pay-roll. You know, we've no undertow at Waikiki, but all my life I've had to worry about the overhead."

He laughed. "You talk like a brother Kiwanian. By the way, has anything happened? You seem considerably cheered."

"I am," she replied. "I went to see poor dad this morning in that horrible place—and when I left someone else was going in to visit him. A stranger."

"A stranger?"

"Yes—and the handsomest thing you ever saw—tall, gray, capable-looking. He had such a friendly air, too—I felt better the moment I saw him."

"Who was he?" John Quincy inquired, with sudden interest.

"I'd never seen him before, but one of the men told me he was Captain Cope, of the British Admiralty."

"Why should Captain Cope want to see your father?"

"I haven't a notion. Do you know him?"

"Yes—I've met him," John Quincy told her.

"Don't you think he's wonderful-looking?" Her dark eyes glowed.

"Oh, he's all right," replied John Quincy without enthusiasm. "You know, I can't help feeling that things are looking up for you."

"I feel that too," she said.

"What do you say we celebrate?" he suggested. "Go out among 'em and get a little taste of night life. I'm a bit fed up on the police station. What do people do here in the evening? The movies?"

"Just at present," the girl told him, "everybody visits Punahou to see the night-blooming cereus. It's the season now, you know."

"Sounds like a big evening," John Quincy laughed. "Go and look at the flowers. Well, I'm for it. Will you come?"

"Of course." She gave a few directions to the clerk, then joined him by the door. "I can run down and get the roadster," he offered.

"Oh, no," she smiled. "I'm sure I'll never own a motor-car, and it might make me discontented to ride in one. The trolley's my carriage—and it's lots of fun. One meets so many interesting people."

On the stone walls surrounding the campus of Oahu College, the strange flower that blooms only on a summer night was heaped in snowy splendor. John Quincy had been a bit lukewarm regarding the expedition when they set out, but he saw his error now. For here was beauty, breath-taking and rare. Before the walls paraded a throng of sight-seers; they joined the procession. The girl was a charming companion, her spirits had revived and she chatted vivaciously. Not about Shaw and the art galleries, true enough, but bright human talk that John Quincy liked to hear.

He persuaded her to go to the city for a maidenly ice-cream soda, and it was ten o'clock when they returned to the beach. They left the trolley at a stop some distance down the avenue from the Reef and Palm, and strolled slowly toward the hotel. The sidewalk was lined at their right by dense foliage, almost impenetrable. The night was calm; the street lamps shone brightly; the paved street gleamed white in the moonlight. John Quincy was talking of Boston.

"I think you'd like it there. It's old and settled, but—"

From the foliage beside them came the flash of a pistol, and John Quincy heard a bullet sing close to his head. Another flash, another bullet. The girl gave a startled little cry.

John Quincy circled round her and plunged into the bushes. Angry branches stung his cheek. He stopped; he couldn't leave the girl alone. He returned to her side.

"What did that mean?" he asked, amazed. He stared in wonder at the peaceful scene before him.

"I—I don't know." She took his arm. "Come—hurry!"

"Don't be afraid," he said reassuringly.

"Not for myself," she answered.

They went on to the hotel, greatly puzzled. But when they entered the lobby, they had something else to think about. Captain Arthur Temple Cope was standing by the desk, and he came at once to meet them.

"This is Miss Egan, I believe. Ah, Winterslip, how are you?" He turned again to the girl. "I've taken a room here, if you don't mind."

"Why, not at all," she gasped.

"I talked with your father this morning. I didn't know about his trouble until I had boarded a ship for the Fanning Islands. I came back as quickly as I could."

"You came back—" She stared at him.

"Yes. I came back to help him."

"That's very kind of you," the girl said. "But I'm afraid I don't understand—"

"Oh, no, you don't understand. Naturally." The captain smiled down at her. "You see, Jim's my young brother. You're my niece, and your name is Carlota Maria Cope. I fancy I've persuaded old Jim to own up to us at last."

The girl's dark eyes were wide. "I—I think you're a very nice uncle," she said at last.

"Do you really?" The captain bowed. "I aim to be," he added.

John Quincy stepped forward. "Pardon me," he said. "I'm afraid I'm intruding. Goodnight, Captain."

"Goodnight, my boy," Cope answered.

The girl went with John Quincy to the balcony. "I—don't know what to make of it," she said.

"Things are coming rather fast," John Quincy admitted. He remembered the Corsican cigarette. "I wouldn't trust him too far," he admonished.

"But he's so wonderful—"

"Oh, he's all right, probably. But looks are often deceptive. I'll go along now and let you talk with him."

She laid one slim tanned hand on his white-clad arm "Do be careful!"

"Oh, I'm all right," he told her.

"But someone shot at you."

"Yes, and a very poor aim he had, too. Don't worry about me." She was very close, her eyes glowing in the dark. "You said you weren't afraid for yourself," he added. "Did you mean—"

"I meant—I was afraid—for you."

The moon, of course, was shining. The cocoa-palms turned their heads away at the suggestion of the trades. The warm waters of Waikiki murmured near by. John Quincy Winterslip, from Boston and immune, drew the girl to him and kissed her. Not a cousinly kiss, either—but why should it have been? She wasn't his cousin.

"Thank you, my dear," he said. He seemed to be floating dizzily in space. It came to him that he might reach out and pluck her a handful of stars.

It came to him a second later that, despite his firm resolve, he had done it again. Kissed another girl. Three—that made three with whom he was sort of entangled.

"Goodnight," he said huskily, and leaping over the rail, fled hastily through the garden.

Three girls now—but he hadn't a single regret. He was living at last. As he hurried through the dark along the beach, his heart was light. Once he fancied he was being followed, but he gave it little thought. What of it?

On the bureau in his room he found an envelope with his name typewritten on the outside. The note within was typewritten too. He read:

"You are too busy out here. Hawaii can manage her affairs without the interference of a malihini. Boats sail almost daily. If you are still here forty-eight hours after you get this—look out! Tonight's shots were fired into the air. The aim will quickly improve!"

Delighted, John Quincy tossed the note aside. Threatening him, eh? His activities as a detective were bearing fruit. He recalled the glowering face of Kaohla when he said: "You did this. I don't forget." And a remark of Dan Winterslip's his aunt had quoted: "Civilized—yes. But far underneath there are deep dark waters flowing still."

Boats were sailing almost daily, were they? Well, let them sail. He would be on one some day—but not until he had brought Dan Winterslip's murderer to justice.

Life had a new glamour now. Look out? He'd be looking—and enjoying it, too. He smiled happily to himself as he took off his coat. This was better than selling bonds in Boston.

XVIII

A CABLE FROM THE MAINLAND

John Quincy awoke at nine the following morning, and slipped from under his mosquito netting eager to face the responsibilities of a new day. On the floor near his bureau lay the letter designed to speed the parting guest. He picked it up and read it again with manifest enjoyment.

When he reached the dining-room Haku informed him that Miss Minerva and Barbara had breakfasted early and gone to the city on a shopping tour.

"Look here, Haku," the boy said. "A letter came for me late last night?"

"Yes-s," admitted Haku.

"Who delivered it?"

"Cannot say. It were found on floor of hall close by big front door."

"Who found it?"

"Kamaikui."

"Oh, yes—Kamaikui."

"I tell her to put in your sleeping room."

"Did Kamaikui see the person who brought it?"

"Nobody see him. Nobody on place."

"All right," John Quincy said.

He spent a leisurely hour on the lanai with his pipe and the morning paper. At about half past ten he got out the roadster and drove to the police station.

Hallet and Chan, he was told, were in a conference with the prosecutor. He sat down to wait, and in a few moments word came for him to join them. Entering Greene's office, he saw the three men seated gloomily about the prosecutor's desk.

"Well, I guess I'm some detective," he announced.

Greene looked up quickly. "Found anything new?"

"Not precisely," John Quincy admitted. "But last night when I was walking along Kalakaua Avenue with a young woman, somebody took a couple of wild shots at me from the bushes. And when I got home I found this letter waiting."

He handed the epistle to Hallet, who read it with evident disgust, then passed it on to the prosecutor "That doesn't get us anywhere," the captain said.

"It may get me somewhere, if I'm not careful," John Quincy replied. "However, I'm rather proud of it. Sort of goes to show that my detective work is hitting home."

"Maybe," answered Hallet, carelessly.

Greene laid the letter on his desk. "My advice to you," he said, "is to carry a gun. That's unofficial, of course."

"Nonsense, I'm not afraid," John Quincy told him. "I've got a pretty good idea who sent this thing."

"You have?" Greene said.

"Yes. He's a friend of Captain Hallet's. Dick Kaohla."

"What do you mean he's a friend of mine?" flared Hallet.

"Well, you certainly treated him pretty tenderly the other night."

"I knew what I was doing," said Hallet grouchily.

"I hope you did. But if he puts a bullet in me some lovely evening, I'm going to be pretty annoyed with you."

"Oh, you're in no danger," Hallet answered. "Only a coward writes anonymous letters."

"Yes, and only a coward shoots from ambush. But that isn't saying he can't take a good aim."

Hallet picked up the letter. "I'll keep this. It may prove to be evidence."

"Surely," agreed John Quincy. "And you haven't got any too much evidence, as I see it."

"Is that so?" growled Hallet. "We've made a rather important discovery about that Corsican cigarette."

"Oh, I'm not saying Charlie isn't good," smiled John Quincy. "I was with him when he worked that out."

A uniformed man appeared at the door. "Egan and his daughter and Captain Cope," he announced to Greene. "Want to see them now, sir?"

"Send them in," ordered the prosecutor.

"I'd like to stay, if you don't mind," John Quincy suggested.

"Oh, by all means," Greene answered. "We couldn't get along without you."

The policeman brought Egan to the door, and the proprietor of the Reef and Palm came into the room. His face was haggard and pale; his long siege with the authorities had begun to tell. But a stubborn light still flamed in his eyes. After him came Carlota Egan, fresh and beautiful, and with a new air of confidence about her. Captain Cope followed, tall, haughty, a man of evident power and determination.

"This is the prosecutor, I believe?" he said. "Ah, Mr Winterslip; I find you everywhere I go."

"You don't mind my staying?" inquired John Quincy.

"Not in the least, my boy. Our business here will take but a moment." He turned to Greene. "Just as a preliminary," he continued, "I am Captain Arthur Temple Cope of the British Admiralty, and this gentleman"—he nodded toward the proprietor of the Reef and Palm— "is my brother."

"Really?" said Greene. "His name is Egan, as I understand it."

"His name is James Egan Cope," the captain replied. "He dropped the Cope many years ago for reasons that do not concern us now. I am here simply to say, sir, that you are holding my brother on the flimsiest pretext I have ever encountered in the course of my rather extensive travels. If necessary, I propose to engage the best lawyer in Honolulu and have him free by night. But I'm giving you this last chance to release him and avoid a somewhat painful expose of the sort of nonsense you go in for."

John Quincy glanced at Carlota Egan. Her eyes were shining but not on him. They were on her uncle.

Greene flushed slightly. "A good bluff, Captain, is always worth trying," he said.

"Oh, then you admit you've been bluffing," said Cope quickly.

"I was referring to your attitude, sir," Greene replied.

"Oh, I see," Cope said. "I'll sit down, if you don't mind. As I understand it, you have two things against old Jim here. One is that he visited Dan Winterslip on the night of the murder, and now refuses to divulge the nature of that call. The other is the stub of a Corsican cigarette which was found by the walk outside the door of Winterslip's living-room."

Greene shook his head. "Only the first," he responded. "The Corsican cigarette is no longer evidence against Egan." He leaned suddenly across his desk. "It is, my dear Captain Cope, evidence against you."

Cope met his look unflinchingly. "Really?" he remarked.

John Quincy noted a flash of startled bewilderment in Carlota Egan's eyes.

"That's what I said," Greene continued. "I'm very glad you dropped in this morning, sir. I've been wanting to talk to you. I've been told that you were heard to express a strong dislike for Dan Winterslip."

"I may have. I certainly felt it."

"Why?"

"As a midshipman on a British war-ship, I was familiar with Australian gossip in the eighties. Mr Dan Winterslip had an unsavory reputation. It was rumored on good authority that he rifled the sea chest of his dead captain on the *Maid of Shiloh*. Perhaps we're a bit squeamish, but that is the sort of thing we sailors cannot forgive. There were other quaint deeds in connection with his blackbirding activities. Yes, my dear sir, I heartily disliked Dan Winterslip, and if I haven't said so before, I say it now."

"You arrived in Honolulu a week ago yesterday," Greene continued. "At noon—Monday noon. You left the following day. Did you, by any chance, call on Dan Winterslip during that period?"

"I did not."

"Ah, yes. I may tell you, sir, that the Corsican cigarettes found in Egan's case were of Turkish tobacco. The stub found near the scene of Dan Winterslip's murder was of Virginia tobacco. So also, my dear Captain Cope, was the Corsican cigarette you gave our man Charlie Chan in the lobby of the Alexander Young Hotel last Sunday night."

Cope looked at Chan, and smiled. "Always the detective, eh?" he said.

"Never mind that!" Greene cried. "I'm asking for an explanation."

"The explanation is very simple," Cope replied. "I was about to give it to you when you launched into this silly cross-examination. The Corsican cigarette found by Dan Winterslip's door was, naturally, of Virginia tobacco. I never smoke any other kind."

"What!"

"There can be no question about it, sir. I dropped that cigarette there myself."

"But you just told me you didn't call on Dan Winterslip."

"That was true. I didn't. I called on Miss Minerva Winterslip, of Boston, who is a guest in the house. As a matter of fact, I had tea with her last Monday at five o'clock. You may verify that by telephoning the lady."

Greene glanced at Hallet, who glanced at the telephone, then turned angrily to John Quincy. "Why the devil didn't she tell me that?" he demanded.

John Quincy smiled. "I don't know, sir. Possibly because she never thought of Captain Cope in connection with the murder."

"She'd hardly be likely to," Cope said. "Miss Winterslip and I had tea in the living-room, then went out and sat on a bench in the garden, chatting over old times. When I returned to the house I was smoking a cigarette. I dropped it just outside the living-room door. Whether Miss Winterslip noted my action or not, I don't know. She probably didn't, it isn't the sort of thing one remembers. You may call her on the telephone if you wish, sir."

Again Greene looked at Hallet, who shook his head. "I'll talk with her later," announced the Captain of Detectives. Evidently Miss Minerva had an unpleasant interview ahead.

"At any rate," Cope continued to the prosecutor, "you had yourself disposed of the cigarette as evidence against old Jim. That leaves only the fact of his silence—"

"His silence, yes," Greene cut in, "and the fact that Winterslip had been heard to express a fear of Jim Egan."

Cope frowned. "Had he, really?" He considered a moment. "Well, what of it? Winterslip had good reason to fear a great many honest men. No, my dear sir, you have nothing save my brother's silence against him, and that is not enough. I demand—"

Greene raised his hand. "Just a minute. I said you were bluffing, and I still think so. Any other assumption would be an insult to your intelligence. Surely you know enough about the law to understand that your brother's refusal to tell me his business with Winterslip, added to the fact that he was presumably the last person to see Winterslip alive, is sufficient excuse for holding him. I can hold him on those grounds, I am holding him, and, my dear Captain, I shall continue to hold him until hell freezes over."

"Very good," said Cope, rising. "I shall engage a capable lawyer—"

"That is, of course, your privilege," snapped Greene. "Goodmorning."

Cope hesitated. He turned to Egan. "It means more publicity, Jim," he said. "Delay, too. More unhappiness for Carlota here. And since everything you did was done for her—"

"How did you know that?" asked Egan quickly.

"I've guessed it. I can put two and two together, Jim. Carlota was to return with me for a bit of schooling in England. You said you had the money, but you hadn't. That was your pride again, Jim. It's got you into a lifetime of trouble. You cast about for the funds, and you remembered Winterslip. I'm beginning to see it all now. You had something on Dan Winterslip, and you went to his house that night to—er—"

"To blackmail him," suggested Greene.

"It wasn't a pretty thing to do, Jim," Cope went on. "But you weren't doing it for yourself. Carlota and I know you would have died first. You did it for your girl, and we both forgive you." He turned to Carlota. "Don't we, my dear?"

The girl's eyes were wet. She rose and kissed her father. "Dear old dad," she said.

"Come on, Jim," pleaded Captain Cope. "Forget your pride for once. Speak up, and we'll take you home with us. I'm sure the prosecutor will keep the thing from the newspapers—"

"We've promised him that a thousand times," Greene said.

Egan lifted his head. "I don't care anything about the newspapers," he explained. "It's you, Arthur—you and Cary—

I didn't want you two to know. But since you've guessed, and Cary knows too—I may as well tell everything."

John Quincy stood up. "Mr Egan," he said. "I'll leave the room, if you wish."

"Sit down, my boy," Egan replied. "Cary's told me of your kindness to her. Besides, you saw the check—"

"What check was that?" cried Hallet. He leaped to his feet and stood over John Quincy.

"I was honor bound not to tell," explained the boy gently.

"You don't say so!" Hallet bellowed. "You're a fine pair, you and that aunt of yours—"

"One minute, Hallet," cut in Greene. "Now, Egan, or Cope, or whatever your name happens to be—I'm waiting to hear from you."

Egan nodded. "Back in the eighties I was teller in a bank in Melbourne, Australia," he said. "One day a young man came to my window—Williams or some such name he called himself. He had a green hide bag full of gold pieces—Mexican, Spanish and English coins, some of them crusted with dirt—and he wanted to exchange them for bank-notes. I made the exchange for him. He appeared several times with similar bags, and the transaction was repeated. I thought little of it at the time, though the fact that he tried to give me a large tip did rather rouse my suspicion.

"A year later, when I had left the bank and gone to Sydney, I heard rumors of what Dan Winterslip had done on the *Maid of Shiloh*. It occurred to me that Williams and Winterslip were probably the same man. But no one seemed to be prosecuting the case, the general feeling was that it was blood money anyhow, that Tom Brade had not come by it honestly himself. So I said nothing.

"Twelve years later I came to Hawaii, and Dan Winterslip was pointed out to me. He was Williams, right enough. And he knew me, too. But I'm not a black-mailer—I've been in some tight places, Arthur, but I've always played fair—so I let the matter drop. For more than twenty years nothing happened.

"Then, a few months ago, my family located me at last, and Arthur here wrote me that he was coming to Honolulu and would look me up. I'd always felt that I'd not done the right thing by my girl—that she was not taking the place in the world to which she was entitled. I wanted her to visit my old mother and get a bit of English training. I wrote to Arthur and it was arranged. But I couldn't let her go as a charity child—I couldn't admit I'd failed and was unable to do anything for her—I said I'd pay her way. And I—I didn't have a cent.

"And then Brade came. It seemed providential. I might have sold my information to him, but when I talked with him I found he had very little money, and I felt that Winterslip would beat him in the end. No, Winterslip was my man—Winterslip with his rotten wealth. I don't know just what happened—I was quite mad, I fancy—the world owed me that, I figured, just for my girl, not for me. I called Winterslip up and made an appointment for that Monday night.

"But somehow—the standards of a lifetime—it's difficult to change. The moment I had called him, I regretted it. I tried to slip out of it—I told myself there must be some other way—perhaps I could sell the Reef and Palm—anyhow, I called him again and said I wasn't coming. But he insisted, and I went.

"I didn't have to tell him what I wanted. He knew. He had a check ready for me—a check for five thousand dollars. It was Cary's happiness, her chance. I took it, and came away—but I was ashamed. I'm not trying to excuse my action; however, I don't believe I would ever have cashed it. When Cary found it in my desk and brought it to me, I tore it up. That's all." He turned his tired eyes toward his daughter. "I did it for you, Cary, but I didn't want you to know." She went over and put her arm about his shoulder, and stood smiling down at him through her tears.

"If you'd told us that in the first place," said Greene, "you could have saved everybody a lot of trouble, yourself included."

Cope stood up. "Well, Mr Prosecutor, there you are. You're not going to hold him now?"

Greene rose briskly. "No. I'll arrange for his release at once." He and Egan went out together, then Hallet and Cope. John Quincy held out his hand to Carlota Egan—for by that name he thought of her still.

"I'm mighty glad for you," he said.

"You'll come and see me soon?" she asked. "You'll find a very different girl. More like the one you met on the Oakland ferry."

"She was very charming," John Quincy replied. "But then, she was bound to be—she had your eyes." He suddenly remembered Agatha Parker. "However, you've got your father now," he added. "You won't need me."

She looked up at him and smiled. "I wonder," she said, and went out.

John Quincy turned to Chan. "Well, that's that," he remarked. "Where are we now?"

"Speaking personally for myself," grinned Chan, "I am static in same place as usual. Never did have fondly feeling for Egan theory."

"But Hallet did," John Quincy answered. "A black morning for him."

In the small anteroom they encountered the Captain of Detectives. He appeared disgruntled.

"We were just remarking," said John Quincy pleasantly, "that there goes your little old Egan theory. What have you left?"

"Oh, I've got plenty," growled Hallet.

"Yes, you have. One by one your clues have gone up in smoke. The page from the guest book, the brooch, the torn newspaper, the ohia wood box, and now Egan and the Corsican cigarette."

"Oh, Egan isn't out of it. We may not be able to hold him, but I'm not forgetting Mr Egan."

"Nonsense," smiled John Quincy. "I asked what you had left. A little button from a glove—useless. The glove was destroyed long ago. A wrist watch with an illuminated dial and a damaged numeral two—"

Chan's amber eyes narrowed. "Essential clue," he murmured. "Remember how I said it."

Hallet banged his fist on a table. "That's it—the wrist watch! If the person who wore it knows anyone saw it, it's probably where we'll never find it now. But we've kept it pretty dark—perhaps he doesn't know. That's our only chance." He turned to Chan. "I've combed these islands once hunting that watch," he cried, "now I'm going to start all over again. The jewelry stores, the pawn shops, every nook and corner. You go out, Charlie, and start the ball rolling."

Chan moved with alacrity despite his weight. "I will give it one powerful push," he promised, and disappeared.

"Well, good luck," said John Quincy, moving on.

Hallet grunted. "You tell that aunt of yours I'm pretty sore," he remarked. He was not in the mood for elegance of diction.

John Quincy's opportunity to deliver the message did not come at lunch, for Miss Minerva remained with Barbara in the city. After dinner that evening he led his aunt out to sit on the bench under the hau tree.

"By the way," he said, "Captain Hallet is very much annoyed with you."

"I'm very much annoyed with Captain Hallet," she replied, "so that makes us even. What's his particular grievance now?"

"He believes you knew all the time the name of the man who dropped that Corsican cigarette."

She was silent for a moment. "Not all the time," she said at length. "What has happened?"

John Quincy sketched briefly the events of the morning at the police station. When he had finished he looked at her inquiringly.

"In the first excitement I didn't remember, or I should have spoken," she explained. "It was several days before the thing came to me. I saw it clearly then—Arthur—Captain Cope—tossing that cigarette aside as we reentered the house. But I said nothing about it."

"Why?"

"Well, I thought it would be a good test for the police. Let them discover it for themselves."

"That's a pretty weak explanation," remarked John Quincy severely. "You've been responsible for a lot of wasted time."

"It—it wasn't my only reason," said Miss Minerva softly.

"Oh—I'm glad to hear that. Go on."

"Somehow, I couldn't bring myself to link up that call of Captain Cope's with—a murder mystery."

Another silence. And suddenly—he was never dense—John Quincy understood.

"He told me you were very beautiful in the eighties," said the boy gently. "The captain, I mean. When I met him in that San Francisco club."

Miss Minerva laid her own hand on the boy's. When she spoke her voice, which he had always thought firm and sharp, trembled a little. "On this beach in my girl-hood," she said, "happiness was within my grasp. I had only to reach out and take it. But somehow—Boston—Boston held me back. I let my happiness slip away."

"Not too late yet," suggested John Quincy.

She shook her head. "So he tried to tell me that Monday afternoon. But there was something in his tone—I may be in Hawaii, but I'm not quite mad. Youth, John Quincy, youth doesn't return, whatever they may say out here." She pressed his hand, and stood. "If your chance comes, dear boy," she added, "don't be such a fool."

She moved hastily away through the garden, and John Quincy looked after her with a new affection in his eyes.

Presently he saw the yellow glare of a match beyond the wire. Amos again, still loitering under his algaroba tree. John Quincy rose and strolled over to him.

"Hello, Cousin Amos," he said. "When are you going to take down this fence?"

"Oh, I'll get round to it some time," Amos answered. "By the way, I wanted to ask you. Any new developments?"

"Several," John Quincy told him. "But nothing that gets us anywhere. So far as I can see, the case has blown up completely."

"Well, I've been thinking it over," Amos said. "Maybe that would be the best outcome, after all. Suppose they do discover who did for Dan—it may only reveal a new scandal, worse than any of the others."

"I'll take a chance on that," replied John Quincy. "For my part, I intend to see this thing through—"

Haku came briskly through the garden. "Cable message for Mr John Quincy Winterslip. Boy say collect. Requests money."

John Quincy followed quickly to the front door. A bored small boy awaited him. He paid the sum due and tore open the cable. It was signed by the postmaster at Des Moines, and it read:

"No one named Saladine ever heard of here."

John Quincy dashed to the telephone. Someone on duty at the station informed him that Chan had gone home, and gave him an address on Punchbowl Hill. He got out the roadster, and in five minutes more was speeding toward the city.

XIX

GOODBYE, PETE!

Charlie Chan lived in a bungalow that clung precariously to the side of Punchbowl Hill. Pausing a moment at the Chinaman's gate, John Quincy looked down on Honolulu, one great gorgeous garden set in an amphitheater of mountains. A beautiful picture, but he had no time for beauty now. He hurried up the brief walk that lay in the shadow of the palm trees.

A Chinese woman—a servant, she seemed—ushered him into Chan's dimly-lighted living-room. The detective was seated at a table playing chess; he rose with dignity when he saw his visitor. In this, his hour of ease, he wore a long loose robe of dark purple silk, which fitted closely at the neck and had wide sleeves. Beneath it showed wide trousers of the same material, and on his feet were shoes of silk, with thick felt soles. He was all Oriental now, suave and ingratiating but remote, and for the first time John Quincy was really conscious of the great gulf across which he and Chan shook hands.

"You do my lowly house immense honor," Charlie said. "This proud moment are made still more proud by opportunity to introduce my eldest son." He motioned for his opponent at chess to step forward, a slim sallow boy with amber eyes—Chan himself before he put on weight. "Mr John Quincy Winterslip, of Boston, kindly condescend to notice Henry Chan. When you appear I am giving him lesson at chess so he may play in such manner as not to tarnish honored name."

The boy bowed low; evidently he was one member of the younger generation who had a deep respect for his elders. John Quincy also bowed. "Your father is my very good friend," he said. "And from now on, you are too."

Chan beamed with pleasure. "Condescend to sit on this atrocious chair. Is it possible you bring news?"

"It certainly is," smiled John Quincy. He handed over the message from the postmaster at Des Moines.

"Most interesting," said Chan. "Do I hear impressive chug of rich automobile engine in street?"

"Yes, I came in the car," John Quincy replied.

"Good. We will hasten at once to home of Captain Hallet, not far away. I beg of you to pardon my disappearance while I don more appropriate costume."

Left alone with the boy, John Quincy sought a topic of conversation. "Play baseball?" he asked.

The boy's eyes glowed. "Not very good, but I hope to improve. My cousin Willie Chan is great expert at that game. He has promised to teach me."

John Quincy glanced about the room. On the back wall hung a scroll with felicitations, the gift of some friend of the family at New Year's. Opposite him, on another wall, was a single picture, painted on silk, representing a bird on an apple bough. Charmed by its simplicity, he went over to examine it. "That's beautiful," he said.

"Quoting old Chinese saying, a picture is a voiceless poem," replied the boy.

Beneath the picture stood a square table, flanked by straight, low-backed armchairs. On other elaborately carved teakwood stands distributed about the room were blue and white vases, porcelain wine jars, dwarfed trees. Pale golden lanterns hung from the ceiling; a soft-toned rug lay on the floor. John Quincy felt again the gulf between himself and Charlie Chan.

But when the detective returned, he wore the conventional garb of Los Angeles or Detroit, and the gulf did not seem so wide. They went out together and entering the roadster, drove to Hallet's house on Iolani Avenue.

The captain lolled in pajamas on his lanai. He greeted his callers with interest.

"You boys are out late," he said. "Something doing?"

"Certainly is," replied John Quincy, taking a proffered chair. "There's a man named Saladine—"

At mention of the name, Hallet looked at him keenly. John Quincy went on to tell what he knew of Saladine, his alleged place of residence, his business, the tragedy of the lost teeth.

"Some time ago we got on to the fact that every time Kaohla figured in the investigation, Saladine was interested. He managed to be at the desk of the Reef and Palm the day Kaohla inquired for Brade. On the night Kaohla was questioned by your men, Miss Egan saw Mr Saladine crouching outside the window. So Charlie and I thought it a good scheme to send a cable of inquiry to the postmaster at Des Moines, where Saladine claimed to be in the wholesale grocery business." He handed an envelope to Hallet. "That answer arrived tonight," he added.

An odd smile had appeared on Hallet's usually solemn face. He took the cable and read it, then slowly tore it into bits.

"Forget it, boys," he said calmly.

"Wha—what!" gasped John Quincy.

"I said forget it. I like your enterprise, but you're on the wrong trail there."

John Quincy was greatly annoyed. "I demand an explanation," he cried.

"I can't give it to you," Hallet answered. "You'll have to take my word for it."

"I've taken your word for a good many things," said John Quincy hotly. "This begins to look rather suspicious to me. Are you trying to shield somebody?"

Hallet rose and laid his hand on John Quincy's shoulder. "I've had a hard day," he remarked, "and I'm not going to get angry with you. I'm not trying to shield anybody. I'm as anxious as you are to discover who killed Dan Winterslip. More anxious, perhaps."

"Yet when we bring you evidence you tear it up—"

"Bring me the right evidence," said Hallet. "Bring me that wrist watch. I can promise you action then."

John Quincy was impressed by the sincerity in his tone. But he was sadly puzzled, too. "All right," he said, "that's that. I'm sorry if we've troubled you with this trivial matter—"

"Don't talk like that," Hallet broke in. "I'm glad of your help. But as far as Mr Saladine is concerned—" he looked at Chan—"let him alone."

Chan bowed. "You are undisputable chief," he replied.

They went back to Punchbowl Hill in the roadster, both rather dejected. As Chan alighted at his gate, John Quincy spoke: "Well, I'm pau. Saladine was my last hope."

The Chinaman stared for a moment at the moonlit Pacific that lay beyond the waterfront lamps. "Stone wall surround us," he said dreamily. "But we circle about, seeking loophole. Moment of discovery will come."

"I wish I thought so," replied John Quincy.

Chan smiled. "Patience are a very lovely virtue," he remarked. "Seem that way to me. But maybe that are my Oriental mind. Your race, I perceive, regard patience with ever-swelling disfavor."

It was with swelling disfavor that John Quincy regarded it as he drove back to Waikiki. Yet he had great need of patience in the days immediately following. For nothing happened.

The forty-eight-hour period given him to leave Hawaii expired, but the writer of that threatening letter failed to come forward and relieve the tedium. Thursday arrived, a calm day like the others; Thursday night, peaceful and serene.

On Friday afternoon Agatha Parker broke the monotony by a cable sent from the Wyoming ranch.

"You must be quite mad. I find the West crude and impossible."

John Quincy smiled; he could picture her as she wrote it, proud, haughty, unyielding. She must have been popular with the man who transmitted the message. Or was he, too, an exile from the East?

And perhaps the girl was right. Perhaps he was mad, after all. He sat on Dan Winterslip's lanai, trying to think things out. Boston, the office, the art gallery, the theaters. The Common on a winter's day, with the air bracing and full of life. The thrill of a new issue of bonds, like the thrill of a theatrical first night—would it get over big or flop at his feet? Tennis at Longwood, long evenings on the Charles, golf with people of his own kind at Magnolia. Tea out of exquisite cups in dim old drawing-rooms. Wasn't he mad to think of giving up all that? But what had Miss Minerva said? "If your chance ever comes—"

The problem was a big one, and big problems were annoying out here where the lotus grew. He yawned, and went aimlessly downtown. Drifting into the public library, he saw Charlie Chan hunched over a table that held an enormous volume. John Quincy went closer. The book was made up of back numbers of the Honolulu morning paper, and it was open at a time-yellowed sporting page.

"Hello, Chan. What are you up to?"

The Chinaman gave him a smile of greeting. "Hello. Little bit of careless reading while I gallop about seeking loophole." He closed the big volume casually. "You seem in the best of health."

"Oh, I'm all right."

"No more fierce shots out of bushes?"

"Not a trigger pulled. I imagine that was a big bluff—nothing more."

"What do you say—bluff?"

"I mean the fellow's a coward, after all."

Chan shook his head solemnly. "Pardon humble suggestion—do not lose carefulness. Hot heads plenty in hot climate."

"I'll look before I leap," John Quincy promised. "But I'm afraid I interrupted you."

"Ridiculous thought," protested Chan.

"I'll go along. Let me know if anything breaks."

"Most certainly. Up to present, everything are intact."

John Quincy paused at the door of the reference room Charlie Chan had promptly opened the big book, and was again bending over it with every show of interest.

Returning to Waikiki, John Quincy faced a dull evening. Barbara had gone to the island of Kauai for a visit with old friends of the family. He had not been sorry when she went, for he didn't feel quite at ease in her presence. The estrangement between the girl and Jennison continued; the lawyer had not been at the dock to see her off. Yes, John Quincy had parted from her gladly, but her absence cast a pall of loneliness over the house on Kalia Road.

After dinner, he sat with his pipe on the lanai. Down the beach at the Reef and Palm pleasant company was available—but he hesitated. He had seen Carlota Egan several times by day, on the beach or in the water. She was very happy now, though somewhat appalled at thought of her approaching visit to England. They'd had several talks about that—daylight talks. John Quincy was a bit afraid to entrust himself—as Chan had said in speaking of his stone idol—of an evening. After all, there was Agatha, there was Boston. There was Barbara, too.

Being entangled with three girls at once was a rather wearing experience. He rose, and went downtown to the movies.

On Saturday morning he was awakened early by the whir of aeroplanes above the house. The American fleet was in the offing, and the little brothers of the air service hastened out to hover overhead in friendly welcome. That day a spirit of carnival prevailed in Honolulu, flags floated from every masthead, and the streets bloomed, as Barbara had predicted, with handsome boys in spotless uniforms. They were everywhere, swarming in the souvenir stores, besieging the soda fountains, sky-larking on the trolley-cars. Evening brought a great ball at the beach hotel, and John Quincy, out for a walk, saw that every spic and span uniform moved toward Waikiki, accompanied by a fair young thing who was only too happy to serve as sweetheart in that particular port.

John Quincy felt, suddenly, rather out of things. Each pretty girl he saw recalled Carlota Egan. He turned his wandering footsteps toward the Reef and Palm, and oddly enough, his pace quickened at once.

The proprietor himself was behind the desk, his eyes calm and untroubled now.

"Good evening, Mr Egan—or should I say Mr Cope," remarked John Quincy.

"Oh, we'll stick to the Egan, I guess," the man replied. "Sort of got out of the hang of the other. Mr Winterslip, I'm happy to set you. Cary will be down in a moment."

John Quincy gazed about the big public room. It was a scene of confusion, spattered ladders, buckets of paint, rolls of new wall-paper. "What's going on?" he inquired.

"Freshening things up a bit," Egan answered. "You know, we're in society now." He laughed. "Yes, sir, the old Reef and Palm has been standing here a long time without so much as a glance from the better element of Honolulu. But now they know I'm related to the British Admiralty, they've suddenly discovered it's a quaint and interesting place. They're dropping in for tea. Just fancy. But that's Honolulu."

"That's Boston, too," John Quincy assured him.

"Yes—and precisely the sort of thing I ran away from England to escape, a good many years ago. I'd tell them all to go to the devil—but there's Cary. Somehow, women feel differently about those things. It will warm her heart a bit to have these dowagers smile upon her. And they're smiling—you know, they've even dug up the fact that my Cousin George has been knighted for making a particularly efficient brand of soap." He grimaced. "It's nothing I'd have mentioned myself—a family skeleton, as I see it. But society has odd standards. And I mustn't be hard on poor old George. As Arthur says, making soap is good clean fun."

"Is your brother still with you?"

"No. He's gone back to finish his job in the Fanning Group. When he returns, I'm sending Cary to England for a long stop. Yes, that's right—*I'm* sending her," he added quickly. "I'm paying for these repairs, too. You see, I've been able to add a second mortgage to the one already on the poor tottering Reef and Palm. That's another outcome of my new-found connection with the British Admiralty and the silly old soap business. Here's Cary now."

John Quincy turned. And he was glad he had, for he would not willingly have missed the picture of Carlota on the stairs. Carlota in an evening gown of some shimmering material, her dark hair dressed in a new and amazingly effective way, her white shoulders gleaming, her eyes happy at last. As she came quickly toward him he caught his breath, never had he seen her look so beautiful. She must have heard his voice in the office, he reflected, and with surprising speed arrayed herself thus to greet him. He was deeply grateful as he took her hand.

"Stranger," she rebuked. "We thought you'd deserted us."

"I'd never do that," he answered. "But I've been rather busy—"

A step sounded behind him. He turned, and there stood one of those ubiquitous navy boys, a tall, blond Adonis who held his cap in his hand and smiled in a devastating way.

"Hello, Johnnie," Carlota said. "Mr Winterslip, of Boston, this is Lieutenant Booth, of Richmond, Virginia."

"How are you," nodded the boy, without removing his eyes from the girl's face. Just one of the guests, this Winterslip, no account at all—such was obviously the lieutenant's idea. "All ready, Cary? The car's outside."

"I'm frightfully sorry, Mr Winterslip," said the girl, "but we're off to the dance. This weekend belongs to the navy, you know. You'll come again, won't you?"

"Of course," John Quincy replied. "Don't let me keep you."

She smiled at him and fled with Johnnie at her side. Looking after them, John Quincy felt his heart sink to his boots, an unaccountable sensation of age and helplessness. Youth, youth was going through that door, and he was left behind.

"A great pity she had to run," said Egan in a kindly voice.

"Why, that's all right," John Quincy assured him. "Old friend of the family, this Lieutenant Booth?"

"Not at all. Just a lad Cary met at parties in San Francisco. Won't you sit down and have a smoke with me?"

"Some other time, thanks," John Quincy said wearily. "I must hurry back to the house."

He wanted to escape, to get out into the calm lovely night, the night that was ruined for him now. He walked along the beach, savagely kicking his toes into the white sand. "Johnnie!" She had called him Johnnie. And the way she had looked at him, too! Again John Quincy felt that sharp pang in his heart. Foolish, foolish; better go back to Boston and forget. Peaceful old Boston, that was where he belonged. He was an old man out here—thirty, nearly. Better go away and leave these children to love and the moonlit beach.

Miss Minerva had gone in the big car to call on friends, and the house was quiet as the tomb. John Quincy wandered aimlessly about the rooms, gloomy and bereft. Down at the Moana an Hawaiian orchestra was playing and Lieutenant Booth, of Richmond, was holding Carlota close in the intimate manner affected these days by the young. Bah! If he hadn't been ordered to leave Hawaii, by gad, he'd go tomorrow.

The telephone rang. None of the servants appeared to answer it, so John Quincy went himself.

"Charlie Chan speaking," said a voice. "That is you, Mr Winterslip? Good. Big events will come to pass very quick. Meet me drug and grocery emporium of Liu Yin, number 927 River Street, soon as you can do so. You savvy locality?"

"I'll find it," cried John Quincy, delighted.

"By bank of stream. I will await. Goodbye."

Action—action at last! John Quincy's heart beat fast. Action was what he wanted tonight. As usually happens in a crisis, there was no automobile available; the roadster was at a garage undergoing repairs, and the other car was in use. He hastened over to Kalakaua Avenue intending to rent a machine, but a trolley approaching at the moment altered his plans and he swung aboard.

Never had a trolley moved at so reluctant a pace. When they reached the corner of Fort Street in the center of the city, he left it and proceeded on foot. The hour was still fairly early, but the scene was one of somnolent calm. A couple of tourists drifted aimlessly by. About the bright doorway of a shooting gallery loitered a group of soldiers from the fort, with a sprinkling of enlisted navy men. John Quincy hurried on down King Street, past Chinese noodle cafés and pawn shops, and turned presently off into River Street.

On his left was the river, on his right an array of shabby stores. He paused at the door of number 927, the establishment of Liu Yin. Inside, seated behind a screen that revealed only their heads, a number of Chinese were engrossed in a friendly little game. John Quincy opened the door; a bell tinkled, and he stepped into an odor of must and decay. Curious sights met his quick eye, dried roots and herbs, jars of sea-horse skeletons, dejected ducks flattened out and varnished to tempt the palate, gobbets of pork. An old Chinaman rose and came forward.

"I'm looking for Mr Charlie Chan," said John Quincy.

The old man nodded and led the way to a red curtain across the rear of the shop. He lifted it, and indicated that John Quincy was to pass. The boy did so, and came into a bare room furnished with a cot, a table on which an oil lamp burned dimly behind a smoky chimney, and a couple of chairs. A man who had been sitting on one of the chairs rose suddenly; a huge red-haired man with the smell of the sea about him.

"Hello," he said.

"Is Mr Chan here?" John Quincy inquired.

"Not yet. He'll be along in a minute. What say to a drink while we're waiting. Hey, Liu, a coupla glasses that rotten rice wine!"

The Chinaman withdrew. "Sit down," said the man. John Quincy obeyed; the sailor sat too. One of his eye-lids drooped wickedly; he rested his hands on the table—enormous hairy hands. "Charlie'll be here pretty quick," he said. "Then I got a little story to tell the two of you."

"Yes?" John Quincy replied. He glanced about the little vile-smelling room. There was a door, a closed door, at the back. He looked again at the red-haired man. He wondered how he was going to get out of there.

For he knew now that Charlie Chan had not called him on the telephone. It came to him belatedly that the voice was never Charlie's. "You savvy locality?" the voice had said. A clumsy attempt at Chan's style, but Chan was a student of English; he dragged his words painfully from the poets; he was careful to use nothing that savored of "pidgin." No, the detective had not telephoned; he was no doubt at home now bending over his chess-board, and here was John Quincy shut up in a little room on the fringe of the River District with a husky sailorman who leered at him knowingly.

The old Chinaman returned with two small glasses into which the liquor had already been poured. He set them on the table. The red-haired man lifted one of them. "Your health, sir," he said.

John Quincy took up the other glass and raised it to his lips. There was a suspicious eagerness in the sailor's one good eye. John Quincy put the glass back on the table. "I'm sorry," he said. "I don't want a drink, thank you."

The great face with its stubble of red beard leaned close to his. "Y' mean you won't drink with me?" said the red-haired man belligerently.

"That's just what I mean," John Quincy answered. Might as well get it over with, he felt; anything was better than this suspense. He stood up. "I'll be going along," he announced.

He took a step toward the red curtain. The sailor, evidently a fellow of few words, rose and got in his way. John Quincy, himself feeling the futility of talk, said nothing, but struck the man in the face. The sailor struck back with efficiency and promptness. In another second the room was full of battle, and John Quincy saw red everywhere, red curtain, red hair, red lamp flame, great red hairy hands cunningly seeking his face. What was it Roger had said? "Ever fought with a ship's officer—the old-fashioned kind with fists like flying hams?" No, he hadn't up to then, but that sweet experience was his now, and it came to John Quincy pleasantly that he was doing rather well at his new trade.

This was better than the attic; here he was prepared and had a chance. Time and again he got his hands on the red curtain, only to be dragged back and subjected to a new attack. The sailor was seeking to knock him out, and though many of his blows went home, that happy result—from the standpoint of the red-haired man—was unaccountably delayed. John Quincy had a similar aim in life; they lunged noisily about the room, while the surprising Orientals in the front of the shop continued their quiet game.

John Quincy felt himself growing weary; his breath came painfully; he realized that his adversary had not yet begun to fight. Standing with his back to the table in an idle moment while the red-haired man made plans for the future, the boy hit on a plan of his own. He overturned the table; the lamp crashed down; darkness fell over the world. In the final glimmer of light he saw the big man coming for him and dropping to his knees he tackled in the approved manner of Soldiers' Field, Cambridge, Massachusetts. Culture prevailed; the sailor went on his head with a resounding thump; John Quincy let go of him and sought the nearest exit. It happened to be the door at the rear, and it was unlocked.

He passed hurriedly through a cluttered back yard and climbing a fence, found himself in the neighborhood known as the River District. There in crazy alleys that have no names, no sidewalks, no beginning and no end, five races live together in the dark. Some houses were above the walk level, some below, all were out of alignment. John Quincy felt he had wandered into a futurist drawing. As he paused he heard the whine and clatter of Chinese music, the clicking of a typewriter, the rasp of a cheap phonograph playing American jazz, the distant scream of an auto horn, a child wailing Japanese lamentations. Footsteps in the yard beyond the fence roused him, and he fled.

He must get out of this mystic maze of mean alleys, and at once. Odd painted faces loomed in the dusk: pasty-white faces with just a suggestion of queer costumes beneath. A babel of tongues, queer eyes that glittered, once a lean hand on his arm. A group of moon-faced Chinese children under a lamp who scattered at his approach. And when he paused again, out of breath, the patter of many feet, bare feet, sandaled feet, the clatter of wooden clogs, the squeak of cheap shoes made in his own Massachusetts. Then suddenly the thump of large feet such as might belong to a husky sailor. He moved on.

Presently he came into the comparative quiet of River Street, and realized that he had traveled in a circle, for there was Liu Yin's shop again. As he hurried on toward King Street, he saw, over his shoulder, that the red-haired man still followed. A big touring car, with curtains drawn, waited by the curb. John Quincy leaped in beside the driver.

"Get out of here, quick!" he panted.

A sleepy Japanese face looked at him through the gloom. "Busy now."

"I don't care if you are—" began John Quincy, and glanced down at one of the man's arms resting on the wheel. His heart stood still. In the dusk he saw a wrist watch with an illuminated dial, and the numeral two was very dim.

Even as he looked, strong hands seized him by the collar and dragged him into the dark tonneau. At the same instant, the red-haired man arrived.

"Got him, Mike? Say, that's luck!" He leaped into the rear of the car. Quick able work went forward, John Quincy's hands were bound behind his back, a vile-tasting gag was put in his mouth. "Damned if this bird didn't land me one in the eye," said the red-haired man. "I'll pay him for it when we get aboard. Hey you—Pier 78. Show us some speed!"

The car leaped forward. John Quincy lay on the dusty floor, bound and helpless. To the docks? But he wasn't thinking of that, he was thinking of the watch on the driver's wrist.

A brief run, and they halted in the shadow of a pier-shed. John Quincy was lifted and propelled none too gently from the car. His cheek was jammed against one of the buttons holding the side curtain, and he had sufficient presence of mind to catch the gag on it and loosen it. As they left the car he tried to get a glimpse of its license plate, but he was able to ascertain only the first two figures—33—before it sped away.

His two huge chaperons hurried him along the dock. Some distance off he saw a little group of men, three in white uniforms, one in a darker garb. The latter was smoking a pipe. John Quincy's heart leaped. He maneuvered the loosened gag with his teeth, so that it dropped about his collar. "Goodbye, Pete!" he shouted at the top of his lungs, and launched at once into a terrific struggle to break away from his startled captors.

There was a moment's delay, and then the clatter of feet along the dock. A stocky boy in a white uniform began an enthusiastic debate with Mike, and the other two were prompt to claim the attention of the red-haired man. Pete Mayberry was at John Quincy's back, cutting the rope on his wrists.

"Well, I'll be damned, Mr Winterslip," he cried.

"Same here," laughed John Quincy. "Shanghaied in another minute but for you." He leaped forward to join the battle, but the red-haired man and his friend had already succumbed to youth and superior forces, and were in full retreat. John Quincy followed joyously along the dock, and planted his fist back of his old adversary's ear. The sailor staggered, but regained his balance and went on.

John Quincy returned to his rescuers. "The last blow is the sweetest," he remarked.

"I can place those guys," said Mayberry. "They're off that tramp steamer that's been lying out in the harbor the past week. An opium runner, I'll gamble on it. You go to the police station right away—"

"Yes," said John Quincy, "I must. But I want to thank you, Mr Mayberry. And"—he turned to the white uniforms— "you fellows too."

The stocky lad was picking up his cap. "Why, that's all right," he said. "A real pleasure, if you ask me. But look here, old timer," he added, addressing Mayberry, "how about your Honolulu waterfront and its lost romance? You go tell that to the marines."

As John Quincy hurried away Pete Mayberry was busily explaining that the thing was unheard of—not in twenty years—maybe more than that—his voice died in the distance.

Hallet was in his room, and John Quincy detailed his evening's adventure. The captain was incredulous, but when the boy came to the wrist watch on the driver of the car, he sat up and took notice.

"Now you're talking," he cried. "I'll start the force after that car tonight. First two figures 33, you say. I'll send somebody aboard that tramp, too. They can't get away with stuff like that around here."

"Oh, never mind them," said John Quincy magnanimously. "Concentrate on the watch."

Back in the quiet town he walked with his head up, his heart full of the joy of battle. And while he thought of it, he stepped into the cable office. The message he sent was addressed to Agatha Parker on that Wyoming ranch. "San Francisco or nothing," was all it said.

As he walked down the deserted street on his way to the corner to wait for his trolley, he heard quick footsteps on his trail again. Who now? He was sore and weary, a bit fed up on fighting for one evening. He quickened his pace. The steps quickened too. He went even faster. So did his pursuer. Oh, well, might as well stop and face him.

John Quincy turned. A young man rushed up, a lean young man in a cap.

"Mr Winterslip, ain't it?" He thrust a dark brown object into John Quincy's hand. "Your July *Atlantic*, sir. Came in on the *Maui* this morning."

"Oh," said John Quincy limply. "Well, I'll take it. My aunt might like to look at it. Keep the change."

"Thank you, sir," said the newsman, touching his cap.

John Quincy rode out to Waikiki on the last seat of the car. His face was swollen and cut, every muscle ached. Under his arm, clasped tightly, he held the July *Atlantic*. But he didn't so much as look at the table of contents. "We move, we advance," he told himself exultantly. For he had seen the watch with the illuminated dial—the dial on which the numeral two was very dim.

XX

THE STORY OF LAU HO

Early Sunday morning John Quincy was awakened by a sharp knock on his door. Rising sleepily and donning dressing-gown and slippers, he opened it to admit his Aunt Minerva. She had a worried air.

"Are you all right, John Quincy?" she inquired.

"Surely. That is, I would be if I hadn't been dragged out of bed a full hour before I intended to get up."

"I'm sorry, but I had to have a look at you." She took a newspaper from under her arm and handed it to him. "What's all this?"

An eight-column head on the first page caught even John Quincy's sleepy eye. "Boston Man has Strange Adventure on Waterfront." Smaller heads announced that Mr John Quincy Winterslip had been rescued from an unwelcome trip to China, "in the nick of time" by three midshipmen from the *Oregon*. Poor Pete Mayberry! He had been the real hero of the affair, but his own paper would not come out again until Monday evening, and rivals had beaten him to the story.

John Quincy yawned. "All true, my dear," he said. "I was on the verge of leaving you when the navy saved me. Life, you perceive, has become a musical comedy."

"But why should anyone want to shanghai you?" cried Miss Minerva.

"Ah, I hoped you'd ask me that. It happens that your nephew has a brain. His keen analytical work as a detective is getting someone's goat. He admitted as much in a letter he sent me the night he took a few shots at my head."

"Someone shot at you!" gasped Miss Minerva.

"I'll say so. You rather fancy yourself as a sleuth, but is anybody taking aim at you from behind bushes? Answer me that."

Miss Minerva sat down weakly on a chair. "You're going home on the next boat," she announced.

He laughed. "About two weeks ago I made that suggestion to you. And what was your reply? Ah, my dear, the tables are turned. I'm not going home on the next boat. I may never go home. This gay, care-free, sudden country begins to appeal to me. Let me read about myself."

He returned to the paper. "The clock was turned back thirty years on the Honolulu waterfront last night," began the somewhat imaginative account. It closed with the news that the tramp steamer *Mary S. Allison* had left port before the police could board her. Evidently she'd had steam up and papers ready, and was only awaiting the return of the red-haired man and his victim. John Quincy handed the newspaper back to his aunt.

"Too bad," he remarked. "They slipped through Hallet's fingers."

"Of course they did," she snapped. "Everybody does. I'd like a talk with Captain Hallet. If I could only tell him what I think of him, I'd feel better."

"Save that paper," John Quincy said. "I want to send it to mother."

She stared at him. "Are you mad? Poor Grace—she'd have a nervous breakdown. I only hope she doesn't hear of this until you're back in Boston safe and sound."

"Oh, yes—Boston," laughed John Quincy. "Quaint old town, they tell me. I must visit there some day. Now if you'll leave me a minute, I'll prepare to join you at breakfast and relate the story of my adventurous life."

"Very well," agreed Miss Minerva, rising. She paused at the door. "A little witch-hazel might help your face."

"The scars of honorable battle," said her nephew. "Why remove them?"

"Honorable fiddlesticks," Miss Minerva answered. "After all, the Back Bay has its good points." But in the hall outside she smiled a delighted little smile.

When John Quincy and his aunt were leaving the dining-room after breakfast Kamaikui, stiff and dignified in a freshly-laundered holoku, approached the boy.

"So very happy to see you safe this morning," she announced.

"Why, thank you, Kamaikui," he answered. He wondered. Was Kaohla responsible for his troubles, and if so, did this huge silent woman know of her grandson's activities?

"Poor thing," Miss Minerva said as they entered the living-room. "She's been quite downcast since Dan went. I'm sorry for her. I've always liked her."

"Naturally," smiled John Quincy. "There's a bond between you."

"What's that?"

"Two vanishing races, yours and hers. The Boston Brahman and the pure Hawaiian."

Later in the morning Carlota Egan telephoned him, greatly excited. She had just seen the Sunday paper.

"All true," he admitted. "While you were dancing your heart out, I was struggling to sidestep a Cook's tour of the Orient."

"I shouldn't have had a happy moment if I'd known."

"Then I'm glad you didn't. Big party, I suppose?"

"Yes. You know, I've been terribly worried about you ever since that night on the avenue. I want to talk with you. Will you come to see me?"

"Will I? I'm on my way already."

He hung up the receiver and hastened down the beach. Carlota was sitting on the white sand not far from the Reef and Palm, all in white herself. A serious wide-eyed Carlota quite different from the gay girl who had been hurrying to a party the night before.

John Quincy dropped down beside her, and for a time they talked of the dance and of his adventure. Suddenly she turned to him.

"I have no right to ask it, I know, but—I want you to do something for me."

"It will make me very happy—anything you ask."

"Go back to Boston."

"What! Not that. I was wrong—that wouldn't make me happy."

"Yes, it would. You don't think so now, perhaps. You're dazzled by the sun out here, but this isn't your kind of place. We're not your kind of people. You think you like us, but you'd soon forget. Back among your own sort—the sort who are interested in the things that interest you. Please go."

"It would be retreating under fire," he objected.

"But you proved your courage, last night. I'm afraid for you. Someone out here has a terrible grudge against you. I'd never forgive Hawaii if—if anything happened to you."

"That's sweet of you." He moved closer. But—confound it—there was Agatha. Bound to Agatha by all the ties of honor. He edged away again. "I'll think about it," he agreed.

"I'm leaving Honolulu too, you know," she reminded him.

"I know. You'll have a wonderful time in England."

She shook her head. "Oh, I dread the whole idea. Dad's heart is set on it, and I shall go to please him. But I shan't enjoy it. I'm not up to England."

"Nonsense."

"No, I'm not. I'm unsophisticated—crude, really—just a girl of the Islands."

"But you wouldn't care to stay here all your life?"

"No, indeed. It's a beautiful spot—to loll about in. But I've too much northern blood to be satisfied with that. One of these days I want dad to sell and we'll go to the mainland. I could get some sort of work—"

"Any particular place on the mainland?"

"Well, I haven't been about much, of course. But all the time I was at school I kept thinking I'd rather live in San Francisco than anywhere else in the world—"

"Good," John Quincy cried. "That's my choice too. You remember that morning on the ferry, how you held out your hand to me and said: 'Welcome to your city—'"

"But you corrected me at once. You said you belonged in Boston."

"I see my error now."

She shook her head. "A moment's madness, but you'll recover. You're an easterner, and you could never be happy anywhere else."

"Oh, yes, I could," he assured her. "I'm a Winterslip, a wandering Winterslip. Any old place we hang our hats—" This time he did lean rather close. "I could be happy anywhere—" he began. He wanted to add "with you." But Agatha's slim patrician hand was on his shoulder. "Anywhere," he repeated, with a different inflection. A gong sounded from the Reef and Palm.

Carlota rose. "That's lunch." John Quincy stood too. "It's beside the point—where you go," she went on. "I asked you to do something for me."

"I know. If you'd asked anything else in the world, I'd be up to my neck in it now. But what you suggest would take a bit of doing. To leave Hawaii—and say goodbye to you—"

"I meant to be very firm about it," she broke in.

"But I must have a little time to consider. Will you wait?"

She smiled up at him. "You're so much wiser than I am," she said. "Yes—I'll wait."

He went slowly along the beach. Unsophisticated, yes—and charming. "You're so much wiser than I am." Where on the mainland could one encounter a girl nowadays who'd say that? He had quite forgotten that she smiled when she said it.

In the afternoon, John Quincy visited the police station. Hallet was in his room in rather a grouchy mood. Chan was out somewhere hunting the watch. No, they hadn't found it yet.

John Quincy was mildly reproving. "Well, you saw it, didn't you?" growled Hallet. "Why in Sam Hill didn't you grab it?"

"Because they tied my hands," John Quincy reminded him. "I've narrowed the search, down for you to the taxi drivers of Honolulu."

"Hundreds of them, my boy."

"More than that, I've given you the first two numbers on the license plate of the car. If you're any good at all, you ought to be able to land that watch now."

"Oh, we'll land it," Hallet said. "Give us time."

Time was just what John Quincy had to give them. Monday came and went. Miss Minerva was bitterly sarcastic.

"Patience are a very lovely virtue," John Quincy told her. "I got that from Charlie."

"At any rate," she snapped, "it are a virtue very much needed with Captain Hallet in charge."

In another direction, too, John Quincy was called upon to exercise patience. Agatha Parker was unaccountably silent regarding that short peremptory cable he had sent on his big night in town. Was she offended? The Parkers were notoriously not a family who accepted dictation. But in such a vital matter as this, a girl should be willing to listen to reason.

Late Tuesday afternoon Chan telephoned from the station-house—unquestionably Chan this time. Would John Quincy do him the great honor to join him for an early dinner at the Alexander Young café?

"Something doing, Charlie?" cried the boy eagerly.

"Maybe it might be," answered Chan, "and maybe also not. At six o'clock in hotel lobby, if you will so far condescend."

"I'll be there," John Quincy promised, and he was.

He greeted Chan with anxious, inquiring eyes, but the Chinaman was suave and entirely non-committal. He led John Quincy to the dining-room and carefully selected a table by a front window.

"Do me the great favor to recline," he suggested.

John Quincy reclined. "Charlie, don't keep me in suspense," he pleaded.

Chan smiled. "Let us not shade the feast with gloomy murder talk," he replied. "This are social meeting. Is it that you are in the mood to dry up plate of soup?"

"Why, yes, of course," John Quincy answered. Politeness, he saw, dictated that he hide his curiosity.

"Two of the soup," ordered Chan of a white-jacketed waiter. A car drew up to the door of the Alexander Young. Chan half rose, staring at it keenly. He dropped back to his seat. "It is my high delight to entertain you thus humbly before you are restored to Boston. Converse at some length of Boston. I feel interested."

"Really?" smiled the boy.

"Undubitably. Gentleman I meet once say Boston are like China. The future of both, he say, lies in graveyards where repose useless bodies of honored guests on high. I am fogged as to meaning."

"He meant both places live in the past," John Quincy explained. "And he was right, in a way. Boston, like China, boasts a glorious history. But that's not saying the Boston of today isn't progressive. Why, do you know—"

He talked eloquently of his native city. Chan listened, rapt.

"Always," he sighed, when John Quincy finished, "I have unlimited yearning for travel." He paused to watch another car draw up before the hotel. "But it are unavailable. I am policeman on small remuneration. In my youth, rambling on evening hillside or by moonly ocean, I dream of more lofty position. Not so now. But that other American citizen, my eldest son, he are dreaming too. Maybe for him dreams eventuate. Perhaps he become second Baby Ruth, home run emperor, applause of thousands making him deaf. Who knows it?"

The dinner passed, unshaded by gloomy talk, and they went outside. Chan proffered a cigar of which he spoke in the most belittling fashion. He suggested that they stand for a time before the hotel door.

"Waiting for somebody?" inquired John Quincy, unable longer to dissemble.

"Precisely the fact. Barely dare to mention it, however. Great disappointment may drive up here any minute now."

An open car stopped before the hotel entrance. John Quincy's eyes sought the license plate, and he got an immediate thrill. The first two figures were 33.

A party of tourists, a man and two women, alighted. The doorman ran forward and busied himself with luggage. Chan casually strolled across the walk, and as the Japanese driver shifted his gears preparatory to driving away, put a restraining hand on the car door.

"One moment, please." The Japanese turned, fright in his eyes. "You are Okuda, from auto stand across way?"

"Yes-s," hissed the driver.

"You are now returned from exploring island with party of tourists? You leave this spot early Sunday morning?"

"Yes-s."

"Is it possible that you wear wrist watch, please?"

"Yes-s."

"Deign to reveal face of same."

The Japanese hesitated. Chan leaned far over into the car and thrust aside the man's coat sleeve. He came back, a pleased light in his eyes, and held open the rear door. "Kindly embark into tonneau, Mr Winterslip." Obediently John Quincy got in. Chan took his place by the driver's side. "The police station, if you will be so kind." The car leaped forward.

The essential clue! They had it at last. John Quincy's heart beat fast there in the rear of the car where, only a few nights before, he had been bound and gagged.

Captain Hallet's grim face relaxed into happy lines when he met them at the door of his room. "You got him, eh? Good work." He glanced at the prisoner's wrist. "Rip that watch off him, Charlie."

Charlie obeyed. He examined the watch for a moment, then handed it to his chief.

"Inexpensive time-piece of noted brand," he announced. "Numeral two faint and far away. One other fact emerge into light. This Japanese here have small wrist. Yet worn place on strap convey impression of being worn by man with wrist of vastly larger circumference."

Hallet nodded. "Yes, that's right. Some other man has owned this watch. He had a big wrist—but most men in Honolulu have, you know. Sit down, Okuda. I want to hear from you. You understand what it means to lie to me?"

"I do not lie, sir."

"No, you bet your sweet life you don't. First, tell me who engaged your car last Saturday night."

"Saturday night?"

"That's what I said!"

"Ah, yes. Two sailors from ship. Engage for evening paying large cash at once. I drive to shop on River Street, wait long time. Then off we go to dock with extra passenger in back."

"Know the names of those sailors?"

"Could not say."

"What ship were they from?"

"How can I know? Not told."

"All right. I'm coming to the important thing. Understand? The truth—that's what I want! Where did you get this watch?"

Chan and John Quincy leaned forward eagerly. "I buy him," said the Japanese.

"You bought him? Where?"

"At jewel store of Chinese Lau Ho on Maunakea Street."

Hallet turned to Chan. "Know the place, Charlie?"

Chan nodded. "Yes, indeed."

"Open now?"

"Open until hour of ten, maybe more."

"Good," said Hallet. "Come along, Okuda. You can drive us there."

Lau Ho, a little wizened Chinaman, sat back of his work bench with a microscope screwed into one dim old eye. The four men who entered his tiny store filled it to overflowing, but he gave them barely a glance.

"Come on, Ho—wake up," Hallet cried. "I want to talk to you."

With the utmost deliberation the Chinaman descended from his stool and approached the counter. He regarded Hallet with a hostile eye. The captain laid the wrist watch on top of a showcase in which reposed many trays of jade.

"Ever see that before?" he inquired.

Lau Ho regarded it casually. Slowly he raised his eyes. "Maybe so. Cannot say," he replied in a high squeaky voice.

Hallet reddened. "Nonsense. You had it here in the store, and you sold it to this Japanese. Now, didn't you?"

Lau Ho dreamily regarded the taxi driver. "Maybe so. Cannot say."

"Damn it!" cried Hallet. "You know who I am?"

"Policeman, maybe."

"Policeman maybe yes! And I want you to tell me about this watch. Now wake up and come across or by the Lord Harry—"

Chan laid a deferential hand on his chief's arm. "Humbly suggest I attempt this," he said.

Hallet nodded. "All right, he's your meat, Charlie." He drew back.

Chan bowed with a great show of politeness. He launched into a long story in Chinese. Lau Ho looked at him with slight interest. Presently he squeaked a brief reply. Chan resumed his flow of talk. Occasionally he paused, and Lau Ho spoke. In a few moments Chan turned beaming.

"Story are now completely extracted like aching tooth," he said. "Wrist watch was brought to Lau Ho on Thursday, same week as murder. Offered him on sale by young man darkly colored with small knife scar marring cheek. Lau Ho buy and repair watch, interior works being in injured state. Saturday morning he sell at seemly profit to Japanese, presumably this Okuda here but Lau Ho will not swear. Saturday night dark young man appear much overwhelmed with excitement and demand watch again, please. Lau Ho say it is sold to Japanese. Which Japanese? Lau Ho is not aware of name, and cannot describe, all Japanese faces being uninteresting outlook for him. Dark young man curse and fly. Appear frequently demanding any news, but Lau Ho is unable to oblige. Such are story of this jewel merchant here."

They went out on the street. Hallet scowled at the Japanese. "All right—run along. I'll keep the watch."

"Very thankful," said the taxi driver, and leaped into his car.

Hallet turned to Chan. "A dark young man with a scar?" he queried.

"Clear enough to me," Chan answered. "Same are the Spaniard José Cabrera, careless man about town with reputation not so savory. Mr Winterslip, is it that you have forgotten him?"

John Quincy started. "Me? Did I ever see him?"

"Recall," said Chan. "It are the night following murder. You and I linger in All American Restaurant engaged in debate regarding hygiene of pie. Door open, admitting Bowker, steward on *President Tyler*, joyously full of okolehau. With him are dark young man—this José Cabrera himself."

"Oh, I remember now," John Quincy answered.

"Well, the Spaniard's easy to pick up," said Hallet. "I'll have him inside an hour—"

"One moment, please," interposed Chan. "Tomorrow morning at nine o'clock the *President Tyler* return from Orient. No gambler myself but will wager incredditable sum Spaniard waits on dock for Mr Bowker. If you present no fierce objection, I have a yearning to arrest him at that very moment."

"Why, of course," agreed Hallet. He looked keenly at Charlie Chan. "Charlie, you old rascal, you've got the scent at last."

"Who—me?" grinned Chan. "With your gracious permission I would alter the picture. Stone walls are crumbling now like dust. Through many loopholes light stream in like rosy streaks of dawn."

XXI

THE STONE WALLS CRUMBLE

The stone walls were crumbling and the light streaming through—but only for Chan. John Quincy was still groping in the dark, and his reflections were a little bitter as he returned to the house at Waikiki. Chan and he had worked together, but now that they approached the crisis of their efforts, the detective evidently preferred to push on alone, leaving his fellow-worker to follow if he could. Well, so be it—but John Quincy's pride was touched.

He had suddenly a keen desire to show Chan that he could not be left behind like that. If only he could, by some inspirational flash of deductive reasoning, arrive at the solution of the mystery simultaneously with the detective. For the honor of Boston and the Winterslips.

Frowning deeply, he considered all the old discarded clues again. The people who had been under suspicion and then dropped—Egan, the Compton woman, Brade, Kaohla, Leatherbee, Saladine, Cope. He even considered several the investigation had not touched. Presently he came to Bowker. What did Bowker's reappearance mean?

For the first time in two weeks he thought of the little man with the fierce pompadour and the gold-rimmed eye-glasses. Bowker with his sorrowful talk of vanished bar-rooms and lost friends behind the bar. How was the steward on the *President Tyler* connected with the murder of Dan Winterslip? He had not done it himself, that was obvious, but in some way he was linked up with the crime. John Quincy spent a long and painful period seeking to join Bowker up with one or another of the suspects. It couldn't be done.

All through that Tuesday evening the boy puzzled, so silent and distrait that Miss Minerva finally gave him up and retired to her room with a book. He awoke on Wednesday morning with the problem no nearer solution.

Barbara was due to arrive at ten o'clock from Kauai, and taking the small car, John Quincy went downtown to meet her. Pausing at the bank to cash a check, he encountered his old shipmate on the *President Tyler*, the sprightly Madame Maynard.

"I really shouldn't speak to you," she said. "You never come to see me."

"I know," he answered. "But I've been so very busy."

"So I hear. Running round with policemen and their victims. I have no doubt you'll go back to Boston and report we're all criminals and cutthroats out here."

"Oh, hardly that."

"Yes, you will. You're getting a very biased view of Honolulu. Why not stoop to associate with a respectable person now and then?"

"I'd enjoy it—if they're all like you."

"Like me? They're much more intelligent and charming than I am. Some of them are dropping in at my house tonight for an informal little party. A bit of a chat, and then a moonlight swim. Won't you come too?"

"I want to, of course," John Quincy replied. "But there's Cousin Dan—"

Her eyes flashed. "I'll say it, even if he was your relative. Ten minutes of mourning for Cousin Dan is ample. I'll be looking for you."

John Quincy laughed. "I'll come."

"Do," she answered. "And bring your Aunt Minerva. Tell her I said she might as well be dead as hogtied by convention."

John Quincy went out to the corner of Fort and King Streets, near which he had parked the car. As he was about to climb into it, he paused. A familiar figure was jauntily crossing the street. The figure of Bowker, the steward, and with him was Willie Chan, demon back-stopper of the Pacific.

"Hello, Bowker," John Quincy called.

Mr Bowker came blithely to join him. "Well, well, well. My old friend Mr Winterslip. Shake hands with William Chan, the local Ty Cobb."

"Mr Chan and I have met before," John Quincy told him.

"Know all the celebrities, eh? That's good. Well, we missed you on the *President Tyler*."

Bowker was evidently quite sober. "Just got in, I take it," John Quincy remarked.

"A few minutes ago. How about joining us?" He came closer and lowered his voice. "This intelligent young man tells me he knows a taxi-stand out near the beach where one may obtain a superior brand of fusel oil with a very pretty label on the bottle."

"Sorry," John Quincy answered. "My cousin's coming in shortly on an Inter-island boat, and I'm elected to meet her."

"I'm sorry, too," said the graduate of Dublin University. "If my strength holds out I'm aiming to stage quite a little party, and I'd like to have you in on it. Yes, a rather large affair—in memory of Tim, and as a last long lingering farewell to the seven seas."

"What? You're pau?"

"Pau it is. When I sail out of here tonight at nine on the old *P.T.* I'm through for ever. You don't happen to know a good country newspaper that can be bought for—well, say ten grand."

"This is rather sudden, isn't it?" John Quincy inquired.

"This is sudden country out here, sir. Well, we must roll along. Sorry you can't join us. If the going's not too rough and I can find a nice smooth table top, I intend to turn down an empty glass. For poor old Tim. So long, sir—and happy days."

He nodded to Willie Chan, and they went on down the street. John Quincy stood staring after them, a puzzled expression on his face.

Barbara seemed paler and thinner than ever, but she announced that her visit had been an enjoyable one, and on the ride to the beach appeared to be making a distinct effort to be gay and sprightly. When they reached the house, John Quincy repeated to his aunt Mrs Maynard's invitation.

"Better come along," he urged.

"Perhaps I will," she answered. "I'll see."

The day passed quietly, and it was not until evening that the monotony was broken. Leaving the dining-room with his aunt and Barbara, John Quincy was handed a cablegram. He hastily opened it. It had been sent from Boston; evidently Agatha Parker, overwhelmed by the crude impossibility of the West, had fled home again, and John Quincy's brief "San Francisco or nothing" had followed her there. Hence the delay.

The cablegram said simply: "Nothing. Agatha." John Quincy crushed it in his hand; he tried to suffer a little, but it was no use. He was a mighty happy man. The end of a romance—no. There had never been any nonsense of that kind between them—just an affectionate regard too slight to stand the strain of parting. Agatha was younger than he, she would marry some nice proper boy who had no desire to roam. And John Quincy Winterslip would read of her wedding—in the San Francisco papers.

He found Miss Minerva alone in the living-room. "It's none of my business," she said, "but I'm wondering what was in your cablegram."

"Nothing," he answered truthfully.

"All the same, you were very pleased to get it."

He nodded. "Yes. I imagine nobody was ever so happy over nothing before."

"Good heavens," she cried. "Have you given up grammar, too?"

"I'm thinking of it. How about going down the beach with me?"

She shook her head. "Someone is coming to look at the house—a leading lawyer, I believe he is. He's thinking of buying, and I feel I should be here to show him about. Barbara appears so listless and disinterested. Tell Sally Maynard I may drop in later."

At a quarter to eight, John Quincy took his bathing suit and wandered down Kalia Road. It was another of those nights; a bright moon was riding high; from a bungalow buried under purple alamander came the soft croon of Hawaiian music. Through the hedges of flaming hibiscus he caught again the exquisite odors of this exotic island.

Mrs Maynard's big house was a particularly unlovely type of New England architecture, but a hundred flowering vines did much to conceal that fact. John Quincy found his hostess enthroned in her great airy drawing-room, surrounded by a handsome laughing group of the best people. Pleasant people, too; as she introduced him he began to wonder if he hadn't been missing a great deal of congenial companionship.

"I dragged him here against his will," the old lady explained. "I felt I owed it to Hawaii. He's been associating with the riff-raff long enough."

They insisted that he take an enormous chair, pressed cigarettes upon him, showered him with hospitable attentions. As he sat down and the chatter was resumed, he reflected that here was as civilized a company as Boston itself could offer. And why not? Most of these families came originally from New England, and had kept in their exile the old ideals of culture and caste.

"It might interest Beacon Street to know," Mrs Maynard said, "that long before the days of forty-nine the people of California were sending their children over here to be educated in the missionary schools. And importing their wheat from here, too."

"Go on, tell him the other one, Aunt Sally," laughed a pretty girl in blue. "That about the first printing press in San Francisco being brought over from Honolulu."

Madame Maynard shrugged her shoulders. "Oh, what's the use? We're so far away, New England will never get us straight."

John Quincy looked up to see Carlota Egan in the doorway. A moment later Lieutenant Booth, of Richmond, appeared at her side. It occurred to the young man from Boston that the fleet was rather overdoing its stop at Honolulu.

Mrs Maynard rose to greet the girl. "Come in, my dear. You know most of these people." She turned to the others. "This is Miss Egan, a neighbor of mine on the beach."

It was amusing to note that most of these people knew Carlota too. John Quincy smiled—the British Admiralty and the soap business. It must have been rather an ordeal for the girl, but she saw it through with a sweet graciousness that led John Quincy to reflect that she would be at home in England—if she went there.

Carlota sat down on a sofa, and while Lieutenant Booth was busily arranging a cushion at her back, John Quincy dropped down beside her. The sofa was, fortunately, too small for three.

"I rather expected to see you," he said in a low voice. "I was brought here to meet the best people of Honolulu, and the way I see it, you're the best of all."

She smiled at him, and again the chatter of small talk filled the room. Presently the voice of a tall young man with glasses rose above the general hubbub.

"They got a cable from Joe Clark out at the Country Club this afternoon," he announced.

The din ceased, and everyone listened with interest. "Clark's our professional," explained the young man to John Quincy. "He went over a month ago to play in the British Open."

"Did he win?" asked the girl in blue.

"He was put out by Hagen in the semi-finals," the young man said. "But he had the distinction of driving the longest ball ever seen on the St. Andrews course."

"Why shouldn't he?" asked an older man. "He's got the strongest wrists I ever saw on anybody?"

John Quincy sat up, suddenly interested. "How do you account for that?" he asked.

The older man smiled. "We've all got pretty big wrists out here," he answered. "Surf-boarding—that's what does it. Joe Clark was a champion at one time—body-surfing and board-surfing too. He used to disappear for hours in the rollers out by the reef. The result was a marvelous wrist development. I've seen him drive a golf ball three hundred and eighty yards. Yes, sir, I'll bet he made those Englishmen sit up and take notice."

While John Quincy was thinking this over, someone suggested that it was time for the swim, and confusion reigned. A Chinese servant led the way to the dressing-rooms, which opened off the lanai, and the young people trouped joyously after him.

"I'll be waiting for you on the beach," John Quincy said to Carlota Egan.

"I came with Johnnie, you know," she reminded him.

"I know all about it," he answered. "But it was the weekend you promised to the navy. People who try to stretch their weekend through the following Wednesday night deserve all they get."

She laughed. "I'll look for you," she agreed.

He donned his bathing suit hastily in a room filled with flying clothes and great waving brown arms. Lieutenant Booth, he noted with satisfaction, was proceeding at a leisurely pace.

Hurrying through a door that opened directly on the beach, he waited under a nearby hau tree. Presently Carlota came, slender and fragile-looking in the moonlight.

"Ah, here you are," John Quincy cried. "The farthest float."

"The farthest float it is," she answered.

They dashed into the warm silvery water and swam gaily off. Five minutes later they sat on the float together. The light on Diamond Head was winking; the lanterns of sampans twinkled out beyond the reef; the shore line of Honolulu was outlined by a procession of blinking stars controlled by dynamos. In the bright heavens hung a lunar rainbow, one colorful end in the Pacific and the other tumbling into the foliage ashore.

A gorgeous setting in which to be young and in love, and free to speak at last. John Quincy moved closer to the girl's side.

"Great night, isn't it?" he said.

"Wonderful," she answered softly.

"Cary, I want to tell you something, and that's why I brought you out here away from the others—"

"Somehow," she interrupted, "it doesn't seem quite fair to Johnnie."

"Never mind him. Has it ever occurred to you that my name's Johnnie, too."

She laughed. "Oh, but it couldn't be."

"What do you mean?"

"I mean I simply couldn't call you that. You're too dignified and—and remote. John Quincy—I believe I could call you John Quincy—"

"Well, make up your mind. You'll have to call me something, because I'm going to be hanging round pretty constantly in the future. Yes, my dear, I'll probably turn out to be about the least remote person in the world. That is, if I can make you see the future the way I see it. Cary dearest—"

A gurgle sounded behind them, and they turned around. Lieutenant Booth was climbing on to the raft. "Swam the last fifty yards under water to surprise you," he sputtered.

"Well, you succeeded," said John Quincy without enthusiasm.

The lieutenant sat down with the manner of one booked to remain indefinitely. "I'll tell the world it's some night," he offered.

"Speaking of the world, when do you fellows leave Honolulu?" asked John Quincy.

"I don't know. Tomorrow, I guess. Me, I don't care if we never go. Hawaii's not so easy to leave. Is it, Cary?"

She shook her head. "Hardest place I know of, Johnnie. I shall have to be sailing presently, and I know what a wrench it will be. Perhaps I'll follow the example of Waioli the swimmer, and leave the boat when it passes Waikiki."

They lolled for a moment in silence. Suddenly John Quincy sat up. "What was that you said?" he asked.

"About Waioli? Didn't I ever tell you? He was one of our best swimmers, and for years they tried to get him to go to the mainland to take part in athletic meets, like Duke Kahanamoku. But he was a sentimentalist—he couldn't bring himself to leave Hawaii. Finally they persuaded him, and one sunny morning he sailed on the *Matsonia*, with a very sad face. When the ship was opposite Waikiki he slipped overboard and swam ashore. And that was that. He never got on a ship again. You see—"

John Quincy was on his feet. "What time was it when we left the beach?" he asked in a low tense voice.

"About eight-thirty," said Booth.

John Quincy talked very fast. "That means I've got just thirty minutes to get ashore, dress, and reach the dock before the *President Tyler* sails. I'm sorry to go, but it's vital—vital. Cary, I'd started to tell you something. I don't know when I'll get back, but I must see you when I do, either at Mrs Maynard's or the hotel. Will you wait up for me?"

She was startled by the seriousness of his tone. "Yes, I'll be waiting," she told him.

"That's great." He hesitated a moment; it is a risky business to leave the girl you love on a float in the moonlight with a handsome naval officer. But it had to be done. "I'm off," he said, and dove.

When he came up he heard the lieutenant's voice. "Say, old man, that dive was all wrong. You let me show you—"

"Go to the devil," muttered John Quincy wetly, and swam with long powerful strokes toward the shore. Mad with haste, he plunged into the dressing-room, donned his clothes, then dashed out again. No time for apologies to his hostess. He ran along the beach to the Winterslip house. Haku was dozing in the hall.

"Wikiwiki," shouted John Quincy. "Tell the chauffeur to get the roadster into the drive and start the engine. Wake up! Travel! Where's Miss Barbara?"

"Last seen on beach—" began the startled Haku.

On the bench under the hau tree he found Barbara sitting alone. He stood panting before her.

"My dear," he said. "I know at last who killed your father—"

She was on her feet. "You do?"

"Yes—shall I tell you?"

"No," she said. "No—I can't bear to hear. It's too horrible."

"Then you've suspected?"

"Yes—just suspicion—a feeling—intuition. I couldn't believe it—I didn't want to believe it. I went away to get it out of my mind. It's all too terrible—"

He put his hand on her shoulder. "Poor Barbara. Don't you worry. You won't appear in this in any way. I'll keep you out of it."

"What—what has happened?"

"Can't stop now. Tell you later." He ran toward the drive. Miss Minerva appeared from the house. "Haven't time to talk," he cried, leaping into the roadster.

"But John Quincy—a curious thing has happened—that lawyer who was here to look at the house—he said that Dan, just a week before he died, spoke to him about a new will—"

"That's good! That's evidence!" John Quincy cried.

"But why a new will? Surely Barbara was all he had—"

"Listen to me," cut in John Quincy. "You've delayed me already. Get the big car and go to the station—tell that to Hallet. Tell him too that I'm on the *President Tyler* and to send Chan there at once."

He stepped on the gas. By the clock in the automobile he had just seventeen minutes to reach the dock before the *President Tyler* would sail. He shot like a madman through the brilliant Hawaiian night. Kalakaua Avenue, smooth and deserted, proved a glorious speedway. It took him just eight minutes to travel the three miles to the dock. A bit of traffic and an angry policeman in the center of the city caused the delay.

A scattering of people in the dim pier-shed waited for the imminent sailing of the liner. John Quincy dashed through them and up the gangplank. The second officer, Hepworth, stood at the top.

"Hello, Mr Winterslip," he said. "You sailing?"

"No. But let me aboard!"

"I'm sorry. We're about to draw in the plank."

"No, no—you mustn't. This is life and death. Hold off just a few minutes. There's a steward named Bowker—I must find him at once. Life and death, I tell you."

Hepworth stood aside. "Oh, well, in that case. But please hurry, sir—"

"I will." John Quincy passed him on the run. He was on his way to the cabins presided over by Bowker when a tall figure caught his eye. A man in a long green ulster and a battered green hat—a hat John Quincy had last seen on the links of the Oahu Country Club.

The tall figure moved on up a stairway to the topmost deck. John Quincy followed. He saw the ulster disappear into one of the de luxe cabins. Still he followed, and pushed open the cabin door. The man in the ulster was back to, but he swung round suddenly.

"Ah, Mr Jennison," John Quincy cried. "Were you thinking of sailing on this boat?"

For an instant Jennison stared at him. "I was," he said quietly.

"Forget it," John Quincy answered. "You're going ashore with me."

"Really? What is your authority?"

"No authority whatever," said the boy grimly. "I'm taking you, that's all."

Jennison smiled, but there was a gleam of hate behind it. And in John Quincy's heart, usually so gentle and civilized, there was hate too as he faced this man. He thought of Dan Winterslip, dead on his cot. He thought of Jennison walking down the gangplank with them that morning they landed, Jennison putting his arm about poor Barbara when she faltered under the blow. He thought of the shots fired at him from the bush, of the red-haired man battering him in that red room. Well, he must fight again. No way out of it. The siren of the *President Tyler* sounded a sharp warning.

"You get out of here," said Jennison through his teeth. "I'll go with you to the gangplank—"

He stopped, as the disadvantages of that plan came home to him. His right hand went swiftly to his pocket. Inspired, John Quincy seized a filled water bottle and hurled it at the man's head. Jennison dodged; the bottle crashed through one of the windows. The clatter of glass rang through the night, but no one appeared. John Quincy saw Jennison leap toward him, something gleaming in his hand. Stepping aside, he threw himself on the man's back and forced him to his knees. He seized the wrist of Jennison's right hand, which held the automatic, in a firm grip. They kept that posture for a moment, and then Jennison began slowly to rise to his feet. The hand that held the pistol began to tear away. John Quincy shut his teeth and sought to maintain his grip. But he was up against a more powerful antagonist than the red-haired sailor, he was outclassed, and the realization of it crept over him with a sickening force.

Jennison was on his feet now, the right hand nearly free. Another moment—what then, John Quincy wondered? This man had no intention of letting him go ashore; he had changed that plan the moment he put it into words. A muffled shot, and later in the night when the ship was well out on the Pacific—John Quincy thought of Boston, his mother. He thought of Carlota waiting his return. He summoned his strength for one last desperate effort to renew his grip.

A serene, ivory-colored face appeared suddenly at the broken window. An arm with a weapon was extended through the jagged opening.

"Relinquish the firearms, Mr Jennison," commanded Charlie Chan, "or I am forced to make fatal insertion in vital organ belonging to you."

Jennison's pistol dropped to the floor, and John Quincy staggered back against the berth. At that instant the door opened and Hallet, followed by the detective, Spencer, came in.

"Hello, Winterslip, what are you doing here?" the captain said. He thrust a paper into one of the pockets of the green ulster. "Come along, Jennison," he said. "We want you."

Limply John Quincy followed them from the stateroom. Outside they were joined by Chan. At the top of the gangplank Hallet paused. "We'll wait a minute for Hepworth," he said.

John Quincy put his hand on Chan's shoulder. "Charlie, how can I ever thank you? You saved my life."

Chan bowed. "My own pleasure is not to be worded. I have saved a life here and there, but never before one that had beginning in cultured city of Boston. Always a happy item on the golden scroll of memory."

Hepworth came up. "It's all right," he said. "The captain has agreed to delay our sailing one hour. I'll go to the station with you."

On the way down the gangplank, Chan turned to John Quincy. "Speaking heartily for myself, I congratulate your bravery. It is clear you leaped upon this Jennison with vigorous and triumphant mood of heart. But he would have pushed you down. He would have conquered. And why? The answer is, such powerful wrists."

"A great surf-boarder, eh?" John Quincy said.

Chan looked at him keenly. "You are no person's fool. Ten years ago this Harry Jennison are champion swimmer in all Hawaii. I extract that news from ancient sporting pages of Honolulu journal. But he have not been in the water much here lately. Pursuing the truth further, not since the night he killed Dan Winterslip."

XXII

THE LIGHT STREAMS THROUGH

They moved on through the pier-shed to the street, where Hepworth, Jennison and the three policemen got into Hallet's car. The captain turned to John Quincy.

"You coming, Mr Winterslip?" he inquired.

"I've got my own car," the boy explained. "I'll follow you in that."

The roadster was not performing at its best, and he reached the station house a good five minutes after the policemen. He noted Dan Winterslip's big limousine parked in the street outside.

In Hallet's room he found the captain and Chan closeted with a third man. It took a second glance at the latter to identify him as Mr Saladine, for the little man of the lost teeth now appeared a great deal younger than John Quincy had thought him.

"Ah, Mr Winterslip," remarked Hallet. He turned to Saladine. "Say, Larry, you've got me into a heap of trouble with this boy. He accused me of trying to shield you. I wish you'd loosen up for him."

Saladine smiled. "Why, I don't mind. My job out here is about finished. Of course, Mr Winterslip will keep what I tell him under his hat?"

"Naturally," replied John Quincy. He noticed that the man spoke with no trace of a lisp. "I perceive you've found your teeth," he added.

"Oh, yes—I found them in my trunk, where I put them the day I arrived at Waikiki," answered Saladine. "When my teeth were knocked out twenty years ago in a football game, I was broken-hearted, but the loss has been a great help to me in my work. A man hunting his bridge work in the water is a figure of ridicule and mirth. No one ever thinks of connecting him with serious affairs. He can prowl about a beach to his heart's content. Mr Winterslip, I am a special agent of the Treasury Department sent out here to break up the opium ring. My name, of course, is not Saladine."

"Oh," said John Quincy, "I understand at last."

"I'm glad you do," remarked Hallet. "I don't know whether you're familiar with the way our opium smugglers work. The dope is brought in from the Orient on tramp steamers—the *Mary S. Allison*, for example. When they arrive off Waikiki they knock together a few small rafts and load 'em with tins of the stuff. A fleet of little boats, supposedly out there for the fishing, pick up these rafts and bring the dope ashore. It's taken downtown and hidden on ships bound for 'Frisco—usually those that ply only between here and the mainland, because they're not so closely watched at the other end. But it just happened that the quartermaster of the *President Tyler* is one of their go-betweens. We searched his cabin this evening and found it packed with the stuff."

"The quartermaster of the *President Tyler*," repeated John Quincy. "That's Dick Kaohla's friend."

"Yeah—I'm coming to Dick. He's been in charge of the pick-up fleet here. He was out on that business the night of the murder. Saladine saw him and told me all about it in that note, which was my reason for letting the boy go."

"I owe you an apology," John Quincy said.

"Oh, that's all right." Hallet was in great good humor. "Larry here has got some of the higher-ups, too. For instance, he's discovered that Jennison is the lawyer for the ring, defending any of them who are caught and brought before the commissioner. The fact has no bearing on Dan Winterslip's murder—unless Winterslip knew about it, and that was one of the reasons he didn't want Jennison to marry his girl."

Saladine stood up. "I'll turn the quartermaster over to you," he said. "In view of this other charge, you can of course have Jennison too. That's all for me. I'll go along."

"See you tomorrow, Larry," Hallet answered. Saladine went out, and the captain turned to John Quincy. "Well, my boy, this is our big night. I don't know what you were doing in Jennison's cabin, but if you'd picked him for the murderer, I'll say you're good."

"That's just what I'd done," John Quincy told him. "By the way, have you seen my aunt? She's got hold of a rather interesting bit of information—"

"I've seen her," Hallet said. "She's with the prosecutor now, telling it to him. By the way, Greene's waiting for us. Come along."

They went into the prosecutor's office. Greene was alert and eager, a stenographer was at his elbow, and Miss Minerva sat near his desk.

"Hello, Mr Winterslip," he said. "What do you think of our police force now? Pretty good, eh, pretty good. Sit down, won't you?" He glanced through some papers on his desk while John Quincy, Hallet and Chan found chairs. "I don't mind telling you, this thing has knocked me all in a heap. Harry Jennison and I are old friends; I had lunch with him at the club only yesterday. I'm going to proceed a little differently than I would with an ordinary criminal."

John Quincy half rose from his chair. "Don't get excited," Greene smiled. "Jennison will get all that's coming to him, friendship or no friendship. What I mean is that if I can save the territory the expense of a long trial by dragging a confession out of him at once, I intend to do it. He's coming in here in a moment, and I propose to reveal my whole hand to him, from start to finish. That may seem foolish, but it isn't. For I hold aces, all aces, and he'll know it as quickly as anyone."

The door opened. Spencer ushered Jennison into the room, and then withdrew. The accused man stood there, proud, haughty, defiant, a viking of the tropics, a blond giant at bay but unafraid.

"Hello, Jennison," Greene said. "I'm mighty sorry about this—"

"You ought to be," Jennison replied. "You're making an awful fool of yourself. What is this damned nonsense, anyhow—"

"Sit down," said the prosecutor sharply. He indicated a chair on the opposite side of the desk. He had already turned the shade on his desk lamp so the light would shine full in the face of anyone sitting there. "That lamp bother you, Harry?" he asked.

"Why should it?" Jennison demanded.

"Good," smiled Greene. "I believe Captain Hallet served you with a warrant on the boat. Have you looked at it, by any chance?"

"I have."

The prosecutor leaned across the desk. "Murder, Jennison!"

Jennison's expression did not change. "Damned nonsense, as I told you. Why should I murder anyone?"

"Ah, the motive," Greene replied. "You're quite right, we should begin with that. Do you wish to be represented here by counsel?"

Jennison shook his head. "I guess I'm lawyer enough to puncture this silly business," he replied.

"Very well." Greene turned to his stenographer. "Get this." The man nodded, and the prosecutor addressed Miss Minerva. "Miss Winterslip, we'll start with you."

Miss Minerva leaned forward. "Mr Dan Winterslip's house on the beach has, as I told you, been offered for sale by his daughter. After dinner this evening a gentleman came to look at it—a prominent lawyer named Hailey. As we went over the house, Mr Hailey mentioned that he had met Dan Winterslip on the street a week before his death, and that my cousin had spoken to him about coming in shortly to draw up a new will. He did not say what the provisions of the will were to be, nor did he ever carry out his intention."

"Ah yes," said Greene. "But Mr Jennison here was your cousin's lawyer?"

"He was."

"If he wanted to draw a new will, he wouldn't ordinarily have gone to a stranger for that purpose."

"Not ordinarily. Unless he had some good reason."

"Precisely. Unless, for instance, the will had some connection with Harry Jennison."

"I object," Jennison cried. "This is mere conjecture."

"So it is," Greene answered. "But we're not in court. We can conjecture if we like. Suppose, Miss Winterslip, the will was concerned with Jennison in some way. What do you imagine the connection to have been?"

"I don't have to imagine," replied Miss Minerva. "I know."

"Ah, that's good. You know. Go on."

"Before I came down here tonight, I had a talk with my niece. She admitted that her father knew she and Jennison were in love, and that he had bitterly opposed the match. He had even gone so far as to say he would disinherit her if she went through with it."

"Then the new will Dan Winterslip intended to make would probably have been to the effect that in the event his daughter married Jennison, she was not to inherit a penny of his money?"

"There isn't any doubt of it," said Miss Minerva firmly.

"You asked for a motive, Jennison," Greene said. "That's motive enough for me. Everybody knows you're money mad. You wanted to marry Winterslip's daughter, the richest girl in the Islands. He said you couldn't have her—not with the money too. But you're not the sort to make a penniless marriage. You were determined to get both Barbara Winterslip and her father's property. Only one person stood in your way—Dan Winterslip. And that's how you happened to be on his lanai that Monday night—"

"Wait a minute," Jennison protested. "I wasn't on his lanai. I was on board the *President Tyler*, and everybody knows that ship didn't land its passengers until nine the following morning—"

"I'm coming to that," Greene told him. "Just now—by the way, what time is it?"

Jennison took from his pocket a watch on the end of a slender chain. "It's a quarter past nine."

"Ah, yes. Is that the watch you usually carry?"

"It is."

"Ever wear a wrist watch?"

Jennison hesitated. "Occasionally."

"Only occasionally." The prosecutor rose and came round his desk. "Let me see your left wrist, please."

Jennison held out his arm. It was tanned a deep brown, but on the wrist was etched in white the outline of a watch and its encircling strap.

Greene smiled. "Yes, you have worn a wrist watch—and you've worn it pretty constantly, from the look of things." He took a small object from his pocket and held it in front of Jennison. "This watch, perhaps?" Jennison regarded it stonily. "Ever see it before?" Greene asked. "No? Well, suppose we try it on, anyhow." He put the watch in position and fastened it. "I can't help noting, Harry," he continued, "that it fits rather neatly over that white outline on your wrist. And the prong of the buckle falls naturally into the most worn of the holes on the strap."

"What of that?" asked Jennison.

"Oh, coincidence, probably. You have abnormally large wrists, however. Surf-boarding, swimming, eh? But that's something else I'll speak of later." He turned to Miss Minerva. "Will you please come over here, Miss Winterslip."

She came, and as she reached his side, the prosecutor suddenly bent over and switched off the light on his desk. Save for a faint glimmer through a transom, the room was in darkness. Miss Minerva was conscious of dim huddled figures, a circle of white faces, a tense silence. The prosecutor was lifting something slowly toward her startled eyes. A watch, worn on a human wrist—a watch with an illuminated dial on which the figure two was almost obliterated.

"Look at that and tell me," came the prosecutor's voice. "You have seen it before?"

"I have," she answered firmly.

"Where?"

"In the dark in Dan Winterslip's living-room just after midnight the thirtieth of June."

Greene flashed on the light. "Thank you, Miss Winterslip." He retired behind his desk and pressed a button. "You identify it by some distinguishing mark, I presume?"

"I do. The numeral two, which is pretty well obscured."

Spencer appeared at the door. "Send the Spaniard in," Greene ordered. "That is all for the present, Miss Winterslip."

Cabrera entered, and his eyes were frightened as they looked at Jennison. At a nod from the prosecutor, Chan removed the wrist watch and handed it to the Spaniard.

"You know that watch, José?" Greene asked.

"I—I—yes," answered the boy.

"Don't be afraid," Greene urged. "Nobody's going to hurt you. I want you to repeat the story you told me this afternoon.

You have no regular job. You're a sort of confidential errand boy for Mr Jennison here."

"I was."

"Yes—that's all over now. You can speak out. On the morning of Wednesday, July second, you were in Mr Jennison's office. He gave you this wrist watch and told you to take it out and get it repaired. Something was the matter with it. It wasn't running. You took it to a big jewelry store. What happened?"

"The man said it is very badly hurt. To fix it would cost more than a new watch. I go back and tell Mr Jennison. He laugh and say it is mine as a gift."

"Precisely." Greene referred to a paper on his desk. "Late in the afternoon of Thursday, July third, you sold the watch. To whom?"

"To Lau Ho, Chinese jeweler in Maunakea Street. On Saturday evening maybe six o'clock Mr Jennison telephone my home, much excited. Must have watch again, and will pay any price. I speed to Lau Ho's store. Watch is sold once more, now to unknown Japanese. Late at night I see Mr Jennison and he curse me with anger. Get the watch, he says. I have been hunting, but I could not find it."

Greene turned to Jennison. "You were a little careless with that watch, Harry. But no doubt you figured you were pretty safe—you had your alibi. Then, too, when Hallet detailed the clues to you on Winterslip's lanai the morning after the crime, he forgot to mention that someone had seen the watch. It was one of those happy accidents that are all we have to count on in this work. By Saturday night you realized your danger—just how you discovered it I don't know—"

"I do," John Quincy interrupted.

"What! What's that?" said Greene.

"On Saturday afternoon," John Quincy told him, "I played golf with Mr Jennison. On our way back to town, we talked over the clues in this case, and I happened to mention the wrist watch. I can see now it was the first he had heard of it. He was to dine with us at the beach, but he asked to be put down at his office to sign a few letters. I waited below. It must have been then that he called up this young man in an effort to locate the watch."

"Great stuff," said Greene enthusiastically. "That finishes the watch, Jennison. I'm surprised you wore it, but you probably knew that it would be vital to you to keep track of the time, and you figured, rightly, that it would not be immediately affected by the salt water—"

"What the devil are you talking about?" demanded Jennison.

Again Greene pressed a button on his desk. Spencer appeared at once. "Take this Spaniard," the prosecutor directed, "and bring in Hepworth and the quartermaster." He turned again to Jennison. "I'll show you what I'm talking about in just a minute. On the night of June thirtieth you were a passenger on the *President Tyler*, which was lying by until dawn out near the channel entrance?"

"I was."

"No passengers were landed from that ship until the following morning?"

"That's a matter of record."

"Very well." The second officer of the *President Tyler* came in, followed by a big hulking sailorman John Quincy recognized as the quartermaster of that vessel. He was interested to note a ring on the man's right hand, and his mind went back to that encounter in the San Francisco attic.

"Mr Hepworth," the prosecutor began, "on the night of June thirtieth your ship reached this port too late to dock. You anchored off Waikiki. On such an occasion, who is on deck—say, from midnight on?"

"The second officer," Hepworth told him. "In this case, myself. Also the quartermaster."

"The accommodation ladder is let down the night before?"

"Usually, yes. It was let down that night."

"Who is stationed near it?"

"The quartermaster."

"Ah, yes. You were in charge then on the night of June thirtieth. Did you notice anything unusual on that occasion?"

Hepworth nodded. "I did. The quartermaster appeared to be under the influence of liquor. At three o'clock I found him dozing near the accommodation ladder. I roused him. When I came back from checking up the anchor bearings before turning in at dawn—about four-thirty—he was dead to the world. I put him in his cabin, and the following morning I of course reported him."

"You noticed nothing else out of the ordinary?"

"Nothing, sir," Hepworth replied.

"Thank you very much. Now, you—" Greene turned to the quartermaster. "You were drunk on duty the night of June thirtieth. Where did you get the booze?" The man hesitated. "Before you say anything, let me give you a bit of advice. The truth, my man. You're in pretty bad already. I'm not making any promises, but if you talk straight here it may help you in that other matter. If you lie, it will go that much harder with you."

"I ain't going to lie," promised the quartermaster.

"All right. Where did you get your liquor?"

The man nodded toward Jennison. "He gave it to me."

"He did, eh? Tell me all about it."

"I met him on deck just after midnight—we was still moving. I knew him before—him and me—"

"In the opium game, both of you. I understand that. You met him on deck—"

"I did, and he says, you're on watch tonight, eh, and I says I am. So he slips me a little bottle an' says, this will help you pass the time. I ain't a drinking man, so help me I ain't, an' I took just a nip, but there was something in that whisky, I'll swear to it. My head was all funny like, an' the next I knew I was waked up in my cabin with the bad news I was wanted above."

"What became of that bottle?"

"I dropped it overboard on my way to see the captain. I didn't want nobody to find it."

"Did you see anything the night of June thirtieth? Anything peculiar?"

"I seen plenty, sir—but it was that drink. Nothing you would want to hear about."

"All right." The prosecutor turned to Jennison. "Well, Harry—you drugged him, didn't you? Why? Because you were going ashore, eh? Because you knew he'd be on duty at that ladder when you returned, and you didn't want him to see you. So you dropped something into that whiskey—"

"Guess work," cut in Jennison, still unruffled. "I used to have some respect for you as a lawyer, but it's all gone now. If this is the best you can offer—"

"But it isn't," said Greene pleasantly. Again he pushed the button. "I've something much better, Harry, if you'll only wait." He turned to Hepworth. "There's a steward on your ship named Bowker," he began, and John Quincy thought that Jennison stiffened. "How has he been behaving lately?"

"Well, he got pretty drunk in Hong Kong," Hepworth answered. "But that, of course, was the money."

"What money?"

"It's this way. The last time we sailed out of Honolulu harbor for the Orient, over two weeks ago, I was in the purser's office. It was just as we were passing Diamond Head. Bowker came in, and he had a big fat envelope that he wanted to deposit in the purser's safe. He said it contained a lot of money. The purser wouldn't be responsible for it without seeing it, so Bowker slit the envelope—and there were ten one hundred dollar bills. The purser made another package of it and put it in the safe.

He told me Bowker took out a couple of the bills when we reached Hong Kong."

"Where would a man like Bowker get all that money?"

"I can't imagine. He said he'd put over a business deal in Honolulu but—well, we knew Bowker."

The door opened. Evidently Spencer guessed who was wanted this time, for he pushed Bowker into the room. The steward of the *President Tyler* was bedraggled and bleary.

"Hello, Bowker," said the prosecutor. "Sober now, aren't you?"

"I'll tell the world I am," replied Bowker. "They've walked me to San Francisco and back. Can—can I sit down?"

"Of course," Greene smiled. "This afternoon, while you were still drunk, you told a story to Willie Chan, out at Okamoto's auto stand on Kalakaua Avenue. Later on, early this evening, you repeated it to Captain Hallet and me. I'll have to ask you to go over it again."

Bowker glanced toward Jennison, then quickly looked away. "Always ready to oblige," he answered.

"You're a steward on the *President Tyler*," Greene continued. "On your last trip over here from the mainland Mr Jennison occupied one of your rooms—number 97. He was alone in it, I believe?"

"All alone. He paid extra for the privilege, I hear. Always traveled that way."

"Room 97 was on the main deck, not far from the accommodation ladder?"

"Yes, that's right."

"Tell us what happened after you anchored off Waikiki the night of June thirtieth."

Bowker adjusted his gold-rimmed glasses with the gesture of a man about to make an after-dinner speech. "Well, I was up pretty late that night. Mr Winterslip here had loaned me some books—there was one I was particularly interested in.

I wanted to finish it so I could give it to him to take ashore in the morning. It was nearly two o'clock when I finally got through it, and I was feeling stuffy, so I went on deck for a breath of air."

"You stopped not far from the accommodation ladder?"

"Yes sir, I did."

"Did you notice the quartermaster?"

"Yes—he was sound asleep in a deck chair. I went over and leaned on the rail, the ladder was just beneath me. I'd been standing there a few minutes when suddenly somebody came up out of the water and put his hands on the lowest rung. I drew back quickly and stood in a shadow.

"Well, pretty soon this man comes creeping up the ladder to the deck. He was barefooted, and all in black—black pants and shirt. I watched him. He went over and bent above the quartermaster, then started toward me down the deck. He was walking on tiptoe, but even then I didn't get wise to the fact anything was wrong.

"I stepped out of the shadow. 'Fine night for a swim, Mr Jennison,' I said. And I saw at once that I'd made a social error. He gave one jump in my direction and his hands closed on my throat. I thought my time had come."

"He was wet, wasn't he?" Greene asked.

"Dripping. He left a trail of water on the deck."

"Did you notice a watch on his wrist?"

"Yes, but you can bet I didn't make any study of it. I had other things to think about just then. I managed to sort of ooze out of his grip, and I told him to cut it out or I'd yell. 'Look here,' he says, 'you and I can talk business, I guess. Come into my cabin.'

"But I wasn't wanting any tête-à-tête with him in any cabin. I said I'd see him in the morning, and after I'd promised to say nothing to anybody, he let me go. I went to bed, pretty much puzzled.

"The next morning, when I went into his cabin, there he was all fresh and rosy and smiling. If I'd had so much as a whiff of booze the night before, I'd have thought I never saw what I did. I went in there thinking I might get a hundred dollars out of the affair, but the minute he spoke I began to smell important money. He said no one must know about his swim the night before. How much did I want? Well, I held my breath and said ten thousand dollars. And I nearly dropped dead when he answered I could have it."

Bowker turned to John Quincy. "I don't know what you'll think of me. I don't know what Tim would think. I'm not a crook by nature. But I was fed up and choking over that steward job. I wanted a little newspaper of my own, and up to that minute I couldn't see myself getting it. And you must remember that I didn't know then what was in the air—murder. Later, when I did find out, I was scared to breathe. I didn't know what they could do to me." He turned to Greene. "That's all fixed," he said.

"I've promised you immunity," the prosecutor answered. "I'll keep my word. Go on—you agreed to accept the ten thousand?"

"I did. I went to his office at twelve. One of the conditions was that I could stay on the *President Tyler* until she got back to San Francisco, and after that I was never to show my face out this way again. It suited me. Mr Jennison introduced me to this Cabrera, who was to chaperon me the rest of that day. I'll say he did. When I went aboard the ship, he handed me a thousand dollars in an envelope.

"When I came back this time, I was to spend the day with Cabrera and get the other nine grand when I sailed. This morning when we tied up I saw the Spaniard on the dock, but by the time I'd landed he had disappeared. I met this Willie Chan and we had a large day. This fusel oil they sell out here loosened my tongue, but I'm not sorry. Of course, the rosy dream has faded, and it's my flat feet on the deck from now to the end of time. But the shore isn't so much any more, with all the bar-rooms under cover, and this sea life keeps a man out in the open air. As I say, I'm not sorry I talked. I can look any man in the eye again and tell him to go to—" He glanced at Miss Minerva. "Madam, I will not name the precise locality."

Greene stood. "Well, Jennison, there's my case. I've tipped it all off to you, but I wanted you to see for yourself how air-tight it is. There are two courses open to you—you can let this go to trial with a plea of not guilty. A long humiliating ordeal for you. Or you can confess here and now and throw yourself on the mercy of the court. If you're the sensible man I think you are, that's what you'll do."

Jennison did not answer, did not even look at the prosecutor. "It was a very neat idea," Greene went on. "I'll grant you that. Only one thing puzzles me—did it come as the inspiration of the moment, or did you plan it all out in advance? You've been over to the mainland rather often of late—were you waiting your chance? Anyhow, it came, didn't it—it came at last. And for a swimmer like you, child's play. You didn't need that ladder when you left the vessel—perhaps you went overboard while the *President Tyler* was still moving. A quick silent dive, a little way under water in case anyone was watching from the deck, and then a long but easy swim ashore. And there you were, on the beach at Waikiki. Not far away Dan Winterslip was asleep on his lanai, with not so much as a locked door between you. Dan Winterslip, who stood between you and what you wanted. A little struggle—a quick thrust of your knife. Come on, Jennison, don't be a fool. It's the best way out for you now. A full confession."

Jennison leaped to his feet, his eyes flashing. "I'll see you in hell first!" he cried.

"Very well—if you feel that way about it—" Greene turned his back upon him and began a low-toned conversation with Hallet. Jennison and Charlie Chan were together on one side of the desk. Chan took out a pencil and accidentally dropped it on the floor. He stooped to pick it up.

John Quincy saw that the butt of a pistol carried in Chan's hip pocket protruded from under his coat. He saw Jennison spring forward and snatch the gun. With a cry John Quincy moved nearer, but Greene seized his arm and held him. Charlie Chan seemed unaccountably oblivious to what was going on.

Jennison put the muzzle of the pistol to his forehead and pulled the trigger. A sharp click—and that was all. The pistol fell from his hand.

"That's it!" cried Greene triumphantly. "That's my confession, and not a word spoken. I've witnesses, Jennison—they all saw you—you couldn't stand the disgrace—a man in your position—you tried to kill yourself. With an empty gun." He went over and patted Chan on the shoulder. "A great idea, Charlie," he said. "Chan thought of it," he added to Jennison. "The Oriental mind, Harry. Rather subtle, isn't it?"

But Jennison had dropped back into his chair and buried his face in his hands.

"I'm sorry," said Greene gently. "But we've got you. Maybe you'll talk now."

Jennison looked up slowly. The defiance was gone from his face; it was lined and old.

"Maybe I will," he said hoarsely.

XXIII

MOONLIGHT AT THE CROSSROADS

They filed out, leaving Jennison with Greene and the stenographer. In the anteroom Chan approached John Quincy.

"You go home decked in the shining garments of success," he said. "One thought are tantalizing me. At simultaneous moment you arrive at same conclusion we do. To reach there you must have leaped across considerable cavity."

John Quincy laughed. "I'll say I did. It came to me tonight. First, someone mentioned a golf professional with big wrists who drove a long ball. I had a quick flash of Jennison on the links here, and his terrific drives. Big wrists, they told me, meant that a man was proficient in the water. Then someone else—a young woman—spoke of a champion swimmer who left a ship off Waikiki. That was the first time the idea of such a thing had occurred to me. I was pretty warm then, and I felt Bowker was the man who could verify my suspicion. When I rushed aboard the *President Tyler* to find him, I saw Jennison about to sail, and that confirmed my theory. I went after him."

"A brave performance," commented Chan.

"But as you can see, Charlie, I didn't have an iota of real evidence. Just guesswork. You were the one who furnished the proof."

"Proof are essential in this business," Chan replied.

"I'm tantalized too, Charlie. I remember you in the library. You were on the track long before I was. How come?"

Chan grinned. "Seated at our ease in All American restaurant that first night, you will recall I spoke of Chinese people as sensitives, like camera film. A look, a laugh, a gesture, something go click. Bowker enters and hovering above, says with alcoholic accent; 'I'm my own mashter, ain't I?' In my mind, the click. He is not own master. I follow to dock, behold when Spaniard present envelope. But for days I am fogged. I can only learn Cabrera and Jennison are very close. Clues continue to burst in our countenance. The occasion remains suspensive. At the library I read of Jennison the fine swimmer. After that, the watch, and triumph."

Miss Minerva moved on toward the door. "May I have great honor to accompany you to car?" asked Chan.

Outside, John Quincy directed the chauffeur to return alone to Waikiki with the limousine. "You're riding out with me," he told his aunt. "I want to talk with you."

She turned to Charlie Chan. "I congratulate you. You've got brains, and they count."

He bowed low. "From you that compliment glows rosy red. At this moment of parting, my heart droops. My final wish—the snowy chilling days of winter and the scorching windless days of summer—may they all be the springtime for you."

"You're very kind," she said softly.

John Quincy took his hand. "It's been great fun knowing you, Charlie," he remarked.

"You will go again to the mainland," Chan said. "The angry ocean rolling between us. Still I shall carry the memory of your friendship like a flower in my heart." John Quincy climbed into the car. "And the parting may not be eternal," Chan added cheerfully. "The joy of travel may yet be mine. I shall look forward to the day when I may call upon you in your home and shake a healthy hand."

John Quincy started the car and slipping away, they left Charlie Chan standing like a great Buddha on the curb.

"Poor Barbara," said Miss Minerva presently. "I dread to face her with this news. But then, it's not altogether news at that. She told me she'd been conscious of something wrong between her and Jennison ever since they landed. She didn't think he killed her father, but she believed he was involved in it somehow. She is planning to settle with Brade tomorrow and leave the next day, probably for ever. I've persuaded her to come to Boston for a long visit. You'll see her there."

John Quincy shook his head. "No, I shan't. But thanks for reminding me. I must go to the cable office at once."

When he emerged from the office and again entered the car, he was smiling happily.

"In San Francisco," he explained, "Roger accused me of being a Puritan survival. He ran over a little list of adventures he said had never happened to me. Well, most of them have happened now, and I cabled to tell him so. I also said I'd take that job with him."

Miss Minerva frowned. "Think it over carefully," she warned. "San Francisco isn't Boston. The cultural standard is, I fancy, much lower. You'll be lonely there—"

"Oh, no, I shan't. Someone will be there with me. At least, I hope she will."

"Agatha?"

"No, not Agatha. The cultural standard was too low for her. She's broken our engagement."

"Barbara, then?"

"Not Barbara, either."

"But I have sometimes thought—"

"You thought Barbara sent Jennison packing because of me. Jennison thought so too—it's all clear now. That was why he tried to frighten me into leaving Honolulu, and set his opium running friends on me when I wouldn't go. But Barbara is not in love with me. We understand now why she broke her engagement."

"Neither Agatha nor Barbara," repeated Miss Minerva. "Then who—"

"You haven't met her yet, but that happy privilege will be yours before you sleep. The sweetest girl in the Islands—or in the world. The daughter of Jim Egan, whom you have been heard to refer to as a glorified beach-comber."

Again Miss Minerva frowned. "It's a great risk, John Quincy. She hasn't our background—"

"No, and that's a pleasant change. She's the niece of your old friend—you knew that?"

"I did," answered Miss Minerva softly.

"Your dear friend of the eighties. What was it you said to me? If your chance ever comes—"

"I hope you will be very happy," his aunt said. "When you write it to your mother, be sure and mention Captain Cope of the British Admiralty. Poor Grace! That will be all she'll have to cling to—after the wreck."

"What wreck?"

"The wreck of all her hopes for you."

"Nonsense. Mother will understand. She knows I'm a roaming Winterslip, and when we roam, we roam."

They found Madame Maynard seated in her living-room with a few of her more elderly guests. From the beach came the sound of youthful revelry.

"Well, my boy," the old woman cried, "it appears you couldn't stay away from your policemen friends one single evening, after all. I give you up."

John Quincy laughed. "I'm pau now. By the way, Carlota Egan—is she—"

"They're all out there somewhere," the hostess said. "They came in for a bit of supper—by the way, there are sandwiches in the dining-room and—"

"Not just now," said John Quincy. "Thank you so much. I'll see you again, of course—"

He dashed out on the sand. A group of young people under the hau tree informed him that Carlota Egan was on the farthest float. Alone? Well, no—that naval lieutenant—

He was, he reflected as he hurried on toward the water, a bit fed up with the navy. That was hardly the attitude he should have taken, considering all the navy had done for him. But it was human. And John Quincy was human at last.

For an instant he stood at the water's edge. His bathing suit was in the dressing-room, but he never gave it a thought. He kicked off his shoes, tossed aside his coat, and plunged into the breakers. The blood of the wandering Winterslips was racing through his veins; hot blood that tropical waters had ever been powerless to cool.

Sure enough, Carlota Egan and Lieutenant Booth were together on the float. John Quincy climbed up beside them.

"Well, I'm back," he announced.

"I'll tell the world you're back," said the lieutenant. "And all wet, too."

They sat there. Across a thousand miles of warm water the trade winds came to fan their cheeks. Just above the horizon hung the Southern Cross; the Island lights trembled along the shore; the yellow eye on Diamond Head was winking. A gorgeous setting. Only one thing was wrong with it. It seemed rather crowded.

John Quincy had an inspiration. "Just as I hit the water," he remarked, "I thought I heard you say something about my dive. Didn't you like it?"

"It was rotten," replied the lieutenant amiably.

"You offered to show me what was wrong with it, I believe?"

"Sure. If you want me to."

"By all means," said John Quincy. "Learn one thing every day. That's my motto."

Lieutenant Booth went to the end of the springboard. "In the first place, always keep your ankles close together—like this."

"I've got you," answered John Quincy.

"And hold your arms tight against your ears."

"The tighter the better, as far as I'm concerned."

"Then double up like a jackknife," continued the instructor. He doubled up like a jackknife and rose into the air.

At the same instant John Quincy seized the girl's hands. "Listen to me. I can't wait another second. I want to tell you that I love you—"

"You're mad," she cried.

"Mad about you. Ever since that day on the ferry—"

"But your people?"

"What about my people? It's just you and I—we'll live in San Francisco—that is, if you love me—"

"Well, I—"

"In heaven's name, be quick. That human submarine is floating around here under us. You love me, don't you? You'll marry me?"

"Yes."

He took her in his arms and kissed her. Only the wandering Winterslips could kiss like that. The stay-at-homes had always secretly begrudged them the accomplishment.

The girl broke away at last, breathless. "Johnnie!" she cried.

A sputter beside them, and Lieutenant Booth climbed on to the float, moist and panting. "Wha's that?" he gurgled.

"She was speaking to me," cried John Quincy triumphantly.

The Chinese Parrot

CONTENTS

I

THE PHILLIMORE PEARLS

Alexander Eden stepped from the misty street into the great marble-pillared room where the firm of Meek and Eden offered its wares. Immediately, behind showcases gorgeous with precious stones or bright with silver, platinum, and gold, forty resplendent clerks stood at attention. Their morning coats were impeccable, lacking the slightest suspicion of a wrinkle, and in the left lapel of each was a pink carnation, as fresh and perfect as though it had grown there.

Eden nodded affably to right and left and went on his way, his heels clicking cheerily on the spotless tile floor. He was a small man, grey-haired and immaculate, with a quick, keen eye and the imperious manner that so well became his position. For the clan of Meek, having duly inherited the earth, had relinquished that inheritance and passed to the great beyond, leaving Alexander Eden the sole owner of the best-known jewellery store west of the Rockies.

Arriving at the rear of the shop, he ascended a brief stairway to the luxurious suite of offices on the mezzanine floor where he spent his days. In the anteroom of the suite he encountered his secretary.

"Ah, good morning, Miss Chase," he said.

The girl answered with a smile. Eden's eye for beauty, developed by long experience in the jewel trade, had not failed him when he picked Miss Chase. She was an ash blonde with violet eyes; her manners were exquisite; so was her gown. Bob Eden, reluctant heir to the business, had been heard to remark that entering his father's office was like arriving for tea in a very exclusive drawing-room.

Alexander Eden glanced at his watch. "In about ten minutes," he announced, "I expect a caller – an old friend of mine – Madame Jordan, of Honolulu. When she arrives show her in at once."

"Yes, Mr Eden," replied the girl.

He passed on into his own room, where he hung up his hat, coat, and stick. On his broad, gleaming desk lay the morning mail; he glanced at it idly, but his mind was elsewhere. In a moment he strolled to one of the windows and stood there gazing at the *façade* of the building across the way.

The day was not far advanced, and the fog that had blanketed San Francisco the night before still lingered in the streets. Staring into that dull grey mist, Eden saw a picture, a picture that was incongruously all colour and light and life. His thoughts had travelled back down the long corridor of the years, and in that imagined scene outside the window he himself moved, a slim, dark boy of seventeen.

Forty years ago – a night in Honolulu, the gay, happy Honolulu of the monarchy. Behind a bank of ferns in one corner of the great Phillimore living-room Berger's band was playing, and over the polished floor young Alec Eden and Sally Phillimore danced together. The boy stumbled now and then, for the dance was a newfangled one called the two-step, lately introduced into Hawaii by a young ensign from the *Nipsic*. But perhaps it was not entirely his unfamiliarity with the two-step that muddled him, for he knew that in his arms he held the darling of the islands.

Some few are favoured by fortune out of all reason, and Sally Phillimore was one of these. Above and beyond her beauty, which would have been sufficient in itself, she seemed, in that simple Honolulu society, the heiress of all the ages. The Phillimore fortunes were at their peak, Phillimore ships sailed the seven seas, on thousands of Phillimore acres the sugar-cane ripened toward a sweet, golden harvest. Looking down, Alec Eden saw hanging about the girl's white throat, a symbol of her place and wealth, the famous pearl necklace Marc Phillimore had brought home from London, and for which he had paid a price that made all Honolulu gasp.

Eden, of Meek and Eden, continued to stare into the fog. It was pleasant to relive that night in Hawaii, a night filled with magic and the scent of exotic blossoms, to hear again the giddy laughter, the distant murmur of the surf, the soft croon of island music. Dimly he recalled Sally's blue eyes shining up at him. More vividly – for he was nearly sixty now, and a business man – he saw again the big lustrous pearls that lay on her breast, reflecting the light with a warm glow....

Oh, well – he shrugged his shoulders. All that was forty years ago, and much had happened since. Sally's marriage to Fred Jordan, for example, and then, a few years later, the birth of her only child, Victor. Eden smiled grimly. How ill-advised she had been when she named that foolish, wayward boy!

He went over to his desk and sat down. No doubt it was some escapade of Victor, he reflected, that was responsible for the scene shortly to be enacted here in this office in Post Street. Yes, of course, that was it. Victor, lurking in the wings, was about to ring down the final curtain on the drama of the Phillimore pearls.

He was deep in his mail when, a few moments later, his secretary opened the door and announced: "Madame Jordan is calling."

Eden rose. Sally Jordan was coming toward him over the Chinese rug. Gay and sprightly as ever – how valiantly she had battled with the years! "Alec – my dear old friend—"

He took both her fragile hands in his. "Sally! I'm mighty glad to see you. Here." He drew a big leather chair close to his desk. "The post of honor for you. Always."

Smiling, she sat down. Eden went to his accustomed place behind his desk. He took up a paper-knife and balanced it; for a man of his poise he appeared rather ill at ease. "Ah – er – how long have you been in town?"

"Two weeks – I think – yes, two weeks last Monday."

"You're not living up to your promise, Sally. You didn't let me know."

"But I've had such a gay round," she protested. "Victor is always so good to me."

"Ah, yes – Victor – he's well, I hope." Eden looked away, out the window. "Fog's lifting, isn't it? A fine day, after all—"

"Dear old Alec." She shook her head. "No good beating round the bush. Never did believe in it. Get down to business – that's my motto. It's as I told you the other day over the telephone. I've made up my mind to sell the Phillimore pearls."

He nodded. "And why not? What good are they, anyhow?"

"No, no," she objected. "It's perfectly true – they're no good to me. I'm a great believer in what's fitting – and those gorgeous pearls were meant for youth. However, that's not the reason I'm selling. I'd hang on to them if I could. But I can't. I – I'm broke, Alec."

He looked out the window again.

"Sounds absurd, doesn't it?" she went on. "All the Phillimore ships – the Phillimore acres – vanished into thin air. The big house on the beach – mortgaged to the hilt. You see – Victor – he's made some unfortunate investments—"

"I see," said Eden softly.

"Oh, I know what you're thinking, Alec. Victor's a bad, bad boy. Foolish and careless and – worse, perhaps. But he's all I've got, since Fred went. And I'm sticking by him."

"Like the good sport you are," he smiled. "No, I wasn't thinking unkindly of Victor, Sally. I – I have a son myself."

"Forgive me," she said. "I should have asked before. How's Bob?"

"Why, he's all right, I guess. He may come in before you leave – if he happens to have had an early breakfast."

"Is he with you in the business?"

Eden shrugged. "Not precisely. Bob's been out of college three years now. One of those years was spent in the South Seas, another in Europe, and the third – from what I can gather – in the card-room of his club. However, his career does seem to be worrying him a bit. The last I heard he was thinking of the newspaper game. He has friends on the papers." The jeweler waved his hand about the office. "This sort of thing, Sally – this thing I've given my life to – it's a great bore to Bob."

"Poor Alec," said Sally Jordan softly. "The new generation is so hard to understand. But – it's my own troubles I came to talk about. Broke, as I told you. Those pearls are all I have in the world."

"Well – they're a good deal," Eden told her.

"Enough to help Victor out of the hole he's in. Enough for the few years left me, perhaps. Father paid ninety thousand for them. It was a fortune at that time – but today—"

"Today," Eden repeated. "You don't seem to realize, Sally. Like everything else, pearls have greatly appreciated since the eighties. Today that string is worth three hundred thousand if it's worth a cent."

She gasped. "Why, it can't be. Are you sure? You've never seen the necklace—"

"Ah – I was wondering if you'd remember," he chided. "I see you don't. Just before you came in I was thinking back – back to a night forty years ago, when I was visiting my uncle in the Islands. Seventeen – that's all I was – but I came to your dance, and you taught me the two-step. The pearls were about your throat. One of the memorable nights of my life."

"And of mine," she nodded. "I remember now. Father had just brought the necklace from London, and it was the first time I'd worn it. Forty years ago – ah, Alec, let's hurry back to the present. Memories – sometimes they hurt." She was silent for a moment. "Three hundred thousand, you say."

"I don't guarantee I can get that much," he told her. "I said the necklace was worth it. But it isn't always easy to find a buyer who will meet your terms. The man I have in mind—"

"Oh – you've found someone—"

"Well – yes – I have. But he refuses to go above two hundred and twenty thousand. Of course, if you're in a hurry to sell—"

"I am," she answered. "Who is this Midas?"

"Madden," he said. "P.J. Madden."

"Not the big Wall Street man? The Plunger?"

"Yes. You know him?"

"Only through the newspapers. He's famous, of course, but I've never seen him."

Eden frowned. "That's curious," he said. "He appeared to know you. I had heard he was in town, and when you telephoned me the other day I went at once to his hotel. He admitted he was on the look-out for a string as a present for his daughter, but he was pretty cold at first. However, when I mentioned the Phillimore pearls he laughed. 'Sally Phillimore's pearls,' he said. 'I'll take them.' 'Three hundred thousand,' I said. 'Two hundred and twenty and not a penny more,' he answered. And looked at me with those eyes of his – as well try to bargain with this fellow here." He indicated a small bronze Buddha on his desk.

Sally Jordan seemed puzzled. "But Alec – he couldn't know me. I don't understand. However, he's offering a fortune, and

I want it badly. Please hurry and close with him before he leaves town."

Again the door opened at the secretary's touch. "Mr Madden, of New York," said the girl.

"Yes," said Eden. "We'll see him at once." He turned to his old friend. "I asked him to come here this morning and meet you. Now take my advice and don't be too eager. We may be able to boost him a bit, though I doubt it. He's a hard man, Sally, a hard man. The newspaper stories about him are only too true."

He broke off suddenly, for the hard man he spoke of stood upon his rug. P.J. himself, the great Madden, the hero of a thousand Wall Street battles, six feet and over and looming like a tower of granite in the grey clothes he always affected. His cold blue eyes swept the room like an Arctic blast.

"Ah, Mr Madden, come in," said Eden, rising. Madden advanced farther into the room, and after him came a tall, languid girl in expensive furs and a lean, precise-looking man in a dark blue suit.

"Madame Jordan, this is Mr Madden, of whom we have just been speaking," Eden said.

"Madame Jordan," repeated Madden, bowing slightly. He had dealt so much in steel that it had got somehow into his voice. "I've brought along my daughter Evelyn, and my secretary, Martin Thorn."

"Charmed, I'm sure," Eden answered. He stood for a moment gazing at this interesting group that had invaded his quiet office – the famous financier, cool, competent, conscious of his power, the slender, haughty girl upon whom, it was reported, Madden lavished all the affection of his later years, the thin, intense secretary, subserviently in the background, but for some reason not so negligible as he might have been. "Won't you all sit down, please?" the jeweler continued. He arranged chairs. Madden drew his close to the desk; the air seemed charged with his presence; he dwarfed them all.

"No need of any preamble," said the millionaire. "We've come to see those pearls."

Eden started. "My dear sir – I'm afraid I gave you the wrong impression. The pearls are not in San Francisco at present."

Madden stared at him. "But when you told me to come here and meet the owner—"

"I'm so sorry – I meant just that."

Sally Jordan helped him out. "You see, Mr Madden, I had no intention of selling the necklace when I came here from Honolulu. I was moved to that decision by events after I reached here. But I have sent for it—"

The girl spoke. She had thrown back the fur about her neck, and she was beautiful in her way, but cold and hard like her father – and just now, evidently, unutterably bored. "I thought, of course, the pearls were here," she said, "or I should not have come."

"Well, it isn't going to hurt you," her father snapped. "Mrs Jordan, you say you've sent for the necklace?"

"Yes. It will leave Honolulu tonight, if all goes well. It should be here in six days."

"No good," said Madden. "My daughter's starting tonight for Denver. I go South in the morning, and in a week I expect to join her in Eldorado and we'll travel East together. No good, you see."

"I will agree to deliver the necklace anywhere you say," suggested Eden.

"Yes – I guess you will." Madden considered. He turned to Madame Jordan. "This is the identical string of pearls you were wearing at the old Palace Hotel in 1889?" he asked.

She looked at him in surprise. "The same string," she answered.

"And even more beautiful than it was then, I'll wager," Eden smiled. "You know, Mr Madden, there is an old superstition in the jewellery trade that pearls assume the personality of their wearer and become sombre or bright, according to the mood of the one they adorn. If that is true, this string has grown more lovely through the years."

"Bunk," said Madden rudely. "Oh, excuse me – I don't mean that the lady isn't charming. But I have no sympathy with the silly superstitions of your trade – or of any other trade. Well, I'm a busy man. I'll take the string – at the price I named."

Eden shook his head. "It's worth at least three hundred thousand, as I told you."

"Not to me. Two hundred and twenty – twenty now to bind it and the balance within thirty days after the delivery of the string. Take it or leave it."

He rose and stared down at the jeweler. Eden was an adept at bargaining, but somehow all his cunning left him as he faced this Gibraltar of a man. He looked helplessly toward his old friend.

"It's all right, Alec," Madame Jordan said. "I accept."

"Very good," Eden sighed. "But you are getting a great bargain, Mr Madden."

"I always get a great bargain," replied Madden. "Or I don't buy." He took out his cheque-book. "Twenty thousand now, as I agreed."

For the first time the secretary spoke; his voice was thin and cold and disturbingly polite. "You say the pearls will arrive in six days?"

"Six days or thereabouts," Madame Jordan answered.

"Ah, yes." An ingratiating note crept in. "They are coming by—"

"By a private messenger," said Eden sharply. He was taking a belated survey of Martin Thorn. A pale, high forehead, pale green eyes that now and then stared disconcertingly, long, pale, grasping hands. Not the jolliest sort of playmate to have around, he reflected. "A private messenger," he repeated firmly.

"Of course," said Thorn. Madden had written the cheque and laid it on the jeweler's desk. "I was thinking, chief – just a suggestion," Thorn went on. "If Miss Evelyn is to return and spend the balance of the winter in Pasadena she will want to wear the necklace there. We'll still be in that neighborhood six days from now, and it seems to me—"

"Who's buying this necklace?" cut in Madden. "I'm not going to have the thing carried back and forth across the country. It's too risky in these days when every other man is a crook."

"But, Father," said the girl, "it's quite true that I'd like to wear it this winter—"

She stopped. P.J. Madden's crimson face had gone purple, and he was tossing his great head. It was a quaint habit he had when opposed, the newspapers said. "The necklace will be delivered to me in New York," he remarked to Eden, ignoring his daughter and Thorn. "I'll be in the South for some time – got a place in Pasadena and a ranch on the desert, four miles from Eldorado. Haven't been down there for quite a while, and unless you look in on these caretakers occasionally they get slack. As soon as I'm back in New York I'll wire you, and you can deliver the necklace at my office. You'll have my cheque for the balance within thirty days."

"That's perfectly agreeable to me," Eden said. "If you'll wait just a moment I'll have a bill of sale drawn, outlining the terms. Business is business – as you of all men understand."

"Of course," nodded Madden. The jeweler went out.

Evelyn Madden rose. "I'll meet you downstairs, Father. I want to look over their stock of jade." She turned to Madame Jordan. "You know, one finds better jade in San Francisco than anywhere else."

"Yes, indeed," smiled the older woman. She rose and took the girl's hands. "Such a lovely throat, my dear – I was saying just before you came – the Phillimore pearls need youth. Well, they're to have it at last. I hope you will wear them through many happy years."

"Why – why, thank you," said the girl, and went.

Madden glanced at his secretary. "Wait for me in the car," he ordered. Alone with Madame Jordan, he looked at her grimly. "You never saw me before, did you?" he inquired.

"I'm so sorry. Have I?"

"No – I suppose not. But I saw you. Oh, we're well along in years now, and it does no harm to speak of these things. I want you to know it will be a great satisfaction to me to own that necklace. A deep wound and an old one is healed this morning."

She stared at him. "I don't understand."

"No, of course you don't. But in the eighties you used to come from the Islands with your family and stop at the Palace Hotel. And I – I was a bell-hop at that same hotel. I often saw you there – I saw you once when you were wearing that famous necklace. I thought you were the most beautiful girl in the world – oh, why not – we're both – er—"

"We're both old now," she said softly.

"Yes – that's what I mean. I worshipped you, but I – I was a bell-hop – you looked through me – you never saw me. A bit of furniture, that's all I was to you. Oh, I tell you, it hurt my pride – a deep wound, as I said. I swore I'd get on – I knew it, even then. I'd marry you. We can both smile at that now. It didn't work out – even some of *my* schemes never worked out. But today I own your pearls – they'll hang about my daughter's neck. It's the next best thing. I've bought you out. A deep wound in my pride, but healed at last."

She looked at him, and shook her head. Once she might have resented this, but not now. "You're a strange man," she said.

"I am what I am," he answered. "I had to tell you. Otherwise the triumph would not have been complete."

Eden came in. "Here you are, Mr Madden. If you'll sign this – thank you."

"You'll get a wire," said Madden. "In New York, remember, and nowhere else. Good day." He turned to Madame Jordan and held out his hand.

She took it, smiling. "Goodbye. I'm not looking through you now. I see you at last."

"And what do you see?"

"A terribly vain man. But a likable one."

"Thank you. I'll remember that. Goodbye."

He left them. Eden sank wearily into a chair. "Well, that's that. He rather wears one out. I wanted to stick for a higher figure, but it looked hopeless. Somehow I knew he always wins."

"Yes," said Madame Jordan, "he always wins."

"By the way, Sally, I didn't want you to tell that secretary who was bringing the pearls. But you'd better tell me."

"Why, of course. Charlie's bringing them."

"Charlie?"

"Detective-Sergeant Chan, of the Honolulu police. Long ago, in the big house on the beach, he was our number one boy."

"Chan. A Chinese?"

"Yes. Charlie left us to join the police force, and he's made a fine record there. He's always wanted to come to the mainland, so I've had it all arranged – his leave of absence, his status as a citizen, everything. And he's coming with the pearls. Where could I have found a better messenger? Why – I'd trust Charlie with my life – no, that isn't very precious any more. I'd trust him with the life of the one I loved dearest in the world."

"He's leaving tonight, you said."

"Yes – on the *President Pierce*. It's due late next Thursday afternoon."

The door opened, and a good-looking young man stood on the threshold. His face was lean and tanned, his manner poised and confident, and his smile had just left Miss Chase daydreaming in the outer office. "Oh, I'm sorry, Dad – if you're busy. Why – look who's here!"

"Bob," cried Madame Jordan. "You rascal – I was hoping to see you. How are you?"

"Just waking into glorious life," he told her. "How are you, and all the other young folks out your way?"

"Fine, thanks. By the way, you dawdled too long over breakfast. Just missed meeting a very pretty girl."

"No, I didn't. Not if you mean Evelyn Madden. Saw her downstairs as I came in – she was talking to one of those exiled Grand Dukes we employ to wait on the customers. I didn't linger – she's an old story now. Been seeing her everywhere I went for the past week."

"I thought her very charming," Madame Jordan said.

"But an iceberg," objected the boy. "B-r-r – how the wintry winds do blow in her vicinity! However, I guess she comes by it honestly. I passed the great P.J. himself on the stairs."

"Nonsense. Have you ever tried that smile of yours on her?"

"In a way. Nothing special – just the old trade smile. But look here – I'm on to you. You want to interest me in the obsolete institution of marriage."

"It's what you need. It's what all young men need."

"What for?"

"As an incentive. Something to spur you on to get the most out of life."

Bob Eden laughed. "Listen, my dear. When the fog begins to drift in through the Gate, and the lights begin to twinkle on O'Farrell Street – well, I don't want to be hampered by no incentive, lady. Besides, the girls aren't what they were when you were breaking hearts."

"Rot," she answered. "They're very much nicer. The young men are growing silly. Alec, I'll go along."

"I'll get in touch with you next Thursday," the elder Eden said. "By the way – I'm sorry it wasn't more, for your sake."

"It was an amazing lot," she replied. "I'm very happy." Her eyes filled. "Dear Dad – he's taking care of me still," she added, and went quickly out.

Eden turned to his son. "I judge you haven't taken a newspaper job yet?"

"Not yet." The boy lighted a cigarette. "Of course, the editors are all after me. But I've been fighting them off."

"Well, fight them off a little longer. I want you to be free for the next two or three weeks. I've a little job for you myself."

"Why, of course, Dad." He tossed a match into a priceless K'ang-Hsi vase. "What sort of job? What do I do?"

"First of all, you meet the *President Pierce* late next Thursday afternoon."

"Sounds promising. I presume a young woman, heavily veiled, comes ashore—"

"No. A Chinese comes ashore."

"A what?"

"A Chinese detective from Honolulu, carrying in his pocket a pearl necklace worth over a quarter of a million dollars."

Bob Eden nodded. "Yes. And after that—"

"After that," said Alexander Eden thoughtfully, "who can say! That may be only the beginning."

II

THE DETECTIVE FROM HAWAII

At six o'clock on the following Thursday evening Alexander Eden drove to the Stewart Hotel. All day a February rain had spattered over the town, bringing an early dusk. For a moment Eden stood in the doorway of the hotel, staring at the parade of bobbing umbrellas and at the lights along Geary Street, glowing a dim yellow in the dripping mist. In San Francisco age does not matter – much, and he felt like a boy again as he rode up in the elevator to Sally Jordan's suite.

She was waiting for him in the doorway of her sitting-room, lovely as a girl in a soft, clinging dinner-gown of grey. Caste tells, particularly when one has reached the sixties, Eden thought as he took her hand.

"Ah, Alec," she smiled. "Come in. You remember Victor?"

Victor stepped forward eagerly, and Eden looked at him with interest. He had not seen Sally Jordan's son for some years, and he noted that, at thirty-five, Victor began to show the strain of his giddy career as man about town. His brown eyes were tired, as though they had looked at the bright lights too long, his face a little puffy, his waistline far too generous. But his attire was perfection; evidently his tailor had yet to hear of the failing Phillimore fortunes.

"Come in, come in," said Victor gaily. His heart was light, for he saw important money in the offing. "As I understand it, tonight's the night."

"And I'm glad it is," Sally Jordan added. "I shall be happy to get that necklace off my mind. Too great a burden at my age."

Eden sat down. "Bob's gone to the dock to meet the *President Pierce*", he remarked. "I told him to come here at once with your Chinese friend."

"Ah, yes," said Sally Jordan.

"Have a cocktail," suggested Victor.

"No, thanks," Eden replied. Abruptly he rose and strode about the room.

Mrs Jordan regarded him with concern. "Has anything happened?" she inquired.

The jeweler returned to his chair. "Well, yes – something has happened," he admitted. "Something – well, something rather odd."

"About the necklace, you mean?" asked Victor, with interest.

"Yes," said Eden. He turned to Sally Jordan. "You remember what Madden told us, Sally? Almost his last words. 'New York, and nowhere else.'"

"Why, yes – I remember," she replied.

"Well, he's changed his mind," frowned the jeweler. "Somehow, it doesn't seem like Madden. He called me up this morning from his ranch down on the desert, and he wants the necklace delivered there."

"On the desert?" she repeated, amazed.

"Precisely. Naturally, I was surprised. But his instructions were emphatic, and you know the sort of man he is. One doesn't argue with him. I listened to what he had to say, and agreed. But after he had rung off I got to thinking. What he had said that morning at my office, you know. I asked myself – was it really Madden talking? The voice had an authentic ring – but even so – well, I determined to take no chances."

"Quite right, too," nodded Sally Jordan.

"So I called him back. I had a devil of a time finding his number, but I finally got it from a business associate of his here in town. Eldorado seven six. I asked for P.J. Madden and I got him. Oh, it was Madden right enough."

"And what did he say?"

"He commended me for my caution, but his orders were even more emphatic than before. He said he had heard certain things that made him think it risky to take the necklace to New York at this time. He didn't explain what he meant by that. But he added that he'd come to the conclusion that the desert was an ideal place for a transaction of this sort. The last place in the world anyone would come looking for a chance to steal a quarter of a million dollar necklace. Of course, he didn't say all that over the wire, but that was what I gathered."

"He's absolutely right, too," said Victor.

"Well, yes – in a way, he is. I've spent a lot of time on the desert myself. In spite of the story-writers, it's the most law-abiding place in America today. Nobody ever locks a door, or so much as thinks of thieves. Ask the average rancher about police protection, and he'll look surprised and murmur something about a sheriff several hundred miles away. But for all that—"

Eden got up again and walked anxiously about the room. "For all that – or rather, for those very reasons, I don't like the idea at all. Suppose somebody did want to play a crooked game – what a setting for it! Away out there on that ocean of sand, with only the Joshua-trees for neighbors. Suppose I send Bob down there with your necklace, and he walks into a trap. Madden may not be at that lonely ranch. He may have gone East. He may even, by the time Bob gets there, have gone West – as they said in the War. Lying out on the desert, with a bullet in him—"

Victor laughed derisively. "Look here, your imagination is running away with you," he cried.

Eden smiled. "Maybe it is," he admitted. "Begins to look as though I were growing old, eh, Sally?" He took out his watch. "But where's Bob? Ought to be here by now. If you don't mind, I'll use your telephone."

He called the dock, and came away from the 'phone with a still more worried look. "The *President Pierce* got in a full forty-five minutes ago," he announced. "Half an hour should bring them here."

"Traffic's rather thick at this hour," Victor reminded him.

"Yes – that's right too," Eden agreed. "Well, Sally, I've told you the situation. What do you think?"

"What should she think?" Victor cut in. "Madden's bought the necklace and wants it delivered on the desert. It isn't up to us to question his orders. If we do he may get annoyed and call the whole deal off. No, our job is to deliver the pearls, get his receipt, and wait for his cheque." His puffy white hands twitched eagerly.

Eden turned to his old friend. "Is that your opinion, Sally?"

"Why, yes, Alec," she said. "I fancy Victor is right." She looked at her son proudly. Eden also looked at him, but with a vastly different expression.

"Very good," he answered. "Then there is no time to be lost. Madden is in a great hurry, as he wants to start for New York very soon. I shall send Bob with the necklace at eleven o'clock tonight – but I absolutely refuse to send him alone."

"I'll go along," Victor offered.

Eden shook his head. "No," he objected, "I prefer a policeman, even though he does belong to a force as far away as Honolulu. This Charlie Chan – do you think, Sally, that you could persuade him to go with Bob?"

She nodded. "I'm sure of it. Charlie would do anything for me."

"All right – that's settled. But where the devil are they? I tell you, I'm worried—"

The telephone interrupted him, and Madame Jordan went to answer it. "Oh – hello, Charlie," she said. "Come right up. We're on the fourth floor – number four nine two. Yes. Are you alone?" She hung up the receiver and turned back into the room. "He says he is alone," she announced.

"Alone," repeated Eden. "Why – I don't understand that—" He sank weakly into a chair.

A moment later he looked up with interest at the chubby little man his hostess and her son were greeting warmly at the door. The detective from Honolulu stepped farther into the room, an undistinguished figure in his Western clothes. He had round fat cheeks, an ivory skin, but the thing about him that caught Eden's attention was the expression in his eyes, a look of keen brightness that made the pupils gleam like black buttons in the yellow light.

"Alec," said Sally Jordan, "this is my old friend Charlie Chan. Charlie – Mr Eden."

Chan bowed low. "Honors crowd close on this mainland," he said. "First I am Miss Sally's old friend, and now I meet Mr Eden."

Eden rose. "How do you do?" he said.

"Have a good crossing, Charlie?" Victor asked.

Chan shrugged. "All time big Pacific Ocean suffer sharp pain down below, and toss about to prove it. Maybe from sympathy, I am in same fix."

Eden came forward. "Pardon me if I'm a little abrupt – but my son – he was to meet your ship—"

"So sorry," Chan said, regarding him gravely. "The fault must indubitably be mine. Kindly overlook my stupidity, but there was no meeting at dock."

"I can't understand it," Eden complained again.

"For some few minutes I linger round gang-board," Chan continued. "No one ventures to approach out of rainy night. Therefore I engage taxi and hurry to this spot."

"You've got the necklace?" Victor demanded.

"Beyond any question," Chan replied. "Already I have procured room in this hotel, partly disrobing to remove same from money-belt about waist." He tossed an innocent-looking string of beads down upon the table. "Regard the Phillimore pearls at journey's end," he grinned. "And now a great burden drops from my shoulders with a most delectable thud."

Eden, the jeweler, stepped forward and lifted the string in his hands. "Beautiful," he murmured, "beautiful. Sally, we should never have let Madden have them at the price. They're perfectly matched – I don't know that I ever saw—" He stared for a moment into the rosy glow of the pearls, then laid them again on the table. "But Bob – where is Bob?"

"Oh, he'll be along," remarked Victor, taking up the necklace. "Just a case of missing each other."

"I am the faulty one," insisted Chan. "Shamed by my blunder—"

"Maybe," said Eden. "But – now that you have the pearls, Sally, I'll tell you something else. I didn't want to worry you before. This afternoon at four o'clock someone called me – Madden again, he said. But something in his voice – anyhow, I was wary. Pearls were coming on the *President Pierce*, were they? Yes. And the name of the messenger? Why should I tell him that, I inquired. Well, he had just got hold of some inside facts that made him feel the string was in danger, and he didn't want anything to happen. He was in a position to help in the matter. He insisted, so I finally said: 'Very good, Mr Madden. Hang up your receiver and I'll call you back in ten minutes with the information you want.' There was a pause, then I heard him hang up. But I didn't 'phone the desert. Instead I had that call traced, and I found it came from a pay-station in a cigar-store at the corner of Sutter and Kearny Streets."

Eden paused. He saw Charlie Chan regarding him with deep interest.

"Can you wonder I'm worried about Bob?" the jeweler continued. "There's some funny business going on, and I tell you I don't like it—"

A knock sounded on the door, and Eden himself opened it. His son stepped into the room, debonair and smiling. At sight of him, as so often happens in such a situation, the anxious father's worry gave way to a deep rage.

"You're a hell of a business man," he cried.

"Now, Father – no compliments," laughed Bob Eden. "And me wandering all over San Francisco in your service."

"I suppose so. That's about what you would be doing, when it was your job to meet Mr Chan at the dock."

"Just a moment, Dad." Bob Eden removed a glistening raincoat. "Hello, Victor. Madame Jordan. And this, I imagine, is Mr Chan."

"So sorry to miss meeting at dock," murmured Chan. "All my fault, I am sure—"

"Nonsense," cried the jeweler. "His fault, as usual. When, in heaven's name, are you going to show a sense of responsibility?"

"Now, Dad. And a sense of responsibility just what I've only this minute stopped showing nothing else but."

"Good Lord – what language is that? You didn't meet Mr Chan, did you?"

"Well, in a way I didn't—"

"In a way? In a way!"

"Precisely. It's a long story, and I'll tell it if you'll stop interrupting with these unwarranted attacks on my character. I'll sit down, if I may. I've been about a bit, and I'm tired."

He lighted a cigarette. "When I came out of the club about five to go to the dock there was nothing in sight but a battered old taxi that had seen better days. I jumped in. When I got down on the Embarcadero I noticed that the driver was a pretty disreputable lad with a scar on one cheek and a cauliflower ear. He said he'd wait for me, and he said it with a lot of enthusiasm.

I went into the pier-shed. There was the *President Pierce* out in the harbour, fumbling round trying to dock. In a few minutes I noticed a man standing near me – a thin, chilly-looking lad with an overcoat, the collar up about his ears, and a pair of black spectacles. I guess I'm psychic – he didn't look good to me. I couldn't tell, but somehow he seemed to be looking at me behind those smoked windows. I moved to the other side of the shed. So did he. I went to the street. He followed. Well, I drifted back to the gang-plank, and old Chilly Bill came along."

Bob Eden paused, smiling genially about him. "Right then and there I came to a quick decision. I'm remarkable that way. I didn't have the pearls, but Mr Chan did. Why tip off the world to Mr Chan? So I just stood there staring hopefully at the crowd landing from the old *P.P.* Presently I saw the man I took to be Mr Chan come down the plank, but I never stirred. I watched him while he looked about, then I saw him go out to the street. Still the mysterious gent behind the windows stuck closer than a bill-collector. After everybody was ashore, I went back to my taxi and paid off the driver. 'Was you expecting somebody on the ship?' he asked. 'Yes,' I told him. 'I came down to meet the Dowager Empress of China, but they tell me she's dead.' He gave me a dirty look. As I hurried away the man with the dark glasses came up. 'Taxi, mister?' said Cauliflower Ear. And old Glasses got in. I had to meander through the rain all the way to the S. P. station before I could find another cab. Just as I drove away from the station along came Cauliflower Ear in his splendid equipage. He followed along behind, down Third, up Market to Powell, and finally to the Saint Francis. I went in the front door of the hotel and out the side, on to Post. And there was Cauliflower Ear and his fare, drifting by our store. As I went in the front door of the club my dear old friends drew up across the street. I escaped by way of the kitchen, and slipped over here. I fancy they're still in front of the club – they loved me like a brother." He paused. "And that, Dad, is the long but thrilling story of why I did not meet Mr Chan."

Eden smiled. "By Jove, you've got more brains than I thought. You were perfectly right. But look here, Sally – I like this less than ever. That necklace of yours isn't a well-known string. It's been in Honolulu for years. Easy as the devil to dispose of it, once it's stolen. If you'll take my advice you'll certainly not send it off to the desert—"

"Why not?" broke in Victor. "The desert's the very place to send it. Certainly this town doesn't look any too good."

"Alec," said Sally Jordan, "we need the money. If Mr Madden is down at Eldorado, and asks for the necklace there, then let's send it to him immediately and get his receipt. After that – well, it's his look-out. His worry. Certainly I want it off my hands as soon as may be."

Eden sighed. "All right. It's for you to decide. Bob will take it at eleven, as we planned. Provided – well, provided you make the arrangement you promised – provided he doesn't go alone." He looked toward Charlie Chan, who was standing at the window watching, fascinated, the noisy life of Geary Street far below.

"Charlie," said Sally Jordan.

"Yes, Miss Sally." He turned, smiling, to face her.

"What was that you said about the burden dropping from your shoulders? The delectable thud?"

"Now vacation begins," he said. "All my life I have unlimited yearning to face the wonders of this mainland. Moment are now at hand. Care-free and happy, not like crossing on ship. There all time pearls rest heavy on stomach, most undigestible, like sour rice. Not so now."

Madame Jordan shook her head. "I'm sorry, Charlie," she said. "I'm going to ask you to eat one more bowl of sour rice. For me – for auld lang syne."

"I do not quite grasp meaning," he told her.

She outlined the plan to send him with Bob Eden to the desert. His expression did not change.

"I will go," he promised gravely.

"Thank you, Charlie," said Sally Jordan softly.

"In my youth," he continued, "I am houseboy in the Phillimore mansion. Still in my heart like old-time garden bloom memories of kindness never to be repaid." He saw Sally Jordan's eyes bright and shining with tears. "Life would be dreary waste," he finished, "if there was no thing called loyalty."

Very flowery, thought Alexander Eden. He sought to introduce a more practical note. "All your expenses will be paid, of course. And that vacation is just postponed for a few days. You'd better carry the pearls – you have the belt, and, besides, no one knows your connexion with the affair. Thank heaven for that."

"I will carry them," Chan agreed. He took up the string from the table. "Miss Sally, toss all worry out of mind. When this young man and I encounter proper person pearls will be delivered. Until then I guard them well."

"I'm sure you will," smiled Madame Jordan.

"Well, that's settled," said Eden. "Mr Chan, you and my son will take the eleven o'clock ferry to Richmond, which connects with the train to Barstow. There you'll have to change to another train for Eldorado, but you should reach Madden's ranch tomorrow evening. If he is there and everything seems in order—"

"Why should everything be in order?" broke in Victor. "If he's there – that's enough."

"Well, of course, we don't want to take any undue risk," Eden went on. "But you two will know what to do when you reach there. If Madden's at the ranch give him the string and get his receipt. That lets us out. Mr Chan, we will pick you up here at ten-thirty. Until then you are free to follow your own inclination."

"Present inclination," smiled Chan, "means tub filled with water, steaming hot. At ten-thirty in entrance-hall of hotel I will be waiting, undigestible pearls on stomach, as before. Goodbye. Goodbye." He bobbed to each in turn and went out.

"I've been in business thirty-five years," said Eden, "but I never employed a messenger quite like him before."

"Dear Charlie," said Sally Jordan. "He'll protect those pearls with his life."

Bob Eden laughed. "I hope it doesn't go as far as that," he remarked. "I've got a life too, and I'd like to hang on to it."

"Won't you both stay to dinner?" suggested Sally Jordan.

"Some other time, thanks," Alexander Eden answered. "I don't think it wise we should keep together tonight. Bob and I will go home – he has a bag to pack, I imagine. I don't intend to let him out of my sight until train-time."

"One last word," said Victor. "Don't be too squeamish when you get down on that ranch. If Madden's in danger that's no affair of ours. Put those pearls in his hand and get his receipt. That's all."

Eden shook his head. "I don't like the look of this, Sally. I don't like this thing at all."

"Don't worry," she smiled. "I have every confidence in Charlie – and in Bob."

"Such popularity must be deserved," said Bob Eden. "I promise I'll do my best. Only I hope that lad in the overcoat doesn't decide to come down to the desert and warm up. Somehow I'm not so sure I'd be a match for him – once he warmed up."

III

AT CHAN KEE LIM'S

An hour later Charlie Chan rode down in the elevator to the bright lobby of his hotel. A feeling of heavy responsibility again weighed upon him, for he had restored to the money-belt about his bulging waist the pearls that alone remained of all the Phillimore fortune. After a quick glance about the lobby he went out into Geary Street.

The rain no longer fell and for a moment he stood on the kerb, a little, wistful, wide-eyed stranger, gazing at a world as new and strange to him as though he had wakened to find himself on Mars. The pavement was crowded with theatregoers; taxis honked in the narrow street; at intervals sounded the flippant warning of cable-car bells, which is a tune heard only in San Francisco, a city with a voice and a gesture all its own.

Unexplored country to Charlie Chan, this mainland, and he was thrilled by the electric gaiety of the scene before him. Old-timers would have told him that what he saw was only a dim imitation of the night life of other days, but he had no memories of the past, and hence nothing to mourn. Seated on a stool at a lunch-counter, he ate his evening meal – a stool and a lunch-counter, but it was adventure enough for one who had never known Billy Bogan's Louvre Café, on the site of which now stands the Bank of Italy – adventure enough for one who had no happy recollections of Delmonico's on O'Farrell Street or of the Odeon or the Pup or the Black Cat, bright spots blotted out for ever now. He partook heartily of the white man's cooking, and drank three cups of steaming tea.

A young man, from his appearance perhaps a clerk, was eating a modest dinner at Chan's side. After a few words concerned with the sugar-bowl, Chan ventured to address him further.

"Please pardon the abrupt advance of a newcomer," he said. "For three hours I am free to wander the damp but interesting streets of your city. Kindly mention what I ought to see."

"Why – I don't know," said the young man, surprised. "Not much doing any more. San Francisco's not what it used to be."

"The Barbary Coast, maybe," suggested Chan.

The young man snorted. "Gone for ever. The Thalia, the Elko, the Midway – say, they're just memories now. Spider Kelley is over in Arizona, dealing in land. Yes, sir – all those old dance-halls are just garages today – or maybe ten-cent flop-houses. But look here – this is New Year's Eve in Chinatown. However—" He laughed. "I guess I don't need to tell you that."

Chan nodded. "Ah, yes – the twelfth of February. New Year's Eve."

Presently he was back on the pavement, his keen eyes sparkling with excitement. He thought of the somnolent thoroughfares of Honolulu by night – Honolulu, where everyone goes home at six, and stays there. How different here in this mainland city! The driver of a sight-seeing bus approached him and also spoke of Chinatown. "Show you the old opium dens and the fan-tan joints," he promised, but after a closer look moved off and said no more of his spurious wares.

At a little after eight the detective from the Islands left the friendly glow of Union Square and, drifting down into the darker stretches of Post Street, came presently to Grant Avenue.

A loiterer on the corner directed him to the left, and he strolled on. In a few moments he came to a row of shops displaying cheap Oriental goods for the tourist eye. His pace quickened; he passed the church on the crest of the hill and moved on down into the real Chinatown.

Here a spirit of carnival filled the air. The *façade* of every *tong* house, outlined by hundreds of glowing incandescent lamps, shone in yellow splendour through the misty night. Throngs crowded on the narrow pavements – white sightseers, dapper young Chinese lads in college-cut clothes escorting Chinese flappers attired in their best, older Chinese shuffling along on felt-clad feet, each secure in the knowledge that his debts were paid, his house scoured and scrubbed, the new year auspiciously begun.

At Washington Street Chan turned up the hill. Across the way loomed an impressive building – four gaudy stories of light and cheer. Gilt letters in the transom over the door proclaimed it the home of the Chan Family Society. For a moment the detective stood, family pride uppermost in his thoughts.

A moment later he was walking down the dim, almost deserted pavement of Waverly Place. A bright-eyed boy of his own race offered him a copy of the *Chinese Daily Times*. He bought it and moved on, his gaze intent on dim house-numbers above darkened doorways.

Presently he found the number he sought, and climbed a shadowy stair. At a landing where crimson and gold-lettered strips of paper served as a warning to evil spirits he paused, and knocked loudly at the door. It was opened, and against the light from within stood the figure of a Chinese, tall, with a grey, meagre beard and a loose-fitting, embroidered blouse of black satin.

For a moment neither spoke. Then Chan smiled. "Good evening, illustrious Chan Kee Lim," he said in pure Cantonese.

"Is it that you do not know your unworthy cousin from the Islands?"

A light shone in the narrow eyes of Kee Lim. "For a moment, no," he replied, "since you come in the garb of a foreign-devil, and knock on my door with the knuckles, as rude foreign devils do. A thousand welcomes. Deign to enter my contemptible house."

Still smiling, the little detective went inside. The room was anything but contemptible, as he saw at once. It was rich with tapestries of Hang-chiu silk, the furniture was of teakwood, elaborately carved. Fresh flowers bloomed before the ancestral shrine, and everywhere were Chinese lilies, the pale, pungent *sui-sin-fah*, symbol of the dawning year. On the mantel, beside a tiny Buddha of Ningpo-wood, an American alarm clock ticked noisily.

"Please sit in this wretched chair," Kee Lim said. "You arrive unexpectedly as August rain. But I am happy to see you." He clapped his hands and a woman entered. "My wife, Chan So," the host explained. "Bring rice-cakes, and my Dew of Roses wine," he ordered.

He sat down opposite Charlie Chan, and regarded him across a teakwood table on which were sprays of fresh almond-blossoms. "There was no news of your coming," he remarked.

Chan shrugged. "No. It was better so. I come on a mission. On business," he added, in his best Rotary Club manner.

Kee Lim's eyes narrowed. "Yes – I have heard of your business," he said.

The detective was slightly uncomfortable. "You do not approve?" he ventured.

"It is too much to say that I do not approve," Kee Lim returned. "But I do not quite understand. The foreign-devil police – what has a Chinese in common with them?"

Charlie smiled. "There are times, honorable cousin," he admitted, "when I do not quite understand myself."

The reed curtains at the rear parted, and a girl came into the room. Her eyes were dark and bright; her face pretty as a doll's. Tonight, in deference to the holiday, she wore the silken trousers and embroidered jacket of her people, but her hair was bobbed and her walk, her gestures, her whole manner, all too obviously copied from her American sisters. She carried a tray piled high with New Year delicacies.

"My daughter Rose," Kee Lim announced. "Behold, our famous cousin from Hawaii." He turned to Charlie Chan. "She too would be an American, insolent as the daughters of the foolish white men."

The girl laughed. "Why not? I was born here. I went to American grammar schools. And now I work American fashion."

"Work?" repeated Charlie, with interest.

"The Classics of Girlhood are forgotten," explained Kee Lim. "All day she sits in the Chinatown telephone exchange, shamelessly talking to a wall of teakwood that flashes red and yellow eyes."

"Is that so terrible?" asked the girl, with a laughing glance at her cousin.

"A most interesting labour," surmised Charlie.

"I'll tell the world it is," answered the girl in English, and went out. A moment later she returned with a battered old wine-jug. Into Swatow bowls she poured two hot libations – then, taking a seat on the far side of the room, she gazed curiously at this notable relative from across the seas. Once she had read of his exploits in the San Francisco papers.

For an hour or more Chan sat, talking with his cousin of the distant days when they were children in China. Finally he glanced toward the mantel. "Does that clock speak the truth?" he asked.

Kee Lim shrugged. "It is a foreign-devil clock," he said. "And therefore a great liar."

Chan consulted his watch. "With the keenest regret," he announced, "I find I must walk my way. Tonight my business carries me far from here – to the desert that lies in the South. I have had the presumption, honest and industrious cousin, to direct my wife to send to your house any letters of importance addressed to me. Should a message arrive in my absence, you will be good enough to hold it here awaiting my return. In a few days, at most, I will walk this way again. Meanwhile I go beyond the reach of messengers."

The girl rose and came forward. "Even on the desert," she said, "there are telephones."

Charlie looked at her with sudden interest. "On the desert," he repeated.

"Most assuredly. Only two days ago I had a long-distance call for a ranch near Eldorado. A ranch named – but I do not remember."

"Perhaps – the ranch of Madden," said Chan hopefully.

She nodded. "Yes – that was the name. It was a most unusual call."

"And it came from Chinatown."

"Of course. From the bowl-shop of Wong Ching, in Jackson Street. He desired to speak to his relative, Louie Wong, caretaker on Madden's ranch. The number, Eldorado seven six."

Chan dissembled his eagerness, but his heart was beating faster. He was of the foreign-devil police now. "Perhaps you heard what was said?"

"Louie Wong must come to San Francisco at once. Much money and a fine position awaited him here—"

"*Haie!*" cut in Kee Lim. "It is not fitting that you reveal thus the secrets of your white-devil profession. Even to one of the family of Chan."

"You are right, ever-wise cousin," Charlie agreed. He turned to the girl. "You and I, little blossom, will meet again. Even though the desert has telephones, I am beyond reach there. Now, to my great regret, I must go."

Kee Lim followed him to the door. He stood there on the reed mat, stroking his thin beard and blinking. "Farewell, notable cousin. On that long journey of yours upon which you now set out – walk slowly."

"Farewell," Charlie answered. "All my good wishes for happiness in the new year." Suddenly he found himself speaking English. "See you later," he called, and hurried down the stairs.

Once in the street, however, he obeyed his cousin's parting injunction, and walked slowly indeed. A startling bit of news, this, from Rose, the telephone-operator. Louie Wong was wanted in San Francisco – wanted by his relative Wong Ching, the bowl merchant. Why?

An old Chinese on a corner directed him to Jackson Street, and he climbed its steep pavement until he reached the shop of Wong Ching. The brightly lighted window was filled with Swatow cups and bowls, a rather beautiful display, but evidently during this holiday season the place was not open for business, for the curtains on the door were drawn. Chan rattled the latch for a full minute, but no one came.

He crossed the street, and took up a post in a dark doorway opposite. Sooner or later his summons would be answered. On a nearby balcony a Chinese orchestra was playing – the whanging flute, the shrill plink of the *moon-kwan*, the rasping cymbals, and the drums filled the night with a blissful dissonance. Presently the musicians ceased, the din died away, and Chan heard only the click of American heels and the stealthy swish of felt slippers passing his hiding-place.

In about ten minutes the door of Wong Ching's shop opened and a man came out. He stood looking cautiously up and down the dim street. A thin man in an overcoat which was buttoned close about him – a chilly-seeming man. His hat was low over his eyes, and as a further means of deceit he wore dark spectacles. Charlie Chan permitted a faint flash of interest to cross his chubby face.

The chilly man walked briskly down the hill, and, stepping quickly from the doorway, Chan followed at a distance. They emerged into Grant Avenue; the dark-spectacled one turned to the right. Still Chan followed; this was child's play for him. One block, two, three. They came to a cheap hotel, the Killarney, on one of Grant Avenue's corners, and the man in the overcoat went inside.

Glancing at his watch, Chan decided to let his quarry escape, and turned in the direction of Union Square. His mind was troubled. "This much even a fool could grasp," he thought. "We move toward a trap. But with eyes open – with eyes keenly open."

Back in his tiny hotel room, he restored to his inexpensive suitcase the few articles he had previously removed. Returning to the desk, he found that his trunk had reached the hotel, but had not yet been taken upstairs. He arranged for its storage until his return, paid his bill, and sitting down in a great leather chair in the lobby, with his suitcase at his feet, he waited patiently.

At precisely ten-thirty Bob Eden stepped inside the door of the hotel and beckoned. Following the young man to the street, Chan saw a big limousine drawn up to the kerb.

"Jump in, Mr Chan," said the boy, taking his bag. As the detective entered the darkened interior Alexander Eden greeted him from the gloom. "Tell Michael to drive slowly – I want to talk," called the older man to his son. Bob Eden spoke to the chauffeur, then leaped into the car, and it moved off down Geary Street.

"Mr Chan," said the jeweler in a low voice, "I am very much disturbed."

"More events have taken place?" suggested Chan.

"Decidedly," Eden replied. "You were in the room this afternoon when I spoke of a telephone-call I had received from a pay-station at Sutter and Kearny Streets." He repeated the details. "This evening I called into consultation Al Draycott, head of the Gale Detective Agency, with which I have affiliations. I asked him to investigate and, if possible, find that man in the overcoat Bob saw at the dock. An hour ago he reported that he had located our man with no great difficulty. He has discovered him—"

"At the Killarney Hotel, perhaps, on Grant Avenue," suggested Chan, dissembling a deep triumph.

"Good Lord," gasped Eden. "You found him too. Why – that's amazing—"

"Amazing luck," said Chan. "Please pardon rude interruption. Will not occur again."

"Well, Draycott located this fellow, and reports that he is Shaky Phil Maydorf, one of the Maydorf brothers, as slick a pair of crooks as ever left New York for their health. The fellow suffers from malaria, I believe, but otherwise he is in good form and, it seems, very much interested in our little affairs. But, Mr Chan – your own story – how in the world did you find him too?"

Chan shrugged. "Successful detective," he said, "is plenty often man on whom luck turns smiling face. This evening I bask in most heart-warming grin." He told of his visit to Chan Lee Kim, of the telephone-call to the desert from Wong's bowl-shop, and of his seeing the man in the overcoat leaving the shop. "After that, simple matter to hound him to hotel," he finished.

"Well, I'm more disturbed than ever," Eden said. "They have called the caretaker away from Madden's ranch. Why? I tell you I don't like this business—"

"Nonsense, Father," Bob Eden protested. "It's rather interesting."

"Not to me. I don't welcome the attention of these Maydorfs – and where, by the way, is the other one? They are not the modern type of crook that relies entirely on a gun. They are men of brains – old-fashioned outlaws who are regarded with respect by the police whom they have fought for many years. I called Sally Jordan and tried to abandon the whole proceeding – but that son of hers! He's itching to get the money, and he's urging her to go ahead. So what can I do? If it was anyone else I'd certainly drop out of the deal – but Sally Jordan – well, she's an old friend. And as you said this afternoon, Mr Chan, there is such a thing as loyalty in the world. But I tell you I'm sending you two down there with the deepest reluctance."

"Don't you worry, Dad. It's going to be great fun, I'm sure. All my life I've wanted to be mixed up in a good exciting murder. As a spectator, of course."

"What are you talking about?" the father demanded.

"Why, Mr Chan here is a detective, isn't he? A detective on a vacation. If you've ever read a mystery story you know that a detective never works so hard as when he's on vacation. He's like the postman who goes for a long walk on his day off. Here we are, all set. We've got our bright and shining mark, our millionaire – P.J. Madden, one of the most famous financiers in America. I tell you, poor P.J. is doomed. Ten to one Mr Chan and I will walk into that ranch-house and find him dead on the first rug we come to."

"This is no joking matter," Eden rebuked severely. "Mr Chan – you seem to be a man of considerable ability. Have you anything to suggest?"

Charlie smiled in the dark car. "Flattery sounds sweet to any ear," he remarked. "I have, it is true, inclination for making humble suggestion."

"Then for heaven's sake make it," Eden said.

"Pray give the future a thought. Young Mr Eden and I walk hand in hand, like brothers, on to desert ranch. What will spectator say? Aha, they bring pearls. If not, why come together for strength?"

"Absolutely true," Eden agreed.

"Then why travel side by side?" Charlie continued. "It is my humble hint that Mr Bob Eden arrive alone at ranch. Answering all inquiries he says no, he does not carry pearls. So many dark clouds shade the scene, he is sent by honorable father to learn if all is well. When he is sure of that he will telegraph necklace be sent at once, please."

"A good idea," Eden said. "Meanwhile— "

"At somewhat same hour," Chan went on, "there stumble on to ranch weary old Chinese, seeking employment. One whose clothes are of a notable shabbiness, a wanderer over sand, a what you call – a desert rat. Who would dream that on the stomach of such a one repose those valuable Phillimore pearls?"

"Say – that's immense," cried Bob Eden enthusiastically.

"Might be," admitted Chan. "Both you and old Chinese look carefully about. If all is well, together you approach this Madden and hand over necklace. Even then, others need not know."

"Fine," said the boy. "We'll separate when we board the train. If you're in doubt at any time just keep your eye on me, and tag along. We're due in Barstow tomorrow at one-fifteen, and there's a train to Eldorado at three-twenty, which arrives about six. I'm taking it, and you'd better do the same. One of my newspaper friends here has given me a letter to a fellow named Will Holley, who's editor of a little paper at Eldorado. I'm going to invite him to have dinner with me, then I'll drive out to Madden's. You, of course, will get out some other way. As somebody may be watching us, we won't speak on our journey. Friends once, but strangers now. That's the idea, isn't it?"

"Precisely the notion," agreed Chan.

The car had stopped before the ferry building. "I have your tickets here," Alexander Eden said, handing over a couple of envelopes. "You have lower berths, in the same car, but at different ends. You'll find a little money there for expenses, Mr Chan. I may say that I think your plan is excellent – but for heaven's sake be careful, both of you. Bob, my boy – you're all I've got. I may have spoken harshly to you, but I – I – take care of yourself."

"Don't you worry, Dad," Bob Eden said. "Though you'll never believe it, I'm grown up. And I've got a good man with me."

"Mr Chan," Eden said, "good luck. And thank you a thousand times."

"Don't talk about it," smiled Charlie. "Happiest walk of postman's life is on his holiday. I will serve you well. Goodbye."

He followed Bob Eden through the gates and on to the ferry-boat. A moment later they had slipped out upon the black waters of the harbour. The rain was gone, the sky spattered with stars, but a chill wind blew through the Gate. Charlie stood alone by the rail; the dream of his life had come true; he knew the great mainland at last. The flaming ball atop the ferry building receded; the yellow lamps of the city marched up the hills and down again. He thought of the tiny island that was his home, of the house on Punch Bowl Hill where his wife and children patiently awaited his return. Suddenly he was appalled at the distance he had come.

Bob Eden joined him there in the dark, and waved his hand toward the glow in the sky above Grant Avenue. "A big night in Chinatown," he said.

"Very large night," agreed Chan. "And why not? Tomorrow is the first day of the new year. Of the year four thousand eight hundred and sixty-nine."

"Great Scott," smiled Eden. "How time flies. A Happy New Year to you."

"Similar one to you," said Chan.

The boat ploughed on. From the prison island of Alcatraz a cruel, relentless searchlight swept at intervals the inky waters. The wind was bitter now.

"I'm going inside," shivered Bob Eden. "This is goodbye, I guess."

"Better so," admitted Charlie. "When you are finally at Madden's ranch, look about for that desert rat."

Alone, he continued to stare at the lamps of the city, cold and distant now, like the stars.

"A desert rat," he repeated softly, "with no fondly feeling for a trap."

IV

THE OASIS SPECIAL

Dusk was falling in the desert town of Eldorado when, on Friday evening, Bob Eden alighted from the train at a station that looked like a little red schoolhouse gone wrong. His journey down from San Francisco to Barstow had been quite without incident. At that town, however, a rather disquieting thing had happened. He had lost all trace of Charlie Chan.

It was in the Barstow lunch-room that he had last seen the detective from the Islands, busy with a cup of steaming tea. The hour of three-twenty and the Eldorado train being some distance off, he had gone for a stroll through the town. Returning about three, he had looked in vain for the little Chinese policeman. Alone he had boarded the train, and now, as he stared up and down the dreary railroad tracks, he perceived that he had been the only passenger to alight at this unpromising spot.

Thinking of the fortune in "undigestible" pearls on the detective's person, he was vaguely alarmed. Had Chan met with some unfortunate accident? Or perhaps – who could say? What did they really know about this Charlie Chan? Every man is said to have his price, and this was an overwhelming temptation to put in the way of an underpaid detective from Honolulu. But no – Bob Eden recalled the look in Chan's eyes when he had promised Sally Jordan to guard those pearls well.

The Jordans no doubt had good reason for their faith in an old friend. But suppose Shaky Phil Maydorf was no longer in San Francisco—

Resolutely Bob Eden put these thoughts aside and, rounding the station, entered a narrow strip of ground which was, rather pathetically, intended for a park. February had done its worst, and up above the chill evening wind from the desert blew through the stark branches of Carolina poplars and cottonwoods. Crossing a gravel path almost hidden by a mass of yellow leaves, he stood on the kerb of the only pavement in Eldorado.

Against the background of bare brown hills, he saw practically the entire town at a glance. Across the way a row of scraggly buildings proclaimed yet another Main Street – a bank, a picture theatre, the Spot Cash Store, the News Bureau, the post-office, and, towering above the rest, a two-storey building that announced itself as the Desert Edge Hotel. Eden crossed the street, and, threading his way between dusty automobiles parked head on at the kerb, approached the door of the latter. On the double seat of a shoe-shining stand two ranchers lolled at ease, and stared at him with mild interest as he went inside.

An electric lamp of modest candle-power burned above the desk of the Desert Edge, and a kindly old man read a Los Angeles paper in its dim company.

"Good evening," said Bob Eden.

"Evenin'," answered the old man.

"I wonder if I might leave this suitcase in your check-room for a while?" the boy inquired.

"Check-room, hell," replied the old man. "Just throw her down anywhere. Ain't lookin' fer a room, I suppose. Make you a special rate."

"No," said Eden. "I'm sorry."

"'Sall right," answered the proprietor. "Not many are."

"I'd like to find the office of the *Eldorado Times*," Eden informed him.

"Round corner on First," murmured the old man, deep in his pink newspaper again.

Bob Eden went to the corner, and turned off. His feet at once left Eldorado's solitary pavement for soft-crunching sand. He passed a few buildings even meaner than those on Main Street, a plumber's shop, a grocer's, and came to a little yellow shack which bore on its window the fading legend: "*The Eldorado Times*. Job Printing Neatly Done." There was no light inside, and crossing a narrow, dilapidated porch, he saw a placard on the door. Straining his eyes in the dusk, he read:

Back in an hour –

God knows why.

WILL HOLLEY

Smiling, Eden returned to the Desert Edge. "How about dinner?" he inquired.

"Wonderin' about it myself," admitted the old man. "We don't serve meals here. Lose a little less that way."

"But there must be a restaurant—"

"Sure there is. This is an up-todate town." He nodded over his shoulder. "Down beyond the bank – the Oasis Café."

Thanking him, Bob Eden departed. Behind unwashed windows he found the Oasis dispensing its dubious cheer. A long, high counter and a soiled mirror running the length of it suggested that in other days this had been an oasis indeed.

The boy climbed on to one of the perilously high stools. At his right, too close for comfort, sat a man in overalls and jumper, with a week's growth of beard on his lean, hard face. At his left, equally close but somehow not so much in the way, was a trim girl in khaki riding-breeches and blouse.

A youth made up to resemble a motion-picture sheik demanded his order, and from a soiled menu he chose the Oasis Special – "steak and onions, French fries bread and butter and coffee. Eighty cents." The sheik departed languidly.

Awaiting the special, Bob Eden glanced into the smoky mirror at the face of the girl beside him. Not so bad, even in that dim reflection. Corn-yellow hair curling from under the brim of a felt hat; a complexion that no beauty parlour had originated. He held his left elbow close so that she might have more room for the business that engrossed her.

His dinner arrived, a plenteous platter of food – but no plate. He glanced at his neighbors. Evidently plates were an affectation frowned upon in the Oasis. Taking up a tarnished knife and fork, he pushed aside the underbrush of onions and came face to face with his steak.

First impressions are important, and Bob Eden knew at once that this was no meek, complacent opponent that confronted him. The steak looked back at him with an air of defiance that was amply justified by what followed. After a few moments of unsuccessful battling, he summoned the sheik. "How about a steel knife?" he inquired.

"Only got three and they're all in use," the waiter replied.

Bob Eden resumed the battle, his elbows held close, his muscles swelling. With set teeth and grim face he bore down and cut deep. There was a terrific screech as his knife skidded along the platter, and to his horror he saw the steak rise from its bed of gravy and onions and fly from him. It travelled the grimy counter for a second, then dropped on to the knees of the girl and thence to the floor.

Eden turned to meet her blue eyes filled with laughter.

"Oh, I'm so sorry," he said. "I thought it was a steak, and it seems to be a lap-dog."

"And I hadn't any lap," she cried. She looked down at her riding-breeches. "Can you ever forgive me? I might have caught it for you. It only goes to show – women should be womanly."

"I wouldn't have you any different," Bob Eden responded gallantly. He turned to the sheik. "Bring me something a little less ferocious," he ordered.

"How about the pot roast?" asked the youth.

"Well, how about it?" Eden repeated. "Fetch it along and I'll fight another round. I claim a foul on that one. And say – bring this young woman a napkin."

"A what? A napkin. We ain't got any. I'll bring her a towel."

"Oh, no – please don't," cried the girl. "I'm all right, really."

The sheik departed.

"Somehow," she added to Eden, "I think it wiser not to introduce an Oasis towel into this affair."

"You're probably right," he nodded. "I'll pay for the damage, of course."

She was still smiling. "Nonsense. I ought to pay for the steak. It wasn't your fault. One needs long practice to eat in the crowded arena of the Oasis."

He looked at her, his interest growing every minute. "You've had long practice?" he inquired.

"Oh, yes. My work often brings me this way."

"Your – er – your work?"

"Yes. Since your steak seems to have introduced us, I may tell you I'm with the moving-pictures."

Of course, thought Eden. The desert was filled with movie people these days. "Ah – have I ever seen you in the films?" he ventured.

She shrugged. "You have not – and you never will. I'm not an actress. My job's much more interesting. I'm a location-finder."

Bob Eden's pot roast arrived, mercifully cut into small pieces by some blunt instrument behind the scenes. "A location finder? I ought to know what that is."

"You certainly ought to. It's just what it sounds like. I travel about hunting backgrounds. By the Vandeventer Trail to Piñon Flat, down to the Salton Sea or up to the Morongos – all the time trying to find something new, something the dear old public will mistake for Algeria, Araby, the South Seas."

"Sounds mighty interesting."

"It is, indeed. Particularly when one loves this country as I do."

"You were born here, perhaps?"

"Oh, no. I came out with Dad to Doctor Whitcomb's – it's five miles from here, just beyond the Madden ranch – some years ago. When – when Dad left me I had to get a job, and – but look here, I'm telling you the story of my life."

"Why not?" asked Eden. "Women and children always confide in me. I've got such a fatherly face. By the way, this coffee is terrible."

"Yes, isn't it?" she agreed. "What will you have for dessert? There are two kinds of pie – apple, and the other's out. Make your selection."

"I've made it," he replied. "I'm taking the one that's out." He demanded his check. "Now, if you'll let me pay for your dinner—"

"Nothing of the sort," she protested.

"But after the way my steak attacked you."

"Forget it. I've an expense account, you know. If you say any more I'll pay your check."

Ignoring the jar of toothpicks hospitably offered by a friendly cashier, Bob Eden followed her to the street. Night had fallen; the pavement was deserted. On the false front of a long, low building with sides of corrugated tin, a sad little string of electric lights proclaimed that gaiety was afoot.

"Whither away?" Bob Eden said. "The movies?"

"Heavens, no. I remember that one. It took ten years off my young life. Tell me, what are you doing here? People confide in me too. Stranger, you don't belong."

"No, I'm afraid I don't," Eden admitted. "It's a complicated story, but I'll inflict it on you, anyhow, some day. Just at present I'm looking for the editor of the *Eldorado Times*. I've got a letter to him in my pocket."

"Will Holley?"

"Yes. You know him?"

"Everybody knows him. Come with me. He ought to be in his office now."

They turned down First Street. Bob Eden was pleasantly conscious of the slim, lithe figure walking at his side. He had never before met a girl so modestly confident, so aware of life and unafraid of it. These desert towns were delightful.

A light was burning in the newspaper office, and under it a frail figure sat hunched over a typewriter. As they entered Will Holley rose, removing a green shade from his eyes. He was a thin, tall man of thirty-five or so, with prematurely grey hair and wistful eyes.

"Hello, Paula," he said.

"Hello, Will. See what *I* found at the Oasis Café?"

Holley smiled. "You would find him," he said. "You're the only one I know who can discover anything worth while in Eldorado. My boy, I don't know who you are, but run away before this desert gets you."

"I've a letter to you, Mr Holley," Eden said. He took it from his pocket. "It's from an old friend of yours – Harry Fladgate."

"Harry Fladgate," repeated Holley softly. He read the letter through. "A voice from the past," he said. "The past when we were boys together on the old *Sun*, in New York. Say – that was a newspaper!" He was silent for a moment, staring out at the desert night. "Harry says you're here on business of some sort," he added.

"Why, yes," Eden replied. "I'll tell you about it later. Just at present I want to hire a car to take me out to the Madden ranch."

"You want to see P.J. himself?"

"Yes, just as soon as possible. He's out there, isn't he?"

Holley nodded. "Yes – he's supposed to be. However, I haven't seen him. It's rumoured he came by motor the other day from Barstow. This young woman can tell you more about him than I can. By the way, have you two met each other, or are you just taking a stroll together in the moonlight?"

"Well, the fact is—" smiled Eden. "Miss – er – she just let a steak of mine get away from her in the Oasis. I had to credit her with an error in the infield, but she made a splendid try. However, as to names – and all that—"

"So I perceive," said Holley. "Miss Paula Wendell, may I present Mr Bob Eden? Let us not forget our book of etiquette, even here in the devil's garden."

"Thanks, old man," remarked Eden. "No one has ever done me a greater kindness. Now that we've been introduced, Miss Wendell, and I can speak to you at last, tell me – do you know Mr Madden?"

"Not exactly," she replied. "It isn't given such humble folk to know the great Madden. But several years ago my company took some pictures at his ranch – he has rather a handsome house there, with a darling *patio*. The other day we got hold of a script that fairly screamed for the Madden *patio*. I wrote him, asking permission to use his place, and he answered – from San Francisco – that he was coming down and would be glad to grant our request. His letter was really most kind."

The girl sat down on the edge of Holley's typewriter table. "I got to Eldorado two nights ago, and drove out to Madden's at once. And – well, it was rather queer – what happened. Do you want to hear all this?"

"I certainly do," Bob Eden assured her.

"The gate was open, and I drove into the yard. The lights of my car flashed suddenly on the barn door, and I saw a bent old man with a black beard and a pack on his back – evidently an old-time prospector such as one meets occasionally, even today, in this desert country. It was his expression that startled me. He stood like a frightened rabbit in the spotlight, then darted away. I knocked at the ranch-house door. There was a long delay, then finally a man came, a pale, excited-looking man – Madden's secretary, Thorn, he said he was. I give you my word – Will's heard this before – he was trembling all over. I told him my business with Madden, and he was very rude. He informed me that I positively could not see the great P.J. 'Come back in a week,' he said, over and over. I argued and pleaded – and he shut the door in my face."

"You couldn't see Madden," repeated Bob Eden slowly. "Anything else?"

"Not much. I drove back to town. A short distance down the road my lights picked up the little old prospector again. But when I got to where I thought he was he'd disappeared utterly. I didn't investigate – I just stepped on the gas. My love for the desert isn't so keen after dark."

Bob Eden took out a cigarette. "I'm awfully obliged," he said. "Mr Holley, I must get out to Madden's at once. If you'll direct me to a garage—"

"I'll do nothing of the sort," Holley replied. "An old flivver that answers to the name of Horace Greeley happens to be among my possessions at the moment, and I'm going to drive you out."

"I couldn't think of taking you away from your work."

"Oh, don't joke like that. You're breaking my heart. My work! Here I am, trying to string one good day's work along over all eternity, and you drift in and start to kid me—"

"I'm sorry," said Eden. "Come to think of it, I did see your placard on the door."

Holley shrugged. "I suppose that was just cheap cynicism. I try to steer clear of it. But sometimes – sometimes..."

They went together out of the office, and Holley locked the door. The deserted, sad little street stretched off to nowhere in each direction. The editor waved his hand at the somnolent picture.

"You'll find us all about out here," he said, "the exiles of the world. Of course, the desert is grand, and we love it – but once let a doctor say 'You can go' and you couldn't see us for the dust. I don't mind the daytime so much – the hot, friendly day – but the nights – the cold, lonely nights."

"Oh, it isn't so bad, Will," said the girl gently.

"Oh, no, it isn't so bad," he admitted. "Not since the radio – and the pictures. Night after night I sit over there in that movie theatre, and sometimes, in a news-reel or perhaps in a feature, I see Fifth Avenue again, Fifth Avenue at Forty-second, with the motors, and the lions in front of the library, and the women in furs. But I never see Park Row." The three of them walked along in silence through the sand. "If you love me, Paula," added Will Holley softly, "there's a location you'll find. A story about Park Row, with the crowds under the El, and the wagons backed up to the rear door of the post-office, and Perry's Drug Store, and the gold dome of the World. Give me a film of that, and I'll sit in the Strand watching it over and over until these old eyes go blind."

"I'd like to," said the girl. "But those crowds under the Elevated wouldn't care for it. What they want is the desert – the broad, open spaces away from the roar of the town."

Holley nodded. "I know. It's a feeling that's spread over America these past few years like some dread epidemic. I must write an editorial about it. The French have a proverb that describes it: 'Wherever one is not, that is where the heart is.'"

The girl held out her hand. "Mr Eden, I'm leaving you here – leaving you for a happy night at the Desert Edge Hotel."

"But I'll see you again," Bob Eden said quickly. "I must."

"You surely will. I'm coming out to Madden's ranch tomorrow. I have that letter of his, and this time I'll see him – you bet I'll see him if he's there."

"If he's there," repeated Bob Eden thoughtfully. "Good night. But before you go – how do you like your steaks?"

"Rare," she laughed.

"Yes – I guess one was enough. However, I'm very grateful to that one."

"It was a lovely steak," she said. "Good night."

Will Holley led the way to an aged car parked before the hotel. "Jump in," he said. "It's only a short run."

"Just a moment – I must get my bag," Eden replied. He entered the hotel and returned in a moment with his suitcase, which he tossed into the tonneau. "Horace Greeley's ready," Holley said. "Come west, young man."

Eden climbed in, and the little car clattered down Main Street. "This is mighty kind of you," the boy said.

"It's a lot of fun," Holley answered. "You know, I've been thinking. Old P.J. never gives an interview, but you can't tell – I might be able to persuade him. These famous men sometimes let down a little when they get out here. It would be a big feather in my cap. They'd hear of me on Park Row again."

"I'll do all I can to help," Bob Eden promised.

"That's good of you," Holley answered. The faint yellow lights of Eldorado grew even fainter behind them. They ascended a rough road between two small hills – barren, unlovely piles of badly assorted rocks. "Well, I'm going to try it," the editor added. "But I hope I have more luck than the last time."

"Oh – then you've seen Madden before?" Eden asked with interest.

"Just once," Holley replied. "Twelve years ago, when I was a reporter in New York. I'd managed to get into a gambling-house in Forty-fourth Street, a few doors east of Delmonico's. It didn't have a very good reputation, that joint, but there was the great P.J. Madden himself, all dolled up in evening clothes, betting his head off. They said that after he'd gambled all day in Wall Street, he couldn't let it alone – hung round the roulette-wheels in that house every night."

"And you tried to interview him?"

"I did. I was a fool kid, with lots of nerve. He had a big railroad merger in the air at the time, and I decided to ask him about it. So I went up to him during a lull in the betting. I told him I was on a newspaper – and that was as far as I got. 'Get the hell out of here,' he roared. 'You know I never give interviews.'" Holley laughed. "That was my first and only meeting with P.J. Madden. It wasn't a very propitious beginning, but what I started that night on Forty-fourth Street I'm going to try to finish out here tonight."

They reached the top of the grade, the rocky hills dropped behind them, and they were in a mammoth doorway leading to a strange new world. Up amid the platinum stars a thin slice of moon rode high, and far below in that meagre light lay the great grey desert, lonely and mysterious.

V

MADDEN'S RANCH

Carefully Will Holley guided his car down the steep, rock-strewn grade. "Go easy, Horace," he murmured. Presently they were on the floor of the desert, the road but a pair of faint wheel-tracks amid the creosote brush and mesquite. Once their headlights caught a jack-rabbit, sitting firmly on the right of way; the next instant he was gone for ever.

Bob Eden saw a brief stretch of palm-trees behind a barbed-wire fence, and down the lane between the trees the glow of a lonely window.

"Alfalfa Ranch," Will Holley explained.

"Why, in heaven's name, do people live out here?" Eden asked.

"Some of them because they can't live anywhere else," the editor answered. "And at that – well, you know it isn't a bad place to ranch it. Apples, lemons, pears—"

"But how about water?"

"It's only a desert because not many people have taken the trouble to bore for water. Just go down a way, and you strike it. Some go down a couple of hundred feet – Madden only had to go thirty odd. But that was Madden luck. He's near the bed of an underground river."

They came to another fence; above it were painted signs and flags fluttering yellow in the moonlight.

"Don't tell me that's a subdivision," Eden said.

Holley laughed. "Date City," he announced. "Here in California the subdivider, like the poor, is always with us. Date City where, if you believe all you're told, every dime is a baby dollar. No one lives there yet – but who knows? We're a growing community – see my editorial in last week's issue."

The car ploughed on. It staggered a bit now, but Holley's hands were firm on the wheel. Here and there a Joshua-tree stretched out hungry black arms as though to seize these travelers by night, and over that grey waste a dismal wind moaned constantly, chill and keen and biting. Bob Eden turned up the collar of his top coat.

"I can't help thinking of that old song," he said. "You know – about the lad who guaranteed to love somebody 'until the sands of the desert grow cold.'"

"It wasn't much of a promise," agreed Holley. "Either he was a great kidder, or he'd never been on the desert at night. But look here – is this your first experience with this country? What kind of a Californian are you?"

"Golden Gate brand," smiled Eden. "Yes, it's true, I've never been down here before. Something tells me I've missed a lot."

"You sure have. I hope you won't rush off in a hurry. By the way, how long do you expect to be here?"

"I don't know," replied Eden. He was silent for a moment; his friend at home had told him that Holley could be trusted, but he really did not need that assurance. One look into the editor's friendly grey eyes was sufficient. "Holley, I may as well tell you why I've come," he continued. "But I rely on your discretion. This isn't an interview."

"Suit yourself," Holley answered. "I can keep a secret if I have to. But tell me or not, just as you prefer."

"I prefer to tell you," Eden said. He recounted Madden's purchase of the Phillimore pearls, his request for their delivery in New York, and then his sudden, unexpected switch to the desert. "That, in itself, was rather disturbing," he added.

"Odd, yes," agreed Holley.

"But that wasn't all," Bob Eden went on. Omitting only Charlie Chan's connexion with the affair, he told the whole story – the telephone-call from the cigar-store in San Francisco, the loving solicitude at the dock and after of the man with the dark glasses, the subsequent discovery that this was Shaky Phil Maydorf, a guest at the Killarney Hotel, and, last of all, the fact that Louie Wong had been summoned from the Madden ranch by his relative in Chinatown. As he related all this out there on that lonesome desert, it began to take on a new and ominous aspect, the future loomed dark and thrilling. Had that great opening between the hills been, in reality, the gateway to adventure? Certainly it looked the part. "What do you think?" he finished.

"Me?" said Holley. "I think I'm not going to get that interview."

"You don't believe Madden is at the ranch?"

"I certainly don't. Look at Paula's experience the other night. Why couldn't she see him? Why didn't he hear her at the door and come to find out what the row was about? Because he wasn't there. My lad, I'm glad you didn't venture out here alone. Particularly if you've brought the pearls – as I presume you have."

"Well, in a way, I've got them. About this Louie Wong? You know him, I suppose?"

"Yes. And I saw him at the station the other morning. Look at tomorrow's *Eldorado Times* and you'll find the big story, under the personals. 'Our respected fellow-townsman, Mr Louie Wong, went to San Francisco on business last Wednesday.'"

"Wednesday, eh? What sort of lad is Louie?"

"Why – he's just a Chinaman. Been in these parts a long time. For the past five years he's stayed at Madden's ranch the year round, as caretaker. I don't know a great deal about him. He's never talked much to anyone round here – except the parrot."

"The parrot? What parrot?"

"His only companion on the ranch. A little grey Australian bird that some sea-captain gave Madden several years ago. Madden brought the bird – its name is Tony – here to be company for the old caretaker. A rough party, Tony – used to hang out in a bar-room on an Australian boat. Some of his language when he first came was far from pretty. But they're clever, those Australian parrots. You know, from associating with Louie, this one has learned to speak Chinese."

"Amazing," said Bob Eden.

"Oh, not so amazing as it sounds. A bird of that sort will repeat anything it hears. So Tony rattles along in two languages. A regular linguist. The ranchers round here call him the Chinese parrot." They had reached a little group of cottonwoods and pepper-trees sheltering a handsome adobe ranch-house – an oasis on the bare plain. "Here we are at Madden's," Holley said. "By the way – have you got a gun?"

"Why, no," Bob Eden replied. "I didn't bring any. I thought that Charlie—"

"What's that?"

"No matter. I'm unarmed."

"So am I. Walk softly, son. By the way, you might open that gate, if you will."

Bob Eden got out and, unlatching the gate, swung it open. When Holley had steered Horace Greeley inside the yard, Eden shut the gate behind him. The editor brought his car to a stop twenty feet away, and alighted.

The ranch-house was a one-storey structure, eloquent of the old Spanish days in California before Iowa came. Across the front ran a long, low veranda, the roof of which sheltered four windows that were glowing warmly in the chill night. Holley and the boy crossed the tile floor of the porch, and came to a big front door, strong and forbidding.

Eden knocked loudly. There was a long wait. Finally the door opened a scant foot, and a pale face looked out.

"What is it? What do you want?" inquired a querulous voice. From inside the room came the gay lilt of a fox-trot.

"I want to see Mr Madden," Bob Eden said. "Mr P.J. Madden."

"Who are you?"

"Never mind. I'll tell Madden who I am. Is he here?"

The door closed a few inches. "He's here, but he isn't seeing anyone."

"He'll see me, Thorn," said Eden sharply. "You're Thorn, I take it. Please tell Madden that a messenger from Post Street, San Francisco, is waiting."

The door swung instantly open, and Martin Thorn was as near to beaming as his meagre face permitted.

"Oh, pardon me. Come in at once. We've been expecting you. Come in – ah – er – gentlemen." His face clouded as he saw Holley. "Excuse me just a moment."

The secretary disappeared through a door at the rear, and left the two callers standing in the great living-room of the ranch-house. To step from the desert into a room like this was a revelation. Its walls were of paneled oak; rare etchings hung upon them; there were softly shaded lamps standing by tables on which lay the latest magazines – even a recent edition of a New York Sunday newspaper. At one end, in a huge fireplace, a pile of logs was blazing, and in a distant corner a loud-speaker ground out dance music from some distant orchestra.

"Say, this is home, sweet home," Bob Eden remarked. He nodded to the wall at the opposite end of the room from the fireplace. "And speaking of being unarmed—"

"That's Madden's collection of guns," Holley explained. "Wong showed it to me once. They're loaded. If you have to back away go in that direction." He looked dubiously about. "You know, that sleek lad didn't say he was going for Madden."

"I know he didn't," Eden replied. He studied the room thoughtfully. One great question worried him – where was Charlie Chan?

They stood there, waiting. A tall clock at the rear of the room struck the hour of nine, slowly, deliberately. The fire sputtered; the metallic tinkle of jazz flowed on.

Suddenly the door through which Thorn had gone opened suddenly behind them, and they swung quickly about. In the doorway, standing like a tower of granite in the grey clothes he always affected, was the man Bob Eden had last seen on the stairs descending from his father's office – Madden, the great financier – P.J. himself.

Bob Eden's first reaction was one of intense relief, as of a burden dropping from his shoulders with a "most delectable thud." But almost immediately after came a feeling of disappointment. He was young, and he craved excitement. Here was the big desert mystery crashing about his ears, Madden alive and well, and all their fears and premonitions proving groundless. Just a tame handing over of the pearls – when Charlie came – and then back to the old rut again. He saw Will Holley smiling.

"Good evening, gentlemen," Madden was saying. "I'm very glad to see you. Martin," he added to his secretary, who had followed him in, "turn off that confounded racket. An orchestra, gentlemen – an orchestra in the ballroom of a hotel in Denver. Who says the day of miracles is past?" Thorn silenced the jazz; it died with a gurgle of protest. "Now," inquired Madden, "which of you comes from Post Street?"

The boy stepped forward. "I am Bob Eden, Mr Madden. Alexander Eden is my father. This is my friend, a neighbor of yours, Mr Will Holley of the *Eldorado Times*. He very kindly drove me out here."

"Ah, yes." Madden's manner was genial. He shook hands. "Draw up to the fire, both of you. Thorn – cigars, please." With his own celebrated hands he placed chairs before the fireplace.

"I'll sit down just a moment," Holley said. "I'm not stopping. I realize that Mr Eden has some business with you, and I'll not intrude. But before I go, Mr Madden—"

"Yes," said Madden sharply, biting the end from a cigar.

"I – I don't suppose you remember me," Holley continued.

Madden's big hand poised with the lighted match. "I never forget a face. I've seen yours before. Was it in Eldorado?"

Holley shook his head. "No – it was twelve years ago – on Forty-fourth Street, New York. At" – Madden was watching him closely – "at a gambling-house just east of Delmonico's. One winter's night—"

"Wait a minute," cut in the millionaire. "Some people say I'm getting old – but listen to this. You came to me as a newspaper reporter, asking an interview. And I told you to get the hell out of there."

"Splendid," laughed Holley.

"Oh, the old memory isn't so bad, eh? I remember perfectly. I used to spend many evenings in that place – until I discovered the game was fixed. Yes, I dropped a lot of spare change there. Why didn't you tell me it was a crooked joint?"

Holley shrugged. "Well, your manner didn't encourage confidences. But what I'm getting at, Mr Madden – I'm still in the newspaper game, and an interview from you—"

"I never give 'em," snapped the millionaire.

"I'm sorry," said Holley. "An old friend of mine runs a news-bureau in New York, and it would be a big triumph for me if I could wire him something from you. On the financial outlook, for example. The first interview from P.J. Madden."

"Impossible," answered Madden.

"I'm sorry to hear you say that, Mr Madden," Bob Eden remarked. "Holley here has been very kind to me, and I was hoping with all my heart you would overlook your rule this once."

Madden leaned back, and blew a ring of smoke toward the paneled ceiling. "Well," he said, and his voice was somehow gentler, "you've taken a lot of trouble for me, Mr Eden, and I'd like to oblige you." He turned to Holley. "Look here – nothing much, you know. Just a few words about business prospects for the present year."

"That would be extremely kind of you, Mr Madden."

"Oh, it's all right. I'm away out here, and I feel a bit differently about the newspapers than I do at home. I'll dictate something to Thorn – suppose you run out here tomorrow about noon."

"I certainly will," said Holley, rising. "You don't know what this means to me, sir. I must hurry back to town." He shook hands with the millionaire, then with Bob Eden. His eyes as he looked at the latter said: "Well, everything's all right, after all. I'm glad." He paused at the door. "Goodbye – until tomorrow," he added. Thorn let him out.

The door had barely closed behind the editor when Madden leaned forward eagerly. His manner had changed; suddenly, like an electric shock, the boy felt the force of this famous personality. "Now, Mr Eden," he began briskly, "you've got the pearls, of course?"

Eden felt extremely silly. All their fears seemed so futile here in this bright, home-like room. "Well, as a matter of fact—" he stammered.

A glass door at the rear of the room opened, and someone entered. Eden did not look round; he waited. Presently the newcomer stepped between him and the fire. He saw a plump little Chinese servant, with worn trousers and velvet slippers, and a loose jacket of Canton *crêpe*. In his arms he carried a couple of logs. "Maybe you wantee catch 'um moah fiah, hey, boss?" he said in a dull voice. His face was quite expressionless. He threw the logs into the fireplace, and as he turned gave Bob Eden a quick look. His eyes were momentarily sharp and bright – like black buttons in the yellow light. The eyes of Charlie Chan.

The little servant went noiselessly out. "The pearls," insisted Madden quickly. "What about the pearls?" Martin Thorn came closer.

"I haven't got them," said Bob Eden slowly.

"What! You didn't bring them?"

"I did not."

The huge red face of Madden purpled suddenly, and he tossed his great head – the old gesture of annoyance of which the newspapers often spoke. "In heaven's name, what's the matter with you fellows, anyhow?" he cried. "Those pearls are mine – I've bought them, haven't I? I've asked for them here – I want them."

"Call your servant." The words were on the tip of Bob Eden's tongue. But something in that look Charlie Chan had given him moved him to hesitate. No, he must first have a word with the little detective.

"Your final instructions to my father were that the pearls must be delivered in New York," he reminded Madden.

"Well, what if they were? I can change my mind, can't I?"

"Nevertheless, my father felt that the whole affair called for caution. One or two things happened—"

"What things?"

Eden paused. Why go over all that? It would sound silly, perhaps – in any case, was it wise to make a confidant of this cold, hard man who was glaring at him with such evident disgust? "It is enough to say, Mr Madden, that my father refused to send that necklace down here into what might be a well-laid trap."

"Your father's a fool," cried Madden.

Bob Eden rose, his face flushed. "Very well – if you want to call the deal off—"

"No, no. I'm sorry. I spoke too quickly. I apologize. Sit down." The boy resumed his chair. "But I'm very much annoyed. So your father sent you here to reconnoitre?"

"He did. He felt something might have happened to you."

"Nothing ever happens to me unless I want it to," returned Madden, and the remark had the ring of truth. "Well, you're here now. You see everything's all right. What do you propose to do?"

"I shall call my father on the telephone in the morning, and tell him to send the string at once. If I may, I'd like to stay here until it comes."

Again Madden tossed his head. "Delay – delay – I don't like it. I must hurry back East. I'd planned to leave here for Pasadena early in the morning, put the pearls in a vault there, and then take a train to New York."

"Ah," said Eden. "Then you never intended to give that interview to Holley?"

Madden's eyes narrowed. "What if I didn't? He's of no importance, is he?" Brusquely he stood up. "Well, if you haven't got the pearls, you haven't got them. You can stay here, of course. But you're going to call your father in the morning – early – I warn you I won't stand for any more delay."

"I agree to that," replied Eden. "And now, if you don't mind – I've had a hard day—"

Madden went to the door and called. Charlie Chan came in.

"Ah Kim," said Madden, "this gentleman has the bedroom at the end of the left wing. Over here." He pointed. "Take his suitcase."

"Allight, boss," replied the newly christened Ah Kim. He picked up Eden's bag.

"Good night," said Madden. "If you want anything, this boy will look after you. He's new here, but I guess he knows the ropes. You can reach your room from the *patio*. I trust you'll sleep well."

"I know I shall," said Eden. "Thank you so much. Good night."

He crossed the *patio* behind the shuffling figure of the Chinese. Above, white and cool, hung the desert stars. The wind blew keener than ever. As he entered the room assigned him he was glad to see that a fire had been laid. He stooped to light it.

"Humbly begging pardon," said Chan. "That are my work."

Eden glanced toward the closed door. "What became of you? I lost you at Barstow."

"Thinking deep about the matter," said Chan softly, "I decide not to await train. On auto-truck belonging to one of my countrymen, among many other vegetables, I ride out of Barstow. Much better I arrive on ranch in warm daylight. Not so shady look to it. I am Ah Kim, the cook. How fortunate I mastered that art in far-away youth!"

"You're darned good," laughed Eden.

Chan shrugged. "All my life," he complained, "I study to speak fine English words. Now I must strangle all such in my throat, lest suspicion rouse up. Not a happy situation for me."

"Well, it won't last long," replied Eden. "Everything's all right, evidently."

Again Chan shrugged, and did not answer.

"It is all right, isn't it?" Eden asked with sudden interest.

"Humbly offering my own poor opinion," said Chan, "it are not so right as I would be pleased to have it."

Eden stared at him. "Why – what have you found out?"

"I have found nothing whatever."

"Well, then—"

"Pardon me," Chan broke in. "Maybe you know – Chinese are very psychic people. Cannot say in ringing words what is wrong here. But deep down in heart—"

"Oh, forget that," cut in Eden. "We can't go by instinct now. We came to deliver a string of pearls to Madden, if he proved to be here, and get his receipt. He's here, and our course is simple. For my part, I'm not taking any chances. I'm going to give him those pearls now."

Chan looked distressed. "No, no, please! Speaking humbly for myself—"

"Now, see here, Charlie – if I may call you that?"

"Greatly honored, to be sure."

"Let's not be foolish, just because we're far from home on a desert. Chinese may be psychic people, as you say. But I see myself trying to explain that to Victor Jordan – and to Dad. All we were to find out was whether Madden was here or not. He is. Please go to Madden at once and tell him I want to see him in his bedroom in twenty minutes. When I go in you wait outside his door, and when I call you – come. We'll hand over our burden then and there."

"An appalling mistake," objected Chan.

"Why? Can you give me one definite reason?"

"Not in words, which are difficult. But—"

"Then I'm very sorry, but I'll have to use my own judgment. I'll take the full responsibility. Now, really, I think you'd better go—"

Reluctantly, Charlie went. Bob Eden lighted a cigarette and sat down before the fire. Silence had closed down like a curtain of fog over the house, over the desert, over the world. An uncanny silence that nothing, seemingly, would ever break.

Eden thought deeply. What had Charlie Chan been talking about, anyhow? Rot and nonsense. They loved to dramatize things, these Chinese. Loved to dramatize themselves. Here was Chan playing a novel *rôle*, and his complaint against it was not sincere. He wanted to go on playing it, to spy around and imagine vain things. Well, that wasn't the American way. It wasn't Bob Eden's way.

The boy looked at his watch. Ten minutes since Charlie had left him; in ten minutes more he would go to Madden's room and get those pearls off his hands for ever. He rose and walked about. From his window opposite the *patio* he looked out across the dim grey desert to the black bulk of distant hills. Ye gods, what a country. Not for him, he thought. Rather street-lamps shining on the pavements, the clamour of cable cars, crowds, crowds of people. Confusion and – noise. Something terrible about this silence. This lonely silence—

A horrible cry shattered the night. Bob Eden stood, frozen. Again the cry, and then a queer, choked voice: "Help! Help! Murder!" The cry. "Help! Put down that gun! Help! Help!"

Bob Eden ran out into the *patio*. As he did so he saw Thorn and Charlie Chan coming from the other side. Madden – where was Madden? But again his suspicion proved incorrect – Madden emerged from the living-room and joined them.

Again came the cry. And now Bob Eden saw, on a perch ten feet away, the source of the weird outburst. A little grey Australian parrot was hanging there uncertainly, screeching its head off.

"That damn bird," cried Madden angrily. "I'm sorry, Mr Eden – I forgot to tell you about him. It's only Tony, and he's had a wild past, as you may imagine."

The parrot stopped screaming and blinked solemnly at the little group before him. "One at a time, gentlemen, please," he squawked.

Madden laughed. "That goes back to his bar-room days," he said. "Picked it up from some bar-tender, I suppose."

"One at a time, gentlemen, please."

"It's all right, Tony," Madden continued. "We're not lined up for drinks. And you keep quiet. I hope you weren't unduly alarmed, Mr Eden. There seems to have been a killing or two in those bar-rooms where Tony used to hang out. Martin," – he turned to his secretary – "take him to the barn and lock him up."

Thorn came forward. Bob Eden thought that the secretary's face was even paler than usual in the moonlight. He held out his hands to the parrot. Did Eden imagine it, or were the hands really trembling? "Here, Tony," said Thorn. "Nice Tony. You come with me." Gingerly he unfastened the chain from Tony's leg.

"You wanted to see me, didn't you?" Madden said. He led the way to his bedroom, and closed the door behind them. "What is it? Have you got those pearls after all?"

The door opened, and the Chinese shuffled into the room.

"What the devil do you want?" cried Madden.

"You allight, boss?"

"Of course I'm all right. Get out of here."

"Tomallah," said Charlie Chan in his *rôle* of Ah Kim, and a glance that was full of meaning passed between him and Bob Eden. "Tomallah nice day, you bet. See you tomallah, gentlemen."

He departed, leaving the door open. Eden saw him moving across the *patio* on silent feet. He was not waiting outside Madden's door.

"What was it you wanted?" Madden persisted.

Bob Eden thought quickly. "I wanted to see you alone for just a moment. This Thorn – you can trust him, can't you?"

Madden snorted. "You give me a pain," he said. "Anyone would think you were bringing me the Bank of England. Of course Thorn's all right. He's been with me for fifteen years."

"I just wanted to be sure," Eden answered. "I'll get hold of Dad early in the morning. Good night."

He returned to the *patio*. The secretary was hurrying in from his unwelcome errand. "Good night, Mr Thorn," Eden said.

"Oh – er – good night, Mr Eden," answered the man. He passed furtively from sight.

Back in his room, Eden began to undress. He was both puzzled and disturbed. Was this adventure to be as tame as it looked? Still in his ears rang the unearthly scream of the parrot. After all, had it been in a bar-room that Tony picked up that hideous cry for help?

VI

TONY'S HAPPY NEW YEAR

Forgetting the promise he had made to rise and telephone his father early in the morning, Bob Eden lingered on in the pleasant company of his couch. The magnificent desert sunrise, famous wherever books are sold, came and went without the seal of his approval, and a haze of heat spread over the barren world. It was nine o'clock when he awoke from a most satisfactory sleep and sat up in bed.

Staring about the room, he gradually located himself on the map of California. One by one the events of the night before came back to him. First of all the scene at the Oasis – that agile steak eluding him with diabolic cunning – the girl whose charming presence made the dreary *café* an oasis indeed. The ride over the desert with Will Holley, the bright and cheery living-room of the ranch-house, the fox-trot from a Denver orchestra. Madden, leaning close and breathing hard, demanding the Phillimore pearls. Chan, in his velvet slippers, whispering of psychic fears and dark premonitions. And then the shrill cry of the parrot out of the desert night.

Now, however, the tense troubled feeling with which he had gone to bed was melting away in the yellow sunshine of the morning. The boy began to suspect that he had made rather a fool of himself in listening to the little detective from the Islands.

Chan was an Oriental, also a policeman. Such a combination was bound to look at almost any situation with a jaundiced eye. After all, he, Bob Eden, was here as the representative of Meek and Eden, and he must act as he saw fit. Was Chan in charge of this expedition, or was he?

The door opened, and on the threshold stood Ah Kim, in the person of Charlie Chan.

"You come 'long, boss," said his confederate loudly. "You ac' lazy bimeby you no catch 'um bleckfast."

Having said which, Charlie gently closed the door and came in, grimacing as one who felt a keen distaste.

"Silly talk like that hard business for me," he complained. "Chinese without accustomed dignity is like man without clothes, naked and ashamed. You enjoy long, restful sleep, I think."

Eden yawned. "Compared to me last night, Rip Van Winkle had insomnia."

"That's good. Humbly suggest you tear yourself out of that bed now. The great Madden indulges in nervous fit on living-room rug."

Eden laughed. "Suffering, is he? Well, we'll have to stop that." He tossed aside the covers.

Chan was busy at the curtains. "Favour me by taking a look from windows," he remarked. "On every side desert stretches off like floor of eternity. Plenty acres of unlimitable sand."

Bob Eden glanced out. "Yes, it's the desert, and there's plenty of it, that's a fact. But look here – we ought to talk fast while we have the chance. Last night you made a sudden change in our plans."

"Presuming greatly – yes."

"Why?"

Chan stared at him. "Why not? You yourself hear parrot scream out of the dark. 'Murder. Help. Help. Put down gun.'"

Eden nodded. "I know. But that probably meant nothing."

Charlie Chan shrugged. "You understand parrot does not invent talk. Merely repeats what others have remarked."

"Of course," Eden agreed. "And Tony was no doubt repeating something he heard in Australia, or on a boat. I happen to know that all Madden said of the bird's past was the truth. And I may as well tell you, Charlie, that, looking at things in the bright light of the morning, I feel we acted rather foolishly last night. I'm going to give those pearls to Madden before breakfast."

Chan was silent for a moment. "If I might presume again, I would speak a few hearty words in praise of patience. Youth, pardon me, is too hot around the head. Take my advice, please, and wait."

"Wait. Wait for what?"

"Wait until I have snatched more conversation out of Tony. Tony very smart bird – he speaks Chinese. I am not so smart – but so do I."

"And what do you think Tony would tell you?"

"Tony might reveal just what is wrong on this ranch," suggested Chan.

"I don't believe any thing's wrong," objected Eden.

Chan shook his head. "Not very happy position for me," he said, "that I must argue with bright boy like you are."

"But listen, Charlie," Eden protested. "I promised to call my father this morning. And Madden isn't an easy man to handle."

"*Hoo malimali*," responded Chan.

"No doubt you're right," Eden said. "But I don't understand Chinese."

"You have made natural error," Chan answered. "Pardon me while I correct you. That are not Chinese. It are Hawaiian talk. Well known in Islands – *hoo malimali* – make Madden feel good by a little harmless deception. As my cousin Willie Chan, captain of All Chinese baseball team, translate, with his vulgarity, kid him along."

"Easier said than done," replied Eden.

"But you are clever boy. You could perfect it. Just a few hours, while I have talk with the smart Tony."

Eden considered. Paula Wendell was coming out this morning. Too bad to rush off without seeing her again. "Tell you what I'll do," he said. "I'll wait until two o'clock. But when the clock strikes two, if nothing has happened in the interval, we hand over those pearls. Is that understood?"

"Maybe," nodded Chan.

"You mean maybe, it's understood?"

"Not precisely. I mean maybe we hand over pearls." Eden looked into the stubborn eyes of the Chinese, and felt rather helpless. "However," Chan added, "accept my glowing thanks. You are pretty good. Now proceed toward the miserable breakfast I have prepared."

"Tell Madden I'll be there very soon."

Chan grimaced. "With your kind permission, I will alter that message slightly, losing the word very. In memory of old times, there remains little I would not do for Miss Sally. My life, perhaps – but by the bones of my honorable ancestors, I will not say 'velly.'" He went out.

On his perch in the *patio*, opposite Eden's window, Tony was busy with his own breakfast. The boy saw Chan approach the bird, and pause. "*Hoo la ma*," cried the detective.

Tony looked up, and cocked his head on one side. "*Hoo la ma*," he replied, in a shrill, harsh voice.

Chan went nearer, and began to talk rapidly in Chinese. Now and then he paused, and the bird replied amazingly with some phrase out of Chan's speech. It was, Bob Eden reflected, as good as a show.

Suddenly from the door on the other side of the *patio* the man Thorn emerged. His pale face was clouded with anger.

"Here," he cried loudly. "What the devil are you doing?"

"Solly, boss," said the Chinese. "Tony nice litta fellah. Maybe I take 'um to cookhouse."

"You keep away from him," Thorn ordered. "Get me – keep away from that bird."

Chan shuffled off. For a long moment Thorn stood staring after him, anger and apprehension mingled in his look. As Bob Eden turned away he was deep in thought. Was there something in Chan's attitude, after all?

He hurried into the bath, which lay between his room and the vacant bedroom beyond. When he finally joined Madden he thought he perceived the afterglow of that nervous fit still on the millionaire's face.

"I'm sorry to be late," he apologized. "But this desert air—"

"I know," said Madden. "It's all right – we haven't lost any time. I've already put in that call for your father."

"Good idea," replied the boy, without any enthusiasm. "Called his office, I suppose?"

"Naturally."

Suddenly Eden remembered. This was Saturday morning, and, unless it was raining in San Francisco, Alexander Eden was by now well on his way to the golf-links at Burlingame. There he would remain until late tonight at least – perhaps over Sunday. Oh, for a bright day in the North!

Thorn came in, sedate and solemn in his blue serge suit, and looked with hungry eyes toward the table standing before the fire. They sat down to the breakfast prepared by the new servant, Ah Kim. A good breakfast it was, for Charlie Chan had not forgotten his early training in the Phillimore household. As it progressed, Madden mellowed a bit.

"I hope you weren't alarmed last night by Tony's screeching," he said presently.

"Well – for a minute," admitted Eden. "Of course, as soon as I found out the source of the racket I felt better."

Madden nodded. "Tony's a colourless little beast, but he's had a scarlet past," he remarked.

"Like some of the rest of us," Eden suggested.

Madden looked at him keenly. "The bird was given me by a sea-captain in the Australian trade. I brought him here to be company for my caretaker, Louie Wong."

"I thought your boy's name was Ah Kim," said Eden innocently.

"Oh – this one. This isn't Wong. Louie was called suddenly to San Francisco the other day. This Ah Kim just happened to drift in most opportunely yesterday. He's merely a stop-gap until Louie comes back."

"You're lucky," Eden remarked. "Such good cooks as Ah Kim are rare."

"Oh, he'll do," Madden admitted. "When I come West to stay I bring a staff with me. This is a rather unexpected visit."

"Your real headquarters out here are in Pasadena, I believe?" Eden inquired.

"Yes – I've got a house there, on Orange Grove Avenue. I just keep this place for an occasional weekend – when my asthma threatens. And it's good to get away from the mob, now and then." The millionaire pushed back from the table, and looked at his watch. "Ought to hear from San Francisco any minute now," he added hopefully.

Eden glanced toward the telephone in a far corner. "Did you put the call in for my father, or just for the office?" he asked.

"Just for the office," Madden replied. "I figured that if he was out we could leave a message."

Thorn came forward. "Chief, how about that interview for Holley?" he inquired.

"Oh, the devil!" Madden said. "Why did I let myself in for that?"

"I could bring the typewriter in here," began the secretary.

"No – we'll go to your room. Mr Eden, if the telephone rings, please answer it."

The two went out. Ah Kim arrived on noiseless feet to clear away the breakfast. Eden lighted a cigarette, and dropped into a chair before the fire, which the blazing sun outside made rather superfluous.

Twenty minutes later the telephone rang. Eden leaped to it, but before he reached the table where it stood, Madden was at his side. He had hoped to be alone for this ordeal, and sighed wearily. At the other end of the wire he was relieved to hear the cool, melodious voice of his father's well-chosen secretary.

"Hello," he said. "This is Bob Eden, at Madden's ranch down on the desert. And how are you this bright and shining morning?"

"What makes you think it's a bright and shining morning up here?" asked the girl.

Eden's heart sank. "Don't tell me it isn't. I'd be broken-hearted."

"Why?"

"Why! Because, while you're beautiful at any time, I like to think of you with the sunlight on your hair—"

Madden laid a heavy hand on his shoulder. "What the blazes do you think you're doing – making a date with a chorus girl? Get down to business."

"Excuse it, please," said Eden. "Miss Chase, is my father there?"

"No. This is Saturday, you know. Golf."

"Oh, yes – of course. Then it *is* a nice day. Well, tell him to call me here if he comes in. Eldorado seven six."

"Where is he?" demanded Madden eagerly.

"Out playing golf," the boy answered.

"Where? What links?"

Bob sighed. "I suppose he's at Burlingame," he said over the wire.

Then – oh, excellent young woman, thought the boy – the secretary answered: "Not today. He went with some friends to another links. He didn't say which."

"Thank you so much," Eden said. "Just leave the message on his desk, please." He rang off.

"Too bad," he remarked cheerfully. "Gone off to play golf somewhere, and nobody knows where."

Madden swore. "The old simpleton. Why doesn't he attend to his business—"

"Look here, Mr Madden—" Eden began.

"Golf, golf, golf," stormed Madden. "It's ruined more good men than whisky. I tell you, if I'd fooled round on golf-links I wouldn't be where I am today. If your father had any sense—"

"I've heard about enough," said Eden, rising.

Madden's manner changed suddenly. "I'm sorry," he said. "But this is annoying, you must admit. I wanted that necklace to start today."

"The day's young," Eden reminded him. "It may get off yet."

"I hope so," Madden frowned. "I'm not accustomed to this sort of dilly-dallying, I can tell you that."

His great head was tossing angrily as he went out. Bob Eden looked after him, thoughtfully. Madden, master of many millions, was putting what seemed an undue emphasis on a little pearl necklace. The boy wondered. His father was getting on in years – he was far from the New York markets. Had he made some glaring mistake in setting a value on that necklace? Was it, perhaps, worth a great deal more than he had asked, and was Madden fuming to get hold of it before the jeweler learned his error and perhaps called off the deal? Of course, Alexander Eden had given his word, but, even so, Madden might fear some hitch in the transaction.

The boy strolled idly out into the *patio*. The chill night wind had vanished, and he saw the desert of song and story baking under a relentless sun. In the sandy little yard of the ranch-house life was humming along. Plump chickens and haughty turkeys strutted behind wire enclosures. He paused for a moment to stare with interest at a bed of strawberries, red and tempting. Up above, on the bare branches of the cottonwoods, he saw unmistakable buds, mute promise of a grateful shade not far away.

Odd how things lived and grew here in this desolate country. He took a turn about the grounds. In one corner was a great reservoir half filled with water – a pleasant sight that must be on an August afternoon. Coming back to the *patio*, he stopped to speak to Tony, who was sitting rather dejectedly on his perch.

"*Hoo la ma*," he said.

Tony perked up. "*Sung kai yat bo*," he remarked.

"Yes, and a great pity, too," replied Eden facetiously.

"*Gee fung low hop*," added Tony, somewhat feebly.

"Perhaps, but I heard different," said Eden, and moved on. He wondered what Chan was doing. Evidently the detective thought it best to obey Thorn's command that he keep away from the bird. This was not surprising, for the windows of the secretary's room looked out on Tony's perch.

Back in the living-room, Eden took up a book. At a few minutes before twelve he heard the asthmatic cough of Horace Greeley in the yard, and, rising, he admitted Will Holley. The editor was smiling and alert.

"Hello," Eden said. "Madden's in there with Thorn, getting out the interview. Sit down." He came close. "And please remember that I haven't brought these pearls. My business with Madden is still unfinished."

Holley looked at him with sudden interest. "I get you. But I thought last night that everything was lovely. Do you mean—"

"Tell you later," interrupted Eden. "I may be in town this afternoon." He spoke in a louder tone. "I'm glad you came along. I was finding the desert a bit flat when you flivvered in."

Holley smiled. "Cheer up. I've got something for you. A veritable storehouse of wit and wisdom." He handed over a paper. "This week's issue of the *Eldorado Times*, damp from the presses. Read about Louie Wong's big trip to San Francisco. All the news to fit the print."

Eden took the proffered paper – eight small pages of mingled news and advertisements. He sank into a chair. "Well," he said, "it seems that the Ladies' Aid Supper last Tuesday night was notably successful. Not only that, but the ladies responsible for the affair laboured assiduously and deserve much credit."

"Yes, but the real excitement's inside," remarked Holley. "On page three. There you'll learn that coyotes are getting pretty bad in the valley. A number of people are putting out traps."

"Under those circumstances," Eden said, "how fortunate that Henry Grattan is caring for Mr Dickey's chickens during the latter's absence in Los Angeles."

Holley rose, and stared for a moment down at his tiny newspaper. "And once I worked with Mitchell on the *New York Sun*," he misquoted sadly. "Don't let Harry Fladgate see that, will you? When Harry knew me I was a newspaper man." He moved off across the room. "By the way, has Madden shown you his collection of firearms?"

Bob Eden rose, and followed. "Why no – he hasn't."

"It's rather interesting. But dusty – say, I guess Louie was afraid to touch them. Nearly everyone of these guns has a history. See – there's a typewritten card above each one. 'Presented to P.J. Madden by Til Taylor' – Taylor was one of the best sheriffs Oregon ever had. And here – look at this one – it's a beauty. Given to Madden by Bill Tilghman. That gun, my boy, saw action on Front Street in the old Dodge City days."

"What's the one with all the notches?" Eden asked.

"Used to belong to Billy the Kid," said Holley. "Ask them about Billy over in New Mexico. And here's one Bat Masterson used to tote. But the star of the collection" – Holley's eyes ran over the wall – "the beauty of the lot—" He turned to Eden. "It isn't there," he said.

"There's a gun missing?" inquired Eden slowly.

"Seems to be. One of the first Colts made – a forty-five – it was presented to Madden by Bill Hart, who's staged a lot of pictures round here." He pointed to an open space on the wall. "There's where it used to be," he added, and was moving away.

Eden caught his coat sleeve. "Wait a minute," he said in a low, tense voice. "Let me get this. A gun missing. And the card's gone, too. You can see where the tacks held it in place."

"Well, what's all the excitement—" began Holley, surprised.

Eden ran his finger over the wall. "There's no dust where that card should be. What does that mean? That Bill Hart's gun has been removed within the last few days."

"My boy," said Holley. "What are you talking about?"

"Hush," warned Eden. The door opened and Madden, followed by Thorn, entered the room. For a moment the millionaire stood regarding them intently.

"Good morning, Mr Holley," he said. "I've got your interview here. You're wiring it to New York, you say?"

"Yes. I've queried my friend there about it this morning. I know he'll want it."

"Well, it's nothing startling. I hope you'll mention in the course of it where you got it. That will help to soothe the feelings of the boys I've turned down so often in New York. And you won't change what I've said?"

"Not a comma," smiled Holley. "I must hurry back to town now. Thank you again, Mr Madden."

"That's all right," said Madden. "Glad to help you out."

Eden followed Holley to the yard. Out of earshot of the house, the editor stopped.

"You seemed a little het up about that gun. What's doing?"

"Oh, nothing, I suppose," said Eden. "On the other hand—"

"What?"

"Well, Holley, it strikes me that something queer may have happened lately on this ranch."

Holley stared. "It doesn't sound possible. However, don't keep me in suspense."

"I've got to. It's a long story, and Madden mustn't see us getting too chummy. I'll come in this afternoon, as I promised."

Holley climbed into his car. "All right," he said. "I can wait, I guess. See you later, then."

Eden was sorry to watch Horace Greeley stagger down the dusty road. Somehow the newspaper man brought a warm, human atmosphere to the ranch, an atmosphere that was needed there. But a moment later he was sorry no longer, for a little speck of brown in the distance became a smart roadster, and at its wheel he saw the girl of the Oasis, Paula Wendell.

He held open the gate, and with a cheery wave of her hand the girl drove past him into the yard.

"Hello," he said as she alighted. "I was beginning to fear you weren't coming."

"I overslept," she explained. "Always do in this desert country. Have you noticed the air? People who are in a position to know tell me it's like wine."

"Had a merry breakfast, I suppose?"

"I certainly did. At the Oasis."

"You poor child. That coffee."

"I didn't mind. Will Holley says that Madden's here."

"Madden? That's right – you do want to see Madden, don't you? Well, come along inside."

Thorn was alone in the living-room. He regarded the girl with a fishy eye. Not many men could have managed that, but Thorn was different.

"Thorn," said Eden. "Here's a young woman who wants to see Mr Madden."

"I have a letter from him," the girl explained, "offering me the use of the ranch to take some pictures. You may remember – I was here Wednesday night."

"I remember," said Thorn sourly. "And I regret very much that Mr Madden cannot see you. He also asks me to say that unfortunately he must withdraw the permission he gave you in his letter."

"I'll accept that word from no one but Mr Madden himself," returned the girl, and a steely light flamed suddenly in her eyes.

"I repeat – he will not see you," persisted Thorn.

The girl sat down. "Tell Mr Madden his ranch is charming," she said. "Tell him I am seated in a chair in his living-room and that I shall certainly continue to sit here until he comes and speaks to me himself."

Thorn hesitated a moment, glaring angrily. Then he went out.

"I say – you're all right," Eden laughed.

"I aim to be," the girl answered, "and I've been on my own too long to take any nonsense from a mere secretary."

Madden blustered in. "What is all this—"

"Mr Madden," the girl said, rising and smiling with amazing sweetness, "I was sure you'd see me. I have here a letter you wrote me from San Francisco. You recall it, of course."

Madden took the letter and glanced at it. "Yes, yes – of course. I'm very sorry, Miss Wendell, but since I wrote that certain matters have come up – I have a business deal on—" He glanced at Eden. "In short, it would be most inconvenient for me to have the ranch overrun with picture people at this time. I can't tell you how I regret it."

The girl's smile vanished. "Very well," she said, "but it means a black mark against me with the company. The people I work for don't accept excuses – only results. I have told them everything was arranged."

"Well, you were a little premature, weren't you?"

"I don't see why. I had the word of P.J. Madden. I believed – foolishly, perhaps – the old rumour that the word of Madden was never broken."

The millionaire looked decidedly uncomfortable. "Well – I – er – of course I never break my word. When did you want to bring your people here?"

"It's all arranged for Monday," said the girl.

"Out of the question," replied Madden. "But if you could postpone it a few days – say, until Thursday." Once more he looked at Eden. "Our business should be settled by Thursday," he added.

"Unquestionably," agreed Eden, glad to help.

"Very well," said Madden. He looked at the girl, and his eyes were kindly. He was no Thorn. "Make it Thursday, and the place is yours. I may not be here then myself, but I'll leave word to that effect."

"Mr Madden, you're a dear," she told him. "I knew I could rely on you."

With a disgusted look at his employer's back, Thorn went out.

"You bet you can," said Madden, smiling pleasantly. He was melting fast. "And the record of P.J. Madden is intact. His word is as good as his bond – isn't that so?"

"If anyone doubts it let him ask me," replied the girl.

"It's nearly lunch-time," Madden said. "You'll stay?"

"Well – I – really, Mr Madden—"

"Of course she'll stay," Bob Eden broke in. "She's eating at a place in Eldorado called the Oasis, and if she doesn't stay, then she's just gone and lost her mind."

The girl laughed. "You're all so good to me," she said.

"Why not?" inquired Madden. "Then it's settled. We need someone like you around to brighten things up. Ah Kim," he added, as the Chinese entered, "another place for lunch. In about ten minutes, Miss Wendell."

He went out. The girl looked at Bob Eden. "Well, that's that. I knew it would be all right, if only he would see me."

"Naturally," said Eden. "Everything in this world would be all right, if every man in it could only see you."

"Sounds like a compliment," she smiled.

"Meant to be," replied the boy. "But what makes it sound so cumbersome? I must brush up on my social chatter."

"Oh – then it was only chatter?"

"Please – don't look too closely at what I say. I may tell you I've got a lot on my mind just now. I'm trying to be a business man, and it's some strain."

"Then you're not a real business man?"

"Not a real anything. Just sort of drifting. You know, you made me think last night."

"I'm proud of that."

"Now – don't spoof me. I got to thinking – here you are, earning your living – luxurious pot roasts at the Oasis and all that – while I'm just Father's little boy. I shouldn't be surprised if you inspired me to turn over a new leaf."

"Then I shan't have lived in vain." She nodded toward the far side of the room. "What in the world is the meaning of that arsenal?"

"Oh – that's gentle old Madden's collection of firearms. A hobby of his. Come on over and I'll teach you to call each one by name."

Presently Madden and Thorn returned, and Ah Kim served a perfect lunch. At the table Thorn said nothing, but his employer, under the spell of the girl's bright eyes, talked volubly and well. As they finished coffee Bob Eden suddenly awoke to the fact that the big clock near the *patio* windows marked the hour as five minutes of two. At two o'clock! There was that arrangement with Chan regarding two o'clock. What were they to do? The impassive face of the Oriental as he served lunch had told the boy nothing.

Madden was in the midst of a long story about his early struggle toward wealth, when the Chinese came suddenly into the room. He stood there, and, though he did not speak, his manner halted the millionaire as effectively as a pistol-shot.

"Well, well, what is it?" Madden demanded.

"Death," said Ah Kim solemnly in his high-pitched voice. "Death unevitable end. No wolly. No solly."

"What in Sam Hill are you talking about?" Madden inquired. Thorn's pale green eyes were bulging.

"Poah litta Tony," went on Ah Kim.

"What about Tony?"

"Poah litta Tony enjoy happly noo yeah in Hadesland," finished Ah Kim.

Madden was instantly on his feet, and led the way to the *patio*. On the stone floor beneath his perch lay the lifeless body of the Chinese parrot.

The millionaire stooped and picked up the bird. "Why – poor old Tony," he said. "He's gone west. He's dead."

Eden's eyes were on Thorn. For the first time since he met that gentleman he thought he detected the ghost of a smile on the secretary's pale face.

"Well, Tony was old," continued Madden. "A very old boy. And as Ah Kim says, death is inevitable—" He stopped, and looked keenly at the expressionless face of the Chinese. "I've been expecting this," he added. "Tony hasn't seemed very well of late. Here, Ah Kim" – he handed over all that was mortal of Tony – "you take and bury him somewhere."

"I take 'um," said Ah Kim, and did so.

In the big living-room the clock struck twice, loud and clear. Ah Kim, in the person of Charlie Chan, was moving slowly away, the bird in his arms. He was muttering glibly in Chinese. Suddenly he looked back over his shoulder.

"*Hoo malimali,*" he said clearly.

Bob Eden remembered his Hawaiian.

VII

THE POSTMAN SETS OUT

The three men and the girl returned to the living-room but Madden's flow of small talk was stilled, and the sparkle was gone from his luncheon party.

"Poor Tony," the millionaire said when they had sat down. "It's like the passing of an old friend. Five years ago he came to me." He was silent for a long time, staring into space.

Presently the girl rose. "I really must be getting back to town," she announced. "It was thoughtful of you to invite me to lunch, Mr Madden, and I appreciate it. I can count on Thursday, then?"

"Yes – if nothing new comes up. In that case, where could I reach you?"

"I'll be at the Desert Edge – but nothing must come up. I'm relying on the word of P.J. Madden."

"Nothing will, I'm sure. Sorry you have to go."

Bob Eden came forward. "I think I'll take a little fling at city life myself," he said. "If you don't mind, I'd like to ride into Eldorado with you."

"Delighted," she smiled. "But I'm not sure I can bring you back."

"Oh, no – I don't want you to. I'll walk back."

"You needn't do that," said Madden. "It seems that Ah Kim can drive a flivver – a rather remarkable boy, Ah Kim." He was thoughtfully silent for a moment. "I'm sending him to town later in the afternoon for supplies. Our larder's rather low. He'll pick you up." The Chinese entered to clear away. "Ah Kim, you're to bring Mr Eden back with you this evening."

"Allight. I bling 'um," said Ah Kim, without interest.

"I'll meet you in front of the hotel any time you say," suggested Eden.

Ah Kim regarded him sourly. "Maybe flive 'clock," he said.

"Fine. At five, then."

"You late, you no catch 'um lide," warned the Chinese.

"I'll be there," the boy promised. He went to his room and got a cap. When he returned Madden was waiting.

"In case your father calls this afternoon, I'll tell him you want that matter rushed through," he said.

Eden's heart sank. He hadn't thought of that. Suppose his father returned to the office unexpectedly – but no, that was unlikely. And it wouldn't do to show alarm and change his plans now.

"Surely," he remarked carelessly. "If he isn't satisfied without a word from me, tell him to call again about six."

When he stepped into the yard the girl was skilfully turning her car about. He officiated at the gate, and joined her in the sandy road.

The car moved off and Eden got his first unimpeded look at this queer world Holley had called the devil's garden. "Plenty acres of unlimitable sand," Chan had said, and that about summed it up. Far in the distance was a touch of beauty – a cobalt sky above snow-capped mountains. But elsewhere he saw only desert, a great grey interminable blanket spattered with creosote brush. All the trees, all the bushes, were barbed and cruel and menacing – a biznaga, pointing like a finger of scorn toward the sky, an unkempt palo verde, the eternal

Joshua-trees, like charred stumps that had stood in the path of a fire. Over this vast waste played odd tricks of light and shade, and up above hung the sun, a living flame, merciless, ineffably pure, and somehow terrible.

"Well, what do you think of it?" asked the girl.

Eden shrugged. "Hell's burnt out and left the embers," he remarked.

She smiled. "The desert is an acquired taste," she explained. "No one likes it at first. I remember the night, long ago, when I got off the train at Eldorado with poor Dad. A little girl from a Philadelphia suburb – a place that was old and settled and civilized. And there I stood in the midst of this savage-looking world. My heart broke."

"Poor kid," said Eden. "But you like it now."

"Yes – after a while – well, there's a sort of weird beauty in this sun-drenched country. You waken to it in the course of time. And in the spring, after the rains – I'd like to take you over round Palm Springs then. The verbena is like a carpet of old rose, and the ugliest trees put forth the most delicate and lovely blossoms. And at any time of the year there's always the desert nights, with the pale stars overhead, and the air full of peace and calm and rest."

"Oh, no doubt it's a great place to rest," Eden agreed. "But as it happens, I wasn't very tired."

"Who knows?" she said. "Perhaps before we say goodbye I can initiate you into the Very Ancient Order of Lovers of the Desert. The requirements for membership are very strict. A sensitive soul, a quick eye for beauty – oh, a very select group, you may be sure. No riff-raff on our rolls."

A blatant sign hung before them. "Stop! Have you bought your lot in Date City?" From the steps of a tiny real-estate office a rather shabby young man leaped to life. He came into the road and held up his hand. Obligingly the girl stopped her car.

"Howdy, folks," said the young man. "Here's the big opportunity of your life – don't pass it by. Let me show you a lot in Date City, the future metropolis of the desert."

Bob Eden stared at the dreary landscape. "Not interested," he said.

"Yeah. Think of the poor devils who once said that about the corner of Spring and Sixth, Los Angeles. Not interested – and they could have bought it for a song. Look ahead. Can you picture this street ten years hence?"

"I think I can," Eden replied. "It looks just the way it does today."

"Blind!" rebuked the young man. "Blind! This won't be the desert for ever. Look!" He pointed to a small lead pipe surrounded by a circle of rocks and trying to act like a fountain. From its top gurgled an anæmic stream. "What's that! Water, my boy, water, the pure, life-giving elixir, gushing madly from the sandy soil. What does that mean? I see a great city rising on this spot, skyscrapers and movie palaces, land five thousand a front foot – land you can buy today for a paltry two dollars."

"I'll take a dollar's worth," remarked Eden.

"I appeal to the young lady," continued the real-estate man. "If that ring on the third finger of her left hand means anything, it means a wedding." Startled, Bob Eden looked, and saw a big emerald set in platinum. "You, miss – you have vision. Suppose you two bought a lot today and held it for your – er – for future generations. Wealth, wealth untold – I'm right, ain't I, miss?"

The girl looked away. "Perhaps you are," she admitted. "But you've made a mistake. This gentleman is not my *fiancé*."

"Oh," said the youth, deflating.

"I'm only a stranger, passing through," Eden told him.

The salesman pulled himself together for a new attack. "That's it – you're a stranger. You don't understand. You can't realize that Los Angeles looked like this once."

"It still does – to some people," suggested Bob Eden gently.

The young man gave him a hard look. "Oh – I get you," he said. "You're from San Francisco." He turned to the girl. "So this ain't your *fiancé*, eh, lady? Well – hearty congratulations."

Eden laughed. "Sorry," he said.

"I'm sorry, too," returned the salesman. "Sorry for you, when I think of what you're passing up. However, you may see the light yet, and if you ever do, don't forget me. I'm here Saturdays and Sundays, and we have an office in Eldorado. Opportunity's knocking, but of course if you're from 'Frisco you're doing the same. Glad to have met you, anyhow."

They left him by his weak little fountain, a sad but hopeful figure.

"Poor fellow," the girl remarked, as the car moved forward. "The pioneer has a hard time of it."

Eden did not speak for a moment. "I'm an observing little chap, aren't I?" he said at last.

"What do you mean?"

"That ring. I never noticed it. Engaged, I suppose?"

"It looks that way, doesn't it?"

"Don't tell me you're going to marry some movie actor who carries a vanity case."

"You should know me better than that."

"I do, of course. But describe this lucky lad. What's he like?"

"He likes me."

"Naturally." Eden lapsed into silence.

"Not angry, are you?" asked the girl.

"Not angry," he grinned, "but terribly, terribly hurt. I perceive you don't want to talk about the matter."

"Well – some incidents in my life I really should keep to myself. On such short acquaintance."

"As you wish," agreed Eden. The car sped on. "Lady," he said presently, "I've known this desert country, man and boy, going on twenty-four hours. And believe me when I tell you, miss, it's a cruel land – a cruel land."

They climbed the road that lay between the two piles of brown rock pretending to be mountains, and before them lay Eldorado, huddled about the little red station. The town looked tiny and helpless and forlorn. As they alighted before the Desert Edge Hotel, Eden said:

"When shall I see you again?"

"Thursday, perhaps."

"Nonsense. I shall probably be gone by then; I must see you soon."

"I'll be out your way in the morning. If you like, I'll pick you up."

"That's kind of you – but morning's a long way off," he said. "I'll think of you tonight, eating at the Oasis. Give my love to that steak, if you see it. Until tomorrow, then – and can't I buy you an alarm clock?"

"I shan't oversleep – much," she laughed. "Goodbye."

"Goodbye," answered Eden. "Thanks for the buggy ride."

He crossed the road to the railroad-station, which was also the telegraph-office. In the little cubby-hole occupied by the agent Will Holley stood, a sheaf of copy paper in his hand.

"Hello," he said. "Just getting that interview on the wire. Were you looking for me?"

"Yes, I was," Eden replied. "But first I want to send a wire of my own."

The agent, a husky youth with sandy hair, looked up. "Say, mister, no can do. Mr Holley here's tied up things for ever."

Holley laughed. "That's all right. You can cut in with Mr Eden's message, and then go back."

Frowning, Eden considered the wording of his rather difficult telegram. How to let his father know the situation without revealing it to the world? Finally he wrote:

Buyer here, but certain conditions make it advisable we treat him to a little *hoo malimali*. Mrs Jordan will translate. When I talk with you over telephone promise to send valuable package at once, then forget it. Any confidential message for me care Will Holley, *Eldorado Times*. They have nice desert down here but too full of mystery for frank and open young business man like your loving son

BOB

He turned the yellow slip over to the worried telegrapher, with instructions to send it to his father's office, and in duplicate to his house. "How much?" he asked.

After some fumbling with a book the agent named a sum, which Eden paid. He added a tip, upsetting the boy still further.

"Say, this is some day here," announced the telegrapher. "Always wanted a little excitement in my life, but now it's come I guess I ain't ready for it. Yes, sir – I'll send it twice – I know – I get you—"

Holley gave the boy a few directions about the Madden interview, and returned with Bob Eden to Main Street.

"Let's drop over to the office," the editor said. "Nobody there now, and I'm keen to know what's doing out at Madden's."

In the bare little home of the *Eldorado Times* Eden took a chair that was already partly filled with exchanges, close to the editor's desk. Holley removed his hat and replaced it with an eye-shade. He dropped down beside his typewriter.

"My friend in New York grabbed at that story," he said. "It was good of Madden to let me have it. I understand they're going to allow me to sign it, too – the name of Will Holley back in the big papers again. But look here – I was surprised by what you hinted out at the ranch this morning. It seemed to me last night that everything was O.K. You didn't say whether you had that necklace with you or not, but I gathered you had—"

"I haven't," cut in Eden.

"Oh – it's still in San Francisco?"

"No. My confederate has it."

"Your what?"

"Holley, I know that if Harry Fladgate says you're all right, you are. So I'm going the whole way in the matter of trusting you."

"That's flattering – but suit yourself."

"Something tells me we'll need your help," Eden remarked. With a glance round the deserted office, he described the real identity of the servant, Ah Kim.

Holley grinned. "Well, that's amusing, isn't it? But go on. I get the impression that although you arrived at the ranch last night to find Madden there and everything, on the surface, serene, such was not the case. What happened?"

"First of all, Charlie thought something was wrong. He sensed it. You know the Chinese are a very psychic race."

Holley laughed. "Is that so? Surely you didn't fall for that guff. Oh, pardon me – I presume you had some better reason for delay?"

"I'll admit it sounded like guff to me – at the start. I laughed at Chan, and prepared to hand over the pearls at once. Suddenly out of the night came the weirdest cry for help I ever expect to hear."

"What! Really? From whom?"

"From your friend the Chinese parrot. From Tony."

"Oh – of course," said Holley. "I'd forgotten him. Well, that probably meant nothing."

"But a parrot doesn't invent," Eden reminded him. "It merely repeats. I may have acted like a fool, but I hesitated to produce those pearls." He went on to tell how, in the morning, he had agreed to wait until two o'clock while Chan had further talk with Tony, and ended with the death of the bird just after lunch. "And there the matter rests," he finished.

"Are you asking my advice?" said Holley. "I hope you are, because I've simply got to give it to you."

"Shoot," Eden replied.

Holley smiled at him in a fatherly way. "Don't think for a moment I wouldn't like to believe there's some big melodrama afoot at Madden's ranch. Heaven knows little enough happens round here, and a thing like that would be manna from above. But as I look at it, my boy, you've let a jumpy Chinese lead you astray into a bad case of nerves."

"Charlie's absolutely sincere," protested Eden.

"No doubt of that," agreed Holley. "But he's an Oriental, and a detective, and he's simply got to detect. There's nothing wrong at Madden's ranch. True, Tony lets out weird cries in the night – but he always has."

"You've heard him, then?"

"Well, I never heard him say anything about help and murder, but when he first came I was living out at Doctor Whitcomb's, and I used to hang round the Madden ranch a good deal. Tony had some strange words in his small head. He'd spent his days amid violence and crime. It's nothing to wonder at that he screamed as he did last night. The setting on the desert, the dark, Charlie's psychic talk – all that combined to make a mountain out of a molehill, in your eyes."

"And Tony's sudden death this noon?"

"Just as Madden said. Tony was as old as the hills – even a parrot doesn't live for ever. A coincidence, yes – but I'm afraid your father won't be pleased with you, my boy. First thing you know P.J. Madden, who is hot and impetuous, will kick you out and call the transaction off. And I can see you back home explaining that you didn't close the deal because a parrot on the place dropped dead. My boy, my boy – I trust your father is a gentle soul. Otherwise he's liable to annihilate you."

Eden considered. "How about that missing gun?"

Holley shrugged. "You can find something queer almost anywhere, if you look for it. The gun was gone – yes. What of it? Madden may have sold it, given it away, taken it to his room."

Bob Eden leaned back in his chair. "I guess you're right, at that. Yes, the more I think about it, here in the bright light of afternoon, the more foolish I feel." Through a side window he saw a car swing up before the grocery store next door, and Charlie Chan alight. He went out on to the porch.

"Ah Kim," he called.

The plump little Chinese detective approached and, without a word, entered the office.

"Charlie," said Bob Eden, "this is a friend of mine, Mr Will Holley. Holley, meet Detective-Sergeant Chan, of the Honolulu police."

At mention of his name Chan's eyes narrowed. "How do you do?" he said coldly.

"It's all right," Eden assured him. "Mr Holley can be trusted – absolutely. I've told him everything."

"I am far away in strange land," returned Chan. "Maybe I would choose to trust no one – but that, no doubt, are my heathen churlishness. Mr Holley will pardon, I am sure."

"Don't worry," said Holley. "I give you my word. I'll tell no one."

Chan made no reply, in his mind, perhaps, the memory of other white men who had given their word.

"It doesn't matter, anyhow," Eden remarked. "Charlie, I've come to the decision that we're chasing ghosts. I've talked things over with Mr Holley, and from what he says, I see that there's really nothing wrong out at the ranch. When we go back this evening we'll hand over those pearls and head for home." Chan's face fell. "Cheer up," added the boy. "You yourself must admit that we've been acting like a couple of old women."

An expression of deeply offended dignity appeared on the little round face. "Just one moment. Permit this old woman more nonsense. Some hours ago parrot drops from perch into vast eternity. Dead, like Cæsar."

"What of it?" said Eden wearily. "He died of old age. Don't let's argue about it, Charlie—"

"Who argues?" asked Chan. "I myself enjoy keen distaste for that pastime. Old woman though I am, I now deal with facts – undubitable facts." He spread a white sheet of paper on Holley's desk, and removing an envelope from his pocket, poured its contents on to the paper. "Examine," he directed. "What you see here are partial contents of food basin beside the perch of Tony. Kindly tell me what you look at."

"Hemp-seed," said Eden. "A parrot's natural food."

"Ah, yes," agreed Chan. "Seed of the hemp. But that other – the fine greyish-white powder that seem so plentiful."

"By gad," cried Holley.

"No argument here," continued Chan. "Before seeking grocer I pause at drug emporium on corner. Wise man about powders make most careful test for me. And what does he say?"

"Arsenic," suggested Holley.

"Arsenic, indeed. Much sold to ranchers hereabouts as rat-killer. Parrot-killer too."

Eden and Holley looked at each other in amazement.

"Poor Tony very sick before he go on long journey," Chan continued. "Very silent and very sick. In my time I am on track of many murders, but I must come to this peculiar mainland to ferret out parrot-murder. Ah, well – all my life I hear about wonders on this mainland."

"They poisoned him," Bob Eden cried. "Why?"

"Why not?" shrugged Chan. "Very true rumour says 'dead men tell no tales'! Dead parrots are in same fix, I think. Tony speaks Chinese like me. Tony and me never speak together again."

Eden put his head in his hands. "Well, I'm getting dizzy," he said. "What in heaven's name is it all about?"

"Reflect," urged Chan. "As I have said before, parrot not able to perpetrate original remarks. He repeats. When Tony cry out in night, 'Help, murder, put down gun,' even old woman might be pardoned to think he repeats something recently heard. He repeats because words are recalled to him by – what?"

"Go on, Charlie," Eden said.

"Recalled by event just preceding cry. What event? I think deep – how is this? Recalled, maybe, by sudden flashing on of lights in bedroom occupied by Martin Thorn, the secretary."

"Charlie, what more do you know?" Eden asked.

"This morning I am about my old-woman duties in bedroom of Thorn. I see on wall stained outline same size and shape as handsome picture of desert scene nearby. I investigate. Picture has been moved, I note, and not so long ago. Why was picture moved? I lift it in my hands and underneath I see little hole that could only be made by flying bullet."

Eden gasped. "A bullet?"

"Precisely the fact. A bullet embedded deep in wall. One bullet that has gone astray and not found resting place in body of that unhappy man Tony heard cry for help some recent night."

Again Eden and Holley looked at each other. "Well," said the editor, "there was that gun, you know. Bill Hart's gun – the one that's gone from the living-room. We must tell Mr Chan about that."

Chan shrugged. "Spare yourself trouble," he advised. "Already last night I have noted empty locality deserted by that weapon. I also found this in waste-basket." He took a small crumpled card from his pocket, a typewritten card, which read, "Presented to P.J. Madden by William S. Hart. September 29, 1923." Will Holley nodded and handed it back. "All day," continued Chan, "I search for missing movie pistol. Without success – so far."

Will Holley rose, and warmly shook Chan's hand. "Mr Chan," he said, "permit me to go on record here and now to the effect that you're all right." He turned to Bob Eden. "Don't ever come to me for advice again. You follow Mr Chan."

Eden nodded. "I think I will," he said.

"Think more deeply," suggested Chan. "To follow an old woman. Where is the honor there?"

Eden laughed. "Oh, forget it, Charlie. I apologize with all my heart."

Chan beamed. "Thanks warmly. Then all is settled? We do not hand over pearls tonight, I think?"

"No, of course we don't," agreed Eden. "We're on the trail of something – heaven knows what. It's all up to you, Charlie, from now on. I follow where you lead."

"You were number one prophet, after all," said Chan. "Postman on vacation goes for long walk. Here on broad desert I cannot forget profession. We return to Madden's ranch and find what we shall find. Some might say, Madden is there, give him necklace. Our duty as splendid American citizens does not permit. If we deliver necklace, we go away, truth is strangled, guilty escape. Necklace deal falls now into second place." He gathered up the evidence in the matter of Tony and restored it to his pocket. "Poor Tony. Only this morning he tell me I talk too much. Now, like boom – boomerang, remark returns and smites him. It is my pressing duty to negotiate with food-merchant. Meet me in fifteen minutes before hotel door."

When he had gone out Holley and Eden were silent for a moment. "Well," said the editor at last, "I was wrong – all wrong. There's something doing out at Madden's ranch."

Eden nodded. "Sure there is. But what?"

"All day," continued Holley, "I've been wondering about that interview Madden gave me. For no apparent reason he broke one of the strictest rules of his life. Why?"

"If you're asking me, save your breath," advised Eden.

"I'm not asking you – I've got my own solution. Quoting Charlie, I think deep about matter – how is this? Madden knows that at any moment something may break and this thing that has happened at his ranch be spread all over the newspapers. Looking ahead, he sees he may need friends among the reporters. So he's come down from his high horse at last. Am I right?"

"Oh, it sounds logical," agreed Eden. "I'm glad something does. You know, I told Dad before I left San Francisco that I was keen to get mixed up in a murder mystery. But this – this is more than I bargained for. No dead body, no weapon, no motive, no murder. Nothing. Why, we can't even prove anybody has been killed." He stood up. "Well, I'd better be moving back to the ranch. The ranch and – what? Whither am I drifting?"

"You stick to your Chinese pal," advised Holley. "The boy's good. Something tells me he'll see you through."

"I hope so," Eden replied.

"Keep your eyes open," added Holley. "And take no chances. If you need help out there don't forget Will Holley."

"You bet I won't," Bob Eden answered. "So long. Maybe I'll see you tomorrow."

He went out and stood on the kerb before the Desert Edge Hotel. It was Saturday evening, and Eldorado was crowded with ranchers, lean, bronzed, work-stained men in khaki riding-breeches and gaudy lumber-jack blouses – simple men to whom this was the city. Through the window of the combined barber-shop and pool-room he saw a group of them shaking dice. Others leaned against the trunks of the cottonwoods, talking of the roads, of crops, of politics. Bob Eden felt like a visitor from Mars.

Presently Chan passed, swung round in the street, and halted the little touring car opposite the boy. As Eden climbed in he saw the detective's keen eyes fixed on the hotel doorway. Seating himself, he followed Chan's gaze.

A man had emerged from the Desert Edge Hotel – a man who looked strangely out of place among the roughly clad ranchers. He wore an overcoat buttoned tightly about his throat, and a felt hat was low over his eyes, which were hidden by dark spectacles.

"See who's here," said Eden.

"Yes, indeed," answered Chan, as they moved down the street. "I think the Killarney Hotel has lost one very important guest. Their loss our gain – maybe."

They left the all-too-brief pavement of Main Street, and a look of satisfaction spread slowly over Charlie Chan's face.

"Much work to do," he said. "Deep mysteries to solve. How sweet, though far from home, to feel myself in company of old friend."

Surprised, Bob Eden looked at him. "An old friend?" he repeated.

Chan smiled. "In garage on Punch Bowl Hill lonesome car like this awaits my return. With flivver shuddering beneath me I can think myself on familiar Honolulu streets again."

They climbed between the mountains, and before them lay the soft glory of the desert sunset. Ignoring the rough road, Chan threw the throttle wide.

"Wow, Charlie," cried Eden, as his head nearly pierced the top. "What's the idea?"

"Pardon, please," said Chan, slowing a bit. "No good, I guess. For a minute I think maybe this little car can bounce the homesick feeling from my heart."

VIII

A FRIENDLY LITTLE GAME

For a time the little brother of the car on Punch Bowl Hill ploughed valiantly on, and neither the detective nor Bob Eden spoke. The yellow glare of the sun was cooling on the grey livery of the desert; the shadows cast by the occasional trees grew steadily longer. The far-off mountains purpled and the wind bestirred itself.

"Charlie," said Bob Eden. "What do you think of this country?"

"This desert land?" asked Charlie.

Eden nodded.

"Happy to have seen it. All my time I yearn to encounter change. Certainly have encountered that here."

"Yes, I guess you have. Not much like Hawaii, is it?"

"I will say so. Hawaii lie like handful of Phillimore pearls on heaving breast of ocean. Oahu little island with very wet neighborhood all about. Moisture hangs in air all time, rain called liquid sunshine, breath of ocean pretty damp. Here I climb round to other side of picture. Air is dry like last year's newspaper."

"They tell me you can love this country if you try."

Chan shrugged. "For my part, I reserve my efforts in that line for other locality. Very much impressed by desert, thank you, but will move on at earliest opportunity."

"Here, too," Eden laughed. "Comes the night, and I long for lights about me that are bright. A little restaurant on O'Farrell Street, a few good fellows, a bottle of mineral water on the table. Human companionship, if it's not asking too much."

"Natural you feel that way," Chan agreed. "Youth is in your heart like a song. Because of you I am hoping we can soon leave Madden's ranch."

"Well, what do you think? What are we going to do now?"

"Watch and wait. Youth, I am thinking, does not like that business. But it must be. Speaking personally for myself, I am not having one happy fine time either. Act of cooking food not precisely my idea of merry vacation."

"Well, Charlie, I can stick it if you can," Eden said.

"Plenty fine sport you are," Chan replied. "Problems that we face are not without interest, for that matter. Most peculiar situation. At home I am called to look at crime, clear-cut like heathen idol's face. Somebody killed, maybe. Clues are plenty, I push little car down one path, I sway about, seeking another. Not so here. Starting forth to solve big mystery, I must first ask myself, just what are this big mystery I am starting forth to solve?"

"You've said it," Eden laughed.

"Yet one big fact gleams clear like snow on distant mountain. On recent night, at Madden's ranch, unknown person was murdered. Who unknown was, why he was killed, and who officiated at the homicide – these are simple little matters remaining to be cleared."

"And what have we to go on?" Eden asked helplessly.

"A parrot's cry at night. The rude removal of that unhappy bird. A bullet-hole hiding back of picture recently changed about. An aged pistol gone from dusty wall. All the more honor for us if we unravel from such puny clues."

"One thing I can't figure out – among others," said Eden. "What about Madden? Does he know? Or is that sly little Thorn pulling something off alone?"

"Important questions," Chan agreed. "In time we learn the answers, maybe. Meanwhile best to make no friend of Madden. You have told him nothing about San Francisco, I hope. Shaky Phil Maydorf and his queer behaviour."

"No, oddly enough, I haven't. I was wondering whether I hadn't better, now that Maydorf has shown up in Eldorado."

"Why? Pearls are in no danger. Did I hear you say in newspaper office you would greatly honor by following me?"

"You certainly did."

"Then, for Madden, more of the *hoo malimali*. Nothing to be gained by other course, much maybe lost. You tell him of Maydorf, and he might answer, deal is off here, bring pearls to New York. What then? You go away, he goes away, I go way. Mystery of recent event at ranch-house never solved."

"I guess you're right," said Eden. They sped on through the gathering dusk, past the little office of the Date City optimist, deserted now. "By the way," added the boy, "this thing you think has happened at the ranch – it may have occurred last Wednesday night?"

"You have fondly feeling for Wednesday night?" asked Chan. "Why?"

Briefly Bob Eden related Paula Wendell's story of that night – Thorn's obvious excitement when he met her at the door, his insistence that Madden could not speak to her, and, most important of all, the little prospector with the black beard whom the girl saw in the yard. Chan listened with interest.

"Now you talk," he commented. "Here is one fine new clue for us. He may be most important, that black-bearded one. A desert rat, I think. The young woman goes much about this country? Am I correct?"

"Yes, she does."

"She can retain secrets, maybe?"

"You bet – this girl can."

"Don't trust her. We talk all over place we may get sorry after while. However, venture so far as to ask please that she keep her pretty eyes open for that black-bearded rat. Who knows? Maybe he is vital link in our chain." They were approaching the little oasis Madden had set on the desert's dusty face. "Go in now," Chan continued, "and act innocent like very new baby. When you talk with Father over telephone, you will find he is prepared. I have sent him telegraph."

"You have?" said Eden. "So did I. I sent him a couple of them."

"Then he is all prepared. Among other matters, I presumed to remind him voice coming over wire is often grasped by others in room as well as him who reclines at telephone."

"Say – that's a good idea. I guess you think of everything, Charlie."

The gate was open, and Chan turned the car into the yard. "Guess I do," he sighed. "Now, with depressing reluctance, I must think of dinner. Recall, we watch and wait. And when we meet alone, the greatest care. No one must pierce my identity. Only this noon I could well have applied to myself resounding kick. That word unevitable too luxurious for poor old Ah Kim. In future I must pick over words like lettuce for salad. Goodbye, and splendid luck."

In the living-room a fire was already blazing in the huge fireplace. Madden sat at a broad, flat-topped desk, signing letters. He looked up as Bob Eden entered.

"Hello," he said. "Have a pleasant afternoon?"

"Quite," the boy replied. "I trust you had the same."

"I did not," Madden answered. "Even here I can't get away from business. Been catching up with a three day's accumulation of mail. There you are, Martin," he added, as the secretary entered. "I believe you'll have time to take them in to the post-office before dinner. And here are the telegrams – get them off too. Take the little car – it'll make better speed over these roads."

Thorn gathered up the letters, and with expert hands began folding them and placing them in envelopes. Madden rose, stretched, and came over to the fire. "Ah Kim brought you back?" he inquired.

"He did," Bob Eden answered.

"Knows how to drive a car all right?" persisted Madden.

"Perfectly."

"An unusual boy, Ah Kim."

"Oh, not very," Eden said carelessly. "He told me he used to drive a vegetable truck in Los Angeles. I got that much out of him, but that's about all."

"Silent, eh?"

Eden nodded. "Silent as a lawyer from Northampton, Massachusetts," he remarked.

Madden laughed. "By the way," he said, as Thorn went out, "your father didn't call."

"No? Well, he isn't likely to get home until evening. I'll try the house tonight, if you want me to."

"I wish you would," Madden said. "I don't want to seem inhospitable, my boy, but I'm very anxious to get away from here. Certain matters in the mail today – you understand – "

"Of course," Bob Eden answered. "I'll do all I can to help."

"That's mighty good of you," Madden told him, and the boy felt a bit guilty. "I think I'll take a nap before dinner. I find, nowadays, it's a great aid to digestion." The famous millionaire was more human than Bob Eden had yet seen him. He stood looking down at the boy wistfully. "A matter you can't grasp, just yet," he added. "You're so damned young – I envy you."

He went out, leaving Bob Eden to a Los Angeles paper he had picked up in Eldorado. From time to time, as the boy read, the quaint little figure of Ah Kim passed noiselessly. He was setting the table for dinner.

An hour later, there on the lonely desert, they again sat down to Ah Kim's cooking. Very different from the restaurant of which Bob Eden thought with longing, but if the company was far from lively, the food was excellent, for the Chinese had negotiated well. When the servant came in with coffee Madden said:

"Light the fire in the *patio*, Ah Kim. We'll sit out there awhile."

The Chinese went to comply with this order, and Eden saw Madden regarding him expectantly. He smiled and rose.

"Well, Dad ought to be struggling in from his hard day on the links any minute now," he said. "I'll put in that call."

Madden leapt up. "Let me do it," he suggested. "Just tell me the number."

The boy told him, and Madden spoke over the telephone in a voice to command respect.

"By the way," he said, when he had finished, "last night you intimated that certain things happened in San Francisco – things that made your father cautious. What – if you don't mind telling me?"

Bob Eden thought rapidly. "Oh, it may all have been a detective's pipe-dream. I'm inclined to think now that it was. You see—"

"Detective? What detective?"

"Well, naturally Dad has a tie-up with various private detective agencies. An operative of one of them reported that a famous crook had arrived in town and was showing an undue interest in our store. Of course, it may have meant nothing—"

"A famous crook, eh? Who?"

Never a good liar, Bob Eden hesitated. "I – I don't know that I remember the name. English, I believe – the Liverpool Kid, or something like that," he invented lamely.

Madden shrugged. "Well, if anything's leaked out about those pearls, it came from your side of the deal," he said. "My daughter, Thorn, and I have certainly been discretion itself. However, I'm inclined to think it's all a pipe-dream, as you say."

"Probably is," agreed Eden.

"Come outside," the millionaire invited. He led the way through the glass doors to the *patio*. There, a huge fire roared in the outdoor fireplace, glowing red on the stone floor and on wicker chairs. "Sit down," suggested Madden. "A cigar – no, you prefer your cigarette, eh?" He lighted up, and, leaning back in his chair, stared up at the dark roof above – the far-off roof of the sky. "I like it out here best," he went on. "A bit chilly, maybe, but you get close to the desert. Ever notice how white the stars are in this country?"

Eden looked at him with surprise. "Sure – I've noticed," he said. "But I never dreamed you had, old boy," he added to himself.

Inside Thorn was busy at the wireless receiver. A horrible medley of bedtime stories, violin solos, and lectures on health and beauty drifted out to them. And then the shrill voice of a woman, urging sinners to repent.

"Get Denver," Madden called loudly.

"I'm trying, chief," answered Thorn.

"If I must listen to the confounded thing," Madden added to the boy, "I want what I hear to come from far away. Over the mountains and the plains – there's romance in that." The crackling of the loud-speaker swept suddenly into a brisk band tune. "That's it," nodded Madden. "The orchestra at the Brown Palace in Denver – perhaps my girl is dancing to that very music at this moment. Poor kid – she'll wonder what's become of me. I promised to be there two days ago. Thorn!"

The secretary appeared at the door. "Yes, chief?"

"Remind me to send Evelyn a wire in the morning."

"I'll do that, chief," said Thorn, and vanished.

"And the band played on," remarked Madden. "All the way from Denver, mile high amid the Rockies. I tell you, man's getting too clever. He's riding for a fall. Probably a sign of age, Mr Eden, but I find myself longing for the older, simpler days. When I was a boy on the farm, winter mornings, the little schoolhouse in the valley. That sledge I wanted – hard times, yes, but times that made men. Oh, well, I mustn't get started on that."

They listened in silence, but presently a bedtime story brought a bellow of rage from the millionaire, and Thorn, getting his cue, shut off the machine.

Madden stirred restlessly in his chair. "We haven't enough for bridge," he remarked. "How about a little poker to pass the time, my boy?"

"Why – that would be fine," Eden replied. "I'm afraid you're pretty speedy company for me, however."

"Oh, that's all right – we'll put a limit on it."

Madden was on his feet, eager for action. "Come along."

They went into the living-room and closed the doors. A few moments later the three of them sat about a big round table under a brilliant light.

"Jacks or better," Madden said. "Quarter limit, eh?"

"Well—" replied Eden dubiously.

He had good reason to be dubious, for he was instantly plunged into the poker game of his life. He had played at college, and was even able to take care of himself in newspaper circles in San Francisco, but all that was child's play by comparison. Madden was no longer the man who noticed how white the stars were. He noticed how red, white, and blue the chips were, and he caressed them with loving hands. He was Madden, the plunger, the gambler with railroads and steel mills and the fortunes of little nations abroad, the Madden who, after he had played all day in Wall Street, was wont to seek the roulette-wheels on Forty-fourth Street at night.

"Aces," he cried. "Three of them. What have you got, Eden?"

"Apoplexy," remarked Eden, tossing aside his hand. "Right here and now I offer to sell my chances in this game for a cancelled postage stamp, or what have you?"

"Good experience for you," Madden replied. "Martin – it's your deal."

A knock sounded suddenly on the door, loud and clear. Bob Eden felt a strange sinking of the heart. Out of the desert dark, out of the vast, uninhabited wastes of the world, someone spoke and demanded to come in.

"Who can that be?" Madden frowned.

"Police," suggested Eden hopefully. "The joint is pinched." No such luck, he reflected.

Thorn was dealing, and Madden himself went to the door and swung it open. From where he sat Eden had a clear view of the dark desert – and of the man who stood in the light. A thin man in an overcoat, a man he had seen first in a San Francisco pier-shed, and later in front of the Desert Edge Hotel. Shaky Phil Maydorf himself, but now without the dark glasses hiding his eyes.

"Good evening," said Maydorf, and his voice too was thin and cold. "This is Mr Madden's ranch, I believe?"

"I'm Madden. What can I do for you?"

"I'm looking for an old friend of mine – your secretary, Martin Thorn."

Thorn rose and came round the table. "Oh, hello," he said, with slight enthusiasm.

"You remember me, don't you?" said the thin man. "McCallum – Henry McCallum. I met you at a dinner in New York a year ago."

"Yes, of course," answered Thorn. "Come in, won't you? This is Mr Madden."

"A great honor," said Shaky Phil.

"And Mr Eden, of San Francisco."

Eden rose, and faced Shaky Phil Maydorf. The man's eyes without the glasses were barbed and cruel, like the desert foliage. For a long moment he stared insolently at the boy. Did he realize, Eden wondered, that his movements on the dock at San Francisco had not gone unnoticed? If he did his nerve was excellent.

"Glad to know you, Mr Eden," he said.

"Mr McCallum," returned the boy gravely.

Maydorf turned again to Madden. "I hope I'm not intruding," he remarked with a wan smile. "Fact is, I'm stopping down the road at Doctor Whitcomb's – bronchitis, that's my trouble. It's lonesome as the devil round here, and when I heard Mr Thorn was in the neighborhood I couldn't resist the temptation to drop in."

"Glad you did," Madden said, but his tone belied the words.

"Don't let me interrupt your game," Maydorf went on. "Poker, eh? Is this a private scrap, or can anybody get into it?"

"Take off your coat," Madden responded sourly, "and sit up. Martin, give the gentleman a stack of chips."

"This is living again," said the newcomer, accepting briskly. "Well, and how have you been, Thorn, old man?"

Thorn, with his usual lack of warmth, admitted that he had been pretty good, and the game was resumed. If Bob Eden had feared for his immediate future before, he now gave up all hope. Sitting in a poker game with Shaky Phil – well, he was certainly travelling and seeing the world.

"Gimme four cards," said Mr Maydorf, through his teeth.

If it had been a bitter, brutal struggle before, it now became a battle to the death. New talent had come in – more than talent, positive genius. Maydorf held the cards close against his chest; his face was carved in stone. As though he realized what he was up against, Madden grew wary, but determined. These two fought it out, while Thorn and the boy trailed along, like non-combatants involved in a battle of the giants.

Presently Ah Kim entered with logs for the fire, and if the amazing picture on which his keen eyes lighted startled him he gave no sign. Madden ordered him to bring highballs, and as he set the glasses on the table Bob Eden noted with a secret thrill that the stomach of the detective was less than twelve inches from the long, capable hands of Shaky Phil. If the redoubtable Mr Maydorf only knew—

But Maydorf's thoughts were elsewhere than on the Phillimore pearls. "Dealer – one card," he demanded.

The telephone rang out sharply in the room. Bob Eden's heart missed a beat. He had forgotten that – and now—After the long wait he was finally to speak with his father – while Shaky Phil Maydorf sat only a few feet away! He saw Madden staring at him, and he rose.

"For me, I guess," he said carelessly. He tossed his cards on the table. "I'm out of it, anyhow." Crossing the room to the telephone, he took down the receiver. "Hello. Hello, Dad. Is that you?"

"Aces and trays," said Maydorf. "All mine?" Madden laid down a hand without looking at his opponent's, and Shaky Phil gathered in another pot.

"Yes, Dad – this is Bob," Eden was saying. "I arrived all right – stopping with Mr Madden for a few days. Just wanted you to know where I was. Yes – that's all. Everything. I may call you in the morning. Have a good game? Too bad. Goodbye!"

Madden was on his feet, his face purple. "Wait a minute," he cried.

"Just wanted Dad to know where I am," Eden said brightly. He dropped back into his chair. "Whose deal is it, anyhow?"

Madden strangled a sentence in his throat, and once more the game was on. Eden was chuckling inwardly. More delay – and not his fault this time. The joke was on P.J. Madden.

His third stack was melting rapidly away, and he reflected with apprehension that the night was young, and time of no importance on the desert, anyhow. "One more hand and I drop out," he said firmly.

"One more hand and we all drop out," barked Madden. Something seemed to have annoyed him.

"Let's make it a good one, then," said Maydorf. "The limit's off, gentlemen."

It was a good one, unexpectedly a contest between Maydorf and Bob Eden. Drawing with the faint hope of completing two pairs, the boy was thrilled to encounter four nines in his hand. Perhaps he should have noted that Maydorf was dealing, but he didn't – he bet heavily, and was finally called. Laying down his hand, he saw an evil smile on Shaky Phil's face.

"Four queens," remarked Maydorf, spreading them out with an expert gesture. "Always was lucky with the ladies. I think you gentlemen pay me."

They did. Bob Eden contributed forty-seven dollars reluctantly. All on the expense account, however, he reflected.

Mr Maydorf was in a not unaccountable good humour. "A very pleasant evening," he remarked, as he put on his overcoat. "I'll drop in again, if I may."

"Good night," snapped Madden.

Thorn took a flashlight from the desk. "I'll see you to the gate," he announced. Bob Eden smiled. A flashlight – with a bright moon overhead.

"Mighty good of you," the outsider said. "Good night, gentlemen, and thank you very much." He was smiling grimly as he followed the secretary out.

Madden snatched up a cigar, and savagely bit the end from it. "Well?" he cried.

"Well," said Eden calmly.

"You made a lot of progress with your father, didn't you?"

The boy smiled. "What did you expect me to do? Spill the whole thing in front of that bird?"

"No – but you needn't have rung off so quick. I was going to get him out of the room. Now you can go over there and call your father again."

"Nothing of the sort," answered Eden. "He's gone to bed, and I won't disturb him till morning."

Madden's face purpled. "I insist. And my orders are usually obeyed."

"Is that so?" remarked Eden. "Well, this is one that won't be."

Madden glared at him. "You young – you – er – young—"

"I know," Eden said. "But this was all your fault. If you will insist on cluttering up the ranch with strangers you must take the consequences."

"Who cluttered up the ranch?" Madden demanded. "I didn't invite that poor fool here. Where the devil did Thorn pick him up, anyhow? You know, the secretary of a man like me is always besieged by a lot of four-flushers – tip-hunters and the like. And Thorn's an idiot sometimes." The secretary entered and laid the flashlight on the desk. His employer regarded him with keen distaste. "Well, your little playmate certainly queered things," he said.

Thorn shrugged. "I know. I'm sorry, chief. But I couldn't help it. You saw how he horned in."

"Your fault for knowing him. Who is he, anyhow?"

"Oh, he's a broker, or something like that. I give you my word, chief, I never encouraged him. You know how those fellows are."

"Well, you go out tomorrow and tie a can to him. Tell him I'm busy here and don't want any visitors. Tell him for me that if he calls here again I'll throw him out."

"All right. I'll go down to the doctor's in the morning and let him know – in a diplomatic way."

"Diplomatic nothing," snorted Madden. "Don't waste diplomacy on a man like that. I won't, if I see him again."

"Well, gentlemen, I think I'll turn in," Eden remarked.

"Good night," said Madden, and the boy went out.

In his bedroom he found Ah Kim engaged in lighting the fire. He closed the door carefully behind him.

"Well, Charlie, I've just been in a poker game."

"A fact already noted by me," smiled Chan.

"Shaky Phil has made a start on us, anyhow. He got forty-seven precious iron men this quiet evening."

"Humbly suggest you be careful," advised Chan.

"Humbly believe you're right," laughed Eden. "I was hoping you were in the offing when Thorn and our friend went to the gate."

"Indeed I was," remarked Chan. "But moonlight so fierce, near approach was not possible."

"Well, I'm pretty sure of one thing after tonight," Eden told him. "P.J. Madden never saw Shaky Phil before. Either that, or he's the finest actor since Edwin Booth."

"Thorn, however—"

"Oh, Thorn knew him all right. But he wasn't the least bit glad to see him. You know, Thorn's whole manner suggested to me that Shaky Phil has something on him."

"That might be possible," agreed Chan. "Especially come to think of my latest discovery."

"You've found something new, Charlie? What?"

"This evening, when Thorn haste to town in little car and I hear noisome snores of Madden, who sleep on bed, I make explicit search in secretary's room."

"Yes – go on – quick. We might be interrupted."

"Under mountain of white shirts in Thorn's bureau reposes – what? Missing forty-five we call Bill Hart's gun."

"Good work! Thorn – the little rat—"

"Undubitably. Two chambers of that gun are quite unoccupied. Reflect on that."

"I'm reflecting. Two empty chambers."

"Humbly suggest you sleep now, gathering strength for what may be most excited tomorrow." The little detective paused at the door. "Two bullets gone, who knows where?" he said in a low voice. "Answer is, we know where one went. Went crazy, landing in wall at spot now covered by desert picture."

"And the other?" said Bob Eden thoughtfully.

"Other hit mark, I think. What mark? We watch and wait, and maybe we discover. Good night, with plenty happy dreams."

IX

A RIDE IN THE DARK

On Sunday morning Bob Eden rose at what was, for him, an amazingly early hour. Various factors conspired to induce this strange phenomenon – the desert sun, an extremely capable planet, filling his room with light, the roosters of P.J. Madden, loudly vocal in the dawn. At eight o'clock he was standing in the ranch-house yard, ready for whatever the day might bring forth.

Whatever it brought, the day was superb. Now the desert was at its best, the chill of night still lingering in the magic air. He looked out over an opal sea, at changing colours of sand and cloud and mountain-top that shamed by their brilliance those glittering showcases in the jewellery shop of Meek and Eden. Though it was the fashion of his age to pretend otherwise, he was not oblivious to beauty, and he set out for a stroll about the ranch with a feeling of awe in his heart.

Turning a rear corner of the barn, he came unexpectedly upon a jarring picture. Martin Thorn was busy beside a basket, digging a deep hole in the sand. In his dark clothes, with his pale face glistening from his unaccustomed exertion, he looked not unlike some prosperous sexton.

"Hello," said Eden. "Who are you burying this fine morning?"

Thorn stopped. Beads of perspiration gleamed on his high white forehead.

"Somebody has to do it," he complained. "That new boy's too lazy. And if you let this refuse accumulate the place begins to look like a deserted picnic grounds."

He nodded toward the basket, filled with old tin cans.

"Wanted, private secretary to bury rubbish back of barn," smiled Eden. "A new sidelight on your profession, Thorn. Good idea to get them out of the way, at that," he added, leaning over and taking up a can. "Especially this one, which I perceive lately held arsenic."

"Arsenic?" repeated Thorn. He passed a dark coat sleeve across his brow. "Oh, yes – we use a lot of that. Rats, you know."

"Rats," remarked Eden, with an odd inflection, restoring the can to its place.

Thorn emptied the contents of the basket into the hole, and began to fill it in. Eden, playing well his *rôle* of innocent bystander, watched him idly.

"There – that's better," said the secretary, smoothing the sand over the recent excavation. "You know – I've always had a passion for neatness." He picked up the basket. "By the way," he added, "if you don't mind, I'd like to give you a little advice."

"Glad to have it," Eden replied, walking along beside him.

"I don't know how anxious you people are to sell that necklace. But I've been with the chief fifteen years, and I can tell you he's not the sort of man you can keep waiting with impunity. The first thing you know, young man, that deal for the pearls will be off."

"I'm doing my best," Eden told him. "Besides, Madden's getting a big bargain, and he must know it – if he stops to think—"

"Once P.J. Madden loses his temper," said Thorn, "he doesn't stop to think. I'm warning you, that's all."

"Mighty kind of you," answered Eden carelessly. Thorn dropped his spade and basket by the cookhouse, from which came the pleasant odour of bacon frying. Walking slowly, the secretary moved on toward the *patio*. Ah Kim emerged from his work-room, his cheeks flushed from close juxtaposition to a cooking-stove.

"Hello, boss," he said. "You takee look-see at sunlise thisee mawnin'?"

"Up pretty early, but not as early as that," the boy replied. He saw the secretary vanish into the house. "Just been watching our dear friend Thorn bury some rubbish back of the barn," he added. "Among other items, a can that lately contained arsenic."

Chan dropped the *rôle* of Ah Kim. "Mr Thorn plenty busy man," he said. "Maybe he get more busy as time goes by. One wrong deed leads on to other wrong deeds, like unending chain. Chinese have saying that applies: 'He who rides on tiger cannot dismount.'"

Madden appeared in the *patio*, full of pep and power. "Hey, Eden," he called. "Your father's on the wire."

"Dad's up early," remarked Eden, hurrying to join him.

"I called him," said Madden. "I've had enough delay."

Reaching the telephone, Bob Eden took up the receiver. "Hello, Dad. I can talk freely this morning. I want to tell you everything's all right down here. Mr Madden? Yes – he's fine – standing right beside me now. And he's in a tearing hurry for that necklace."

"Very well – we'll get it to him at once," the elder Eden said. Bob Eden sighed with relief. His telegram had arrived.

"Ask him to get it off today," Madden commanded.

"Mr Madden wants to know if it can start today," the boy said.

"Impossible," replied the jeweler. "I haven't got it."

"Not today," Bob Eden said to Madden. "He hasn't got—"

"I heard him," roared Madden. "Here – give me that 'phone. Look here, Eden – what do you mean, you haven't got it?"

Bob Eden could hear his father's replies. "Ah – Mr Madden – how are you? The pearls were in a quite disreputable condition – I couldn't possibly let them go as they were. So I'm having them cleaned – they're with another firm—"

"Just a minute, Eden," bellowed the millionaire. "I want to ask you something – can you understand the English language, or can't you? Keep still – I'll talk. I told you I wanted the pearls now – at once – *pronto* – what the devil language do you speak? I don't give a hang about having them cleaned. Good Lord, I thought you understood."

"So sorry," responded Bob Eden's gentle father. "I'll get them in the morning, and they'll start tomorrow night."

"Yeah – that means Tuesday evening at the ranch. Eden, you make me sick. I've a good mind to call the whole thing off—" Madden paused, and Bob Eden held his breath. "However, if you promise the pearls will start tomorrow sure—"

"I give you my word," said the jeweler. "They will start tomorrow, at the very latest."

"All right. I'll have to wait, I suppose. But this is the last time I deal with you, my friend. I'll be on the look-out for your man on Tuesday. Goodbye."

In a towering rage, Madden hung up. His ill-humour continued through breakfast, and Eden's gay attempts at conversation fell on barren ground. After the meal was finished Thorn took the little car and disappeared down the road. Bob Eden loafed expectantly about the front yard.

Much sooner than he had dared to hope his vigil was ended. Paula Wendell, fresh and lovely as the California morning, drove up in her smart roadster and waited outside the barbed-wire fence.

"Hello," she said. "Jump in. You act as though you were glad to see me."

"Glad! Lady, you're a life-saver. Relations are sort of strained this morning at the old homestead. You'll find it hard to believe, but P.J. Madden doesn't love me."

She let in the clutch. "The man's mad," she laughed.

"I'll say he's mad. Ever eat breakfast with a rattlesnake that's had bad news?"

"Not yet. The company at the Oasis is mixed, but not so mixed as that. Well, what do you think of the view this morning? Ever see such colouring before?"

"Never. And it's not out of a drug-store, either."

"I'm talking about the desert. Look at those snow-capped peaks."

"Lovely. But, if you don't mind, I prefer to look closer. No doubt he's told you you're beautiful."

"Who?"

"Wilbur, your *fiancé*."

"His name is Jack. Don't jump on a good man when he's down."

"Of course he's a good man, or you wouldn't have picked him." They ploughed along the sandy road. "But even so – look here, lady. Listen to a man of the world. Marriage is the last resort of feeble minds."

"Think so?"

"I know it. Oh, I've given the matter some thought. I've had to. There's my own case. Now and then I've met a girl whose eyes said, 'Well, I might.' But I've been cautious. Hold fast, my lad – that's my motto."

"And you've held fast?"

"You bet. Glad of it, too. I'm free. I'm having a swell time. When evening comes, and the air's full of zip and zowie, and the lights flicker round Union Square, I just reach for my hat. And who says, in a gentle, patient voice: 'Where are you going, my dear? I'll go with you'?"

"Nobody."

"Not a living soul. It's grand. And you – your case is just like mine. Of course there are millions of girls who have nothing better to do than marriage. All right for them. But you – why – you've got a wonderful job. The desert, the hills, the canyons – and you're willing to give all that up for a gas-range in the rear room of an apartment?"

"Perhaps we can afford a maid."

"Lots of people can – but where to get one nowadays? I'm warning you – think it over well. You're having a great time now – that will end with marriage. Mending Wilbur's socks—"

"I tell you his name is Jack."

"What of it? He'll be just as hard on the socks. I hate to think of a girl like you, tied down somewhere—"

"There's a lot in what you say," Paula Wendell admitted.

"I've only scratched the surface," Eden assured her.

The girl steered her car off the road through an open gate. Eden saw a huge, rambling ranch-house surrounded by a group of tiny cottages. "Here we are at Doctor Whitcomb's," remarked Paula Wendell. "Wonderful person, the doctor. I want you two to meet."

She led the way through a screen-door into a large living-room, not so beautifully furnished as Madden's, but bespeaking even greater comfort. A grey-haired woman was rocking contentedly near a window. Her face was kindly, her eyes calm and comforting. "Hello, doctor," said the girl. "I've brought someone to call on you."

The woman rose, and her smile seemed to fill the room. "Hello, young man," she said, and took Bob Eden's hand.

"You – you're the doctor?" he stammered.

"Sure am," the woman replied. "But you don't need me. You're all right."

"So are you," he answered. "I can see that."

"Fifty-five years old," returned the doctor, "but I can still get a kick out of that kind of talk from a nice young man. Sit down. The place is yours. Where are you staying?"

"I'm down the road at Madden's."

"Oh, yes – I heard he was here. Not much of a neighbor, this P.J. Madden. I've called on him occasionally, but he's never come to see me. Stand-offish – and that sort of thing doesn't go in the desert. We're all friends here."

"You've been a friend to a good many," said Paula Wendell.

"Why not?" shrugged Doctor Whitcomb. "What's life for, if not to help one another? I've done my best – I only wish it had been more."

Bob Eden felt suddenly humble in this woman's presence.

"Come on – I'll show you round my place," invited the doctor. "I've made the desert bloom – put that on my tombstone. You should have seen this neighborhood when I came. Just a rifle and a cat – that's all I had at first. And the cat wouldn't stay. My first house here I built with my own hands. Five miles to Eldorado – I walked in and back every day. Mr Ford hadn't been heard of then."

She led the way into the yard, in and out among the little cottages. Tired faces brightened at her approach, weary eyes gleamed with sudden hope.

"They've come to her from all over the country," Paula Wendell said. "Broken-hearted, sick, discouraged. And she's given them new life—"

"Nonsense," cried the doctor. "I've just been friendly. It's a pretty hard world. Being friendly – that works wonders."

In the doorway of one of the cottages they came upon Martin Thorn, deep in converse with Shaky Phil Maydorf. Even Maydorf mellowed during a few words with the doctor.

Finally, when they reluctantly left, Doctor Whitcomb followed them to the gate. "Come often," she said. "You will, won't you?"

"I hope to," answered Bob Eden. He held her great rough hand a moment. "You know – I'm beginning to sense the beauty of the desert," he added.

The doctor smiled. "The desert is old and weary and wise," she said. "There's beauty in that, if you can see it. Not everybody can. The latch-string's always out at Doctor Whitcomb's. Remember, boy."

Paula Wendell swung the car about, and in silence they headed home.

"I feel as though I'd been out to old Aunt Mary's," said Eden presently. "I sort of expected her to give me a cookie when I left."

"She's a wonderful woman," said the girl softly. "I ought to know. It was the light in her window I saw my first night on the desert. And the light in her eyes – I shall never forget. All the great people are not in the cities."

They rode on. About them the desert blazed stark and empty in the midday heat; a thin haze cloaked the distant dunes and the far-away slopes of the hills. Bob Eden's mind returned to the strange problems that confronted him. "You've never asked me why I'm here," he remarked.

"I know," the girl answered. "I felt that pretty soon you'd realize we're all friends on the desert – and tell me."

"I want to – some day. Just at present – well, I can't. But going back to that night you first visited Madden's ranch – you felt that something was wrong there?"

"I did."

"Well, I can tell you this much – you were probably right." She glanced at him quickly. "And it's my job to find out if you were. That old prospector – I'd give a good deal to meet him. Isn't there a chance that you may run across him again?"

"Just a chance," she replied.

"Well, if you do, would you mind getting in touch with me at once? If it's not asking too much—"

"Not at all," she told him. "I'll be glad to. Of course, the old man may be clear over in Arizona by now. When I last saw him he was moving fast!"

"All the more reason for wanting to find him," Eden said. "I – I wish I could explain. It isn't that I don't trust you, you know. But – it's not altogether my secret."

She nodded. "I understand. I don't want to know."

"You grow more wonderful every minute," he told her.

The minutes passed. After a time the car halted before Madden's ranch, and Bob Eden alighted. He stood looking into the girl's eyes – somehow they were like the eyes of Doctor Whitcomb – restful and comforting and kind. He smiled.

"You know," he said, "I may as well confess it – I've been sort of disliking Wilbur. And now it comes to me suddenly – if I really mean all that about loving my freedom – then Wilbur has done me the greatest service possible. I ought not to dislike him any more. I ought to thank him from the bottom of my heart."

"What in the world are you talking about?"

"Don't you understand? I've just realized that I'm up against the big temptation of my life. But I don't have to fight it. Wilbur has saved me. Good old Wilbur. Give him my love when next you write."

She threw her car into gear. "Don't you worry," she advised. "Even if there hadn't been a Wilbur, your freedom wouldn't have been in the slightest danger. I would have seen to that."

"Somehow, I don't care for that remark," Eden said. "It ought to reassure me, but as a matter of fact I don't like it at all. Well, I owe you for another buggy ride. Sorry to see you go – it looks like a dull Sunday out here. Would you mind if I drifted into town this afternoon?"

"I probably wouldn't even know it," said the girl. "Goodbye."

Bob Eden's prediction about Sunday proved true – it was long and dull. At four in the afternoon he could stand it no longer. The blazing heat was dying, a restless wind had risen, and with the permission of Madden, who was still ill-humoured and evidently restless too, he took the little car and sped toward the excitement of Eldorado.

Not much diversion there. In the window of the Desert Edge Hotel the proprietor waded grimly through an interminable Sunday paper. Main Street was hot and deserted. Leaving the car before the hotel, the boy went to Holley's office.

The editor came to the door to meet him. “Hello,” he said. “I was hoping you'd come along. Kind of lonesome in the great open spaces this afternoon. By the way, there's a telegram here for you.”

Eden took the yellow envelope and hurriedly tore it open. The message was from his father:

I don't understand what it's all about but I am most disturbed. For the present I will follow your instructions. I am trusting you two utterly but I must remind you that it would be most embarrassing for me if sale fell through. Jordans are eager to consummate deal and Victor threatens to come down there any moment. Keep me advised.

“Huh,” said Bob Eden. “That would be fine.”

“What would?” asked Holley.

“Victor threatens to come – the son of the woman who owns the pearls. All we need here to wreck the works is that amiable bonehead and his spats.”

“What's new?” asked Holley, as they sat down.

“Several things,” Bob Eden replied. “To start with the big tragedy, I'm out forty-seven dollars.” He told of the poker game. “In addition, Mr Thorn has been observed burying a can that once held arsenic. Furthermore, Charlie has found that missing pistol in Thorn's bureau – with two chambers empty.”

Holley whistled. “Has he really? You know, I believe your friend Chan is going to put Thorn back of the bars before he's through.”

“Perhaps,” admitted Eden. “Got a long way to go, though. You can't convict a man of murder without a body to show for it.”

"Oh – Chan will dig that up."

Eden shrugged. "Well, if he does he can have all the credit. And do all the digging. Somehow, it's not the sort of thing that appeals to me. I like excitement, but I like it nice and neat. Heard from your interview?"

"Yes. It's to be released in New York tomorrow." The tired eyes of Will Holley brightened. "I was sitting here getting a thrill out of the idea when you came in." He pointed to a big scrap-book on his desk. "Some of the stories I wrote on the old *Sun*," he explained. "Not bad, if I do say it myself."

Bob Eden picked up the book, and turned the pages with interest. "I've been thinking of getting a job on a newspaper myself," he said.

Holley looked at him quickly. "Think twice," he advised. "You, with a good business waiting for you – what has the newspaper game to offer you? Great while you're young, maybe – great even now when the old order is changing and the picture paper is making a monkey out of a grand profession. But when you're old—" He got up and laid a hand on the boy's shoulder. "When you're old – and you're old at forty – then what? The copy desk, and some day the owner comes in, and sees a streak of grey in your hair, and he says: 'Throw that doddering fool out. I want young men here.' No, my boy – not the newspaper game. You and I must have a long talk."

They had it. It was five by the little clock on Holley's desk when the editor finally stood up, and closed his scrap-book. "Come on," he said. "I'm taking you to the Oasis for dinner."

Eden went gladly. At one of the tables opposite the narrow counter Paula Wendell sat alone.

"Hello," she greeted them. "Come over here. I felt in an expansive mood tonight – had to have the prestige of a table."

They sat down opposite her. "Did you find the day as dull as you expected?" inquired the girl of Eden.

"Very dull by contrast, after you left me," he answered.

"Try the chicken," she advised. "Born and raised right here at home, and the desert hen is no weak sister. Not so bad, however."

They accepted her suggestion. When the generously filled platters were placed before them Bob Eden squared his shoulders.

"Take to the lifeboats," he said. "I'm about to carve, and when I carve it's a case of women and children first."

Holley stared down at his dinner. "Looks like the same old chicken," he sighed. "What wouldn't I give for a little home cooking?"

"Ought to get married," smiled the girl. "Am I right, Mr Eden?"

Eden shrugged. "I've known several poor fellows who got married hoping to enjoy a bit of home cooking. Now they're back in the restaurants, and the only difference is they've got the little woman along. Double the check and half the pleasure."

"Why all this cynicism?" asked Holley.

"Oh, Mr Eden is very much opposed to marriage," the girl said. "He was telling me today."

"Just trying to save her," Eden explained. "By the way, do you know this Wilbur who's won her innocent, trusting heart?"

"Wilbur?" asked Holley blankly.

"He will persist in calling Jack out of his name," the girl said. "It's his disrespectful way of referring to my *fiancé*."

Holley glanced at the ring. "No, I don't know him," he announced. "I certainly congratulate him, though."

"So do I," Eden returned. "On his nerve. However, I oughtn't to knock Wilbur. As I was saying only this noon—"

"Never mind," put in the girl. "Wake up, Will. What are you thinking about?"

Holley started. "I was thinking of a dinner I had once at Mouquin's," he replied. "Closed up now, I hear. Gone – like all the other old landmarks – the happy stations on the five o'clock cocktail route. You know, I wonder sometimes if I'd like New York today—"

He talked of the old Manhattan he had known. In what seemed to Bob Eden no time at all the dinner hour had passed. As they were standing at the cashier's desk the boy noted, for the first time, a stranger lighting a cigar near by. He was, from his dress, no native – a small, studious-looking man with piercing eyes.

"Good evening, neighbor," Holley said.

"How are you?" answered the stranger.

"Come down to look us over?" the editor asked, thinking of his next issue.

"Dropped in for a call on the kangaroo-rat," replied the man. "I understand there's a local variety whose tail measures three millimetres longer than any hitherto recorded."

"Oh," returned Holley. "One of those fellows, eh? We get them all – beetle men and butterfly men, mouse and gopher men. Drop round to the office of the *Times* some day and we'll have a chat."

"Delighted," said the little naturalist.

"Well, look who's here," cried Holley suddenly. Bob Eden turned, and saw entering the door of the Oasis a thin little Chinese who seemed as old as the desert. His face was the colour of a beloved meerschaum pipe, his eyes beady and bright. "Louie Wong," Holley explained. "Back from San Francisco, eh, Louie?"

"Hello, boss," said Louie, in a high, shrill voice. "My come back."

"Didn't you like it up there?" Holley persisted.

"San Flancisco no good," answered Louie. "All time lain dlop on nose. My like 'um heah."

"Going back to Madden's, eh?" Holley inquired. Louie nodded. "Well, here's a bit of luck for you, Louie. Mr Eden is going out to the ranch presently, and you can ride with him."

"Of course," assented Eden.

"Catch 'um hot tea. You wait jus' litta time, boss," said Louie, sitting down at the counter.

"We'll be down in front of the hotel," Holley told him. The three of them went out. The little naturalist followed, and slipped by them, disappearing in the night.

Neither Holley nor Eden spoke. When they reached the hotel they stopped.

"I'm leaving you now," Paula Wendell said. "I have some letters to write."

"Ah, yes," Eden remarked. "Well – don't forget. My love to Wilbur."

"These are business letters," she answered severely. "Good night."

The girl went inside. "So Louie's back," Eden said. "That makes a pretty situation."

"What's the matter?" Holley said. "Louie may have a lot to tell."

"Perhaps. But when he shows up at his old job – what about Charlie? He'll be kicked out, and I'll be alone on the big scene. Somehow, I don't feel I know my lines."

"I never thought of that," replied the editor. "However, there's plenty of work for two boys out there when Madden's in residence. I imagine he'll keep them both. And what a chance for Charlie to pump old Louie dry. You and I could ask him questions from now until doomsday and never learn a thing. But Charlie – that's another matter."

They waited, and presently Louie Wong came shuffling down the street, a cheap little suitcase in one hand and a full paper bag in the other.

"What you got there, Louie?" Holley asked. He examined the bag. "Bananas, eh?"

"Tony like 'um banana," the old man explained. "Pleasant foah Tony."

Eden and Holley looked at each other. "Louie," said the editor gently, "poor Tony's dead."

Anyone who believes the Chinese face is always expressionless should have seen Louie's then. A look of mingled pain and anger contorted it, and he burst at once into a flood of language that needed no translator. It was profane and terrifying.

"Poor old Louie," Holley said. "He's reviling the street, as they say in China."

"Do you suppose he knows?" asked Eden. "That Tony was murdered, I mean."

"Search me," answered Holley. "It certainly looks that way, doesn't it?" Still loudly vocal, Louie Wong climbed into the back seat of the car, and Bob Eden took his place at the wheel. "Watch your step, boy," advised Holley. "See you soon. Good night."

Bob Eden started the car, and with old Louie Wong set out on the strangest ride of his life.

The moon had not yet risen; the stars, wan and far-off and unfriendly, were devoid of light. They climbed between the mountains, and that mammoth doorway led seemingly to a black and threatening inferno that Eden could sense but could not see. Down the rocky road and on to the sandy floor of the desert they crept along; out of the dark beside the way gleamed little yellow eyes, flashing hatefully for a moment, then vanishing for ever. Like the ugly ghosts of trees that had died the Joshuas writhed in agony, casting deformed, appealing arms aloft. And constantly as they rode on muttered the weird voice of the old Chinese in the back seat, mourning the passing of his friend, the death of Tony.

Bob Eden's nerves were steady, but he was glad when the lights of Madden's ranch shone with a friendly glow ahead. He left the car in the road and went to open the gate. A stray twig was caught in the latch, but finally he got it open, and, returning to the car, swung it into the yard. With a feeling of deep relief, he swept up before the barn. Charlie Chan was waiting in the glow of the headlights.

"Hello, Ah Kim," Eden called. "Got a little playmate for you in the back seat. Louie Wong has come back to his desert." He leaped to the ground. All was silence in the rear of the car. "Come on, Louie," he cried. "Here we are."

He stopped, a sudden thrill of horror in his heart. In the dim light he saw that Louie had slipped to his knees, and that his head hung limply over the door at the left.

"My God!" cried Eden.

"Wait," said Charlie Chan. "I get flashlight."

He went, while Bob Eden stood fixed and frightened in his tracks. Quickly the efficient Charlie returned, and made a hasty examination with the light. Bob Eden saw a gash in the side of Louie's old coat – a gash that was bordered with something wet and dark.

"Stabbed in the side," said Charlie calmly. "Dead – like Tony."

"Dead – when?" gasped Eden. "In the minute I left the car at the gate. Why – it's impossible—"

Out of the shadows came Martin Thorn, his pale face gleaming in the dusk. "What's all this?" he asked. "Why – it's Louie. What's happened to Louie?"

He bent over the door of the car, and the busy flashlight in the hand of Charlie Chan shone for a moment on his back. Across the dark coat was a long tear – a tear such as might have been made in the coat of one climbing hurriedly through a barbed-wire fence.

"This is terrible," Thorn said. "Just a minute – I must get Mr Madden."

He ran to the house, and Bob Eden stood with Charlie Chan by the body of Louie Wong.

"Charlie," whispered the boy huskily, "you saw that rip in Thorn's coat?"

"Most certainly," answered Chan. "I observed it. What did I quote to you this morning? Old saying of Chinese. 'He who rides on tiger cannot dismount.'"

X

BLISS OF THE HOMICIDE SQUAD

In another moment Madden was with them there by the car, and they felt rather than saw a quivering, suppressed fury in every inch of the millionaire's huge frame. With an oath he snatched a flashlight from the hand of Charlie Chan and bent over the silent form in the back of the car. The glow from the lamp illuminated faintly his big red face, his searching eyes, and Bob Eden watched him with interest.

There in that dusty car lay the lifeless shape of one who had served Madden faithfully for many years. Yet no sign either of compassion or regret was apparent in the millionaire's face – nothing save a constantly growing anger. Yes, Bob Eden reflected, those who reported Madden lacked a heart spoke nothing but the truth.

Madden straightened, and flashed the light into the pale face of his secretary.

"Fine business!" he snarled.

"Well, what are you staring at me for?" cried Thorn, his voice trembling.

"I'll stare at you if I choose – though God knows I'm sick of the sight of your silly face—"

"I've had about enough from you," warned Thorn, and the tremor in his voice was rage. For a moment they regarded each other while Bob Eden watched them, amazed. For the first time he realized that under the mask of their daily relations these two were anything but friends.

Suddenly Madden turned the light on Charlie Chan. "Look here, Ah Kim – this was Louie Wong – the boy you replaced here – savvy? You've got to stay on the ranch now – after I've gone too – how about it?"

"I think I stay, boss."

"Good. You're the only bit of luck I've had since I came to this accursed place. Bring Louie into the living-room – on the couch. I'll call Eldorado."

He stalked off through the *patio* to the house, and after a moment's hesitation Chan and the secretary picked up the frail body of Louie Wong. Slowly Bob Eden followed that odd procession. In the living-room Madden was talking briskly on the telephone. Presently he hung up the receiver.

"Nothing to do but wait," he said. "There's a sort of constable in town – he'll be along pretty soon with the coroner. Oh, it's fine business. They'll overrun the place – and I came here for a rest."

"I suppose you want to know what happened," Eden began. "I met Louie Wong in town, at the Oasis Café. Mr Holley pointed him out to me, and—"

Madden waved a great hand. "Oh, save all that for some half-witted cop. Fine business, this is."

He took to pacing the floor like a lion with the toothache. Eden dropped into a chair before the fire. Chan had gone out, and Thorn was sitting silently near by. Madden continued to pace. Bob Eden stared at the blazing logs. What sort of affair had he got into, anyhow? What desperate game was afoot here on Madden's ranch, far out on the lonely desert? He began to wish himself out of it, back in town where the lights were bright and there was no constant undercurrent of hatred and suspicion and mystery.

He was still thinking in this vein when the clatter of a car sounded in the yard. Madden himself opened the door, and two of Eldorado's prominent citizens entered.

"Come in, gentlemen," Madden said, amiable with an effort. "Had a little accident out here."

One of the two, a lean man with a brown, weather-beaten face, stepped forward.

"Howdy, Mr Madden, I know you, but you don't know me. I'm Constable Brackett, and this is our coroner, Doctor Simms. A murder, you said on the 'phone."

"Well," replied Madden, "I suppose you could call it that. But fortunately no one was hurt. No white man, I mean. Just my old Chink, Louie Wong." Ah Kim had entered in time to hear this speech, and his eyes blazed for a moment as they rested on the callous face of the millionaire.

"Louie?" said the constable. He went over to the couch. "Why, poor old Louie. Harmless as they come, he was. Can't figure who'd have anything against old Louie."

The coroner, a brisk young man, also went to the couch and began an examination. Constable Brackett turned to Madden. "Now, we'll make just as little trouble as we can, Mr Madden," he promised. Evidently he was much in awe of this great man. "But I don't like this. It reflects on me. I got to ask a few questions. You see that, don't you?"

"Of course," answered Madden. "Fire away. I'm sorry, but I can't tell you a thing. I was in my room when my secretary" – he indicated Thorn – "came in and said that Mr Eden here had just driven into the yard with the dead body of Louie in the car."

The constable turned with interest to Eden. "Where'd you find him?" he inquired.

"He was perfectly all right when I picked him up," Eden explained. He launched into his story – the meeting with Louie at the Oasis, the ride across the desert, the stop at the gate, and finally the gruesome discovery in the yard. The constable shook his head.

"All sounds mighty mysterious to me," he admitted. "You say you think he was killed while you was openin' the gate. What makes you think so?"

"He was talking practically all the way out here," Eden replied. "Muttering to himself there in the back seat. I heard him when I got out to unfasten the gate."

"What was he sayin'?"

"He was talking in Chinese. I'm sorry, but I'm no sinologue."

"I ain't accused you of anything, have I?"

"A sinologue is a man who understands the Chinese language," Bob Eden smiled.

"Oh." The constable scratched his head. "This here secretary, now—"

Thorn came forward. He had been in his room, he said, when he heard a disturbance in the yard, and went outside. Absolutely nothing to offer. Bob Eden's glance fell on the tear across the back of Thorn's coat. He looked at Charlie Chan, but the detective shook his head. Say nothing, his eyes directed.

The constable turned to Madden. "Who else is on the place?" he wanted to know.

"Nobody but Ah Kim here. He's all right."

The officer shook his head. "Can't always tell," he averred. "All these *tong* wars, you know." He raised his voice to a terrific bellow. "Come here, you," he cried.

Ah Kim, lately Detective-Sergeant Chan of the Honolulu police, came with expressionless face and stood before the constable. How often he had played the opposite *rôle* in such a scene – played it far better than this mainland officer ever would!

"Ever see this Louie Wong before?" thundered the constable.

"Me, boss? No, boss, I no see 'um."

"New round here, ain't you?"

"Come las' Fliday, boss."

"Where did you work before this?"

"All place, boss. Big town, litta town."

"I mean where'd you work last?"

"Lailload, I think, boss. Santa Fé lailload. Lay sticks on glound."

"Ah – er – well, doggone." The constable had run out of questions. "Ain't had much practice at this sort of thing," he apologized. "Been so busy confiscatin' licker these last few years I sort of lost the knack for police work. This is sheriff's stuff. I called him before we come out, an' he's sendin' Captain Bliss of the Homicide Squad down tomorrow mornin'. So we won't bother you no more tonight, Mr Madden."

The coroner came forward. "We'll take the body in town, Mr Madden," he said. "I'll have the inquest in there, but I may want to bring my jurors out here some time tomorrow."

"Oh, sure," replied Madden. "Just attend to anything that comes up, and send all the bills to me. Believe me, I'm sorry this thing has happened."

"So am I," said the constable. "Louie was a good old scout."

"Yes – and – well, I don't like it. It's annoying to have something like this happen."

"All mighty mysterious to me," the constable admitted again. "My wife told me I never ought to take this job. Well, so long, Mr Madden – great pleasure to meet a man like you."

When Bob Eden retired to his room Madden and Thorn were facing each other on the hearth. Something in the expression of each made him wish he could overhear the scene about to be enacted in that room.

Ah Kim was waiting beside a crackling fire. "I make 'um burn, boss," he said. Eden closed the door and sank into a chair.

"Charlie, in heaven's name what's going on here?" he inquired helplessly.

Chan shrugged. "Plenty goes on," he said. "Two nights now gone since in this room I hint to you Chinese are psychic people. On your face then I see well-bred sneer."

"I apologize," Eden returned. "No sneering after this, even the well-bred kind. But I'm certainly stumped. This thing tonight—"

"Most unfortunate, this thing tonight," said Chan thoughtfully. "Humbly suggest you be very careful, or everything spoils. Local police come thumping on to scene, not dreaming in their slight brains that murder of Louie are of no importance in the least."

"Not important, you say?"

"No, indeed. Not when compared to other matters."

"Well, it was pretty important to Louie, I guess," said Eden.

"Guess so too. But murder of Louie just like death of parrot – one more dark deed covering up very black deed occurring here before we arrive on mysterious scene. Before parrot go, before Louie make unexpected exit, unknown person dies screaming unanswered cries for help. Who? Maybe in time we learn."

"Then you think Louie was killed because he knew too much?"

"Just like Tony, yes. Poor Louie very foolish, does not stay in San Francisco when summoned there. Comes with sad blunder back to desert. Most bitterly unwelcome here. One thing puzzles me."

"Only one thing?" asked Eden.

"One at present. Other puzzles put aside for moment. Louie goes on Wednesday morning, probably before black deed was done. How then does he know? Did act have echo in San Francisco? I am most sad not to have talk with him. But there are other paths to follow."

"I hope so," sighed Bob Eden. "But I don't see them. This is too much for me."

"Plenty for me too," agreed Chan. "Pretty quick I go home, lifelong yearning for travel for ever quenched. Keep in mind, much better police do not find who killed Louie Wong. If they do our fruit may be picked when not yet ripe. We should handle case. Officers of law must be encouraged off of ranch at earliest possible time, having found nothing."

"Well, the constable was easy enough," smiled Eden.

"All looked plenty mysterious to him," answered Chan, smiling too.

"I sympathized with him in that," Eden admitted. "But this Captain Bliss probably won't be so simple. You watch your step, Charlie, or they'll lock you up."

Chan nodded. "New experiences crowd close on this mainland," he said. "Detective-Sergeant Chan a murder suspect. Maybe I laugh at that, when I get home again. Just now, laugh won't come. A warm good night—"

"Wait a minute," interrupted Eden. "How about Tuesday afternoon? Madden's expecting the messenger with the pearls then, and somehow I haven't a stall left in me."

Chan shrugged. "Two days yet. Stop the worry. Much may manage to occur before Tuesday afternoon." He went out softly.

Just as they finished breakfast on Monday morning, a knock sounded on the door of the ranch-house, and Thorn admitted Will Holley.

"Oh," said Madden sourly. His manner had not improved overnight. "So you're here again?"

"Naturally," replied Holley. "Being a good newspaper man, I'm not overlooking the first murder we've had round here in years." He handed a newspaper to the millionaire. "By the way, here's a Los Angeles morning paper. Our interview is on the front page."

Madden took it without much interest. Over his shoulder Bob Eden caught a glimpse of the headlines:

ERA OF PROSPERITY DUE, SAYS FAMED MAGNATE

P.J. MADDEN, INTERVIEWED ON DESERT RANCH, PREDICTS BUSINESS BOOM

Madden glanced idly through the article. When he had finished he said: "In the New York papers, I suppose?"

"Of course," Holley answered. "All over the country this morning. You and I are famous, Mr Madden. But what's this about poor old Louie?"

"Don't ask me," frowned Madden. "Some fool bumped him off. Your friend Eden can tell you more than I can." He got up and strode from the room.

Eden and Holley stared at each other for a moment, then went together into the yard.

"Pretty raw stuff," remarked Holley. "It makes me hot. Louie was a kindly old soul. Killed in the car, I understand."

Eden related what had happened. They moved farther away from the house.

"Well, who do you think?" Holley inquired.

"I think Thorn," Eden answered. "However, Charlie says Louie's passing was just a minor incident, and it will be better all round if his murderer isn't found just at present. Of course he's right."

"Of course he is. And there isn't much danger they'll catch the guilty man, at that. The constable is a helpless old fellow."

"How about this Captain Bliss?"

"Oh, he's a big, noisy bluff with a fatal facility for getting the wrong man. The sheriff's a regular fellow, with brains, but he may not come round. Let's stroll out and look over the ground where you left the car last night. I've got something to slip you, a telegram – from your father, I imagine."

As they went through the gate the telegram changed hands. Holding it so it could not be seen from the house, Bob Eden read it through.

"Well, Dad says he's going to put up the bluff to Madden that he's sending Draycott with the pearls tonight."

"Draycott?" asked Holley.

"He's a private detective Dad uses in San Francisco. As good a name as any, I suppose. When Draycott fails to arrive, Dad's going to be very much upset." The boy considered for a moment. "I guess it's about the best he can do – but I hate all this deception. And I certainly don't like the job of keeping Madden cool. However, something may happen before then."

They examined the ground where Bob Eden had halted the car while he opened the gate the night before. The tracks of many cars passing in the road were evident – but no sign of any footsteps. "Even my footsteps are gone," remarked Eden. "Do you suppose it was the wind drifting the sand—"

Holley shrugged. "No," he said. "It was not. Somebody has been out here with a broom, my boy, and obliterated every trace of footsteps about that car."

Eden nodded. "You're right. Somebody – but who? Our old friend Thorn, of course."

They stepped aside as a car swung by them and entered Madden's yard.

"There's Bliss now, with the constable," Holley remarked. "Well, they get no help from us, eh?"

"Not a bit," replied Eden. "Encourage them off the ranch at earliest possible moment. That's Charlie's suggestion."

They returned to the yard and waited. Inside the living-room they heard Thorn and Madden talking with the two officers. After a time Bliss came out, followed by the millionaire and Constable Brackett. He greeted Holley as an old friend, and the editor introduced Bob Eden.

"Oh, yes, Mr Eden," said the captain. "Want to talk to you. What's your version of this funny business?"

Bob Eden looked at him with distaste. He was a big, flat-footed policeman of the usual type, and no great intelligence shone in his eyes. The boy gave him a carefully edited story of the night before.

"Humph," said Bliss. "Sounds queer to me."

"Yes?" smiled Eden. "To me too. But it happens to be the truth."

"Well, I'll have a look at the ground out there," remarked Bliss.

"You'll find nothing," said Holley. "Except the footprints of this young man and myself. We've just been taking a squint round."

"Oh, you have, have you?" replied Bliss grimly. He strode through the gate, the constable tagging after him. After a perfunctory examination the two returned.

"This is sure some puzzle," said Constable Brackett.

"Is that so?" Bliss sneered. "Well, get on to yourself. How about this Chink, Ah Kim? Had a good job here, didn't he? Louie Wong comes back. What does that mean? Ah Kim loses his job."

"Nonsense," protested Madden.

"Think so, do you?" remarked Bliss. "Well, I don't. I tell you I know these Chinks. They think nothing of sticking knives in each other. Nothing at all." Ah Kim emerged from round the side of the house. "Hey, you," cried Captain Bliss. Bob Eden began to worry.

Ah Kim came up. "You wantum me, boss?"

"You bet I want you. Going to lock you up."

"Why foah, boss?"

"For knifing Louie Wong. You can't get away with that stuff round here."

The Chinese regarded this crude practitioner of his own arts with a lifeless eye. "You clazy, boss," he said.

"Is that so?" Bliss's face hardened. "I'll show you just how crazy I am. Better tell me the whole story now. It'll go a lot easier with you if you do."

"What stoahy, boss?"

"How you sneaked out and put a knife in Louie last night."

"Maybe you catch 'um knife, hey, boss?" asked Ah Kim maliciously.

"Never mind about that!"

"Poah old Ah Kim's fingah plints on knife, hey, boss?"

"Oh, shut up," said Bliss.

"Maybe you takee look-see, find velvet-slippah plints in sand, hey, boss?" Bliss glared at him in silence. "What I tell you – you clazy cop, hey, boss?"

Holley and Eden looked at each other with keen enjoyment. Madden broke in: "Oh, come now, captain, you haven't got a thing against him, and you know it. You take my cook away from me without any evidence, and I'll make you sweat for it."

"Well – I —" Bliss hesitated. "I know he did it, and I'll prove it later." His eyes lighted. "How'd you get into this country?" he demanded.

"'Melican citizen, boss. Boahn San Flancisco. Foahty-flive yeah old now."

"Born here, eh? Is that so? Then you've got your chock-gee, I suppose. Let me see it."

Bob Eden's heart sank to his boots. Though many Chinese were without chock-gees, he knew that the lack of one would be sufficient excuse for this stupid policeman to arrest Chan at once. Another moment, and they'd all be done for....

"Come on," bellowed Bliss.

"What you say, boss?" parried Ah Kim.

"You know what I said. Your chock-gee – certificate – hand it over, or by heaven I'll lock you up so quick—"

"Oh, boss – ce'tiflicate – allight, boss." And before Eden's startled gaze the Chinese took from his blouse a worn slip of paper about the size of a banknote, and handed it to Bliss.

The captain read it sourly and handed it back. "All right – but I ain't through with you yet," he said.

"Thanks, boss," returned Ah Kim, brightening. "You plenty clazy, boss. Thasaw? Goo'bye." And he shuffled away.

"I told you it looked terrible mysterious to me," commented the constable.

"Oh, for Pete's sake, shut up," cried Bliss. "Mr Madden, I'll have to admit I'm stumped for the time being. But that condition don't last long with me. I'll get to the bottom of this yet. You'll see me again."

"Run out any time," Madden invited, with deep insincerity. "If I happen on anything, I'll call Constable Brackett."

Bliss and the constable got into their car and rode away. Madden returned to the house.

"Oh, excellent Chan," said Will Holley softly. "Where in Sam Hill did he get that chock-gee?"

"It looked as though we were done for," Eden admitted. "But good old Charlie thinks of everything."

Holley climbed into his car. "Well, I guess Madden isn't going to invite me to lunch. I'll go along. You know, I'm keener than ever to get the answer to this puzzle. Louie was my friend. It's a rotten shame."

"I don't know where we're going, but we're on our way," Eden answered. "I'd feel pretty helpless if I didn't have Charlie with me."

"Oh, you've got a few brains too," Holley assured him.

"You're clazy, boss," Eden laughed, as the editor drove away.

Returning to his room, he found Ah Kim calmly making the bed.

"Charlie, you're a peach," said the boy, closing the door. "I thought we were sunk without warning. Whose chock-gee did you have, anyhow?"

"Ah Kim's chock-gee, to be sure," smiled Chan.

"Who's Ah Kim?"

"Ah Kim humble vegetable merchant who drive me amidst other garden truck from Barstow to Eldorado. I make simple arrangement to rent chock-gee short while.

"Happy to note long wear in pockets make photograph look like image of anybody. Came to me in bright flash Madden might ask for identification certificate before engaging me for honorable tasks. Madden did not do so, but thing fit in plenty neat all the same."

"It certainly did," Eden agreed. "You're a brick to do all this for the Jordans – and for Dad. I hope they pay you handsomely."

Chan shook his head. "What you say in car riding to ferry? Postman on holiday itches to try long stretch of road. All this sincere pleasure for me. When I untie knots and find answer, that will be fine reward." He bowed and departed.

Some hours later, while they waited for lunch, Bob Eden and Madden sat talking in the big living-room. The millionaire was reiterating his desire to return East at the earliest possible moment. He was sitting facing the door. Suddenly on his big red face appeared a look of displeasure so intense it startled the boy. Turning about, Eden saw standing in the doorway the slight figure of a man, a stooped, studious-looking man who carried a suitcase in one hand. The little naturalist of the Oasis Café.

"Mr Madden?" inquired the newcomer.

"I'm Madden," said the millionaire. "What is it?"

"Ah, yes." The stranger came into the room, and set down his bag. "My name, sir, is Gamble, Thaddeus Gamble, and I am keenly interested in certain fauna surrounding your desert home. I have here a letter from an old friend of yours, the president of a college that has received many benefactions at your hands. If you will be so kind as to look it over—"

He offered the letter, and Madden took it, glaring at him in a most unfriendly manner. When the millionaire had read the brief epistle he tore it into bits and, rising, tossed them into the fireplace.

"You want to stop here a few days?" he said.

"It would be most convenient if I could," answered Gamble. "Of course, I should like to pay for my accommodation—"

Madden waved his hand. Ah Kim came in, headed for the luncheon-table. "Another place, Ah Kim," ordered Madden. "And show Mr Gamble to the room in the left wing – the one next to Mr Eden's."

"Very kind of you, I'm sure," remarked Gamble suavely. "I shall try to make as little trouble as may be. Luncheon impends, I take it. Not unwelcome, either. This – er – this desert air, sir – er – I'll return in a moment."

He followed Ah Kim out. Madden glared after him, his face purple. Bob Eden realized that a new puzzle had arrived.

"The devil with him," cried Madden. "But I had to be polite. That letter." He shrugged. "Gad, I hope I get out of here soon."

Bob Eden continued to wonder. Who was Mr Gamble? What did he want at Madden's ranch?

XI

THORN GOES ON A MISSION

Whatever Mr Gamble's mission at the ranch, Bob Eden reflected during lunch, it was obviously a peaceful one. Seldom had he encountered a milder-mannered little chap. All through the meal the newcomer talked volubly and well, with the gentle, cultivated accent of a scholar. Madden was sour and unresponsive; evidently he still resented the intrusion of this stranger. Thorn as usual sat silent and aloof, a depressing figure in the black suit he had today donned to replace the one torn so mysteriously the night before. It fell to Bob Eden to come to Mr Gamble's aid and keep the conversation going.

The luncheon over, Gamble rose and went to the door. For a moment he stood staring out across the blazing sand in the direction of the cool, white tops of the mountains, far away.

"Magnificent," he commented. "I wonder, Mr Madden, if you realize the true grandeur of this setting for your ranch-house? The desert, the broad, lonely desert, that has from time immemorial cast its weird spell on the souls of men. Some find it bleak and disquieting, but as for myself—"

"Be here long?" cut in Madden.

"Ah, that depends. I sincerely hope so. I want to see this country after the spring rains – the verbena and the primroses in bloom. The thought enchants me. What says the prophet

Isaiah? 'And the desert shall rejoice, and blossom as the rose. And the parched ground shall become a pool, and the thirsty land springs of water.' You know Isaiah, Mr Madden?"

"No, I don't. I know too many people now," responded Madden grimly.

"I believe you said you were interested in the fauna round here, professor?" Bob Eden remarked.

Gamble looked at him quickly. "You give me my title," he said. "You are an observant young man. Yes, there are certain researches I intend to pursue – the tail of the kangaroo-rat, which attains here a phenomenal length. The maxillary arch in the short-nosed pocket-mouse, I understand, has also reached in this neighborhood an eccentric development."

The telephone rang, and Madden himself answered it. Listening carefully, Bob Eden heard: "Telegram for Mr Madden." At this point the millionaire pressed the receiver close to his ear, and the rest of the message was an indistinct blur.

Eden was sorry for that, for he perceived that as Madden listened an expression of keen distress came over his face. When finally he put the receiver slowly back on to its hook he sat for a long time looking straight before him, obviously very much perplexed.

"What do you grow here in this sandy soil, Mr Madden?" Professor Gamble inquired.

"Er – er—" Madden came gradually back to the scene. "What do I grow? A lot of things. You'd be surprised, and so would Isaiah." Gamble was smiling at him in a kindly way, and the millionaire warmed up a little. "Come out, since you're interested, and I'll show you round."

"Very good of you, sir," replied Gamble, and meekly followed into the *patio*. Thorn rose and joined them. Quickly Eden went to the telephone and got Will Holley on the wire.

"Look here," he said in a low voice, "Madden has just taken a telegram over the 'phone, and it seemed to worry him considerably. I couldn't make out what it was, but I'd like to know at once. Do you stand well enough with the operator to find out – without rousing suspicion, of course?"

"Sure," Holley replied. "That kid will tell me anything. Are you alone there? Can I call you back in a few minutes?"

"I'm alone just now," Eden responded. "If I shouldn't be when you call back, I'll pretend you want Madden and turn you over to him. You can fake something to say. But if you hurry that may not be necessary. Speed, brother, speed!"

As he turned away Ah Kim came in to gather up the luncheon things.

"Well, Charlie," Eden remarked. "Another guest at our little hotel, eh?"

Chan shrugged. "Such news comes plenty quick to cookhouse," he said.

Eden smiled. "You're the one who wanted to watch and wait," he reminded the detective. "If you're threatened with housemaid's knee don't blame me."

"This Gamble," mused Chan. "Seems harmless like May morning, I think."

"Oh, very. A Bible student. And it strikes me there's a fair opening for a good Bible student round here."

"Undangerous and mild," continued Chan. "Yet hidden in his scant luggage is one pretty new pistol completely loaded."

"Going to shoot the tails off the rats most likely," Eden smiled. "Now, don't get suspicious of him, Charlie. He's probably just a tenderfoot who believes the movies, and so came to this wild country armed to defend himself. By the way, Madden just got a telegram over the 'phone, and it was, judging by appearances, another bit of unwelcome news for our dear old friend. Holley's looking it up for me. If the telephone rings go to the *patio*, and be ready to tip me off in case anyone is coming."

Silently Ah Kim resumed his work at the table. In a few moments, loud and clear, came the ring of Holley on the wire.

Running to the telephone, Eden put his hand over the bell, muffling it. Chan stepped into the *patio*.

"Hello, Holley," said the boy softly. "Yes. Yes. O.K. Shoot. Um.... Say, that's interesting, isn't it? Coming tonight, eh? Thanks, old man."

He hung up, and Charlie returned. "A bit of news," said Eden, rising. "That telegram was from Miss Evelyn Madden. Got tired of waiting in Denver, I guess. The message was sent from Barstow. The lady arrives tonight at Eldorado on the six-forty. Looks as though I may have to give up my room and check out."

"Miss Evelyn Madden?" repeated Chan.

"That's right – you don't know, do you? She's Madden's only child. A proud beauty too – I met her in San Francisco. Well, it's no wonder Madden was perplexed, is it?"

"Certainly not," agreed Chan. "Murderous ranch like this no place for refined young woman."

Eden sighed. "Just one more complication," he said. "Things move, but we don't seem to get anywhere."

"Once more," returned Chan, "I call to your attention that much unused virtue, patience. Aspect will be brighter here now. A woman's touch—"

"This woman's touch means frost-bite," smiled Eden. "Charlie, I'll bet you a million – not even the desert will thaw out Evelyn Madden."

Chan departed to his duties in the cookhouse. Madden and Thorn drifted in after a time; Gamble, it appeared, had retired to his room. The long, hot afternoon dragged by, baking hours of deathly calm, during which the desert lived up to its reputation. Madden disappeared, and presently his "noisome" snores filled the air. A good idea, Bob Eden decided.

In a recumbent position on his bed he found that time passed more swiftly. In fact, he didn't know it was passing.

Toward evening he awoke, hot and muddled of mind, but a cold shower made him feel human again.

At six o'clock he crossed the *patio* to the living-room. In the yard before the barn he saw Madden's big car standing ready for action, and remembered. The millionaire was no doubt about to meet his daughter in town, and the haughty Evelyn was not to be affronted with the unpretentious runabout.

But when he reached the living-room Eden saw that it was evidently Thorn who had been selected for the trip to Eldorado. The secretary stood there in his gloomy clothes, a black slouch hat accentuating the paleness of his face. As Eden entered what was obviously a serious conversation between Thorn and the millionaire came to a sudden halt.

"Ah, good evening," said Eden. "Not leaving us, Mr Thorn?"

"Business in town," returned Thorn. "Well, chief, I'll go along."

Again the telephone rang. Madden leaped to it. For a moment he listened, and history repeated itself on his face. "Bad news all the time," Eden thought.

Madden put his great hand over the mouthpiece, and spoke to his secretary. "It's that old bore down the road, Doctor Whitcomb," he announced, and Eden felt a flash of hot resentment at this characterization. "She wants to see me this evening – says she has something very important to tell me."

"Say you're busy," suggested Thorn.

"I'm sorry, doctor," Madden began over the 'phone, "but I am very much occupied—"

He stopped, evidently interrupted by a flood of conversation. Again he put his hand over the transmitter. "She insists, confound it," he complained.

"Well, you'll have to see her, then," said Thorn.

"All right, doctor," Madden capitulated. "Come about eight."

Thorn went out, and the big car roared off toward the road and Evelyn Madden's train. Mr Gamble entered, refreshed and ready with a few apt quotations. Eden amused himself with the wireless apparatus.

At the usual hour, much to Eden's surprise, they dined. Thorn's chair was empty, and there was, oddly enough, no place for Evelyn; nor did the millionaire make any arrangements regarding a room for his daughter. Strange, Eden thought.

After dinner Madden led them to the *patio*. Again he had arranged for a fire out there, and the blaze glowed red on the stone floor, on the adobe walls of the house, and on the nearby perch of Tony, now empty and forlorn.

"This is living," remarked Gamble, when they had sat down and he had lighted one of Madden's cigars. "The poor fools cooped up in cities – they don't know what they're missing. I could stay here for ever."

His final sentence made no hit with the host, and silence fell. At a little past eight they heard the sound of a car entering the yard. Thorn and the girl, perhaps – but evidently Madden didn't think so, for he said:

"That's the doctor. Ah Kim!" The servant appeared. "Show the lady out here."

"Well, she doesn't want to see me," Gamble said, getting up. "I'll go in and find a book."

Madden looked at Bob Eden, but the boy remained where he was. "The doctor's a friend of mine," he explained.

"Is that so?" growled Madden.

"Yes – I met her yesterday morning. A wonderful woman."

Doctor Whitcomb appeared. "Well, Mr Madden?" She shook hands. "It's a great pleasure to have you with us again."

"Thanks," said Madden coolly. "You know Mr Eden, I believe?"

"Oh, hello!" smiled the woman. "Glad to see you. Not very pleased with you, however. You didn't drop in today."

"Rather busy," Eden replied. "Won't you sit down, please?"

He brought forward a chair; it seemed that Madden needed a hint or two on hospitality. The guest sank into it. Madden, his manner very haughty and aloof, sat down some distance away, and waited.

"Mr Madden," said Doctor Whitcomb, "I'm sorry if I seem to intrude – I know that you are here to rest, and that you don't welcome visitors. But this is not a social call. I came here about – about this terrible thing that has happened on your place."

For a moment Madden did not reply. "You – mean—" he said slowly.

"I mean the murder of poor Louie Wong," the woman answered.

"Oh." Was there relief in Madden's voice? "Yes – of course."

"Louie was my friend – he often came to see me. I was so sorry when I heard. And you – he served you faithfully, Mr Madden. Naturally you're doing everything possible to run down his murderer?"

"Everything," replied Madden carelessly.

"Whether what I have to tell has any connexion with the killing of Louie – that's for policemen to decide," went on the doctor. "You can hand my story on to them – if you will."

"Gladly," replied the millionaire. "What is your story, doctor?"

"On Saturday evening a man arrived at my place who said his name was McCallum, Henry McCallum," began Doctor Whitcomb, "and that he came from New York. He told me he suffered from bronchitis, though I must say I saw no symptoms of it. He took one of my cabins and settled down for a stay – so I thought."

"Yes," nodded Madden. "Go on."

"At dark Sunday night – a short time before the hour when poor Louie was killed – someone drove up in a big car before my place and blew the horn. One of my boys went out, and the stranger asked for McCallum. McCallum came, talked with the man in the car for a moment, then got in and rode off with him – in this direction. That was the last I've seen of

Mr McCallum. He left a suitcase filled with clothes in his cabin, but he has not returned."

"And you think he killed Louie?" asked Madden, with a note of polite incredulity in his voice.

"I don't think anything about it. How should I know? I simply regard it as a matter that should be called to the attention of the police. As you are much closer to the investigation than I am, I'm asking you to tell them about it. They can come down and examine McCallum's property if they wish."

"All right," said Madden, rising pointedly. "I'll tell them. Though if you're asking my opinion, I don't think—"

"Thank you," smiled the doctor. "I wasn't asking your opinion, Mr Madden." She too stood. "Our interview, I see, is ended. I'm sorry if I've intruded—"

"Why, you didn't intrude," protested Madden. "That's all right. Maybe your information is valuable. Who knows?"

"Very good of you to say so," returned the doctor, with gentle sarcasm. She glanced toward the parrot's perch "How's Tony? He, at least, must miss Louie a lot."

"Tony's dead," said Madden brusquely.

"What! Tony too!" The doctor was silent for a moment. "A rather memorable visit, this one of yours," she said slowly. "Please give my regards to your daughter. She is not with you?"

"No," returned Madden. "She is not with me." That was all.

"A great pity," Doctor Whitcomb replied. "I thought her a charming girl."

"Thank you," Madden said. "Just a moment. My boy will show you to your car."

"Don't trouble," put in Bob Eden. "I'll attend to that." He led the way through the bright living-room, past Mr Gamble deep in a huge book. In the yard the doctor turned to him.

"What a man!" she said. "As hard as granite. I don't believe the death of Louie means a thing to him."

"Very little, I'm afraid," Eden agreed.

"Well, I rely on you. If he doesn't repeat my story to the sheriff, you must."

The boy hesitated. "I'll tell you something – in confidence," he said. "Everything possible is being done to find the murderer of Louie. Not by Madden – but by – others."

The doctor sat silent for a moment in the dark car under the dark, star-spangled sky. "I think I understand," she said softly. "With all my heart, I wish you luck, my boy."

Eden took her hand. "If I shouldn't see you again, doctor – I want you to know. Just meeting you has been a privilege."

"I'll remember that," she answered. "Good night."

The boy watched her back the car through the open gate. When he returned to the living-room Madden and Gamble were together there. "Confounded old busybody," Madden said.

"Wait a minute," Eden said hotly. "That woman with just her two hands has done more good in the world than you with all your money. And don't you forget it."

"Does that give her a licence to butt into my affairs?" demanded Madden.

Further warm words were on the tip of the boy's tongue, but he restrained himself. However, he reflected that he was about fed-up with this arrogant, callous millionaire.

He looked toward the clock. A quarter to nine, and still no sign of Thorn and Evelyn Madden. Was the girl's train late? Hardly likely.

Though he did not feel particularly welcome in the room, he waited on. He would see this latest development through. At ten o'clock Mr Gamble rose and, commenting favourably on the desert air, went to his room.

At five minutes past ten the roar of the big car in the yard broke the intense stillness. Bob Eden sat erect, his eager eyes straying from one door to another. Presently the glass doors leading to the *patio* opened. Martin Thorn came in alone.

Without a word to his chief, the secretary threw down his hat and dropped wearily into a chair. The silence became oppressive.

"Got your business attended to, eh?" suggested Eden cheerfully.

"Yes," said Thorn – no more. Eden rose.

"Well, I guess I'll turn in," he said, and went to his room. As he entered he heard the splash of Mr Gamble in the bath that lay between his apartment and that occupied by the professor. His seclusion was ended. Have to be more careful in the future.

Shortly after his lights were on Ah Kim appeared at the door. Eden, finger on lips, indicated the bath. The Chinese nodded. They stepped to the far side of the bedroom and spoke in low tones.

"Well, where's little Evelyn?" asked the boy.

Chan shrugged. "More mystery," he whispered.

"Just what has our friend Thorn been doing for the past four hours?" Eden wondered.

"Enjoying moonlit ride on desert, I think," Chan returned. "When big car go out, I note speedometer. Twelve thousand eight hundred and forty miles. Four miles necessary to travel to town, and four to return with. But when big car arrives home, speedometer announces quietly twelve thousand eight hundred and seventy-nine miles."

"Charlie, you think of everything," Eden said admiringly.

"Strange place this Thorn has been," Charlie added. "Much red clay on ground." He exhibited a fragment of earth. "Scraped off on accelerator," he explained. "Maybe you have seen such place round here?"

"Nothing like it," Eden replied. "You don't suppose he's harmed the gal – but no, Madden seems to be in on it, and she's his darling."

"Just one more little problem rising up," said Chan.

Eden nodded. "Lord, I haven't met so many problems since I gave up algebra. And by the way, tomorrow's Tuesday. The pearls are coming, hurrah, hurrah. At least, old P.J. thinks they are. He's going to be hard to handle tomorrow."

A faint knock sounded on the door to the *patio*, and Chan had just time to get to the fireplace and busy himself there when it was opened and Madden, oddly noiseless for him, entered.

"Why, hello—" began Eden.

"Hush!" said Madden. He looked toward the bathroom. "Go easy, will you? Ah Kim, get out of here."

"Allight, boss," said Ah Kim, and went.

Madden stepped to the bathroom door and listened. He tried it gently; it opened at his touch. He went in, locked the door leading into the room occupied by Gamble, and returned, shutting the door behind him.

"Now," he began, "I want to see you. Keep your voice down. I've finally got hold of your father on the telephone, and he tells me a man named Draycott will arrive with the pearls at Barstow tomorrow noon."

Eden's heart sank. "Ah – er – that ought to bring him here tomorrow night—"

Madden leaned close, and spoke in a hoarse undertone. "Whatever happens," he said, "I don't want that fellow to come to the ranch."

Eden stared at him in amazement. "Well, Mr Madden, I'll be—"

"Hush! Leave my name out of it."

"But after all our preparation—"

"I tell you I've changed my mind. I don't want the pearls brought to the ranch at all. I want you to go to Barstow tomorrow, meet this Draycott, and order him to go on to Pasadena. I'm going down there on Wednesday. Tell him to meet me at the door of the Garfield National Bank in Pasadena at noon, sharp,

Wednesday. I'll take the pearls then – and I'll put them where they'll be safe."

Bob Eden smiled. "All right," he agreed. "You're the boss."

"Good," said Madden. "I'll have Ah Kim drive you into town in the morning, and you can catch the Barstow train. But remember – this is between you and me. Not a word to anybody. Not to Gamble – of course. Not even to Thorn."

"I get you," Eden answered.

"Fine! Then it's set. Good night."

Madden went softly out. For a long time Eden stared after him, more puzzled than ever.

"Well, anyhow," he said at last, "it means another day grace. For this relief, much thanks."

XII

THE TRAMCAR IN THE DESERT

A new day dawned, and over the stunted, bizarre shapes of that land of drought the sun resumed its merciless vigil. Bob Eden was early abroad; it was getting to be a habit with him. Before breakfast was served he had a full hour for reflection, and it could not be denied that he had much upon which to reflect. One by one he recalled the queer things that had happened since he came to the ranch. Foremost in his thoughts was the problem of Evelyn Madden. Where was that haughty lady now? No morning mists on the landscape here, but in his mind a constantly increasing fog. If only something definite would occur, something they could understand.

After breakfast he rose from the table and lighted a cigarette. He knew that Madden was eagerly waiting for him to speak.

"Mr Madden," he said, "I find that I must go to Barstow this morning on rather important business. It's an imposition, I know. But if Ah Kim could drive me to town in time for the ten-fifteen train—"

Thorn's green eyes widened with sudden interest. Madden looked at the boy with ill-concealed approval.

"Why, that's all right," he replied. "I'll be glad to arrange it for you. Ah Kim – you drive Mr Eden in town in half an hour. Savvy?"

"All time moah job," complained Ah Kim. "Gettum up sunlise, woik, woik till sun him dlop. You want 'um taxi-dliver why you no say so?"

"What's that?" cried Madden.

Ah Kim shrugged. "Allight, boss. I dlive 'um."

When, later on, Eden sat in the car beside the Chinese and the ranch was well behind them Chan regarded him questioningly.

"Now you produce big mystery," he said. "Barstow on business has somewhat unexpected sound to me."

Eden laughed. "Orders from the big chief," he replied. "I'm to go down there and meet Al Draycott – and the pearls."

For a moment Chan's free hand rested on his waist and the "undigestible" burden that still lay there.

"Madden changes fickle mind again?" he inquired.

"That's just what he's done." Eden related the purport of the millionaire's call on him the night before.

"What you know concerning that!" exclaimed Chan wonderingly.

"Well, I know this much," Eden answered. "It gives us one more day for the good old *hoo malimali*. Outside of that it's just another problem for us to puzzle over. By the way, I didn't tell you why Doctor Whitcomb came to see us last night."

"No necessity," Chan replied. "I am loafing idle inside door close by and hear it all."

"Oh, you were? Then you know it may have been Shaky Phil, and not Thorn, who killed Louie?"

"Shaky Phil – or maybe stranger in car who drive up and call him into the road. Must admit that stranger interests me very deep. Who was he? Was it maybe him who carried news of Louie's approach out on to dreary desert?"

"Well, if you're starting to ask me questions," replied Eden, "then the big mystery is over and we may as well wash up and go home. For I haven't got an answer in me." Eldorado lay before them, its roofs gleaming under the morning sun. "By the way, let's drop in and see Holley. The train isn't due yet – I suppose I'd better take it, somebody might be watching. In the interval Holley may have news."

The editor was busy at his desk. "Hello, you're up and around pretty early this morning," he said. He pushed aside his typewriter. "Just dashing off poor old Louie's obit. What's new out at Mystery Ranch?"

Bob Eden told him of Doctor Whitcomb's call, also of Madden's latest switch regarding the pearls, and his own imminent wild-goose chase to Barstow.

Holley smiled, "Cheer up – a little travel will broaden you," he remarked. "What did you think of Miss Evelyn? But then I believe you had met her before."

"Think of Miss Evelyn? What do you mean?" asked Eden, surprised.

"Why, she came last night, didn't she?"

"Not so anybody could notice it. No sign of her at the ranch."

Holley rose and walked up and down for a moment. "That's odd. That's very odd. She certainly arrived on the six-forty train."

"You're sure of that?" Eden asked.

"Of course I am. I saw her." Holley sat down again. "I wasn't very much occupied last night – it was one of my free nights – I have three hundred and sixty-five of them every year. So I strolled over to the station and met the six-forty. Thorn was there too. A tall, handsome girl got off the train, and I heard Thorn address her as Miss Evelyn. 'How's Dad?' she asked. 'Get in,' said Thorn, 'and I'll tell you about him. He wasn't able to come and meet you himself.' The girl entered the car, and they drove away. Naturally. I thought she was brightening your life long before this."

Eden shook his head. "Funny business," he commented. "Thorn got back to the ranch a little after ten, and when he came he was alone. Charlie here discovered, with his usual acumen, that the car had travelled some thirty-nine miles."

"Also clinging to accelerator, as though scraped off from shoe of Thorn, small fragment of red clay," added Chan. "You are accustomed round here, Mr Holley. Maybe you can mention home of red clay."

"Not offhand," replied Holley. "There are several places— But say, this thing gets deeper and deeper. Oh – I was forgetting – there's a letter here for you, Eden."

He handed over a neat missive addressed in an old-fashioned hand. Eden inspected it with interest. It was from Madame Jordan, a rather touching appeal not to let the deal for the pearls fall through. He went back and began to read it aloud. Mrs Jordan could not understand. Madden was there, he had bought the pearls – why the delay? The loss of that money would be serious for her.

When he had finished Eden looked accusingly at Chan, then tore the letter to bits and threw them into a wastepaper-basket. "I'm about through," he said. "That woman is one of the dearest old souls that ever lived, and it strikes me we're treating her shamefully. After all, what's happening out at Madden's ranch is none of our business. Our duty to Madame Jordan—"

"Pardon me," broke in Chan, "but coming to that, I have sense of duty most acute myself. Loyalty blooms in my heart for ever—"

"Well, and what do you think we ought to do?" demanded Eden.

"Watch and wait."

"But, good Lord – we've done that. I was thinking about it this morning. One inexplicable event after another, and never anything definite, anything we can get our teeth into. Such a state of affairs may go on for ever. I tell you, I'm fed-up."

"Patience," said Chan, "are a very lovely virtue. Through long centuries Chinese cultivate patience like kind gardener tending flowers. White men leap about similar to bug in bottle. Which are better method, I inquire?"

"But listen, Charlie. All this stuff we've discovered out at the ranch – that's for the police."

"For stupid Captain Bliss, maybe. He with the feet of large extensiveness."

"I can't help the size of his feet. What's that got to do with it? No, sir – I can't see why we don't give Madden the pearls, get his receipt, and then send for the sheriff and tell him the whole story. After that, he can worry about who was killed at Madden's ranch."

"He would solve the problem," scoffed Chan. "Great mind, no doubt, like Captain Bliss. Your thought has, from me, nothing but hot opposition."

"Well, but I'm considering Madame Jordan. I've got her interests at heart."

Chan patted him on the back. "Who can question that? You fine young fellow, loyal and kind. But listen now to older heads. Mr Holley, you have inclination to intrude your car?"

"I certainly have," smiled Holley. "I'm all on the side of Chan, Eden. It would be a pity to drop this thing now. The sheriff's a good sort, but all this would be too deep for him. No, wait just a little while—"

"All right," sighed Eden. "I'll wait. Provided you tell me one thing. What are we waiting for?"

"Madden goes to Pasadena tomorrow," Chan suggested. "No doubt Thorn will accompany, and we quench this Gamble somehow. Great time for us. All our search at ranch up to now hasty and breathless, like man pursuing trolley-car. Tomorrow we dig deep."

"You can do it," replied Eden. "I'm not eager to dig for the sort of prize you want." He paused. "At that, I must admit I'm pretty curious myself. Charlie, you're an old friend of the Jordans, and you can take the responsibility for this delay."

"Right here on shoulders," Chan agreed, "responsibility reclines. Same way necklace reposes on stomach. Seem to coddle there now, those Phillimore pearls, happy and content. Humbly suggest you take this aimless journey to Barstow."

Eden looked at his watch. "I suppose I might as well. Bit of city life never did anybody any harm. But I warn you that when I come back I want a little light. If any more dark, mysterious things happen at that ranch I certainly will run right out into the middle of the desert and scream."

Taking the train proved an excellent plan, for on the station platform he met Paula Wendell, who evidently had the same idea. She was trim and charming in riding habit, and her eyes sparkled with life.

"Hello," she said. "Where are you bound?"

"Going to Barstow, on business," Eden explained.

"Is it important?"

"Naturally. Wouldn't squander my vast talents on any other kind."

A train wandered in, and they found a seat together in one of its two cars.

"Sorry to hear you're needed in Barstow," remarked the girl. "I'm getting off a few stations down. Going to rent a horse and take a long ride up into Lonely Canyon. It wouldn't have been so lonely if you could have come along."

Eden smiled happily. Certainly one had few opportunities to look into eyes like hers. "What station do we get off at?" he inquired.

"We? I thought you said—"

"The truth isn't in me these days. Barstow doesn't need my presence any more than you need a beauty doctor. Lonely Canyon, after today, will have to change its name."

"Good," she answered. "We get off at Seven Palms. The old rancher who rents me a horse will find one for you, I'm sure."

"I'm not precisely dressed for the *rôle*," admitted Eden. "But I trust it will be all the same to the horse."

The horse didn't appear to mind. His rather dejected manner suggested that he had expected something like this. They left the tiny settlement known as Seven Palms and cantered off across the desert.

"For to admire an' for to see, for to be'old this world so wide," said Eden. "Never realized how very wide it was until I came down here."

"Beginning to like the desert?" the girl inquired.

"Well, there's something about it," he admitted. "It grows on you, that's a fact. I don't know that I could put the feeling into words."

"I'm sure I can't," she answered. "Oh, I envy you, coming here for the first time. If only I could look at this country again with a fresh, disinterested eye. But it's just location to me. I see all about me the cowboys, the cavalcades, the *caballeros* of Hollywood. Tragedies and feats of daring, rescues and escapes. I tell you, these dunes and canyons have seen more movies than Will Hays."

"Hunting locations today?" Eden asked.

"Always hunting," she sighed. "They've just sent me a new script – as new as those mountains over there. All about the rough cowpuncher and the millionaire's dainty daughter from the East – you know."

"I certainly do. Girl's fed up on those Society orgies, isn't she?"

"Who wouldn't be? However, the orgies are given in full, with the swimming-pool working overtime, as always. But that part doesn't concern me. It's after she comes out here, sort of hungering to meet a real man, that I must start worrying. Need I add, she meets him? Her horse runs away over the desert, and tosses her off amid the sage-brush. In the nick of time the cowpuncher finds her. Despite their different stations, love blossoms here in the wastelands. Sometimes I'm almost glad that mine is beginning to be an obsolete profession."

"Is it? How come?"

"Oh, the movies move. A few years back the location-finder was a rather important person. Today most of this country has been explored and charted, and every studio is equipped with big albums full of pictures. So every time a new efficiency expert comes along – which is about once a week – and starts lopping off heads, it's the people in my line who are the first to go. In a little while we'll be as extinct as the dodo."

"You may be extinct," Eden answered. "But there the similarity between you and the dodo will stop abruptly."

The girl halted her horse. "Just a minute. I want to take a few pictures here. It looks to me like a bit of desert we haven't used yet. Just the sort of thing to thrill the shop-girls and the bookkeepers back there where the East hangs out." When she had swung again into the saddle she added: "It isn't strange they love it, those tired people in the cities. Each one thinks, 'Oh, if only I could go there.'"

"Yes, and if they got here once they'd die of loneliness the first night," Bob Eden said. "Just pass out in agony moaning for the subway and the comics in the evening paper."

"I know they would," the girl replied. "But fortunately they'll never come."

They rode on, and the girl began to point out the various unfriendly-looking plants of the desert, naming them one by one. Arrow-weed, bitter-brush, mesquite, desert plantain, catclaw, thistle-sage.

"That's a cholla," she announced. "Another variety of cactus. There are seventeen thousand in all."

"All right," Eden replied. "I'll take your word for it. You needn't name them." His head was beginning to ache with all this learning.

Presently sumac and Canterbury bell proclaimed their nearness to the canyon, and they cantered out of the desert heat into the cathedral-like coolness of the hills. In and out over almost hidden trails the horses went. Wild plum glowed on the slopes, and far below under native palms a narrow stream tinkled invitingly.

Life seemed very simple and pleasant there in Lonely Canyon, and Bob Eden felt suddenly close indeed to this lively girl with the eager eyes. All a lie that there were crowded cities. The world was new, unsullied and unspoiled, and they were alone in it.

They descended by way of a rather treacherous path, and in the shelter of the palms that fringed the tiny stream dismounted for a lunch which Paula Wendell claimed to have concealed in her knapsack.

"Wonderfully restful here," Bob Eden said.

"But you said the other day you weren't tired," the girl reminded him.

"Well, I'm not. But somehow I like this, anyhow. However, I guess it isn't all a matter of geography. It's not so much the place you're in – it's who you're with. After which highly original remark, I hasten to add that I really can't eat a thing."

"You were right," she laughed. "The truth isn't in you. I know what you're thinking – I didn't bring enough for two. But these Oasis sandwiches are meant for ranchers, and one is my limit. There are four of them – I must have had a premonition. We'll divide the milk equally."

"But look here – it's your lunch. I should have thought to get something at Seven Palms."

"There's a roast-beef sandwich. Try that, and maybe you won't feel so talkative."

"Well, I – um – gumph—"

"What did I tell you? Oh, the Oasis aims to fill. Milk?"

"Ashamed of myself," mumbled Eden. But he was easily persuaded.

"You haven't eaten a thing," he said finally.

"Oh, yes, I have. More than I usually do. I'm one of those dainty eaters."

"Good news for Wilbur," replied Eden. "The upkeep won't be high. Though if he has any sense he'll know that, whatever the upkeep on a girl like you, it will be worth it."

"I sent him your love," said the girl.

"Is that so? Well, I'm sorry you did, in a way. I'm no hypocrite, and, try as I may, I can't discover any lurking fondness for Wilbur. Oddly enough, the boy begins to annoy me."

"But you said—"

"I know. But isn't it just possible that I've overrated this freedom stuff? I'm young, and the young are often mistaken. Stop me if you've heard this one, but the more I see of you—"

"Stop. I've heard it."

"I'll bet you have. Many times."

"And my suggestion is that we get back to business. If we don't that horse of yours is going to eat too much Bermuda grass."

Through the long afternoon, amid the hot yellow dunes, the wind-blown foothills of that sandy waste, they rode back to Seven Palms by a roundabout route. The sun was sinking, the rose-and-gold wonder of the skies reflected on snow and glistening sand, when finally they headed for the village.

"If only I could find a novel setting for the final love scene," sighed the girl.

"Whose final love scene?"

"The cowpuncher's and the poor little rich girl's. So many times they've just wandered off into the sunset, hand in hand. Really need a little more kick in it than that."

Eden heard a clank as of a horse's hoofs on steel. His mount stumbled, and he reined it in sharply.

"What in Sam Hill's that?" he asked.

"Oh – that! It's one of the half-buried rails of the old branch road – a memento of a dream that never came true. Years ago they started to build a town over there under those cottonwoods, and the railroad laid down fifteen miles of track from the main line. A busy metropolis of the desert – that's what they meant it to be – and there's just one little old ruined house standing today. But that was the time of great expectations. They brought out crowds of people, and sold six hundred lots one hectic afternoon."

"And the railroad?"

"Ran just one train – and stopped. All they had was an engine and two old street-cars brought down from San Francisco. One of the cars has been demolished and the timber carried away, but the wreck of the other is still standing not far from here."

Presently they mounted a ridge, and Bob Eden cried: "What do you know about that?"

There before them on the lonely desert, partly buried in the drifting sand, stood the remnant of a tramcar. It was tilted rakishly to one side, its windows were yellow with dust, but on the front, faintly decipherable still, was the legend "Market Street."

At that familiar sight, Bob Eden felt a keen pang of nostalgia. He reined in his horse and sat staring at this symbol of the desert's triumph over the proud schemes of man. Man had thought he could conquer, he had come with his engines and his dreams, and now an old battered tramcar stood alone as a warning and a threat.

"There's your setting," he said. "They drive out together and sit there on the steps, your lovers. What a background – a car that once trundled from Twin Peaks to the Ferry, standing lonely and forlorn amid the cactus-plants!"

"Fine," the girl answered. "I'm going to hire you to help me after this."

They rode close to the car and dismounted. The girl unlimbered her camera and held it steady. "Don't you want me in the picture?" Eden asked. "Just as a sample lover, you know."

"No samples needed," she laughed. The camera clicked. As it did so the two young people stood rooted to the desert in amazement. An old man had stepped suddenly from the interior of the car – a bent old man with a coal-black beard.

Eden's eyes sought those of the girl. "Last Wednesday night at Madden's?" he inquired in a low voice.

She nodded. "The old prospector," she replied.

The black-bearded one did not speak, but stood with a startled air on the front platform of that lost car, under the legend "Market Street."

XIII

WHAT MR CHERRY SAW

Bob Eden stepped forward. "Good evening," he said. "I hope we haven't disturbed you."

Moving with some difficulty, the old man descended from the platform to the sandy floor of the desert. "How do?" he said gravely, shaking hands. He also shook hands with Paula Wendell. "How do, miss? No, you didn't disturb me none. Just takin' my forty winks – I ain't so spry as I used to be."

"We happened to be passing—" Eden began.

"Ain't many pass this way," returned the old man. "Cherry's my name – William I. Cherry. Make yourselves at home. Parlour chairs is kind o' scarce, miss."

"Of course," said the girl.

"We'll stop a minute, if we may," suggested Eden.

"It's comin' on supper-time," the old man replied hospitably. "How about grub? There's a can o' beans, an' a mite o' bacon—"

"Couldn't think of it," Eden told him. "You're mighty kind, but we'll be back in Seven Palms shortly." Paula Wendell sat down on the car-steps, and Eden took a seat on the warm sand. The old man went to the rear of the tram and returned with an empty soap-box. After an unsuccessful attempt to persuade Eden to accept it as a chair he put it to that use himself.

"Pretty nice home you've picked out for yourself," Eden remarked.

"Home?" The old man surveyed the tramcar critically. "Home, boy? I ain't had no home these thirty years. Temporary quarters, you might say."

"Been here long?" asked Eden.

"Three – four days. Rheumatism's been actin' up. But I'm movin' on tomorrey."

"Moving on? Where?"

"Why – over yonder."

"Just where is that?" Eden smiled.

"Where it's allus been. Over yonder. Somewhere else."

"Just looking, eh?"

"Jest lookin'. You've hit it. Goin' on over yonder an' jest lookin'." His tired old eyes were on the mountaintops.

"What do you expect to find?" inquired Paula Wendell.

"Struck a vein o' copper once, miss," Mr Cherry said. "But they got her away from me. Howsomever, I'm lookin' still."

"Been on the desert a long time?" Eden asked.

"Twenty – twenty-five years. One desert or another."

"And before that?"

"Prospected in West Australia from Hannans to Hall's Creek – through the Territory into Queensland. Drove cattle from the gulf country into New South Wales. Then I worked in the stokehole on ocean liners."

"Born in Australia, eh?" Eden suggested.

"Who – me?" Mr Cherry shook his head. "Born in South Africa – English descent. Been all up and down the Congo an' Zambesi – all through British Central Africa."

"How in the world did you get to Australia?" Eden wondered.

"Oh, I don't know, boy. I was filibusterin' down along the South American continent for a while, an' then I drifted into a Mexican campaign. Seems like there was somethin' I wanted in Australia – anyhow, I got there. Jest the way I got here. It was over yonder, an' I went."

Eden shook his head. "Ye gods, I'll bet you've seen a lot!"

"I guess I have, boy. Doctor over in Redlands was tellin' me t'other day – you need spectacles, he says. 'Hell, doc,' I says, 'what fer? I've seen everything,' I says, and I come away."

Silence fell. Bob Eden wasn't exactly sure how to go about this business; he wished he had Chan at his elbow. But his duty was clear.

"You – er – you've been here for three or four days, you say?"

"'Bout that, I reckon."

"Do you happen to recall where you were last Wednesday night?"

The old man's eyes were keen enough as he glanced sharply at the boy. "What if I do?"

"I was only going to say that if you don't I can refresh your memory. You were at Madden's ranch-house, over near Eldorado."

Slowly Mr Cherry removed his slouch hat. With gnarled, bent fingers he extracted a toothpick from the band. He stuck it defiantly in his mouth. "Maybe I was. What then?"

"Well – I'd like to have a little talk with you about that night."

Cherry surveyed him closely. "You're a new one on me," he said. "An' I thought I knew every sheriff an' deputy west o' the Rockies."

"Then you'll admit something happened at Madden's that might interest a sheriff?" returned Eden quickly.

"I ain't admittin' nothin'," answered the old prospector.

"You have information regarding last Wednesday night at Madden's," Eden persisted. "Vital information. I must have it."

"Nothin' to say," replied Cherry stubbornly.

Eden took another tack. "Just what was your business at Madden's ranch?"

Mr Cherry rolled the aged toothpick in his mouth. "No business at all. I jest dropped in. Been wanderin' the desert a long time, like I said, an' now an' agin I drifted in at Madden's.

Me an' the old caretaker, Louie Wong, was friends. When I'd come along he'd stake me to a bit o' grub an' a bed in the barn. Sort o' company fer him, I was. He was lonesome-like at the ranch – only a Chink, but lonesome-like, same as if he'd been white."

"A kindly old soul, Louie," suggested Eden.

"One o' the best, boy, an' that's no lie."

Eden spoke slowly. "Louie Wong has been murdered," he said.

"What's that?"

"Stabbed in the side last Sunday night near the ranch gate. Stabbed – by some unknown person."

"Some dirty dog," said Mr Cherry indignantly.

"That's just how I feel about it. I'm not a policeman, but I'm doing my best to find the guilty man. The thing you saw that night at the ranch, Mr Cherry, no doubt has a decided bearing on the killing of Louie. I need your help. Now, will you talk?"

Mr Cherry removed the toothpick from his mouth and, holding it before him, regarded it thoughtfully. "Yes," he said, "I will. I was hopin' to keep out o' this. Judges an' courts an' all that truck ain't fer me. I give 'em a wide berth. But I'm a decent man, an' I ain't got nothin' to hide. I'll talk, but I don't hardly know how to begin."

"I'll help you," Eden answered, delighted. "The other night when you were at Madden's ranch perhaps you heard a man cry: 'Help! Help! Murder! Put down that gun. Help.' Something like that, eh?"

"I ain't got nothin' to hide. That's jest what I heard."

Eden's heart leaped. "And after that – you saw something—"

The old man nodded. "I saw plenty, boy. Louie Wong wasn't the first to be killed at Madden's ranch. I saw murder done."

Eden gasped inwardly. He saw Paula Wendell's eyes wide and startled. "Of course you did," he said. "Now go on and tell me all about it."

Mr Cherry restored the toothpick to its predestined place in his mouth, but it interfered in no way with his speech.

"Life's funny," he began. "Full o' queer twists an' turns. I thought this was jest one more secret fer me an' the desert together. Nobody knows about you, I says. Nobody ain't goin' to question you. But I was wrong, I see, an' I might as well speak up. It's nothin' to me, one way or t'other, though I would like to keep out o' courtrooms—"

"Well, maybe I can help you," Eden suggested. "Go on. You say you saw murder—"

"Jest hold yer horses, boy," Mr Cherry advised. "As I was sayin', last Wednesday after dark I drifts in at Madden's as usual. But the minute I comes into the yard, I see there's something doin' there. The boss has come. Lights in most o' the windows, an' a big car in the barn, longside Louie's old flivver. Howsomever, I'm tired, an' I figures I'll jest wait round fer Louie, keepin' out o' sight o' the big fellow. A little supper an' a bed, maybe, kin be negotiated without gettin' too conspicuous.

"So I puts my pack down in the barn, an' steps over to the cookhouse. Louie ain't there. Jest as I'm comin' out o' the place, I hears a cry from the house – a man's voice, loud an' clear. 'Help,' he says. 'Put down that gun. I know your game. Help. Help.' Jest as you said. Well, I ain't lookin' fer no trouble, an' I stands there a minute, uncertain. An' then the cry comes again, almost the same words – but not the man this time. It's Tony, the Chinese parrot, on his perch in the *patio*, an' from him the words is shrill an' piercin' – more terrible, somehow. An' then I hears a sharp report – the gun is workin'. The racket seems to come from a lighted room in one ell – a window is open. I creeps closer, an' there goes the gun agin. There's a sort of groan. It's hit, sure enough. I goes up to the window an' looks in."

He paused. "Then what?" Bob Eden asked breathlessly.

"Well, it's a bedroom, an' he's standin' there with the smokin' gun in his hand, lookin' fierce but frightened-like. An' there's somebody on the floor, t'other side of the bed – all I kin see is his shoes. He turns toward the window, the gun still in his hand—"

"Who?" cried Bob Eden. "Who was it with the gun in his hand? You're talking about Martin Thorn?"

"Thorn? You mean that little sneakin' secretary? No – I ain't speakin' o' Thorn. I'm speakin' o' him—"

"Who?"

"The big boss. Madden. P.J. Madden himself."

There was a moment of tense silence. "Good Lord," gasped Eden. "Madden? You mean to say that Madden was—Why, it's impossible. How did you know? Are you sure?"

"O' course I'm sure. I know Madden well enough. I seen him three years ago at the ranch. A big man, red-faced, thin grey hair – I couldn't make no mistake about Madden. There he was standin', the gun in his hand, an' he looks toward the window. I ducks back. An' at that minute this Thorn you're speakin' of – he comes tearin' into the room. 'What have you done now?' he says. 'I've killed him,' says Madden, 'that's what I've done.' 'You poor fool,' says Thorn. 'It wasn't necessary.' Madden throws down the gun. 'Why not?' he wants to know. 'I was afraid of him.' Thorn sneers. 'You was always afraid of him,' he says. 'You dirty coward. That time in New York—' Madden gives him a look. 'Shut up,' he says. 'Shut up an' fergit it. I was afraid o' him an' I killed him. Now git busy an' think what we better do.'"

The old prospector paused, and regarded his wide-eyed audience. "Well, mister," he continued, "an' miss – I come away. What else was there to be done? It was no affair o' mine, an' I wasn't hungerin' fer no court-room an' all that. Jest slip away into the night, I tells myself, the good old night that's been yer friend these many years. Slip away an' let others worry. I runs to the barn an' gits my pack, an' when I comes out, a car is drivin' into the yard. I crawls through the fence an' moseys down the road. I thought I was out o' it an' safe, an' how you got on to me is a mystery. But I'm decent, an' I ain't hidin' anything. That's my story – the truth, s' help me."

Bob Eden rose and paced the sand. "Man alive," he said, "this is serious business."

"Think so?" inquired the old prospector.

"Think so! You know who Madden is, don't you? One of the biggest men in America—"

"Sure he is. An' what does that mean? You'll never git him fer what he done. He'll slide out o' it some way. Self-defense—"

"Oh, no, he won't. Not if you tell your story. You've got to go back with me to Eldorado—"

"Wait a minute," cut in Cherry. "That's something I don't aim to do – go an' stifle in no city. Leastways, not till it's absolutely necessary. I've told my story, an' I'll tell it agin, any time I'm asked. But I ain't goin' back to Eldorado – bank on that, boy."

"But listen—"

"Listen to me. How much more information you got? Know who that man was, layin' behind the bed? Found his body yet?"

"No, we haven't, but—"

"I thought so. Well, you're jest startin' on this job. What's my word agin the word o' P.J. Madden – an' no other evidence to show? You got to dig some up."

"Well, perhaps you're right."

"Sure I am. I've done you a favour – now you do one fer me. Take this here information an' go back an' make the most o' it. Leave me out entirely if you kin. If you can't – well, I'll keep in touch. Be round down Needles in about a week – goin' to make a stop there with my old friend, Slim Jones. Porter J. Jones, Real Estate – you kin git me there. I'm makin' you a fair proposition – don't you say so, miss?"

The girl smiled at him. "Seems fair to me," she admitted.

"It's hardly according to Hoyle," said Eden. "But you have been mighty kind. I don't want to see you stifle in a city –

though I find it hard to believe you and I are talking about the same Eldorado. However, we're going to part friends, Mr Cherry. I'll take your suggestion – I'll go back with what you've told me – it's certainly very enlightening. And I'll keep you out of it – if I can."

The old man got painfully to his feet. "Shake," he said. "You're a white man, an' no mistake. I ain't tryin' to save Madden – I'll go on the stand if I have to. But with what I've told you, maybe you can land him without me figurin' in it."

"We'll have to go along," Eden told him. He laughed. "I don't care what the book of etiquette says – Mr Cherry, I'm very pleased to have met you."

"Same here," returned Cherry. "Like a talk now an' then with a good listener. An' the chance to look at a pretty gal – well, say, I don't need no specs to enjoy that."

They said goodbye, and left the lonely old man standing by the tramcar there on the barren desert. For a long moment they rode in silence.

"Well," said Eden finally, "you've heard something, lady."

"I certainly have. Something I find it difficult to believe."

"Perhaps you won't find it so difficult if I go back and tell you a few things. You've been drawn into the big mystery at Madden's at last, and there's no reason why you shouldn't know as much as I do about it. So I'm going to talk."

"I'm keen to hear," she admitted.

"Naturally, after today. Well, I came down here to transact a bit of business with P.J. – I needn't go into that, it has no particular bearing. The first night I was on the ranch—" He proceeded to detail one by one the mysterious sequence of events that began with the scream of the parrot from the dark. "Now you know. Someone had been killed, that was evident. Someone before Louie. But who? We don't know yet. And by whom? Today gave us that answer, anyhow."

"It seems incredible."

"You don't believe Cherry's story?" he suggested.

"Well – these old boys who wander the desert get queer sometimes. And there was that about his eyes – the doctor at Redlands, you know—"

"I know. But, all the same, I think Cherry told the truth. After a few days with Madden I consider him capable of anything. He's a hard man, and if anyone stood in his way – good night. Some poor devil stood there – but not for long. Who? We'll find out. We must."

"We?"

"Yes, you're in on this thing too. Have to be, after this, whether you like it or not."

"I think I'm going to like it," Paula Wendell said.

They returned their tired horses to the stable at Seven Palms, and after a sketchy dinner at the local hotel caught the Eldorado train. When they alighted Charlie and Will Holley were waiting.

"Hello," said the editor. "Why, hello, Paula – where you been? Eden, here's Ah Kim. Madden sent him in for you."

"Hello, gentlemen," cried Eden gaily. "Before Ah Kim and I head for the ranch we're all going over to the office of that grand old sheet the *Eldorado Times*. I have something to impart."

When they reached the newspaper office – which Ah Kim entered with obvious reluctance – Eden closed the door and faced them. "Well, folks," he announced, "the clouds are breaking. I've finally got hold of something definite. But before I go any further – Miss Wendell, may I present Ah Kim? So we sometimes call him, after our quaint fashion. In reality, you are now enjoying the priceless opportunity of meeting Detective-Sergeant Charlie Chan of the Honolulu police."

Chan bowed. "I'm so glad to know you, sergeant," said the girl, and took up her favourite perch on Holley's typewriter table.

"Don't look at me like that, Charlie," laughed Eden. "You're breaking my heart. We can rely on Miss Wendell absolutely. And you can't freeze her out any longer, because she now knows more about your case than you do. As they say on the stage – won't you – sit down?"

Puzzled and wondering, Chan and Will Holley found chairs. "I said this morning I wanted a little light," Eden continued. "I've got it already – how's that for service? Aimless trip to Barstow, Charlie, proved to be all aim. Miss Wendell and I turned aside for a canter over the desert, and we have met and interviewed that little black-bearded one – our desert rat."

"Boy – now you're talking," cried Holley.

Chan's eyes lighted.

"Chinese are psychic people, Charlie," Eden went on. "I'll tell the world. You were right. Before we arrived at Madden's ranch someone staged a little murder there. And I know who did it."

"Thorn," suggested Holley.

"Thorn nothing! No piker like Thorn. No, gentlemen, it was the big chief – Madden himself – the great P.J. Last Wednesday night at his ranch Madden killed a man. Add favourite pastimes of big millionaires."

"Nonsense," objected Holley.

"You think so, eh? Listen." Eden repeated the story Cherry had told.

Chan and Holley heard him out in amazed silence.

"And what are present whereabouts of old prospector?" inquired Chan when he had finished.

"I know, Charlie," answered Eden. "That's the flaw in my armour. I let him go. He's on his way – over yonder. But I know where he's going and we can get hold of him when we need him. We've got other matters to look after first."

"We certainly have," agreed Holley. "Madden! I can hardly believe it."

Chan considered. "Most peculiar case ever shoved on my attention," he admitted. "It marches now, but look how it marches backwards. Mostly murder means dead body on the rug, and from clues surrounding I must find who did it. Not so here. I sense something wrong; after long pause light breaks and I hear name of guilty man who killed. But who was killed? The reason, please? There is work to be done – much work."

"You don't think," suggested Eden, "that we ought to call in the sheriff—"

"What then?" frowned Chan. "Captain Bliss arrives on extensive feet, committing blunder with every step. Sheriff faces strange situation, all unprepared. Madden awes them with greatness, and escapes Scotch-free. None of the sheriff, please – unless maybe you lose faith in Detective-Sergeant Chan."

"Never for a minute, Charlie," Eden answered. "Wipe out that suggestion. The case is yours."

Chan bowed. "You're pretty good, thanks. Such a tipsy-turvy puzzle rouses professional pride. I will get to bottom of it or lose entire face. Be good enough to watch me."

"I'll be watching," Eden answered. "Well, shall we go along?"

In front of the Desert Edge Hotel Bob Eden held out his hand to the girl. "The end of a perfect day," he said. "Except for one thing."

"Yes? What thing?"

"Wilbur. I'm beginning to find the thought of him intolerable."

"Poor Jack. You're so hard on him. Good night – and—"

"And what?"

"Be careful, won't you? Out at the ranch I mean."

"Always careful – on ranches – everywhere. Good night."

As they sped over the dark road to Madden's, Chan was thoughtfully silent. He and Eden parted in the yard. When the boy entered the *patio* he saw Madden sitting alone, wrapped in an overcoat, before a dying fire.

The millionaire leaped to his feet. "Hello," he said. "Well?"

"Well?" replied Eden. He had completely forgotten his mission to Barstow.

"You saw Draycott?" Madden whispered.

"Oh!" The boy remembered with a start. More deception – would it ever end? "Tomorrow at the door of the bank in Pasadena," he said softly. "Noon sharp."

"Good," answered Madden. "I'll be off before you're up. Not turning in already?"

"I think I will," responded Eden. "I've had a busy day."

"Is that so?" said Madden carelessly, and strode into the living-room. Bob Eden stood staring after the big, broad shoulders, the huge frame of this powerful man. A man who seemed to have the world in his grasp, but who had killed because he was afraid.

XIV

THE THIRD MAN

As soon as he was fully awake the following morning, Bob Eden's active brain returned to the problem with which it had been concerned when he dropped off to sleep. Madden had killed a man. Cool, confident, and self-possessed though he always seemed, the millionaire had lost his head for once. Ignoring the possible effect of such an act on his fame, his high position, he had with murderous intent pulled the trigger on the gun Bill Hart had given him. His plight must have been desperate indeed.

Whom had he killed? That was something yet to be discovered. Why had he done it? By his own confession, because he was afraid. Madden, whose very name struck terror to many, and into whose presence lesser men came with awe and trembling, had himself known the emotion of fear. Ridiculous, but "You were always afraid of him," Thorn had said.

Some hidden door in the millionaire's past must be found and opened. First of all, the identity of the man who had been killed last Wednesday night on this lonely ranch must be ascertained. Well, at least the mystery was beginning to clear, the long sequence of inexplicable, maddening events since they came to the desert was broken for a moment by a tangible bit of explanation. Here was a start, something into which they could get their teeth. From this they must push on to – what?

Chan was waiting in the *patio* when Bob Eden came out. His face was decorated with a broad grin.

"Breakfast reposes on the table," he announced. "Consume it speedily. Before us stretches splendid day for investigation with no prying eyes."

"What's that?" asked Eden. "Nobody here? How about Gamble?"

Chan led the way to the living-room, and held Bob Eden's chair. "Oh, cut that, Charlie," the boy said. "You're not Ah Kim today. Do you mean to say that Gamble has also left us?"

Chan nodded. "Gamble develops keen yearning to visit Pasadena," he replied. "On which journey he is welcome as one of his long-tailed rats."

Eden quaffed his orange juice. "Madden didn't want him, eh?"

"Not much," Chan answered. "I rise before day breaks and prepare breakfast, which are last night's orders. Madden and Thorn arrive, brushing persistent sleep out of eyes. Suddenly enters this Professor Gamble, plentifully awake and singing happy praise for desert sunrise. 'You are up early,' says Madden, growling like a dissatisfied dog. 'Decided to take little journey to Pasadena along with you,' announces Gamble. Madden purples like distant hills when evening comes, but regards me and quenches his reply. When he and Thorn enter big car, behold Mr Gamble climbing into rear seat. If looks could assassinate Madden would then and there have rendered him extinct, but such are not the case. Car rolls off on to sunny road with Professor Gamble smiling pleasantly in back. Welcome as long-tailed rat, but not going to worry about it, thank you."

Eden chuckled. "Well, it's a good thing from our standpoint, Charlie. I was wondering what we were going to do with Gamble nosing round. Big load off our shoulders right away."

"Very true," agreed Chan. "Alone here, we relax all over place and find what is to find. How you like oatmeal, boy? Not so lumpy, if I may be permitted the immodesty."

"Charlie, the world lost a great chef when you became a policeman. But – the devil! Who's that driving in?"

Chan went to the door. "No alarm necessary," he remarked. "Only Mr Holley."

The editor appeared. "Here I am, up with the lark and ready for action," he announced. "Want to be in on the big hunt, if you don't mind."

"Certainly don't," said Eden. "Glad to have you. We've had a bit of luck already." He explained about Gamble's departure.

Holley nodded wisely. "Of course Gamble went to Pasadena," he remarked. "He's not going to let Madden out of his sight. You know, I've had some flashes of inspiration about this matter out here."

"Good for you," replied Eden. "For instance—"

"Oh, just wait a while. I'll dazzle you with them at the proper moment. You see, I used to do a lot of police reporting. Little Bright Eyes I was often called."

"Pretty name," laughed Eden.

"Little Bright Eyes is here to look about," Holley continued. "First of all, we ought to decide what we're looking for."

"I guess we know that, don't we?" Eden asked.

"Oh, in a general way, but let's be explicit. To go back and start at the beginning – that's the proper method, isn't it, Chan?"

Charlie shrugged. "Always done – in books," he said. "In real life, not so much so."

Holley smiled. "That's right – dampen my young enthusiasm. However, I am now going to recall a few facts. We needn't stress the side issues at present – the pearls, the activities of Shaky Phil in San Francisco, the murder of Louie, the disappearance of Madden's daughter – all these will be explained when we get the big answer. We are concerned today chiefly with the story of the old prospector."

"Who may have been lying or mistaken," Eden suggested.

"Yes – his tale seems unbelievable, I admit. Without any evidence to back it up, I wouldn't pay much attention to it. However, we have that evidence. Don't forget Tony's impassioned remarks, and his subsequent taking off. More important still, there is Bill Hart's gun, with two empty chambers. Also the bullet-hole in the wall. What more do you want?"

"Oh, it seems to be well substantiated," Eden agreed.

"It is. No doubt about it – somebody was shot at this place Wednesday night. We thought at first Thorn was the killer, now we switch to Madden. Madden lured somebody to Thorn's room, or cornered him there, and killed him. Why? Because he was afraid of him? We think hard about Wednesday night – and what do we want to know? We want to know – who was the third man?"

"The third man?" Eden repeated.

"Precisely. Ignore the prospector – who was at the ranch? Madden and Thorn – yes. And one other. A man who, seeing his life in danger, called loudly for help. A man who, a moment later, lay on the floor beyond the bed, and whose shoes alone were visible from where the prospector stood. Who was he? Where did he come from? When did he arrive? What was his business? Why was Madden afraid of him? These are questions to which we must now seek answers. Am I right, Sergeant Chan?"

"Undubitably," Charlie replied. "And how shall we find those answers? By searching, perhaps. Humbly suggest we search."

"Every nook and corner of this ranch," agreed Holley. "We'll begin with Madden's desk. Some stray bit of correspondence may throw unexpected light. It's locked, of course. But I've brought along a pocketful of old keys – got them from a locksmith in town."

"You act like number one detective," Chan remarked.

"Thanks," answered Holley. He went over to the big, flat-topped desk belonging to the millionaire and began to experiment with various keys. In a few moments he found the proper one and all the drawers stood open.

"Splendid work," said Chan.

"Not much here, though," Holley declared. He removed the papers from the top left-hand drawer and laid them on the blotting-pad. Bob Eden lighted a cigarette and strolled away. Somehow this idea of inspecting Madden's mail did not appeal to him.

The representatives of the police and the Press, however, were not so delicately minded. For more than half an hour Chan and the editor studied the contents of Madden's desk. They found nothing, save harmless and understandable data of business deals, not a solitary scrap that could by the widest stretch of the imagination throw any light on the identity or meaning of the third man. Finally, perspiring and baffled, they gave up and the drawers were relocked.

"Well," said Holley, "not so good, eh? Mark the desk off our list and let's move on."

"With your permission," Chan remarked, "we divide the labours. For you gentlemen the inside of the house. I myself have fondly feeling for outdoors." He disappeared. One by one Holley and Eden searched the rooms. In the bedroom occupied by the secretary they saw for themselves the bullet-hole in the wall. An investigation of the bureau, however, revealed the fact that Bill Hart's pistol was no longer there. This was their sole discovery of any interest.

"We're up against it," admitted Holley at length, his cheerful manner waning. "Madden's a clever man, and he didn't leave a warm trail, of course. But somehow – somewhere —"

They returned to the living-room. Chan, hot and puffing, appeared suddenly at the door. He dropped into a chair.

"What luck, Charlie?" Eden inquired.

"None whatever," admitted Chan gloomily. "Heavy disappointment causes my heart to sag. No gambler myself, but would have offered huge wager something buried on this ranch. When Madden, having shot, remarked, 'Shut up and forget. I was afraid and I killed. Now, think quick what we had better do,' I would expect first thought is – burial. How else to dispose of dead? So just now I have examined every inch of ground, with highest hope. No good. If burial made, it was not here. I see by your faces you have similar bafflement to report."

"Haven't found a thing," Eden replied.

Chan sighed. "I drag the announcement forth in pain," he said. "But I now gaze solemnly at stone wall."

They sat in helpless silence. "Well, let's not give up yet," Bob Eden remarked. He leaned back in his chair and blew a ring of smoke toward the paneled ceiling. "By the way, has it ever occurred to you that there must be some sort of attic above this room?"

Chan was instantly on his feet. "Clever suggestion," he cried. "Attic, yes, but how to ascend?" He stood staring at the ceiling a moment, then went quickly to a large closet in the rear of the room. "Somewhat humiliated situation for me," he announced. Crowding close beside him in the dim closet, the other two looked aloft at an unmistakable trap-door.

Bob Eden was selected for the climb, and with the aid of a step-ladder Chan brought from the barn he managed it easily. Holley and the detective waited below. For a moment Eden stood in the attic, his head bent low, cobwebs caressing his face, while he sought to accustom his eyes to the faint light.

"Nothing here, I'm afraid," he called. "Oh, yes, there is. Wait a minute."

They heard him walking gingerly above, and clouds of dust descended on their heads. Presently he was lowering a bulky object through the narrow trap – a battered old Gladstone bag.

"Seems to be something in it," Eden announced.

They took it with eager hands, and set it on the desk in the sunny living-room. Bob Eden joined them.

"By gad," the boy said, "not much dust on it, is there? Must have been put there recently. Holley, here's where your keys come in handy."

It proved a simple matter for Holley to master the lock. The three men crowded close.

Chan lifted out a cheap toilet-case, with the usual articles – a comb and brush, razors, shaving-cream, tooth-paste, shirts, socks, handkerchiefs. He examined the laundry mark.

"D – thirty-four," he announced.

"Meaning nothing," Eden said.

Chan was lifting a brown suit of clothes from the bottom of the bag.

"Made to order by tailor in New York," he said, after an inspection of the inner coat-pocket. "Name of purchaser, however, is blotted out by too much wearing." He took from the side-pockets a box of matches and a half-empty packet of inexpensive cigarettes. "Finishing the coat," he added.

He turned his attention to the waistcoat, and luck smiled upon him. From the lower right-hand pocket he removed an old-fashioned watch, attached to a heavy chain. The timepiece was silent; evidently it had been unwound for some time. Quickly he pried open the back case, and a little grunt of satisfaction escaped him. He passed the watch to Bob Eden.

"Presented to Jerry Delaney by his old friend, Honest Jack McGuire," read Eden in a voice of triumph. "And the date – August twenty-sixth, 1913."

"Jerry Delaney!" cried Holley. "By heaven, we're getting on now. The name of the third man was Jerry Delaney."

"Yet to be proved he was the third man," Chan cautioned. "This, however, may help."

He produced a soiled scrap of coloured paper – a passenger's receipt for a Pullman compartment. "Compartment B – car one nine eight," he read. "Chicago to Barstow." He turned it over. "Date when used, February eighth, present year."

Bob Eden turned to a calendar. "Great stuff," he cried. "Jerry Delaney left Chicago on February eighth – a week ago on Sunday night. That got him into Barstow last Wednesday morning, February eleventh – the morning of the day he was killed. Some detectives, we are."

Chan was still busy with the waistcoat. He brought forth a key-ring with a few keys, then a worn newspaper clipping. The latter he handed to Eden.

"Read it, please?" he suggested.

Bob Eden read:

"Theatre-goers of Los Angeles will be delighted to know that in the cast of *One Night in June*, the musical comedy opening at the Mason next Monday night, will be Miss Norma Fitzgerald. She has the *rôle* of Marcia, which calls for a rich soprano voice, and her vast army of admirers hereabouts know in advance how well she will acquit herself in such a part. Miss Fitzgerald has been on the stage twenty years – she went on as a mere child – and has appeared in such productions as *The Love Cure*."

Eden paused. "There's a long list." He resumed reading:

"Matinées of *One Night in June* will be on Wednesdays and Saturdays, and for this engagement a special scale of prices has been inaugurated."

Eden put the clipping down on the table. "Well, that's one more fact about Jerry Delaney. He was interested in a soprano. So many men are – but still, it may lead somewhere."

"Poor Jerry," said Holley, looking down at the rather pitiful pile of the man's possessions. "He won't need a hairbrush, or a razor, or a gold watch where he's gone." He took up the watch and regarded it thoughtfully. "Honest Jack McGuire. I seem to have heard that name somewhere."

Chan was investigating the trousers-pockets. He turned them out one by one, but found nothing.

"Search is now complete," he announced. "Humbly suggest we put all back as we found it. We have made delightful progress."

"I'll say we have," cried Eden, with enthusiasm. "More progress than I ever thought possible. Last night we knew only that Madden had killed a man. Today we know the name of the man." He paused. "I don't suppose there can be any doubt about it?" he inquired.

"Hardly," Holley replied. "A man doesn't part with such personal possessions as a hairbrush and a razor as long as he has any further use for them. If he's through with them he's through with life. Poor devil!"

"Let's go over it all again before we put these things away," said Eden. "We've learned that the man Madden feared, the man he killed, was Jerry Delaney. What do we know of Delaney? He was not in very affluent circumstances, though he did have his clothes made by a tailor. Not a smart tailor, judging by the address. He smoked Corsican cigarettes. Honest Jack McGuire, whoever he may be, was an old friend of his, and thought so highly of him he gave Jerry a watch. What else? Delaney was interested in an actress named Norma Fitzgerald. A week ago last Sunday he left Chicago at eight P.M. – the Limited – for Barstow, riding in compartment B, car one nine eight. And that, I guess, about sums up what we know of Jerry Delaney."

Charlie Chan smiled. "Very good," he said. "A splendid list, rich with promise. But one fact you have missed complete."

"What's that?" inquired Eden.

"One very easy fact," continued Chan. "Take this vest once on Jerry Delaney. Examine close – what do you discover?"

Carefully Eden looked over the waistcoat, then with a puzzled air handed it to Holley, who did the same. Holley shook his head.

"Nothing?" asked Chan, laughing silently. "Can it be you are not such able detectives as I thought? Here – place hand in pocket."

Bob Eden thrust his fingers into the pocket indicated by Chan. "It's chamois-lined," he said. "The watch-pocket, that's all."

"True enough," answered Chan. "And on the left, I presume."

Eden looked foolish. "Oh," he admitted, "I get you. The watch-pocket is on the right."

"And why?" persisted Charlie. "With coat buttoned, certain man cannot reach watch easily when it reposes at left. Therefore he instructs tailor, make pocket for watch on right, please." He began to fold up the clothes in order to return them to the bag. "One other fact we know about Jerry Delaney, and it may be used in tracing his movements the day he came to this ranch. Jerry Delaney had peculiarity to be left-handed."

"Great Scott!" cried Holley suddenly. They turned to him. He had picked up the watch again and was staring at it. "Honest Jack McGuire – I remember now."

"You know this McGuire?" inquired Chan quickly.

"I met him long ago," Holley replied. "The first night I brought Mr Eden out here to the ranch he asked me if I'd ever seen P.J. Madden before. I said that twelve years ago I saw Madden in a gambling-house on East Forty-fourth Street, New York, dolled up like a prince and betting his head off. Madden himself remembered the occasion when I spoke to him about it."

"But McGuire?" Chan wanted to know.

"I recall now that the name of the man who ran that gambling-house was Jack McGuire. Honest Jack, he had the nerve to call himself. It was a queer joint – that was later proved. But Jack McGuire was Delaney's old friend – he gave Jerry a watch as a token of their friendship. Gentlemen, this is interesting. McGuire's gambling-house on Forty-fourth Street comes back into the life of P.J. Madden."

XV

WILL HOLLEY'S THEORY

When the bag was completely repacked and again securely locked, Bob Eden climbed with it to the dusty attic. He reappeared, the trap-door was closed, and the step-ladder removed. The three men faced one another, pleased with their morning's work.

"It's after twelve," said Holley. "I must hurry back to town."

"About to make heartfelt suggestion, you remain at lunch," remarked Chan.

Holley shook his head. "That's kind of you, Charlie, but I wouldn't think of it. You must be about fed-up on this cooking proposition, and I won't spoil your first chance for a little vacation. You take my advice, and make Eden rustle his own grub today."

Chan nodded. "True enough that I was planning a modest repast," he returned. "Cooking business begins to get tiresome like the company of a Japanese. However, fitting punishment for a postman who walks another man's beat. If Mr Eden will pardon I relax to the extent of sandwiches and tea this noon."

"Sure," said Eden. "We'll dig up something together. Holley, you'd better change your mind."

"No," replied Holley. "I'm going to town to make a few inquiries. Just by way of substantiating what we found here today. If Jerry Delaney came out here last Wednesday he must have left some sort of trail through the town. Someone may have seen him. Was he alone? I'll speak to the boys at the gas-station, the hotel proprietor—"

"Humbly suggest utmost discretion," said Chan.

"Oh, I understand the need of that. But there's really no danger. Madden has no connexion whatever with the life of the town. He won't hear of it. Just the same, I'll be discretion itself. Trust me. I'll come out here again later in the day."

When he had gone Chan and Eden ate a cold lunch in the cookhouse, and resumed their search. Nothing of any moment rewarded their efforts, however. At four that afternoon Holley drove into the yard. With him was a lean, sad-looking youth whom Eden recognized as the real-estate salesman of Date City.

As they entered the room Chan withdrew, leaving Eden to greet them. Holley introduced the youth as Mr De Lisle.

"I've met De Lisle," smiled Bob Eden. "He tried to sell me a corner lot on the desert."

"Yeah," said Mr De Lisle. "And some day, when the United Cigar Stores and Woolworth are fighting for that stuff, you'll kick yourself up and down every hill in 'Frisco. However, that's your funeral."

"I brought Mr De Lisle along," explained Holley, "because I want you to hear the story he's just told me. About last Wednesday night."

"Mr De Lisle understands that this is confidential—" began Eden.

"Oh, sure," said the young man. "Will's explained all that. You needn't worry. Madden and I ain't exactly pals – not after the way he talked to me."

"You saw him last Wednesday night?" Eden suggested.

"No, not that night. It was somebody else I saw then. I was here at the development until after dark, waiting for a prospect – he never showed up, the lowlife. Anyhow, along about seven o'clock, just as I was closing up the office, a big sedan stopped out in front. I went out. There was a little guy driving and another man in the back seat. 'Good evening,' said the little fellow. 'Can you tell me, please, if we're on the road to Madden's ranch?' I said sure, to keep right on straight. The man in the back spoke up. 'How far is it?' he wants to know. 'Shut up, Jerry,' says the little guy. 'I'll attend to this.' He shifted the gears, and then he got kind of literary. '"And an highway shall be there, and a way,"' he says. 'Not any too clearly defined, Isaiah.' And he drove off. Now why do you suppose he called me Isaiah?"

Eden smiled. "Did you get a good look at him?"

"Pretty good, considering the dark. A thin, pale man with sort of greyish lips – no colour in them at all. Talked kind of slow and precise – awful neat English, like he was a professor or something."

"And the man in the back seat?"

"Couldn't see him very well."

"Ah, yes. And when did you meet Madden?"

"I'll come to that. After I got home I began to think – Madden was out at the ranch, it seemed. And I got a big idea. Things ain't been going so well here lately – Florida's been nabbing all the easy – all the good prospects – and I said to myself, how about Madden? There's big money. Why not try and interest Madden in Date City? Get him behind it. Worth a shot, anyhow. So bright and early Thursday morning I came out to the ranch."

"About what time?"

"Oh, it must have been a little after eight. I'm full of pep at that hour of the day, and I knew I'd need it. I knocked at the front door, but nobody answered. I tried it – it was locked. I came around to the back and the place was deserted. Not a soul in sight."

"Nobody here?" repeated Eden, wonderingly.

"Not a living thing but the chickens and the turkeys. And the Chinese parrot, Tony. He was sitting on his perch. 'Hello, Tony,' I said. 'You're a damn crook,' he answers. Now I ask you, is that any way to greet a hard-working, honest real-estate man? Wait a minute – don't try to be funny."

"I won't," Eden laughed. "But Madden—"

"Well, just then Madden drove into the yard with that secretary of his. I knew the old man right away from his pictures. He looked tired and ugly, and he needed a shave. 'What are you doing here?' he wanted to know. 'Mr Madden,' I said, 'have you ever stopped to consider the possibilities of this land round here?' And I waltzed right into my selling talk. But I didn't get far. He stopped me, and then he started. Say – the things he called me. I'm not used to that sort of thing – abuse by an expert, and that's what it was. I saw his psychology was all wrong, so I walked out on him. That's the best way – when the old psychology ain't working."

"And that's all?" Eden inquired.

"That's my story, and I'll stick to it," replied Mr De Lisle.

"I'm very much obliged," Eden said. "Of course, this is all between ourselves. And I may add that if I ever do decide to buy a lot on the desert—"

"You'll consider my stuff, won't you?"

"I certainly will. Just at present the desert doesn't look very good to me."

Mr De Lisle leaned close. "Whisper it not in Eldorado," he said. "I sometimes wish I was back in good old Chi myself. If I ever hit the Loop again I'm going to nail myself down there."

"If you'll wait outside a few minutes, De Lisle—" Holley began.

"I get you. I'll just mosey down to the development and see if the fountain's working. You can pick me up there."

The young man went out. Chan came quickly from behind a nearby door.

"Get all that, Charlie?" Eden inquired.

"Yes, indeed. Most interesting."

"We move right on," said Holley. "Jerry Delaney came out to the ranch about seven o'clock Wednesday night, and he didn't come alone. For the first time a fourth man enters the picture. Who? Sounded to me very much like Professor Gamble."

"No doubt about that," replied Eden. "He's an old friend of the prophet Isaiah's – he admitted it here Monday after lunch."

"Fine," commented Holley. "We begin to place Mr Gamble. Here's another thing – someone drove up to the doctor's Sunday night and carried Shaky Phil away. Couldn't that have been Gamble, too? What do you say, Charlie?"

Chan nodded. "Possible. That person knew of Louie's return. If we could only discover—"

"By George," Eden cried. "Gamble was at the desk of the Oasis when Louie came in. You remember, Holley?"

The editor smiled. "All fits in very neatly. Gamble sped out here like some sinister version of Paul Revere with the news of Louie's arrival. He and Shaky Phil were at the gate when you drove up."

"But Thorn. That tear in Thorn's coat?"

"We must have been on the wrong trail there. This new theory sounds too good. What else have we learned from De Lisle? After the misadventure with Delaney Madden and Thorn were out all night. Where?"

Chan sighed. "Not such good news, that. Body of Delaney was carried far from this spot."

"I'm afraid it was," admitted Holley. "We'll never find it without help from somebody who knows. There are a hundred lonely canyons round here where poor Delaney could have been tossed aside and nobody any the wiser. We'll have to go ahead and perfect our case without the vital bit of evidence –

the body of Delaney. But there are a lot of people in on this, and before we get through somebody is going to squeal."

Chan was sitting at Madden's desk, idly toying with the big blotting-pad that lay on top. Suddenly his eyes lighted, and he began to separate the sheets of blotting-paper.

"What is this?" he said.

They looked, and saw in the detective's pudgy hand a large sheet of paper, partly filled with writing. Chan perused the missive carefully, and handed it to Eden. The latter was written in a man's strong hand. "It's dated last Wednesday night," Eden remarked to Holley. He read:

"DEAR EVELYN,

"I want you to know of certain developments here at the ranch. As I have told you before, Martin Thorn and I have been on very bad terms for the past year. This afternoon the big blow-off finally arrived, and I dismissed him from my service. Tomorrow morning I'm going with him to Pasadena, and when we get there we part for all time. Of course, he knows a lot of things I wish he didn't – otherwise I'd have scrapped him a year ago. He may make trouble, and I am warning you in case he shows up in Denver. I'm going to take this letter in town myself and mail it tonight, as I don't want Thorn to know anything about it—"

The letter stopped abruptly at that point.

"Better and better," said Holley. "Another sidelight on what happened here last Wednesday night. We can picture the scene for ourselves. Madden is sitting at his desk, writing that letter to his daughter. The door opens – someone comes in. Say it's Delaney – Delaney, the man P.J.'s feared for years. Madden hastily slips the letter between the leaves of the blotter. He gets to his feet, knowing that he's in for it now. A quarrel ensues, and by the time it's over they've got into Thorn's room somehow and Delaney is dead on the floor. Then – the problem of what to do with the body, not solved until morning. Madden comes back to the ranch tired and worn, realizing that he can't dismiss Thorn now. He must make his peace with the secretary. Thorn knows too much. How about it, Charlie?"

"It has plenty logic," Chan admitted.

"I said this morning I had some ideas on this affair out here," the editor continued, "and everything that has happened today has tended to confirm them. I'm ready to spring my theory now – that is, if you care to listen."

"Shoot," said Eden.

"To me, it's all as clear as a desert sunrise," Holley went on. "Just let me go over it for you. Reconstruct it, as the French do. To begin with, Madden is afraid of Delaney. Why? Why is a rich man afraid of anybody? Blackmail, of course. Delaney has something on him – maybe something that dates back to that gambling-house in New York. Thorn can't be depended on – they've been rowing, and he hates his employer. Perhaps he has even gone so far as to link up with Delaney and his friends. Madden buys the pearls, and the gang hears of it and decides to spring. What better place than way out here on the desert? Shaky Phil goes to San Francisco; Delaney and the professor come South. Louie, the faithful old retainer, is lured away by Shaky Phil. The stage is set. Delaney arrives with his threat. He demands the pearls, money, both. An argument follows, and in the end Delaney, the blackmailer, is killed by Madden. Am I right so far?"

"Sounds plausible," Eden admitted.

"Well, imagine what followed. When Madden killed Delaney he probably thought Jerry had come alone. Now he discovers there are others in the gang. They have not only the information with which Delaney was threatening him, but they have something else on him too. Murder! The pack is on him – he must buy them off. They clamour for money – and the pearls. They force Madden to call up and order the Phillimore necklace sent down here at once. When did he do that, Eden?"

"Last Thursday morning," Eden replied.

"See – what did I tell you? Last Thursday morning, when he got back from his grisly midnight trip. They were on him then – they were blackmailing him to the limit. That's the answer to our puzzle. They're blackmailing him now. At first Madden was just as eager as they were for the necklace – he wanted to settle the thing and get away. It isn't pleasant to linger round the spot where you've done murder. The past few days his courage has begun to return, he's temporizing, seeking a way out. I'm a little sorry for him, I really am." Holley paused. "Well, that's my idea. What do you think, Charlie? Am I right?"

Chan sat turning Madden's unfinished letter slowly in his hand.

"Sounds good," admitted the detective. "However, here and there objections arise."

"For example?" Holley demanded.

"Madden is big man. Delaney and these others nobody much. He could announce he killed blackmailer in self-defense."

"So he could – if Thorn were friendly and would back him up. But the secretary is hostile and might threaten to tell a different story. Besides, remember it isn't only the killing of Delaney they have against him. There's the information Delaney has been holding over his head."

Chan nodded. "So very true. One other fact, and then I cease my brutal fault-finding. Louie, long in confidence of Chinese parrot, is killed. Yet Louie depart for San Francisco on Wednesday morning, twelve hours before tragic night. Is not his murder then a useless gesturing?"

Holley considered. "Well, that is a point. But he was Madden's friend, which was a pretty good reason for not wanting him here. They preferred their victim alone and helpless. A rather weak explanation, perhaps. Otherwise I'm strong for my theory. You're not so keen on it."

Chan shook his head. "For one reason only. Long experience has taught fatal consequence may follow if I get too addicted to a theory. Then I try and see, can I make everything fit? I can, and first thing I know theory explodes in my countenance with loud bang. Much better, I have found, to keep mind free and open."

"Then you haven't any idea on all this to set up against mine?" Holley asked.

"No solitary one. Frankly speaking, I am completely in the dark." He glanced at the letter in his hand. "Or nearly so," he added. "We watch and wait, and maybe I clutch something soon."

"That's all right," said Eden, "but I have a feeling we don't watch and wait much longer at Madden's ranch. Remember, I promised that Draycott would meet him today in Pasadena. He'll be back soon, asking how come?"

"Unfortunate incident," shrugged Chan. "Draycott and he have failed to connect. Many times that has happened when two strangers make appointment. It can happen again."

Eden sighed. "I suppose so. But I hope P.J. Madden's feeling good-natured when he comes home from Pasadena tonight. There's a chance that he's toting Bill Hart's gun again, and I don't like the idea of lying behind a bed with nothing showing but my shoes. I haven't had a shine for a week."

XVI

THE MOVIES ARE IN TOWN

The sun set behind far peaks of snow; the desert purpled under a sprinkling of stars. In the thermometer that hung on a *patio* wall the mercury began its quick, relentless fall, a sharp wind swept over the desolate waste, and loneliness settled on the world.

"Warm food needed now," remarked Chan. "With your permission I will open numerous cans."

"Anything but the arsenic," Eden told him. He departed for the cookhouse.

Holley had long since gone, and Bob Eden sat alone by the window, looking out at a vast silence. Lots of room left in America yet, he reflected. Did they think of that, those throngs of people packed into subways at this hour, seeking tables in noisy restaurants, waiting at jammed corners for the traffic signal, climbing weary and worn at last to the pigeon-holes they called home? Elbow room on the desert; room to expand the chest. But a feeling of disquiet, too, a haunting realization of one man's ridiculous unimportance in the scheme of things.

Chan entered with a tray on which the dishes were piled high. He set down on the table two steaming plates of soup.

"Deign to join me," he suggested. "First course is now served with the kind assistance of the can-opener."

"Aged in the tin, eh, Charlie?" smiled Eden, drawing up. "Well, I'll bet it's good at that. You're a bit of a magician in the kitchen." They began to eat. "Charlie, I've been thinking," the boy continued. "I know now why I have this sense of unrest on the desert. It's because I feel so blamed small. Look at me, and then look out the window, and tell me where I get off to strut like a somebody through the world."

"Not bad feeling for the white man to experience," Chan assured him. "Chinese has it all time. Chinese knows he is one minute grain of sand on seashore of eternity. With what result? He is calm and quiet and humble. No nerves, like hopping, skipping Caucasian. Life for him not so much ordeal."

"Yes, and he's happier too," said Eden.

"Sure," replied Chan. He produced a platter of canned salmon. "All time in San Francisco I behold white men hot and excited. Life like a fever, always getting worse. What for? Where does it end? Same place as Chinese life, I think."

When they had finished Eden attempted to help with the dishes, but was politely restrained. He sat down and turned on the wireless set. The strong voice of a leather-lunged announcer rang out in the quiet room.

"Now, folks, we got a real treat for you this balmy, typical California evening. Miss Norma Fitzgerald, of the *One Night in June* company, now playing at the Mason, is going to sing – er – what are you going to sing, Norma? Norma says wait and find out."

At mention of the girl's name Bob Eden called to the detective, who entered and stood expectantly. "Hello, folks," came Miss Fitzgerald's greeting. "I certainly am glad to be back in good old L. A."

"Hello, Norma," Eden said, "never mind the songs. Two gentlemen out on the desert would like a word with you. Tell us about Jerry Delaney."

She couldn't have heard him, for she began to sing in a clear, beautiful soprano voice. Chan and the boy listened in silence.

"More of the white man's mysteries," Charlie remarked when she had finished. "So near to her, and yet so far away. Seems to me that we must visit this lady soon."

"Ah, yes – but how?" inquired Eden.

"It will be arranged," Chan said, and vanished.

Eden tried a book. An hour later he was interrupted by the peal of the telephone-bell, and a cheery voice answered his hello.

"Still pining for the bright lights?"

"I sure am," he replied.

"Well, the movies are in town," said Paula Wendell. "Come on in."

He hurried to his room. Chan had built a fire in the *patio*, and was sitting before it, the warm light flickering on his chubby, impassive face. When Eden returned with his hat he paused beside the detective.

"Getting some new ideas?" he asked.

"About our puzzle?" Chan shook his head. "No. At this moment I am far from Madden's ranch. I am in Honolulu, where nights are soft and sweet, not like chilly desert dark. Must admit my heart is weighed a little with homesick qualms. I picture my humble house on Punch Bowl Hill, where lanterns glow and my ten children are gathered round."

"Ten!" cried Eden. "Great Scott – you *are* a father."

"Very proud one," assented Chan. "You are going from here?"

"I'm running in town for a while. Miss Wendell called up – it seems the picture people have arrived. By the way, I just remembered – tomorrow is the day Madden promised they could come out here. I bet the old man's clean forgot it."

"Most likely. Better not to tell him, he might refuse permission. I have unlimited yearning to see movies in throes of being born. Should I go home and report that experience to my eldest daughter, who is all time sunk in movie magazines, ancestor-worship breaks out plenty strong at my house."

Eden laughed. "Well, then, let's hope you get the chance. I'll be back early."

A few minutes later he was again in the small runabout, under the platinum stars. He thought fleetingly of Louie Wong, buried now in the bleak little graveyard beyond Eldorado, but his mind turned quickly to happier things. With a lively feeling of anticipation he climbed between the twin hills at the gateway, and the yellow lights of the desert town were winking at him.

The moment he crossed the threshold of the Desert Edge Hotel, he knew this was no ordinary night in Eldorado. From the parlour at the left came the strains of giddy, inharmonious music, laughter, and a medley of voices. Paula Wendell met him and led him in.

The stuffy little room, dated by heavy mission furniture and bits of broken plaster hanging crazily from the ceiling, was renewing its youth in pleasant company. Bob Eden met the movies in their hours of ease, childlike, happy people, seemingly without a care in the world. A very pretty girl gave him a hand which recalled his father's jewellery shop, and then restored it to the ukelele she was playing. A tall young man designated as Rannie, whose clothes were perfection and whose collar and shirt shamed the blue of California's sky, desisted briefly from his torture of a saxophone.

"Hello, old-timer," he remarked. "I hope you brought your harp." And instantly ran amuck on the saxophone again.

A middle-aged actor with a bronzed, rather hard face was officiating at the piano. In a far corner a grand dame and an old man with snow-white hair sat apart from the crowd, and Eden dropped down beside them.

"What was the name?" asked the old man, his hand behind his ear. "Ah, yes, I'm glad to meet any friend of Paula's. We're a little clamorous here tonight, Mr Eden. It's like the early days when I was trouping – how we used to skylark on station platforms! We were happy then – no movies. Eh, my dear?" he added to the woman.

She bent a little. "Yes – but I never trouped much. Thank heaven I was usually able to steer clear of those terrible towns where Main Street is upstairs. Mr Belasco rarely asked me to leave New York." She turned to Eden. "I was in Belasco companies fifteen years," she explained.

"Wonderful experience, no doubt," the boy replied.

"Greatest school in the world," she said. "Mr Belasco thought very highly of my work. I remember once at a dress rehearsal he told me he could never have put on the piece without me, and he gave me a big red apple. You know that was Mr Belasco's way of—"

The din had momentarily stopped, and the leading man cried:

"Suffering cats! She's telling him about the apple, and the poor guy only just got here. Go on, Fanny, spring the one about the time you played Portia. What Charlie Frohman said – as soon as he came to, I mean."

"Humph," shrugged Fanny. "If you young people in this profession had a few traditions like us, the pictures wouldn't be such a joke. I thank my stars—"

"Hush, everybody," put in Paula Wendell. "Introducing Miss Diane Day on Hollywood's favourite instrument, the ukulele."

The girl she referred to smiled and, amid a sudden silence, launched into a London music-hall song. Like most of its *genre*, its import was not such as to recommend it for a church social, but she did it well, with a note of haunting sweetness in her voice. After another of the same sort she switched suddenly into *Way down upon the Swanee River*, and there were tears in her voice now, a poignant sadness in the room. It was too solemn for Rannie.

"Mr Eddie Boston at the piano, Mr Randolph Renault handling the saxophone," he shouted, "will now offer for your approval that touching ballad, *So's Your Old Mandarin*. Let her go, professor."

"Don't think they're always like this," Paula Wendell said to Eden above the racket. "It's only when they have a hotel to themselves, as they usually have here."

They had it indeed to themselves, save for the lads of the village, who suddenly found pressing business in the lobby, and passed and repassed the parlour door, open-mouthed with wonder.

The approval shown the instrumental duet was scant indeed, due, Mr Renault suggested, to professional jealousy.

"The next number on our very generous programme," he announced, "will follow immediately. It's called *Let's Talk about my Sweetie Now*. On your mark – Eddie."

"Nothing doing," cried the girl known as Diane. "I haven't had my Charleston lesson today, and it's getting late. Eddie – kindly oblige."

Eddie obliged. In another moment everyone save the two old people in the corner had leaped into action. The framed autographed portraits that other film celebrities had bestowed on the proprietor of the Desert Edge rattled on the walls. The windows shook. Suddenly in the doorway appeared a bald man with a gloomy eye.

"Good Lord," he shouted, "how do you expect me to get my rest?"

"Hello, Mike," cried Rannie. "What is it you want to rest from?"

"You direct a gang like this for a while, and you'll know," replied Mike sourly. "It's ten o'clock. If you'll take my advice for once, you'll turn in. Everybody's to report in costume here in the lobby tomorrow morning at eight-thirty."

This news was greeted with a chorus of low moans. "Nine-thirty, you say?" Rannie inquired.

"Eight-thirty. You heard me. And anybody who's late pays a good stiff fine. Now please go to bed and let decent people sleep."

"Decent people?" repeated Rannie softly, as the director vanished. "He's flattering himself again." But the party was over, and the company moved reluctantly up the stairs to the second floor. Mr Renault returned the saxophone to the desk.

"Say, landlord, there's a sour note in this thing," he complained. "Have it fixed before I come again."

"Sure will, Mr Renault," promised the proprietor.

"Too early for bed, no matter what Mike says," remarked Eden, piloting Paula Wendell to the street. "Let's take a walk. Eldorado doesn't look much like Union Square, but night air is night air wherever you find it."

"Lucky for me it isn't Union Square," said the girl. "I wouldn't be tagging along if it was."

"Is that so?"

They strolled down Main Street, white and empty in the moonlight. In a lighted window of the Spot Cash Store hung a brilliant patchwork quilt.

"To be raffled off by the ladies of the Orange Blossom Club for the benefit of the Orphans' Home," Eden read. "Think I'll take a chance on that tomorrow."

"Better not get mixed up with any Orange Blossom Club," suggested Paula Wendell.

"Oh, I can take care of myself. And it's the orphans I'm thinking of, you know."

"That's your kind heart," she answered. They climbed a narrow, sandy road. Yellow lamplight in the front window of a bungalow was suddenly blotted out.

"Look at that moon," said Eden. "Looks like a slice of honeydew melon just off the ice."

"Fond of food, aren't you?" remarked the girl. "I'll always think of you wrestling with that steak."

"A man must eat. And if it hadn't been for the steak we might never have met."

"What if we hadn't?" she asked.

"Pretty lonesome for me down here in that event." They turned about in silence. "You know, I've been thinking," Eden continued. "We're bound to come to the end of things at the ranch presently. And I'll have to go back—"

"Back to your freedom. That will be nice."

"You bet it will. All the same, I don't want you to forget me after I've gone. I want to go on being your – er – your friend. Or what have you?"

"Splendid. One always needs friends."

"Write to me occasionally. I'll want to know how Wilbur is. You never can tell – is he careful crossing the streets?"

"Wilbur will always be fine, I'm sure." They stopped before the hotel. "Good night," said the girl.

"Just a minute. If there hadn't been a Wilbur—"

"But there was. Don't commit yourself. I'm afraid it's the moon, looking so much like a slice of melon—"

"It's not the moon. It's you."

The proprietor of the Desert Edge came to the door. Dim lights burned in the interior of the hotel.

"Lord, Miss Wendell," he said. "I nearly locked you out."

"I'm coming," returned the girl. "See you at the ranch tomorrow, Mr Eden."

"Fine," answered Eden. He nodded to the landlord, and the front door of the hotel banged to in his face.

As he drove out across the lonely desert he began to wonder what he was going to say to the restless P.J. Madden when he reached the ranch. The millionaire would be home from Pasadena now; he had expected to meet Draycott there. And Draycott was in San Francisco, little dreaming of the part his name was playing in the drama of the Phillimore pearls. P.J. would be furious; he would demand an explanation.

But nothing like that happened. The ranch-house was in darkness and only Ah Kim was in evidence about the place.

"Madden and others in bed now," explained the Chinese. "Came home tired and very much dusted and at once retired to rooms."

"Well, I've got it on good authority that tomorrow is another day," replied Eden. "I'll turn in too."

When he reached the breakfast-table on Thursday morning the three men were there before him. "Everything run off smoothly in Pasadena yesterday?" he inquired brightly.

Thorn and Gamble stared at him, and Madden frowned. "Yes, yes, of course," he said. He added a look which clearly meant, "Shut up."

After breakfast Madden joined the boy in the yard. "Keep that matter of Draycott to yourself," he ordered.

"You saw him, I suppose?" Eden inquired.

"I did not."

"What! Why, that's too bad. But not knowing each other I suppose—"

"No sign of anybody that looked like your man to me. You know, I'm beginning to wonder about you—"

"But, Mr Madden, I told him to be there."

"Well, as a matter of fact, I didn't care especially. Things didn't work out as I expected. I think now you'd better get hold of him and tell him to come to Eldorado. Did he call you up?"

"He may have. I was in town last night. At any rate, he's sure to call soon."

"Well, if he doesn't you'd better go over to Pasadena and get hold of him—"

A truck filled with motion-picture camera-men, props, and actors in weird costumes stopped before the ranch. Two other cars followed. Someone alighted to open the gate.

"What's this?" cried Madden.

"This is Thursday," answered Eden. "Have you forgotten—"

"Forgot it completely," said Madden. "Thorn! Where's Thorn?"

The secretary emerged from the house. "It's the movies, chief. This was the day—"

"Damnation!" growled Madden. "Well, we'll have to go through with it. Martin, you look after things." He went inside.

The movies were all business this morning, in contrast to the careless gaiety of the night before. The cameras were set up in the open end of the *patio*. The actors, in Spanish costume, stood ready. Bob Eden went over to Paula Wendell.

"Good morning," she said. "I came along in case Madden tried to renig on his promise. You see, I know so much about him now—"

The director passed. "This will be O.K.," he remarked to the girl.

"Pleased him for once," she smiled to Eden. "That ought to get into the papers."

The script was a story of old California, and presently they were grinding away at a big scene in the *patio*.

"No, no, no," wailed the director. "What ails you this morning, Rannie? You're saying goodbye to the girl – you love her – love her – love her. You'll probably never see her again."

"The hell I won't," replied the actor. "Then the thing's a flop right now."

"You know what I mean – you think you'll never see her again. Her father has just kicked you out of the house for ever. A bit of a critic, the father. But come on – this is the big farewell. Your heart is broken. Broken, my boy – what are you grinning about?"

"Come on, Diane," said the actor. "I'm never going to see you again, and I'm supposed to be sorry about it. Ye gods, the things these script-writers imagine. However, here goes. My art's equal to anything."

Eden strolled over to where the white-haired patriarch and Eddie Boston were sitting together on a pile of lumber beside the barn. Near at hand Ah Kim hovered, all eyes for these queer antics of the white men.

Boston leaned back and lighted a pipe. “Speaking of Madden,” he remarked, “makes me think of Jerry Delaney. Ever know Jerry, Pop?”

Startled, Eden moved nearer. The old man put his hand behind his ear.

“Who’s that?” he inquired.

“Delaney,” shouted Boston. Chan also edged closer. “Jerry Delaney. There was one smooth worker in his line, Pop. I hope I get a chance – I’m going to ask Madden if he remembers—”

A loud outcry for Mr Boston arose in the *patio*, and he laid down his pipe and fled. Chan and Bob Eden looked at each other.

The company worked steadily until the lunch hour arrived. Then, scattered about the yard and the *patio*, they busied themselves with the generous sandwiches of the Oasis and with coffee served from thermos bottles. Suddenly Madden appeared in the doorway of the living-room. He was in a genial mood.

“Just a word of welcome,” he said. “Make yourselves at home.” He shook hands with the director and, moving about, spoke a few moments with each member of the company in turn. The girl named Diane held his attention for some time.

Presently he came to Eddie Boston. Casually Eden managed it so that he was near by during that interview.

“Boston’s the name,” said the actor. His hard face lighted. “I was hoping to meet you, Mr Madden. I wanted to ask if you remember an old friend of mine – Jerry Delaney, of New York?”

Madden’s eyes narrowed, but the poker face triumphed.

“Delaney?” he repeated vacantly.

"Yes – Jerry Delaney, who used to hang out at Jack McGuire's place on Forty-fourth Street," Boston persisted. "You know, he—"

"I don't recall him," said Madden. He was moving away. "I meet so many people."

"Maybe you don't want to recall him," said Boston, and there was an odd note in his voice. "I can't say I blame you either, sir. No, I guess you wouldn't care much for Delaney. It was a crime what he did to you—"

Madden looked anxiously about. "What do you know about Delaney?" he asked in a low tone.

"I know a lot about him," Boston replied. He came close, and Bob Eden could barely distinguish the words. "I know all about Delaney, Mr Madden."

For a moment they stood staring at each other.

"Come inside, Mr Boston," Madden suggested, and Eden watched them disappear through the door into the living-room.

Ah Kim came into the *patio* with a tray on which were cigars and cigarettes, the offering of the host. As he paused before the director, that gentleman looked at him keenly. "By gad, here's a type," he cried. "Say, John – how'd you like to act in the pictures?"

"You clazy, boss," grinned Ah Kim.

"No, I'm not. We could use you in Hollywood."

"Him lookee like you make 'um big joke."

"Nothing of the kind. You think it over. Here." He wrote on a card. "You change your mind, you come and see me. Savvy?"

"Maybe nuddah day, boss. Plenty happly heah now." He moved along with his tray.

Bob Eden sat down beside Paula Wendell. He was, for all his outward calm, in a very perturbed state of mind.

"Look here," he began, "something has happened, and you can help us again." He explained about Jerry Delaney, and repeated the conversation he had just overheard between

Madden and Eddie Boston. The girl's eyes were wide. "It wouldn't do for Chan or me to make any inquiries," he added. "What sort of fellow is this Boston?"

"Rather unpleasant person," she said. "I've never liked him."

"Well, suppose you ask him a few questions, the first chance you have. I presume that won't come until you get back to town. Find out all he knows about Jerry Delaney, but do it in a way that won't rouse his suspicions, if you can."

"I'll certainly try," she answered. "I'm not very clever – "

"Who says you're not? You're mighty clever – and kind too. Call me up as soon as you've talked with him, and I'll hurry in town."

The director was on his feet. "Come on – let's get this thing finished. Is everybody here? Eddie! Where's Eddie?"

Mr Boston emerged from the living-room, his face a mask, telling nothing. Not going to be an easy matter, Bob Eden reflected, to pump Eddie Boston.

An hour later the movies vanished down the road in a cloud of dust, with Paula Wendell's roadster trailing. Bob Eden sought out Charlie Chan. In the seclusion behind the cookhouse, he again went over Boston's surprising remarks to Madden. The detective's little black eyes shone.

"We march again," he said. "Eddie Boston becomes with sudden flash our one best wager. He must be made to talk. But how?"

"Paula Wendell's going to have a try at it," Eden replied.

Chan nodded. "Fine idea, I think. In presence of pretty girl what man keeps silent? We pin our eager hopes on that."

XVII

IN MADDEN'S FOOTSTEPS

An hour later Bob Eden answered a ring on the telephone. Happily the living-room was deserted. Paula Wendell was on the wire.

"What luck?" asked the boy in a low voice.

"Not so good," she answered. "Eddie was in a terrific rush when we got back to town. He packed his things, paid his bill, and was running out of the hotel when I caught him. 'Listen, Eddie – I want to ask you—' I began, but that was as far as I got. He pointed to the station. 'Can't talk now, Paula,' he said. 'Catching the Los Angeles train.' And he managed to swing aboard it just as it was pulling out."

Eden was silent for a moment. "That's odd. He'd naturally have gone back with the company, wouldn't he? By automobile?"

"Of course. He came that way. Well, I'm awfully sorry, chief. I've fallen down on the job. I guess there's nothing for me to do but turn in my shield and nightstick—"

"Nothing of the sort. You did your best."

"But it wasn't good enough. I'm sorry. I'm forced to start for Hollywood in my car in about an hour. Shall you be here when I come back?"

Eden sighed. “Me? It begins to look as though I’d be here for ever.”

“How terrible!”

“What sort of speech is that?”

“For you, I mean.”

“Oh! Well, thank you very much. I’ll hope to see you soon.”

He hung up the receiver and went into the yard. Ah Kim was loitering near the cookhouse. Together they strolled into the barn.

“We pinned our eager hopes on empty air,” said Eden. He repeated his conversation with Paula Wendell.

Chan nodded, unperturbed. “I would have made fat wager same would happen. Eddie Boston knows all about Delaney, and admits the fact to Madden. What the use we try to see Boston then? Madden has seen him first.”

Bob Eden dropped down on a battered old settee that had been exiled from the house. He put his head in his hands.

“Well, I’m discouraged,” he admitted. “We’re up against a stone wall, Charlie.”

“Many times in my life I find myself in that precise locality,” returned the detective. “What happens? I batter old head until it feels sore, and then a splendid idea assails me. I go around.”

“What do you suggest?”

“Possibilities of ranch now exhausted and drooping. We must look elsewhere. Names of three cities gallop into mind – Pasadena, Los Angeles, Hollywood.”

“All very fine – but how to get there? By gad – I think I can manage it at that. Madden was saying this morning I ought to go to Pasadena and look up Draycott. It seems that for some strange reason they didn’t meet yesterday.”

Chan smiled. “Did he display peevish feeling as result?”

“No, oddly enough, he didn’t. I don’t think he wanted to meet Draycott, with the professor tagging along. Paula

Wendell's going over that way shortly in her car. If I hurry, I may be able to ride with her."

"Which, to my thinking, would be joyful travelling," agreed Chan. "Hasten along. We have more talk when I act part of taxi-driver and carry you to Eldorado."

Bob Eden went at once to Madden's bedroom. The door was open, and he saw the huge figure of the millionaire stretched on the bed, his snores shattering the calm afternoon. He hammered loudly on the panel of the door.

Madden leaped from the bed with startling suddenness, his eyes instantly wide and staring. He seemed like one expecting trouble. For a moment Eden pitied the great man. Beyond all question Madden was caught in some inexplicable net; he was harassed and worn, but fighting still. Not a happy figure, for all his millions.

"I'm awfully sorry to disturb you, sir," Eden said. "But the fact is I have a chance to ride over to Pasadena with some of the movie people, and I think I'd better go. Draycott hasn't called, and—"

"Hush," said Madden sharply. He closed the door. "The matter of Draycott is between you and me. I suppose you wonder what it's all about, but I can't tell you – except to say that this fellow Gamble doesn't strike me as being what he pretends. And—"

"Yes, sir," said Eden hopefully, as the millionaire paused.

"Well, I won't go into that. You locate Draycott and tell him to come to Eldorado. Tell him to put up at the Desert Edge and keep his mouth shut. I'll get in touch with him shortly. Until I do he's to lie low. Is that understood?"

"Perfectly, Mr Madden. I'm sorry this thing has dragged out as it has—"

"Oh, that's all right. You go and tell Ah Kim I said he was to drive you to Eldorado – unless your movie friends are coming out here for you."

"No – I shall have to enlist Ah Kim again. Thank you, sir. I'll be back soon."

"Good luck," answered Madden.

Hastily Eden threw a few things into his suitcase, and waited in the yard for Ah Kim and the car. Gamble appeared.

"Not leaving us, Mr Eden?" he inquired in his mild way.

"No such luck – for you," the boy replied. "Just a short trip."

"On business, perhaps?" persisted the professor gently.

"Perhaps," smiled Eden, and the car with its Chinese chauffeur appearing at that moment, he leaped in.

Again he and Chan were abroad in the yellow glory of a desert sunset. "Well, Charlie," Eden said, "I'm a little new at this detective business. What am I to do first?"

"Toss all worry out of mind. I shall hover round your elbow, doing prompt work."

"You? How are you going to get away?"

"Easy thing. Tomorrow morning I announce I take day off to visit sick brother in Los Angeles. Very ancient plea of all Chinese servants. Madden will be angry, but he will not suspect. Train leaves Eldorado at seven in the morning, going to Pasadena. I am aboard, reaching there at eleven. You will, I hope, condescend to meet me at station?"

"With the greatest pleasure. We take Pasadena first, eh?"

"So I would plan it. We ascertain Madden's movements there on Wednesday. What happened at bank? Did he visit home? Then Hollywood, and maybe Eddie Boston. After that, we ask the lady soprano to desist from singing and talk a little time."

"All right, but we're going to be a fine pair," Eden replied, "with no authority to question anybody. You may be a policeman in Honolulu, but that isn't likely to go very big in Southern California."

Chan shrugged. "Ways will open. Paths will clear."

"I hope so," the boy answered. "And here's another thing. Aren't we taking a big chance? Suppose Madden hears of our antics? Risky, isn't it?"

"Risky pretty good word for it," agreed Chan. "But we are desperate now. We take long gambles."

"I'll say we're desperate," sighed Eden. "Me, I'm getting desperater every minute. I may as well tell you that if we come back from this trip with no definite light on things, I'll be strongly tempted to lift a big burden from your stomach – and my mind."

"Patience very nice virtue," smiled Chan.

"Well, you ought to know," Eden said. "You've got a bigger supply on hand than any man I ever met."

When they reached the Desert Edge Hotel Eden was relieved to see Paula Wendell's car parked in front. They waited by the little roadster, and while they did so Will Holley came along. They told him of their plans.

"I can help you a bit," said the editor. "Madden has a caretaker at his Pasadena house – a fine old chap named Peter Fogg. He's been down here several times, and I know him rather well." He wrote on a card. "Give him that, and tell him I sent you."

"Thanks," said Eden. "We'll need it, or I'm much mistaken."

Paula Wendell appeared.

"Great news for you," Eden announced. "I'm riding with you as far as Pasadena."

"Fine," she replied. "Jump in."

Eden climbed into the roadster. "See you boys later," he called, and the car started.

"You ought to get a regular taxi, with a meter," Eden suggested.

"Nonsense. I'm glad to have you."

"Are you really?"

"Certainly am. Your weight will help to keep the car on the road."

"Lady, you surely can flatter," he told her. "I'll drive, if you like."

"No, thanks – I guess I'd better. I know the roads."

"You're always so efficient, you make me nervous," he commented.

"I wasn't so efficient when it came to Eddie Boston. I'm sorry about that."

"Don't you worry. Eddie's a tough bird. Chan and I will try him presently."

"Where does the big mystery stand now?" asked the girl.

"It stands there leering at us," the boy replied. "Just as it always has." For a time they speculated on Madden's unexplained murder of Delaney. Meanwhile they were climbing between the hills, while the night gathered about them. Presently they dropped down into a green fertile valley, fragrant with the scent of blossoms.

"Um," sighed Eden, breathing deep. "Smells pretty. What is it?"

The girl glanced at him. "You poor, benighted soul. Orange blossoms."

"Oh! Well, naturally I couldn't be expected to know that."

"Of course not."

"The condemned man gets a rather pleasant whiff in his last moments, doesn't he? I suppose it acts like ether – and when he comes to he's married." A reckless driver raced toward them on the wrong side of the road. "Look out!"

"I saw him coming," said the girl. "You're safe with me. How many times must I tell you that?"

They had dinner and a dance or two at an inn in Riverside, and all too soon, it seemed to Eden, arrived at Pasadena. The girl drove up before the Maryland Hotel, prepared to drop him.

"But look here," he protested. "I'll see you safely to Hollywood, of course."

"No need of that," she smiled. "I'm like you. I can take care of myself."

"Is that so?"

"Want to see me tomorrow?"

"Always want to see you tomorrow. Chan and I are coming over your way. Where can we find you?"

She told him she would be at the picture studio at one o'clock, and with a gay goodbye disappeared down the brightly lighted stretch of Colorado Street. Eden went in to a quiet night at the hotel.

After breakfast in the morning he recalled that an old college friend named Spike Bristol was reported in the class histories as living now in Pasadena. The telephone directory furnished Bristol's address, and Eden set out to find him. His friend turned out to be one of the more decorative features of a bond office.

"Bond salesman, eh?" said Eden, when the greetings were over.

"Yes – it was either that or real-estate," replied Bristol. "I was undecided for some time. Finally I picked this."

"Of course," laughed Eden. "As any class history proves, gentlemen prefer bonds. How are you getting on?"

"Fine. All my old friends are buying from me."

"Ah, now I know why you were so glad to see me."

"Sure was. We have some very pretty first mortgage sixes—"

"I'll bet you have – and you can keep them. I'm here on business, Spike – private business. Keep what I say under your hat."

"Never wear one," answered Spike brightly. "That's the beauty of this climate—"

"You can't sell me the climate, either. Spike, you know P.J. Madden, don't you?"

"Well – we're not very chummy. He hasn't asked me to dinner. But of course all of us big financiers are acquainted. As for Madden, I did him a service only a couple of days ago."

"Elucidate."

"This is just between us. Madden came in here Wednesday morning with a hundred and ten thousand dollars' worth of negotiable bonds – mostly Liberties – and we sold them for him the same day. Paid him in cash too."

"Precisely what I wanted to know. Spike, I'd like to talk with somebody at Madden's bank about his actions there Wednesday."

"Who are you – Sherlock Holmes?"

"Well—" Eden thought of Chan. "I am connected with the police temporarily." Spike whistled. "I may go as far as to say – and for heaven's sake keep it to yourself – that Madden is in trouble. At the present moment I'm stopping at his ranch on the desert, and I have every reason to believe he's being blackmailed."

Spike looked at him. "What if he is? That ought to be his business."

"It ought to be, but it isn't. A certain transaction with my father is involved. Do you know anybody at the Garfield Bank?"

"One of my best friends is cashier there. But you know these bankers – hard-boiled eggs. However, we'll have a try."

They went together to the marble precincts of the Garfield Bank. Spike held a long and earnest conversation with his friend. Presently he called Eden over and introduced him.

"How do you do?" said the banker. "You realize that what Spike here suggests is quite irregular. But if he vouches for you I suppose—What is it you want to know?"

"Madden was here on Wednesday. Just what happened?"

"Yes, Mr Madden came in on Wednesday. We hadn't seen him for two years, and his coming caused quite a stir. He visited the safe-deposit vaults and spent some time going through his box."

"Was he alone?"

"No, he wasn't," the banker replied. "His secretary, Thorn, who is well known to us, was with him. Also a little, middle-aged man whom I don't recall very clearly."

"Ah, yes. He examined his safety deposit box. Was that all?"

The banker hesitated. "No. He had wired his office in New York to deposit a rather large sum of money to our credit with the Federal Reserve Bank – but I'd really rather not say any more."

"You paid over to him that large sum of money?"

"I'm not saying we did. I'm afraid I've said too much already."

"You've been very kind," Eden replied. "I promise you won't regret it. Thank you very much."

He and Bristol returned to the street. "Thanks for your help, Spike," Eden remarked. "I'm leaving you here."

"Cast off like an old coat," complained Bristol. "How about lunch?"

"Sorry. Some other time. I must run along now. The station's down here, isn't it? I leave you to your climate."

"Sour grapes," returned Spike. "Don't go home and get lost in the fog. So long."

From the eleven o'clock train a quite different Charlie Chan alighted. He was dressed as Eden had seen him in San Francisco.

"Hello, Dapper Dan," the boy said.

Chan smiled. "Feel respected again," he explained. "Visited Barstow and rescued proper clothes. No cooking today, which makes life very pretty."

"Madden put up a fight when you left?"

"How could he do so? I leave before his awakening, dropping quaintly worded note at door. No doubt now his heart is heavy, thinking I have deserted for ever. Happy surprise for him when Ah Kim returns to home nest."

"Well, Charlie, I've been busy," said Eden. He went over his activities of the morning. "When the old boy came back to the ranch the other night he must have been oozing cash at every pore. I tell you, Holley's right. He's being blackmailed."

"Seems that way," agreed Chan. "Here is another thought. Madden has killed a man, and fears discovery. He gets huge sum together so if necessity arouses he can flee with plenty cash until affair blows overhead. How is that?"

"By George – it's possible," admitted Eden.

"To be considered," replied Chan. "Suggest now we visit caretaker at local home."

A yellow taxi carried them to Orange Grove Avenue. Chan's black eyes sparkled as they drove through the cheerful, handsome city. When they turned off under the shade of the pepper-trees lining the favourite street of the millionaires, the detective regarded the big houses with awe.

"Impressive sight for one born in thatched hut by side of muddy river," he announced. "Rich men here live like emperors. Does it bring content?"

"Charlie," said Eden, "I'm worried about this caretaker business. Suppose he reports our call to Madden. We're sunk."

"Without bubble showing. But what did I say – we accept long chance and hope for happy luck."

"Is it really necessary to see him?"

"Important to see everybody knowing Madden. This caretaker may turn out useful find."

"What shall we say to him?"

"The thing that appears to be true. Madden in much trouble – blackmail. We are police on trail of crime."

"Fine. And how can you prove that?"

"Quick flash of Honolulu badge, which I have pinned to vest. All police badges much alike, unless person has suspicion to read close."

"Well, you're the doctor, Charlie. I follow on."

The taxi halted before the largest house on the street – or in the world, it seemed. Chan and Eden walked up the broad driveway to find a man engaged in training roses on a pergola. He was a scholarly-looking man even in his overalls, with keen eyes and a pleasant smile.

"Mr Fogg?" inquired Eden.

"That's my name," the man said. Bob Eden offered Holley's card, and Fogg's smile broadened.

"Glad to meet any friend of Holley's," he remarked. "Come over to the side veranda and sit down. What can I do for you?"

"We're going to ask a few questions, Mr Fogg," Eden began. "They may seem odd – you can answer them or not, as you prefer. In the first place, Mr Madden was in Pasadena last Wednesday?"

"Why, yes – of course he was."

"You saw him then?"

"For a few minutes – yes. He drove up to the door in that Requa car he uses out here. That was about six o'clock. I talked with him for a while, but he didn't get out of the car."

"What did he say?"

"Just asked me if everything was all right, and added that he might be back shortly for a brief stay here – with his daughter."

"With his daughter, eh?"

"Yes."

"Did you make any inquiries about the daughter?"

"Why, yes – the usual polite hope that she was well. He said she was quite well, and anxious to get here."

"Was Madden alone in the car?"

"No. Thorn was with him – as always. And another man whom I had never seen before."

"They didn't go into the house?"

"No. I had the feeling Mr Madden intended to, but changed his mind."

Bob Eden looked at Charlie Chan. "Mr Fogg – did you notice anything about Madden's manner? Was he just as always?"

Fogg's brow wrinkled. "Well, I got to thinking about it after he left. He did act extremely nervous and sort of – er – harassed."

"I'm going to tell you something, Mr Fogg, and I rely entirely on your discretion. You know that if we weren't all right Will Holley would not have sent us. Mr Madden *is* nervous – he *is* harassed. We have every reason to believe that he is the victim of a gang of blackmailers. Mr Chan—" Chan opened his coat for a brief second, and the celebrated California sun flashed on a silver badge.

Peter Fogg nodded. "I'm not surprised," he said seriously. "But I'm sorry to hear it, just the same. I've always liked Madden. Not many people do – but he has certainly been a friend to me. As you may imagine, this work I'm doing here is hardly in my line. I was a lawyer back East. Then my health broke, and I had to come out here. It was a case of taking anything I could get. Yes, sir, Madden has been kind to me, and I'll help you any way I can."

"You say you're not surprised. Have you any reason for that statement?"

"No particular reason – but a man as famous as Madden – and as rich – well, it seems to me inevitable."

For the first time Charlie Chan spoke. "One more question, sir. Is it possible you have idea why Mr Madden should fear a certain man? A man named – Jerry Delaney?"

Fogg looked at him quickly, but did not speak.

"Jerry Delaney," repeated Bob Eden. "You've heard that name, Mr Fogg?"

"I can tell you this," answered Fogg. "The chief is rather friendly at times. Some years ago he had this house gone over and a complete set of burglar-alarms installed. I met him in the hall while the men were busy at the windows. 'I guess that'll give us plenty of notice if anybody tries to break in,' he said. 'I imagine a big man like you has plenty of enemies, chief,' said I. He looked at me kind of funny. 'There's only one man in the world I'm afraid of, Fogg,' he answered. 'Just one.' I got sort of nervy. 'Who's that, chief?' I asked. 'His name is Jerry Delaney,' he said. 'Remember that, if anything happens.' I told him I would. He was moving off. 'And why are you afraid of this Delaney, chief?' I asked him. It was a cheeky thing to say, and he didn't answer at first."

"But he did answer?" suggested Bob Eden.

"Yes. He looked at me for a minute, and he said: 'Jerry Delaney follows one of the queer professions, Fogg. And he's too damn good at it.' Then he walked away into the library, and I knew better than to ask him anything more."

XVIII

THE BARSTOW TRAIN

A few moments later they left Peter Fogg standing on the trimly kept lawn beside P.J. Madden's empty palace. In silence they rode down the avenue, then turned toward the more lively business district.

"Well, what did we get out of that?" Bob Eden wanted to know. "Not much, if you ask me."

Chan shrugged. "Trifles, mostly. But trifles sometimes blossom big. Detective business consist of one unsignificant detail placed beside other of the same. Then with sudden dazzle light begins to dawn."

"Bring on your dazzle," said Eden. "We've learned that Madden visited his house here on Wednesday, but did not go inside. When questioned about his daughter he replied that she was well and would be along soon. What else? A thing we knew before – that Madden was afraid of Delaney."

"Also that Delaney followed queer profession."

"What profession? Be more explicit."

Chan frowned. "If only I could boast expert knowledge of mainland ways. How about you? Please do a little speculating."

Eden shook his head. "Promised my father I'd never speculate. Just as well too, for in this case I'd get nowhere. My brain – if you'll pardon the mention of one more insignificant detail – is numb. Too many puzzles make Jack a dull boy."

The taxi landed them at the station whence hourly buses ran to Hollywood, and they were just in time to connect with the twelve o'clock run. Back up the hill and over the bridge spanning the Arroyo they sped. A cheery world lay about them, tiny stucco bungalows tinted pink or green, or gleaming white, innumerable service stations. In time they came to the outskirts of the film city, where gaily coloured mansions perched tipsily on miniature hills. Then down a long street that seemed to stretch off into eternity, into the maelstrom of Hollywood's business district.

Expensive cars honked deliriously about the corner where they alighted, and on the pavement crowded a busy throng, most of them living examples of what the well-dressed man or woman will wear if not carefully watched. They crossed the street.

"Watch your step, Charlie," Eden advised. "You're in the auto salesman's paradise." He gazed curiously about him. "The most picturesque factory town in the world. Everything is here except the smoking chimneys."

Paula Wendell was waiting for them in the reception-room of the studio with which she was connected. "Come along," she said. "I'll take you to lunch at the cafeteria, and then perhaps you'd like to look round a bit."

Chan's eyes sparkled as she led them down a street lined with the false fronts of imaginary dwellings. "My oldest girl would exchange the favour of the gods to be on this spot with me," he remarked. "I shall have much to relate when I return to Punch Bowl Hill."

They lunched among the film players, grotesque in make-up and odd costumes. "No postman before," said Chan, over his chicken-pie, "ever encountered such interesting walk on his holiday. Pardon, please, if I eat with unashamed enjoyment and too much gusto. New experience for me to encounter food I have not perspired over myself in person."

"They're taking a picture on Stage Twelve," the girl explained, when lunch was finished. "It's against the rules, but if you're not too boisterous I can get you in for a look."

They passed out of the dazzling sunshine into the dim interior of a great building that looked like a warehouse. Another moment, and they reached the set, built to represent a smart foreign restaurant. Rich hangings were in the background, beautiful carpets on the floor. Along the walls were many tables with pink-shaded lights, and a resplendent headwaiter stood haughtily at the entrance.

The sequence being shot at the moment involved, evidently, the use of many extras, and a huge crowd stood about, waiting patiently. The faces of most of them were vital and alive, unforgettable. Here were people who had known life – and not too much happiness – in many odd corners of the world. Nearly all the men were in uniform – a war picture, no doubt. Bob Eden heard snatches of French, German, Spanish; he saw in the eyes about him a hundred stories more real and tragic than any these people would ever act on the silver screen.

"Leading men and women are standardized, more or less," said Paula Wendell, "but the extras – they're different. If you talked with some of them you'd be amazed. Brains and refinement – remarkable pasts – and on the bargain counter now at five dollars a day."

A call sounded, and the extras filed on to the set and took their allotted stations at the various tables. Chan watched fascinated; evidently he could stay here for ever. But Bob Eden, sadly lacking in that lovely virtue, patience, became restless.

"This is all very well," he said. "But we have work to do. How about Eddie Boston?"

"I have his address for you," the girl replied. "I doubt whether you'll find him in at this hour, but you can try."

An old man appeared in the shadowy space behind the cameras. Eden recognized the veteran player who had been yesterday at Madden's ranch – the actor known as "Pop."

"Hello," cried Paula Wendell. "Maybe Pop can help you." She hailed him. "Know where we can find Eddie Boston?" she inquired.

As Pop joined them Charlie Chan stepped back into a dark corner.

"Why – how are you, Mr Eden?" the old man said. "You want to see Eddie Boston, you say?"

"I'd like to – yes."

"That's too bad. You won't find him in Hollywood."

"Why not? Where is he?"

"On his way to San Francisco by this time," Pop answered. "At least, that was where he was going when I saw him late last night."

"San Francisco? What's he going there for?" asked Eden, amazed.

"One grand outbreak, to hear him tell it. You know, it looks to me like Eddie's come into a bit of money."

"He has, has he?" Eden's eyes narrowed.

"I met him on the street last night when we got in from the desert. He'd come by train, and I asked him why. 'Had some rush business to attend to, Pop,' he says. 'I'm off to 'Frisco in the morning. Things are looking up. Now the picture's finished I aim to take a little jaunt for my health.' Said he hadn't been in 'Frisco since the nineties and was hungry to see it again."

Eden nodded. "Well, thank you very much." With Paula Wendell he moved toward the door, and Chan, his hat low over his eyes, followed.

At the foot of the runway in the bright world outside Eden paused. "That's that," he said. "One more disappointment. Will we ever get to the end of this? Well, Charlie – Boston's beat it. Our bird has flown."

"Why not?" said Chan. "Madden pays him to go, of course. Did Boston not say he knew all about Delaney?"

"Which must mean he knows Delaney's dead. But how could he? Was he on the desert that Wednesday night? Ye gods!" The boy put his hand to his forehead. "You haven't any smelling-salts, have you?" he added to Paula Wendell.

She laughed. "Never use 'em."

They moved out to the street.

"Well, we must push on," said Eden. "The night is dark and we are far from home." He turned to the girl. "When do you go back to Eldorado?"

"This afternoon," she replied. "I'm working on another script – one that calls for a ghost city this time."

"A ghost city?"

"Yes – you know. A deserted mining town. So it's me for the Petticoat Mine again."

"Where's that?"

"Up in the hills about seventeen miles from Eldorado. Petticoat Mine had three thousand citizens ten years ago, but there's not a living soul there today. Just ruins, like Pompeii. I'll have to show it to you – it's mighty interesting."

"That's a promise," Eden returned. "We'll see you back on your dear old desert."

"Warmest thanks for permitting close inspection of picture factory," Chan remarked. "Always a glowing item on the scroll of memory."

"It was fun for me," answered the girl. "Sorry you must go."

On the car bound for Los Angeles Eden turned to the Chinese. "Don't you ever get discouraged, Charlie?" he inquired.

"Not while work remains to do," the detective replied. "This Miss Fitzgerald. Songbird, perhaps, but she will not have flown."

"You'd better talk with her—" Eden began.

But Chan shook his head.

"No, I will not accompany on that errand. Easy to see my presence brings embarrassed pause. I am hard to explain, like black eye."

"Well, I shouldn't have called you that," smiled the boy.

"Go alone to see this woman. Inquire all she knows about the dead man – Delaney."

Eden sighed. "I'll do my best. But my once proud faith in myself is ebbing fast."

At the stage-door of the deserted theatre Eden slipped a dollar into the hand of the doorman, and was permitted to step inside and examine the call-board. As he expected, the local addresses of the troupe were posted up, and he located Miss Fitzgerald at the Wynnwood Hotel.

"You have aspect of experienced person," ventured Chan.

Eden laughed. "Oh, I've known a few chorus-girls in my time. Regular man of the world, I am."

Chan took up his post on a bench in Pershing Square, while the boy went on alone to the Wynnwood Hotel. He sent up his name, and after a long wait in the cheap lobby the actress joined him. She was at least thirty, probably more, but her eyes were young and sparkling. At sight of Bob Eden she adopted a rather coquettish manner.

"You Mr Eden?" she said. "I'm glad to see you, though why I see you's a mystery to me."

"Well, just so long as it's a pleasant mystery—" Eden smiled.

"I'll say it is – so far. You in the profession?"

"Not precisely. First of all, I want to say that I heard you sing over the radio the other night, and I was enchanted. You've a wonderful voice."

She beamed. "Say, I like to hear you talk like that. But I had a cold – I've had one ever since I struck this town. You ought to hear me when I'm going good."

"You were going good enough for me. With a voice like yours you ought to be in grand opera."

"I know – that's what all my friends say. And it ain't that I haven't had the chance. But I love the theatre. Been on the stage since I was a teeny-weeny girl."

"Only yesterday that must have been."

"Say, boy – you're good," she told him. "You don't happen to be scouting for the Metropolitan, do you?"

"No – I wish I were." Eden paused. "Miss Fitzgerald, I'm an old pal of a friend of yours."

"Which friend? I've got so many."

"I'll bet you have. I'm speaking of Jerry Delaney. You know Jerry?"

"Do I? I've known him for years." She frowned suddenly. "Have you any news of Jerry?"

"No, I haven't," Eden answered. "That's why I've come to you. I'm terribly anxious to locate him, and I thought maybe you could help."

She was suddenly cautious. "Old pal of his, you say?"

"Sure. Used to work with him at Jack McGuire's place on Forty-fourth Street."

"Did you really?" The caution vanished. "Well, you know just as much about Jerry's whereabouts as I do. Two weeks ago he wrote me from Chicago – I got it in Seattle. He was kind of mysterious. Said he hoped to see me out this way before long."

"He didn't tell you about the deal he had on?"

"What deal?"

"Well, if you don't know – Jerry was about to pick up a nice little bit of change."

"Is that so? I'm glad to hear it. Things ain't been any too jake with Jerry since those old days at McGuire's."

"That's true enough, I guess. By the way, did Jerry ever talk to you about the men he met at McGuire's? The swells. You know, we used to get some pretty big trade there."

"No, he never talked about it much. Why?"

"I was wondering whether he ever mentioned to you the name of P.J. Madden."

She turned upon the boy a baby stare, wide-eyed and innocent. "Who's P.J. Madden?" she inquired.

"Why, he's one of the biggest financiers in the country. If you ever read the papers—"

"But I don't. My work takes so much time. You've no idea the long hours I put in—"

"I can imagine it. But look here – the question is, where's Jerry now? I may say I'm worried about him."

"Worried? Why?"

"Oh – there's risk in Jerry's business, you know."

"I don't know anything of the sort. Why should there be?"

"We won't go into that. The fact remains that Jerry Delaney arrived at Barstow a week ago last Wednesday morning, and shortly afterwards he disappeared off the face of the earth."

A startled look came into the woman's eyes. "You don't think he's had an – an accident?"

"I'm very much afraid he has. You know the sort Jerry was. Reckless—"

The woman was silent for a moment. "I know," she nodded. "Such a temper. These red-headed Irishmen—"

"Precisely," said Eden, a little too soon.

The green eyes of Miss Norma Fitzgerald narrowed. "Knew Jerry at McGuire's, you say?"

"Of course."

She stood up. "And since when has he had red hair?" Her friendly manner was gone. "I was thinking only last night – I saw a cop at the corner of Sixth and Hill – such a handsome boy. You certainly got fine-looking fellows on your force out here."

"What are you talking about?" demanded Eden.

"Go peddle your papers," advised Miss Fitzgerald. "If Jerry Delaney's in trouble I don't hold with it, but I'm not tipping anything off. A friend's a friend."

"You've got me all wrong," protested Eden.

"Oh, no, I haven't. I've got you all right – and you can find Jerry without any help from me. As a matter of fact, I haven't any idea where he is, and that's the truth. Now run along."

Eden stood up. "Anyhow, I did enjoy your singing," he smiled.

"Yeah. Such nice cops – and so gallant. Well, listen in any time – the radio's open to all."

Bob Eden went glumly back to Pershing Square. He dropped down on the bench beside Chan.

"Luck was poor," remarked the detective. "I see it in your face."

"You don't know the half of it," returned the boy. He related what had happened. "I certainly made a bloomer of it," he finished. "She called me a cop, but she flattered me. The kindergarten class of rookies would disown me."

"Stop the worry," advised Chan. "Woman a little too smart, that is all."

"That's enough," Eden answered. "After this, you officiate. As a detective, I'm a great little jeweler."

They dined at a hotel, and took the five-thirty train to Barstow. As they sped on through the gathering dusk Bob Eden looked at his companion.

"Well, it's over, Charlie," he said. "The day from which we hoped for so much. And what have we gained? Nothing. Am I right?"

"Pretty close to right," admitted Chan.

"I tell you, Charlie, we can't go on. Our position is hopeless. We'll have to go to the sheriff—"

"With what! Pardon that I interrupt. But realize, please, that all our evidence is hazy, like flowers seen in a pool. Madden is big man, his word law to many." The train paused at a station. "We go to sheriff with queer talk – a dead parrot, tale of a desert rat, half-blind and maybe crazy, suitcase in attic filled with old clothes. Can we prove famous man guilty of murder on such foolish grounds? Where is body? Few policemen alive who would not laugh at us—"

Chan broke off suddenly, and Eden followed his gaze. In the aisle of the car stood Captain Bliss of the Homicide Squad, staring at them.

Eden's heart sank. The captain's little eyes slowly took in every detail of Chan's attire, then were turned for a moment on the boy. Without a sign, he turned about and went down the aisle and into the car behind.

"Good night!" said Eden.

Chan shrugged. "Fret no longer," he remarked. "We need not go to sheriff – sheriff will come to us. Our time is brief at Madden's ranch. Poor old Ah Kim may yet be arrested for the murder of Louie Wong."

XIX

THE VOICE ON THE AIR

They arrived at Barstow at half-past ten, and Bob Eden announced his intention of stopping for the night at the station hotel. After a brief talk with the man at the ticket-window Chan rejoined him.

"I take room that neighbors the one occupied by you," he said. "Next train for Eldorado leaves at five o'clock in morning. I am on her when she goes. Much better you await subsequent train at eleven-ten. Not so good if we return to ranch like Siamese twins. Soon enough that blundering Bliss will reveal our connexion."

"Suit yourself, Charlie," returned Eden. "If you've got the strength of character to get up and take a five o'clock train you'll have my best wishes. And those wishes, I may add, will be extended in my sleep."

Chan got his suitcase from the parcel-room, and they went upstairs. But Eden did not at once prepare for bed. Instead he sat down, his head in his hands, and tried to think.

The door between the two rooms opened suddenly, and Chan stood on the threshold. He held in his hand a luminous string of pearls.

"Just to reassure," he smiled. "The Phillimore fortune is still safe."

He laid the pearls on the table, under a brilliant light. Bob Eden reached over, and thoughtfully ran them through his fingers.

"Lovely, aren't they?" he said. "Look here, Charlie – you and I must have a frank talk." Chan nodded. "Tell me, and tell me the truth – have you got the faintest glimmering as to what's doing out at Madden's ranch?"

"One recent day," said Chan, "I thought—"

"Yes?"

"But I was wrong."

"Precisely. I know it's a tough thing for a detective to admit, but you're absolutely stumped, aren't you?"

"You have stumped feeling yourself, maybe—"

"All right – I'll answer the question for you. You are. You're up against it, and we can't go on. Tomorrow afternoon I come back to the ranch. I'm supposed to have seen Draycott – more lies, more deception. I'm sick of it, and, besides, something tells me it won't work any longer. No, Charlie – we're at the zero hour. We've got to give up the pearls."

Chan's face saddened. "Please do not say so," he pleaded. "At any moment—"

"I know – you want more time. Your professional pride is touched. I can understand, and I'm sorry."

"Just a few hours," suggested Chan.

Eden looked for a long moment at the kindly face of the Chinese. He shook his head. "It's not only me – it's Bliss. Bliss will come thumping in presently. We're at the end of our rope. I'll make one last concession – I'll give you until eight o'clock tomorrow night. That's provided Bliss doesn't show up in the interval. Do you agree?"

"I must," said Chan.

"Very good. You'll have all day tomorrow. When I come back I won't bother with that bunk about Draycott. I'll simply say: 'Mr Madden, the pearls will be here at eight o'clock.' At that hour, if nothing has happened, we'll hand them over and go. On our way home we'll put our story before the sheriff, and if he laughs at us we've at least done our duty." Eden sighed with relief. He stood up. "Thank heaven, that's settled."

Gloomily Chan picked up the pearls. "Not happy position for me," he said, "that I must come to this mainland and be sunk in bafflement." His face brightened. "But another day. Much may happen."

Eden patted his broad back. "Lord knows I wish you luck," he said. "Good night."

When Eden awakened to consciousness the following morning the sun was gleaming on the tracks outside his window. He took the train for Eldorado and dropped in at Holley's office.

"Hello," said the editor. "Back at last, eh? Your little pal is keener on the job than you are. He went through here early this morning."

"Oh, Chan's ambitious," Eden replied. "You saw him, did you?"

"Yes." Holley nodded toward a suitcase in the corner. "He left his regular clothes with me. Expects to put 'em on in a day or two, I gather."

"Probably going to wear them to jail," replied Eden glumly. "I suppose he told you about Bliss."

"He did. And I'm afraid it means trouble."

"I'm sure it does. As you probably know, we dug up very little down in the valley."

Holley nodded. "Yes – and what you did dig up was mostly in support of my blackmail theory. Something has happened here too that goes to confirm my suspicions."

"What's that?"

"Madden's New York office has arranged to send him another fifty thousand, through the bank here. I was just talking to the president. He doesn't think he can produce all that in cash before tomorrow, and Madden has agreed to wait."

Eden considered. "No doubt your theory's the right one. The old boy's being blackmailed. Though Chan has made a rather good suggestion – he thinks Madden may be getting this money together—"

"I know – he told me. But that doesn't explain Shaky Phil and the professor. No, I prefer my version. Though I must admit it's the most appalling puzzle—"

"I'll say it is," Eden replied. "And to my mind we've done all that's humanly possible to solve it. I'm handing over the pearls tonight. I presume Chan told you that?"

Holley nodded. "Yes – you're breaking his heart. But from your viewpoint you're absolutely right. There's a limit to everything, and you seem to have reached it. However, I'm praying something happens before tonight."

"So am I," said Eden. "If it doesn't I don't see how I can bring myself to – but doggone it! There's Madame Jordan. It's nothing to her that Madden's killed a man."

"It's been a difficult position for you, my boy," Holley replied. "You've handled it well. I'll pray my hardest – and I did hear once of a newspaper man whose prayers were answered. But that was years ago."

Eden stood up. "I must get back to the ranch. Seen Paula Wendell today?"

"Saw her at breakfast down at the Oasis. She was on the point of starting for the Petticoat Mine." Holley smiled. "But don't worry – I'll take you out to Madden's."

"No, you won't. I'll hire a car—"

"Forget it. Paper's off the press now, and I'm at an even looser end than usual. Come along."

Once more Horace Greeley carried them up the rough road between the hills. As they rattled down to the blazing floor of the desert the editor yawned.

"I didn't sleep much last night," he explained.

"Thinking about Jerry Delaney?" asked the boy.

Holley shook his head. "No – something has happened – something that concerns me alone. That interview with Madden has inspired my old friend in New York to offer me a job there – a mighty good job. Yesterday afternoon I had a doctor in Eldorado look me over – and he told me I could go."

"That's great!" Eden cried. "I'm mighty happy for your sake."

An odd look had come into Holley's eyes. "Yes," he said, "the prison door swings open, after all these years. I've dreamed of this moment, longed for it – and now—"

"What?"

"The prisoner hesitates. He's frightened at the thought of leaving his nice quiet cell. New York! Not the old New York I knew. Could I tackle it again, and win? I wonder."

"Nonsense," Eden answered. "Of course you could."

A determined look passed over Holley's face. "I'll try it," he said. "I'll go. Why the devil should I throw my life away out here? Yes – I'll tackle Park Row again."

He left Eden at the ranch. The boy went at once to his room, and, as soon as he had freshened up a bit, stepped into the *patio*. Ah Kim passed.

"Anything new?" whispered Eden.

"Thorn and Gamble away all day in big car," the Chinese replied. "Nothing more." It was obvious he was still "sunk in bafflement."

In the living-room Eden found the millionaire sitting aimless and lonely. Madden perked up at the boy's arrival. "Back safe, eh?" he said. "Did you find Draycott? You can speak out. We're alone here."

Eden dropped into a chair. "It's all set, sir. I'll give you the Phillimore pearls at eight o'clock tonight."

"Where?"

"Here at the ranch."

Madden frowned. "I'd rather it had been at Eldorado. You mean Draycott's coming here—"

"No, I don't. I'll have the pearls at eight o'clock, and I'll give them to you. If you want the transaction kept private that can be arranged."

"Good." Madden looked at him. "Maybe you've got them now?" he suggested.

"No. But I'll have them at eight."

"Well, I'm certainly glad to hear it," Madden replied. "But I want to tell you right here that if you're stalling again—"

"What do you mean – stalling?"

"You heard me. Do you think I'm a fool? Ever since you came you've been stalling about that necklace. Haven't you?"

Eden hesitated. The moment had come for a bit of frankness, it seemed. "I have," he admitted.

"Why?"

"Because, Mr Madden, I thought there was something wrong here."

"Why did you think that?"

"Before I tell you – what made you change your mind in the first place? In San Francisco you wanted the necklace delivered in New York. Why did you switch to Southern California?"

"A simple reason," Madden replied. "I thought up there that my daughter was going East with me. Her plans are altered – she's going at once to Pasadena for the balance of the season. And I propose to put the necklace in safety deposit there for her use when she wants it."

"I met your daughter in San Francisco," Eden said. "She's a very charming girl."

Madden looked at him keenly. "You think so, do you?"

"I do. I presume she is still in Denver?"

For a moment Madden was silent, regarding him. "No," he admitted finally, "she is not in Denver now."

"Indeed. If you don't mind telling me—"

"She is in Los Angeles, visiting friends."

At this surprising information Eden's eyes opened wide.

"How long has she been there?" he inquired.

"Since last Tuesday," Madden answered. "I think it was Tuesday – I got a wire saying she was coming here. I didn't want her here, for certain reasons, so I sent Thorn in to meet her, with instructions to take her back to Barstow and put her on the Los Angeles train."

Eden thought fast. Barstow was about the proper distance away to account for the mileage on the big car. But where was the red clay on station platforms hereabouts?

"You're certain she reached Los Angeles safely?" he asked.

"Of course. I saw her there on Wednesday. Now, I've answered all your questions. It's your turn. Why did you think something was wrong here?"

"What has become of Shaky Phil Maydorf?" countered Eden.

"Who?"

"Shaky Phil – the lad who called himself McCallum, and who won forty-seven dollars from me at poker here the other night?"

"You mean his name was really Maydorf?" inquired Madden with interest.

"I certainly do. I had some experience with Maydorf in San Francisco."

"In what way?"

"He acted as though he was trying to annex the Phillimore pearls."

Madden's face was purple again. "Is that so? Would you mind telling me about it?"

"Not at all," replied Eden. He narrated Maydorf's activities at the pier, but failed to mention the connexion with Louie Wong.

"Why didn't you tell me sooner?" demanded Madden.

"Because I thought you knew it. I still think so."

"You're crazy."

"Maybe. We won't go into that. But when I saw Maydorf down here it was natural to suspect something was wrong. I'm not convinced yet that it isn't. Why not go back to the original plan and deliver the pearls in New York?"

Madden shook his head. "No. I've set out to get them here, and I'll go through with it. Anybody will tell you I'm no quitter."

"Then at least tell me what the trouble is."

"There is no trouble," Madden replied. "At least, none that I can't handle myself. It's my own affair. I've bought the pearls, and I want them. I give you my word that you'll be paid, which is all that need concern you."

"Mr Madden," said the boy, "I'm not blind. You're in a jam of some sort, and I'd like to help you."

Madden turned, and his tired, harassed face was ample proof of Eden's statement. "I'll get out of it," he said. "I've got out of worse holes. I thank you for your kind intentions, but don't you worry about me. At eight o'clock then – I'm relying on you. Now, if you'll excuse me I think I'll lie down. I anticipate a rather busy evening."

He went from the room, and Bob Eden stared after him, perplexed and at sea. Had he gone too far with the millionaire – told him too much? And how about this news of Evelyn Madden? Could it be true? Was she really in Los Angeles? It sounded plausible enough, and her father's manner when he spoke of her seemed frankness itself.

Oh, well – the heat on the desert was now a tangible thing, wave on wave of filmy haze. Eden was weary with his many problems. He followed Madden's example, and slept the afternoon away.

When he rose the sun was sinking and the cool night coming on. He heard Gamble in the bathroom. Gamble – who was Gamble? Why was he allowed to remain on Madden's ranch?

In the *patio* the boy had a few whispered words with Ah Kim, telling him the news about Evelyn Madden.

"Thorn and professor home now," the detective said. "I notice mileage – thirty-nine, as before. And bits of red clay on floor of car."

Eden shook his head. "Time is passing," he remarked.

Chan shrugged. "If I could arrest it I would do so," he replied.

At the dinner-table Professor Gamble was amiability personified.

"Well, well, Mr Eden, we're glad to have you back with us. Sorry to have you miss any of this desert air. Your business – if I may presume – your business prospered?"

"Sure did," smiled Eden. "And how does yours go?"

The professor looked at him quickly. "I – er – I am happy to say I have had a most gratifying day. I found the very rat I was looking for."

"Fine for you, but hard on the rat," said Eden, and the dinner proceeded in silence.

When they rose from the table Madden lighted a cigar and dropped into his favourite chair before the fire. Gamble sat down with a magazine beside a lamp. Eden took out a packet of cigarettes, lighted one, wandered about. Thorn also selected a magazine. The big clock struck the hour of seven, and then an air of almost intolerable quiet settled over the room.

Eden paused at the wireless set. "Never could see the sense of these things until I came down here," he explained to Madden. "I realize now there are times when even a lecture on the habits of the hookworm may seem enchanting. How about a bedtime story for the kiddies?"

He tuned in. Ah Kim entered and busied himself at the table. The sharp voice of an announcer in Los Angeles filled the room:

"...next number on our programme – Miss Norma Fitzgerald, who is appearing in the musical show at the Mason, will sing a couple of selections."

Madden leaned forward and tapped the ash from his cigar. Thorn and Gamble looked up with languid interest.

"Hello, folks," came the voice of the woman Bob Eden had talked with the day before. "Here I am again. And right at the start I want to thank all you good friends for the loads and loads of letters I've had since I went on the air out here. I found a lovely bunch at the studio tonight. I haven't had time to read them all, but I want to tell Sadie French, if she's listening in, that I was glad to know she's in Santa Monica, and I'll sure call her up. Another letter that brought me happiness was from my old pal, Jerry Delaney...."

Eden's heart stopped beating. Madden leaned forward, Thorn's mouth opened and stayed that way, and the eyes of the professor narrowed. Ah Kim, at the table, worked without a sound.

"I've been a little worried about Jerry," the woman went on, "and it was great to know that he's alive and well. I'm looking forward to seeing him soon. Now I must go on with my programme, because I'm due at the theatre in half an hour. I hope you good people will all come and see us, for we've certainly got a dandy little show, and—"

"Oh, shut the confounded thing off," said Madden. "Advertising, nine-tenths of these radio programmes. Makes me sick."

Norma Fitzgerald had burst into song, and Bob Eden shut the confounded thing off. A long look passed between him and Ah Kim. A voice had come to the desert, come over the bare brown hills and the dreary miles of sage-brush and sand – a voice that said Jerry Delaney was alive and well. Alive and well – and all their fine theories came crashing down.

The man Madden killed was not Jerry Delaney! Then whose was the voice calling for help that tragic night at the ranch? Who uttered the cry that was heard and echoed by Tony, the Chinese Parrot?

XX

PETTICOAT MINE

Ah Kim, carrying a heavy tray of dishes, left the room. Madden leaned back at ease in his chair, his eyes closed, and blew thick rings of smoke toward the ceiling. The professor and Thorn resumed their placid reading, one on each side of the lamp. A touching scene of domestic peace!

But Bob Eden did not share that peace. His heart was beating fast – his mind was dazed. He rose and slipped quietly outdoors. In the cookhouse Ah Kim was at the sink, busily washing dishes. To look at the impassive face of the Chinese no one would have guessed that this was not his regular employment.

"Charlie," said Eden softly.

Chan hastily dried his hands and came to the door. "Humbly begging pardon, do not come in here." He led the way to the shadows beside the barn. "What are trouble now?" he asked gently.

"Trouble!" said Eden. "You heard, didn't you? We've been on the wrong track entirely. Jerry Delaney is alive and well."

"Most interesting, to be sure," admitted Chan.

"Interesting! Say – what are you made of, anyhow?" Chan's calm was a bit disturbing. "Our theory blows up completely, and you—"

"Old habit of theories," said Chan. "Not the first to shatter in my countenance. Pardon me if I fail to experience thrill like you."

"But what shall we do now?"

"What should we do? We hand over pearls. You have made foolish promise, which I heartily rebuked. Nothing to do but carry out."

"And go away without learning what happened here! I don't see how I can—"

"What is to be, will be. The words of the infinitely wise Kong Fu Tse—"

"But listen, Charlie – have you thought of this? Perhaps nothing happened. Maybe we've been on a false trail from the start—"

A little car came tearing down the road, and they heard it stop with a wild shriek of the brakes before the ranch. They hurried round the house. The moon was low and the scene in semi-darkness. A familiar figure alighted and, without pausing to open the gate, leaped over it. Eden ran forward.

"Hello, Holley," he said.

Holley turned suddenly.

"Good Lord – you scared me. But you're the man I'm looking for." He was panting, obviously excited.

"What's wrong?" Eden asked.

"I don't know. But I'm worried. Paula Wendell—"

Eden's heart sank. "What about Paula Wendell?"

"You haven't heard from her – or seen her?"

"No, of course not."

"Well, she never came back from the Petticoat Mine. It's only a short run up there, and she left just after breakfast. She should have been back long ago. She promised to have dinner with me, and we were going to see the picture at the theatre tonight. It's one she's particularly interested in."

Eden was moving toward the road. "Come along – in heaven's name – hurry—"

Chan stepped forward. Something gleamed in his hand.

"My automatic," he explained. "I rescued it from suitcase this morning. Take it with you—"

"I won't need that," said Eden. "Keep it. You may have use for it—"

"I humbly beg of you—"

"Thanks, Charlie. I don't want it. All right, Holley—"

"The pearls," suggested Chan.

"Oh, I'll be back by eight. This is more important—"

As he climbed into the car by Holley's side Eden saw the front door of the ranch-house open, and the huge figure of Madden framed in the doorway.

"Hey!" cried the millionaire.

"Hey yourself!" muttered Eden. The editor was backing his car, and with amazing speed he swung it round. They were off down the road, the throttle wide open.

"What could have happened?" Eden asked.

"I don't know. It's a dangerous place, that old mine. Shafts sunk all over – the mouths of some of them hidden by underbrush. Shafts several hundred feet deep—"

"Faster!" pleaded Eden.

"Going the limit now," Holley replied. "Madden seemed interested in your departure, didn't he? I take it you haven't given him the pearls."

"No. Something new broke tonight." Eden told of the voice over the wireless. "Ever strike you that we may have been cuckoo from the start? No one even slightly damaged at the ranch, after all?"

"Quite possible," the editor admitted.

"Well, that can wait. It's Paula Wendell now."

Another car was coming toward them with reckless speed. Holley swung out, and the two cars grazed in passing.

"Who was that?" wondered Eden.

"A taxi from the station," Holley returned. "I think I recognized the driver. There was someone in the back seat."

"I know," said Eden. "Someone headed for Madden's ranch perhaps."

"Perhaps," agreed Holley. He turned off the main road into the perilous, half-obliterated highway that led to the long-abandoned mine. "Have to go slower, I'm afraid," he said.

"Oh, hit it up," urged Eden. "You can't hurt old Horace Greeley." Holley again opened the throttle wide, and, the front wheel on the left coming at that moment in violent contact with a rock, their heads nearly pierced the top of the car.

"It's all wrong, Holley," remarked Eden with feeling.

"What's all wrong?"

"A pretty, charming girl like Paula Wendell running about alone in this desert country. Why in heaven's name doesn't somebody marry her and take her away from it?"

"Not a chance," replied Holley. "She hasn't any use for marriage. 'The last resort of feeble minds' is what she calls it."

"Is that so?"

"Never coop her up in a kitchenette, she told me, after the life of freedom she's enjoyed."

"Then why did she go and get engaged to this guy?"

"What guy?"

"Wilbur – or whatever his name is. The lad who gave her the ring."

Holley laughed – then was silent for a minute. "I don't suppose she'll like it," he said at last, "but I'm going to tell you, anyhow. It would be a pity if you didn't find out. That emerald is an old one that belonged to her mother. She's had it put in a more modern setting, and she wears it as a sort of protection."

"Protection?"

"Yes. So every mush-head she meets won't pester her to marry him."

"Oh," said Eden. A long silence. "Is that the way she characterizes me?" asked the boy finally.

"How?"

"As a mush-head."

"Oh, no. She said you had the same ideas on marriage that she had. Refreshing to meet a sensible man like you, is the way she put it." Another long silence. "What's on your mind?" asked the editor.

"Plenty," said Eden grimly. "I suppose, at my age, it's still possible to make over a wasted life?"

"It ought to be," Holley assured him.

"I've been acting like a fool. Going to give good old Dad the surprise of his life when I get home. Take over the business, like he's wanted me to, and work hard. So far I haven't known what I wanted. Been as weak and vacillating as a – a woman."

"Some simile," replied Holley. "I don't know that I ever heard a worse one. Show me the woman who doesn't know what she wants – and, knowing, fails to go after it."

"Oh, well – you get what I mean. How much farther is it?"

"We're getting there. Five miles more."

"Gad – I hope nothing's happened to her."

They rattled on, closer and closer to the low hills, brick red under the rays of the slowly rising moon. The road entered a narrow canyon; it almost disappeared, but like a homing thing Horace Greeley followed it intuitively.

"Got a flashlight?" Eden inquired.

"Yes. Why?"

"Stop a minute, and let me have it. I've an idea."

He descended with the light, and carefully examined the road ahead. "She's been along here," he announced. "That's the tread of her tyres – I'd know it anywhere – I changed one of them for her. She's – she's up there somewhere too. The car has been this way but once."

He leaped back beside Holley, and the car sped on, round hairpin turns, and along the edge of a precipice. Presently it turned a final corner, and before them, nestled in the hills, was the ghost city of Petticoat Mine.

Bob Eden caught his breath. Under the friendly moon lay the remnants of a town, here a chimney and there a wall, street after street of houses crumbled now to dust. Once the mine had boomed and the crowd had come, they had built their homes here where the shafts sank deep; silver had fallen in price, and the crowd had gone, leaving Petticoat Mine to the most deadly bombardment of all, the patient, silent bombardment of the empty years.

They rode down Main Street, weaving in and out among black, gaping holes that might have been made by bursting shells. Between the cracks of the pavements, thronged once on a Saturday night, grew patches of pale green basket-grass. Of the 'business blocks' but two remained, and one of these was listing with the wind.

"Cheery sight," remarked Eden.

"The building that's on the verge of toppling is the old Silver Star Saloon," said Holley. "The other one – it never will topple. They built it of stone – built it to stand – and they needed it too, I guess. That's the old jail."

"The jail," Eden repeated.

Holley's voice grew cautious. "Is that a light in the Silver Star?"

"Seems to be," Eden answered. "Look here – we're at rather a disadvantage – unarmed, you know. I'll just stow away in the tonneau, and appear when needed. The element of surprise may make up for our lack of a weapon."

"Good idea," agreed Holley, and Eden climbed into the rear of the car and hid himself. They stopped before the Silver Star. A tall man appeared suddenly in the doorway, and walked briskly up to the car.

"Well, what do you want?" he asked, and Bob Eden thrilled to hear again the thin, high voice of Shaky Phil Maydorf.

"Hello, stranger," said Holley. "This is a surprise. I thought old Petticoat was deserted."

"Company's thinking of opening up the mine soon," returned Maydorf. "I'm here to do a little assaying."

"Find anything?" inquired Holley casually.

"The silver's pretty well worked out. But there's copper in those hills to the left. You're a long way off the main road."

"I know that. I'm looking for a young woman who came up here this morning. Maybe you saw her."

"There hasn't been anyone here for a week, except me."

"Really? Well, you may be mistaken. If you don't mind, I'll have a look round—"

"And if I do mind?" snarled Shaky Phil.

"Why should you—"

"I do. I'm alone here, and I'm not taking any chances. You swing that car of yours around—"

"Now, wait a minute," said Holley. "Put away that gun. I come as a friend—"

"Yeah. Well, as a friend you turn and beat it. Understand." He was close to the car. "I tell you there's nobody here—"

He stopped as a figure rose suddenly from the tonneau and fell upon him. The gun exploded, but harmlessly into the road, for Bob Eden was bearing down upon it hard.

For a brief moment, there on that deserted street before the Silver Star, the two struggled desperately. Shaky Phil was no longer young, but he offered a spirited resistance. However, it was not prolonged, and by the time Holley had alighted Bob Eden was on top and held Maydorf's weapon in his hand.

"Get up," the boy directed. "And lead the way. Give me your keys. There's a brand-new lock on that jail door, and we have a yearning to see what's inside." Shaky Phil rose to his feet and looked helplessly about. "Hurry!" cried Eden. "I've been longing to meet you again, and I don't feel any too gentle. There's that forty-seven dollars – to say nothing of all the trouble you put me to the night the *President Pierce* docked in San Francisco."

"There's nothing in the jail," said Maydorf. "I haven't got the key—"

"Go through him, Holley," suggested the boy.

A quick search produced a bunch of keys, and Eden, taking them, handed Holley the gun. "I give old Shaky Phil into your keeping. If he tries to run shoot him down like a rabbit."

He took the flashlight from the car, and, going over, unlocked the outer door of the jail. Stepping inside, he found himself in what had once been a sort of office. The moonlight pouring in from the street, fell upon a dusty desk and chair, an old safe, and a shelf with a few tattered books. On the desk lay a newspaper. He flashed his light on the date – only a week old.

At the rear were two heavy doors, both with new locks. Searching among his keys, he unlocked the one at the left. In a small, cell-like room with high, barred windows his flashlight revealed the tall figure of a girl. With no great surprise he recognized Evelyn Madden. She came toward him swiftly. "Bob Eden!" she cried, and then, her old haughtiness gone, she burst into tears.

"There – there," said Eden. "You're all right now." Another girl appeared suddenly in the doorway – Paula Wendell, bright and smiling.

"Hello," she remarked calmly. "I rather thought you'd come along."

"Thanks for the ad," replied Eden. "Say, you might get hurt running about like this. What happened, anyhow?"

"Nothing much. I came up to look round, and he" – she nodded to Shaky Phil in the moonlit street – "told me I couldn't. I argued it with him, and ended up in here. He said I'd have to stay overnight. He was polite, but firm."

"Lucky for him he was polite," remarked Eden grimly. He took the arm of Evelyn Madden. "Come along," he said gently. "I guess we're through here—"

He stopped. Someone was hammering on the inside of the second door. Amazed, the boy looked toward Paula Wendell.

She nodded. "Unlock it," she told him.

He unfastened the door and, swinging it open, peered inside. In the semi-darkness he saw the dim figure of a man.

Eden gasped, and fell back against the desk for support.

"Ghost city!" he cried. "Well, that's what it is all right."

XXI

END OF THE POSTMAN'S JOURNEY

If Bob Eden had known the identity of the passenger in the taxi that he and Holley passed on their way to the mine, it is possible that, despite his concern for Paula Wendell, he would have turned back to Madden's ranch. But he drove on unknowing; nor did the passenger, though he stared with interest at the passing car, recognize Eden. The car from the Eldorado station went on its appointed way, and finally drew up before the ranch-house.

The driver alighted and was fumbling with the gate, when his fare leaped to the ground.

"Never mind that," he said. "I'll leave you here. How much do I owe you?" He was a plump little man, about thirty-five years old, attired in the height of fashion and with a pompous manner. The driver named a sum, and, paying him off, the passenger entered the yard. Walking importantly up to the front door of the house, he knocked loudly.

Madden, talking with Thorn and Gamble by the fire, looked up in annoyance. "Now who the devil—" he began. Thorn went over and opened the door. The plump little man at once pushed his way inside.

"I'm looking for Mr P.J. Madden," he announced.

The millionaire rose. "All right – I'm Madden. What do you want?"

The stranger shook hands. "Glad to meet you, Mr Madden. My name is Victor Jordan, and I'm one of the owners of those pearls you bought in San Francisco."

A delighted smile spread over Madden's face. "Oh – I'm glad to see you," he said. "Mr Eden told me you were coming—"

"How could he?" demanded Victor. "He didn't know it himself."

"Well, he didn't mention you. But he informed me the pearls would be here at eight o'clock—"

Victor stared. "Be here at eight o'clock?" he repeated. "Say, just what has Bob Eden been up to down here, anyhow? The pearls left San Francisco a week ago, when Eden did."

"What!" Purple again in Madden's face. "He had them all the time! Why, the young scoundrel! I'll break him in two for this. I'll wring his neck—" He stopped. "But he's gone. I just saw him driving away."

"Really?" returned Victor. "Well, that may not be so serious as it looks. When I say the pearls left San Francisco with Eden, I don't mean he was carrying them. Charlie had them."

"Charlie who?"

"Why, Charlie Chan, of the Honolulu police. The man who brought them from Hawaii."

Madden was thoughtful. "Chan – a Chinaman?"

"Of course. He's here too, isn't he? I understood he was."

A wicked light came into Madden's eyes. "Yes, he's here. You think he still has the pearls?"

"I'm sure he has. In a money-belt about his waist. Get him here and I'll order him to hand them over at once."

"Fine – fine!" chuckled Madden. "If you'll step into this room for a moment, Mr Jordan, I'll call you presently."

"Yes, sir – of course," agreed Victor, who was always polite to the rich. Madden led him by the inside passage to his bedroom. When the millionaire returned, his spirits were high.

"Bit of luck, this is," he remarked. "And to think that blooming cook—" He went to the door leading on to the *patio*, and called loudly, "Ah Kim!"

The Chinese shuffled in. He looked at Madden blankly. "Wha's matta, boss?" he inquired.

"I want to have a little talk with you." Madden's manner was genial, even kindly. "Where did you work before you came here?"

"Get 'um woik all place, boss. Maybe lay sticks on gloun' foah lailload—"

"What town – what town did you work in last?"

"No got 'um town, boss. Jus' outdoahs no place, laying sticks—"

"You mean you were laying ties for the railroad on the desert?"

"Yes, boss. You light now."

Madden leaned back and put his thumbs in the arm-holes of his waistcoat. "Ah Kim – you're a damned liar," he said.

"Wha's matter, boss?"

"I'll show you what's the matter. I don't know what your game here has been, but it's all over now." Madden rose and stepped to the door. "Come in, sir," he called, and Victor Jordan strode into the room. Chan's eyes narrowed.

"Charlie, what is all this nonsense?" demanded Victor. "What are you doing in that melodramatic outfit?"

Chan did not answer. Madden laughed. "All over, as I told you, Charlie – if that's your name. This is Mr Jordan, one of the owners of those pearls you're carrying in your money-belt."

Chan shrugged. "Mr Jordan juggles truth," he replied, dropping his dialect with a sigh of relief. "He has no claim on pearls. They are property of his mother, to whom I give promise I would guard them with life."

"See here, Charlie," cried Victor angrily, "don't tell me I lie. I'm sick and tired of this delay down here, and I've come with my mother's authority to put an end to it. If you don't believe me, read that."

He handed over a brief note in Madame Jordan's old-fashioned script. Chan read it. "One only answer," he remarked. "I must release the pearls." He glanced toward the clock, ticking busily by the *patio* window. "Though I am much preferring to wait Mr Eden's come back—"

"Never mind Eden," said Victor. "Produce that necklace."

Chan bowed and, turning, fumbled for a moment at his waist. The Phillimore necklace was in his hand.

Madden took it eagerly. "At last," he said.

Gamble was staring over his shoulder. "Beautiful," murmured the professor.

"One minute," said Chan. "A receipt, if you will be so kind."

Madden nodded, and sat at his desk. "I got one ready this afternoon. Just have to sign it." He laid the pearls on the blotter, and took a typewritten sheet from the top drawer. Slowly he wrote his name. "Mr Jordan," he was saying, "I'm deeply grateful to you for coming down here and ending this. Now that it's settled I'm leaving at once—" He offered the receipt to Chan.

A strange look had come into the usually impassive eyes of Charlie Chan. He reached out toward the sheet of paper offered him, then with the speed of a tiger he snatched for the pearls. Madden snatched too, but he was a little late. The necklace disappeared into Chan's voluminous sleeve.

"What's this?" bellowed Madden, on his feet. "Why, you crazy—"

"Hush," said Chan. "I will retain the pearls."

"You will, will you?" Madden whipped out a pistol. "We'll see about that—"

There was a loud report and a flash of fire – but they did not come from Madden's gun. They came from the silken sleeve of Charlie Chan. Madden's weapon clattered to the floor, and there was blood on his hand.

"Do not stoop!" warned Chan, and his voice was suddenly high and shrill. "Postman has been on such long walk, but now at last he has reached journey's end. Do not stoop, or I put bullet in somewhat valuable head!"

"Charlie – are you mad?" cried Victor.

"Not very," smiled Chan. "Kindly favour me by backing away, Mr Madden." He picked up the pistol from the floor – Bill Hart's present, it seemed to be. "Very nice gun, I use it now." Swinging Madden round, he searched him, then placed a chair in the centre of the room. "Be seated here, if you will so far condescend—" he said.

"The hell I will," cried Madden.

"Recline!" said Chan.

The great Madden looked at him a second, then dropped sullenly down upon the chair. "Mr Gamble," called Chan. He ran over the slim person of the professor. "You have left pretty little weapon in room. That is good. This will be your chair. And not to forget Mr Thorn, also unarmed. Comfortable chair for you too." He backed away, facing them. "Victor, I make humble suggestion that you add yourself to group. You are plenty foolish boy, always. I remember – in Honolulu—" His tone hardened. "Sit quickly, or I puncture you and lift big load from mother's mind!"

He drew up a chair between them and the exhibition of guns on the wall. "I also will venture to recline," he announced. He glanced at the clock. "Our wait may be a long one. Mr Thorn, another suggestion occurs. Take handkerchief and bind up wounded hand of chief."

Thorn produced a handkerchief and Madden held out his hand. "What the devil are we waiting for?" snarled the millionaire.

"We await come back of Mr Bob Eden," replied Chan. "I am having much to impart when he arrives."

Thorn completed his act of mercy, and slunk back to his chair. The tall clock by the *patio* windows ticked on. With the patience characteristic of his race Chan sat staring at his odd assortment of captives. Fifteen minutes passed, a half-hour, the minute hand began its slow advance toward the hour of nine.

Victor Jordan shifted uneasily in his chair. Such disrespect to a man worth millions! "You're clear out of your mind, Charlie," he protested.

"Maybe," admitted Chan. "We wait and see."

Presently a car rattled into the yard. Chan nodded. "Long wait nearly over," he announced. "Now Mr Eden comes."

His expression altered as a knock sounded on the door. It was pushed open, and a man strode brusquely in. A stocky, red-faced, determined man – Captain Bliss of the Homicide Squad. After him came another, a lean, wiry individual in a two-quart hat. They stood amazed at the scene before them.

Madden leaped to his feet. "Captain Bliss. By gad, I'm delighted to see you. You're just in time."

"What's all this?" inquired the lean man.

"Mr Madden," said Bliss, "I've brought along Harley Cox, sheriff of the county. I guess you need us here."

"We sure do," replied Madden. "This Chinaman has gone crazy. Take that gun away from him and put him under arrest."

The sheriff stepped up to Charlie Chan. "Give me the firearms, John," he ordered. "You know what that means – a Chinaman with a gun in California. Deportation. Good Lord – he's got two of them."

"Sheriff," said Charlie with dignity. "Permit me the honor that I introduce myself. I am Detective-Sergeant Chan, of the Honolulu police."

The sheriff laughed. "You don't say. Well, I'm the Queen of Sheba. Are you going to give me that other gun, or do you want a charge of resisting an officer?"

"I do not resist," said Chan. He gave up his own weapon. "I only call to your attention I am fellow-policeman, and I yearn to save you from an error you will have bitter cause to regret."

"I'll take the chance. Now, what's going on here?" The sheriff turned to Madden. "We came about that Louie Wong killing. Bliss saw this Chinaman on a train last night with the fellow named Eden, all dolled up in regular clothes and as chummy as a brother."

"You're on the right trail now, Sheriff," Madden assured him. "There's no doubt he killed Louie. And just at present he has somewhere about him a string of pearls belonging to me. Please take them away from him."

"Sure, Mr Madden," replied the sheriff. He advanced to make a search, but Chan forestalled him. He handed him the necklace.

"I give it to your keeping," he said. "You are officer of law and responsible. Attend your step."

Cox regarded the pearls. "Some string, ain't it? Kinda pretty, Mr Madden. You say it belongs to you?"

"It certainly does— "

"Sheriff," pleaded Charlie, with a glance at the clock, "if I may make humble suggestion, go slow. You will kick yourself angrily over vast expanse of desert should you make blunder now."

"But if Mr Madden says these pearls are his— "

"They are," said Madden. "I bought them from a jeweler named Eden in San Francisco ten days ago. They belonged to the mother of Mr Jordan here."

"That's quite correct," admitted Victor.

"It's enough for me," remarked the sheriff.

"I tell you I am of the Honolulu police— " protested Chan.

"Maybe so, but do you think I'd take your word against that of a man like P.J. Madden? Mr Madden, here are your pearls— "

"One moment," cried Chan. "This Madden says he is the same who bought the necklace at San Francisco jeweler's. Ask him, please, location of jeweler's store."

"On Post Street," said Madden.

"What part Post Street? Famous building across way. What building?"

"Officer," objected Madden, "must I submit to this from a Chinese cook? I refuse to answer. The pearls are mine—"

Victor Jordan's eyes were open wide. "Hold on," he said. "Let me in this. Mr Madden, my mother told me of the time when you first saw her. You were employed then – where – in what position?"

Madden's face purpled. "That's my affair."

The sheriff removed his ample hat and scratched his head. "Well, maybe I better keep this trinket for a minute," he reflected. "Look here, John – or – er – Sergeant Chan, if that's your name – what the devil are you driving at, anyhow?"

He turned suddenly at a cry from Madden. The man had edged his way to the array of guns on the wall, and stood there now, with one of them in his bandaged hand.

"Come on," he cried, "I've had enough of this. Up with your hands – Sheriff, that means you! Gamble – get that necklace! Thorn – get the bag in my room!"

With a magnificent disregard for his own safety, Chan leaped upon him and seized the arm holding the pistol. He gave it a sharp twist, and the weapon fell to the floor.

"Only thing I am ever able to learn from Japanese," he said. "Captain Bliss, prove yourself real policeman by putting handcuffs on Thorn and the professor. If the sheriff will so kindly return my personal automatic, which I employ as detective in Hawaii, I will be responsible for this Madden here."

"Sure, I'll return it," said Cox. "And I want to congratulate you. I don't know as I ever saw a finer exhibition of courage—"

Chan grinned. "Pardon me if I make slight correction. One recent morning at dawn I have busy time removing all cartridges from this splendid collection of old-time pistols on the wall. Long, dusty job, but I am glad I did it." He turned suddenly to the big man beside him. "Put up the hands, Delaney," he cried.

"Delaney?" repeated the sheriff.

"Undubitably," replied Chan. "You have questioned value of my speech against word of P.J. Madden. Happy to say that situation does not arise. This is not P.J. Madden. His name is Jerry Delaney."

Bob Eden had entered quietly from the *patio*. "Good work, Charlie," he said. "You've got it now. But how in Sam Hill did you know?"

"Not long ago," answered Chan, "I shoot gun from his grasp. Observe the bandage on his hand, and note it is the left. Once in this room I told you Delaney was left-handed."

Through the open door behind Eden came a huge, powerful, but weary-looking man. One of his arms was in a sling, and his face was pale beneath a ten days' growth of beard. But there was about him an air of authority and poise; he loomed like a tower of granite, though the grey suit was sadly rumpled now. He stared grimly at Delaney.

"Well, Jerry," he said, "you're pretty good. But they always told me you were – the men who ran across you at Jack McGuire's. Yes – very good, indeed. Standing in my house, wearing my clothes, you look more like me than I do myself."

XXII

THE ROAD TO ELDORADO

The man at the door came farther into the room and looked inquiringly about him. His eyes fell on Thorn.

"Hello, Martin," he said. "I warned you it wouldn't work. Which of you gentlemen is the sheriff?"

Cox came forward. "Right here, sir. I suppose you're P.J. Madden?"

Madden nodded. "I suppose so. I've always thought I was. We telephoned the constable from a ranch down the road, and he told us you were here. So we've brought along another little item to add to your collection." He indicated the *patio* door, through which Holley came at that moment leading Shaky Phil by the arm. Maydorf's hands were tied behind him. Paula Wendell and Evelyn Madden also entered.

"You'd better handcuff this newcomer to Delaney, Sheriff," suggested Madden. "And then I'll run over a little list of charges against the crowd that I think will hold them for a while."

"Sure, Mr Madden," agreed the sheriff. As he stepped forward Chan halted him.

"Just one minute. You have string of pearls—"

"Oh, yes – that's right," replied the sheriff. He held out the Phillimore necklace. Chan took it and placed it in the hand of P.J. Madden.

"Fully aware you wanted it in New York," he remarked, "but you will perform vast kindness to accept it here. I have carried it to outside limit of present endurance. Receipt at your convenience, thank you."

Madden smiled. "All right, I'll take it." He put the necklace in his pocket. "You're Mr Chan, I imagine. Mr Eden was telling me about you on the way down from the mine. I'm mighty glad you've been here."

"Happy to serve," bowed Chan.

The sheriff turned. "There you are, sir. The charge, I guess, is attempted theft—"

"And a lot of other things," Madden added, "including assault with intent to kill." He indicated his limp arm. "I'll run over my story as quickly as I can – but I'll do it sitting down." He went to his desk. "I'm a little weak – I've been having a rough time of it. You know in a general way what has happened, but you don't know the background, the history, of this affair. I'll have to go back – back to a gambling-house on Forty-fourth Street, New York. Are you familiar with New York gamblers and their ways, Sheriff?"

"Been to New York just once," said the sheriff. "Didn't like it."

"No, I don't imagine you would," replied Madden. He looked about. "Where are my cigars? Ah – here. Thanks, Delaney – you left me a couple, didn't you? Well, Sheriff, in order that you may understand what's been going on here, I must tell you about a favourite stunt of shady gamblers and confidence men in New York – a stunt that was flourishing there twelve or fifteen years ago. It was a well-known fact at the time that, in the richly furnished houses where they lay in wait for trusting out-of-town suckers, certain members of the ring were assigned to impersonate widely known millionaires, such as Frank Gould, Cornelius Vanderbilt, Mr Astor – myself. The greatest care was exercised – photographs of these men were studied; wherever possible they themselves were closely observed in every feature of height, build, carriage, dress. The way they brushed their hair, the kind of glasses they wore, their peculiar mannerisms – no detail was too insignificant to escape attention. The intended dupe must be utterly taken in, so he might feel that he was among the best people, and that the game was honest."

Madden paused a moment. "Of course, some of these impersonations were rather flimsy, but it was my bad luck that Mr Delaney here, who had been an actor, was more or less of an artist. Starting with a rather superficial resemblance to me, he built up an impersonation that got better and better as time went on. I began to hear rumours that I was seen nightly at the gambling-house of one Jack McGuire, in Forty-fourth Street. I sent my secretary, Martin Thorn, to investigate. He reported that Delaney was making a good job of it – not, of course, so good that he could deceive anyone really close to me, but good enough to fool people who knew me only from photographs. I put my lawyer on the matter, and he came back and said that Delaney had agreed to desist, on threat of arrest.

"And I imagine he did drop it – in the gambling-houses. What happened afterward I can only conjecture, but I guess I can hit it pretty close. These two Maydorf boys, Shaky Phil and" – he nodded at Gamble – "his brother, who is known to the police as the Professor, were the brains of the particular gang at McGuire's. They must long ago have conceived the plan of having Delaney impersonate me somewhere, some time. They could do nothing without the aid of my secretary, Thorn, but they evidently found him willing. Finally they hit on the desert as the proper locale for the enterprise. It was an excellent selection. I come here rarely; meet few people when I do come. Once they could get me here alone, without my family, it was a simple matter. All they had to do was to put me out of the way, and then P.J. Madden appears with his secretary, who is better known locally than he is – no one is going to dream of questioning his identity, particularly as he looks just like his pictures."

Madden puffed thoughtfully on his cigar. "I've been expecting some such move for years. I feared no man in the world – except Delaney. The possibilities of the harm he might do me were enormous. Once I saw him in a restaurant, studying me. Well – they had a long wait, but their kind is patient. Two weeks ago I came here with Thorn, and the minute I got here I sensed there was something in the air. A week ago last Wednesday night I was sitting here writing a letter to my daughter Evelyn – it's probably still between the leaves of this blotter where I put it when I heard Thorn cry out sharply from his bedroom. 'Come quick, chief,' he called. He was typing letters for me, and I couldn't imagine what had happened. I rose and went to his room – and there he was, with an old gun of mine – a gun Bill Hart had given me – in his fist. 'Put up your hands,' he said. Someone entered from the *patio*. It was Delaney.

"'Now don't get excited, chief,' said Thorn, and I saw the little rat was in on the game. 'We're going to take you for a ride to a place where you can have a nice little rest. I'll go and pack a few things for you. Here, Jerry – you watch him.' And he handed Delaney the gun.

"There we stood, Delaney and I, and I saw that Jerry was nervous – the game was a little rich for his blood. Thorn was busy in my room. I began to call for help at the top of my voice – why? Who would come? I didn't know, but a friend might hear – Louie might have got home – someone might be passing on the road. Delaney told me to shut up. His hand trembled like a leaf. In the *patio* outside I heard an answering voice – but it was only Tony, the parrot. I knew well enough what was afoot, and I decided to take a chance. I started for Delaney; he fired and missed. He fired again, and I felt a sort of sting in my shoulder, and fell.

"I must have been unconscious for a second, but when I came to Thorn was in the room, and I heard Delaney say he'd killed me. In a minute, of course, they discovered I was alive, and my good friend Jerry was all for finishing the job. But Thorn wouldn't let him – he insisted on going through with the original plan. He saved my life – I'll have to admit it – the contemptible little traitor. Cowardice, I imagine, but he saved me. Well, they put me in a car, and drove me up to the jail at Petticoat Mine. In the morning they left – all except the Professor, who had joined our happy party. He stayed behind, dressed my wound, fed me after a fashion. On Sunday afternoon he went away and came back late at night with Shaky Phil. Monday morning the Professor left, and Shaky Phil was my jailer after that. Not so kind as his brother.

"What was going on at the ranch you gentlemen know better than I do. On Tuesday my daughter wired that she was coming, and of course the game was up if she reached here. So Thorn met her in Eldorado, told her I was injured and up at the mine, and took her there. Naturally, she trusted him. Since then she has been there with me, and we'd be there now if Mr Eden and Mr Holley had not come up tonight, searching for this other young woman who had, unfortunately for her, stumbled on the affair earlier in the day."

Madden rose. "That's my story, Sheriff. Do you wonder that I want to see this gang behind the bars? I'll sleep better then."

"Well, I reckon it's easy arranged," returned the sheriff. "I'll take 'em along and we can fix the warrants later. Guess I'll see 'em safe in the jail at the county-seat – Eldorado can't offer 'em all the comforts of a first-class cell."

"One thing," said Madden. "Thorn, I heard you say the other night to Delaney: 'You were always afraid of him – that time in New York—' What did that mean? You tried this thing before?"

Thorn looked up with stricken face, which had been hidden in his hands. "Chief, I'm sorry about this. I'll talk. We had it all set to pull it once at the office in New York when you were away on a hunting-trip. But if you were afraid of Delaney, he was a lot more afraid of you. He got cold feet – backed out at the last minute—"

"And why wouldn't I back out?" snarled Delaney. "I couldn't trust any of you. A bunch of yellow dogs—"

"Is that so?" cried Shaky Phil. "Are you talking about me?"

"Sure I'm talking about you. I suppose you didn't try to cop the pearls in 'Frisco when we sent you up there to draw Louie Wong away? Oh, I know all about that—"

"Why wouldn't I try to cop them?" demanded Shaky Phil. "You been trying to cop them, haven't you? When you thought Draycott was bringing them what did you try to pull? Oh, brother Henry's been on to you—"

"I sure have," put in the Professor. "Trying to sneak off and meet Draycott alone. If you thought I wasn't wise you must be a fool. But of course that's what you are – a poor fool that writes letters to actresses—"

"Shut up!" bellowed Delaney. "Who had a better right to those pearls? What could you have done if it hadn't been for me? A lot of help you were – mooning round with your tall talk. And you" – he turned back to Shaky Phil – "you pulled some brilliant stuff. Putting a knife in Louie Wong right on the door-step—"

"Who put a knife in Louie Wong?" cried Shaky Phil.

"You did," shouted Thorn. "I was with you and I saw you. I'll – swear to that – "

"An accessory, eh?" grinned the sheriff. "By gad, just let this gang loose at one another, and they'll hang themselves."

"Boys, boys," said the Professor gently. "Cut it out. We'll never get anywhere that way. Sheriff, we are ready—"

"One moment," said Charlie Chan. He disappeared briefly, and returned with a small black bag, which he set before Madden. "I have pleasure calling your attention to this," he announced. "You will find inside vast crowds of currency. Money from sale of bonds, money sent from New York office. Pretty much intact – but not quite. I ask Delaney."

"It's all there," Delaney growled.

Chan shook his head. "I grieve to differ even with rascal like you are. But there was Eddie Boston—"

"Yes," replied Delaney. "It's true – I gave Boston five thousand dollars. He recognized me the other day in the yard. Go after him and get it back – the dirty crook."

The sheriff laughed. "Speaking of crooks," he said, "that sounds to me like your cue, boys. We'd better be getting along, Bliss. We can swear in a deputy or two in Eldorado. Mr Madden, I'll see you tomorrow."

Bob Eden went up to Delaney. "Well, Jerry," he smiled, "I'm afraid this is goodbye. You've been my host down here, and my mother told me I must always say I've had a very nice time—"

"Oh, go to the devil," said Delaney.

The sheriff and Bliss herded their captives out into the desert night, and Eden went over to Paula Wendell.

"Exit the Delaney quartette," he remarked. "I guess my stalling days at the ranch are ended. I'm taking the ten-thirty train to Barstow, and—"

"Better call up for a taxi," she suggested.

"Not while you and the roadster are on the job. If you'll wait while I pack – I want a word with you, anyhow. About Wilbur."

"One happy thought runs through my mind," Will Holley was saying. "I'm the author of a famous interview with you, Mr Madden. One you never gave."

"Really?" replied Madden. "Well, don't worry. I'll stand behind you."

"Thanks," answered the editor. "I wonder why they gave out that story," he mused.

"Simple to guess," said Chan. "They are wiring New York office money be sent, please. How better to establish fact Madden is at desert ranch than to blaze same forth in newspapers? Printed word has ring of convincing truth."

"I imagine you're right," nodded Holley. "By the way, Charlie, we thought we'd have a big surprise for you when we got back from the mine. But you beat us to it, after all."

"By a hair's width," replied Chan. "Now that I have leisure I bow my head and do considerable blushing. Must admit I was plenty slow to grasp apparent fact. Only tonight light shone. To please this Victor, I hand over pearls. Madden is signing receipt – he writes slow and painful. Suddenly I think – he does all things slow and painful with that right hand. Why? I recall Delaney's vest, built for left-handed man. Inwardly, out of sight, I gasp. To make a test, I snatch at pearls. Madden, to call him that, snatches too. But guard is down – he snatches with left hand. He rips out pistol – left hand again. The fact is proved. I know."

"Well, that was quick thinking," Holley said.

Chan sadly shook his head. "Why not? Poor old brain must have been plenty rested. Not at work for many days. When I arrange these dishonest ones in chairs to wait for you, I have much time for bitter self-incriminations. Why have I experienced this stupid sinking spell? All time it was clear as desert morning. A man writes important letter, hides in blotter, goes away. Returning, he never touches same. Why? He did not return. Other easy clues – Madden, calling him so again, receives Doctor Whitcomb in dusk of *patio*. Why? She has seen him before. He talks with caretaker in Pasadena – when? Six o'clock, when dark has fallen. Also he fears to alight from car. Oh, as I sit here I give myself many resounding mental kicks. Why have I been so thick? I blame this climate of South

California. Plenty quick I hurry back to Honolulu, where I belong."

"You're too hard on yourself," said P.J. Madden. "If it hadn't been for you, Mr Eden tells me, the necklace would have been delivered long ago, and this crowd off to the Orient or somewhere else far away. I owe you a lot, and if mere thanks—"

"Stop thanking me," urged Chan. "Thank Tony. If Tony didn't speak that opening night, where would necklace be now? Poor Tony, buried at this moment in rear of barn." He turned to Victor Jordan, who had been lurking modestly in the background. "Victor, before returning North, it is fitting that you place wreath of blossoms on grave of Tony, the Chinese parrot. Tony died, but he lived to splendid purpose. Before he passed he saved the Phillimore pearls."

Victor nodded. "Anything you say, Charlie. I'll leave a standing order with my florist. I wonder if someone will give me a lift back to town?"

"I'll take you," Holley said. "I want to get this thing on the wire. Charlie – shall I see you again—"

"Leaving on next train," replied Chan. "I am calling at your office to collect more fitting clothes. Do not wait, however. Miss Wendell has kindly offered use of her car."

"I'm waiting for Paula too," Eden said. "I'll see you at the station." Holley and Victor said their goodbyes to Madden and his daughter, and departed. Bob Eden consulted his watch. "Well, the old home-week crowd is thinning out. Just one thing more, Charlie. When Mr Madden here came in tonight you weren't a bit surprised. Yet, recognizing Delaney, your first thought must have been that Madden had been killed."

Chan laughed noiselessly. "I observe you have ignorance concerning detective customs. Surprised detective might as well put on iron collar and leap from dock. He is finished. Mr Madden's appearance staggering blow for me, but I am not letting rival policemen know it, thank you. It is apparent we keep

Miss Wendell waiting. I have some property in cookhouse – just one moment."

"The cookhouse," cried P.J. Madden. "By the Lord Harry, I'm hungry. I haven't had anything but canned food for days."

An apprehensive look flitted over Chan's face. "Such a pity," he said. "Present cook on ranch has resumed former profession. Miss Wendell, I am with you in five seconds." He went hastily out.

Evelyn Madden put her arm about her father. "Cheer up, Dad," she advised. "I'll drive you in town and we'll stop at the hotel tonight. You must have a doctor look at your shoulder at once." She turned to Bob Eden. "Of course, there's a restaurant in Eldorado?"

"Of course," smiled Eden. "It's called the Oasis, but it isn't. However, I can heartily recommend the steaks."

P.J. Madden was on his feet, himself again. "All right, Evelyn. Call up the hotel and reserve a suite – five rooms – no, make it a floor. Tell the proprietor I want supper served in my sitting-room – two porterhouse steaks, and everything else they've got. Tell him to have the best doctor in town there when I arrive. Help me find the telegraph blanks. Put in five long-distance calls – no, that had better wait until we reach the hotel. Find out if there's anybody in Eldorado who can take dictation. Call up the leading real-estate man and put this place on the market. I never want to see it again. And oh, yes – don't let that Chinese detective get away without seeing me. I'm not through with him. Make a note to call a secretarial bureau in Los Angeles at eight in the morning—"

Bob Eden hurried to his room, and packed his suitcase. When he returned Chan was standing in Madden's presence, holding crisp banknotes in his hand.

"Mr Madden has given receipt for necklace," said the Chinese. "He has also enforced on me this vast sum of money, which I am somewhat loathsome to accept."

"Nonsense," Eden replied. "You take it, Charlie. You've earned it."

"Just what I told him," Madden declared.

Chan put the banknotes carefully away. "Free to remark the sum represents two and one-half years' salary in Honolulu. This mainland climate not so bad after all."

"Goodbye, Mr Eden," Madden said. "I've thanked Mr Chan – but what shall I say to you? You've been through a lot down here—"

"Been through some of the happiest moments in my life," Eden replied.

Madden shook his head. "Well, I can't say I understand that—"

"I think I do," said his daughter. "Good luck, Bob, and thank you a thousand times."

The desert wind was cool and bracing as they went out to the little roadster, waiting patiently in the yard. Paula Wendell climbed in behind the wheel. "Get in, Mr Chan," she invited. Chan took his place beside her. Bob Eden tossed his suitcase into the luggage compartment at the back, and returned to the car door.

"Squeeze in there, Charlie," he said. "Don't make a fool of the advertisements. This is a three-seater car."

Charlie squeezed. "Moment of gentle embarrassment for me," he remarked. "The vast extensiveness of my area becomes painfully apparent."

They were out on the road. The Joshua-trees waved them a weird farewell in the white moonlight.

"Charlie," said Eden, "I suppose you don't dream why you are in this party?"

"Miss Wendell very kind," remarked Chan.

"Kind – and cautious," laughed Eden. "You're here as a Wilbur – a sort of buffer between this young woman and the dread institution of marriage. She doesn't believe in marriage,

Charlie. Now where do you suppose she picked up that foolish notion?"

"Plenty foolish," agreed Chan. "She should be argued at."

"She will be argued at. She brought you along because she knows I'm mad about her. She's seen it in my great trusting eyes. She knows that since I've met her that precious freedom of mine seems rather a stale joke. She realizes that I'll never give up – that I intend to take her away from the desert – but she thought I wouldn't mention it if you were along."

"I begin to feel like skeleton at feast," remarked Chan.

"Cheer up – you certainly don't feel like that to me," Eden assured him. "Yes, she thought I'd fail to speak of the matter – but we'll fool her. I'll speak of it, anyhow. Charlie, I love this girl."

"Natural you do," agreed Chan.

"I intend to marry her."

"Imminently fitting purpose," assented Chan. "But she has said no word."

Paula Wendell laughed. "Marriage," she said. "The last resort of feeble minds. I'm having a great time, thanks. I love my freedom. I mean to hang on to it."

"Sorry to hear that," said Chan. "Permit me if I speak a few words in favour of married state. I am one who knows. Where is the better place than a new home? Truly an earthly paradise where cares vanish, where the heavenly melody of wife's voice vibrates everything in a strange symphony."

"Sounds pretty good to me," remarked Eden.

"The ramble hand in hand with wife on evening streets, the stroll by moonly seaside. I recollect the happy spring of my own marriage with unlimited yearning."

"How does it sound to you, Paula?" Eden persisted.

"And this young man," continued Chan. "I am unable to grasp why you resist. To me he is plenty fine fellow. I have for him a great likeness." Paula Wendell said nothing. "A very great likeness," added Chan.

"Well," admitted the girl, "if it comes to that, I have a little likeness for him myself."

Chan dug his elbow deep into Eden's side. They climbed between the dark hills and the lights of Eldorado shone before them. As they drove up to the hotel Holley and Victor Jordan greeted them.

"Here you are," said the editor. "Your bag is in the office, Charlie. The door's unlocked."

"Many thanks," returned Chan, and fled.

Holley looked up at the white stars. "Sorry you're going, Eden," he said. "It'll be a bit lonesome down here without you."

"But you'll be in New York," suggested Eden.

Holley shook his head and smiled. "Oh, no, I won't. I sent a telegram this evening. A few years ago, perhaps – but not now. I can't go now. Somehow, this desert country – well, it's got me, I guess. I'll have to take my New York in pictures from this on."

Far off across the dreary waste of sand the whistle of the Barstow train broke the desert silence. Charlie came round the corner; the coat and waistcoat of Sergeant Chan had replaced the Canton *crêpe* blouse of Ah Kim.

"Hoarse voice of railroad proclaims end of our adventure," he remarked. He took Paula Wendell's hand. "Accept last wish from somewhat weary postman. May this be for you beginning of life's greatest adventure! And happiest!"

They crossed the empty street. "Goodbye," Eden said, as he and the girl paused in the shadow of the station. Something in the warm clasp of her slender, strong fingers told him all he wanted to know, and his heart beat faster. He drew her close.

"I'm coming back soon," he promised. He transferred the emerald ring to her right hand. "Just by way of a reminder," he added. "When I return I'll bring a substitute – the glittering pick of the finest stock on the coast. Our stock."

"Our stock?"

"Yes." The branch-line train had clattered in, and Chan was calling to him from the car steps. "You don't know it yet, but for you the dream of every woman's life has come true. You're going to marry a man who owns a jewellery store."

Behind That Curtain

To the Only Critic I Love – MY WIFE

CONTENTS

I

THE MAN FROM SCOTLAND YARD

Bill Rankin sat motionless before his typewriter, grimly seeking a lead for the interview he was about to write. A black shadow shot past his elbow and materialized with a soft thud on his desk. Bill's heart leaped into his throat and choked him.

But it was only Egbert, the office cat. Pretty lonesome round here, seemed to be Egbert's idea. How about a bit of play? Rankin glared at the cat with deep disgust. Absurd to be so upset by a mere Egbert, but when one has been talking with a great man for over an hour and the subject of the talk has been murder, one is apt to be a trifle jumpy.

He reached out and pushed Egbert to the floor. "Go away," he said. "What do you mean, scaring me out of a year's growth? Can't you see I'm busy?"

His dignity offended, Egbert stalked off through the desert of typewriter tables and empty chairs. Bill Rankin watched him disappear at last through the door leading into the hallway. The hour was five thirty; the street ten stories below was filled with home-going throngs, but up here in the city room of the *Globe* a momentary quiet reigned. Alone of all the green-shaded lamps in the room, the one above Rankin's typewriter was alight, shedding a ghastly radiance on the blank sheet of paper in his machine. Even the copy desk was deserted. In his cubby-hole at the rear sat the *Globe's* city editor, the only other human thing in sight. And he was not, if you believed the young men who worked for him, so very human at that.

Bill Rankin turned back to his interview. For a brief moment he sat wrapped in thought; then his long, capable fingers sought the keys. He wrote:

"The flights of genius and miracles of science which solve most of the crimes in detective stories have no real part in detective work. This is the verdict of Sir Frederic Bruce, former head of the Criminal Investigation Department at Scotland Yard.

"Sir Frederic, who is stopping over for two weeks in San Francisco during the course of a trip around the world, is qualified to give an expert opinion. For nearly seventeen years he acted as Deputy-Commissioner at the head of the most famous detective organization in existence, and though he has now retired, his interest in crime detection is as keen as ever. Sir Frederic is a big man, with a kindly twinkle in his gray eyes, but occasionally those eyes have a steely look that made this reporter nervous. If we had killed the old Earl of Featherstonehaugh on his rare Persian rug, we would not care to have Sir Frederic on our trail. For the great detective is that type of Scotchman who is a stranger to defeat. He would never abandon the scent.

"'I read a great deal of detective fiction,' Sir Frederic said. 'It amuses me, but there is usually nothing for a detective to learn from it. Except for the fingerprint system and work in the chemical laboratory on stains, scientific research has furnished little assistance to crime detection. Murder mysteries and other difficult criminal cases are solved by intelligence, hard work and luck, with little help from the delicate scientific devices so dear to the authors of—'"

Suddenly Bill Rankin stopped writing and sat erect in his uncomfortable chair. There was a familiar ring to the ideas he was setting down on paper; he had heard them before, and recently. Opinions identical with these, expressed not in the polished English of Sir Frederic, but in a quite different idiom—Ah yes. He smiled, recalling that pudgy little man he had interviewed three days ago in the lobby of the Stewart Hotel.

The reporter rose from his chair and, lighting a cigarette, began to pace the floor. He spoke aloud: "Of course – and I never thought of it. A corking feature story staring me right in the face, and I was blind – blind. I must be losing my grip." He looked anxiously at the clock, tossed aside his cigarette and resumed his chair. Completing the sentence which he had interrupted midway, he continued:

"Sir Frederic was asked what he considered the greatest piece of detective work within his knowledge.

"'I cannot answer that because of the important part played by chance,' he replied. 'As I have just said, most criminal cases are solved by varying proportions of hard work, intelligence and luck, and I am sorry I must add that of these three, luck is the greatest by far.

"'Hard, methodical work, however, has brought results in many instances. For example, it unraveled the famous Crippen mystery. The first intimation we had of something wrong in that case came when we heard that the woman treasurer of a music-hall—'"

Bill Rankin wrote on, with lightning speed now, for he was eager to finish. The thing he was doing had suddenly become a minor matter. A far better story was running through his head. His fingers flew over the keys; when he paused, at rare intervals, it was to turn an inquiring gaze on the clock.

He ripped the final sheet of paper from his machine, snatched up the story, and hurried toward the city editor's nook. The lone man in charge of the copy desk, just returned from a bitter argument with the composing-room foreman, watched him sourly as he passed, and grimly sharpened a blue pencil.

"Wha's 'at?" inquired the city editor, as Bill Rankin threw the story down before him.

"Interview with Sir Frederic Bruce," Bill reminded him.

"Oh, you found him, did you?"

"We all found him. The room was full of reporters."

"Where was he?"

"He's putting up at Barry Kirk's bungalow. Kirk knew his son in London. I tried the hotels until my feet ached."

The editor snorted. "The more fool you. No Englishman ever stops at a hotel if he can wangle board and room from somebody. You've been sent out to find enough lecturing British authors to know that."

"The interview's blah," said Rankin. "Every paper in town will have it. But while I was writing it, an idea for a feature hit me hard. It'll be a hum-dinger – if I can only put it over on Sir Frederic. I thought I'd go back up there and see what I can do."

"A feature?" The editor frowned. "If you happen on a bit of news in the course of your literary work, you'll let me know, won't you? Here I am, trying to get out a newspaper, and all I get from you fellows is an avalanche of pretty little essays. I suspect you're all hoping that some day you'll be tapped for the *Atlantic Monthly*."

"But this feature's good," Rankin protested. "I must hurry along—"

"Just a minute. I'm only your editor, of course. I don't want to pry into your plans—"

Rankin laughed. He was an able man, and privileged. "I'm sorry, sir, but I can't stop to explain now. Someone may beat me to it yet. Gleason of the *Herald* was up there today and he'll get the same hunch as sure as fate. So if you don't mind—"

The editor shrugged. "All right – go to it. Hurry up to the Kirk Building. And don't let this sudden attack of energy die there. Hurry back, too."

"Yes, sir," agreed the reporter. "Of course, I'll need a bit of dinner—"

"*I* never eat," growled his charming employer.

Bill Rankin sped across the city room. His fellow reporters were drifting in now from their afternoon assignments, and the place was coming to life. Near the door, Egbert, black as the night from pole to pole, crossed Rankin's path with haughty, aloof manner and dignified stride.

Descending to the street, the reporter stood for a moment undecided. The Kirk Building was not far away; he could walk there – but time was precious. Suppose he arrived to be met by the news that Sir Frederic was dressing for dinner. With this famous and correct Englishman, the act would be a sacred rite not to be lightly interrupted by panting pressmen. No, he must reach Sir Frederic before the detective reached for his black pearl studs. He hailed a passing taxi.

As the car drew up to the curb, a red-cheeked boy, one of the *Globe's* younger reporters, emerged from the crowd and with a deep bow, held open the taxi door.

"To the Royal Opera, my good man," he shouted, "and an extra gold sovereign for you if we pass the Duke's car on the way."

Rankin pushed the facetious one aside. "Don't interfere with your betters, my lad," he remarked, and added, to the driver: "The Kirk Building, on California Street."

The taxi swung out into Market Street, followed the intricate car tracks for a few blocks, and turned off into Montgomery. In another moment they were in the financial district of San Francisco, now wrapped in its accustomed evening calm. The huge buildings of trust companies, investment houses and banks stood solemn and solid in the dusk; across the doorways of many, forbidding bronze gates were already shut. Gilded signs met Rankin's eye – "The Yokohama Bank"; on another window, "The Shanghai Trading Company"; one may not forget the Orient in the city by the Gate. Presently the taxi drew up before a twenty-story office building, and Rankin alighted.

The Kirk Building was architecturally perfect, in the excellent taste that had marked the family ever since the first Dawson Kirk had made his millions and gone his way. Now it was the particular hobby of young Barry Kirk, who lived in bachelor splendor in the spacious but breezy bungalow on its roof. Its pure white lobby was immaculate; its elevator girls trim and pretty in neat uniforms; its elevator starter resplendent as an Admiral of the Fleet. At this hour the fever of the day was ended and cleaning women knelt reverently on the marble floor. One elevator was still running, and into this Bill Rankin stepped.

"All the way," he said to the girl.

He alighted at the twentieth floor, the final stop. A narrow stair led to Barry Kirk's bungalow, and the reporter ascended two steps at a time. Pausing before an imposing door, he rang. The door opened and Paradise, Kirk's English butler, stood like a bishop barring Rankin's path.

"Ah – er – I'm back," panted Rankin.

"So I see, sir." Very like a bishop indeed, with that great shock of snow-white hair. His manner was not cordial. Earlier that day he had admitted many reporters, but with misgivings.

"I must see Sir Frederic at once. Is he in?"

"Sir Frederic is in the offices, on the floor below. I fancy he is busy, but I will announce you—"

"No – please don't trouble," said Rankin quickly. Running down to the twentieth floor, he noted a door with Barry Kirk's name on the frosted glass. As he moved toward it, it opened suddenly, and a young woman came out.

Rankin stopped in his tracks. A remarkably pretty young woman – that much was obvious even in the dim light on the twentieth floor. One of those greatly preferred blondes, with a slender figure trim in a green dress of some knitted material. Not precisely tall, but—

What was this? The young woman was weeping. Silently, without fuss, but indubitably weeping. Tears not alone of grief, but, if Rankin was any judge, of anger and exasperation, too. With a startled glance at the reporter, she hastily crossed the hall and disappeared through a door that bore the sign "Calcutta Importers, Inc."

Bill Rankin pushed on into Barry Kirk's office. He entered a sort of reception-room, but a door beyond stood open, and the newspaper man went confidently forward. In the second room, Sir Frederic Bruce, former head of the C. I. D., sat at a big, flat-topped desk. He swung around, and his gray eyes were stern and dangerous.

"Oh," he said. "It's you."

"I must apologize for intruding on you again, Sir Frederic," Bill Rankin began. "But – I – er – may I sit down?"

"Certainly." The great detective slowly gathered up some papers on the desk.

"The fact is—" Rankin's confidence was ebbing. An inner voice told him that this was not the genial gentleman of the afternoon interview in the bungalow upstairs. Not the gracious visitor to San Francisco, but Sir Frederic Bruce of Scotland Yard, unbending, cold and awe-inspiring. "The fact is," continued the reporter lamely, "an idea has struck me."

"Really?" Those eyes – they looked right through you.

"What you told us this afternoon, Sir Frederic—Your opinion of the value of scientific devices in the detection of crime, as against luck and hard work—" Rankin paused. He seemed unable to finish his sentences. "I was reminded, when I came to write my story, that oddly enough I had heard that same opinion only a few days ago."

"Yes? Well, I made no claim to originality." Sir Frederic threw his papers into a drawer.

"Oh, I haven't come to complain about it," smiled Rankin, regaining a trace of his jaunty spirit. "Under ordinary conditions, it wouldn't mean anything, but I heard your ideas from the lips of a rather unusual man, Sir Frederic. A humble worker in your own field, a detective who has evolved his theories far from Scotland Yard. I heard them from Detective-Sergeant Charlie Chan, of the Honolulu police."

Sir Frederic's bushy eyebrows rose. "Really? Then I must applaud the judgment of Sergeant Chan – whoever he may be."

"Chan is a detective who has done some good work in the islands. He happens to be in San Francisco at the moment, on his way home. Came to the mainland on a simple errand, which developed into quite a case before he had finished with it. I believe he acquitted himself with credit. He's not very impressive to look at, but—"

Sir Frederic interrupted. "A Chinese, I take it?"

"Yes, sir."

The great man nodded. "And why not? A Chinese should make an excellent detective. The patience of the East, you know."

"Precisely," agreed Bill Rankin. "He's got that. And modesty—"

Sir Frederic shook his head. "Not such a valuable asset, modesty. Self-assurance, a deep faith in one's self – they help. But Sergeant Chan is modest?"

"Is he? 'Falling hurts least those who fly low' – that's the way he put it to me. And Sergeant Chan flies so low he skims the daisies."

Sir Frederic rose and stepped to the window. He gazed down at the spatter of lights flung like a handful of stars over the darkening town. For a moment he said nothing. Then he turned to the reporter.

"A modest detective," he said, with a grim smile. "That's a novelty, at any rate. I should like very much to meet this Sergeant Chan."

Bill Rankin sighed with relief. His task was unbelievably easy, after all.

"That's exactly what I came here to suggest," he said briskly. "I'd like to bring you and Charlie Chan together – hear you go over your methods and experiences – you know, just a real good talk. I was wondering if you would do us the great honor to join Mr Chan and me at lunch tomorrow?"

The former head of the C. I. D. hesitated. "Thank you very much. But I am more or less in Mr Kirk's hands. He is giving a dinner tomorrow night, and I believe he said something about luncheon tomorrow, too. Much as I should like to accept at once, decidedly we must consult Mr Kirk."

"Well, let's find him. Where is he?" Bill Rankin was all business.

"I fancy he is up in the bungalow." Sir Frederic turned and, swinging shut the door of a big wall safe, swiftly twirled the knob.

"You did that just like an American business man, Sir Frederic," Rankin smiled.

The detective nodded. "Mr Kirk has kindly allowed me to use his office while I am his guest."

"Ah – then you're not altogether on a pleasure trip," said Bill Rankin quickly.

The gray eyes hardened. "Absolutely – a pleasure trip. But there are certain matters – private business – I am writing my *Memoirs*—"

"Ah yes – of course," apologized the reporter.

The door opened, and a cleaning woman entered. Sir Frederic turned to her. "Good evening," he said. "You understand that no papers on this desk – or in it – are to be interfered with in any way?"

"Oh, yes, sir," the woman answered.

"Very good. Now, Mr – er – Mr—"

"Rankin, Sir Frederic."

"Of course. There is a stairs in this rear room leading up to the bungalow. If you will come with me—"

They entered the third and last room of the office suite, and Bill Rankin followed the huge figure of the Englishman aloft. The stairs ended in a dark passageway on the floor above. Throwing open the nearest door, Sir Frederic flooded the place with light, and Bill Rankin stepped into the great living-room of the bungalow. Paradise was alone in the room; he received the reporter with cold disdain. Barry Kirk, it appeared, was dressing for dinner, and the butler went reluctantly to inform him of the newspaper man's unseemly presence.

Kirk appeared at once, in his shirt-sleeves and with the ends of a white tie dangling about his neck. He was a handsome, lean young man in the late twenties, whose manner spoke of sophistication, and spoke true. For he had traveled to the far corners of the earth seeking to discover what the Kirk fortune would purchase there, and life held no surprises for him any more.

"Ah yes – Mr Rankin of the *Globe*," he said pleasantly. "What can I do for you?"

Paradise hastened forward to officiate with the tie, and over the servant's shoulder Bill Rankin explained his mission. Kirk nodded.

"A bully idea," he remarked. "I have a lot of friends in Honolulu, and I've heard about Charlie Chan. I'd like to meet him myself."

"Very happy to have you join us," said the reporter.

"Can't be done. You must join me."

"But – the suggestion of the lunch was mine—" began Rankin uncomfortably.

Kirk waved a hand in the airy manner of the rich in such a situation. "My dear fellow – I've already arranged a luncheon for tomorrow. Some chap in the district attorney's office wrote me a letter. He's interested in criminology and wants to meet Sir Frederic. As I explained to Sir Frederic, I couldn't very well ignore it. We never know when we'll need a friend in the district attorney's office, these days."

"One of the deputies?" inquired Rankin.

"Yes. A fellow named Morrow – J. V. Morrow. Perhaps you know him?"

Rankin nodded. "I do," he said.

"Well, that's the scenario," went on Kirk. "We're to meet this lad at the St. Francis tomorrow at one. The topic of the day will be murder, and I'm sure your friend from Honolulu will fit in admirably. You must pick up Mr Chan and join us."

"Thank you very much," said Rankin. "You're extremely kind. We'll be there. I – I won't keep you any longer."

Paradise came forward with alacrity to let him out. At the foot of the stairs on the twentieth floor he met his old rival, Gleason of the *Herald*. He chuckled with delight.

"Turn right around," he said. "You're too late. I thought of it first."

"Thought of what?" asked Gleason, with assumed innocence.

"I'm getting Sir Frederic and Charlie Chan together, and the idea's copyrighted. Lay off."

Gloomily Mr Gleason turned about, and accompanied Bill Rankin to the elevators. As they waited for the car, the girl in the green dress emerged from the office of the Calcutta Importers and joined them. They rode down together. The girl's tears had vanished, and had happily left no trace. Blue eyes – that completed the picture. A charming picture. Mr Gleason was also showing signs of interest.

In the street Gleason spoke. “I never thought of it until dinner,” he said sourly.

“With me, my career comes first,” Rankin responded. “Did you finish your dinner?”

“I did, worse luck. Well, I hope you get a whale of a story – a knock-out, a classic.”

“Thanks, old man.”

“And I hope you can’t print one damn word of it.”

Rankin did not reply as his friend hurried off into the dusk. He was watching the girl in the green dress disappear up California Street. Why had she left the presence of Sir Frederic Bruce to weep outside that office door? What had Sir Frederic said to her? Might ask Sir Frederic about it tomorrow. He laughed mirthlessly. He saw himself – or any other man – prying into the private affairs of Sir Frederic Bruce.

II

WHAT HAPPENED TO EVE DURAND?

The next day at one Sir Frederic Bruce stood in the lobby of the St. Francis, a commanding figure in a gray tweed suit. By his side, as immaculate as his guest, stood Barry Kirk, looking out on the busy scene with the amused tolerance befitting a young man of vast leisure and not a care in the world. Kirk hung his stick on his arm, and took a letter from his pocket.

"By the way, I had this note from J. V. Morrow in the morning's mail," he said. "Thanks me very politely for my invitation, and says that I'll know him when he shows up because he'll be wearing a green hat. One of those green plush hats, I suppose. Hardly the sort of thing I'd put on my head if I were a deputy district attorney."

Sir Frederic did not reply. He was watching Bill Rankin approach rapidly across the floor. At the reporter's side walked, surprisingly light of step, an unimpressive little man with a bulging waistband and a very earnest expression on his chubby face.

"Here we are," Rankin said. "Sir Frederic Bruce – may I present Detective-Sergeant Chan, of the Honolulu police?"

Charlie Chan bent quickly like a jack-knife. "The honor," he said, "is unbelievably immense. In Sir Frederic's reflected glory I am happy to bask. The tiger has condescended to the fly."

Somewhat at a loss, the Englishman caressed his mustache and smiled down on the detective from Hawaii. As a keen judge of men, already he saw something in those black restless eyes that held his attention.

"I'm happy to know you, Sergeant Chan," he said. "It seems we think alike on certain important points. We should get on well together."

Rankin introduced Chan to the host, who greeted the little Chinese with obvious approval. "Good of you to come," he said.

"A four-horse chariot could not have dragged me in an opposite direction," Chan assured him.

Kirk looked at his watch. "All here but J. V. Morrow," he remarked. "He wrote me this morning that he's coming in at the Post Street entrance. If you'll excuse me, I'll have a look around."

He strolled down the corridor toward Post Street. Near the door, on a velvet davenport, sat a strikingly attractive young woman. No other seat was available, and with an interested glance at the girl Kirk also dropped down on the davenport. "If you don't mind—" he murmured.

"Not at all," she replied, in a voice that somehow suited her.

They sat in silence. Presently Kirk was aware that she was looking at him. He glanced up, to meet her smile.

"People are always late," he ventured.

"Aren't they?"

"No reason for it, usually. Just too inefficient to make the grade. Nothing annoys me more."

"I feel the same way," the girl nodded.

Another silence. The girl was still smiling at him.

"Go out of your way to invite somebody you don't know to lunch," Kirk continued, "and he isn't even courteous enough to arrive on time."

"Abominable," she agreed. "You have all my sympathy – Mr Kirk."

He started. "Oh – you know me?"

She nodded. "Somebody once pointed you out to me – at a charity bazaar," she explained.

"Well," he sighed, "their charity didn't extend to me. Nobody pointed you out." He looked at his watch.

"This person you're expecting—" began the girl.

"A lawyer," he answered. "I hate all lawyers. They're always telling you something you'd rather not know."

"Yes – aren't they?"

"Messing around with other people's troubles. What a life."

"Frightful." Another silence. "You say you don't know this lawyer?" A rather unkempt young man came in and hurried past. "How do you expect to recognize him?"

"He wrote me he'd be wearing a green hat. Imagine! Why not a rose behind his ear?"

"A green hat." The girl's smile grew even brighter. Charming, thought Kirk. Suddenly he stared at her in amazement. "Good lord – you're wearing a green hat!" he cried.

"I'm afraid I am."

"Don't tell me—"

"Yes – it's true. I'm the lawyer. And you hate all lawyers. What a pity."

"But I didn't dream—"

"J. V. Morrow," she went on. "The first name is June."

"And I thought it was Jim," he cried. "Please forgive me."

"You'd never have invited me if you'd known – would you?"

"On the contrary – I wouldn't have invited anybody else. But come along. There are a lot of murder experts in the lobby dying to meet you."

They rose, and walked rapidly down the corridor, "You're interested in murder?" Kirk inquired.

"Among other things," she smiled.

"Must take it up myself," Kirk murmured.

Men turned to look at her a second time, he noticed. There was an alertness in her dark eyes that resembled the look in Chan's, her manner was brisk and businesslike, but for all that she was feminine, alluring.

He introduced her to the surprised Sir Frederic, then to Charlie Chan. The expression on the face of the little Chinese did not alter. He bowed low.

"The moment has charm," he remarked.

Kirk turned to Rankin. "And all the time," he accused, "you knew who J. V. Morrow was."

The reporter shrugged. "I thought I'd let you find it out for yourself. Life holds so few pleasant surprises."

"It never held a pleasanter one for me," Kirk answered. They went in to the table he had engaged, which stood in a secluded corner.

When they were seated, the girl turned to her host. "This was so good of you. And of Sir Frederic, too. I know how busy he must be."

The Englishman bowed. "A fortunate moment for me," he smiled, "when I decided I was not too busy to meet J. V. Morrow. I had heard that in the States young women were emancipated—"

"Of course, you don't approve," she said.

"Oh – but I do," he murmured.

"And Mr Chan. I'm sure Mr Chan disapproves of me."

Chan regarded her blankly. "Does the elephant disapprove of the butterfly? And who cares?"

"No answer at all," smiled the girl. "You are returning to Honolulu soon, Mr Chan?"

A delighted expression appeared on the blank face. "Tomorrow at noon the *Maui* receives my humble person. We churn over to Hawaii together."

"I see you are eager to go," said the girl.

"The brightest eyes are sometimes blind," replied Chan. "Not true in your case. It is now three weeks since I arrived on the mainland, thinking to taste the joys of holiday. Before I am aware events engulf me, and like the postman who has day of rest I foolishly set out on long, tiresome walk. Happy to say that walk are ended now. With beating heart I turn toward little home on Punchbowl Hill."

"I know how you feel," said Miss Morrow.

"Humbly begging pardon to mention it, you do not. I have hesitation in adding to your ear that one thing calls me home with unbearable force. I am soon to be happy father."

"For the first time?" asked Barry Kirk.

"The eleventh occasion of the kind," Chan answered.

"Must be sort of an old story by now," Bill Rankin suggested.

"That is one story which does not get aged," Chan replied. "You will learn. But my trivial affairs have no place here. We are met to honor a distinguished guest." He looked toward Sir Frederic.

Bill Rankin thought of his coming story. "I was moved to get you two together," he said, "because I found you think alike. Sir Frederic is also scornful of science as an aid to crime detection."

"I have formed that view from my experience," remarked Sir Frederic.

"A great pleasure," Chan beamed, "to hear that huge mind like Sir Frederic's moves in same groove as my poor head-piece. Intricate mechanics good in books, in real life not so much so. My experience tell me to think deep about human people. Human passions. Back of murder what, always? Hate, greed, revenge, need to make silent the slain one. Study human people at all times."

"Precisely," agreed Sir Frederic. "The human element – that is what counts. I have had no luck with scientific devices. Take the dictaphone – it has been a complete washout at the

Yard." He talked on, while the luncheon progressed. Finally he turned to Chan. "And what have your methods gained you, Sergeant? You have been successful, I hear."

Chan shrugged. "Luck – always happy luck."

"You're too modest," said Rankin. "That won't get you anywhere."

"The question now arises – where do I want to go?"

"But surely you're ambitious?" Miss Morrow suggested.

Chan turned to her gravely. "Coarse food to eat, water to drink, and the bended arm for a pillow – that is an old definition of happiness in my country. What is ambition? A canker that eats at the heart of the white man, denying him the joys of contentment. Is it also attacking the heart of white woman? I hope not." The girl looked away. "I fear I am victim of crude philosophy from Orient. Man – what is he? Merely one link in a great chain binding the past with the future. All times I remember I am link. Unsignificant link joining those ancestors whose bones repose on far distant hillsides with the ten children – it may now be eleven – in my house on Punchbowl Hill."

"A comforting creed," Barry Kirk commented.

"So, waiting the end, I do my duty as it rises. I tread the path that opens." He turned to Sir Frederic. "On one point, from my reading, I am curious. In your work at Scotland Yard, you follow only one clue. What you call the essential clue."

Sir Frederic nodded. "Such is usually our custom. When we fail, our critics ascribe it to that. They say, for example, that our obsession over the essential clue is the reason why we never solved the famous Ely Place murder."

They all sat up with interest. Bill Rankin beamed. Now things were getting somewhere. "I'm afraid we never heard of the Ely Place murder, Sir Frederic," he hinted.

"I sincerely wish I never had," the Englishman replied. "It was the first serious case that came to me when I took charge of the C. I. D. over sixteen years ago. I am chagrined to say I have never been able to fathom it."

He finished his salad, and pushed away the plate. "Since I have gone so far, I perceive I must go farther. Hilary Galt was the senior partner in the firm of Pennock and Galt, solicitors, with offices in Ely Place, Holborn. The business this firm carried on for more than a generation was unique of its kind. Troubled people in the highest ranks of society went to them for shrewd professional advice and Mr Hilary Galt and his father-in-law, Pennock, who died some twenty years ago, were entrusted with more numerous and romantic secrets than any other firm of solicitors in London. They knew the hidden history of every rascal in Europe, and they rescued many persons from the clutches of blackmailers. It was their boast that they never kept records of any sort."

Dessert was brought, and after this interruption, Sir Frederic continued.

"One foggy January night sixteen years ago, a caretaker entered Mr Hilary Galt's private office, presumably deserted for the day. The gas lights were ablaze, the windows shut and locked; there was no sign of any disturbance. But on the floor lay Hilary Galt, with a bullet in his brain.

"There was just one clue, and over that we puzzled for many weary months at the Yard. Hilary Galt was a meticulous dresser, his attire was perfect, always. It was perfect on this occasion – with one striking exception. His highly polished boots – I presume you call them shoes over here – were removed and standing on a pile of papers on top of his desk. And on his feet he wore a pair of velvet slippers, embellished with a curious design.

"These, of course, seemed to the Yard the essential clue, and we set to work. We traced those slippers to the Chinese Legation in Portland Place. Mr Galt had been of some trifling service to the Chinese minister, and early on the day of his murder the slippers had arrived as a gift from that gentleman. Galt had shown them to his office staff, and they were last seen wrapped loosely in their covering near his hat and stick. That was as far as we got.

"For sixteen years I have puzzled over those slippers. Why did Mr Hilary Galt remove his boots, don the slippers, and prepare himself as though for some extraordinary adventure? I don't know to this day. The slippers still haunt me. When I resigned from the Yard, I rescued them from the Black Museum and took them with me as a souvenir of my first case – an unhappy souvenir of failure. I should like to show them to you, Miss Morrow."

"Thrilling," said the girl.

"Annoying," corrected Sir Frederic grimly.

Bill Rankin looked at Charlie Chan. "What's your reaction to that case, Sergeant?" he inquired.

Chan's eyes narrowed in thought. "Humbly begging pardon to inquire," he said, "have you the custom, Sir Frederic, to put yourself in place of murderer?"

"It's a good idea," the Englishman answered, "if you can do it. You mean—"

"A man who has killed – a very clever man – he knows that Scotland Yard has fiercely fixed idea about essential clue. His wits accompany him. He furnishes gladly one essential clue which has no meaning and leads no place at all."

Sir Frederic regarded him keenly. "Excellent," he remarked. "And it has one great virtue – from your point of view. It completely exonerates your countrymen at the Chinese Legation."

"It might do more than that," suggested Barry Kirk.

Sir Frederic thoughtfully ate his dessert. No one spoke for some moments. But Bill Rankin was eager for more material.

"A very interesting case, Sir Frederic," he remarked. "You must have a lot like it up your sleeve. Murders that ended more successfully for Scotland Yard—"

"Hundreds," nodded the detective. "But none that still holds its interest for me like the crime in Ely Place. As a matter of fact, I have never found murder so fascinating as some other things. The murder case came and went and, with a rare exception such as this I have mentioned, was quickly forgotten. But there is one mystery that to me has always been the most exciting in the world."

"And what is that?" asked Rankin, while they waited with deep interest.

"The mystery of the missing," Sir Frederic replied. "The man or woman who steps quietly out of the picture and is never seen again. Hilary Galt, dead in his office, presents a puzzle, of course; still, there is something to get hold of, something tangible, a body on the floor. But if Hilary Galt had disappeared into the fog that gloomy night, leaving no trace – that would have been another story.

"For years I have been enthralled by the stories of the missing," the detective went on. "Even when they were outside my province, I followed many of them. Often the solution was simple, or sordid, but that could never detract from the thrill of the ones that remained unsolved. And of all those unsolved cases, there is one that I have never ceased to think about. Sometimes in the night I wake up and ask myself – what happened to Eve Durand?"

"Eve Durand," repeated Rankin eagerly.

"That was her name. As a matter of fact, I had nothing to do with the case. It happened outside my bailiwick – very far outside. But I followed it with intense interest from the first. There are others, too, who have never forgotten – just before I left England I clipped from a British periodical a brief reference to the matter – I have it here." He removed a bit of paper from his purse. "Miss Morrow – will you be kind enough to read this aloud?"

The girl took the clipping. She began to read, in a low, clear voice:

"A gay crowd of Anglo-Indians gathered one night fifteen years ago on a hill outside Peshawar to watch the moon rise over that isolated frontier town. Among the company were Captain Eric Durand and his wife, just out 'from home.' Eve Durand was young, pretty and well-born – a Miss Mannering, of Devonshire. Someone proposed a game of hide-and-seek before the ride back to Peshawar. The game was never finished. They are still looking for Eve Durand. Eventually all India was enlisted in the game. Jungle and bazaar, walled city and teak forest, were fine-combed for her. Through all the subterranean channels of that no-white-man's land of native life the search was carried by the famous secret service. After five years her husband retired to a life of seclusion in England, and Eve Durand became a legend – a horror tale to be told by ayahs to naughty children, along with the ghost stories of that north country."

The girl ceased reading, and looked at Sir Frederic, wide-eyed. There followed a moment of tense silence.

Bill Rankin broke the spell. "Some little game of hide-and-seek," he said.

"Can you wonder," asked Sir Frederic, "that for fifteen years the disappearance of Eve Durand, like Hilary Galt's slippers, has haunted me? A notably beautiful woman – a child, really – she was but eighteen that mysterious night at Peshawar. A blonde, blue-eyed, helpless child, lost in the dark of those dangerous hills. Where did she go? What became of her? Was she murdered? What happened to Eve Durand?"

"I'd rather like to know myself," remarked Barry Kirk softly.

"All India, as the clipping says, was enlisted in the game. By telegraph and by messenger, inquiries went, forward. Her heart-broken, frantic husband was given leave, and at the risk of his life he scoured that wild country. The secret service did its utmost. Nothing happened. No word ever came back to Peshawar.

"It was like looking for a needle in a haystack, and in time, for most people, the game lost its thrill. The hue and cry died down. All save a few forgot.

"When I retired from the Yard and set out on this trip around the world, India was of course on my itinerary. Though it was far off my track, I resolved to visit Peshawar. I went down to Ripple Court in Devonshire and had a chat with Sir George Mannering, the uncle of Eve Durand. Poor man, he is old before his time. He gave me what information he could – it was pitifully meager. I promised I would try to take up the threads of this old mystery when I reached India."

"And you did?" Rankin inquired.

"I tried – but, my dear fellow, have you ever seen Peshawar? When I reached there the hopelessness of my quest struck me, as Mr Chan might say, with an unbearable force. The Paris of the Pathans, they call it, and its filthy alleys teem with every race in the East. It isn't a city, it's a caravansary, and its population is constantly shifting. The English garrison is changed frequently, and I could find scarcely anyone who was there in the time of Eve Durand.

"As I say, Peshawar appalled me. Anything could happen there. A wicked town – its sins are the sins of opium and hemp and jealousy and intrigue, of battle, murder and sudden death, of gambling and strange intoxications, the lust of revenge. Who can explain the deviltry that gets into men's blood in certain latitudes? I walked the Street of the Story Tellers and wondered in vain over the story of Eve Durand. What a place to bring a woman like that, delicately reared, young, inexperienced."

"You learned nothing?" inquired Barry Kirk.

"What could you expect?" Sir Frederic dropped a small lump of sugar into his coffee. "Fifteen years since that little picnic party rode back to Peshawar, back to the compound of the lonely garrison, leading behind them the riderless pony of Eve Durand. And fifteen years, I may tell you, make a very heavy curtain on India's frontier."

Again Bill Rankin turned to Charlie Chan. "What do you say, Sergeant?" he asked.

Chan considered. "The town named Peshawar stands with great proximity to the Khyber Pass, leading into wilds of Afghanistan," he said.

Sir Frederic nodded. "It does. But every foot of the pass is guarded night and day by British troops, and no European is permitted to leave by that route, save under very special conditions. No, Eve Durand could never have left India by way of the Khyber Pass. The thing would have been impossible. Grant the impossible, and she could not have lived a day among the wild hill men over the border."

Chan gravely regarded the man from Scotland Yard. "It is not to be amazed at," he said, "that you have felt such deep interest. Speaking humbly for myself, I desire with unlimited yearning to look behind that curtain of which you speak."

"That is the curse of our business, Sergeant," Sir Frederic replied. "No matter what our record of successes, there must always remain those curtains behind which we long with unlimited yearning to look – and never do."

Barry Kirk paid the check, and they rose from the table. In the lobby, during the course of the goodbys, the party broke up momentarily into two groups. Rankin, Kirk and the girl went to the door, and after a hurried expression of thanks, the reporter dashed out to the street.

"Mr Kirk – it was wonderful," Miss Morrow said. "Why are all Englishmen so fascinating? Tell me that."

"Oh – are they?" He shrugged. "You tell me. You girls always fall for them, I notice."

"Well – they have an air about them. An atmosphere. They're not provincial, like a Rotarian who wants to tell you about the water-works. He took us traveling, didn't he? London and Peshawar – I could listen to him for hours. Sorry I have to run."

"Wait. You can do something for me."

"After what you've done for me," she smiled, "anything you ask."

"Good. This Chinese – Chan – he strikes me as a gentleman, and a mighty interesting one. I believe he would go big at my dinner tonight. I'd like to ask him, but that would throw my table out of gear. I need another woman. How about it? Will old man Blackstone let you off for the evening?"

"He might."

"Just a small party – my grandmother, and some people Sir Frederic has asked me to invite. And since you find Englishmen so fascinating, there'll be Colonel John Beetham, the famous Asiatic explorer. He's going to show us some movies he took in Tibet – which is the first intimation I've had that anything ever moved in Tibet."

"That will be splendid. I've seen Colonel Beetham's picture in the papers."

"I know – the women are all crazy about him, too. Even poor grandmother – she's thinking of putting up money for his next expedition to the Gobi Desert. You'll come then? Seven thirty."

"I'd love to – but it does seem presumptuous. After what you said about lawyers— "

"Yes – that was careless of me. I'll have to live it down. Give me a chance. My bungalow – you know where it is— "

She laughed. "Thanks. I'll come. Goodby – until tonight."

Meanwhile Sir Frederic Bruce had led Charlie Chan to a sofa in the lobby. "I was eager to meet you, Sergeant," he said, "for many reasons. Tell me, are you familiar with San Francisco's Chinatown?"

"I have slight acquaintance with same," Chan admitted. "My cousin, Chan Kee Lim, is an honored resident of Waverly Place."

"Have you, by any chance, heard of a Chinese down there – a stranger, a tourist – named Li Gung?"

"No doubt there are many so named. I do not know the one you bring up."

"This man is a guest of relatives on Jackson Street. You could do me a great service, Sergeant."

"It would remain," said Chan, "a golden item on the scroll of memory."

"Li Gung has certain information and I want it. I have tried to interview him myself, but naturally with no success."

"Light begins to dawn."

"If you could strike up an acquaintance with him – get into his confidence—"

"Humbly asking pardon, I do not spy on my own race with no good reason."

"The reasons in this case are excellent."

"Only a fool could doubt it. But what you hint would demand a considerable interval of time. My humble affairs have rightly no interest for you, so you have properly overlooked my situation. Tomorrow at noon I hasten to my home."

"You could stay over a week. I would make it greatly worth your while."

A stubborn look came into the little eyes. "One path only is worth my while now. The path to my home on Punchbowl Hill."

"I mean I would pay—"

"Again asking pardon – I have food, I have clothes which cover even the vast area I possess. Beyond that, what is money?"

"Very good. It was only a suggestion."

"I am desolated by acute pain," replied Chan. "But I must refuse."

Barry Kirk joined them. "Mr Chan, I'm going to ask you to do something for me," he began.

Chan sought to keep concern from his face, and succeeded. But what next, he wondered. "I am eagerly at attention," he said. "You are my host."

"I've just invited Miss Morrow to dinner tonight and I need another man. Will you come?"

"Your requests are high honors, which only an ungrate would refuse. But I am now already in your debt. More is going to embarrass me."

"Never mind that. I'll expect you at seven thirty – my bungalow on the Kirk Building."

"Splendid," said Sir Frederic. "We'll have another talk then, Sergeant. My requests are not precisely honors, but I may yet persuade you."

"Chinese funny people," remarked Chan. "They say no, no is what they mean. They say yes, and they are glued to same. With regard to dinner, I say yes, greatly pleased."

"Good," said Barry Kirk.

"Where's that reporter?" Sir Frederic asked.

"He hurried away," Kirk explained. "Anxious to get to his story, I imagine."

"What story?" asked the Englishman blankly.

"Why – the story of our luncheon. Your meeting with Sergeant Chan."

A startled expression crossed the detective's face. "Good lord – you don't mean he's going to put that into print?"

"Why naturally. I supposed you knew—"

"I'm afraid I'm woefully ignorant of American customs. I thought that was merely a social function. I didn't dream—"

"You mean you don't want him to print it?" asked Barry Kirk, surprised.

Sir Frederic turned quickly to Charlie. "Goodby, Sergeant. This has been a real pleasure. I shall see you tonight—"

He hastily shook hands with Chan, and dragged the dazed Barry Kirk to the street. There he motioned for a taxi.

"What paper was that young scoundrel representing?" he inquired.

"The *Globe*," Kirk told him.

"The *Globe* office – and quickly, please," Sir Frederic ordered.

The two got in, and for a moment rode in silence.

"You are curious, perhaps," said Sir Frederic at last.

"I hope you won't think it's unnatural of me," smiled Kirk.

"I know I can rely on your discretion, my boy. I told only a small part of the story of Eve Durand at luncheon, but even that must not reach print just yet. Not here – not now—"

"Great Scott. Do you mean—"

"I mean I am near the end of a long trail. Eve Durand was not murdered in India. She ran away. I know why she ran away. I even suspect the peculiar method of her going. More than that—"

"Yes?" cried Kirk eagerly.

"More than that I cannot tell you at present." The journey was continued in silence, and presently they drew up before the office of the *Globe*.

In the city editor's cubby-hole, Bill Rankin was talking exultantly to his chief. "It's going to be a corking good feature—" he was saying, when he felt a grip of steel on his arm. Turning, he looked into the face of Sir Frederic Bruce. "Why – why – hello," he stammered.

"There has been a slight mistake," said the detective.

"Let me explain," suggested Barry Kirk. He shook hands with the editor and introduced Sir Frederic, who merely nodded, not relaxing his grip on the reporter's paralyzed arm. "Rankin, this is unfortunate," Kirk continued, "but it can't be helped. Sir Frederic is unfamiliar with the ways of the American press, and he did not understand that you were gathering a story at lunch. He thought it a purely social affair. So we have come to ask that you print nothing of the conversation you heard this noon."

Rankin's face fell. "Not print it? Oh – I say—"

"We appeal to you both," added Kirk to the editor.

"My answer must depend on your reason for making the request," said that gentleman.

"My reason would be respected in England," Sir Frederic told him. "Here, I don't know your custom. But I may tell you that if you print any of that conversation, you will seriously impede the course of justice."

The editor bowed. "Very well. We shall print nothing without your permission, Sir Frederic," he said.

"Thank you," replied the detective, releasing Rankin's arm. "That concludes our business here, I fancy." And wheeling, he went out. Having added his own thanks, Kirk followed.

"Well, of all the rotten luck," cried Rankin, sinking into a chair.

Sir Frederic strode on across the city room. A cat may look at a king, and Egbert stood staring with interest at the former head of the C. I. D. Just in front of the door, the Englishman paused. It was either that or a collision with Egbert, moving slowly like a dark shadow across his path.

III

THE BUNGALOW IN THE SKY

Barry Kirk stepped from his living-room through French windows leading into the tiny garden that graced his bungalow in the sky – "my front yard," he called it. He moved over to the rail and stood looking out on a view such as few front yards have ever offered. Twenty stories below lay the alternate glare and gloom of the city; far in the distance the lights of the ferry-boats plodded across the harbor like weary fireflies.

The stars were bright and clear and amazingly close above his head, but he heard the tolling of the fog bell over by Belvedere, and he knew that the sea mist was drifting in through the Gate. By midnight it would whirl and eddy about his lofty home, shutting him off from the world like a veil of filmy tulle. He loved the fog. Heavy with the scent of distant gardens, salt with the breath of the Pacific, it was the trade-mark of his town.

He went back inside, closing the window carefully behind him. For a moment he stood looking about his living-room, which wealth and good taste had combined to furnish charmingly. A huge, deep sofa, many comfortable chairs, a half-dozen floor lamps shedding their warm yellow glow, a brisk fire crackling on a wide hearth – no matter how loudly the wind rattled at the casements, here were comfort and good cheer.

Kirk went on into his dining-room. Paradise was lighting the candles on the big table. The flowers, the snowy linen, the old silver, made a perfect picture, forecasting a perfect dinner. Kirk inspected the ten place cards. He smiled.

"Everything seems to be O.K.," he said. "It's got to be, tonight. Grandmother's coming, and you know what she thinks about a man who lives alone. To hear her tell it, every home needs a woman's touch."

"We shall disillusion her once again, sir," Paradise remarked.

"Such is my aim. Not that it will do any good. When she's made up her mind, that's that."

The door-bell rang, and Paradise moved off with slow, majestic step to answer it. Entering the living-room, Barry Kirk stood for a moment fascinated by the picture he saw there. The deputy district attorney had paused just inside the door leading from the hallway; she wore a simple, orange-colored dinner gown, her dark eyes were smiling.

"Miss Morrow," Kirk came forward eagerly. "If you don't mind my saying so, you don't look much like a lawyer tonight."

"I presume that's intended for a compliment," she answered. Chan appeared at her back. "Here's Mr Chan. We rode up together in the elevator. Heavens – don't tell me we're the first."

"When I was a boy," smiled Kirk, "I always started in by eating the frosting off my cake. Which is just to tell you that with me, the best is always first. Good evening, Mr Chan."

Chan bowed. "I am deeply touched by your kindness. One grand item is added to my mainland memories tonight." He wore a somewhat rusty dinner coat, but his linen gleamed and his manners shone.

Paradise followed with their wraps on his arm, and disappeared through a distant doorway. Another door opened. Sir Frederic Bruce stood on the threshold.

"Good evening, Miss Morrow," he said. "My word – you look charming. And Mr Chan. This is luck – you're the first. You know I promised to show you a souvenir of my dark past."

He turned and reentered his room. Kirk led his guests over to the blazing fire.

"Sit down – do," he said. "People are always asking how I can endure the famous San Francisco zephyrs up here." He waved a hand toward the fireplace. "This is one of my answers."

Sir Frederic rejoined them, a distinguished figure in his evening clothes. He carried a pair of slippers. Their tops were of cut velvet, dark red like old Burgundy, and each bore as decoration a Chinese character surrounded by a design of pomegranate blossoms. He handed one to the girl, and the other to Charlie Chan.

"Beautiful," cried Miss Morrow. "And what a history! The essential clue."

"Not any too essential, as it turned out," shrugged the great detective.

"You know, I venture to presume, the meaning of the character inscribed on velvet?" Chan inquired.

"Yes," said Sir Frederic. "Not any too appropriate, in this case, I believe. I was told it signifies 'Long life and happiness.'"

"Precisely." Chan turned the slipper slowly in his hand. "There exist one hundred and one varieties of this character – one hundred for the people, one reserved for the Emperor. A charming gift. The footwear of a mandarin, fitting only for one high-placed and wealthy."

"Well, they were on Hilary Galt's feet when we found him, murdered on the floor," Sir Frederic said. "'Walk softly, my best of friends' – that was what the Chinese minister wrote in the letter he sent with them. Hilary Galt was walking softly that night – but he never walked again." The Englishman took the slippers. "By the way – I hesitate to ask it – but I'd rather you didn't mention this matter tonight at dinner."

"Why, of course," remarked the girl, surprised.

"And that affair of Eve Durand. Ah – er – I fear I was a little indiscreet this noon. Now that I'm no longer at the Yard, I allow myself too much rope. You understand, Sergeant?"

Chan's little eyes were on him with a keenness that made Sir Frederic slightly uncomfortable. "Getting immodest for a minute," the Chinese said, "I am A 1 honor student in school of discretion."

"I'm sure of that," the great man smiled.

"No impulse to mention these matters would assail me, I am certain," Chan went on. "You bright man, Sir Frederic – you know Chinese are psychic people."

"Really?"

"Undubitably. Something has told me—"

"Ah yes – we needn't go into that," Sir Frederic put in hastily. "I have a moment's business in the offices below. If you will excuse me—"

He disappeared with the slippers into his room. Miss Morrow turned in amazement to Kirk.

"What in the world did he mean? Surely Eve Durand—"

"Mr Chan is psychic," Kirk suggested. "Maybe he can explain it."

Chan grinned. "Sometimes psychic feelings lead positively nowhere," he remarked.

Paradise escorted two more guests through the outer hall into the living-room. A little, bird-like woman was on tiptoe, kissing Barry Kirk.

"Barry, you bad boy. I haven't seen you for ages. Don't tell me you've forgot your poor old grandmother."

"I couldn't do that," he laughed.

"Not while I have my health and strength," she returned. She came toward the fireplace. "How cozy you are—"

"Grandmother – this is Miss Morrow," Kirk said. "Mrs Dawson Kirk."

The old lady took both the girl's hands. "My dear, I'm happy to know you—"

"Miss Morrow is a lawyer," Kirk added.

"Lawyer fiddlesticks," his grandmother cried. "She couldn't be – and look like this."

"Just what I said," nodded Kirk.

The old lady regarded the girl for a brief moment. "Youth and beauty," she remarked. "If I had those, my child, I wouldn't waste time over musty law books." She turned toward Chan. "And this is—"

"Sergeant Chan, of the Honolulu police," Kirk told her.

The old lady gave Charlie a surprisingly warm handclasp. "Know all about you," she said. "I like you very much."

"Flattered and overwhelmed," gasped Chan.

"Needn't be," she answered.

The woman who had accompanied Mrs Kirk stood rather neglected in the background. Kirk hurried forward to present her. She was, it seemed, Mrs Tupper-Brock, Mrs Kirk's secretary and companion. Her manner was cold and distant. Chan gave her a penetrating look and then bowed low before her.

"Paradise will show you into one of the guest rooms," said Kirk to the women. "You'll find a pair of military brushes and every book on football Walter Camp ever wrote. If there's anything else you want, try and get it."

They followed the butler out. The bell rang, and going to the door himself, Kirk admitted another couple. Mr Carrick Enderby, who was employed in the San Francisco office of Thomas Cook and Sons, was a big, slow, blond man with a monocle and nothing much behind it. All the family brilliance seemed to be monopolized by his wife, Eileen, a dark, dashing woman of thirty-five or so, who came in breezily. She joined the women, and the three men stood in the ill-at-ease silence that marks a dinner party in its initial stages.

"We're in for a bit of fog, I fancy," Enderby drawled.

"No doubt of it," Kirk answered.

When the women reappeared, Mrs Dawson Kirk came at once to Chan's side.

"Sally Jordan of Honolulu is an old friend of mine," she told him. "A very good friend. We're both living beyond our time, and there's nothing cements friendship like that. I believe you were once – er – attached—"

Chan bowed. "One of the great honors of my poor life. I was her house-boy, and memories of her kindness will survive while life hangs out."

"Well, she told me how you repaid that kindness recently. A thousandfold, she put it."

Chan shrugged. "My old employer has only one weakness. She exaggerates stupendously."

"Oh, don't be modest," said Mrs Kirk. "Gone out of fashion, long ago. These young people will accuse you of something terrible if you try that tune. However, I like you for it."

A diversion at the door interrupted her. Colonel John Beetham entered the living-room. John Beetham the explorer, whose feet had stood in many dark and lonely places, who knew Tibet and Turkestan, Tsaidam and southern Mongolia. He had lived a year in a house-boat on the largest river in the heart of Asia, had survived two heart-breaking, death-strewn retreats across the snowy plateau of Tibet, had walked amid the ruins of ancient desert cities that had flourished long before Christ was born.

For once, here was a man who looked the part. Lean, tall, bronzed, there was a living flame in his gray eyes. But like Charlie Chan, he came of a modest race, and his manner was shy and aloof as he acknowledged the introductions.

"So glad," he muttered. "So glad." A mere formula.

Suddenly Sir Frederic Bruce was again in the room. He seized Colonel Beetham's hand.

"I met you several years ago," he said. "You wouldn't recall it. You were the lion of the hour, and I a humble spectator. I was present at the dinner of the Royal Geographical Society in London when they gave you that enormous gold doodad – the Founders' Medal – wasn't that it?"

"Ah yes – of course. To be sure," murmured Colonel Beetham.

His eyes bright as buttons in the subdued light, Charlie Chan watched Sir Frederic being presented to the ladies – to Mrs Tupper-Brock and Eileen Enderby. Paradise arrived with something on a tray.

"All here except Miss Garland," Kirk announced. "We'll wait just a moment." The bell rang, and he motioned to his servant that he would go.

When Kirk returned, he was accompanied by a handsome woman whose face was flushed and who carried some burden in her jeweled hands. She hurried to a table, and deposited there a number of loose pearls.

"I had the most ridiculous accident on the stairs," she explained. "The string of my necklace broke, and I simply shed pearls right and left. I do hope I haven't lost any."

One of the pearls rolled to the floor, and Kirk retrieved it. The woman began counting them off into a gold mesh handbag. Finally she stopped.

"Got them all?" Barry Kirk inquired.

"I – I think so. I never can remember the number. And now – you really must forgive my silly entrance. It would be rather effective on the stage, I fancy, but I'm not on the stage now. In real life, I'm afraid it was rather rude."

Paradise took her cloak, and Kirk introduced her. Charlie Chan studied her long and carefully. She was no longer young, but her beauty was still triumphant. It would have to be, for her profession was the stage, and she was well-beloved in the Australian theaters.

At the table, Charlie found himself at Mrs Kirk's right, with June Morrow on his other side. If he was a bit awed by the company in which he had landed, he gave no sign. He listened to several anecdotes of Sally Jordan's past from Mrs Kirk, then turned to the girl beside him. Her eyes were shining.

"I'm thrilled to the depths," she whispered. "Sir Frederic and that marvelous Beetham man all in one evening – and you, too."

Chan smiled, "I am pretty lonely fly in this menagerie of lions," he admitted.

"Tell me – that about being psychic. You don't really think Sir Frederic has found Eve Durand?"

Chan shrugged. "For one word a man may be adjudged wise, and for one word he may be adjudged foolish."

"Oh, please don't be so Oriental. Just think – Eve Durand may be at this table tonight."

"Strange events permit themselves the luxury of occurring," Chan conceded. His eyes traveled slowly about the board, they rested on Mrs Tupper-Brock, silent and aloof, on the vivacious Eileen Enderby, longest of all on the handsome Gloria Garland, now completely recovered from her excitement over the scattered pearls.

"Tell me, Sir Frederic," remarked Mrs Kirk. "How are you making out here in Barry's womanless Eden?"

"Splendidly," smiled the detective. "Mr Kirk has been very kind. I not only have the run of this charming bungalow, but he has also installed me in the offices below." He looked at Kirk. "Which reminds me – I'm afraid I quite forgot to close the safe downstairs."

"Paradise can attend to it," suggested Kirk.

"Oh, no," said Sir Frederic. "Please don't trouble. It doesn't matter – as far as I am concerned."

Carrick Enderby spoke in a loud, booming voice. "I say, Colonel Beetham. I've just read your book, you know."

"Ah, yes – er – which one?" inquired Beetham blandly.

"Don't be a fool, Carry," said Eileen Enderby rather warmly. "Colonel Beetham has written many books. And he's not going to be impressed by the fact that, knowing you were to meet him here tonight, you hastily ran through one of them."

"But it wasn't hastily," protested Enderby. "I gave it my best attention. The *Life*, I mean, you know. All your adventures – and by jove, they were thrilling. Of course, I can't understand you, sir. For me, the cheery old whisky and soda in the comfortable chair by the warm fire. But you – how you do yearn for the desolate places, my word."

Beetham smiled. "It's the white spots – the white spots on the map. They call to me. I – I long to walk there, where no man has walked before. It is an odd idea, isn't it?"

"Well, of course, getting home must be exciting," Enderby admitted. "The Kings and the Presidents pinning decorations on you, and the great dinners, and the eulogies—"

"Quite the most terrible part of it, I assure you," said Beetham.

"Nevertheless, I'd take it in preference to your jolly old deserts," continued Enderby. "That time you were lost on the – er – the—"

"The desert of Takla-makan," finished Beetham. "I was in a bit of a jam, wasn't I? But I wasn't lost, my dear fellow. I had simply embarked on the crossing with insufficient water and supplies."

Mrs Kirk spoke. "I was enthralled by that entry you quoted from your diary. What you thought was the last entry you would ever make. I know it by heart. 'Halted on a high dune, where the camels fell exhausted. We examined the East through the field-glasses; mountains of sand in all directions; not a straw, no life. All, men as well as camels, are extremely weak. God help us.'"

"But it wasn't my last entry, you know," Beetham reminded her. "The next night, in a dying condition, I crept along on my hands and knees until I reached a forest, the bed of a dry river – a pool. Water. I came out much better than I deserved."

"Pardon me if I make slight inquiry," said Charlie Chan. "What of old superstition, Colonel? Mention was made of it by Marco Polo six hundred fifty years ago. When a traveler is moving across desert by night, he hears strange voices calling his name. In bewitched state, he follows ghostly voices to his early doom."

"It is quite obvious," returned Beetham, "that I followed no voices. In fact, I heard none."

Eileen Enderby shuddered. "Well, I never could do it," she said. "I'm frightfully afraid of the dark. It drives me almost insane with fear."

Sir Frederic Bruce looked at her keenly. For the first time in some moments he spoke. "I fancy many women are like that," he said. He turned suddenly to Mrs Kirk's companion. "What has been your experience, Mrs Tupper-Brock?"

"I do not mind the dark," said that lady, in a cool, even tone.

"Miss Garland?" His piercing eyes turned on the actress.

She seemed a little embarrassed. "Why – I – really, I much prefer the spotlight. No, I can't say I fancy darkness."

"Nonsense," said Mrs Dawson Kirk. "Things are the same in the dark as in the light. I never minded it."

Beetham spoke slowly. "Why not ask the gentlemen, Sir Frederic? Fear of the dark is not alone a woman's weakness. Were you to ask me, I should have to make a confession."

Sir Frederic turned on him in amazement. "You, Colonel?"

Beetham nodded. "When I was a little shaver, my life was made miserable by my horror of the dark. Every evening, when I was left alone in my room, I died a thousand deaths."

"By jove," cried Enderby. "And yet you grew up to spend your life in the dark places of the world."

"You conquered that early fear, no doubt?" Sir Frederic suggested.

Beetham shrugged. "Does one ever quite conquer a thing like that? But really – there is too much about me. Mr Kirk has asked me to let you see, after dinner, some pictures I took last year in Tibet. I fear I shall bore you by becoming, as you Americans say, the whole show."

Again they chatted by two and two. Miss Morrow leaned over to Chan.

"Imagine," she said, "that picture of the great explorer, as a little boy, frightened of the dark. It's quite the most charming and human thing I ever heard."

He nodded gravely, his eyes on Eileen Enderby. "The dark drives me almost insane with fear," she had said. How dark it must have been that night in the hills outside Peshawar.

After he had served coffee in the living-room, Paradise appeared with a white, glittering screen which, under the Colonel's direction, he stood on a low table against a Flemish tapestry. Barry Kirk helped Beetham carry in from the hallway a heavy motion-picture projector and several boxes of films.

"Lucky we didn't overlook this," the young man laughed. "A rather embarrassing thing for you if you had to go home without being invited to perform. Like the man who tried to slip away from an evening party with a harp that he hadn't been asked to play."

The machine was finally ready, and the company took their places in comfortable chairs facing the screen.

"We shall want, of course, complete darkness," Beetham said. "Mr Kirk, if you will be so kind—"

"Surely." Barry Kirk turned off the lights, and drew thick curtains over doors and windows. "Is it all right now?"

"The light in the hallway," Beetham suggested.

Kirk also extinguished that. There was a moment of tense silence.

"Heavens – this is creepy," spoke Eileen Enderby out of the blackness. There was a slight note of hysteria in her voice.

Beetham was placing a roll of film in the machine. "On the expedition I am about to describe," he began, "we set out from Darjeeling. As you no doubt know, Darjeeling is a little hill station on the extreme northern frontier of India—"

Sir Frederic interrupted. "You have been in India a great deal, Colonel?"

"Frequently – between journeys—"

"Ah yes – pardon me for breaking in—"

"Not at all." The film began to unwind. "These first pictures are of Darjeeling, where I engaged my men, rounded up supplies, and—" The Colonel was off on his interesting but rather lengthy story.

Time passed, and his voice droned on in the intense darkness. The air was thick with the smoke of cigarettes; now and then there was the stir of someone moving, walking about in the rear, occasionally a curtain parted at a window. But Colonel Beetham gave no heed. He was living again on the high plateau of Tibet; the old fervor to go on had returned; he trekked through snowy passes, leaving men and mules dead in the wasteland, fighting like a fanatic on toward his goal.

A weird feeling of oppression settled down over Charlie Chan, a feeling he attributed to the thick atmosphere of the room. He rose and dodged guiltily out into the roof-top garden. Barry Kirk was standing there, a dim figure in the mist, smoking a cigarette. For it was misty now, the fog bell was tolling its warning, and the roof was wrapped in clouds.

"Hello," said Kirk, in a low voice. "Want a bit of air, too, eh? I hope he's not boring my poor guests to death. Exploring's a big business now, and he's trying to persuade grandmother to put up a lot of money for a little picnic he's planning. An interesting man, isn't he?"

"Most interesting," Chan admitted.

"But a hard one," added Kirk. "He leaves the dead behind with never so much as a look over his shoulder. I suppose that's the scientific type of mind – what's a few dead men when you're wiping out one of those white spots on the map? However, it's not my style. That's my silly American sentimentality."

"It is undubitably the style of Colonel Beetham," Chan returned. "I read same in his eyes."

He went back into the big living-room, and walked about in the rear. A slight sound in the hallway interested him, and he went out there. A man had just entered by the door that led to the floor below. Before he closed it the light outside fell on the blond hair of Carrick Enderby.

"Just having a cigarette on the stairs," he explained in a hoarse whisper. "Didn't want to add any more smoke to the air in there. A bit thick, what?"

He stole back into the living-room, and Chan, following, found a chair. A clatter of dishes sounded from the distant pantry, competing with the noise of the unwinding film and the steady stream of Beetham's story. The tireless man was starting on a new reel.

"Voice is getting a bit weary," the Colonel admitted. "I'll just run this one off without comment. It requires none." He fell back from the dim light by the machine, into the shadows.

In ten minutes the reel had unwound its length, and the indomitable Beetham was on hand. He was preparing to start on what he announced as the final reel, when the curtains over one of the French windows parted suddenly, and the white figure of a woman came into the room. She stood there like a wraith in the misty light at her back.

"Oh, stop it!" she cried. "Stop it and turn up the lights. Quickly! Quickly – please!" There was a real hysteria in Eileen Enderby's voice now.

Barry Kirk leaped to the light switch, and flooded the room. Mrs Enderby stood, pale and swaying slightly, clutching at her throat. "What is it?" Kirk asked. "What's the trouble?"

"A man," she panted. "I couldn't stand the dark – it was driving me mad – I stepped out into the garden. I was standing close to the railing when I saw a man leap from a lighted window on the floor below, out on to the fire-escape. He ran down it into the fog."

"My offices are below," Kirk said quietly. "We had better look into this. Sir Frederic —" His eyes turned from one to the other. "Why – where is Sir Frederic?" he asked.

Paradise had entered from the pantry. "I beg your pardon, sir," he said. "Sir Frederic went down to the offices some ten minutes ago."

"Down to the offices? Why?"

"The burglar alarm by your bed was buzzing, sir. The one connected up downstairs. Just as I discovered it, Sir Frederic entered your room. 'I will investigate this, Paradise,' he said. 'Don't disturb the others.'"

Kirk turned to Charlie Chan. "Sergeant, will you come with me, please?"

Silently Charlie followed him to the stairs, and together they went below. The offices were ablaze with light. The rear room, into which the stairs led, was quite empty. They advanced into the middle room.

A window was open as far as it would go, and in the mist outside Chan noted the iron gratings of a fire-escape. This room too seemed empty. But beyond the desk Barry Kirk, in advance, gave a little cry and dropped to his knees.

Chan stepped around the desk. He was not surprised by what he saw, but he was genuinely sorry. Sir Frederic Bruce lay on the floor, shot cleanly through the heart. By his side lay a thin little volume, bound in bright yellow cloth.

Kirk stood up, dazed. "In my office," he said slowly, as though that were important. "It's – it's horrible. Good God – look!"

He pointed to Sir Frederic. On the detective's feet were black silk stockings – and nothing else. He wore no shoes.

Paradise had followed. He stood for a moment staring at the dead man on the floor, and then turned to Barry Kirk.

"When Sir Frederic came downstairs," he said, "he was wearing a pair of velvet slippers. Sort of heathen-looking slippers they were, sir."

IV

THE RECKONING OF HEAVEN

Barry Kirk stood looking about his office; he found it difficult to believe that into this commonplace, familiar room, tragedy had found its way. Yet there was that silent figure on the floor, a few moments before so full of life and energy.

"Poor Sir Frederic," he said. "Only today he told me he was near the end of a long trail. Nearer than he dreamed, it appears." He stopped. "A long trail, Sergeant – only a few of us know how far back into the past this thing must reach."

Chan nodded. He had been consulting a huge gold watch; now he snapped shut the case and restored it to his pocket. "Death is the reckoning of heaven," he remarked. "On this occasion, a most complicated reckoning."

"Well, what shall we do?" Kirk asked helplessly. "The police, I suppose. But good lord – this is a case beyond any policeman I ever met. Any uniformed man, I mean." He paused, and a grim smile flashed across his face. "It looks very much to me, Mr Chan, as though you would have to take charge and—"

A stubborn light leaped into the little black eyes. "Miss Morrow is above," said Chan. "What a happy chance, since she is from the district attorney's office. If I may humbly suggest—"

"Oh, I never thought of that." Kirk turned to his servant. "Paradise, ask Miss Morrow to come here. Make my excuses to my guests, and ask them to wait."

"Very good, sir," replied Paradise, and departed.

Kirk walked slowly about the room. The drawers of the big desk were open and their contents jumbled. "Somebody's been on a frantic search here," he said. He paused before the safe; its door was slightly ajar.

"Safe stands open," suggested Chan.

"Odd about that," said Kirk. "This afternoon Sir Frederic asked me to take out anything of value and move it upstairs. I did so. He didn't explain."

"Of course," nodded Chan. "And at the dinner table he makes uncalled-for reference to fact that he has not locked safe. The matter struck me at the time. One thing becomes clear – Sir Frederic desired to set a trap. A safe unlocked to tempt marauders." He nodded to the small volume that lay at the dead man's side. "We must disturb nothing. Do not touch, but kindly regard book and tell me where last reposing."

Kirk leaned over. "That? Why, it's the year-book of the Cosmopolitan Club. It was usually in that revolving case on which the telephone stands. It can't mean anything."

"Maybe not. Maybe" – Chan's little eyes narrowed – "a hint from beyond the unknown."

"I wonder," mused Kirk.

"Sir Frederic was guest of Cosmopolitan Club?"

"Yes – I gave him a two weeks' card. He wrote a lot of his letters there. But – but – I can't see—"

"He was clever man. Even in moment of passing, his dying hand would seek to leave behind essential clue."

"Speaking of that," said Kirk, "how about those velvet slippers? Where are they?"

Chan shrugged. "Slippers were essential clue in one case, long ago. What did they lead to? Positively nothing. If I am suiting my own taste, this time I look elsewhere."

Miss Morrow entered the room. Her face was usually full of color – an authentic color that is the gift of the fog to San Francisco's daughters. Now it was deathly pale. Without speaking, she stepped beyond the desk and looked down. For a moment she swayed, and Barry Kirk leaped forward.

"No, no," cried the girl.

"But I thought—" he began.

"You thought I was going to faint. Absurd. This is my work – it has come to me and I shall do it. You believe I can't—"

"Not at all," protested Kirk.

"Oh, yes you do. Everybody will. I'll show them. You've called the police, of course."

"Not yet," Kirk answered.

She sat down resolutely at the desk, and took up the telephone. "Davenport 20," she said. "The Hall of Justice?... Captain Flannery, please... Hello – Captain? Miss Morrow of the district attorney's office speaking. There has been a murder in Mr Kirk's office on the top floor of the Kirk Building. You had better come yourself... Thank you... Yes – I'll attend to that."

She got up, and, going round the desk, bent over Sir Frederic. She noted the book, and her eyes strayed wonderingly to the stocking feet. Inquiringly she turned to Chan.

"The slippers of Hilary Galt," he nodded. "Souvenir of that unhappy case, they adorned his feet when he came down. Here is Paradise – he will explain to you."

The butler had returned, and Miss Morrow faced him. "Tell us what you know, please," she said.

"I was busy in the pantry," Paradise said. "I thought I heard the buzz of the burglar alarm by Mr Kirk's bed – the one connected with the windows and safe in this room. I hastened to make sure, but Sir Frederic was just behind. It was almost as though he had been expecting it. I don't know how I got that impression – I'm odd that way—"

"Go on," said the girl. "Sir Frederic followed you into Mr Kirk's room?"

"Yes, Miss. 'There's someone below, sir,' I said. 'Someone who doesn't belong there.' Sir Frederic looked back into the pitch dark living-room. 'I fancy so, Paradise,' he said. He was smiling. 'I will attend to it. No need to disturb Mr Kirk or his guests.' I followed him into his room. He tossed off his patent leather pumps. 'The stairs are a bit soiled, I fear, sir,' I reminded him. He laughed. 'Ah, yes,' he said. 'But I have the very thing.' The velvet slippers were lying near his bed. He put them on. 'I shall walk softly in these, Paradise,' he told me. At the head of the stairs, I stopped him. A sort of fear was in my heart – I am given to that – to having premonitions—"

"You stopped him," Kirk cut in.

"I did, sir. Respectfully, of course. 'Are you armed, Sir Frederic?' I made bold to inquire. He shook his head. 'No need, Paradise,' he answered. 'I fancy our visitor is of the weaker sex.' And then he went down, sir – to his death."

They were silent for a moment, pondering the servant's story.

"We had better go," said the girl, "and tell the others. Someone must stay here. If it's not asking too much, Mr Chan—"

"I am torn with grief to disagree," Chan answered. "Please pardon me. But for myself, I have keen eagerness to note how this news is taken in the room above."

"Ah, yes. Naturally."

"I shall be glad to stay, Miss," Paradise said.

"Very well," the girl answered. "Please let me know as soon as Captain Flannery arrives." She led the way above, and Kirk and the little detective from Honolulu followed.

Barry Kirk's guests were seated, silent and expectant, in the now brightly lighted living-room. They looked up inquiringly as the three from below entered. Kirk faced them, at a loss how to begin.

"I have dreadful news for you," he said. "An accident – a terrible accident." Chan's eyes moved rapidly about the group and, making their choice, rested finally on the white, drawn face of Eileen Enderby. "Sir Frederic Bruce has been murdered in my office," Kirk finished.

There was a moment's breathless silence, and then Mrs Enderby got to her feet. "It's the dark," she cried in a harsh, shrill voice. "I knew it. I knew something would happen when the lights were turned off. I knew it, I tell you—"

Her husband stepped to her side to quiet her, and Chan stood staring not at her, but at Colonel John Beetham. For one brief instant he thought the mask had dropped from those weary, disillusioned eyes. For one instant only.

They all began to speak at once. Gradually Miss Morrow made herself heard above the din. "We must take this coolly," she said, and Barry Kirk admired her composure. "Naturally, we are all under suspicion. We—"

"What? I like that!" Mrs Dawson Kirk was speaking. "Under suspicion, indeed—"

"The room was in complete darkness," Miss Morrow went on. "There was considerable moving about. I don't like to stress my official position here, but perhaps you would prefer my methods to those of a police captain. How many of you left this room during the showing of Colonel Beetham's pictures?"

An embarrassed silence fell. Mrs Kirk broke it. "I thought the pictures intensely interesting," she said. "True, I did step into the kitchen for a moment—"

"Just to keep an eye on my domestic arrangements," suggested Barry Kirk.

"Nothing of the sort. My throat was dry. I wanted a glass of water."

"You saw nothing wrong?" inquired Miss Morrow.

"Aside from the very wasteful methods that seemed to be in vogue in the kitchen – nothing," replied Mrs Kirk firmly.

"Mrs Tupper-Brock?" said Miss Morrow.

"I was on the sofa with Miss Garland," replied that lady. "Neither of us moved from there at any time." Her voice was cool and steady.

"That's quite true," the actress added.

Another silence. Kirk spoke up. "I'm sure none of us intended a discourtesy to the Colonel," he said. "The entertainment he gave us was delightful, and it was gracious of him to honor us. I myself – er – I was in the room constantly – except for one brief moment in the garden. I saw no one there – save—"

Chan stepped forward. "Speaking for myself, I found huge delight in the pictures. A moment I wish to be alone, in order that I may digest great events flashed before me on silvery screen. So I also invade the garden, and meet Mr Kirk. For a time we marvel at the distinguished Colonel Beetham – his indomitable courage, his deep resource, his service to humanity. Then we rush back, that we may miss no more." He paused. "Before I again recline in sitting posture, noise in hallway offend me. I hurry out there in shushing mood, and behold—"

"Ah – er – the pictures were marvelous," said Carrick Enderby. "I enjoyed them immensely. True enough, I stepped out on the stairs for a cigarette—"

"Carry, you fool," his wife cried. "You would do that."

"But I say – why not? I saw nothing. There was nothing to see. The floor below was quite deserted." He turned to Miss Morrow. "Whoever did this horrible thing left by way of the fire-escape. You've already learned that—"

"Ah, yes," cut in Chan. "We have learned it indeed – from your wife." He glanced at Miss Morrow and their eyes met.

"From my wife – yes," repeated Enderby. "Look here – what do you mean by that? I—"

"No matter," put in Miss Morrow. "Colonel Beetham – you were occupied at the picture machine. Except for one interval of about ten minutes, when you allowed it to run itself."

"Ah, yes," said the Colonel evenly. "I did not leave the room, Miss Morrow."

Eileen Enderby rose. "Mr Kirk – we really must be going. Your dinner was charming – how terrible to have it end in such a tragic way. I—"

"Just a moment," said June Morrow. "I cannot let you go until the captain of police releases you."

"What's that?" the woman cried. "Outrageous. You mean we are prisoners here—"

"Oh – but, Eileen—" protested her husband.

"I'm very sorry," said the girl. "I shall protect you as much as possible from the annoyance of further questioning. But you really must wait."

Mrs Enderby flung angrily away, and a filmy scarf she was wearing dropped from one shoulder and trailed after her. Chan reached out to rescue it. The woman took another step, and he stood with the scarf in his hand. She swung about. The detective's little eyes, she noticed, were fixed with keen interest on the front of her pale blue gown, and following his gaze, she looked down.

"So sorry," said Chan. "So very sorry. I trust your beautiful garment, is not a complete ruin."

"Give me that scarf," she cried, and snatched it rudely from him.

Paradise appeared in the doorway. "Miss Morrow, please," he said. "Captain Flannery is below."

"You will kindly wait here," said the girl. "All of you. I shall arrange for your release at the earliest possible moment."

With Kirk and Charlie Chan, she returned to the twentieth floor. In the central room they found Captain Flannery, a gray-haired, energetic policeman of about fifty. With him were two patrolmen and a police doctor.

"Hello, Miss Morrow," said the Captain. "This is a he – I mean, a terrible thing. Sir Frederic Bruce of Scotland Yard –

we're up against it now. If we don't make good quick we'll have the whole Yard on our necks."

"I'm afraid we shall," admitted Miss Morrow. "Captain Flannery – this is Mr Kirk. And this – Detective-Sergeant Charlie Chan, of Honolulu."

The Captain looked his fellow detective over slowly. "How are you, Sergeant? I've been reading about you in the paper. You got on this job mighty quick."

Chan shrugged. "Not my job, thank you," he replied. "All yours, and very welcome. I am here in society rôle, as guest of kind Mr Kirk."

"Is that so?" The Captain appeared relieved. "Now, Miss Morrow, what have you found out?"

"Very little. Mr Kirk was giving a dinner upstairs." She ran over the list of guests, the showing of the pictures in the dark, and the butler's story of Sir Frederic's descent to the floor below, wearing the velvet slippers. "There are other aspects of the affair that I will take up with you later," she added.

"All right. I guess the D. A. will want to get busy on this himself."

The girl flushed. "Perhaps. He is out of town tonight. I hope he will leave the matter in my hands—"

"Great Scott, Miss Morrow – this is important," said the Captain, oblivious of his rudeness. "You're holding those people upstairs?"

"Naturally."

"Good. I'll look 'em over later. I ordered the night-watchman to lock the front door and bring everybody in the building here. Now, we better fix the time of this. How long's he been dead, Doctor?"

"Not more than half an hour," replied the doctor.

"Humbly begging pardon to intrude," said Chan. "The homicide occurred presumably at ten twenty."

"Sure of that?"

"I have not the habit of light speaking. At ten twenty-five we find body, just five minutes after lady on floor above rush in with news of man escaping from this room by fire-escape."

"Huh. The room seems to have been searched." Flannery turned to Barry Kirk. "Anything missing?"

"I haven't had time to investigate," said Kirk. "If anything has been taken, I fancy it was Sir Frederic's property."

"This is your office, isn't it?"

"Yes. But I had made room here for Sir Frederic. He had various papers and that sort of thing."

"Papers? What was he doing? I thought he'd retired."

"It seems he was still interested in certain cases, Captain," Miss Morrow said. "That is one of the points I shall take up with you later."

"Again interfering with regret," remarked Chan, "if we do not know what was taken, all same we know, what was hunted."

"You don't say." Flannery looked at Chan coldly. "What was that?"

"Sir Frederic English detective, and great one. All English detectives make exhausting records of every case. No question that records of certain case, in which murderer was hotly interested, were sought here."

"Maybe," admitted the Captain. "We'll go over the room later." He turned to the patrolmen. "You boys take a look at the fire-escape." They climbed out into the fog. At that moment the door leading from the reception-room into the hallway opened, and an odd little group came in. A stout, middle-aged man led the procession; he was Mr Cuttle, the night-watchman.

"Here they are, Captain," he said. "I've rounded up everybody in the building, except a few cleaning women who have nothing to do with this floor. You can see 'em later, if you like. This is Mrs Dyke, who takes care of the two top floors."

Mrs Dyke, very frightened, said that she had finished with Kirk's office at seven and gone out, leaving the burglar alarm in working order, as was her custom. She had not been back since. She had seen no one about the building whom she did not recognize.

"And who is this?" inquired the Captain, turning to a pale, sandy-haired young man who appeared extremely nervous.

"I am employed by Brace and Davis, Certified Public Accountants, on the second floor," said the young man. "My name is Samuel Smith. I was working tonight to catch up – I have been ill – when Mr Cuttle informed me I was wanted up here. I know nothing of this horrible affair."

Flannery turned to the fourth and last member of the party, a young woman whose uniform marked her as an operator of one of the elevators. "What's your name?" he asked.

"Grace Lane, sir," she told him.

"Run the elevator, eh?"

"Yes, sir. Mr Kirk had sent word that one of us must work overtime tonight. On account of the party."

"How many people have you brought up since the close of business?"

"I didn't keep count. Quite a few – ladies and gentlemen – Mr Kirk's guests, of course."

"Don't remember anybody who looked like an outsider?"

"No, sir."

"This is a big building," said Flannery. "There must have been others working here tonight besides this fellow Smith. Remember anybody?"

The girl hesitated. "There – there was one other, sir."

"Yes? Who was that?"

"A girl who is employed in the office of the Calcutta Importers, on this floor. Her name is Miss Lila Barr."

"Working here tonight, eh? On this floor. She's not here now?"

"No, sir. She left some time ago."

"How long ago?"

"I can't say exactly, sir. Half an hour – perhaps a little more than that."

"Humph." The Captain took down their names and addresses, and dismissed them. As they went out, the two patrolmen entered from the fire-escape, and, leaving them in charge, Flannery asked to be directed upstairs.

The dinner guests were sitting with rather weary patience in a semicircle in the living-room. Into their midst strode the Captain, with an air of confidence he was far from feeling. He stood looking them over.

"I guess you know what I'm doing here," he said. "Miss Morrow tells me she's had a talk with you, and I won't double back over her tracks. However, I want the name and address of everyone of you." He turned to Mrs Kirk. "I'll start with you."

She stiffened at his tone. "You're very flattering, I'm sure. I am Mrs Dawson Kirk." She added her address.

"You." Flannery turned to the explorer.

"Colonel John Beetham. I am a visitor in the city, stopping at the Fairmont."

Flannery went on down the list. When he had finished, he added:

"Anyone got any light to throw on this affair? If you have, better give it to me now. Things'll be a lot pleasanter all round than if I dig it up for myself later." No one spoke. "Some lady saw a man running down the fire-escape," he prompted.

"Oh – I did," said Eileen Enderby. "I've been all over that with Miss Morrow. I had gone out into the garden—" Again she related her experience.

"What'd this man look like?" demanded Flannery.

"I couldn't say. A very dim figure in the fog."

"All right. You can all go now. I may want to see some of you later." Flannery strode past them into the garden.

One by one they said their strained farewells and departed – Mrs Kirk and her companion, Miss Gloria Garland, then the

Enderbys, and finally the explorer. Charlie Chan also got his hat and coat, while Miss Morrow watched him inquiringly.

"Until dark deed shaded the feast," said Chan, "the evening was an unquestioned joy. Mr Kirk—"

"Oh, but you're not leaving," cried Miss Morrow. "Please. I want to have a talk with you."

"Tomorrow I am sea-going man," Chan reminded her. "The experience weakens me considerably. I have need of sleep, and relaxing—"

"I'll keep you only a moment," she pleaded, and Chan nodded.

Captain Flannery appeared from the garden. "Dark out there," he announced. "But if I'm not mistaken, anyone could have reached the floor below by way of the fire-escape. Is that right?"

"Undoubtedly," replied Kirk.

"An important discovery," approved Chan. "On the gown of one of the lady guests were iron rust stains, which might have been suffered by—But who am I to speak thus to keen man like the Captain? You made note of the fact, of course?"

Flannery reddened. "I – I can't say I did. Which lady?"

"That Mrs Enderby, who witnessed fleeing man. Do not mention it, sir. So happy to be of slightest service."

"Let's go back downstairs," growled Flannery. On the floor below, he stood for a long moment, looking about. "Well, I got to get busy here."

"I will say farewell," remarked Chan.

"Going, eh?" said Flannery, with marked enthusiasm.

"Going far," smiled Chan. "Tomorrow I am directed toward Honolulu. I leave you to the largest problem of your life, Captain. I suffer no envy for you."

"Oh, I'll pull through," replied Flannery.

"Only the witless could doubt it. But you will travel a long road. Consider. Who is great man silent now on couch? A famous detective with a glorious record. The meaning of that? A thousand victories – and a thousand enemies. All over broad world are scattered men who would do him into death with happy hearts. A long road for you, Captain. You have my warmest wishes for bright outcome. May you emerge in the shining garments of success."

"Thanks," said Flannery.

"One last point. You will pardon me if I put in final oar." He took up from the table a little yellow book, and held it out. "Same was at the dead man's elbow when he fell."

Flannery nodded. "I know. The Cosmopolitan Club book. It can't mean a damn thing."

"Maybe. I am stupid Chinese from tiny island. I know nothing. But if this was my case I would think about book, Captain Flannery. I would arouse in the night to think about it. Goodby, and all good wishes already mentioned."

He made a deep bow, and went through the reception-room into the hall. Kirk and the girl followed swiftly. The latter put her hand on Chan's arm.

"Sergeant – you mustn't," she cried despairingly. "You can't desert me now. I need you."

"You rip my heart to fragments," he replied. "However, plans are set."

"But poor Captain Flannery – all this is far beyond him. You know more about the case than he does. Stay, and I'll see that you're given every facility—"

"That's what I say," put in Barry Kirk. "Surely you can't go now. Good lord, man, have you no curiosity?"

"The bluest hills are those farthest away," Chan said. "Bluest of all is Punchbowl Hill, where my little family is gathered, waiting for me—"

"But I was depending on you," pleaded the girl. "I must succeed – I simply must. If you would stay—"

Chan drew away from her. "I am so sorry. Postman on his holiday, they tell me, takes long walk. I have taken same, and I am weary. So very sorry – but I return to Honolulu tomorrow." The elevator door was open. Chan bowed low. "The happiest pleasure to know you both. May we meet again. Goodby."

Like a grim, relentless Buddha he disappeared below. Kirk and the girl reentered the office, where Captain Flannery was eagerly on the hunt.

Chan walked briskly through the fog to the Stewart Hotel. At the desk the clerk handed him a cable, which he read with beaming face. He was still smiling when, in his room, the telephone rang. It was Kirk.

"Look here," Kirk said. "We made the most astonishing discovery in the office after you left."

"Pleased to hear it," Chan replied.

"Under the desk – a pearl from Gloria Garland's necklace!"

"Opening up," said Chan, "a new field of wonderment. Hearty congratulations."

"But see here," Kirk cried, "aren't you interested? Won't you stay and help us get at the bottom of this?"

Again that stubborn look in Charlie's eyes. "Not possible. Only a few minutes back I have a cable that calls me home with unbearable force. Nothing holds me on the mainland now."

"A cable? From whom?"

"From my wife. Glorious news. We are now in receipt of our eleventh child – a boy."

V

THE VOICE IN THE NEXT ROOM

Charlie Chan rose at eight the next morning, and as he scraped the stubble of black beard from his cheeks, he grinned happily at his reflection in the glass. He was thinking of the small, helpless boy-child who no doubt at this moment lay in the battered old crib on Punchbowl Hill. In a few days, the detective promised himself, he would stand beside that crib, and the latest Chan would look up to see, at last, his father's welcoming smile.

He watched a beetle-browed porter wheel his inexpensive little trunk off on the first leg of its journey to the Matson docks, and then neatly placed his toilet articles in his suitcase. With jaunty step he went down to breakfast.

The first page of the morning paper carried the tragic tale of Sir Frederic's passing, and for a moment Chan's eyes narrowed. A complicated mystery, to be sure. Interesting to go to the bottom of it – but that was the difficult task of others. Had it been his duty, he would have approached it gallantly, but, from his point of view, the thing did not concern him. Home – that alone concerned him now.

He laid the paper down, and his thoughts flew back to the little boy in Honolulu. An American citizen, a future boy scout under the American flag, he should have an American name.

Chan had felt himself greatly attracted to his genial host of the night before. Barry Chan – what was the matter with that?

As he was finishing his tea, he saw in the dining-room door the thin, nervous figure of Bill Rankin, the reporter. He signed his check, left a generous tip, and joined Rankin in the lobby.

"Hello," said the reporter. "Well, that was some little affair up at the Kirk Building last night."

"Most distressing," Chan replied. They sat down on a broad sofa, and Rankin lighted a cigarette.

"I've got a bit of information I believe you should have," the newspaper man continued.

"Begging pardon, I think you labor under natural delusion," Chan said.

"Why – what do you mean?"

"I am not concerned with case," Chan calmly informed him.

"You don't mean to say—"

"In three hours I exit through Golden Gate."

Rankin gasped. "Good lord. I knew you'd planned to go, of course, but I supposed—Why, man alive, this is the biggest thing that's broke round here since the fire. Sir Frederic Bruce – it's an international catastrophe. I should think you'd leap at it."

"I am not," smiled Charlie, "a leaping kind of man. Personal affairs call me to Hawaii. The postman refuses to take another walk. Very interesting case, but as I have heard my slanging cousin Willie say, I am not taking any of it."

"I know," said Rankin. "The calm, cool Oriental. Never been excited in your life, I suppose?"

"What could I have gained by that? I have watched the American citizen. His temples throb. His heart pounds. The fibers of his body vibrate. With what result? A year subtracted from his life."

"Well, you're beyond me," said Rankin, leaning back and seeking to relax a bit himself. "I hope I won't be boring you if I go on talking about Sir Frederic. I've been all over our luncheon at the St. Francis in my mind, and do you know what I think?"

"I should be pleased to learn," returned Chan.

"Fifteen years make a very heavy curtain on the Indian frontier, Sir Frederic said. If you ask me, I'd say that in order to solve the mystery of his murder last night, we must look behind that curtain."

"Easy said, but hard to do," suggested Chan.

"Very hard, and that's why you—Oh, well, go on and take your boat ride. But the disappearance of Eve Durand is mixed up in this somehow. So, perhaps, is the murder of Hilary Galt."

"You have reason for thinking this?"

"I certainly have. Just as I was about to sit down and write a nice feature story about that luncheon, Sir Frederic rushed into the *Globe* office and demanded I hush it all up. Why should he do that? I ask you."

"And I pause for your reply."

"You'll get it. Sir Frederic was still working on one, or maybe both, of those cases. More than that, he was getting somewhere. That visit to Peshawar may not have been as lacking in results as he made out. Eve Durand may be in San Francisco now. Someone connected with one of those cases is certainly here – someone who pulled that trigger last night. For myself, I would *cherchez la femme*. That's French—"

"I know," nodded Chan. "You would hunt the woman. Excellent plan. So would I."

"Aha – I knew it. And that's why this information I have is vital. The other night I went up to the Kirk Building to see Sir Frederic. Paradise told me he was in the office. Just as I was approaching the office door, it opened, and a young woman—"

"One moment," Chan cut in. "Begging pardon to interrupt, you should go at once with your story to Miss June Morrow. I am not connected."

Rankin stood up. "All right. But you're certainly beyond me. The man of stone. I wish you a pleasant journey. And if this case is ever solved, I hope you never hear about it."

Chan grinned broadly. "Your kind wishes greatly appreciated. Goodby, and all luck possible."

He watched the reporter as he dashed from the lobby into the street, then going above, he completed his packing. A glance at his watch told him he had plenty of time, so he went to say goodby to his relative in Chinatown. When he returned to the hotel to get his bags, Miss Morrow was waiting for him.

"What happy luck," he said. "Once again I am rewarded by a sight of your most interesting face."

"You certainly are," she replied. "I simply had to see you again. The district attorney has put this whole affair in my hands, and it's my big chance. You are still determined to go home?"

"More than usual." He led her to a sofa. "Last night I have joyous cable—"

"I know. I was there when Mr Kirk telephoned you. A boy, I think he said."

"Heaven's finest gift," nodded Chan.

Miss Morrow sighed. "If it had only been a girl," she said.

"Good luck," Chan told her, "dogs me in such matters. Of eleven opportunities, I am disappointed but three times."

"You're to be congratulated. However, girls are a necessary evil."

"You are unduly harsh. Necessary, of course. In your case, no evil whatever."

Barry Kirk came into the lobby and joined them. "Good morning, father," he smiled. "Well, we're all here to speed the parting guest."

Chan consulted his watch. Miss Morrow smiled. "You've quite a lot of time," she said. "At least give me the benefit of your advice before you leave."

"Happy to do so," agreed Chan. "It is worthless, but you are welcome."

"Captain Flannery is completely stumped, though of course he won't admit it. I told him all about Hilary Galt and Eve Durand, and he just opened his mouth and forgot to close it."

"Better men than the Captain might also pause in yawning doubt."

"Yes – I admit that." Miss Morrow's white forehead wrinkled in perplexity. "It's all so scattered – San Francisco and London and Peshawar – it almost looks as though whoever solved it must make a trip around the world."

Chan shook his head. "Many strings reach back, but solution will lie in San Francisco. Accept my advice, and take heart bravely."

The girl still puzzled. "We know that Hilary Galt was killed sixteen years ago. A long time, but Sir Frederic was the sort who would never abandon a trail. We also know that Sir Frederic was keenly interested in the disappearance of Eve Durand from Peshawar. That might have been a natural curiosity – but if it was, why should he rush to the newspaper office and demand that nothing be printed about it? No – it was more than curiosity. He was on the trail of something."

"And near the end of it," put in Kirk. "He told me that much."

Miss Morrow nodded. "Near the end – what did that mean? Had he found Eve Durand? Was he on the point of exposing her identity? And was there someone – Eve Durand or someone else – who was determined he should never do so? So determined, in fact, that he – or she – would not stop short of murder to silence him?"

"All expressed most clearly," approved Chan.

"Oh – but it isn't clear at all. Was Hilary Galt's murder connected somehow with the disappearance of that young girl from Peshawar? The velvet slippers – where are they now? Did the murderer of Sir Frederic take them? And if so – why?"

"Many questions arise," admitted Chan. "All in good time you get the answers."

"We'll never get them," sighed the girl, "without your help."

Chan smiled. "How sweet your flattery sounds." He considered. "I made no search of the office last night. But Captain Flannery did. What was found? Records? A case-book?"

"Nothing," said Kirk, "that had any bearing on the matter. Nothing that mentioned Hilary Galt or Eve Durand."

Chan frowned. "Yet without question of doubt, Sir Frederic kept records. Were those records the prize for which the killer made frantic search? Doubtless so. Did he – or she – then, find them? That would seem to be true, unless—"

"Unless what?" asked the girl quickly.

"Unless Sir Frederic had removed same to safe and distant place. On face of things, he expected marauder. He may have baited trap with pointless paper. You have hunted his personal effects, in bedroom?"

"Everything," Kirk assured him. "Nothing was found. In the desk downstairs were some newspaper clippings – accounts of the disappearance of other women who walked off into the night. Sir Frederic evidently made such cases his hobby."

"Other women?" Chan was thoughtful.

"Yes. But Flannery thought those clippings meant nothing, and I believe he was right."

"And the cutting about Eve Durand remained in Sir Frederic's purse?" continued Chan.

"By gad!" Kirk looked at the girl. "I never thought of that. The clipping was gone!"

Miss Morrow's dark eyes were filled with dismay. "Oh – how stupid," she cried. "It was gone, and the fact made no impression on me at all. I'm afraid I'm just a poor, weak woman."

"Calm your distress," said Chan soothingly. "It is a matter to note, that is all. It proves that the quest of Eve Durand held important place in murderer's mind. You must, then, *cherchez la femme*. You understand?"

"Hunt the woman," said Miss Morrow.

"You have it. And in such an event, a huntress will be far better than a hunter. Let us think of guests at party. Mr Kirk, you have said a portion of these people are there because Sir Frederic requested their presence. Which?"

"The Enderbys," replied Kirk promptly. "I didn't know them. But Sir Frederic wanted them to come."

"That has deep interest. The Enderbys. Mrs Enderby approached state of hysteria all evening. Fear of dark might mean fear of something else. Is it beyond belief that Eve Durand, with new name, marries again into bigamy?"

"But Eve Durand was a blonde," Miss Morrow reminded him.

"Ah, yes. And Eileen Enderby has hair like night. It is, I am told, a matter that is easily arranged. Color of hair may be altered, but color of eyes – that is different. And Mrs Enderby's eyes are blue, matching oddly raven locks.

"Never miss a trick, do you?" smiled Kirk.

"Mrs Enderby goes to garden, sees man on fire-escape. So she informs us. But does she? Or does she know her husband, smoking cigarette on stairs, has not been so idly occupied? Is man on fire-escape a myth of her invention, to protect her husband? Why are stains on her gown? From leaning with too much hot excitement against garden rail, damp with the fog of night? Or from climbing herself on to fire-escape – you apprehend my drift? What other guests did Sir Frederic request?"

Kirk thought. "He asked me to invite Gloria Garland," the young man announced.

Chan nodded. "I expected it. Gloria Garland – such is not a name likely to fall to human lot. Sounds like a manufacture. And Australia is so placed on map it might be appropriate end of journey from Peshawar. Blonde, blue-eyed, she breaks necklace on the stair. Yet you discover a pearl beneath the office desk."

Miss Morrow nodded. "Yes – Miss Garland certainly is a possibility."

"There remains," continued Chan, "Mrs Tupper-Brock. A somewhat dark lady – but who knows? Sir Frederic did not ask her presence?"

"No – I don't think he knew she existed," said Kirk.

"Yes? But it is wise in our work, Miss Morrow, that even the smallest improbabilities be studied. Men stumble over pebbles, never over mountains. Tell me, Mr Kirk – was Colonel John Beetham the idea of Sir Frederic, too?"

"Not at all. And now that I remember, Sir Frederic seemed a bit taken back when he heard Beetham was coming. But he said nothing."

"We have now traversed the ground. You have, Miss Morrow, three ladies to receive your most attentive study – Mrs Enderby, Miss Garland, Mrs Tupper-Brock. All of proper age, so near as a humble man can guess it in this day of beauty rooms with their appalling tricks. These only of the dinner party—"

"And one outside the dinner party," added the girl, to Chan's surprise.

"Ah – on that point I have only ignorance," he said blankly.

"You remember the elevator operator spoke of a girl employed by the Calcutta Importers, on the twentieth floor? A Miss Lila Barr. She was at work in her office there last night."

"Ah, yes," nodded Chan.

"Well, a newspaper man, Rankin of the *Globe*, came to see me a few minutes ago. He said that the other evening – night before last – he went to call on Sir Frederic, in Mr Kirk's office, rather late. Just as he approached the door, a girl came out. She was crying. Rankin saw her dab at her eyes and disappear into the room of the Calcutta Importers. A blonde girl, he said."

Chan's face was grave. "A fourth lady to require your kind attention. The matter broadens. So much to be done – and you in the midst of it all, like a pearl in a muddy pool." He stood up. "I am sorry. But the *Maui* must even now be straining at her moorings—"

"One other thing," put in the girl. "You made quite a point of that Cosmopolitan Club year-book lying beside Sir Frederic. You thought it important?"

Chan shrugged. "I fear I was in teasing mood. I believed it hardest puzzle of the lot. Therefore I am mean enough to press it on Captain Flannery's mind. What it meant, I cannot guess. Poor Captain Flannery will never do so."

He looked at his watch. The girl rose. "I won't keep you longer," she sighed. "I'm very busy, but somehow I can't let you go. I'm trailing along to the dock with you, if you don't mind. Perhaps I'll think of something else on the way."

"Who am I," smiled Chan, "to win such overwhelming honor? You behold me speechless with delight. Mr Kirk—"

"Oh, I'm going along," said Kirk. "Always like to see a boat pull out. The Lord meant me for a traveling salesman."

Chan got his bag, paid his bill, and the three of them entered Kirk's car, parked round the corner.

"Now that the moment arrives," said Chan, "I withdraw from this teeming mainland with some regret. Fates have been in smiling mood with me here."

"Why go?" suggested Kirk.

"Long experience," replied Chan, "whispers not to strain fates too far. Their smile might fade."

"Want to stop anywhere on the way?" Kirk asked. "You've got thirty minutes until sailing time."

"I am grateful, but all my farewells are said. Only this morning I have visited Chinatown—" He stopped. "So fortunate you still hang on," he added to the girl. "I was forgetting most important information for you. Still another path down which you must travel."

"Oh, dear," she sighed. "I'm dizzy now. What next?"

"You must at once inflict this information on Captain Flannery. He is to find a Chinese, a stranger here, stopping with relatives on Jackson Street. The name, Li Gung."

"Who is Li Gung?" asked Miss Morrow.

"Yesterday, when delicious lunch was ended, I hear of Li Gung from Sir Frederic." He repeated his conversation with the great man. "Li Gung had information much wanted by Sir Frederic. That alone I can say. Captain Flannery must extract this information from Li."

"He'll never get it," replied the girl pessimistically. "Now you, Sergeant—"

Chan drew a deep breath. "I am quite overcome," he remarked, "by the bright loveliness of this morning on which I say farewell to the mainland."

They rode on in silence, while the girl thought hard. If only she could find some way of reaching this stolid man by her side, some appeal that would not roll off like water from a duck's back. She hastily went over in her mind all she had ever read of the Chinese character.

Kirk drove his smart roadster on to the pier, a few feet from the *Maui's* gangplank. The big white ship was gay with the color of women's hats and frocks. Taxis were sweeping up, travelers were alighting, white-jacketed stewards stood in a bored line ready for another sailing. Goodbys and final admonitions filled the air.

A steward stepped forward and took Chan's bag. "Hello, Sergeant," he said. "Going home, eh? What room, please?"

Chan told him, then turned to the young people at his side. "At thought of your kindness," he remarked, "I am choking. Words escape me. I can only say – goodby."

"Give my regards to the youngest Chan," said Kirk. "Perhaps I'll see him some day."

"Reminding me," returned Chan, "that only this morning I scour my brain to name him. With your kind permission, I will denote him Barry Chan."

"I'm very much flattered," Kirk answered gravely. "Wish to heaven I had something to send him – er – a mug – or a what-you-may-call-it. You'll hear from me later."

"I only trust," Chan said, "he grows up worthy of his name. Miss Morrow – I am leaving on this dock my heartiest good wishes—"

She looked at him oddly. "Thank you," she remarked in a cool voice. "I wish you could have stayed, Mr Chan. But of course I realize your point of view. The case was too difficult. For once, Charlie Chan is running away. I'm afraid the famous Sergeant of the Honolulu police has lost face today."

A startled expression crossed that usually bland countenance. For a long moment Chan looked at her with serious eyes, then he bowed, very stiffly. "I wish you goodby," he said, and walked with offended dignity up the gangplank.

Kirk was staring at the girl in amazement. "Don't look at me like that," she cried ruefully. "It was cruel, but it was my last chance. I'd tried everything else. Well, it didn't work. Shall we go?"

"Oh – let's wait," pleaded Kirk. "They're sailing in a minute. I always get a thrill out of it. Look – up there on the top deck." He nodded toward a pretty girl in gray, with a cluster of orchids pinned to her shoulder. "A bride, if you ask me. And I suppose that vacant-faced idiot at her side is the lucky man."

Miss Morrow looked, without interest.

"A great place for a honeymoon, Hawaii," went on Kirk. "I've often thought – I hope I'm not boring you?"

"Not much," she said.

"I know. Brides leave you cold. I suppose divorce is more in your line. You and Blackstone. Well, you shan't blast my romantic young nature." He took out a handkerchief and waved it toward the girl on the top deck. "So long, my dear," he called. "All the luck in the world."

"I don't see Mr Chan," said the young woman from the district attorney's office.

Mr Chan was sitting thoughtfully on the edge of the berth in his stateroom, far below. The great happiness of his long anticipated departure for home had received a rude jolt. Running away – was that it? Afraid of a difficult case? Did Miss Morrow really think that? If she did, then he had lost face indeed.

His gloomy reflections were interrupted by a voice in the next stateroom – a voice he had heard before. His heart stood still as he listened.

"I fancy that's all, Li," said the familiar voice. "You have your passport, your money. You are simply to wait for me in Honolulu. Better lie low there."

"I will do so," replied a high-pitched, singsong voice.

"And if anyone asks any questions, you know nothing. Understand?"

"Yes-s-s. I am silent. I understand."

"Very good. You're a wonderful servant, Li Gung. I don't like to flatter you, you grinning beggar, but I couldn't do without you. Goodby – and a pleasant journey."

Chan was on his feet now, peering out into the dim passageway along which opened the rooms on the lowest deck. In that faint light he saw a familiar figure emerge from the room next door, and disappear in the distance.

The detective stood for a moment, undecided. Of all the guests at Barry Kirk's party one had interested him beyond all others – almost to the exclusion of the others. The tall, grim, silent man who had made his camps throughout the wastelands of the world, who had left a trail of the dead but who had always moved on, relentlessly, toward his goal. Colonel John Beetham, whom he had just seen emerging from the stateroom next to his with a last word of farewell to Li Gung.

Chan looked at his watch. It was never his habit to hurry, but he must hurry now. He sighed a great sigh that rattled the glasses in their rings, and snatched up his bag. On the saloon deck he met the purser.

"Homeward bound, Charlie?" inquired that gentleman breezily.

"So I thought," replied Chan, "but it seems I was mistaken. At the last moment, I am rudely wrenched ashore. Yet I have ticket good only on this boat."

"Oh, they'll fix that up for you at the office. They all know you, Charlie."

"Thanks for the suggestion. My trunk is already loaded. Will you kindly deliver same to my oldest son, who will call for it when you have docked at Honolulu?"

"Sure." The "visitors ashore" call was sounding for the last time. "Don't you linger too long on this wicked mainland, Charlie," the purser admonished.

"One week only," called Chan, over his shoulder. "Until the next boat. I swear it."

On the dock, Miss Morrow seized Kirk's arm. "Look. Coming down the gangplank. Colonel Beetham. What's he doing here?"

"Beetham – sure enough," said Kirk. "Shall I offer him a lift? No – he's got a taxi. Let him go. He's a cold proposition – I like him not." He watched the Colonel enter a cab and ride off.

When he turned back to the *Maui*, two husky sailors were about to draw up the plank. Suddenly between them appeared a chubby little figure, one hand clutching a suitcase. Miss Morrow gave a cry of delight.

"It's Chan," Kirk said. "He's coming ashore."

And ashore Charlie came, while they lifted the plank at his heels. He stood before the two young people, ill at ease.

"Moment of gentle embarrassment for me," he said. "The traveler who said goodby is back before he goes."

"Mr Chan," the girl cried, "you dear! You're going to help us, after all."

Chan nodded. "To the extent of my very slight ability, I am with you to finish, bitter or sweet."

On the top deck of the *Maui* the band began to play – *Aloha,* that most touching of farewells. Long streamers of bright-colored paper filled the air. The last goodbys, the final admonitions – a loud voice calling "Don't forget to write." Charlie Chan watched, a mist before his eyes. Slowly the boat drew away from the pier. The crowd ran along beside it, waving frantically. Charlie's frame shook with another ponderous sigh.

"Poor little Barry Chan," he said. "He would have been happy to see me. Captain Flannery will not be so happy. Let us ride away into the face of our problems."

VI

THE GUEST DETECTIVE

Barry Kirk tossed Chan's suitcase into the luggage compartment of his roadster, and the trio crowded again on to its single seat. The car swung about in the pier shed and emerged into the bright sunlight of the Embarcadero.

"You are partially consumed with wonder at my return?" suggested Chan.

The girl shrugged. "You're back. That's enough for me."

"All the same, I will confess my shame. It seems I have circulated so long with mainland Americans I have now, by contagion, acquired one of their worst faults. I too suffer curiosity. Event comes off on boat which reveals, like heavenly flash, my hidden weakness."

"Something happened on the boat?" Miss Morrow inquired.

"You may believe it did. On my supposed farewell ride through city, I inform you of Li Gung. I tell you he must be questioned. He cannot be questioned now."

"No? Why not?"

"Because he is on *Maui*, churning away. It is not unprobable that shortly he will experience a feeling of acute disfavor in that seat of all wisdom, the stomach."

"Li Gung on the *Maui*?" repeated the girl. Her eyes were wide. "What can that mean?"

"A question," admitted Chan, "which causes the mind to itch. Not only is Li Gung on *Maui*, but he was warmly encouraged away from here by a friend of ours." He repeated the brief conversation he had overheard in the adjoining cabin.

Barry Kirk was the first to speak. "Colonel Beetham, eh?" he said. "Well, I'm not surprised."

"Nonsense," cried Miss Morrow warmly. "Surely he isn't involved? A fine man like that—"

"A fine man," Chan conceded, "and a hard one. Look in his eyes and behold; they are cold and gleaming, like the tiger's. Nothing stands in the way when such eyes are fixed on the goal of large success – stands there long – alive."

The girl did not seem to be convinced. "I won't believe it. But shouldn't we have taken Li Gung off the boat?"

Chan shrugged. "Too late. The opportunity wore rapid wings."

"Then we'll have him questioned in Honolulu," Miss Morrow said.

Chan shook his head. "Pardon me if I say, not that. Chinese character too well known to me. Questioning would yield no result – save one. It would serve to advise Colonel Beetham that we look on him with icy eye. I shudder at the thought – this Colonel clever man. Difficult enough to shadow if he does not suspect. Impossible if he leaps on guard."

"Then what do you suggest?" asked the girl.

"Let Li Gung, unknowing, be watched. If he seeks to proceed beyond Honolulu, rough hands will restrain him. Otherwise we permit him to lie, like winter overcoat in closet during heated term." Chan turned to Barry Kirk. "You are taking me back to hotel?"

"I am not," smiled Kirk. "No more hotel for you. If you're going to look into this little puzzle, the place for you is the Kirk Building, where the matter originated. Don't you say so, Miss Morrow?"

"That's awfully kind of you," said the girl.

"Not at all. It's painfully lonesome up where the fog begins without at least one guest. I'm all out of visitors at the moment – er – ah – I mean Mr Chan will be doing me a real favor." He turned to Charlie. "You shall have Sir Frederic's room," he added.

Chan shrugged. "I can never repay such goodness. Why attempt it?"

"Let's go to my office, first of all," Miss Morrow said. "I want the district attorney to meet Mr Chan. We must all be friends – at the start, anyhow."

"Anywhere you say," Kirk agreed, and headed the car up Market Street, to Kearny. He remained in the roadster, while the girl and Charlie went up to the district attorney's offices. When they entered that gentleman's private room, they found Captain Flannery already on the scene.

"Mr Trant – I've good news for you," the girl began. "Oh – good morning, Captain."

Flannery's Irish eyes were not precisely smiling as they rested on Charlie Chan. "What's this, Sergeant?" he growled. "I thought you were off for Honolulu at twelve?"

Chan grinned. "You will be delighted to learn that my plans are changed. Miss Morrow has persuaded me to remain here and add my minute brain power to your famous capacity in same line."

"Is that so?" mumbled Flannery.

"Yes – isn't it splendid?" cried the girl. "Mr Chan is going to help us." She turned to her chief. "You must give him a temporary appointment as a sort of guest detective connected with this office."

Trant smiled. "Wouldn't that be a bit irregular?" he asked.

"Impossible," said Flannery firmly.

"Not at all," persisted the girl. "It's a very difficult case, and we shall need all the help we can get. Sergeant Chan will not interfere with you, Captain—"

"I'll say he won't," Flannery replied warmly.

"He can act in a sort of advisory capacity. You're a big enough man to take advice, I know."

"When it's any good," the Captain added. The girl looked appealingly at Trant.

"You are on leave of absence from the Honolulu force, Sergeant?" inquired the district attorney.

"One which stretches out like an elastic," nodded Chan.

"Very well. Since Miss Morrow wishes it, I see no reason why you shouldn't lend her your no doubt very useful aid. Remembering, of course, that neither one of you is to interfere with Captain Flannery in any way."

"Better say that again," Flannery told him. He turned to Chan. "That means you're not to butt in and spoil things."

Chan shrugged. "It was the wise K'ung-fu-tsze who said, 'he who is out of office should not meddle with the government.' The labor is all yours. I will merely haunt the background, thinking tensely."

"That suits me," Flannery agreed. "I'll make all the inquiries." He turned to the district attorney. "I'm going to get after that Garland woman right away. The pearl she dropped under Sir Frederic's desk – I want to know all about it."

"Please don't think I'm interfering," Miss Morrow said sweetly. "But as regards the women involved in this case, I feel that perhaps I can get more out of them than you can. Being a woman myself, you know. Will you let me have Miss Garland, please?"

"I can't see it," said Flannery stubbornly.

"I can," remarked Trant, decisively. "Miss Morrow is a clever girl, Captain. Leave the women to her. You take the men."

"What men?" protested Flannery. "It's all women, in this affair."

"Thank you so much," smiled Miss Morrow, assuming his unproffered consent. "I will look up Miss Garland, then.

There's another woman who must be questioned at once – a Miss Lila Barr. I shall have a talk with her at the first possible moment. Of course, I'll keep you advised of all I do."

Flannery threw up his hands. "All right – tell me about it – after it's over. I'm nobody."

"Quite incorrect," said Chan soothingly. "You are everybody. When the moment of triumph comes, who will snatch all credit? And rightly so. Captain Flannery, in charge of the case. Others will fade like fog in local sun."

The girl stood up. "We must go along. I'll be in to see you later, Captain. Come, Sergeant Chan—"

Chan rose. He seemed a bit uncomfortable. "The Captain must pardon me. I fear I afflict him like sore thumb. Natural, too. I would feel the same."

"That's all right," returned Flannery. "You're going to stick in the background, thinking tensely. You've promised. Think all you like – I can't stop that." His face brightened. "Think about that Cosmopolitan Club book. I'll turn the heavy thinking on that over to you. Me, I'll be busy elsewhere. One thing I insist on – you're not to question any of these people under suspicion."

Chan bowed. "I am disciple of famous philosopher, Captain," he remarked. "Old man in China who said, 'The fool questions others, the wise man questions himself.' We shall meet again. Goodby." He followed the girl out.

Flannery, his face brick red, turned to the district attorney. "Fine business," he cried. "The toughest case I ever had, and what sort of help do I draw? A doll-faced girl and a Chinaman! Bah – I – I—" He trailed off into profanity.

Trant was smiling. "Who knows?" he replied. "You may get more help from them than you expect."

"If I get any at all, I'll be surprised." Flannery stood up."A woman and a Chinaman. Hell, I'll be the joke of the force."

The two whom Captain Flannery was disparaging found Barry Kirk waiting impatiently in his car. "An inner craving," he announced, "tells me it's lunch-time. You're both lunching with me at the bungalow. Step lively, please."

Atop the Kirk Building, Paradise was ordered to lay two more places, and Kirk showed Chan to his room. He left the detective there to unpack, and returned to Miss Morrow.

"You seem the perpetual host," she smiled, as he joined her.

"Oh, I'm going to get a lot of fun out of Charlie," he answered. "He's a good scout, and I like him. But, by way of confession, I had other reasons for inviting him here. You and he are going to work together, and that means – what?"

"It means, I hope, that I'm going to learn a lot."

"From associating with Chan?"

"Precisely."

"And if you associate with my guest, you'll be bound to stumble over me occasionally. I'm a wise lad. I saw it coming."

"I don't understand. Why should you want me to stumble over you?"

"Because every time you do I'll leap up and look at you, and that will be another red-letter day in my life."

She shook her head. "I'm afraid you're terribly frivolous. If I see much of you, you'll drag me down and down until I lose my job."

"Look on the other side, lady," he pleaded. "You might drag me up and up. It could be done, you know."

"I doubt it," she told him.

Chan came into the room, and Paradise, unperturbed by the impromptu guests, served a noble luncheon. Toward its close, Kirk spoke seriously.

"I've been thinking about this Barr girl downstairs," he said. "I don't know that I've told you the circumstances under which Sir Frederic came to stay with me. His son happens to be an acquaintance of mine – not a friend, I know him only slightly –

and he wrote me his father was to be in San Francisco. I called on Sir Frederic at his hotel. From the start he appeared keenly interested in the Kirk Building. I couldn't quite figure it out. He asked me a lot of questions, and when he learned that I lived on the roof, I must say he practically invited himself to stop with me. Not that I wasn't delighted to have him, you understand – but somehow there was an undercurrent in the talk – well, I just sensed his eagerness. It was odd, wasn't it?"

"Very," said the girl.

"Well, after he'd been here a couple of days he began to ask questions about the Calcutta Importers, and finally these all seemed to center on Miss Lila Barr. I knew nothing about the firm or about Miss Barr – I'd never even heard of her. Later he found that my secretary, Kinsey, knew the girl, and the questions were all turned in that direction – though I fancied they grew more discreet. One day in the office I heard Kinsey ask Sir Frederic if he'd like to meet Miss Barr, and I also heard Sir Frederic's answer."

"What did he say?" Miss Morrow inquired.

"He said simply, 'Later, perhaps,' with what I thought an assumed carelessness. I don't know whether all this is important or not?"

"In view of the fact that Miss Lila Barr once left Sir Frederic's presence in tears, I should say it is very important," Miss Morrow returned. "Don't you agree, Mr Chan?"

Chan nodded. "Miss Barr has fiercely interesting sound," he agreed. "I long with deep fervor to hear you question her."

The girl rose from the table. "I'll call the office of the Calcutta Importers and ask her to step up here," she announced, and went to the telephone.

Five minutes later Miss Lila Barr entered the living-room under the impeccable chaperonage of Paradise. She stood for a second regarding the three people who awaited her. They noted that she was an extremely pretty girl slightly under middle height, an authentic blonde, with a sort of startled innocence in her blue eyes.

"Thank you for coming." The deputy district attorney rose and smiled at the girl in kindly fashion. "I am Miss Morrow, and this is Mr Charles Chan. And Mr Barry Kirk."

"How do you do," said the girl, in a low voice.

"I wanted to talk with you – I'm from the district attorney's office," Miss Morrow added.

The girl stared at her, an even more startled expression in her eyes. "Ye – es," she said uncertainly.

"Sit down, please." Kirk drew up a chair.

"You know, of course, of the murder that took place on your floor of the building last night?" Miss Morrow went on.

"Of course," replied the girl, her voice barely audible.

"You were working last night in your office?"

"Yes – it's the first of the month, you know. I always have extra work at this time."

"At what hour did you leave the building?"

"I think it was about ten fifteen. I'm not sure. But I went away without knowing anything of – of this – terrible affair."

"Yes. Did you see any strangers about the building last night?"

"No one. No one at all." Her voice was suddenly louder.

"Tell me" – Miss Morrow looked at her keenly – "had you ever met Sir Frederic Bruce?"

"No – I had never met him."

"You had never met him. Please think what you are saying. You didn't meet him night before last – when you visited him in his office?"

The girl started. "Oh – I saw him then, of course. I thought you meant – had I been introduced to him."

"Then you did go into his office night before last?"

"I went into Mr Kirk's office. There was a big man, with a mustache, sitting in the second room. I presume it was Sir Frederic Bruce."

"You presume?"

"Well – of course I know now it was. I saw his picture in this morning's paper."

"He was alone in the office when you went in?"

"Yes."

"Was he the person you went there to see?"

"No, he was not."

"When you left the office, you burst into tears." Again the girl started, and her face flushed. "Was it seeing Sir Frederic made you do that?"

"Oh, no," cried Miss Barr, with more spirit.

"Then what was it made you cry?"

"It was – a purely personal matter. Surely I needn't go into it?"

"I'm afraid you must," Miss Morrow told her. "This is a serious affair, you know."

The girl hesitated. "Well – I—"

"Tell me all that happened night before last."

"Well – it wasn't seeing Sir Frederic made me cry," the girl began. "It was – not seeing someone else."

"Not seeing someone else? Please explain that."

"Very well." The girl moved impulsively toward Miss Morrow. "I can tell you. I'm sure you will understand. Mr Kinsey, Mr Kirk's secretary, and I – we are – well – sort of engaged. Every night Mr Kinsey waits for me, and we have dinner. Then he takes me home. Day before yesterday we had a little quarrel – just over some silly thing – you know how it is—"

"I can imagine," said Miss Morrow solemnly.

"It was about nothing, really. I waited a long time that evening, and he didn't come for me. So I thought maybe I had been in the wrong. I swallowed my pride and went to look for him. I opened the door of Mr Kirk's office and went in. Of course I thought Mr Kinsey would be there. Sir Frederic was alone in the office – Mr Kinsey had gone. I muttered some apology – Sir Frederic didn't say anything, he just looked at me. I hurried out again and – perhaps you know the feeling, Miss Morrow—"

"You burst into tears, because Mr Kinsey hadn't waited?"

"I'm afraid I did. It was silly of me, wasn't it?"

"Well, that doesn't matter." Miss Morrow was silent for a moment. "The company you work for – it imports from India, I believe?"

"Yes – silk and cotton, mostly."

"Have you ever been in India, Miss Barr?"

The girl hesitated. "When I was quite young – I lived there for some years – with my mother and father."

"Where in India?"

"Calcutta, mostly."

"Other places, too?" The girl nodded. "In Peshawar, perhaps?"

"No," answered Miss Barr. "I was never in Peshawar."

Chan coughed rather loudly, and, catching his eye, Miss Morrow dropped the matter of India. "You had never heard of Sir Frederic before he came here?" she asked.

"Oh, no, indeed."

"And you saw him just that once, when he said nothing at all?"

"Only that once."

Miss Morrow rose. "Thank you very much. That is all for the present. I trust Mr Kinsey has apologized?"

The girl smiled. "Oh, yes – that's all right now. Thank you for asking." She went out quickly.

Barry Kirk had disappeared from the room, and now he returned. "Kinsey's on his way up," he announced. "Grab him quick before they can compare notes – that was my idea. Getting to be some little detective myself."

"Excellent," nodded Miss Morrow approvingly. A tall, dark young man, very well dressed, came in.

"You wanted to see me, Mr Kirk?" he inquired.

"Yes. Sorry to butt into your private affairs, Kinsey, but I hear you are sort of engaged to a Miss Lila Barr, who works in one of the offices. Did you know about it?"

Kinsey smiled. "Of course, Mr Kirk. I have been meaning to mention the matter to you, but the opportunity hasn't offered."

"Day before yesterday you had a bit of a quarrel with her?"

"Oh, it was nothing, sir." Kinsey's dark face clouded. "It's all fixed up now."

"That's good. But on that evening, contrary to your custom, you didn't wait to take her home? You walked out on her?"

"I – I'm afraid I did. I was somewhat annoyed—"

"And you wanted to teach her a lesson. What I call the proper spirit. That's all – and please pardon these personal questions."

"Quite all right, sir." Kinsey turned to go, but hesitated. "Mr Kirk—"

"Yes, Kinsey?"

"Nothing, sir," said Kinsey, and disappeared.

Kirk turned to Miss Morrow. "There you are. The story of Miss Lila Barr, duly authenticated."

"Such a reasonable story, too," sighed the girl. "But it gets us nowhere. I must say I'm disappointed. Mr Chan – you thought I went too far – on India?"

Chan shrugged. "In this game, better if the opponent does not know what we are thinking. Assume great innocence is always my aim. Sometimes what I assume is exactly what I've got. Others – I am flying at a low altitude."

"I'm afraid I should have flown at a lower altitude than I did," the girl reflected, frowning. "Her story was perfectly plausible, and yet – I don't know—"

"Well, one thing's certain," remarked Kirk. "She's not Eve Durand."

"How do you know that?" asked Miss Morrow.

"Why, – her age. She's a mere kid."

Miss Morrow laughed. "Lucky a woman is in on this," she said. "You men are so painfully blind where a blonde is concerned."

"What do you mean?"

"I mean there are certain artifices which fool a man, but never fool a woman. Miss Barr is thirty – at the very least."

Kirk whistled. "I must be more careful," he said. "I thought her sweet and twenty."

He turned to find Paradise at his elbow. The butler had entered noiselessly, and was holding out a silver tray in the manner of one offering rich treasure.

"What shall I do with these, sir?" he inquired.

"Do with what?" Kirk asked.

"Letters addressed to Sir Frederic Bruce, sir. They have just been delivered by the local office of Thomas Cook and Sons."

Miss Morrow came eagerly forward. "I'll take charge of them," she said. Paradise bowed, and went out. The girl's eyes sparkled. "We never thought of this, Sergeant. Sir Frederic's mail – it may prove a gold mine." She held up a letter. "Here – the first thing – one from London. The Metropolitan Police, Scotland Yard—"

Quickly she ripped open the envelope and withdrawing a single sheet of paper, spread it out. She gave a little cry of dismay.

Kirk and Charlie Chan came nearer. They stared at the sheet of paper that had arrived in the envelope from Scotland Yard. It was just that – a sheet of paper – completely blank.

VII

MUDDY WATER

Miss Morrow stood, her brows contracted in bewilderment, looking down at the unexpected enclosure she had found in the envelope with the London postmark.

"Oh, dear," she sighed. "There's just one trouble with this detective business. It's so full of mystery."

Chan smiled. "Humbly begging pardon to mention it, I would suggest you iron out countenance. Wrinkles might grow there, which would be a heart-breaking pity. Occasional amazing occurrence keeps life spicy. Accept that opinion from one who knows it."

"But what in the world does this mean?" she asked.

"One thing I am certain it does not mean," Chan replied. "Scotland Yard in sudden playful mood does not post empty paper over six thousand miles of land and water. No, some queer business has blossomed up near at hand, which it is our duty to unveil." The girl began to smooth the blank sheet. Chan stretched out a warning hand. Despite his girth, the hand was thin and narrow, with long, tapering fingers. "I beg of you, do not touch further," he cried. "A great mistake. For although we cannot see, there is something on that paper."

"What?" she inquired.

"Fingerprints," he answered. Gingerly by one corner he removed the paper from her hand. "The fingerprints, dainty and firm, you have made. The fingerprints, also, perhaps not so dainty, of the person who folded it and put it in envelope."

"Oh, of course," said Miss Morrow.

"I am no vast admirer of science in this work," Chan went on. "But fingerprints tell pretty much truth. Happy to say I have made half-hearted study of the art. In Honolulu, where I am faced by little competition, I rejoice in mouth-filling title of fingerprint expert. Mr Kirk, have you a drawer with heavy lock, to which you alone hold key?"

"Surely," replied Kirk. He unlocked a compartment in a handsome Spanish desk, and Chan deposited the paper inside. Kirk turned the key, and removing it from the ring, handed it to Charlie.

"Later," remarked Chan, "with lamp black and camel's hair brush, I perform like the expert I have been pronounced. Maybe we discover who has been opening Sir Frederic's mail." He picked up the empty envelope. "Behold – steam has been applied. The marks unquestionable."

"Steam," cried Barry Kirk. "But who in the world – oh, I say. Sir Frederic's mail came through the local office of Thomas Cook and Sons."

"Precisely," grinned Chan.

"And Mr Carrick Enderby is employed there."

Chan shrugged. "You are bright young man. It is not beyond possibility that the mark of Mr Enderby's large thumb is on that paper. However, speculation is idle thing. Facts must be upearthed. Miss Morrow – may I rudely suggest – the remainder of Sir Frederic's mail?"

"Yes, of course," said the girl. "I feel rather guilty about this, but when duty calls, you know— "

She sat down and went through the other letters. Obviously her search was without any interesting result.

"Well," she said finally, "that's that. I leave the matter of the blank sheet of paper to you, Sergeant. For myself, I am going to turn my attention to Miss Gloria Garland. What was that pearl from her necklace doing under the desk beside which Sir Frederic was killed?"

"A wise question," nodded Chan. "Miss Garland should now be invited to converse. May she prove more pointed talker than Miss Lila Barr."

"Let me call her up and ask her over here," suggested Kirk. "I'll tell her I want to have a talk with her in my office about last night's affair. She may arrive a bit less prepared with an explanation than if she knows it's the police who want to see her."

"Splendid," approved Miss Morrow. "But I'm afraid we're cutting in most frightfully on your business, Mr Kirk. You must say so if we are."

"What business?" he inquired airily. "Like Sergeant Chan, I am now attached to your office. And I'm likely to grow more attached all the time. If you'll pardon me for a moment—"

He went to the telephone and reached Miss Garland at her apartment. The actress agreed to come at once.

As Kirk came away from the telephone, the door-bell rang and Paradise admitted a visitor. Captain Flannery strode into the room.

"Hello," he said. "You're all here, ain't you? I'd like to look round a bit – if I'm not butting in."

"Surely no one could be more warmly welcome," Chan told him.

"Thanks, Sergeant. You solved this problem yet?"

"Not up to date of present speaking," grinned Chan.

"Well, you're a little slow, ain't you?" Captain Flannery was worried, and not in the best of humor. "I thought from what I've read about you, you'd have the guilty man locked up in a closet for me, by this time."

Chan's eyes narrowed. "Challenge is accepted," he answered with spirit. "I have already obliged mainland policemen by filling a few closets with guilty men they could not catch. From my reading in newspapers, there still remains vast amount of work to do in same line."

"Is that so?" Flannery responded. He turned to Miss Morrow. "Did you talk with the Barr woman?"

"I did," said the girl. She repeated Lila Barr's story. Flannery heard her out in silence.

"Well," he remarked when she had finished, "you didn't get much, did you?"

"I'll have to admit I didn't," she replied.

"Maybe not as much as I could have got – and me not a woman, either. I'm going down now and have a talk with her myself. She don't look good to me. Cried because her fellow went and left her? Perhaps. But if you ask me, it takes more than that to make a woman cry nowadays."

"You may be right," Miss Morrow agreed.

"I know I'm right. And let me tell you something else – I'm going to be on hand when you talk with Gloria Garland. Make up your mind to that right now."

"I shall be glad to have you. Miss Garland is on her way here to meet us in the office downstairs."

"Fine. I'll go and take a look at this weepy dame. If the Garland woman comes before I'm back, you let me know. I've been in this game thirty years, young woman, and no district attorney's office can freeze me out. When I conduct an investigation, I conduct it."

He strode from the room. Chan looked after him without enthusiasm. "How loud is the thunder, how little it rains," he murmured beneath his breath.

"We'd better go to the office," suggested Kirk. "Miss Garland is likely to arrive at any moment."

They went below. The sun was blazing brightly in the middle room; the events of the foggy night now passed seemed like a bad dream. Kirk sat down at his desk, opened a drawer, and handed Chan a couple of press clippings.

"Want to look at those?" he inquired. "As I told you this morning, it appears that Sir Frederic was interested, not only in Eve Durand, but in other missing women as well."

Chan read the clippings thoughtfully, and laid them on the desk. He sighed ponderously. "A far-reaching case," he remarked, and was silent for a long time.

"A puzzler, even to you," Kirk said at length.

Chan came to himself with a start. "Pardon, please? What did you say?"

"I said that even the famous Sergeant Chan is up against it this time."

"Oh, yes. Yes, indeed. But I was not thinking of Sir Frederic. A smaller, less important person occupied my mind. Without fail I must go to little Barry Chan on next Wednesday's boat."

"I hope you can," smiled Miss Morrow. "Not many men are as devoted to their families nowadays as you are."

"Ah – you do not understand," said Chan. "You mainland people – I observe what home is to you. An unprivate apartment, a pigeonhole to dive into when the dance or the automobile ride is ended. We Chinese are different. Love, marriage, home, still we cling to unfashionable things like that. Home is a sanctuary into which we retire, the father is high priest, the altar fires burn bright."

"Sounds rather pleasant," remarked Barry Kirk. "Especially that about the father. By the way, I must send my namesake a cablegram and wish him luck."

Miss Gloria Garland appeared in the outer office, and Kinsey escorted her into the middle room. She was not quite so effective in the revealing light of day as she had been at a candle-lighted dinner table. There were lines about her eyes, and age was peering from beneath the heavy make-up.

"Well, here I am, Mr Kirk," she said. "Oh – Miss Morrow – and Mr Chan. I'm a wreck, I know. That thing last night upset me terribly – such a charming man, Sir Frederic. Has – has anything been unearthed – any clue?"

"Nothing much," replied Kirk, "as yet. Please sit down."

"Just a moment," said Miss Morrow. "I must get Captain Flannery."

"I will go, please," Chan told her, and hurried out.

He pushed open the door of the office occupied by the Calcutta Importers. Captain Flannery was standing, red-faced and angry, and before him sat Lila Barr, again in tears. The Captain swung about. "Yes?" he snapped.

"You are wanted, Captain," Chan said. "Miss Garland is here."

"All right." He turned to the weeping girl. "I'll see you again, young woman." She did not reply. He followed Chan to the hall.

"You too have some success as a tear-starter," suggested Chan.

"Yeah – she's the easiest crier I've met this year. I wasn't any too gentle with her. It don't pay."

"Your methods, of course, had amazing success?"

"Oh – she stuck to her story. But you take it from me, she knows more than she's telling. Too many tears for an innocent bystander. I'll bet you a hundred dollars right now that she's Eve Durand."

Chan shrugged. "My race," he said, "possesses great fondness for gambling. Not to go astray into ruin, I am compelled to overlook even easy methods of gain in that line."

Captain Flannery was driven back to his favorite phrase. "Is that so?" he replied, and they entered Kirk's office.

When they were all in the middle room, Barry Kirk shut the door on the interested Mr Kinsey. Captain Flannery faced Gloria Garland.

"I want to see you. You know who I am. I was upstairs last night. So your name's Gloria Garland, is it?"

She looked up at him a bit apprehensively. "Yes, of course."

"Are you telling your real name, lady?"

"Well, it's the name I have used for many years. I—"

"Oh? So it isn't the real one?"

"Not exactly. It's a name I took—"

"I see. You took a name that didn't belong to you." The Captain's tone implied a state's prison offense. "You had reasons, I suppose?"

"I certainly had." The woman looked at him with growing anger. "My name was Ida Pingle, and I didn't think that would go well in the theater. So I called myself Gloria Garland."

"All right. You admit you travel under an assumed name?"

"I don't care for the way you put it. A great many people on the stage have taken more attractive names than their own. I have done nothing to justify your rudeness—"

"I can quite understand your feeling," said Miss Morrow, with a disapproving glance at the Captain. "From this point I will take up the inquiry."

"I wish you would," remarked Miss Garland warmly.

"Had you ever met Sir Frederic Bruce before you came to Mr Kirk's dinner party last night?" the girl inquired.

"No, I had not."

"He was, then, a complete stranger to you?"

"He certainly was. Why should you ask me that?"

"You had no private interview with him last night?"

"No. None."

Captain Flannery stepped forward, his mouth open, about to speak. Miss Morrow raised her hand. "Just a moment, Captain.

Miss Garland, I warn you this is a serious business. You should tell the truth."

"Well—" Her manner became uncertain. "What makes you think I'm—"

"Lying? We know it," exploded Flannery.

"You broke the string of your necklace last night on your way to the bungalow," Miss Morrow continued. "Where did that accident happen?"

"On the stairs – the stairs leading up from the twentieth floor to the roof."

"Did you recover all the pearls?"

"Yes – I think so. I wasn't quite sure of the number. Of course, I needn't tell you they're only imitation. I couldn't afford the real thing."

Miss Morrow opened her hand-bag, and laid a solitary pearl on the desk. "Do you recognize that, Miss Garland?"

"Why – why, yes. It belongs to me, of course. Thank you so much. Where – er – where did you find it?"

"We found it," said Miss Morrow slowly, "under the desk in this room." The woman flushed, and made no reply. There was a moment's strained silence. "Miss Garland," the girl went on, "I think you had better change your tactics. The truth, if you please."

The actress shrugged. "I fancy you're right. I was only trying to keep out of this. It's not the sort of publicity I want. And as a matter of fact, I'm not in it very deep."

"But you really broke the string in this office, where you had come for a talk with Sir Frederic?"

"Yes, that's true. I caught the necklace on a corner of the desk, when I got up to go."

"Please don't start with the moment when you got up to go. Take it from the beginning, if you will."

"Very good. When I said I had never seen Sir Frederic before last night, I was telling the truth. I had left the elevator and was crossing the hallway to the stairs, when the door of these offices opened and a man stood on the threshold. He said: 'You are Miss Garland, I believe?' I told him that was my name, and he said he was Sir Frederic Bruce, Mr Kirk's guest, and that he wanted to have a talk with me, alone, before we met upstairs."

"Yes – go on."

"Well, it seemed odd, but he was such a distinguished-looking man I felt it must be all right, so I followed him in here. We sat down, and he started in to tell me who he was – Scotland Yard, and all that. I'm English, of course, and I have the greatest respect for anyone from the Yard. He talked around for a minute, and then he went to the point."

"Ah, yes," smiled Miss Morrow. "That's what we are waiting for. What was the point?"

"He – he wanted to ask me something."

"Yes? What?"

"He wanted to ask me if I could identify a woman who disappeared a great many years ago. A woman who just stepped off into the night, and was never heard of again."

A tense silence followed these words. Quietly Chan moved a little closer. Barry Kirk's eyes were fixed with interest on Gloria Garland's face. Even Captain Flannery stood eagerly at attention.

"Yes," said Miss Morrow calmly. "And why did Sir Frederic think you could identify this woman?"

"Because I was her best friend. I was the last person who saw her on the night she disappeared."

Miss Morrow nodded. "Then you were present at a picnic party in the hills near Peshawar on a certain night fifteen years ago?"

The woman's eyes opened wide. "Peshawar? That's in India, isn't it? I have never been in India in my life."

Another moment of startled silence. Then Flannery roared at her. "Look here – you promised to tell the truth—"

"I am telling the truth," she protested.

"You are not. That woman he asked you about was Eve Durand, who disappeared from a party one night outside Peshawar—"

Chan cut in on him. "Humbly asking pardon, Captain," he said, "you shouldn't be so agile in jumping upon the lady's story." He picked up a couple of clippings from the desk. "Will you be so kind," he added to Miss Garland, "as to mention name of place from which your friend disappeared?"

"Certainly. She disappeared from Nice."

"Nice? Where the hell's that?" Flannery asked.

"Nice is a resort city on the French Riviera," replied Miss Garland, sweetly. "I am afraid your duties keep you too much at home, Captain."

"Nice," repeated Chan slowly. "Then the name of your friend was perhaps Marie Lantelme?"

"That was her name," the actress replied.

Chan selected a clipping, and handed it to Miss Morrow. "Will you condescend to read words out loud?" he inquired. "Most interesting, to be sure."

Again, as in the dining-room of the St. Francis the day before, Miss Morrow read one of Sir Frederic's treasured clippings.

"What became of Marie Lantelme? It is now eleven years since that moonlit June night when a company under English management played *The Dollar Princess* on the stage of the Theatre de la Jetée-Promenade, in the city of Nice. It was a memorable evening for all concerned. The house was sold out, packed with soldiers on leave, and the manager was frantic. At the last moment word had come that his leading lady was seriously ill and with many misgivings he sent for the understudy, a pretty, inconspicuous little chorus girl named Marie Lantelme. It was her big chance at last. She stepped out on the blazing stage and became a woman transformed. The performance she gave will never be forgotten by anyone who was in that audience – an audience that went wild, that was on its feet cheering for her when the curtain fell.

"After the performance the manager rushed in high glee to Marie Lantelme's dressing-room. She was a discovery, and she was his. He would star her in London, in New York. She listened to him in silence. Then she put on her simple little frock and stepped from the stage door out upon the jetty. Fame and riches were waiting for her, if she chose to take them. Whether she chose or not will never be known. All that is known is that when she left the theater she walked off into nothingness. Eleven years have passed, and from that day to this no one has ever heard from Marie Lantelme."

Miss Morrow stopped reading, her countenance again in great need of ironing out. Captain Flannery stood with open mouth. Only Chan seemed to have retained his cheerful composure.

"Marie Lantelme was your friend?" he said to Miss Garland.

"She was," replied the actress, "and somehow Sir Frederic knew it. I was appearing in that same company. I must say the clipping exaggerates a bit – I suppose they have to do it to make things interesting. It was an adequate performance – that's what I would have called it. I don't remember any cheering. But there isn't any doubt about her making good. She could have had other parts – better ones than she had ever had before. Yet it's true enough – she left the theater, and that was the last of her."

"You had final view of her?" Chan suggested.

"Yes. On my way home, I saw her standing talking to some man on the Promenade des Anglais, at the entrance to the jetty. I went on, thinking nothing of it at the time. Afterward, of course—"

"And it was this girl Sir Frederic asked you about?" Miss Morrow inquired.

"It was. He showed me that clipping, and asked me if I wasn't in the same company. I said I was. He wanted to know if I thought I could identify Marie Lantelme if I met her again, and I said I was quite sure I could. 'Very good,' he said. 'I may call upon you for that service before the evening is over. Please do not leave tonight until we have had another talk.' I told him I wouldn't, but of course, at the end – well, he wasn't talking to anyone any more."

They sat for a moment in silence. Then Miss Morrow spoke.

"I think that is all," she said. "Unless Captain Flannery—"

She glanced at the Captain. An expression of complete bewilderment decorated that great red face. "Me? No – no, I guess not. Nothing more from me, now," he stammered.

"Thank you very much, Miss Garland," the girl continued. "You are going to be in the city for some time?"

"Yes. I've been promised a part at the Alcazar."

"Well, don't leave town without letting me know. You may go now. So good of you to come."

Miss Garland nodded toward the desk. "May I have the pearl?"

"Oh – certainly."

"Thanks. When an actress has been out of a shop for some time, even the imitation jewels are precious. You understand?"

Miss Morrow let her out, and returned to the silent little group in the inner room. "Well?" she remarked.

"It's incredible," cried Barry Kirk. "Another lost lady. Good lord, Eve Durand and Marie Lantelme can't both be hanging out around here. Unless this is the Port of Missing Women. What do you say, Sergeant?"

Chan shrugged. "All time we get in deeper," he admitted. "Free to announce I find myself sunk in bafflement."

"I'll get to the bottom of it," Flannery cried. "You leave it to me. I'll stir things up."

Chan's eyes narrowed. "My race has old saying, Captain," he remarked gently. "'Muddy water, unwisely stirred, grows darker still. Left alone, it clears itself.'"

Flannery glared at him and without a word strode from the room, slamming the outer door behind him.

VIII

WILLIE LI'S GOOD TURN

Thoughtfully Charlie Chan picked up Sir Frederic's clippings from the desk and taking out a huge wallet, stowed them away inside. Barry Kirk's eyes were on the door through which Flannery had taken his unceremonious departure.

"I'm very much afraid," he said, "that the policeman's lot is not a happy one. The dear old Captain seemed a bit – what's a good word for it? Nettled? Ah yes, nettled is a very good word."

Miss Morrow smiled. "He's frightfully puzzled, and that always makes a policeman cross."

"I hope it doesn't have that effect on you."

"If it did, I'd be so cross right at this moment you'd order me out of your life for ever."

"A trifle baffled, eh?"

"Can you wonder? Was there ever a case like this?" She picked up her coat, which she had brought with her from the bungalow. "All that about Marie Lantelme—"

"Humbly making suggestion," remarked Chan, "do not think too much about Marie Lantelme. She is – what you say – an issue from the side. Remember always one big fact – Sir Frederic Bruce dead on this very floor, the velvet shoes absent from his feet. Wandering too far from that, we are lost. Think of Eve Durand, think of Hilary Galt, but think most of all regarding Sir Frederic and last night. Bestow Marie Lantelme in distant pigeonhole of mind. That way alone, we progress, we advance."

The girl sighed. "Shall we ever advance? I doubt it."

"Take cheer," advised Chan. "A wise man said, 'The dark clouds pass, the blue heavens abide.'" He bowed low and disappeared toward the stairs leading up to the bungalow.

Barry Kirk held the girl's coat. As he placed it about her shoulders the words of a familiar advertisement flashed into his mind. "Obey that impulse." But one couldn't go through life obeying every chance impulse.

"'All time we get in deeper,'" he quoted. "It begins to look like a long and very involved case."

"I'm afraid it does," Miss Morrow replied.

"What do you mean, afraid? You and I are very brainy people – thanks for including me – and we should welcome a good stiff test of our powers. Let's get together for a conference very soon."

"Do you think that's necessary?"

"I'm sure of it."

"Then it's all settled," she smiled. "Thanks for the lunch – and goodby."

When Kirk reached the bungalow, Charlie called to him from the room formerly occupied by the man from Scotland Yard. Going in, he found the detective standing thoughtfully before Sir Frederic's luggage, now piled neatly in a corner.

"You have investigated these properties of Sir Frederic?" Chan asked.

Kirk shook his head. "No, I haven't. That's hardly in my line. Flannery went through them last night, and evidently found nothing. He told me to turn them over to the British consul."

"Flannery travels with too much haste," protested Chan. "You have the keys, perhaps? If so, I experience a yearning of my own to look inside."

Kirk handed him the keys, and left him alone. For a long time Chan proceeded with his search. Finally he appeared in the living-room with a great collection of books under his arm.

"Find anything?" Kirk asked.

"Nothing at all," Chan returned, "with these somewhat heavy exceptions. Deign to come closer, if you will be kind enough."

Kirk rose and casually examined the books. His offhand manner vanished, and he cried excitedly: "Great Scott!"

"The same from me," Chan smiled. "You have noted the name of the author of these volumes." He read off the titles. "*Across China and Back. Wanderings in Persia. A Year in the Gobi Desert. Tibet, the Top of the World. My Life as an Explorer.*" His eyes narrowed as he looked at Kirk. "All the work of our good friend, Colonel Beetham. No other books amid Sir Frederic's luggage. Does it not strike you as strange, his keen interest in one solitary author?"

"It certainly does," agreed Kirk. "I wonder—"

"I have never ceased to wonder. When I look into deep eyes of the lonely explorer last night, I ask myself, what make of man is this? No sooner is Sir Frederic low on the floor than my thoughts fly back to that mysterious face. So cold, so calm, but who knows with what hot fires beneath." He selected one enormous volume, the *Life*. "I feel called upon to do some browsing amid Sir Frederic's modest library. I will advance first on this, which will grant me bird's-eye look over an adventurous career."

"A good idea," Kirk nodded.

Before Chan could settle to his reading, the bell rang and Paradise admitted Mrs Dawson Kirk. She came in as blithely as a girl.

"Hello, Barry. Mr Chan, I rather thought I'd find you here. Didn't sail after all, did you?"

Chan sighed. "I have encountered some difficulty in bringing vacation to proper stop. History is a grand repeater."

"Well, I'm glad of it," said Mrs Kirk. "They'll need you here. Frightful thing, this is. And to think, Barry, it happened in your building. The Kirks are not accustomed to scandal. I never slept a wink all night."

"I'm sorry to hear it," her grandson said.

"Oh, you needn't be. Not sleeping much anyhow, of late. Seems I got all my sleeping done, years ago. Well, what's happened? Have they made any progress?"

"Not much," Kirk admitted.

"How could they? That stupid police captain – he annoyed me. No subtlety. Sally Jordan's boy here will show him up."

"Humbly accept the flattery," Chan bowed.

"Flattery – rot. The truth, nothing else. Don't you disappoint me. All my hopes are pinned on you."

"By the way," said Kirk, "I'm glad you came alone. How long has that woman – Mrs Tupper-Brock – been with you?"

"About a year. What's she got to do with it?"

"Well – what do you know about her?"

"Don't be a fool, Barry. I know everything. She's all right."

"You mean all her past is an open book to you?"

"Nothing of the sort. I never asked about it. I didn't have to. I'm a judge of people. One look – that's enough for me."

Kirk laughed. "What a smart lady. As a matter of fact, you don't know a thing about her, do you?"

"Oh, yes I do. She's English – born in Devonshire."

"Devonshire, eh?"

"Yes. Her husband was a clergyman – you'd know that by her starved look. He's dead now."

"And that's the extent of your knowledge?"

"You're barking up the wrong tree – but you would. A nice boy, but never very clever. However, I didn't come here to discuss Helen Tupper-Brock. It has just occurred to me that I didn't tell all I knew last night."

"Concealing evidence, eh?" smiled Kirk.

"I don't know – it may be evidence – probably not. Tell me – have they dug up any connection between Sir Frederic and that little Mrs Enderby?"

"No, they haven't. Have you?"

"Well – it was just after the pictures started. I went out into the kitchen—"

"You would."

"My throat was dry. I didn't see any water in the living-room. But what could I expect in a man-run house? In the passageway I came upon Sir Frederic and Mrs Enderby engaged in what appeared to be a quite serious talk."

"What were they saying?"

"I'm no eavesdropper. Besides, they stopped suddenly when I appeared, and remained silent until I had gone by. When I returned a few moments later, both were gone."

"Well, that may be important," Kirk admitted. "Perhaps not. Odd, though – Sir Frederic told me he had never met Mrs Enderby when he suggested I invite the pair to dinner. I'll turn your information over to Miss Morrow."

"What's Miss Morrow got to do with it?" snapped the old lady.

"She's handling the case for the district attorney's office."

"What! You mean to say they've put an important case like this in the hands of—"

"Calm yourself. Miss Morrow is a very intelligent young woman."

"She couldn't be. She's too good-looking."

"Miracles happen," laughed Kirk.

His grandmother regarded him keenly. "You look out for yourself, my boy."

"What are you talking about?"

"The Kirk men always did have a weakness for clever women – the attraction of opposites, I presume. That's how I came to marry into the family."

"You don't happen to have an inferiority complex about you, do you?"

"No, sir. That's one thing the new generation will never be able to pin on me. Well, go ahead and tell Miss Morrow about Eileen Enderby. But I fancy the important member of the investigating committee has heard it already. I'm speaking of Mr Chan." She rose. "I wrote Sally Jordan this morning that I'd met you," she went on, to the detective. "I said I thought the mainland couldn't spare you just yet."

Chan shrugged. "Mainland enjoys spectacle of weary postman plodding on his holiday walk," he replied. "No offense is carried, but I am longing for Hawaii."

"Well, that's up to you," remarked Mrs Kirk bluntly. "Solve this case quickly and run before the next one breaks. I must go along. I've a club meeting. That's what my life's come to – club meetings. Barry, keep me posted on this thing. First excitement in my neighborhood in twenty years. I don't want to miss any of it."

Kirk let her out, and returned to the living-room. The quick winter dusk was falling, and he switched on the lights.

"All of which," he said, "brings little Eileen into it again. She did seem a bit on edge last night – even before she saw that man on the fire-escape. If she really did see him. I'll put Miss Morrow on her trail, eh?"

Chan looked up from his big book, and nodded without interest. "All you can do."

"She doesn't intrigue you much, does she?" Kirk smiled.

"This Colonel Beetham," responded Chan. "What a man!"

Kirk looked at his watch. "I'm sorry, but I'm dining tonight at the Cosmopolitan Club, with a friend. I made the engagement several days ago."

"Greatly pained," said Chan, "if I interfered with your plans in any way. Tell me – our Colonel Beetham – you have seen him at Cosmopolitan Club?"

"Yes. Somebody's given him a card. I meet him around there occasionally. I must take you over to the club one of these days."

"The honor will be immense," Chan said gravely.

"Paradise will give you dinner," Kirk told him.

"Not to be considered," Chan protested. "Your staff in kitchen deserves holiday after last night's outburst. I am doing too much eating at your gracious board. I too will dine elsewhere – there are little matters into which I would peer inquiringly."

"As you wish," nodded Kirk. He went into his bedroom, leaving Chan to the book.

At six thirty, after Kirk had left, Chan also descended to the street. He had dinner at an inexpensive little place and when it was finished, strolled with what looked like an aimless step in the direction of Chinatown.

The Chinese are a nocturnal race; Grant Avenue's shops were alight and thronged with customers; its sidewalk crowded with idlers who seemed at a loose end for the evening. The younger men were garbed like their white contemporaries; the older, in the black satin blouse and trousers of China, shuffled along on felt shod feet. Here and there walked with ponderous dignity a Chinese matron who had all too obviously never sought to reduce. A sprinkling of bright-eyed flappers lightened the picture.

Chan turned up Washington Street, then off into the gloomy stretch of Waverly Place. He climbed dimly lighted stairs and knocked at a familiar door.

Surprise is not in the lexicon of the race, and Chan Kee Lim admitted him with stolid face. Though they had said farewell only that morning, the detective's call was accepted calmly by his cousin.

"I am here again," Chan said in Cantonese. "It was my thought that I was leaving the mainland, but the fates have decreed otherwise."

"Enter," his cousin said. "Here in my poor house the welcome never cools. Deign to sit on this atrociously ugly stool."

"You are too kind," Charlie returned. "I am, as you must surmise, the victim of my despicable calling. If you will so far condescend, I require information."

Kee Lim's eyes narrowed, and he stroked his thin gray beard. He did not approve of that calling, as Charlie well knew.

"You are involved," he said coldly, "with the white devil police?"

Chan shrugged. "Unfortunately, yes. But I ask no betrayal of confidence from you. A harmless question, only. Perhaps you could tell me of a stranger, a tourist, who has been guest of relatives in Jackson Street? The name Li Gung."

Kee Lim nodded. "I have not met him, but I have heard talk at the Tong House. He is one who has traveled much in foreign lands. For some time he has been domiciled with his cousin Henry Li, the basket importer, who lives American style in the big apartment-house on Jackson Street. The Oriental Apartments, I believe. I have not been inside, but I understand there are bathrooms and other strange developments of what the white devil is pleased to call his civilization."

"You are an acquaintance of Henry Li?" Charlie asked.

Kee Lim's eyes hardened. "I have not the honor," he replied.

Charlie understood. His cousin would have no part in whatever he proposed. He rose from his ebony stool.

"You are extremely kind," he said. "That was the extent of my desire. Duty says I must walk my way."

Kee Lim also rose. "The briefness of your stop makes it essential you come again. There is always a welcome here."

"Only too well do I know it," nodded Charlie. "I am busy man, but we will meet again. I am saying goodby."

His cousin followed to the door. "I hope you have a safe walk," he remarked, and there was, it seemed, something more in his mind than the conventional farewell wish.

Chan set out at once for Jackson Street. Half-way up the hill he encountered the gaudy front of the Oriental Apartments. Here the more prosperous members of the Chinese colony lived in the manner of their adopted country.

He entered the lobby and studied the letter boxes. Henry Li, he discovered, lived on the second floor. Ignoring the push buttons, he tried the door. It was unlocked, and he went inside. He climbed to the third floor, walking softly as he passed the apartment occupied by Henry Li. For a moment he stood at the head of the stairs, then started down. He had proceeded about half-way to the floor below, when suddenly he appeared to lose his footing, and descended with a terrific clatter to the second-floor landing. The door of Henry Li's apartment opened, and a fat little Chinese in a business suit peered out.

"You are concerned in an accident?" he inquired solicitously.

"Haie!" cried Chan, picking himself up, "the evil spirits pursue me. I have lost my footing on these slippery stairs." He tried to walk, but limped painfully. "I fear I have given my ankle a bad turn. If I could sit quietly for a moment— "

The little man threw wide his door. "Condescend to enter my contemptible house. My chairs are plain and uncomfortable, but you must try one."

Profuse in thanks, Chan followed him into an astonishing living-room. Hang-chau silk hangings and a few pieces of teak-wood mingled with blatant plush furniture from some department store. A small boy, about thirteen, was seated at a radio, which ground out dance music. He wore the khaki uniform of a boy scout, with a bright yellow handkerchief about his throat.

"Please sit here," invited Henry Li, indicating a huge chair of green plush. "I trust the pain is not very acute."

"It begins to subside," Chan told him. "You are most kind."

The boy had shut off the radio, and was standing before Charlie Chan with keen interest in his bright eyes.

"A most regrettable thing," explained his father. "The gentleman has turned his ankle on our detestable stairs."

"So sorry," the boy announced. His eyes grew even brighter. "All boy scouts know how to make bandages. I will get my first-aid kit—"

"No, no," protested Chan hastily. "Do not trouble yourself. The injury is not serious."

"It would be no trouble at all," the boy assured him. With some difficulty Charlie dissuaded him, and to the detective's great relief, the boy disappeared.

"I will sit and rest for a moment," Chan said to Henry Li. "I trust I am no great obstacle here. The accident overwhelmed me when I was on the search for an old friend of mine – Li Gung by name."

Henry Li's little eyes rested for a moment on the picture of a middle-aged Chinese in a silver frame on the mantel. "You are a friend of Li Gung?" he inquired.

The moment had been enough for Chan. "I am – and I see his photograph above there, tastefully framed. Is it true, then, that he is stopping here? Has my search ended so fortunately after all?"

"He was here," Li replied, "but only this morning he walked his way."

"Gone!" Chan's face fell. "Alas, then I am too late. Would you be so kind as to tell me where he went?"

Henry Li became discreet. "He disappeared on business of his own, with which I have no concern."

"Of course. But it is a great pity. A friend of mine, an American gentleman who goes on a long, hazardous journey, required his services. The recompense would have been of generous amount."

Li shook his head. "The matter would have held no interest for Gung. He is otherwise occupied."

"Ah, yes. He still remains in the employ of Colonel John Beetham?"

"No doubt he does."

"Still, the reward in this other matter would have been great. But it may be that he is very loyal to Colonel Beetham. A loyalty cemented through many years. I am trying to figure, but I cannot. How long is it your honorable cousin is in Colonel Beetham's service?"

"Long enough to cement loyalty, as you say," returned Li, non-commitally.

"Fifteen years, perhaps?" hazarded Chan.

"It might be."

"Or even longer?"

"As to that, I do not know."

Chan nodded. "When you know, to know that you know, and when you do not know, to know that you do not know – that is true knowledge, as the master said." He moved his foot, and a spasm of pain spread over his fat face. "A great man, Colonel Beetham. A most remarkable man. Li Gung has been fortunate. With Colonel Beetham he has seen Tibet, Persia – even India. He has told you, perhaps, of his visits to India with Colonel Beetham?"

In the slanting eyes of the host a stubborn expression was evident. "He says little, my cousin," Henry Li remarked.

"Which point of character no doubt increases his value to a man like the Colonel," suggested Chan. "I am very sorry he has gone. While I would no doubt have failed, owing to his feeling of loyalty for his present employer, I would nevertheless have liked to try. I promised my friend—"

The outer door opened, and the active little boy scout burst into the room. After him came a serious, prematurely bearded young American with a small black case.

"I have brought a physician," cried Willie Li triumphantly.

Chan gave the ambitious boy a savage look.

"An accident, eh?" said the doctor briskly. "Well – which one of you—"

Henry Li nodded toward Chan. "This gentleman's ankle," he said.

The white man went at once to Chan's side. "Let's have a look at it."

"It is nothing," Chan protested. "Nothing at all."

He held out his foot, and the doctor ripped off shoe and stocking. He made a quick examination with his fingers, turned the foot this way and that, and studied it thoughtfully for a moment. Then he stood up.

"What are you trying to do – kid me?" he said with disgust. "Nothing wrong there."

"I remarked the injury was of the slightest," Chan said.

He looked at Henry Li. An expression of complete understanding lighted the basket merchant's face.

"Five dollars, please," said the doctor sternly.

Chan produced his purse, and counted out the money. With an effort he refrained from looking in the boy's direction.

The white man left abruptly. Chan drew on his stocking, slipped into his shoe, and stood up. His dignity requiring that he still maintain the fiction, he limped elaborately.

"These white devil doctors," he remarked glumly. "All they know is five dollars, please."

Henry Li was looking at him keenly. "I recall," he said, "there was one other who came to ask questions about Li Gung. An Englishman – a large man. They are clever and cool, the English, like a thief amid the fire. Was it not his death I read about in the morning paper?"

"I know nothing of the matter," responded Chan stiffly.

"Of course." Henry Li followed to the door. "If you will accept advice offered in humble spirit," he added, "you will walk softly. What a pity if you encountered a really serious accident."

Mumbling a goodby, Chan went out. By the door he passed young Willie Li, who was grinning broadly. The event had come to an unexpected ending, but none the less the lad was happy. He was a boy scout, and he had done his good turn for the day.

Chan returned to the street, thoroughly upset. Rarely had any of his little deceptions ended so disastrously. His usefulness on the trail of Li Gung was no doubt over for all time. He consigned all boy scouts to limbo with one muttered imprecation.

Entering a drug store, he purchased a quantity of lamp black and a camel's hair brush. Then he went on to the Kirk Building. The night watchman took him up to the bungalow, and he let himself in with a key Kirk had given him. The place was dark and silent. He switched on the lights, and made a round of the rooms. No one seemed to be about.

He unlocked the compartment in Kirk's desk, and carefully removed the sheet of paper that had arrived in the envelope from Scotland Yard. With satisfaction he noted the paper was of a cheap variety, highly glazed. Along the lines where it had been folded, someone's fingers must have pressed hard.

Seated at the desk, with a floor lamp glowing brightly at his side, he cautiously sprinkled the black powder in the most likely place. Then he carefully dusted it with his brush. He was rewarded by the outline of a massive thumb – the thumb of a big man. He considered. Carrick Enderby was a big man. He was employed at Cook's. In some way he must procure impressions of Enderby's thumb.

He returned the paper to the compartment, and with it the tools of his investigation. Turning over ways and means in his mind, he sat down in a comfortable chair, took up Colonel John Beetham's story of his life, and began to read.

About an hour later Paradise came in from outside. He was absent for a moment in the pantry. Then, entering the living-room with his inevitable silver platter, he removed a few letters and laid them on Kirk's desk.

"The last mail is in, sir," he announced. "There is, I believe, a picture postcard for you."

He carried card and tray negligently at his side, as though to express his contempt for picture postcards. Chan looked up in surprise; he had telephoned the hotel to forward any mail to him here, and this was quick work. Paradise offered the tray, and Chan daintily took up the card.

It was from his youngest girl, designed to catch him just before he left. "Hurry home, honorable father," she wrote. "We miss you all the time. There is Kona weather here now, and we have ninety degrees of climate every day. Wishing to see you soon. Your loving daughter, Anna."

Chan turned over the card. He saw a picture of Waikiki, the surf boards riding the waves, Diamond Head beyond. He sighed with homesickness, and sat for a long moment immobile in his chair.

But as Paradise left the room, the little detective leaped nimbly to his feet and returned to the desk. For Paradise had glued the postcard to his tray with one large, moist thumb, a thumb which had fortunately rested on the light blue of Hawaii's lovely sky.

Quickly Chan applied lamp black and brush. Then he removed the blank paper from the compartment, and with the aid of a reading glass, studied the impressions.

He leaned back in his chair with a puzzled frown. He knew now that he need not investigate the fingerprints of Carrick Enderby. The thumbprint of Paradise was on the postcard, and the same print was on the blank sheet of paper that had arrived in the envelope from Scotland Yard. It was Paradise, then, who had tampered with Sir Frederic's mail.

IX

THE PORT OF MISSING WOMEN

Thursday morning dawned bright and fair. Stepping briskly from his bed to the window, Chan saw the sunlight sparkling cheerily on the waters of the harbor. It was a clear, cool world he looked upon, and the sight was invigorating. Nor for ever would he wander amid his present dark doubts and perplexities; one of these days he would see the murderer of Sir Frederic as plainly as he now saw the distant towers of Oakland. After that – the Pacific, the lighthouse on Makapuu Point, Diamond Head and a palm-fringed shore, and finally his beloved town of Honolulu nestling in the emerald cup of the hills.

Calm and unhurried, he prepared himself for another day, and left his bedroom. Barry Kirk, himself immaculate and unperturbed, was seated at the breakfast table reading the morning paper. Chan smiled at thought of the bomb he was about to toss at his gracious host. For he had not seen Kirk the previous night after his discovery. Though he had waited until midnight, the young man had not returned, and Chan had gone sleepily to bed.

"Good morning," Kirk said. "How's the famous sleuth today?"

"Doing as well as could be predicted," Chan replied. "You are tip-top yourself. I see it without the formal inquiring."

"True enough," Kirk answered. "I am full of vim, vigor and ambition, and ready for a new day's discoveries. By the way, I called Miss Morrow last night and gave her my grandmother's story about Eileen Enderby. She's going to arrange an interview with the lady, and you're invited. I hope I won't be left out of the party, either. If I am, it won't be my fault."

Chan nodded. "Interview is certainly indicated," he agreed.

Paradise entered, haughty and dignified as always, and after he had bestowed on each a suave good morning, placed orange juice before them. Kirk lifted his glass.

"Your very good health," he said, "in the wine of the country. California orange juice – of course you read our advertisements. Cures anything from insomnia to a broken heart. How did you spend last evening?"

"Me?" Chan shrugged. "I made slight sally into Chinatown."

"On Li Gung's trail, eh? What luck?"

"The poorest," returned Chan, grimacing at the memory. "I encounter Chinese boy scout panting to do good turn, and he does me one of the worst I ever suffered." He recounted his adventure, to Kirk's amusement.

"Tough luck," laughed the young man. "However, you probably got all you could, at that."

"Later," continued Chan, "the luck betters itself." Paradise came in with the cereal, and Chan watched him in silence. When the butler had gone, he added: "Last night in living-room out there I make astonishing discovery."

"You did? What was that?"

"How much you know about this perfect servant of yours?"

Kirk started. "Paradise? Good lord! You don't mean—"

"He came with references?"

"King George couldn't have brought better. Dukes and earls spoke of him in glowing terms. And why not? He's the best servant in the world."

"Too bad," commented Chan.

"What do you mean, too bad?"

"Too bad best servant in world has weakness for steaming open letters—" He stopped suddenly, for Paradise was entering with bacon and eggs. When he had gone out, Kirk leaned over and spoke in a low tense voice.

"Paradise opened that letter from Scotland Yard? How do you know?"

Briefly Charlie told him, and Kirk's face grew gloomy at the tale.

"I suppose I should have been prepared," he sighed. "The butler is always mixed up in a thing like this. But Paradise! My paragon of all the virtues. Oh well – 'twas ever thus. 'I never loved a young gazelle—' What's the rest of it? What shall I do? Fire him?"

"Oh, no," protested Chan. "For the present, silence only. He must not know we are aware of his weakness. Just watchfully waiting."

"Suits me," agreed Kirk. "I'll hang on to him until you produce the handcuffs. What a pity it will seem to lock up such competent hands as his."

"May not happen," Chan suggested.

"I hope not," Kirk answered fervently.

After breakfast Chan called the *Globe* office, and got Bill Rankin's home address. He routed the reporter from a well-earned sleep, and asked him to come at once to the bungalow.

An hour later Rankin, brisk and full of enthusiasm, arrived on the scene. He grinned broadly as he shook hands.

"Couldn't quite pull it off, eh?" he chided. "The cool, calm Oriental turned back at the dock."

Chan nodded. "Cool, calm Oriental gets too much like mainland Americans from circling in such lowering society. I have remained to assist Captain Flannery, much to his well-concealed delight."

Rankin laughed. "Yes – I talked with him last night. He's tickled pink but he won't admit it, even to himself. Well, what's the dope? Who killed Sir Frederic?"

"A difficult matter to determine," Chan replied. "We must go into the past, upearthing here and there. Just at present I am faced by small problem with which you can assist. So I have ventured to annoy you."

"No annoyance whatever. I'm happy to have you call on me. What are your orders?"

"For the present, keep everything shaded by darkness. No publicity. You understand it?"

"All right – for the present. But when the big moment comes, I'm the fair-haired boy. You understand it?"

Chan smiled. "Yes – you are the chosen one. That will happen. Just now, a little covered investigation. You recall the story of Eve Durand?"

"Will I ever forget it? I don't know when anything has made such an impression on me. Peshawar – the dark hills – the game of hide-and-seek – the little blonde who never came back from the ride. If that isn't what the flappers used to call intriguing, I don't know what is."

"You speak true. Fifteen years ago. Sir Frederic said. But from neither Sir Frederic nor the clipping did I obtain the exact date, and for it I am yearning. On what day of what month, presumably in the year 1913, did Eve Durand wander off into unlimitable darkness of India? Could you supply the fact?"

Rankin nodded. "A story like that must have been in the newspapers all over the world. I'll have a look at our files for 1913 and see what I can find."

"Good enough," said Chan. "Note one other matter, if you please. Suppose you find accounts. Is the name of Colonel John Beetham anywhere mentioned?"

"What! Beetham! That bird? Is he in it?"

"You know him?"

"Sure – I interviewed him. A mysterious sort of guy. If he's in it, the story's even better than I thought."

"He may not be," warned Chan. "I am curious, that is all. You will then explore in files?"

"I certainly will. You'll hear from me *pronto*. I'm on my way now."

The reporter hurried off, leaving Chan to his ponderous book. For a long time he wandered with Colonel Beetham through lonely places, over blazing sands at one moment, at another over wastelands of snow. Men and camels and mules lay dead on the trail, but Beetham pushed on. Nothing stopped him.

During lunch the telephone rang, and Kirk answered. "Hello – oh, Miss Morrow. Of course. Good – he'll be there. So will I—I beg your pardon?... No trouble at all. Mr Chan's a stranger here, and I don't want him to get lost... Yes... Yes, I'm coming, so get resigned, lady, get resigned."

He hung up. "Well, we're invited to Miss Morrow's office at two o'clock to meet the Enderbys. That is, you're invited, and I'm going anyhow."

At two precisely Chan and his host entered the girl's office, a dusty, ill-lighted room piled high with law books. The deputy district attorney rose from behind an orderly desk and greeted them smilingly.

Kirk stood looking about the room. "Great Scott – is this where you spend your days?" He walked to the window. "Charming view of the alley, isn't it? I must take you out in the country some time and show you the grass and the trees. You'd be surprised."

"Oh, this room isn't so bad," the girl answered. "I'm not like some people. I keep my mind on my work."

Flannery came in. "Well, here we are again," he said. "All set for another tall story. Mrs Enderby this time, eh? More women in this case than in the League of Women Voters."

"You still appear in baffled stage," Chan suggested.

"Sure I do," admitted the Captain. "I am. And how about you? I don't hear any very illuminating deductions from you."

"At any moment now," grinned Chan, "I may dazzle you with great light."

"Well, don't hurry on my account," advised Flannery. "We've got all year on this, of course. It's only Sir Frederic Bruce of Scotland Yard who was murdered. Nobody cares – except the whole British Empire."

"You have made progress?" Chan inquired.

"How could I? Every time I get all set to go at the thing in a reasonable way, I have to stop and hunt for a missing woman. I tell you, I'm getting fed up on that end of it. If there's any more nonsense about—"

The door opened, and a clerk admitted Carrick Enderby and his wife. Eileen Enderby, even before she spoke, seemed flustered and nervous. Miss Morrow rose.

"How do you do," she said. "Sit down, please. It was good of you to come."

"Of course we came," Eileen Enderby replied. "Though what it is you want, I for one can't imagine—"

"We must let Miss Morrow tell us what is wanted, Eileen," drawled her husband.

"Oh, naturally," Mrs Enderby's blue eyes turned from one to the other and rested at last on the solid bulk of Captain Flannery.

"We're going to ask a few questions, Mrs Enderby," began Miss Morrow. "Questions that I know you'll be glad to answer. Tell me – had you ever met Sir Frederic Bruce before Mr Kirk's dinner party the other night?"

"I'd never even heard of him," replied the woman firmly.

"Ah, yes. Yet just after Colonel Beetham began to show his pictures, Sir Frederic called you out into a passageway. He wanted to speak to you alone."

Eileen Enderby looked at her husband, who nodded. "Yes," she admitted. "He did. I was never so surprised in my life."

"What did Sir Frederic want to speak to you about?"

"It was a most amazing thing. He mentioned a girl – a girl I once knew very well."

"What about the girl?"

"Well – it was quite a mystery. This girl Sir Frederic spoke of – she disappeared one night. Just walked off into the dark and was never heard of again."

There was a moment's silence. "Did she disappear at Peshawar, in India?" Miss Morrow inquired.

"India? Why, no – not at all," replied Eileen Enderby.

"Oh, I see. Then he was speaking of Marie Lantelme, who disappeared from Nice?"

"Nice? Marie Lantelme? I don't know what you're talking about." Mrs Enderby's pretty forehead wrinkled in amazement.

For the first time, Chan spoke. "It is now how many years," he asked, "since your friend was last seen?"

"Why – it must be – let me think. Seven – yes – seven years."

"She disappeared from New York, perhaps?"

"From New York – yes."

"Her name was Jennie Jerome?"

"Yes. Jennie Jerome."

Chan took out his wallet and removed a clipping. He handed it to Miss Morrow. "Once more, and I am hoping for the last time," he remarked, "I would humbly request that you read aloud a scrap of paper from Sir Frederic's effects."

Miss Morrow took the paper, her eyes wide. Captain Flannery's face was a study in scarlet. The girl began to read:

"What happened to Jennie Jerome? A famous New York modiste and an even more famous New York illustrator are among those who have been asking themselves that question for the past seven years.

"Jennie Jerome was what the French call a mannequin, a model employed by the fashionable house of DuFour et Cie, on Fifth Avenue, in New York. She was something more than a model, a rack for pretty clothes; she was a girl of charming and marked personality and a beauty that will not be forgot in seven times seven years. Though employed but a brief time by DuFour she was the most popular of all their models among the distinguished patrons of the house. A celebrated New York illustrator saw her picture in a newspaper and at once sought her out, offering her a large sum of money to pose for him.

"Jennie Jerome seemed delighted at the opportunity. She invited a number of her friends to a little dinner party at her apartment, to celebrate the event. When these friends arrived, the door of her apartment stood open. They entered. The table was set, the candles lighted, preparations for the dinner apparent. But the hostess was nowhere about.

"The boy at the telephone switchboard in the hall below reported that, a few minutes before, he had seen her run down the stairs and vanish into the night. He was the last person who saw Jennie Jerome. Her employer, Madame DuFour, and the illustrator who had been struck by her beauty, made every possible effort to trace her. These efforts came to nothing. Jennie Jerome had vanished into thin air. Eloped? But no man's name was ever linked with hers. Murdered? Perhaps. No one knows. At any rate, Jennie Jerome had gone without leaving a trace, and there the matter has rested for seven years."

"Another one of 'em," cried Flannery, as Miss Morrow stopped reading. "Great Scott – what are we up against?"

"A puzzle," suggested Chan calmly. He restored the clipping to his pocketbook.

"I'll say so," Flannery growled.

"You knew Jennie Jerome?" Miss Morrow said to Eileen Enderby.

Mrs Enderby nodded. "Yes. I was employed by the same firm – DuFour. One of the models, too. I was working there when I met Mr Enderby, who was in Cook's New York office at the time. I knew Jennie well. If I may say so, that story you just read has been touched up a bit. Jennie Jerome was just an ordinarily pretty girl – nothing to rave about. I believe some illustrator did want her to pose for him. We all got offers like that."

"Leaving her beauty out of it," smiled Miss Morrow, "she did disappear?"

"Oh, yes. I was one of the guests invited to her dinner. That part of it is true enough. She just walked off into the night."

"And it was this girl whom Sir Frederic questioned you about?"

"Yes. Somehow, he knew I was one of her friends – how he knew it, I can't imagine. At any rate, he asked me if I would know Jennie Jerome if I saw her again. I said I thought I would. He said: 'Have you seen her in the Kirk Building this evening?'"

"And you told him—"

"I told him I hadn't. He said to stop and think a minute. I couldn't see the need of that. I hadn't seen her – I was sure of it."

"And you still haven't seen her?"

"No – I haven't."

Miss Morrow rose. "We are greatly obliged to you, Mrs Enderby. That is all, I believe. Captain Flannery—"

"That's all from me," said Flannery.

"Well, if there's any more I can tell you—" Mrs Enderby rose, with evident relief.

Her husband spoke. "Come along, Eileen," he said sternly. They went out. The four left behind in the office stared at one another in wonder.

"There you are," exploded Flannery, rising. "Another missing woman. Eve Durand, Marie Lantelme and Jennie Jerome. Three – count 'em – three – and if you believe your ears, every damn one of 'em was in the Kirk Building night before last. I don't know how it sounds to you, but to me it's all wrong."

"It does sound fishy," Barry Kirk admitted. "The Port of Missing Women – and I thought I was running just an ordinary office building."

"All wrong, I tell you," Flannery went on loudly. "It never happened, that's all. Somebody's kidding us to a fare-ye-well. This last story is one too many—" He stopped, and stared at Charlie Chan. "Well, Sergeant – what's on your mind?" he inquired.

"Plenty," grinned Chan. "On one side of our puzzle, at least, light is beginning to break. This last story illuminates darkness. You follow after me, of course."

"I do not. What are you talking about?"

"You do not? A great pity. In good time, I show you."

"All right – all right," cried Flannery. "I leave these missing women to you and Miss Morrow here. I don't want to hear any more about 'em – I'll go dippy if I do. I'll stick to the main facts. Night before last Sir Frederic Bruce was murdered in an office on the twentieth floor of the Kirk Building. Somebody slipped away from that party, or somebody got in from outside, and did for him. There was a book beside him, and there were marks on the fire-escape – I didn't tell you that, but there were – and the murderer nabbed a pair of velvet shoes off his feet. That's my case, my job, and by heaven I'm going after it, and if anybody comes to me with any more missing women stories—"

He stopped. The outer door had opened, and Eileen Enderby was coming in. At her heels came her husband, stern and grim. The woman appeared very much upset.

"We – we've come back," she said. She sank into a chair. "My husband thinks – he has made me see—"

"I have insisted," said Carrick Enderby, "that my wife tell you the entire story. She has omitted a very important point."

"I'm in a terrible position," the woman protested. "I do hope I'm doing the right thing. Carry – are you sure—"

"I am sure," cut in her husband, "that in a serious matter of this sort, truth is the only sane course."

"But she begged me not to tell," Eileen Enderby reminded him. "She pleaded so hard. I don't want to make trouble for her—"

"You gave no promise," her husband said. "And if the woman's done nothing wrong, I don't see—"

"Look here," broke in Flannery. "You came back to tell us something. What is it?"

"You came back to tell us that you have seen Jennie Jerome?" suggested Miss Morrow.

Mrs Enderby nodded, and began to speak with obvious reluctance.

"Yes – I did see her – but not before I talked with Sir Frederic. I told him the truth. I hadn't seen her then – that is, I had seen her, but I didn't notice – one doesn't, you know—"

"But you noticed later."

"Yes – on our way home. Going down in the elevator. I got a good look at her then, and that was when I realized it. The elevator girl in the Kirk Building night before last was Jennie Jerome."

X

THE LETTER FROM LONDON

Captain Flannery got up and took a turn about the room. He was a simple man and the look on his face suggested that the complexities of his calling were growing irksome. He stopped in front of Eileen Enderby.

"So – the elevator girl in the Kirk Building was Jennie Jerome? Then you lied a few minutes ago when you told Miss Morrow you hadn't seen her?"

"You can't hold that against her," Enderby protested. "She's come back of her own free will to tell you the truth."

"But why didn't she tell it in the first place?"

"One doesn't care to become involved in a matter of this sort. That's only natural."

"All right, all right." Flannery turned back to Mrs Enderby. "You say you recognized this girl when you were going down in the elevator, on your way home after the dinner? And you let her see that you recognized her?"

"Oh, yes. I cried out in surprise: 'Jennie! Jennie Jerome! What are you doing here?'"

"You saw what she was doing, didn't you?"

"It was just one of those questions – it didn't mean anything."

"Yeah. And what did she say?"

"She just smiled quietly and said: 'Hello, Eileen. I was wondering if you'd know me.'"

"Then what?"

"There were a thousand questions I wanted to ask of course. Why she ran away that time – where she had been—But she wouldn't answer, she just shook her head, still smiling, and said maybe some other time she'd tell me everything. And then she asked me if I'd do this – this favor for her."

"You mean, keep still about the fact that you'd seen her?"

"Yes. She said she'd done nothing wrong, but that if the story about how she left New York came out it might create a lot of suspicion—"

"According to your husband, you made no promise?" Flannery said.

"No, I didn't. Under ordinary conditions, of course, I'd have promised at once. But I thought of Sir Frederic's murder, and it seemed to me a very serious thing she was asking. So I just said I'd think it over and let her know when I saw her again."

"And have you seen her again?"

"No, I haven't. It was all so strange. I hardly knew what to do."

"Well, you'd better keep away from her," Flannery suggested.

"I'll keep away from her all right. I feel as though I'd betrayed her." Eileen Enderby glanced accusingly at her husband.

"You were not in her debt," said Enderby. "Lying's a dangerous business in a matter of this kind."

"You're lucky, Mrs Enderby," said the Captain. "You've got a sensible husband. Just listen to him, and you'll be O.K. I guess that's all now. You can go. Only keep this to yourself."

"I'll certainly do that," the woman assured him. She rose.

"If I want you again, I'll let you know," Flannery added.

Chan opened the door for her. "May I be permitted respectful inquiry," he ventured. "The beautiful garment marked by iron rust stains – it was not ruined beyond reclaim?"

"Oh, not at all," she answered. She paused, as though she felt that the matter called for an explanation. "When I saw that man on the fire-escape I became so excited I leaned against the garden railing. It was dripping with fog. Careless of me, wasn't it?"

"In moment of stress, how easy to slip into careless act," returned Chan. Bowing low, he closed the door after the Enderbys.

"Well," said Flannery, "I guess we're getting somewhere at last. Though if you ask me where, I can't tell you. Anyhow, we know that Sir Frederic was looking for Jennie Jerome the night he was killed, and that Jennie Jerome was running an elevator just outside his door. By heaven, I've a notion to lock her up right now."

"But you haven't anything against her," Miss Morrow objected. "You know that."

"No, I haven't. However, the newspapers are howling for an arrest. They always are. I could give 'em Jennie Jerome – a pretty girl – they'd eat it up. Then, if nothing else breaks against her, I could let her off, sort of quiet."

"Such tactics are beneath you, Captain," Miss Morrow said. "I trust that when we make an arrest, it will be based on something more tangible than any evidence we've got so far. Are you with me, Mr Chan?"

"Undubitably," Chan replied. He glanced up at the frowning face of the Captain. "If I may make humble suggestion—"

"Of course," agreed Miss Morrow.

But Chan, it seemed, changed his mind. He kept his humble suggestion to himself. "Patience," he finished lamely, "always brightest plan in these matters. Acting as champion of that lovely virtue, I have fought many fierce battles. American has always the urge to leap too quick. How well it was said, retire a step and you have the advantage."

"But these newspaper men—" protested the Captain.

"I do not wish to infest the picture," Chan smiled, "but I would like to refer to my own habit in similar situation. When newspapers rage, I put nice roll of cotton in the ears. Simmered down to truth, I am responsible party, not newspaper reporter. I tell him with exquisite politeness to fade off and hush down."

"A good plan," laughed Miss Morrow. She turned to Barry Kirk. "By the way, do you know anything about this elevator girl? Grace Lane was, I believe, the name she gave the other night."

Kirk shook his head. "Not a thing. Except that she's the prettiest girl we've ever employed in the building. I'd noticed that, of course."

"I rather thought you had," Miss Morrow said.

"Lady, I'm not blind," he assured her. "I notice beauty anywhere – in elevators, in cable cars – even in a lawyer's office. I tried to talk to this girl once or twice, but I didn't get very far. If you like, I'll try it again."

"No, thanks. You'd probably be away off the subject."

"Well, it all sounds mighty mysterious to me," he admitted. "We thought Sir Frederic was on the trail of Eve Durand, and now it seems it must have been a couple of other women. The poor chap is gone, but he's left a most appalling puzzle on my doorstep. You're all such nice detectives – I don't want to hurt your feelings – but will you kindly tell me whither we are drifting? Where are we getting? Nowhere, if you ask me."

"I'm afraid you're right," Miss Morrow sighed.

"Maybe if I locked this woman up—" began Flannery, attached to the idea.

"No, no," Miss Morrow told him. "We can't do that. But we can shadow her. And since she is one who has some talent for walking off into the night, I suggest that you arrange the matter without delay."

Flannery nodded. "I'll put the boys on her trail. I guess you're right – we might get on to something that way. But Mr Kirk has said it – we're not progressing very fast. If there was only some clue I could get my teeth into—"

Chan cut in. "Thanks for recalling my wandering ideas," he said. "So much has happened the matter was obscure in my mind. I have something here that might furnish excellent teeth-hold." He removed an envelope from his pocket and carefully extracted a folded sheet of paper and a picture postcard. "No doubt, Captain, you have more cleverness with fingerprints than stupid man like me. Could you say – are these thumbprints identically the same?"

Flannery studied the two items. "They look the same to me. I could put our expert on them – but say, what's this all about?"

"Blank sheet of paper," Chan explained, "arrive in envelope marked Scotland Yard. Without question Miss Morrow has told you?"

"Oh, yes – she mentioned that. Somebody tampering with the mail, eh? And this thumb print on the postcard?"

"Bestowed there last night by digit of Paradise, Mr Kirk's butler," Chan informed him.

Flannery jumped up. "Well, why didn't you say so? Now we're getting on. You've got the makings of a detective after all, Sergeant. Paradise, eh – fooling with Uncle Sam's mail. That's good enough for me – I'll have him behind the bars in an hour."

Chan lifted a protesting hand. "Oh, no – my humblest apologies. Again you leap too sudden. We must watch and wait—"

"The hell you say," Flannery cried. "That's not my system. I'll nab him. I'll make him talk—"

"And I," sighed Barry Kirk, "will lose my perfect butler. Shall I write him a reference – or won't they care, at the jail?"

"Captain, pause and listen," pleaded Chan. "We have nothing here to prove Paradise fired fatal bullet into Sir Frederic. Yet somehow he is involved. We watch his every move. Much may be revealed by the unsuspecting. We hunt through his effects. Today, I believe, he enjoys weekly holiday. Is that not so?" He looked at Kirk.

"Yes, it's Black Thursday – the servants' day off," Kirk said. "Paradise is probably at the movies – he adores them. Melodrama – that's his meat."

"Fortunate event," continued Chan. "Cook too is out. We return to bungalow and do some despicable prying into private life of Paradise. Is that not better, Captain, than searching through crowded atmosphere of movie theaters to make foolish arrest?"

Flannery considered. "Well, I guess it is, at that."

"Back to the bungalow," said Kirk, rising. "If Miss Morrow will lend a hand, I'll give you tea."

"Count me out," said Flannery.

"And other liquids," amended Kirk.

"Count me in again," added Flannery. "You got your car?" Kirk nodded. "You take Miss Morrow then, and the Sergeant and I will follow in mine."

In the roadster on their way to the Kirk Building, Barry Kirk glanced at Miss Morrow and smiled.

"Yes?" she inquired.

"I was just thinking. I do, at times."

"Is it necessary?"

"Perhaps not. But I find it exhilarating. I was thinking at that moment about you."

"Oh, please don't trouble."

"No trouble at all. I was wondering. There are so many mysterious women hovering about this case. And no one is asking you any questions."

"Why should they?"

"Why shouldn't they? Who are you? Where did you come from? Since you're not very likely to investigate yourself, perhaps I should take over the job."

"You're very kind."

"I hope you won't object. Of course, you look young and innocent, but I have your word for it that men are easily fooled." He steered round a lumbering truck, then turned to her sternly. "Just what were you doing on the night Eve Durand slipped from sight at Peshawar?"

"I was probably worrying over my home work," the girl replied. "I was always very conscientious, even in the lowest grades."

"I'll bet you were. And where was this great mental effort taking place? Not in San Francisco?"

"No, in Baltimore. That was my home before I came west to law school."

"Yes? Peering further into your dark past – why, in heaven's name, the law school? Disappointed in love, or something?"

She smiled. "Not at all. Father was a judge, and it broke his heart that I wasn't a boy."

"I've noticed how unreasonable judges are. Times when they've talked to me about my automobile driving. So the judge wanted a boy? He didn't know his luck."

"Oh, he gradually discovered I wasn't a total loss. He asked me to study law, and I did."

"What an obedient child," Kirk said.

"I didn't mind – in fact, I rather liked it. You see, frivolous things never have appealed to me."

"I'm afraid that's true. And it worries me."

"Why should it?"

"Because, as it happens, I'm one of those frivolous things."

"But surely you have your serious side?"

"No – I'm afraid that side was just sketched in – never finished. However, I'm working on it. Before I get through you'll be calling me deacon."

"Really? I'm afraid I've never cared much for deacons, either."

"Well, not exactly deacon, then. I'll try to strike a happy medium."

"I'll help you," smiled the girl.

Kirk parked his car in a side street, and they went round the corner to the Kirk Building. It was Grace Lane who took them aloft. Kirk studied her with a new interest. Strands of dark red hair crept out from beneath her cap; her face was pale, but unlined and young. Age uncertain, Kirk thought, but beauty unmistakable. What was the secret of her past? Why had Sir Frederic brought to the Kirk Building that clipping about Jennie Jerome?

"I'll be along in a minute," Miss Morrow said, when the elevator stopped at the twentieth floor. Kirk nodded and preceded her to the roof. She followed almost immediately. "I wanted to ask a question or two," she explained. "You see, I gave Grace Lane very little attention on the night Sir Frederic was killed."

"What do you think of her – now that you've looked again?"

"She's a lady – if you don't mind an overworked word. This job she has now is beneath her."

"Think so?" Kirk took Miss Morrow's coat. "I should have said that most of the time, it's over her head."

The girl shrugged. "That from you, deacon," she said, reproachfully.

Chan and Captain Flannery were at the door, and Kirk let them in. The Captain was all business.

"Hello," he said. "Now if you'll show us that butler's room, Mr Kirk, we'll get busy right away. I've brought a few skeleton keys. We'll go over the place like a vacuum cleaner." Kirk led them into the corridor.

"How about the cook's room?" Flannery added. "We might take a look at that."

"My cook's a Frenchman," Kirk explained. "He sleeps out."

"Humph. He was here the other night at the time of the murder?"

"Yes, of course."

"Well, I'd better have a talk with him some time."

"He speaks very little English," Kirk smiled. "You'll enjoy him." He left the two in the butler's bedroom, and returned to Miss Morrow.

"I suppose you hate the sight of a kitchen," he suggested.

"Why should I?"

"Well – a big lawyer like you—"

"But I've studied cook-books, too. You'd be surprised. I can cook the most delicious—"

"Rarebit," he finished. "I know. And your chocolate fudge was famous at the sorority house. I've heard it before."

"Please let me finish. I was going to say, pot roast. And my lemon pie is not so bad, either."

He stood solemnly regarding her. "Lady," he announced, "you improve on acquaintance. And if that isn't gilding the lily, I don't know what is. Come with me and we'll dig up the tea things."

She followed him to the kitchen. "I've got a little apartment," she said. "And when I'm not too tired, I get my own dinner."

"How are you on Thursday nights?" he asked. "Pretty tired?"

"That depends. Why?"

"Servants' night out. Need I say more?"

Miss Morrow laughed. "I'll remember," she promised. With deft hands she set the water to boiling, and began to arrange the tea tray. "How neat everything is," she remarked. "Paradise is a wonder."

"Tell that to my grandmother," Kirk suggested. "She believes that a man who lives alone wallows in grime and waste. Every home needs a woman's touch, according to her story."

"Absurd," cried the girl.

"Oh, well – grandmother dates back a few years. In her day women were housekeepers. Now they're movie fans, club members, lawyers – what have you? Must have been a rather comfortable age at that."

"For the men, yes."

"And men don't count any more."

"I wouldn't say that. I guess we're ready now."

Kirk carried the tray to the living-room, and placed it on a low table before the fire. Miss Morrow sat down behind it. He threw a couple of logs on to the glowing embers, then, visiting the dining-room, returned with a bottle, a siphon and glasses.

"Mustn't forget that Captain Flannery doesn't approve of tea," he said.

Miss Morrow looked toward the passageway. "They'd better hurry, or they'll be late for the party," she remarked.

But Chan and Flannery did not appear. Outside the March dusk was falling; a sharp wind swept through the little garden and rattled insistently at the casements. Kirk drew the curtains. On the hearth the fresh logs flamed, filling the room with a warm, satisfying glow. He took from Miss Morrow's hand his cup of tea, selected a small cake, and dropped into a chair.

"Cozy – that would be my word for this," he smiled. "To look at you now, no one would ever suspect that old affair between you and Blackstone."

"I'm versatile, anyhow," she said.

"I wonder," he replied.

"Wonder what?"

"I wonder just how versatile you are. It's a matter I intend to investigate further. I may add that I am regarded throughout the world as the greatest living judge of a lemon pie."

"You frighten me," Miss Morrow said.

"If your testimony has been the truth, so help you," he answered, "what is there to be frightened about?"

At that moment Chan and Flannery appeared in the doorway. The Captain seemed very pleased with himself.

"What luck?" Kirk inquired.

"The best," beamed Flannery. He carried a piece of paper in his hand. "Ah – shall I help myself?"

"By all means," Kirk told him. "A congratulatory potion. Mr Chan – what's yours?"

"Tea, if Miss Morrow will be so kind. Three lumps of sugar and the breath of the lemon in passing."

The girl prepared his cup. Flannery dropped into a chair.

"I see you've found something," Kirk suggested.

"I certainly have," the Captain replied. "I've found the letter from Scotland Yard that Paradise nabbed from the mail."

"Good enough," cried Kirk.

"A slick bird, this Paradise," Flannery went on. "Where do you think he had it? All folded up in a little wad and tucked into the toe of a shoe."

"How clever of you to look there," Miss Morrow approved.

Flannery hesitated. "Well – er – come to think of it, I didn't. It was Sergeant Chan here dug it up. Yes, sir – the Sergeant's getting to be a real sleuth."

"Under your brilliant instruction," smiled Chan.

"Well, we can all learn from each other," conceded the Captain. "Anyhow, he found it, and turned it right over to me. The letter that came in the Scotland Yard envelope – no question about it. See – at the top – the Metropolitan Police—"

"If it's not asking too much," said Kirk, "what's in the letter?"

Flannery's face fell. "Not a whole lot. We'll have to admit that. But little by little—"

"With brief steps we advance," put in Chan. "Humbly suggest you read the epistle."

"Well, it's addressed to Sir Frederic, care of Cook's, San Francisco," said Flannery. He read:

"Dear Sir Frederic: I was very glad to get your letter from Shanghai and to know that you are near the end of a long trail. It is indeed surprising news to me that the murder of Hilary Galt and the disappearance of Eve Durand from Peshawar are, in your final analysis, linked together. I know you always contended they were, but much as I admire your talents, I felt sure you were mistaken. I can only apologize most humbly. It is a matter of regret to me that you did not tell me more; what you wrote roused my interest to a high pitch. Believe me, I shall be eager to hear the end of this strange case.

"By the way, Inspector Rupert Duff will be in the States on another matter at about the time you reach San Francisco. You know Duff, of course. A good man. If you should require his help, you have only to wire him at the Hotel Waldorf, New York.

"With all good wishes for a happy outcome to your investigation, I am, sir, always, your obedient servant, Martin Benfield, Deputy-Commissioner."

Flannery stopped reading and looked at the others. "Well, there you are," he said. "The Galt affair and Eve Durand are mixed up together. Of course that ain't exactly news – I've known it right along. What I want to find out now is, why did Paradise try to keep this information from us? What's his stake in the affair? I could arrest him at once, but I'm afraid that if I do, he'll shut up like a clam and that will end it. He doesn't know we're wise to him, so I'm going to put this letter back where we found it and give him a little more rope. The Sergeant here has agreed to keep an eye on him, and I rely on you, too, Mr Kirk, to see that he doesn't get away."

"Don't worry," said Kirk. "I don't want to lose him."

Flannery rose. "Sir Frederic's mail isn't coming here any more?" he inquired of Miss Morrow.

"No, of course not. I arranged to have it sent to my office. There's been nothing of interest – purely personal matters."

"I must put this letter back, and then I'll have to run along," the Captain said. He went into the passageway.

"Well," remarked Kirk, "Paradise hangs on a little longer. I see your handiwork there, Sergeant, and you have my warmest thanks."

"For a brief time, at least," Chan said. "You will perceive I am no person's fool. I do not arrange arrest of butler in house where I am guest. I protect him, and I would do same for the cook."

Flannery returned. "I got to get back to the station," he announced. "Mr Kirk, thanks for your – er – hospitality."

Miss Morrow looked up at him. "You are going to wire to New York for Inspector Duff?" she asked.

"I am not," the Captain said.

"But he might be of great help—"

"Nix," cut in Flannery stubbornly. "I got about all the help I can stand on this case now. Get him here and have him under foot? No, sir – I'm going to find out first who killed Sir Frederic. After that, they can all come. Don't you say so, Sergeant?"

Chan nodded. "You are wise man. The ship with too many steersmen never reaches port."

XI

THE MUDDY WATER CLEARS

Flannery departed, and Miss Morrow picked up her coat. Reluctantly Kirk held it for her. "Must you go?" he protested.

"Back to the office – yes," she said. "I've oceans of work. The district attorney keeps asking me for results in this investigation, and so far all I have been able to report is further mysteries. I wonder if I'll ever have anything else."

"It was my hope," remarked Chan, "that today we take a seven-league step forward. But it is fated otherwise. Not before Monday now."

"Monday," repeated the girl. "What do you mean, Mr Chan?"

"I mean I experience great yearning to bring Miss Gloria Garland to this building again. I have what my cousin Willie Chan, a vulgar speaker, calls a hunch. But this morning when I call Miss Garland on the telephone I learn that she is absent in Del Monte, and will not return until Sunday night."

"Miss Garland? What has she to do with it?"

"Remains to be observed. She may have much, or nothing. Depends on the authentic value of my hunch. Monday will tell."

"But Monday," sighed Miss Morrow. "This is only Thursday."

Chan also sighed. "I too resent that with bitter feelings. Do not forget that I have sworn to be on boat departing Wednesday. My little son demands me."

"Patience," laughed Barry Kirk. "The doctor must take his own medicine."

"I know," shrugged Chan. "I am taking same in plenty large doses. Mostly when I talk of patience, I am forcing it on others. Speaking for myself in this event, I do not much enjoy the flavor."

"You said nothing about your hunch to Captain Flannery," Miss Morrow remarked.

Chan smiled. "Can you speak of the ocean to a well frog, or of ice to a summer insect? The good Captain would sneer – until I prove to him I am exceedingly correct. I am praying to do that on Monday."

"In the meantime, we watch and wait," said Miss Morrow.

"You wait, and I will watch," suggested Chan.

Kirk accompanied Miss Morrow to the door. "*Au revoir*," he said. "And whatever you do, don't lose that lemon pie recipe."

"You needn't keep hinting," she replied. "I won't forget."

Upon Kirk's return, Charlie regarded him keenly. "A most attracting young woman," he remarked.

"Charming," agreed Kirk.

"What a deep pity," Chan continued, "that she squanders glowing youth in a man's pursuit. She should be at mothering work."

Kirk laughed. "You tell her," he suggested.

On Friday, Bill Rankin called Chan on the telephone. He had been through the *Globe's* files for the year 1913, he said – a long, arduous job. His search had been without result; he could find no story about Eve Durand. Evidently cable news had not greatly interested the *Globe's* staff in those days.

"I'm going to the public library for another try," he announced. "No doubt some of the New York papers carried the story. They seem our best bet now. I'm terribly busy, but I'll speed all I can."

"Thanks for your feverish activity," Chan replied. "You are valuable man."

"Just a real good wagon," laughed Rankin. "Here's hoping I don't break down. I'll let you know the minute I find something."

Saturday came; the life at the bungalow was moving forward with unbroken calm. Through it Paradise walked with his accustomed dignity and poise, little dreaming of the dark cloud of suspicion that hovered over his head. Chan was busy with the books of Colonel John Beetham; he had finished the *Life* and was now going methodically through the others as though in search of a clue.

On Saturday night Kirk was dining out, and after his own dinner Chan again went down into Chinatown. There was little he could do there, he knew, but the place drew him none the less. This time he did not visit his cousin, but loitered on the crowded sidewalk of Grant Avenue.

Catching sight of the lights outside the Mandarin Theater, he idly turned his footsteps toward the doorway. The Chinese have been a civilized race for many centuries; they do not care greatly for moving-pictures, preferring the spoken drama. A huge throng was milling about the door of the theater, and Chan paused. There was usually enough drama in real life to satisfy him, but tonight he felt the need of the painted players.

Suddenly in the mob he caught sight of Willie Li, the boy scout whose good deed had thwarted his best laid plans on the previous Wednesday evening. Willie was gazing wistfully at the little frame of actors' pictures in the lobby. Chan went up to him with a friendly smile.

"Ah, we meet again," he said in Cantonese. "How fortunate, since the other night I walked my way churlishly, without offering my thanks for the great kindness you did me in bringing a physician."

The boy's face brightened in recognition. "May I be permitted to hope that the injury is improved?" he said.

"You have a kind heart," Chan replied. "I now walk on the foot with the best of health. Be good enough to tell me, have you performed your kind act for today?"

The boy frowned. "Not yet. Opportunities are so seldom."

"Ah, yes – how true. But if you will deign to come into the theater as my guest, opportunities may increase. Each of the actors, as you know, receives in addition to his salary a bonus of twenty-five cents for every round of applause that is showered upon him. Come, and by frequent applauding you may pile up enough kind acts to spread over several days."

The boy was only too willing, and buying a couple of tickets, Chan led him inside. The horrible din that greeted them they did not find disconcerting. It was, in fact, music to their ears. Even at this early hour the house was crowded. On the stage, with the casual, offhand manner they affected, the Chinese company was enacting a famous historical play. Chan and the boy were fortunate enough to find seats.

Looking about, the detective from Hawaii saw that he was in a gathering of his own race exclusively. The women members of the audience were arrayed in their finest silks; in a stage box sat a slave girl famous in the colony. Little, slant-eyed children played in the aisles; occasionally a mother sent out to the refreshment booth in the lobby a bottle of milk, to be heated for the baby in her arms.

The clatter of the six-piece orchestra never ceased; it played more softly at dramatic moments, but comedy lines were spoken to the accompaniment of a terrific fusillade. Chan became engrossed in the play, for the actors were finished artists, the women players particularly graceful and accomplished. At eleven o'clock he suggested that they had better go, lest the boy's family be troubled about him.

"My father will not worry," said Willie Li. "He knows a boy scout is trustworthy."

Nevertheless Chan led him to the lobby, and there stood treat to a hot dog and a cup of coffee – for the refreshment booth alone was Americanized. As they climbed the empty street to the Oriental Apartments. Charlie looked inquiringly at the boy.

"Tell me," he said, still speaking in Cantonese, "of your plans for the future. You are ambitious. What profession calls you?"

"I would be an explorer, like my cousin Li Gung," the boy answered in the same rather stilted tongue.

"Ah, yes – he who is attached to Colonel John Beetham," nodded Chan. "You have heard from your cousin stories of Colonel Beetham?"

"Many exciting ones," the boy replied.

"You admire the Colonel? You think him very great character?"

"Why not? He is man of iron, stern but just. Discipline is with him important thing, and all boy scouts know that is right thinking. Many examples of this our cousin told us. Sometimes, Li Gung said, the caravan would revolt. Then the Colonel would snatch out gun, facing them with his bravery, alone. The caravan would tremble and proceed."

"They knew, perhaps, that the Colonel would not hesitate to fire?"

"They had seen him do it. One event Li Gung spoke about I can never forget." The boy's voice rose in excitement. "It was on the desert, and the Colonel had told them what they must do, and what they must not do. A dirty keeper of camels, a man of low character, he did a thing which the Colonel had forbidden. In an instant he lay on the sand, with a bullet in his heart."

"Ah, yes," said Chan, "I would expect that. However, it is an incident I have not encountered in any of the Colonel's books."

They were at the door of the apartment-house. "Accept my thanks, please," Willie Li said. "You have done a very kind deed to me."

Chan smiled. "Your company was a real pleasure. I hope we meet again."

"I hope it, too," answered Willie Li warmly. "Good night."

Chan walked slowly back to the Kirk Building. He was thinking of Colonel Beetham. A hard man, a man who did not hesitate to kill those who opposed their will to his. Here was food for thought.

On Sunday Barry Kirk called up Miss Morrow and suggested a ride into the country and dinner at a distant inn. "Just to clear the cobwebs from your brain," he put it.

"Thanks for the ad," she answered. "So that's how my brain strikes you? Cobwebby."

"You know what I mean," he protested. "I want you to keep keen and alert. Nothing must happen to that pie."

They spent a happy, care-free day on roads far from the rush of city traffic. When Kirk helped the girl out of the car before her door that night, he said: "Well, tomorrow morning Charlie springs his hunch."

"What do you imagine he has up his sleeve?"

"I haven't an idea. The more I see of him, the less I know him. But let's hope it's something good."

"And illuminating," added Miss Morrow. "I feel the need of a little light." She held out her hand. "You've been lovely to me today."

"Give me another chance," he said. "Give me lots of 'em. I'll get lovelier and lovelier as time goes on."

"Is that a threat?" she laughed.

"A promise. I hope you don't mind."

"Why should I? Good night." She entered the lobby of her apartment-house.

On Monday morning Chan was brisk and businesslike. He called Gloria Garland and was much relieved to hear her answering voice. She agreed to come to the bungalow at ten o'clock, and Charlie at once got in touch with Miss Morrow and asked her to come at the same hour, bringing Captain Flannery. Then he turned to Kirk.

"Making humble suggestion," he said, "would you be so kind as to dispatch Paradise on lengthy errand just as ten o'clock hour approaches. I do not fancy him in bungalow this morning."

"Surely," agreed Kirk. "I'll send him out for some fishing tackle. I never get time to fish, but a man can't have too much tackle."

At fifteen minutes of ten Chan rose and got his hat. He would, he said, himself escort Miss Garland to the bungalow. Going below, he took up his stand in the doorway of the Kirk Building.

He saw Miss Morrow and Flannery enter, but gave them only a cool nod as they passed. Mystified, they went on upstairs. Kirk met them at the door.

"Here we are," growled Flannery. "I wonder what the Sergeant's up to. If he's got me here on a wild goose chase, I'll deport him to Hawaii. I'm too busy today to feel playful."

"Oh, Chan will make good," Kirk assured him. "By the way, I suppose you've got that elevator girl – Jennie Jerome, or Grace Lane, or whatever her name is – under your eagle eye?"

"Yes. The boys have been shadowing her."

"Find out anything?"

"Not a thing. She's got a room on Powell Street. Stays in nights and minds her own business, as far as I can learn."

Down at the door, Chan was greeting Gloria Garland. "You are promptly on the minute," he approved. "A delectable virtue."

"I'm here, but I don't know what you want," she replied. "I told you everything the other day—"

"Yes, of course. Will you be kind enough to walk after me? We rise aloft."

He took her up in a car run by a black-haired Irish girl, and they entered the living-room of the bungalow.

"Ah, Captain – Miss Morrow – we are all here. That is correct," Charlie said. "Miss Garland, will you kindly recline on chair."

The woman sat down, obviously puzzled. Her eyes sought Flannery's. "What do you want with me now?" she asked.

The Captain shrugged his broad shoulders. "Me – I don't want you. It's Sergeant Chan here. He's had a mysterious hunch."

Chan smiled. "Yes, I am guilty party, Miss Garland. I hope I have not rudely unconvenienced you?"

"Not a bit," she answered.

"One day you told us of the girl Marie Lantelme, who disappeared so oddly out of Nice," Chan continued. "Will you kindly state – you have still not encountered her?"

"No, of course not," the woman replied.

"You are quite sure you would recognize her if you met her?"

"Of course. I knew her well."

Chan's eyes narrowed. "There would be no reason why you would conceal act of recognition from us? I might humbly remind you, this is serious affair."

"No – why should I do that? I'll tell you if I see her – but I'm sure I haven't—"

"Very good. Will you remain in present posture until my return?" Chan went rapidly out to the stairway leading to the floor below.

They looked at one another in wonder, but no one spoke. In a moment, Chan returned. With him came Grace Lane, the elevator girl whom Mrs Enderby had identified as Jennie Jerome.

She came serenely into the room, and stood there. The sunlight fell full upon her, outlining clearly her delicately modeled face. Gloria Garland started, and half rose from her chair.

"Marie!" she cried. "Marie Lantelme! What are you doing here?"

They gasped. A look of triumph shone in Chan's narrow eyes.

The girl's poise did not desert her. "Hello, Gloria," she said softly. "We meet again."

"But where have you been, my dear?" Miss Garland wanted to know. "Where did you go – and why—"

The girl stopped her. "Some other time—" she said.

In a daze, Flannery rose to his feet. "Look here," he began. "Let me get this straight." He moved forward accusingly, "You are Marie Lantelme?"

"I was – once," she nodded.

"You were singing in the same troupe as Miss Garland here – eleven years ago, at Nice? You disappeared?"

"I did."

"Why?"

"I was tired of it. I found I didn't like the stage. If I had stayed, they would have forced me to go on. So I ran away."

"Yeah. And seven years ago you were in New York – a model for a dressmaker. Your name then was Jennie Jerome. You disappeared again?"

"For the same reason. I didn't care for the work. I – I'm restless, I guess—"

"I'll say you're restless. You kept changing names?"

"I wanted to start all over. A new person."

Flannery glared at her. "There's something queer about you, my girl. You know who I am, don't you?"

"You appear to be a policeman."

"Well, that's right. I am."

"I have never done anything wrong. I am not afraid."

"Maybe not. But tell me this – what do you know about Sir Frederic Bruce?"

"I know that he was a famous man from Scotland Yard, who was killed in Mr Kirk's office last Tuesday night."

"Ever see him before he came here?"

"No, sir – I never had."

"Ever hear of him?"

"I don't believe so."

Her even, gentle answers put Flannery at a loss. He stood, considering. His course was far from clear.

"You were running the elevator here last Tuesday night?" he continued.

"Yes, sir, I was."

"Have you any idea why Sir Frederic was hunting for you? For Marie Lantelme, or Jennie Jerome, or whoever you really are?"

She frowned. "Was he hunting for me? How strange. No, sir, – I have no idea at all."

"Well," said Flannery, "let me tell you this. You're a pretty important witness in the matter of Sir Frederic's murder, and I don't intend you shall get away."

The girl smiled. "So I judge. I seem to have been followed rather closely the past few days."

"Well, you'll be followed even more closely from now on. One false move, and I lock you up. You understand that?"

"Perfectly, sir."

"All right. Just tend to your work, and when I want you, I'll tell you so. You can go now."

"Thank you, sir," the girl replied, and went out.

Flannery turned to Miss Garland. "You recognized her the other night, didn't you?" he demanded.

"Oh, but I assure you, I didn't. I recognized her today for the first time."

"Which is plenty time enough," said Chan. "Miss Garland, we are sunk deep in your debt. I permit you now to depart—"

"Yeah – you can go," added Flannery. "Take some other car and keep away from your old friend until this thing's cleared up."

"I'll do that," Miss Garland assured him. "I'm afraid she didn't want me to identify her. I do hope I haven't got her into trouble."

"That depends," answered Flannery, and Kirk showed the actress out.

Chan was beaming. "Hunch plenty good, after all," he chuckled.

"Well, where are we?" Flannery said. "The elevator girl is Jennie Jerome. Then she's Marie Lantelme. What does that mean?"

"It means only one thing," said Miss Morrow softly.

"The Captain is pretending to be dense," suggested Chan. "He could not really be so thick."

"What are you talking about?" Flannery demanded.

"My hunch, which has come so nicely true," Chan told him. "The elevator girl is Jennie Jerome. Next, she is Marie Lantelme. What does it mean, you ask? It means one thing only. She is also Eve Durand."

"By heaven!" Flannery cried.

"Consider how the muddy water clears," Chan went on. "Eve Durand flees from India one dark night fifteen years ago. Four years later she is found in Nice, playing in theater. Something happens – maybe she is seen and recognized – again she runs away. Another four years elapse and we encounter her in New York, walking in model gowns. Again something happens, again she disappears. Where does she go? Eventually, to San Francisco. Here opportunities are not so good, she must take more lowly position. And here Sir Frederic comes, always seeking for Eve Durand."

"It's beautifully clear," approved Miss Morrow.

"Like lake at evening," nodded Chan. "Sir Frederic, though he has looked long for this woman, has never seen her. He can upearth here no one who can identify Eve Durand, but he remembers once she was Marie Lantelme, once Jennie Jerome. In this great city, he learns, are two people who have known her when she was wearing these other names. He asks that they be invited to dinner, hoping that one or both will point out to him the woman he has trailed so long."

Flannery was walking the floor. "Well – I don't know. It's almost too good to be true. But if it is – if she's Eve Durand – then I can't let her wander around loose. I'll have to lock her up this morning. If I could only be sure—"

"I am telling you," persisted Chan.

"I know, but you are guessing. You've identified her as those other two, but as for Eve Durand—"

The telephone rang. Kirk answered, and handed it to Flannery, "For you, Captain," he said.

Flannery took the telephone. "Oh – hello, Chief," he said. "Yeah – yeah. What's that? Oh – oh, he is? Good enough. Thank you, Chief. I sure will."

He hung up the receiver and turned to the others. A broad smile was on his face.

"We're going to find out, Sergeant, just how good a guesser you are," he said. "I'll put a couple of extra men to following this dame, but I won't do anything more until tomorrow. Yes, sir – by tomorrow evening I'll know whether she's Eve Durand or not."

"Your words have obscure sound," Chan told him.

"The Chief of Police has just had a wire," Flannery explained. "Inspector Duff of Scotland Yard is getting in tomorrow afternoon at two thirty. And he's bringing with him the one man in all the world who's sure to know Eve Durand when he sees her. He's bringing the woman's husband, Major Eric Durand."

XII

A MISTY EVENING

When Chan and Kirk were left alone, the little detective sat staring thoughtfully into space. "Now Tuesday becomes the big day for keen anticipation," he remarked. "What will it reveal? Much, I hope, for my time on the mainland becomes a brief space indeed."

Kirk looked at him in wonder. "Surely you won't go on Wednesday, if this thing isn't solved?"

Chan nodded stubbornly. "I have made unspoken promise to Barry Chan. Now I put it into words. Tomorrow Eve Durand's husband arrives. In all the world we could have selected no more opportune person. He will identify this elevator woman as his wife, or he will not. If he does, perhaps case is finished. If he does not" – Charlie shrugged – "then I have done all possible. Let Captain Flannery flounder alone after that."

"Well, we won't cross our oceans until we get to them," Kirk suggested. "A lot may happen before Wednesday. By the way, I've been meaning to take you over to the Cosmopolitan Club. How about lunching there this noon?"

Chan brightened. "I have long nursed desire to see that famous interior. You are most kind."

"All set, then," replied his host. "I have some business in the office. Come downstairs for me at twelve thirty. And when Paradise returns, please tell him we're lunching out."

He took his hat and coat and went below. Chan strolled aimlessly to the window and stood looking down on the glittering city. His eyes strayed to the Matson dock, the pier shed and, beyond, the red funnels of a familiar ship. A ship that was sailing, day after tomorrow, for Honolulu harbor. Would he be on it? He had sworn, yes – and yet—He sighed deeply. The door-bell rang, and he admitted Bill Rankin, the reporter.

"Hello," said Rankin. "Glad to find you in. I spent all day yesterday at the public library, and say, I'll bet I stirred up more dust than the chariot in *Ben Hur*."

"With any luck?" Chan inquired.

"Yes. I finally found the story in the files of the *New York Sun*. A great newspaper in those days – but I won't talk shop. It was just a brief item with the Peshawar date line – I copied it down. Here it is."

Charlie took the sheet of yellow paper, and read a short cable story that told him nothing he did not already know. Eve Durand, the young wife of a certain Captain Eric Durand, had disappeared under mysterious circumstances two nights previously, while on a picnic party in the hills outside Peshawar. The authorities were greatly alarmed, and parties of British soldiers were scouring the wild countryside.

"Item has date, May fifth," remarked Chan. "Then Eve Durand was lost on night of May third, the year 1913. You found nothing else?"

"There were no follow-up stories," Rankin replied. "And no mention of Beetham, as you hoped. Say – what in Sam Hill could he have to do with this?"

"Nothing," said Chan promptly. "It was one of my small mistakes. Even great detective sometimes steps off on wrong foot. My wrong foot often weary from too much use."

"Well, what's going on, anyhow?" Rankin wanted to know. "I've hounded Flannery, and I've tried Miss Morrow, and not a thing do I learn. My city editor is waxing very sarcastic. Can't you give me a tip to help me out?"

Chan shook his head. "It would be plenty poor ethics for me to talk about the case. I am in no authority here, and already Captain Flannery regards me with the same warm feeling he would show pick-pocket from Los Angeles. Pursuing the truth further, there is nothing to tell you, anyhow. We are not as yet close to anything that might indicate happy success."

"I'm sorry to hear it," Rankin said.

"Situation will not continue," Chan assured him. "Light will break. For the present we swim with one foot on the ground, but in good time we will plunge into center of the stream. Should I be on scene when success is looming, I will be happy to give you little secret hint."

"If you're on the scene? What are you talking about?"

"Personal affairs call me home with a loud megaphone. On Wednesday I go whether case is solved or not."

"Yes – like you did last Wednesday," Rankin laughed. "You can't kid me. The patient Oriental isn't going to get impatient at the wrong minute. Well, I must run. Remember your promise about the hint."

"I have lengthy memory," Chan replied. "And already I owe you much. Goodby."

When the reporter had gone, Charlie stood staring at the copy of that cable story. "May third, nineteen hundred thirteen," he said aloud. With a surprisingly quick step he went to a table and took from it the *Life* of Colonel John Beetham. He ran hastily through the pages until he found the thing he sought. Then for a long moment he sat in a chair with the book open on his knee, staring into space.

At precisely twelve thirty he entered Kirk's office. The young man rose and, accepting some papers from his secretary put them into a leather briefcase. "Got to see a lawyer after lunch," he explained. "Not a nice lawyer, either – a man this time." They went to the Cosmopolitan Club.

When they had checked their hats and coats and returned to the lobby in that imposing building, Chan looked about him with deep interest. The Cosmopolitan's fame was widespread; it was the resort of men active in the arts, in finance and in journalism. Kirk's popularity there was proved by many jovial greetings. He introduced Chan to a number of his friends, and the detective was presently the center of a pleasant group. With difficulty they got away to lunch in one corner of the big dining-room.

It was toward the close of the lunch that Chan, looking up, saw approaching the man who interested him most at the moment. Colonel John Beetham's hard-bitten face was more grim than ever, seen in broad daylight. He paused at their table.

"How are you, Kirk?" he said. "And Mr Chan. I'll sit down a moment, if I may."

"By all means," Kirk agreed cordially. "How about lunch? What can I order for you?"

"Thanks, I've just finished," Beetham replied.

"A cigarette, then." Kirk held out his case.

"Good of you." The Colonel took one and lighted it. "I haven't seen you since that beastly dinner. Oh – I beg your pardon – you get my meaning?... What a horrible thing that was – a man like Sir Frederic – by the way, have they any idea who did it?"

Kirk shrugged. "If they have, they're not telling me."

"Sergeant Chan – perhaps you are working on the case?" Beetham suggested.

Chan's eyes narrowed. "The affair concerns mainland police. I am stranger here, like yourself."

"Ah, yes, of course," responded Beetham. "I just happened to recall that you were on the point of leaving, and I thought, seeing you had stayed over—"

"If I can help, I will do so," Chan told him. He was thinking deeply. A man like Colonel Beetham did not note the comings and goings of a Charlie Chan without good reason.

"How's the new expedition shaping up?" Kirk inquired.

"Slowly – rather slowly," Beetham frowned. "Speaking of that, I have wanted a chat with you on the subject. Your grandmother has offered to help with the financing, but I have hesitated – it's a stiff sum."

"How much?"

"I have part of the money. I still need about fifty thousand dollars."

Kirk's eyebrows went up. "Ah, yes – quite a nest-egg. But if grandmother wants to do it – well, it's her own money."

"Glad you feel that way about it," said Beetham. "I was fearful the other members of the family might think I was using undue influence. The whole idea was hers – I give you my word."

"Naturally," Kirk answered. "I'm sure she would enjoy it, at that."

"The results will be most important from a scientific point of view," Beetham continued. "Your grandmother's name would be highly honored. I would see that she had full credit."

"Just what sort of expedition is it?" Kirk asked.

The tired eyes lighted for the first time. "Well, I had a bit of luck when I was last on the Gobi Desert. I stumbled on to the ruins of a city that must have been flourishing early in the first century. Only had time to take a brief look – but I turned up coins that bore the date of 7 A.D. I unearthed the oldest papers in existence – papers that bore the scrawl of little children – arithmetic – seven times seven and the like. Letters written by the military governor of the city, scraps of old garments, jewelry – amazing mementoes of the past. I am keen to go back and make a thorough investigation. Of course, the trouble in China will interfere, rather – but there is always trouble in China. I have waited long enough. I shall get through somehow. I always have."

"Well, I don't envy you," Kirk smiled. "The way I've always felt, when you've seen one desert, you've seen 'em all. But you have my best wishes."

"Thanks. You're frightfully kind," Beetham rose. "I hope to settle the matter in a few days. I am hoping, also, that before I leave, the murderer of Sir Frederic will be found. Struck me as a good chap, Sir Frederic."

Chan looked up quickly. "A great admirer of yours, Colonel Beetham," he said.

"Admirer of mine? Sir Frederic? Was he really?" The Colonel's tone was cool and even.

"Undubitable fact. Among his effects we find many books written by you."

Beetham threw down his cigarette. "That was good of him. I am quite flattered. If by any chance you are concerned in the hunt for the person who killed him, Sergeant Chan, I wish you the best of luck."

He strolled away from the table, while Chan looked after him thoughtfully.

"Reminds me of the snows of Tibet," Kirk said. "Just as warm and human. Except when he spoke of his dead city. That seemed to rouse him. An odd fish, isn't he, Charlie?"

"An odd fish from icy waters," Chan agreed. "I am wondering—"

"Yes?"

"He regrets Sir Frederic's passing. But might it not happen that beneath his weeping eyes are laughing teeth?"

They went to the check-room, where they retrieved their hats and coats and Kirk's briefcase. As they walked down the street, Kirk looked at Chan.

"Just remembered the Cosmopolitan Club year-book," he said. "You don't imagine it meant anything, do you?"

Chan shrugged. "Imagination does not seem to thrive on mainland climate," he replied.

Kirk went off to his lawyer's and Charlie returned home to await a more promising tomorrow.

On Tuesday afternoon Miss Morrow was the first to arrive at the bungalow. She came in about three thirty. The day was dark, with gusts of wind and rain, but the girl was glowing.

Kirk helped her off with her rain-coat. "You seem to be filled with vim and vigor," he said.

"Walked all the way," she told him. "I was too excited to sit calmly in a taxi. Just think – in a few minutes we may see the meeting between Major Durand and his long lost wife."

"The Major has arrived?" Chan inquired.

"Yes – he and Inspector Duff came half an hour ago. Their train was a trifle late. Captain Flannery went to the station to meet them. He telephoned me they'd be along shortly. It seems that, like a true Englishman, the Major didn't care to talk with anybody until he'd gone to a hotel and had his tub."

"Don't blame him, after that trip from Chicago," Kirk said. "I believe little Jennie Jerome Marie Lantelme is on the elevator."

Miss Morrow nodded. "She is. I saw her when I came up. I wonder if she is really Eve Durand? Won't it be thrilling if she is!"

"She's got to be. She's Charlie's hunch."

"Do not be too certain," Chan objected. "In the past it has often happened I was hoarsely barking up incorrect tree."

Kirk stirred the fire, and drew up a wide chair for the girl. "Here you are – a trifle large for you, but you may grow. I'll give you tea later. These Englishmen probably can't do a thing until they've had their Oolong."

The girl sat down, and, dropping into a chair at her side, Kirk began to talk airily of nothing in particular. He was conscious that at his back Chan was nervously walking the floor.

"Better sit down, Charlie," he suggested. "You act like a man in a dentist's waiting-room."

"Feel that way," Chan told him. "Much is at stake now for me. If I have taken wrong turning, I shall have to endure some Flannery sneers."

It was four o'clock, and the dusk was falling outside the lofty windows, when the bell rang. Kirk himself went to the door. He admitted Flannery and a thick-set young Englishman. Two men only – Kirk peered past them down the stairs, but the third man was not in evidence.

"Hello," Flannery said, striding in. "Major Durand not here yet, eh?"

"He is not," Kirk replied. "Don't tell me you've mislaid him."

"Oh, no," Flannery answered. "I'll explain in a minute. Miss Morrow, meet Inspector Duff, of Scotland Yard."

The girl came forward, smiling. "I'm so glad," she said.

"Charmed," remarked Duff, in a hearty, roast-beef-of-Old-England voice. He was surprisingly young, with rosy cheeks, and the look of a farmer about him. And indeed it had been from a farm in Yorkshire that he had come to London and the Metropolitan police.

"The Inspector and I went from the train to my office," Flannery explained. "I wanted to go over the records of our case with him. The Major stopped at the hotel to brush up – he'll be along in a minute. Oh, yes – Mr Kirk, Inspector Duff. And this, Inspector, is Sergeant Charlie Chan, of the Honolulu police."

Chan bowed low. "A moment that will live for ever in my memory," he said.

"Oh – er – really?" Duff replied. "The Captain's told me of you, Sergeant. We're in the same line – some miles apart."

"Many miles apart," conceded Charlie gravely.

"Look here," said Flannery, "it will be just as well if the Major doesn't meet that girl in the elevator until we're all set for it. Somebody should go below and steer him into a different car."

"I will be happy to perform that service," Chan offered.

"No – I know him by sight – I'll do it," Flannery replied. "I want to have a word with the men I've got watching her.

I saw one of them in front of the building when I came in. Inspector – I'll leave you here. You're in good hands." He went out.

Kirk drew up a chair for the English detective. "Give you tea when the Major comes," he said.

"You're very kind, I'm sure," Duff answered.

"You have been all over the case with Captain Flannery?" Miss Morrow inquired.

"I have – from the beginning." Duff replied. "It's a shocking affair – shocking. Sir Frederic was deeply respected – I might even say loved – by all of us. It appears that he was killed in the line of duty, though he had retired and was, supposedly, out of all that. I can assure you that the murder of one of its men is not taken lightly by Scotland Yard. We shall not rest until we have found the guilty person – and in that task, Sergeant, we shall welcome help from every possible source."

Chan bowed. "My abilities are of the slightest, but they are lined up beside your very great ones."

"I had hoped, Inspector," Miss Morrow said, "that you would be able to throw considerable light on this affair."

Duff shook his head. "I'm frightfully sorry. There are so many other men – older men – on our force who would have been of much greater service. Unfortunately I am the only Scotland Yard man in the States at the moment. You see – I'm a bit young—"

"I'd noticed that," smiled the girl.

"All these events that appear to be linked up with Sir Frederic's murder happened before my day. I shall do my best – but—"

"Will you have a cigarette?" Kirk suggested.

"No, thanks. My pipe, if the young lady doesn't object."

"Not at all," said Miss Morrow. "It's quite in the Sherlock Holmes tradition."

Duff smiled. "But the only point of similarity, I fear. As I say, I have been with the Metropolitan police a comparatively brief time – a mere matter of seven years. Of course I have heard of the Hilary Galt murder, though it happened many years ago. As a young policeman I was shown, in the Black Museum, the famous velvet slippers they found Galt wearing that disastrous night. Coming to Eve Durand, I am familiar, in a casual way, with the story of her disappearance. In fact, I had, once, a very slight connection with the case. Five years ago there was a rumor that she had been seen in Paris, and Sir Frederic sent me across the Channel to look into it. It was merely another false alarm, but while making the investigation I chanced to encounter Major Durand, who was also on the ground. Poor chap – that was one of a long series of disappointments for him. I hope he is not to suffer another here tonight."

"How did the Major happen to come to America at this time?" Miss Morrow inquired.

"He came in answer to a cable from Sir Frederic," Duff explained. "Sir Frederic asked his help, and of course he hastened to comply, landing in New York a week ago. When I got off the Twentieth Century in Chicago I discovered Durand had been on the same train. We joined forces and hurried on to San Francisco together."

"Well, he, at least, can help us," Miss Morrow suggested.

"I fancy he can. I repeat, I have been over the case carefully, but I have had no inspiration as yet. One angle of it interests me tremendously – those velvet slippers. Why were they taken? Where are they now? They appear to be again the essential clue. What do you say, Sergeant?"

Chan shrugged. "Slippers were exactly that long time ago," he said. "On which occasion they led positively no place."

"I know," smiled Duff. "But I'm not superstitious. I shall follow them again. By the way, there is one point on which I may be able to offer some help." He turned suddenly to Kirk. "You have a butler named Paradise?" he inquired.

Kirk's heart sank. "Yes – and a very good one," he answered.

"I have been interested in Paradise," said Duff. "And Paradise, I understand, has been interested in Sir Frederic's mail. Where is he now?"

"He's in the kitchen, or his room," Kirk replied. "Do you want to see him?"

"Before I go – yes," Duff said.

Flannery came through the hall, followed by a big, blond man in a dripping Burberry coat. Major Eric Durand, retired, looked to be the sportsman type of Englishman; his cheeks were tanned and weather-beaten, as though from much riding in the open, his blue eyes alert. Indoors, one would picture him sitting in a club with a cigar, a whiskey and soda, and a copy of the *Field*.

"Come in, Major," Flannery said. He introduced the Britisher to the company, and Kirk hurried forward to take the Burberry coat. There followed a moment of awkward silence.

"Major," Flannery began, "we haven't told you why we got you here. You have come to San Francisco in response to a cablegram from Sir Frederic Bruce?"

"I have," said Durand quietly.

"Did he give you any idea of why he wanted you to come?"

"He intimated that he was on the point of finding – my wife."

"I see. Your wife disappeared under unusual circumstances some fifteen years ago, in India?"

"Precisely."

"Did you ever hear of her after that?"

"Never. There were many false reports, of course. We followed them all up, but none of them came to anything in the end."

"You never heard of her at Nice? Or in New York?"

"No – I don't think those were among the places. I'm sure they weren't."

"You would, of course, know her if you saw her now?"

Durand looked up with sudden interest. "I fancy I would. She was only eighteen when she was – lost." Miss Morrow felt a quick twinge of pity for the man. "But one doesn't forget, you know."

"Major," said Flannery slowly, "we have every reason to believe that your wife is in this building tonight."

Durand took a startled step backward. Then he sadly shook his head. "I wish it were true. You've no idea – fifteen years' anxiety – it rather takes it out of a chap. One stops hoping, after a time. Ah, yes – I wish it were true – but there have been so many disappointments. I cannot hope any more."

"Please wait just a minute," Flannery said, and went out.

A strained silence followed his exit. The ticking of a tall clock in a corner became suddenly like the strokes of a hammer. Durand began to pace the floor.

"It can't be," he cried to Duff. "No – it can't be Eve. After all these years – in San Francisco – no, no – I can't believe it."

"We shall know in a moment, old chap," Duff said gently.

The moments lengthened horribly. Chan began to wonder. Durand continued to pace back and forth, silently, over the rug. Still the hammer strokes of the clock. Five minutes – ten –

The outer door was flung open and Flannery burst into the room. His face was crimson, his gray hair disheveled.

"She's gone!" he cried. "Her elevator's standing at the seventh floor, with the door open. She's gone, and no one saw her go!"

Durand gave a little cry and sinking into a chair, buried his face in his hands.

XIII

OLD FRIENDS MEET AGAIN

Major Durand was not the only one to whom Flannery's news came as a shock and a disappointment. On the faces of the four other people in that room dismay was clearly written.

"Gone, and no one saw her go," Chan repeated. He looked reprovingly at the Captain. "Yet she was under watchful eye of clever mainland police."

Flannery snorted. "She was, but we're not supermen. That woman's as slippery as an eel. There were two of my boys on the job – both keen lads – well, no use crying over spilt milk. I'll get her. She can't—"

The door opened and a plain clothes man entered, bringing with him a little old cleaning woman with straggling gray hair.

"Hello, Petersen – what is it?" Flannery asked.

"Listen to this, Chief," said Petersen. "This woman was working in an office on the seventh floor." He turned to her. "Tell the Captain what you told me."

The woman twisted her apron nervously. "In 709 I was, sir. They go home early, and I was alone there at my work. The door opens and this red-headed elevator girl runs in. She's got on a rain-coat, and a hat. 'What's the matter?' I says, but she just runs on into the back room, and sort of wondering, I follow her.

I'm just in time to see her climb on to the fire-escape. Never a word she said, sir – she just disappeared in the night."

"The fire-escape," repeated Flannery. "I thought so. Have you looked at it, Petersen?"

"Yes, sir. It's one of those – you know – a person's weight lets down the last flight of steps to the ground. A simple matter to go like that."

"All right," Flannery answered. "Someone must have seen her when she came out of the alley. We'll go down and have a look round." He turned to the cleaning woman. "That's all. You can go."

The woman passed a second plain clothes man in the hall. He came quickly into the living-room.

"I've got a lead, Captain," he said. "Boy in the cigar store on the corner. He says a girl with a Kirk Building uniform under her coat rushed in a few minutes ago and used his telephone."

"Did he hear the call?"

"No, sir. It's a booth phone. She was there only a few minutes, and then she hurried out again."

"Well, that's something," Flannery said. "You boys wait for me – I've got a car. First of all, I'll send out the alarm. I'll have men at the ferries and the railroad stations – she's a marked woman with that uniform. I'll pick her up before midnight—"

"On what charge?" asked Miss Morrow gently.

"Oh – oh, well – as a witness. I'll take her as a witness. Still that will mean a lot of publicity I don't want at this time. I have it. I'll take her on a charge of stealing. The uniform is your property, Mr Kirk?"

"Yes – but I don't like that," protested Kirk.

"Oh, it's just a fake. We won't press it. I've got to get her on some pretext. Now – if I can use your phone—"

Flannery talked to some purpose to the station house, and the hue and cry after that elusive woman was once more underway. He rose full of energy.

"I'll get her," he promised. "It's a bad set-back to our plans, but it's only for a minute. She can't get away—"

"She is one who has had some success at getting away in the past," Chan reminded him.

"Yeah – but not this time," answered the Captain. "She's never had me on her trail before." He blustered out, followed by his two men.

Major Durand slumped dejectedly in his chair. Inspector Duff was puffing calmly on his well-seasoned pipe.

"It's a bit of hard luck," he remarked. "But patience – that's what counts in this work, eh, Sergeant Chan?"

Charlie beamed. "At last I meet fellow detective who talks same language with me."

Barry Kirk rose and rang the bell. "How about a cup of tea?" he said. He stepped to the window and looked out. Swords of light marking the streets floated dimly in the mist, far below. The wind howled, rain spattered on the panes, the city was shrouded and lost. "It's one of those nights – a little something to warm us up—" He was silent. What a night it was – made to order for the man or woman who sought to slip away and never be seen again.

Paradise entered with calm dignity and stood in the brightly lighted room, his shock of snow-white hair lending him an air of stern respectability.

"You rang, sir?" he said.

"Yes," Kirk replied. "We'll have tea, Paradise. Five of us here—" He stopped. The butler's eyes were on Inspector Duff, and his face was suddenly as white as his hair.

There was a moment of silence. "Hello, Paradise," Duff said quietly.

The butler muttered something, and turned as though to go out.

"Just a moment!" The Inspector's voice was steely cold. "This is a surprise, my man. A surprise for both of us, I fancy.

When I last saw you, you were standing in the dock at Old Bailey." Paradise bowed his head. "Perhaps I shouldn't have been inclined to give you away, Paradise, if you had behaved yourself. But you've been opening mail – haven't you? You've been tampering with a letter addressed to Sir Frederic Bruce?"

"Yes, sir, I have." The servant's voice was very low.

"So I understand," Duff continued. He turned to Barry Kirk. "I'm sorry to distress you, Mr Kirk. I believe Paradise has been a good servant?"

"The best I ever had," Kirk told him.

"He was always a good servant," went on Duff. "As I recall, that fact was brought out clearly at the trial. A competent, faithful man – he had many references to prove it. But unfortunately a few years ago, in England, there was some suspicion that he had put hydrocyanic acid in a lady's tea."

"What an odd place for hydrocyanic acid," said Kirk. "But then, of course, I speak without knowing the lady."

"The lady was his wife," Duff explained. "It seemed to some of us that he had rather overstepped a husband's privileges. He was brought to trial— "

Paradise raised his head. "Nothing was ever proved," he said firmly. "I was acquitted."

"Yes, our case collapsed," admitted Inspector Duff. "That doesn't often happen, Mr Kirk, but it did in this instance. Technically, at least, Paradise cannot be adjudged guilty. In the eyes of the law, I mean. And for that reason I might have been inclined to keep all this to myself, if I had not heard of his queer work with that letter. Tell me, Paradise – do you know anything about Eve Durand?"

"I have never heard the name before, sir."

"Have you any information in the matter of an old murder in Ely Place – the murder of Hilary Galt?"

"None whatever, sir."

"But you opened an envelope addressed to Sir Frederic Bruce and substituted a blank sheet for the letter you found inside. I think you had better explain, my man."

"Yes, sir. I will do so." The servant turned to Barry Kirk. "This is very painful for me, Mr Kirk. In the two years I have been with you I have done nothing dishonorable before – before this act. The gentleman has said that I poisoned my wife. I may call attention to the fact that he has some animus in the matter, as he conducted the investigation and was bitterly disappointed when a jury acquitted me. A natural feeling—"

"Never mind that," said Duff sharply.

"At any rate, sir," the butler continued to Kirk, "I was acquitted, for the very good reason that I was an innocent man. But I knew that, innocent or not, the fact of my having been tried would not be – er – pleasant news for you."

"Anything but," agreed Kirk.

"I thought it would be best if the matter remained in its former oblivion. I have been happy here – it is an excellent post – the very fact of its height above the ground has inspired me. I was always fond of high places. So I was in a bit of a funk, sir, when you told me Sir Frederic Bruce was coming. I had never had the pleasure of his acquaintance, but I'd had my brief moment in the public eye and I feared he might do me the honor to remember me. Well, he arrived and – unfortunately – he recognized me at once. We had a long talk here in this room. I assured him that I had been unjustly accused, that I had never done anything wrong, and that I was living a model life. I begged him to keep my secret. He was a just man. He said he would look into the matter – I presumed he wanted to hear Scotland Yard's opinion of the evidence – and would let me know his decision later. And there the matter stood, sir, on the night Sir Frederic met his unhappy end."

"Ah, yes," said Kirk. "I begin to see."

"What I did later was done from a misguided wish to retain your respect and confidence, sir. A messenger from Cook's put into my hand that packet of letters, and I saw on the top what I thought was the dreaded missive from Scotland Yard. If I may be allowed to say so, I went a bit balmy then. I believed that Sir Frederic had cabled about me to the Yard, and that this was the answer. It would no doubt fall into the hands of the police—"

"It was too early for any answer yet," Kirk told him.

"How could I be sure, sir? In this day of the air-mail and other time-saving devices. I determined to have a look at that letter, and if it did not concern me, to put it back in place—"

"But it didn't concern you, Paradise," said Kirk.

"Not directly, sir. However, it mentioned that Inspector Duff was in New York. I had enjoyed the honor of Inspector Duff's personal attention in my – er – my ordeal, and I was panic-stricken. The local police, reading the letter, might send for him, with results that are all too apparent now. So in my madness I slipped a blank sheet of paper into the envelope and resealed it. It was a clumsy subterfuge, sir, and one I deeply regret. Not the clumsiness, but the deceit, sir – that pains me. Everything has always been above the table with us, sir."

"I should hope it had," said Kirk.

"I am perhaps going too far when I ask you to overlook my defection, Mr Kirk. I assure you, however, that it was my fondness for you, my keen desire to remain in your service, that prompted my rash act. If we could only go back to the old basis, sir – of mutual confidence and esteem—"

Kirk laughed. "I don't know. I shall have to think this over. Are you sure you're fond of me, Paradise?"

"Very, sir."

"Have you analyzed your emotions carefully? No little hidden trace of resentment, or disapproval?"

"None whatever, sir. I give you my word."

Kirk shrugged. “Very well. Then you might go and prepare the – er – the tea. In the usual manner, please.”

“Thank you, sir,” answered Paradise, and departed.

“The poor old dear,” said Miss Morrow. “I’m sure he never did it. He was the victim of circumstances.”

“Perhaps,” admitted Duff. “Personally, however, I thought the evidence very strong. But I was new to the work at that time, and I may have been mistaken. At any rate, I am happy to have been able to eliminate Paradise from our case. It clears the air a bit.”

“He may be eliminated from the case,” Barry Kirk remarked. “But I’m free to admit that to me he is more important than ever.”

“You don’t believe he had anything to do with killing Sir Frederic?” Miss Morrow inquired.

“No – but I’m afraid he may have something to do with killing me. I’m faced by a private and personal problem – and a very pretty one, too. I’d hate to lose Paradise, but I’d hate to lose myself even more. Imagine taking the glass of good old orange juice every morning from a hand that has been up to tricks with hydrocyanic acid. Not so good. Charlie, as a guest here, you’re interested. What do you say?”

Chan shrugged. “It may be he disliked his wife,” he suggested.

“I should hate to think he was fond of her,” Kirk replied. “But at that, he’s a good old soul. And some wives, no doubt, drive a man too far. I think I’ll let him stay a while. However” – he looked at Miss Morrow – ”something tells me I’ll do an awful lot of eating out.”

“Sergeant Chan,” Duff said, “you have not been idle. What discoveries have you made in our case so far?”

“None but the slightest,” Chan told him. “I am very bright in tracking down Paradise here, and we have just seen the value of that. Alas, there are sprouting crops that never ripen into grain.”

"True enough," agreed the Inspector. "But you must have had ideas along other lines, too. I should be interested to hear them."

"Some time we have little talk," Charlie promised. "For the present – I hesitate to speak of it. I am not without tender feeling to my heart, and I know only too well the topic must be one of deep pain to Major Durand. He must pardon my rudeness if I have keen desire to hear something of that far-away night when Eve Durand was lost."

Durand came out of a deep reverie. "Ah, yes – what's that? The night when Eve – of course, it was all so long ago."

"Yet a moment you are not likely to forget," suggested Chan.

Durand smiled ruefully. "I'm afraid not. I have tried to forget – it seemed the best way. But I have never succeeded."

"The date was the third of May, in the year 1913," Chan prompted.

"Precisely. We had been living in Peshawar just six months – I was assigned to a regiment there only a month after our marriage, in England. A God-forsaken place, Peshawar – an outpost of empire, with a vengeance. No place to bring a woman like Eve, who had known nothing save the civilized life of the English countryside."

He paused, deep in thought. "Yet we were very happy. We were young – Eve was eighteen, I was twenty-four – young and tremendously in love. The discomforts of that far garrison meant nothing – we had each other."

"And on this night under question," Chan persisted.

"There was a gay social life at the garrison, and Eve took an important part in it, as was natural. On the evening you ask about, we had arranged a picnic party in the hills. We were to ride our ponies out of the town and up a narrow dirt road to a small plateau from which we could watch the moon rise over the roofs of Peshawar. The plan was rather foolhardy – the hills were full of bandits – I was a bit fearful at the time. But the ladies – they insisted – you know how women are. And there were five men in the party, all fully armed. There seemed no real danger."

Again he paused. "Eve wore her jewels – a pearl necklace her uncle had given her – I remember protesting against it before we set out. She only laughed at me. Sometimes I have thought—But no, I do not like to think that. Was she killed for her necklace, her rings? I have had to face it.

"At any rate, we packed our supper and rode out of the town. Everything went well until the hour arrived to go home. Then someone suggested a game of hide-and-seek—"

"You recall who suggested that?" asked Chan.

"Yes – it was Eve. I objected, but – well, one doesn't like to be a spoil sport, and the party was in a gay humor. The women scattered among the tamarisks – disappeared into the shadows, laughing and chatting. Within the half-hour we had found them all – save one. We have not found her yet."

"How terrible," Miss Morrow cried.

"You can scarcely realize the true horror of it," Durand returned. "Those black hills filled with innumerable dangers – oh, it was a foolish thing, that game. It should never have happened. Of the night that followed – and the long, hot dreadful days after that – I need not go on, I'm sure." He bowed his head.

"There were five men," said Chan. "Yourself already counted."

"Five men, yes," Durand replied. "And five charming girls."

"Five men – the other four officers, like yourself?" Charlie continued.

"Three of them were officers. One was not."

Chan's face lighted. "One was not?"

"No. The party was given in his honor, in a way. You see, he was a famous man – everyone was eager to pay tribute to him. He had just been a guest at the Viceregal Lodge, he'd spoken in the throne-room, and they'd pinned medals and things on him. All India was ringing with his praises. He'd recently come back from a beastly perilous journey through Tibet—"

Chan's eyes narrowed. "He was an explorer?"

"One of the best. A brave man."

"You are referring to Colonel John Beetham?"

"Yes, of course. Then you knew?"

Kirk and Miss Morrow sat up with sudden interest. Chan nodded. "I had guessed," he said. He was silent for a moment. "Colonel Beetham is at this moment in San Francisco," he added.

"Really?" answered the Major. "An odd coincidence. I should like to meet him again. He was most sympathetic."

"The party was in his honor, you have said?" Charlie went on.

"Yes – a sort of farewell. You see, he was leaving the next day. Leaving for home, but not by the conventional route – not Beetham. He was going by caravan through the wilds of Afghanistan and across the great salt desert of Persia to Teheran."

"Through Khyber Pass?" Chan asked.

"Oh, yes – through the Khyber. A dangerous business, but he had a big retinue of servants who had been with him on other expeditions – and the Emir of Afghanistan had invited him. He left early the next morning and I have never seen him since."

"Early the next morning," Chan repeated slowly. "Going home." He stared for a moment at the misty window. "I had hoped to go home in the morning myself. But always something rises up making me break my word to my little son. What a despicable father he will think me. However" – he shrugged – "what is to be, will be."

Paradise came into the room, pompously wheeling a tea-wagon. There was a moment of uncomfortable silence.

"Tea, sir," said the butler.

"I hope so, I'm sure," replied Kirk.

Paradise served Miss Morrow, and then turned to Inspector Duff. "What will you have in yours, sir?" he inquired.

The Inspector looked him firmly in the eye. "One lump of sugar," he said. "And – nothing else."

XIV

DINNER FOR TWO

With a grave face Paradise served the tea, passed sandwiches and cakes, and then silently withdrew. Barry Kirk paused with his cup at his lips, an inquiring look in his eyes. Inspector Duff saw it and smiled.

"I may tell you," he said, "that hydrocyanic acid has a quite distinctive odor. A pungent odor of peach blossoms."

"That's very good of you," answered Kirk. "I shall remember what you say. And you, Charlie – you'd better do the same. At the first intimation that we are in a peach orchard, we call up the employment agency and engage a new butler."

"I have made a note," Chan told him.

"At any rate," Kirk continued, "life's going to be rather a sporting proposition from now on. 'To be, or not to be: that is the question.'"

"We must treat Paradise with kindly consideration," Chan suggested. "We must bear in mind that a good word has heat enough for three winters, while a hard one wounds like six months of cold. It is going to improve our characters."

"I'll say it is," agreed Kirk. He looked at Major Durand and reflected that perhaps the conversation was a bit flippant in view of that gentleman's mission in San Francisco. Poor devil – what a life he must have led. Seeking about to include him in the talk, Kirk was able to hit upon nothing save the aged and obvious bromide. "Tell us, Major," he said. "What do you think of the States?"

"Ah, yes," replied Durand. "My impressions. Well, really, I'm afraid I can't be very original. My sole impression so far is one of – er – bigness. Size, you know. My word – your country is tremendous."

Duff nodded. "We could talk of little else on the train coming out. You can scarcely imagine the effect of America on the minds of men who hail from a country like England. There, a ride of a few miles in any direction and you are on the coast. But here – day after day we looked from the car windows incredulous, amazed. We thought we should never come to the end of our journey."

"No doubt about it," Kirk returned, "there's plenty of the United States. Too much, some people think."

"We haven't said that," Durand reminded him, smiling faintly. "However, the possibilities of such a country seem endless. I may add" – he looked at Miss Morrow – "that I find your young women charming."

"How very polite of you," she smiled.

"Oh, not at all. I really mean it. If you will pardon me – I did not quite catch your connection with this affair?"

"I am in the district attorney's office," she told him.

"Like our crown prosecutor, the district attorney," Duff explained. "This young woman is, I believe, a student of the law."

"My word," said Durand. "Just fancy. Then it surprises me there is not more respect for law in the States."

"Thank you," Miss Morrow answered. "That's flattering to me, if not to the States."

Durand rose. "You must forgive me if I run along," he said. "I have found the long journey somewhat fatiguing – and added to that is the disappointment I suffered a few moments ago.

I pretended, of course, that I had no hope, but it wasn't quite true. As a matter of fact, despite all the false rumors in the past, I still go on hoping. And this time, with the word of a man like Sir Frederic Bruce involved – well, my mind will never be at rest until I have seen the woman who left so suddenly tonight."

"She may yet be found," Duff suggested.

"I hope so, I'm sure. Are you coming, old chap?"

"Of course," Duff replied, rising.

"You and I must have that talk soon, Inspector," Chan said.

Duff stopped. "Well, I've always thought there's no time like the present. You go ahead, Major, and I'll follow."

"Very good," Durand answered. "I have engaged a room for you at the St. Francis Hotel. I trust you'll approve of my choice."

"That was thoughtful of you," Duff told him. "I'll see you shortly."

Durand turned to Barry Kirk. "You've been very hospitable to a stranger."

"Not at all," Kirk said. "You must drop in often. I hope you won't be lonely here. I'll send you a card for a club or two, and if you like, we'll have a little party occasionally."

"Frightfully kind, I'm sure," Durand replied warmly. "A thousand thanks." He added his farewells and went out.

"Poor man," Miss Morrow said.

"A nice chap," Duff remarked. He turned briskly to Charlie. "But this isn't getting us forward, Sergeant. Where shall we begin? I learned from Captain Flannery that no records of any case were found among Sir Frederic's effects?"

"None whatsoever," Chan corroborated.

"Then it looks like theft as well as murder, for unquestionably such records were kept. Somewhere – unless they have been destroyed by the same hand that killed Sir Frederic – there must be in existence detailed accounts of the Hilary Galt case, as well as the disappearance of Eve Durand—"

"You have heard that, in Sir Frederic's thinking, these two matters boast some obscure connection?" Chan asked.

Duff nodded. "Yes, I saw the copy of the letter from my Chief at the Yard. I should say from the sound of it that he's as much in the dark as we are. But I have already cabled him for any information he may have."

"You act with beautiful speed," Chan approved. "One thing this Major Durand has told us puts new face on whole matter. Up to now, it was entirely unknown round here that Colonel John Beetham attended picnic that unforgotten night at Peshawar."

"What about Beetham? He's in San Francisco, you say?"

"Very much so. He was present at dinner. A strange, silent, mind-beguiling man."

Miss Morrow spoke suddenly. "Why, of course," she cried. "Colonel Beetham at the picnic – that means he knew Eve Durand. On the night he came here to dinner, he must have been brought up in the elevator by little Jennie Jerome Marie Lantelme. If she was Eve Durand, he probably recognized her."

"Undubitably," Chan agreed.

"Why, that makes it all very simple," Miss Morrow continued. "I'll get hold of him at once, and ask him—"

Chan raised his hand. "Humbly begging pardon to cut in – would you ask a blind man the road?"

"Why – I – what do you mean?"

"I have known for some days that the Colonel was in neighborhood of Peshawar that early May, 1913. Until tonight I did not dream he was member of picnic party. Even so, the last act I would consider would be to make inquiries."

"Surely you don't think—"

"I have not decided what to think. A member of that party – the fact may mean much, or it may mean nothing at all. On chance that it means much, let us say nothing to the Colonel just yet. To do so might defeat our own ends. There was once a man who pinched the baby while rocking the cradle. His work was not regarded a very large success."

Miss Morrow smiled. "I shall take your advice, of course."

"Thank you. Before we act, permit that I dig about some more amid events of past." Chan turned to the Inspector. "Dropping the Colonel for the moment, I mention those velvet slippers."

"Yes," said Duff. "The velvet slippers. A bit of a mystery, they are. Carried off by the murderer, it seems. But why? And what did he – or she – do with them? It's not unreasonable to suppose they were hurriedly chucked away somewhere. In England, we have a system in such a case – we advertise and offer a reward."

"Splendid idea," agreed Chan.

"Surely Captain Flannery has thought of it?"

Chan shrugged. "Captain acts much like little child caught in cross-woven net. He can only struggle, always getting deeper. But I must restrain my criticism. Free to admit the plan had not occurred even to me."

Duff laughed. "Well, I'll look the Captain up after dinner and suggest that he try it. By the way, I'm quite at a loss – the city is new to me. Could I prevail on you, Sergeant, to dine with me? We can talk things over, and afterward you can show me about, and direct me to Flannery's office."

"Deeply pleased at the invitation," Chan beamed. "I have much to learn. Where better could I study than in your distinguished company?"

"Well – er – that's a bit strong," returned Duff. "However, we'll have a jolly little dinner. Any time you're ready—"

"I procure hat and coat with instant action," Chan replied.

Duff turned to Kirk and the girl. "Great pleasure to meet you both," he said. "Miss Morrow, to work with a charming young woman on a case will be a new experience for me – and a delightful one."

"You must think it an utterly ridiculous situation," she remarked.

"I haven't said so," he smiled.

Chan returned, and he and Duff went out together. Miss Morrow took up her coat.

"Just a minute," Kirk protested. "Where are you going?"

"Home," she told him.

"To a lonely dinner," he suggested.

"You needn't hint. I can't invite you tonight. I shall need loads of time to prepare that pie—"

"Of course. I wasn't hinting. But oddly enough, I've gone sort of cold on the idea of dining here in my cozy little nest. I propose to go where there are lights, laughter, and a waiter I can trust. And unless you prove more cruel than you look, I'm not dining alone."

"But I really should go home – and freshen up."

"Nonsense – you're blooming now. Like a peach tree covered with blossoms – I wonder how I came to think of that? No matter – will you join me?"

"If you want me to."

Kirk rang the bell, and Paradise appeared at once. "Ah – er – I'm dining out tonight," the young man explained.

Paradise looked distressed. "Very good, sir. But if I may make so bold—"

"Yes – what is it?"

"I trust this is not a sign of waning confidence in me, sir? I have been hoping for the old relations between us—"

"Nonsense. I often dine out. You know that."

"Certainly, sir." The butler made a gloomy exit.

"Good lord," sighed Kirk, "I'm afraid he's going sensitive on my hands. I suppose that just to show I trust him, I'll have to give a large dinner and invite all the people of whom I'm especially fond."

"A large dinner?"

"Well – fairly large. My grandmother, and Charlie Chan, and a few old friends from the club. And – er – would you come?"

"If I didn't, it wouldn't be because I was afraid of Paradise."

They descended to the street. It was a night of mist, with occasional fierce rain. Kirk found his car and helping the girl in, drove from the deserted business district to Union Square, where bright lights were gleaming on the wet pavements. The cable-car bells rang cheerily, a flotilla of umbrellas bobbed jauntily along the sidewalk; the spirits of the people of San Francisco, habitually high, are not to be damped by a little rain. "How about Marchetti's?" Kirk inquired.

"Sounds good to me," Miss Morrow answered.

They entered the little restaurant. On the dance floor the first of the cabaret acts was underway; a young, goodlooking chorus pranced about to the strains of a popular air. Barry Kirk was known there, and the result was a good table and an obsequious head waiter. They gave their order.

"I like this place," said Kirk. "They never confuse noise with merriment." A pretty little blonde awarded him a sweet smile in passing. "Awfully cute girls, don't you think?"

"Yes, aren't they?" Miss Morrow answered. "Do you like cute girls?"

"Like to see 'em going by – on the other side. Never cared much for their conversation. It has no weight. Now, you take a lawyer, for instance—"

"Please," she said. "Don't make fun of me. I'm not in the mood for it tonight. I'm tired – and discouraged."

"Tired – that's all right," he replied. "But discouraged – what about? As I understand it, you've been a big success in your work."

"Oh, no I haven't. I've got on – a little way – but am I going any farther? Have you forgotten – this is an anniversary. A week ago tonight—"

"You dined with me for the first time. I hope—"

"A week ago tonight Sir Frederic was killed, and I embarked on my first big case. Up to this minute I haven't contributed a thing to its solution—"

"Oh, yes, you have. Of course, you haven't solved the puzzle, but there's plenty of time—"

"Oh, no, there isn't. At any moment the district attorney may tell me I'm out. I've got to make good quickly – and how can I? Look back – what have we accomplished to date?"

"Well, you've found Eve Durand."

"And lost her. That is – if the little elevator girl was Eve Durand."

"She must be. Charlie says so."

Miss Morrow shook her head. "Charlie's clever, but he's been wrong. He admits it freely. You know, something happened tonight while we were waiting for Captain Flannery to lead that girl into the room. Something inside me. Just a hunch – a woman's intuition – I suddenly felt quite sure that she wasn't Eve Durand after all."

"You don't say. And what basis did you have for that hunch?"

"None whatever. But I felt we were on the wrong trail altogether. She might very well be Jennie Jerome, and Marie Lantelme too, and still not be Durand's lost wife. Don't forget there are many other possibilities for that rôle."

"For example?"

"How about Lila Barr – the girl in the office of the Calcutta Importers? You remember what you told us – how interested Sir Frederic was in her? Just what did that mean?"

"I'd be happy to tell you – if I knew."

"But you don't. Then there's Eileen Enderby and Gloria Garland. In spite of their stories about why Sir Frederic wanted to see them – are they out of it? And Mrs Tupper-Brock. No – we can't be sure that the elevator girl was Eve Durand. We've just been guessing – Chan's been guessing. And we'll never know now."

"Why not? Flannery will find her."

"You don't really believe that? If you do, you've more faith in the poor old Captain than I have. Suppose he does find her, and she is Eve Durand – what of it? She'll simply refuse to talk, and we'll be no nearer knowing who killed Sir Frederic than we ever were."

"I brought you here for an evening of gaiety," Kirk said sternly, "and you sit there thinking black thoughts."

"Just a minute – let me go on. It's such a comfort to talk things over. Who killed Sir Frederic – that's my problem. The identity of Eve Durand may not have as much to do with the matter as we think. It may even prove to have nothing to do with it at all. Who pulled that trigger in your office last Tuesday night? Carrick Enderby? It's quite possible. Eileen Enderby? There were those stains on her frock – did she climb down the fire-escape on some sinister errand? Dismissing the Enderby family, there are others. How about Gloria Garland? Mrs Tupper-Brock?"

"Each of whom, of course, arrived at my dinner with a pistol hidden under her gown?" smiled Kirk.

"Each of whom knew she was to meet Sir Frederic that night. The pistol could have been arranged. To go on with the list – there's Paradise. I like him, but I can't see that his story of this afternoon puts him completely beyond suspicion. On the contrary. Outside the bungalow, there was that pale young man from the accountants' office."

"Oh yes – name of Smith," said Kirk. "I'd forgotten all about him."

"I haven't," Miss Morrow replied. "Then, there's Li Gung. The Chinese who fled to Honolulu next day. What was his hurry? Isn't it possible that he climbed up the fire-escape— Oh, what's the use? The list seems endless." Miss Morrow sighed.

"And incomplete, as you give it," added Kirk.

"You mean—"

"I mean the man who accompanied Li Gung to the dock. Colonel John Beetham."

"Absurd! A man like Colonel Beetham – famous throughout the world – a man who has won all the medals and distinctions there are for gallant conduct – as though he could do anything base, anything despicable."

"Just there," said Kirk, "your sex betrays you. Not one of you women can resist a handsome, distinguished-looking Englishman. Speaking as a less romantic male, I must say that the Colonel doesn't strike me quite so favorably. He has courage, yes – and he has a will that gets him where he wants to go, and damn the consequences. I shouldn't care to be one of his party on the top floor of Tibet and too weak to go on. He'd give me one disgusted look, and leave me. But wait a minute – I believe he'd do me one last kindness before he left."

"What's that?"

"I think he'd pull out a gun and shoot me. Yes, I'm certain he would, and he'd go on his way happy to know there was one weakling who would never trouble him again."

"Yes, he's a hard, determined man," Miss Morrow admitted. "Nevertheless, he wouldn't kill Sir Frederic. Poor Sir Frederic wasn't interfering with his plans in any way."

"Oh, wasn't he? How do you know he wasn't?"

"Well – I can't see—"

"Let's leave Beetham to Chan," Kirk suggested. "The little man has an air about him – I believe he knows what he's doing. And now will you drop all this and dance with me – or must I dance alone?"

"I don't know. In my position, I have to give an impression of being serious – the public—"

"Oh, forget your public. He wouldn't venture out on a night like this. Come along."

Miss Morrow laughed, and they danced together on the tiny floor. For the rest of the evening she permitted Kirk to lead the conversation into more frivolous channels – a task at which he excelled. The change seemed to do her good.

"Well," said Kirk, as he signed the check, "you can be gay, after all. And I must say it becomes you."

"I've forgot all my worries," replied the girl, her eyes sparkling. "I feel as though I should never think of them again."

"That's the talk," Kirk approved.

But before they got out of the room, Miss Morrow's worries were suddenly brought back to her. Along one wall was a series of booths, beside which they walked on their way to the door. Opposite the final booth the girl half stopped, and glanced back over her shoulder at Barry Kirk. In passing he too looked into the compartment, and then hastily moved on. He need not have effaced himself so hurriedly, for the two people who were dining together in the booth were so deep in serious conversation they were oblivious to everything.

In the street Miss Morrow turned to Kirk. "What did I tell you?" she cried. "There are other women involved in this affair besides that poor little elevator girl."

"And what did I tell you," Kirk answered, "about your handsome British hero?"

Miss Morrow nodded. "Tomorrow," she said, "I shall look into this. Just what, I wonder, is the connection between Colonel Beetham and Mrs Helen Tupper-Brock?"

XV

THE DISCREET MR CUTTLE

When Charlie Chan rose on Wednesday morning, the rain was over and the fog was lifting. Bravely struggling through remnants of mist, the sun fell on a sparkling town, washed clean for a new day. Chan stood for a long time looking out at the magnificent panorama over bay and harbor, at the green of Goat Island and the prison fortress of Alcatraz. Along the waterfront stretched a line of great ships as though awaiting a signal that should send them scurrying off to distant treaty ports and coral islands.

Chan's heart was heavy despite the bright morning. At twelve noon would sail the ship on which he had sworn to depart, the ship that would come finally to rest under the tower that bore the word "Aloha." There would be keen disappointment in the little house beneath the algaroba trees on Punchbowl Hill, as there was disappointment in the detective's heart now. He sighed. Would this holiday never end? This holiday so filled with work and baffling problems? This holiday that was no holiday at all?

When he entered the dining-room Barry Kirk was already at the table, but his glass of orange juice stood before him, untouched.

"Hello," said the host. "I waited for you."

"You grow increasingly kind with every dawn," Chan grinned.

"Oh, I don't know. It isn't exactly kindness. Somehow, I don't seem in any hurry to quaff California's favorite beverage this morning. Take a look at it. Does it strike you as being – er – the real thing?"

As Chan sat down, Paradise appeared in the doorway. Without a moment's hesitation, Chan lifted his glass. "Your very good health," he remarked.

Kirk glanced at the butler, and raised his own glass. "I sincerely trust you're right," he murmured, and drank heartily.

Paradise gravely said his good mornings and, setting down two bowls of oatmeal, departed. "Well," Barry Kirk smiled, "we seem to be O.K. so far."

"Suspicion," Chan told him, "is a wicked thing. That is written in many places."

"Yes – and where would you be in your work without it?" Kirk inquired. "By the way, did you get anything out of Duff last night?"

"Nothing that demands heavy thought. One point he elucidated carried slight interest."

"What was that?"

"Begging respectful pardon, for the present I will ponder same with my customary silence. You dined here?"

"No. Miss Morrow and I went to a restaurant."

"Ah – a moment's pleasant recreation," said Chan approvingly.

"That was the idea."

"You enjoy society of this young woman?"

"I do not precisely pine in her presence. You know, she's not so serious as she pretends to be."

"That is good. Women were not invented for heavy thinking. They should decorate scene, like blossom of the plum."

"Yes, but they can't all be movie actresses. I don't mind a girl's having a brain if she doesn't act up-stage about it – and Miss Morrow never does. We had a very light-hearted evening, but we weren't blind. As we left the restaurant, we made a little discovery."

"Good, what was it?"

Kirk shrugged. "Shall I ponder same with my customary silence? No, I won't be as mean as you are, Charlie. We saw your old friend Colonel John Beetham relaxing from the stern realities of life. We saw him dining with a lady."

"Ah, yes. Which lady?"

"A lady we have rather overlooked so far. Mrs Helen Tupper-Brock."

"That has interest. Miss Morrow will investigate?"

"Yes. I'm going to pick up Mrs Tupper-Brock this morning and take her down to the district attorney's office. I don't look for any brilliant results, however. She's cold and distant, like the winter stars. Good lord – I'm getting poetic. You don't suppose it could be something I've had for breakfast?"

"More likely memories of last night," Chan answered.

When the meal was finished, Kirk announced that he was going down to the office to attend to a few letters. Chan rose quickly.

"I will accompany, if I may," he said. "I must produce letter of explanation for my wife, hoping it will yet catch out-going boat. It will be substitute for me – a smaller substitute." He sighed.

"That's right," Kirk remembered. "You were going out on the tide today, weren't you? It's a shame you can't."

"What will little Barry think of me?"

"Oh, he's probably sensible, like his namesake. He'll want you to stay where duty lies. And how proud he'll be – in the future – over your success in running down the murderer of Sir Frederic Bruce."

"Still have some running to do," Chan admitted. "One more week – I give myself that. Then, whatever has happened, I shift mainland dust off my shoes and go. I swear it, and this time I am firm like well-known Gibraltar rock."

"A week," repeated Kirk. "Oh, that will be ample. You'll be sitting pretty then."

"On deck of boat bound for Honolulu," Chan said firmly. "Quoting local conversation, you bet I will."

They went below, and Kirk seated himself at the big desk. Kinsey was out; "collecting rents," Kirk explained. Chan accepted paper and an envelope and took his place at the stenographer's desk by the wall.

But his mind did not seem to be on the letter he was writing. Out of the corner of his eye he watched Kirk's movements carefully. In a moment he rose and came over to Kirk's desk. "Pen enjoys stubborn spasm," he explained. "The ink will not gush. Who calls it fountain pen?"

"There are pens in here," Kirk said, leaning over to open a lower drawer. Chan's keen eyes were on the papers atop the desk. Noted for his courtesy, his actions were odd. He appeared to be spying on his host.

Charlie accepted a pen and returned to his writing. Still he watched Kirk from the corner of his eye.

The young man finished his letter and started another. When he had completed the second, he stamped them both. Simultaneously Chan sealed his own letter, stamped it, and rose quickly to his feet. He held out his long, thin hand.

"Permit me," he said, "that I deposit our mail in the hallway chute."

"Why – thank you," Kirk replied, giving him the letters.

When Charlie returned, Kirk was on his feet, consulting his watch. "Want to hear Mrs Tupper-Brock's life story?" he inquired.

The detective shook his head. "Thanking you all the same, I will not interpolate myself. Miss Morrow is competent for work. Already, I have several times squirmed about in the position of fifth, unnecessary wheel. This once I will loiter elsewhere."

"Suit yourself," Kirk answered carelessly. He took up his hat and coat and disappeared.

When Chan went upstairs by the inner route, he found Bill Rankin waiting for him in the living-room of the bungalow. The reporter looked at him with amusement.

"Good morning," he said. "I presume you're sailing this noon?"

Chan frowned. "Missing boats is now a regular habit for me," he replied. "I cannot go. Too many dark clouds shade the scene."

"I knew it," smiled Rankin. "Before you go you've got to give me a story that will thrill the town. I was sure I could depend on you. A great little people, the Chinese."

"Thanks for advertising my unassuming race," Chan said.

"Now, to get down to business," Rankin continued. "I've brought you a little present this bright morning."

"You are pretty good."

"I'm a clever boy," Rankin admitted. "You know, your rather foggy remarks about Colonel John Beetham have set me thinking. And when I think – get out from under. I have read the Colonel's *Life*, from cover to cover. I imagine I need not tell you that on May fourth, nineteen hundred and thirteen, Beetham set out on an eight months' journey from Peshawar to Teheran, by way of Afghanistan and the Kevir desert of Persia?"

"I too have upearthed that," nodded Chan.

"I thought you had. But did you know that he had written a book – a separate book – about that little jaunt? A bit of a holiday, he called it. Not real exploring, but just his way of going home."

Chan was interested. "I have been unaware of that volume," he replied.

"It isn't as well known as his other books," went on Rankin. "Out of print now. *The Land Beyond the Khyber*, he called it. I tried every book store in town, and finally picked up a copy over in Berkeley."

He produced a volume bound in deep purple. "It's the little present I mentioned," he added.

Chan took it eagerly. "Who shall say? This may be of some value. I am in your debt and sinking all the time."

"Well, I don't know about its value. Maybe you can find something I have overlooked. I've been through it carefully, but I haven't found a thing."

Chan opened the book. "Interesting item flashes up immediately," he said. "Unlike Colonel Beetham's other books, this has dedication." Slowly he read the inscription on the dedicatory page: "To one who will remember, and understand."

"I noticed that," Rankin told him. "It begins to look as though the Colonel has his tender moments, doesn't it? To one who will remember and understand. A boyhood sweetheart, probably. One who will remember the time he kissed her under the lilacs at the gate, and understand that he goes on his daring trips with her image in his heart."

Chan was deep in thought. "Possible," he muttered.

"You know, these Englishmen aren't as hard-boiled as they seem," Rankin continued. "I knew a British aviator in the war – a tough baby, he ate nails for breakfast. Yet he always carried a sprig of heather on his plane – the memento of an old love-affair. A sentimentalist at heart. Perhaps Colonel Beetham is the same type."

"May very well be," Charlie agreed.

Rankin got up. "Well, I suppose my dear old Chief is crying his eyes out because I haven't shown up. He loves me, even though he does threaten to cast me off because I haven't solved the mystery of Sir Frederic's murder."

"You are not alone in that fault," Chan told him.

"I – I don't suppose you could give me any little morsel for our million panting readers?"

"Nothing of note may yet be revealed."

"Well, it does seem high time we were getting a glimpse behind that curtain," Rankin remarked.

Charlie shook his head. "The matter is difficult. If I were in Peshawar – but I am not. I am in San Francisco fifteen years after the event, and I can only guess. I may add, guessing is poor business that often leads to lengthy saunters down the positively wrong path."

"You hang on," advised Rankin. "You'll win yet and when you do, just let me be there, with a direct line to the office at my elbow."

"We will hope that happy picture eventuates," Chan replied.

Rankin went out, leaving Charlie to the book. He sat down before the fire and began to read eagerly. This was better than interviewing Mrs Tupper-Brock.

At about the same time, Barry Kirk was going blithely up the steps of his grandmother's handsome house on Pacific Heights. The old lady greeted him in the drawing-room.

"Hello," she said. "How do you happen to be up and about so early? And wide awake, if I can believe my failing eyesight."

"Detective work," he laughed.

"Good. What can I do for you? I seem to have been left entirely out of things, and it annoys me."

"Well, you're still out, so don't get up any false hopes," he returned. "I'm not here to consult with you, wise as I know you to be. I'm looking for Mrs Tupper-Brock. Where is she?"

"She's upstairs. What do you want with her?"

"I want to take her for a little ride – down to see Miss Morrow."

"Oh, so that young woman is still asking questions? She seems a bit lacking in results, so far."

"Is that so? Well, give her time."

"I rather fancy she'll need a lot of it. Mixing up in affairs that should be left to the men—"

"You're a traitor to your sex. I think it's mighty fine of her to be where she is. Give this little girl a great big hand."

"Oh, I imagine she doesn't lack for applause when you are about. You seem very much taken with her."

"I am, and don't forget it. Now, how about calling Mrs Tupper-Brock? Please tell her to come, and bring her hyphen."

Mrs Kirk gave him a scornful look, and departed. In a few minutes the secretary appeared in the room. Poised and cool, as always, she greeted Barry Kirk without enthusiasm.

"Good morning," he said. "I'm sorry to disturb you, but Miss Morrow – you met her at my dinner – would like to see you. If you can come now, I'll drive you down in my car."

"Why, of course," returned the woman calmly. "I'll be just a moment."

She went out, and Mrs Kirk reappeared. "What's the matter with that boy of Sally Jordan's?" she demanded. "I thought he'd have this thing solved long ago. I've been watching the papers like a bargain hunter."

"Oh, Charlie's all right," Kirk said. "He's slow, but sure."

"He's slow enough," admitted the old lady. "You might tell him that I'm growing impatient."

"That'll speed him up," Kirk smiled.

"I wish something would," his grandmother snapped. "What's all this about Helen? Surely she's not entangled in the case?"

"I'm not free to say, one way or another. Tell me, have you given Colonel Beetham that money yet?"

"No – but I believe I will."

"Take my advice and hold off for a few days."

"What? He isn't in it, is he? Why – he's a gentleman."

"Just take my advice—" began Kirk. Mrs Tupper-Brock was in the hall, waiting for him.

"Now you've got me all excited," complained Mrs Kirk.

"That's bad, at your age," Kirk said. "Calm down."

"What do you mean – my age? I read of a woman the other day who is a hundred and two."

"Well, there's a mark to shoot at," Kirk told her. "So long. See you later."

Mrs Tupper-Brock sat at his side in the roadster, stiff and obviously not inclined to talk. A few remarks on the weather yielding no great flood of conversation, Kirk abandoned the effort. They rode on in silence, and finally he ushered her into Miss Morrow's office.

The deputy district attorney made a charming picture against that gloomy background. Such was not, however, her aim at the moment. Alert and businesslike, she greeted Mrs Tupper-Brock and indicated a chair beside her desk.

"Sit down, please. So good of you to come. I hope I haven't inconvenienced you?"

"Not in the least," the woman replied, seating herself. There was a moment's silence.

"You know, of course, that we are hunting the murderer of Sir Frederic Bruce," Miss Morrow began.

"Naturally," Mrs Tupper-Brock's tone was cool. "Why did you wish to see me?"

"I wondered whether you have any information that might help us."

"That's hardly likely," responded Mrs Tupper-Brock. She took out a lace-edged handkerchief and began to turn it slowly in her hands.

"No, perhaps not," Miss Morrow smiled. "Still, we are not justified in ignoring anyone in this terrible affair. Sir Frederic was a complete stranger to you?"

"Yes, quite. I met him for the first time on that Tuesday night."

"Did you also meet Colonel Beetham for the first time that night?"

The handkerchief was suddenly a tiny ball in her hand. "No – I did not."

"You had met him before?"

"Yes. At Mrs Dawson Kirk's. He had been to the house frequently."

"Of course. You and the Colonel are quite good friends, I hear. Perhaps you knew him before he came to San Francisco?"

"No, I did not."

"While the Colonel was showing his pictures, you remained on the davenport with Miss Garland. You saw nothing of a suspicious nature?"

"Nothing whatever." The handkerchief lay in a crumbled heap in her lap. She took it up and once more began to smooth it.

"Have you ever lived in India?"

"No – I have never been there."

"Did you ever hear of a tragic event that happened in India – at Peshawar? The disappearance of a young woman named Eve Durand?"

Mrs Tupper-Brock considered. "I may have read about it in the newspapers," she admitted. "It has a dimly familiar sound."

"Tell me – did you by any chance notice the elevator girl who took you up to the bungalow the night of Mr Kirk's dinner?"

Again the handkerchief was crushed in the woman's hand. "I did not. Why should I?"

"She was, then, quite unknown to you?"

"I fancy she was. Of course, one doesn't study – er – that sort of person."

"Ah, yes." Miss Morrow sought an inconsequential ending for the interview. "You are English, Mrs Tupper-Brock?"

"English, yes."

"A Londoner?"

"No – I was born in Devonshire. I stayed there until my – my marriage. Then my husband took me to York, where he had a living. He was a clergyman, you know."

"Thank you so much."

"I'm afraid I have been of very little help."

"Oh, but I hardly looked for anything else," Miss Morrow smiled. "These questions are a mere formality. Everyone at the dinner – you understand. It was good of you to come." She rose.

Mrs Tupper-Brock restored the handkerchief to her bag, and also stood up. "That is all, I take it?"

"Oh, quite. It's a lovely day after the rain."

"Beautiful," murmured the woman, and moved toward the door. Kirk came from the corner where he had been lolling.

"Any other little service I can do?" he asked.

"Not at present, thanks. You're immensely valuable."

Mrs Tupper-Brock had reached the outer room. Kirk spoke in a low voice. "No word of the elevator girl?"

"Not a trace," Miss Morrow sighed. "The same old story. But just what I expected."

Kirk looked toward the other room. "And the lady who has just left," he whispered. "A complete dud, wasn't she? I'm awfully sorry. She told you nothing."

The girl came very close, fragrant, young, smiling. Kirk felt a bit dizzy. "You are wrong," she said softly. "The lady who has just left told me a great deal."

"You mean?"

"I mean she's a liar, if I ever met one. A liar, and a poor one. I'm going to prove it, too."

"Bright girl," Kirk smiled, and, hurrying out, caught up with Mrs Tupper-Brock in the hall.

The return ride to Mrs Dawson Kirk's house was another strained, silent affair, and Kirk parted from the dark, mysterious lady with a distinct feeling of relief. He drove back to the Kirk Building and ascended to the twentieth floor. As he got out of the elevator he saw Mr Cuttle trying his office door. Cuttle was not only the night-watchman, but was also assistant superintendent of the building, a title in which he took great pride.

"Hello, Cuttle," Kirk said. "Want to see me?"

"I do, sir," Cuttle answered. "Something that may be important." Kirk unlocked the office and they went in.

"It's about that girl, Grace Lane, sir," Cuttle explained, when they reached the inner room. "The one who disappeared last night."

"Oh, yes." Kirk looked at him with sudden interest. "What about her?"

"The police asked me a lot of questions. Where did I get her, and all that. There was one point on which I was silent. I thought I had better speak to you first, Mr Kirk."

"Well, I don't know, Cuttle. It isn't wise to try to conceal things from the police."

"But on this point, sir—"

"What point?"

"The matter of how I came to hire her. The letter she brought to me from a certain person—"

"From what person?"

"From your grandmother, sir. From Mrs Dawson Kirk."

"Good lord! Grace Lane came to you with a letter from my grandmother?"

"She did. I still have the letter. Perhaps you would like to see it?"

Cuttle produced a gray, expensive-looking envelope. Kirk took out the enclosure and saw that the message was written in his grandmother's cramped, old-fashioned hand. He read:

"My dear Mr Cuttle: The young woman who presents this letter is a good friend of mine, Miss Grace Lane. I should be very pleased if you could find some employment for her in the building – I have thought of the work on the elevators. Miss Lane is far above such work, but she has had a bad time of it, and is eager to take anything that offers. I am sure you will find her willing and competent. I will vouch for her in every way. Sincerely yours, Mary Winthrop Kirk."

Kirk finished, a puzzled frown on his face. "I'll keep this, Cuttle," he remarked, putting the letter in his pocket. "And – I guess it was just as well you said nothing to the police."

"I thought so, sir," replied Cuttle with deep satisfaction, and retired.

XVI

LONG LIFE AND HAPPINESS

Kirk hurried up to the bungalow. He found Charlie Chan seated in a chair by the window, completely engrossed in Colonel John Beetham's description of *The Land Beyond the Khyber.*

"Well," said Kirk, "here's news for you. I've just got on the trail of another suspect in our little case."

"The more the increased merriment," Chan assured him. "Kindly deign to name the newest person who has been performing queer antics."

"Just my grandmother," Kirk returned. "That's all."

Charlie allowed himself the luxury of a moment's surprise. "You overwhelm me with amazement. That dear old lady. What misendeavor has she been up to?"

"It was she who got Grace Lane – or whatever her confounded name is – a job in the Kirk Building." The young man repeated his talk with Cuttle and showed Chan the letter.

Charlie read Mrs Dawson Kirk's warm endorsement with interest. He handed it back, smiling. "Grandmother now becomes a lady to be investigated. Humbly suggest you place Miss Morrow on her track."

Kirk laughed. "I'll do it. The resulting display of fireworks ought to prove a very pretty sight." He called Miss Morrow and, having heard his story, she suggested an interview with Mrs Kirk at the bungalow at two o'clock.

The young man got his grandmother on the wire. "Hello," he said, "this is Barry. Did I understand you to say this morning you'd like to be mixed up in the Bruce murder?"

"Well – in a nice way – I wouldn't mind. In fact, I'd rather enjoy it."

"You've got your wish. Just at present the police are after you."

"Mercy – what have I done?"

"I leave that to you. Think over your sins, and report here at two o'clock. Miss Morrow wants to question you."

"She does, eh? Well, I'm not afraid of her."

"All right. Only come."

"I shall have to leave early. I promised to go to a lecture—"

"Never mind. You'll leave when the law has finished with you. I suggest that you come prepared to tell the truth. If you do, I may yet be able to keep you out of jail."

"You can't frighten me. I'll come – but only from curiosity. I should like to see that young woman in action. I haven't a doubt in the world but what I can hold my own."

"I heard different," replied Kirk. "Remember – two o'clock. Sharp!"

He hung up the receiver and waited impatiently for the hour of the conflict. At a quarter before two Miss Morrow arrived on the scene.

"This is a strange turn," she said, when Kirk had taken her coat. "So your grandmother knows Jennie Jerome Marie Lantelme?"

"Knows her!" replied Kirk. "They're great friends." He handed over the letter. "Read that. Vouches for her in every way. Good old grandmother!"

Miss Morrow smiled. "I must handle her gently," she remarked. "Somehow, I don't believe she approves of me."

"She's reached the age where she doesn't approve of anybody," Kirk explained. "Not even of me. A fine noble character, as you well know. Yet she discovers flaws. Can you imagine!"

"Absurd," cried Miss Morrow.

"Don't be too nice to her," Kirk suggested. "She'll like you better if you walk all over her. Some people are made that way."

Charlie entered from his room. "Ah, Miss Morrow. Again you add decoration to the scene. Am I wrong in presuming that Captain Flannery has apprehended Eve Durand?"

"If you mean the elevator girl, you are quite wrong. Not a trace of her. You still think she was Eve Durand?"

"If she wasn't, then I must bow my head in sack-cloth and ashes," Chan replied.

"Well, that's no place for anybody's head," Kirk remarked.

"None the less, mine has been there," Chan grinned.

Mrs Dawson Kirk bustled in. "Here I am, on time to the minute. Please make a note of that."

"Hello," Kirk greeted her. "You remember Miss Morrow, of course."

"Oh, yes – the lawyer. How do you do. And Mr Chan – look here, why haven't you solved this case?"

"A little more patience," grinned Chan. "We are getting warm now. You are under hovering cloud of suspicion at last."

"So I hear," snapped the old lady. She turned to Miss Morrow. "Well, my dear, Barry said you wanted to cross-question me."

"Nothing cross about it," Miss Morrow said, with a smile. "Just a few polite questions."

"Oh, really. Don't be too polite. I'm always suspicious of too polite people. You don't think I killed poor Sir Frederic, I hope?"

"Not precisely. But you've written a letter— "

"I suppose so. Have a habit of writing indiscreet letters. And old habits are hard to break. But I always put 'burn this' at the bottom. Somebody has failed to follow my instructions, eh?"

Miss Morrow shook her head. "I believe you omitted that admonition in this case." She handed the letter to Mrs Kirk. "You wrote that, didn't you?"

Mrs Kirk glanced it through. "Certainly I wrote it. What of it?"

"This Grace Lane was a good friend of yours?"

"In a way, yes. Of course, I scarcely knew the girl—"

"Oho," cried Barry Kirk. "You vouched for her in every way, yet you scarcely knew her."

"Keep out of this, Barry," advised the old lady. "You're not a lawyer. You haven't the brains."

"Then you knew Grace Lane only slightly, Mrs Kirk?" the girl continued.

"That's what I said."

"Yet you recommended her without reservation? Why did you do that?"

Mrs Kirk hesitated. "If you'll pardon me, I regard it as my own affair."

"I'm sorry," Miss Morrow replied quickly, "but you will have to answer. Please do not be deceived by the setting of this interview. It is not a social function. I am acting for the district attorney's office, and I mean business."

Mrs Kirk's eyes flashed. "I understand. But now, if you don't mind, I'd like to ask a few questions."

"You may do so. And when you have finished, I will resume."

"What has this girl, Grace Lane, to do with the murder of Sir Frederic Bruce?"

"That is what we are trying to determine."

"You mean she had something to do with it?"

"We believe she had. And that is why your recommendation of her is no longer your own affair, Mrs Kirk."

The old lady sat firmly on the edge of her chair. "I shan't say a word until I know where all this is leading us."

"It'll lead you to jail if you don't stop being stubborn," suggested Barry Kirk.

"Indeed? Well, I have friends among the lawyers, too. Miss Morrow, I want to know Grace Lane's connection with Sir Frederic?"

"I have no objection to telling you – if you will keep the matter to yourself."

"She's the most indiscreet woman on the west coast," Kirk warned.

"Hush up, Barry. I can keep still if I have to, Miss Morrow—?"

"When Sir Frederic came here," Miss Morrow explained, "he was seeking a woman named Eve Durand, who disappeared from India fifteen years ago. We suspect Grace Lane was that woman."

"Well, why don't you ask her?"

"We'd be glad to, but we can't. You see, she's disappeared again."

"What! She's gone?"

"Yes. Now I have answered your questions, and I expect you to do as much for me." Miss Morrow became again very businesslike. "Grace Lane was undoubtedly brought to you by a third person – a person you trusted. Who was it?"

Mrs Kirk shook her head. "I'm sorry. I can't tell you."

"You realize, of course, the seriousness of your refusal?"

"I – well, I – good heavens, what have I got mixed up in, anyhow? A respectable woman like me—"

"Precisely," said Miss Morrow sternly. "A woman honored throughout the city, a woman prominent in every forward-looking movement – I must say I am surprised, Mrs Kirk, to find you obstructing the course of justice. And all because this person who brought Grace Lane to you is now asking you to keep the matter secret—"

"I didn't say that."

"But I did. It's true, isn't it?"

"Well – yes – it is. And I must say I think she's asking a good deal of me—"

"She? Then Grace Lane was brought to you by a woman?"

"What? Oh – oh, yes. Of course. I'll admit that."

"You have admitted it," chuckled Barry Kirk.

"Tell me this," Miss Morrow went on, "before you left to come down here, did you let Mrs Tupper-Brock know where you were going?"

"I did."

"Did you tell her you expected to be questioned by me when you got here?"

"Y-yes."

"And was it then that she asked you not to reveal the fact that she was the person who brought Grace Lane to you, with a request that you help the girl?" Mrs Kirk was silent. "You needn't answer," Miss Morrow smiled. "As a matter of fact, you have answered. Your face, you know."

Mrs Kirk shrugged. "You're a clever young woman," she complained.

"Since that is settled, and I now know that it was Mrs Tupper-Brock who introduced the Lane girl to you," Miss Morrow continued, "there is no real reason why you shouldn't give me the details. How long ago did it happen?"

Mrs Kirk hesitated, and then surrendered. "Several months ago," she said. "Helen brought the girl to the house. She told me she had met her on a ferry – that they were old friends – had known each other in Devonshire, a great many years back."

"In Devonshire. Please go on."

"Helen said this girl had been through a lot—"

"What?"

"I didn't ask. I have some delicacy. Also, that she was destitute and in desperate need of work. She was such a pretty, modest, feminine little thing, I took an immediate fancy to her. So I got her the job in this building."

"Without consulting me," Kirk suggested.

"Why should I? It was a matter requiring instant action. You were off somewhere as usual."

"And that's all you know about Grace Lane?" inquired Miss Morrow.

"Yes. I made inquiries, and found she was doing well and was, apparently, happy. When we came up here the other night, we spoke to her. She thanked me, very nicely. I'm sorry she's been hounded out of town."

Miss Morrow smiled. "One thing more. Have you noticed any signs of a close friendship between Mrs Tupper-Brock and Colonel Beetham?"

"I believe they've gone out together occasionally. I don't spy on them."

"Naturally not. I think that is all, Mrs Kirk."

Mrs Kirk stood up. She appeared to be in a rather chastened mood. "Thanks. Fortunately, I can still get to my lecture on time."

"Just one point," added the girl. "I'd rather you didn't repeat this conversation to Mrs Tupper-Brock."

"Me – I won't repeat it to anybody." The old lady smiled grimly. "Somehow I don't seem to have come out of it as well as I expected." She said goodby and made a hasty exit.

"Bully for you," cried Kirk, with an admiring look at Miss Morrow.

She stood, frowning. "What did I tell you this morning? Mrs Tupper-Brock was lying, but I didn't expect confirmation so soon."

"Going to have her on the carpet again?" Kirk asked.

"I am not. What's the good of more lies? Grace Lane was an old friend – which may mean that Grace Lane will write to Mrs Tupper-Brock from wherever she is hiding. I am going to make immediate arrangements with the postal authorities. Mrs Tupper-Brock's mail will reach her through my office from now on."

"Excellent," approved Chan. "You have wise head on pretty shoulders. What an unexpected combination! May I inquire, what is our good friend Flannery doing?"

"The Captain has taken a sudden fancy to Miss Lila Barr. I believe he has ordered her to his office at five this afternoon, for what he calls a grilling. I can't be there, but if I were you, I'd drop in on it."

Chan shrugged. "I fear I will look in vain for welcome inscribed in glowing characters on the mat. However, I will appear with offhand air."

Miss Morrow turned to Barry Kirk. "I do hope your grandmother won't hold my inquisition against me."

"Nonsense. You were splendid, and she's crazy about you. I saw it in her eyes when she went out."

"I didn't," smiled the girl.

"You didn't look carefully. That's where you make a mistake. Examine the eyes about you. You'll find a lot more approval than you suspect."

"Really? I'm afraid I'm too busy – I must leave that sort of thing to the old-fashioned girls. Now, I must run along. There's just a chance I can find Grace Lane for Captain Flannery. Someone must."

"And it might as well be you," quoted Kirk. "I'll hope to see you again soon." He showed her out.

At four thirty Charlie Chan strolled to the Hall of Justice and walked in on Captain Flannery. The Captain appeared to be in rare good humor.

"How are you, Sergeant," he said. "What's new with you?"

"With me, everything has aged look," Chan replied.

"Not getting on as fast as you expected, are you?" Flannery inquired. "Well, this should be a lesson to you. Every frog ought to stick to his own pond. You may be a world-beater in a village like Honolulu, but you're on the big time over here. You're in over your depth."

"How true," Charlie agreed. "I am often dismayed, but I think of you and know you will not permit me to drown. Something has happened to elevate your spirit?"

"It sure has. I've just pulled off a neat little stunt. You see, I had a grand idea. I put an ad in the morning paper for those velvet slippers—"

"Ah, yes," Chan grinned. "Inspector Duff warned me you were about to be hit by that idea."

"Oh, he did, did he? Well, I'm not taking orders from Duff. I was on the point of doing it some days ago, but it slipped my mind. Duff recalled it to me, that's all. I put a very cagy advertisement in the paper, and—"

"Results are already apparent?" Chan finished.

"Are they? I'll say so." Flannery took up something wrapped in a soiled newspaper. The string had already been loosened, and casting it aside, he revealed the contents of the bundle. Before Chan's eyes lay the red velvet slippers from the Chinese Legation, the slippers found on the feet of Hilary Galt that tragic night in London, the slippers in which Sir Frederic Bruce had walked to his death little more than a week ago.

"What happy luck," Charlie said.

"Ain't it?" agreed Flannery. "A soldier from out at the Presidio brought them in less than an hour ago. It seems he was crossing to Oakland to visit his girl last Wednesday noon, and he picked this package up from one of the benches on the ferry-boat. There was nobody about to claim it, so he took it along. Of course, he should have turned it over to the ferry people – but he didn't. I told him that was all right with me."

"On ferry-boat to Oakland," Chan repeated.

"Yes. This guy'd been wondering what to do with his find, and he was mighty pleased when I slipped him a five spot."

Charlie turned the slippers slowly about in his hands. Again he was interested by the Chinese character which promised long life and happiness. A lying promise, that. The slippers had not brought long life and happiness to Hilary Galt. Nor to Sir Frederic Bruce.

"Just where," Chan mused, "do we arrive at now?"

"Well, I'll have to admit that we're still a long ways from home," Flannery replied. "But we're getting on. Last Wednesday, the day after the murder, somebody left these slippers on an Oakland ferry-boat. Left them intentionally, I'll bet – glad enough to be rid of 'em."

"In same identical paper," Charlie inquired, "they were always wrapped?"

"Yes – that's the paper this fellow found them in. An evening paper dated last Wednesday night. A first edition, issued about ten in the morning."

Chan spread out the newspaper and studied it. "You have been carefully over this journal, I suspect?"

"Why – er – I haven't had time," Flannery told him.

"Nothing of note catches the eye," Chan remarked. "Except – ah, yes – here on margin of first page. A few figures, carelessly inscribed in pencil. Paper is torn in that locality, and they are almost obliterated."

Flannery came closer, and Charlie pointed. A small sum in addition had evidently been worked out.

$79. 23. – 103.

"A hundred three," Flannery read. "That's wrong. Seventy-nine and twenty-three don't add up to a hundred three."

"Then we must seek one who is poor scholar of arithmetic," Chan replied. "If you have no inclination for objecting, I will jot figures down."

"Go ahead. Put your big brain on it. But don't forget – I produced the slippers."

"And the newspaper," Charlie added. "The brightest act you have performed to date."

The door opened, and a man in uniform entered. "That dame's outside, Captain," he announced. "She's brought her fellow with her. Shall I fetch 'em in?"

"Sure," Flannery nodded. "It's Miss Lila Barr," he explained to Chan. "I got to thinking about her, and she don't sound so good to me. I'm going to have another talk with her. You can stay, if you want to."

"Overwhelmed by your courtesy," Chan responded.

Miss Lila Barr came timidly through the door. After her came Kinsey, Kirk's secretary. The girl seemed very much worried.

"You wanted me, Captain Flannery?"

"Yeah. Come in. Sit down." He looked at Kinsey. "Who's this?"

"Mr Kinsey – a friend of mine," the girl explained. "I thought you wouldn't mind—"

"Your fellow, eh?"

"Well, – I suppose—"

"The guy you was crying about that night you came out of the office where you saw Sir Frederic?"

"Yes."

"Well, I'm glad to meet him. I'm glad you can prove you've got a fellow, anyhow. But even so – that story of yours sounds pretty fishy to me."

"I can't help how it sounds," returned the girl with spirit. "It's the truth."

"All right. Let it go. It's the next night I want to talk about now. The night Sir Frederic was killed. You were working in your office that night?"

"Yes, sir. Though I must have left before – the thing – happened."

"How do you know you left before it happened?"

"I don't. I was just supposing—"

"Don't suppose with me," bullied Flannery.

"She has good reason for thinking she left before the murder," Kinsey put in. "She heard no shot fired."

Flannery swung on him. "Say – when I want any answers from you, I'll ask for 'em." He turned back to the girl. "You didn't hear any shot?"

"No, sir."

"And you didn't see anybody in the hall when you went home?"

"Well – I – I— "

"Yes? Out with it."

"I'd like to change my testimony on that point."

"Oh, you would, would you?"

"Yes. I have talked it over with Mr Kinsey, and he thinks I was wrong to – to – say what I did— "

"To lie, you mean?"

"But I didn't want to be entangled in it," pleaded the girl. "I saw myself testifying in court – and I didn't think – it just seemed I couldn't— "

"You couldn't help us, eh? Young woman, this is serious business. I could lock you up— "

"Oh, but if I change my testimony? If I tell you the truth now?"

"Well, we'll see. But make sure of one thing – that it's the truth at last. Then there was somebody in the hall?"

"Yes. I started to leave the office, but just as I opened the door, I remembered my umbrella. So I went back. But in that moment at the door, I saw two men standing near the elevators."

"You saw two men. What did they look like?"

"One – one was a Chinese."

Flannery was startled. "A Chinese. Say – it wasn't Mr Chan here?" Charlie smiled.

"Oh, no," the girl continued. "It was an older Chinese. He was talking with a tall, thin man. A man whose picture I have seen in the newspapers."

"Oh, you've seen his picture in the papers? What's his name?"

"His name is Colonel John Beetham, and I believe he is – an explorer."

"I see." Flannery got up and paced the floor. "You saw Beetham talking with a Chinese in the hall just before Sir Frederic was killed. Then you went back to get your umbrella?"

"Yes – and when I came out again they were gone."

"Anything else?"

"No – I guess not."

"Think hard. You've juggled the truth once."

"She was not under oath," protested Kinsey.

"Well, what if she wasn't? She obstructed our work, and that's no joking matter. However, I'll overlook it, now that she's finally come across. You can go. I may want you again."

The girl and Kinsey went out. Flannery walked the floor in high glee.

"Now I'm getting somewhere," he cried. "Beetham! I haven't paid much attention to him, but I'll make up for lost time from here on. Beetham was in the hall talking with a Chinaman a few minutes before the murder. And he was supposed to be upstairs running his magic lantern. A Chinaman – do you get it? Those slippers came from the Chinese Legation. By heaven, it's beginning to tie up at last."

"If I might presume," said Chan, "you now propose to—"

"I propose to get after Colonel Beetham. He told Miss Morrow he didn't leave the room upstairs. Another liar – and a distinguished one this time."

"Humbly asking pardon," Chan ventured, "Colonel Beetham very clever man. Have a care he does not outwit you."

"I'm not afraid of him. He can't fool me. I'm too old at this game."

"Magnificent confidence," Charlie smiled. "Let us hope it is justified by the finish."

"It will be, all right. You just leave Colonel Beetham to me."

"With utmost gladness," agreed Chan. "If you will allot something else to me."

"What's that?" Flannery demanded.

"I refer to faint little figures on newspaper margin."

"Poor arithmetic," snorted Flannery. "And a poor clue."

"Time will reveal," said Chan gently.

XVII

THE WOMAN FROM PESHAWAR

Barry Kirk answered the ring of the telephone the next morning at ten, and was greeted by a voice that, even over the wire, seemed to afford him pleasure.

"Good morning," he said. "I'm glad to hear from you. This is what I call starting the day right."

"Thanks ever so much," Miss Morrow replied. "Now that your day has begun auspiciously, would you mind fading away into the background and giving Mr Chan your place at the telephone?"

"What – you don't want to talk to me?"

"I'm sorry – no. I'm rather busy today."

"Well, I can take a hint as quickly as the next man. I know when I'm not wanted. That's what you meant to convey, isn't it—"

"Please, Mr Kirk."

"Here's Charlie now. I'm not angry, but I'm terribly, terribly hurt—" He handed the telephone to Chan.

"Oh, Mr Chan," the girl said. "Captain Flannery is going to interview Colonel Beetham at eleven o'clock. He's all Beetham today. He's asked me to be on hand to remind the Colonel about his testimony the night of the murder, and I suggest you come too."

"The Captain demands me?" Chan inquired.

"I demand you. Isn't that enough?"

"To me it is delicious plenty," Charlie replied. "I will be there – at Captain Flannery's office, I presume?"

"Yes. Don't fail me," Miss Morrow said, and rang off.

"Something doing?" Kirk asked.

Chan shrugged. "Captain Flannery has hot spasm about Colonel Beetham. He interrogates him at eleven, and I am invited."

"How about me?"

"I am stricken by regret, but you are not mentioned."

"Then I hardly think I'll go," Kirk said.

At a little before eleven, Charlie went to the Hall of Justice. In Flannery's dark office he found Miss Morrow, brightening the dreary corner where she was.

"Good morning," she said. "The Captain is showing Inspector Duff about the building. I'm glad you're here. Somehow I've got the impression Captain Flannery doesn't care much for me this morning."

"Mainland police have stupid sinking spells," Chan informed her.

Flannery came in, followed by Inspector Duff. He stood for a minute glaring at Charlie and the girl.

"Well, a fine pair you are," he roared. "What's the idea, anyhow?"

"What *is* the idea, Captain?" asked Miss Morrow sweetly.

"The idea seems to be to keep me in the dark," Flannery went on. "What do you think I am? A mind-reader? I've just been talking with Inspector Duff about Colonel Beetham, and I discover you two know a lot more about the Colonel than you've ever told me."

"Please understand – I haven't been tale-bearing," smiled Duff. "I mentioned these things thinking of course the Captain knew them."

"Of course you thought I knew them," Flannery exploded. "Why shouldn't I know them? I'm supposed to be in charge of this case, ain't I? Yet you two have been digging up stuff right along and keeping it to yourselves. I tell you, it makes me sore—"

"Oh, I'm so sorry," cried Miss Morrow.

"That helps a lot. What's all this about a servant of the Colonel's – a Chinaman named Li Gung? Are you willing to talk now, Sergeant Chan, or are you still playing button, button, who's got the—"

"I'm the guilty one," the girl cut in. "I should have told you myself. Naturally, Mr Chan must have thought I had."

"Oh, no," Chan protested. "Please shift all guilt from those pretty shoulders to my extensive ones. I have made mistake. It is true I have pondered certain facts in silence, but I was hoping some great light would break—"

"All right, all right," Flannery interrupted. "But will you talk now, that's what I want to know? When did you first hear about Li Gung?"

"At noon of the day Sir Frederic was killed, I have great honor to lunch with him. After lunch he takes me apart and talks of this Li Gung, a stranger visiting relatives in Jackson Street. He suggests I might make cunning inquiries of the man, but I am forced to refuse the task. On morning after murder I am in stateroom of *Maui* boat, foolishly believing I am going to Honolulu, when I hear Colonel Beetham in next cabin saying farewell to one he calls Li Gung. The Colonel directs that Gung lie low in Honolulu, and answer no questions."

"And all that was so unimportant I never heard of it," stormed Flannery. "How about the fact that Beetham was one of the guests at the picnic near Peshawar?"

"We did not learn that until Tuesday night," Miss Morrow informed him.

"Only had about thirty-six hours to tell me, eh. On May fourth, nineteen hundred and thirteen, Colonel Beetham left Peshawar by way of the – er – the Khyber Pass to go to – to – to make a trip—"

"To Teheran by way of Afghanistan and the Kevir Desert of northern Persia," Duff helped him out.

"Yes. You told the Inspector that, Sergeant. But you never told me."

Charlie shrugged. "Why should I trouble you? The matter appears to mean nothing. True enough, I might make a surmise – a most picturesque surmise. But I see you, Captain, floundering about in difficult murder case. Should I ask such a man to come with me and gaze upon the bright tapestry of romance?"

"Whatever that means," Flannery returned. "If I hadn't got that Barr girl in, I'd still be in the dark. I was too smart for you – I hit on Beetham's trail myself – but that doesn't excuse you. I'm disappointed in the pair of you."

"Overwhelmed with painful regret," Chan bowed.

"Oh, forget it." A man in uniform ushered Colonel Beetham into the room.

The Colonel knew a good tailor, a tailor who no doubt rejoiced in the trim, lithe figure of his client. He was faultlessly attired, with a flower in his button-hole, a stick in his gloved hand. For a moment he stood, those tired eyes that had looked on so many lonely corners of the world unusually alert and keen.

"Good morning," he said. He bowed to Miss Morrow and Chan. "Ah – this, I believe, is Captain Flannery—"

"Morning," replied Flannery. "Meet Inspector Duff, of Scotland Yard."

"Delighted," Beetham answered. "I am very happy to see a man from the Yard. No doubt the search for Sir Frederic's murderer will get forward now."

"I guess it will," growled Flannery, "if you answer a few questions for us – and tell the truth—"

The Colonel raised his eyebrows very slightly. "The truth, of course," he remarked, with a wan smile. "I shall do my best. May I sit down?"

"Sure," replied Flannery, indicating a dusty chair. "On the night Sir Frederic was killed, you were giving a magic lantern show on the floor above—"

"I should hardly have called it that. Motion pictures, you know, of Tibet—"

"Yes, yes. You did a lecture with these lantern slides, but toward the end you dropped out and let the performance run itself. Later Miss Morrow here asked you – what was it you asked him, Miss Morrow?"

"I referred to that moment when he left the machine," the girl said. "He assured me that he had not been absent from the room during the interval."

The Captain looked at Beetham. "Is that right, Colonel?"

"Yes – I fancy that is what I told her."

"Why?"

"Why? What do you mean?"

"Why did you tell her that when you knew damn well you had been down on the twentieth floor talking with a Chinaman?"

Beetham laughed softly. "Have you never done anything that you later regretted, Captain? The matter struck me as of no importance – I had seen nothing of note on my brief jaunt below. I had a sort of inborn diffidence about being involved in the scandal. So I very foolishly made a slight – er – misstatement."

"Then you did go down to the twentieth floor?"

"Only for a second. You see, a motion-picture projector and seven reels of film make a rather heavy load. My old boy, Li Gung, had assisted me in bringing the outfit to Mr Kirk's apartment. I thought I should be finished by ten, and I told him to be back then. When I left the machine at fifteen minutes past ten, I realized that I still had another reel to show. I ran downstairs, found Gung waiting on the lower floor, and told him to go home. I said I would carry the machine away myself."

"Ah, yes – and he left?"

"He went at once, in the lift. The lift girl can verify my statement – if—"

"If what?"

"If she will."

"You were going to say – if we can find her."

"Why should I say that. Isn't she about?"

"She is not. In her absence, maybe Li Gung can back up your story?"

"I'm sure he can – if you care to cable him. He is in Honolulu at the moment."

"He left the next noon, on the *Maui*?"

"Yes, he did."

"You saw him off?"

"Naturally. He has been with me more than twenty years. A faithful chap."

"When you said goodby, you told him to lie low over in Hawaii."

"Yes, I – yes, I did. You see, there was some trouble about his passport. I was fearful he might get into difficulties."

"You also told him to answer no questions."

"For the same reason, of course."

"You knew he would have to show his passport on landing. If it wasn't O.K. did you suppose lying low after that would do any good?"

"Show his passport at another American port? Really, you know, I'm frightfully ignorant of your many rules and regulations. Quite confusing, I find them."

"You must – a man who's traveled as little as you have, Colonel."

"Ah, yes. Now you're being sarcastic."

"Oh, don't mind me," Flannery said. "We'll drop Li Gung. But I'm not through yet. I understand you were at Peshawar, in India, on the night of May third, nineteen hundred and thirteen."

Beetham nodded slowly. "That is a matter of record."

"And can't very well be denied, eh? You went out into the hills on a picnic. One of the party was a woman named Eve Durand." Beetham stirred slightly. "That night Eve Durand disappeared and has never been seen since. Have you any idea how she got out of India?"

"If she has never been seen since, how do you know she did get out of India?"

"Never mind. I'm asking you questions. You remember the incident?"

"Naturally. A shocking affair."

Flannery studied him for a moment. "Tell me, Colonel – had you ever met Sir Frederic before the other night at Barry Kirk's bungalow?"

"Never. Stop a bit. I believe he said he had been at a dinner of the Royal Geographical Society in London, and had seen me there. But I did not recall the meeting."

"You didn't know that he had come to San Francisco to find Eve Durand?"

"Had he really? How extraordinary."

"You didn't know it?"

"Of course not."

"Could you have given him any help if you had?"

"I could not," replied Beetham firmly.

"All right, Colonel. You're not thinking of leaving San Francisco soon?"

"In a few days – when I have completed arrangements for my next long expedition."

"You're not leaving until we find out who killed Sir Frederic. Is that understood?"

"But, my dear fellow – surely you don't think—"

"I think your testimony may prove valuable. I'm asking you – is it understood?"

"Perfectly. I shall hope, however, for your early success."

"We all hope for it."

"Of course." Beetham turned to Inspector Duff. "A frightful thing. Sir Frederic was a charming fellow—"

"And much beloved," said Duff evenly. "Please don't worry. Everything possible is being done, Colonel Beetham."

"I am happy to hear that." Beetham rose. "Now – if there's nothing more—"

"Not at present," said Flannery.

"Thank you so much," replied the Colonel, and went debonairly out.

Flannery stared after him. "He lies like a gentleman, don't he?" he remarked.

"Beautifully," sighed Miss Morrow, her eyes on the door through which the explorer had gone.

"Well, he don't fool me," Flannery continued. "He knows more about this than he's telling. If he was anybody but the famous Colonel Beetham, I'd take a chance and lock him up this morning."

"Oh, but you couldn't," the girl cried.

"I suppose not. I'd be mobbed by all the club women in the Bay District. However, I don't need to. He's too well known to make a getaway. But I'd better keep him shadowed, at that. Now, let's get to business. If only Li Gung was here, I'd sweat something out of him. What was that Sir Frederic told you, Sergeant? About Li Gung's relatives in Jackson Street? I might look them up."

"No use," Chan answered. "I have already done so."

"Oh, you have? Without a word to me, of course—"

"Words of no avail. I made most pitiful failure. I am admitted to house, but plans are foiled by kind act of boy scout—"

"A boy scout in the family, eh?"

"Yes – name of Willie Li. The family of Henry Li, Oriental Apartment House."

Flannery considered. "Well, the young generation will talk, if the old one won't. Willie ought to have a chance."

"He has obtained it. He tells me little – save that once on a hard journey Colonel Beetham kills a man."

"He told you that? Then he knows something about Beetham's journeys?"

"Undubitably he does. He has overheard talk—"

Flannery jumped up. "That's enough for me, I'll have Manley of the Chinatown Squad bring the kid here tonight. They're all crazy about Manley, these Chink kids. We'll get something."

The telephone rang. Flannery answered, and then relinquished it to Miss Morrow. As she listened to the news coming over the wire, her eyes brightened with excitement. She hung up the receiver and turned to the others.

"That was the district attorney," she announced. "We've got hold of a letter mailed to Mrs Tupper-Brock from Santa Barbara. It was written by Grace Lane, and it gives her present address."

"Fine business," Flannery cried. "I told you she couldn't get away from me. I'll get a couple of men off in a car right away." He looked at Miss Morrow. "They can stop at your office for the address."

She nodded. "I'm going right back. I'll give it to them."

Flannery rubbed his hands. "Things are looking up at last! Make it seven tonight – I'll have the kid here then. Sergeant – you're coming. I may want your help. And you can look in if you like, Inspector."

"Thanks," Duff said.

"How about me?" asked Miss Morrow.

He frowned at her. "I'm not so pleased with you. All those secrets—"

"But I'm so sorry." She smiled at him. "And I was a little help to you in finding Grace Lane, you know."

"I guess you were, at that. Sure – come along, if you want to."

The party scattered, and Charlie Chan went back to the bungalow, where he found Barry Kirk eagerly awaiting news. When he heard the plan for the evening, Kirk insisted on taking Miss Morrow and Chan to dinner. At six thirty they left the obscure little restaurant he had selected because of its capable chef, and strolled toward the Hall of Justice.

The night was clear and cool, without fog, and the stars were bright as torches overhead. They skirted the fringe of Chinatown and passed on through Portsmouth Square, the old Plaza of romantic history. It was emptied now of its usual derelicts and adventurers; the memorial to R. L. S. stood lonely and serene in the starlight.

Flannery and Duff were waiting in the former's office. The Captain regarded Barry Kirk without enthusiasm.

"We're all here, ain't we?" he inquired.

"I thought you wouldn't mind," smiled Kirk.

"Oh, well – it's all right. I guess it's pretty late now to bar you out." He turned to Miss Morrow. "You saw Petersen, didn't you?"

"Yes. I gave him the address."

"He had Myers with him. Good men, both of them. They'll be in Santa Barbara this evening, and can start back at sunrise. Barring accidents, they'll bring Grace Lane into this office late tomorrow afternoon. And if she gets away from me again, she'll be going some."

They sat down. Presently a huge police officer in plain clothes, with a khaki shirt, came in. He was kindly and smiling, but he had the keen eye of a man who is prepared for any emergency. Flannery introduced him.

"Sergeant Manley," he explained. "Head of the Chinatown Squad for seven years – which is a good many years longer than anyone else has lived to hold that job."

Manley's manner was cordial. "Glad to meet you," he said. "I've got the kid outside, Captain. I picked him up and brought him along without giving him a chance to run home for instructions."

"Good idea," Flannery nodded. "Will he talk?"

"Oh, he'll talk all right. He and I are old friends. I'll bring him in."

He disappeared into the outer office and returned with Willie Li. The boy scout was in civilian clothes, and looked as though he would have welcomed the moral support of his uniform.

"Here you are, Willie," Manley said. "This is Captain Flannery. He's going to ask you to do him a big favor."

"Sure," grinned Willie Li.

"All boy scouts," Manley went on, "are American citizens, and they stand for law and order. That's right, ain't it, Willie?"

"In the oath," replied Willie gravely.

"I've explained to him," Manley continued, "that none of his family is mixed up in this in any way. They won't be harmed by anything he tells you."

"That's right," said Flannery. "You can take my word for it, son."

"Sure," agreed the boy readily.

"Your cousin, Li Gung," Flannery began, "has been a servant of Colonel Beetham's for a long time. He's been all over the world with the Colonel?"

Willie nodded. "Gobi Desert. Kevir Desert. Tibet, India, Afghanistan."

"You've heard Li Gung tell about his adventures with the Colonel?"

"Yes."

"Remember 'em?"

"Never going to forget," replied Willie, his little black eyes shining.

"You told your friend Mr Chan here that the Colonel once shot a man for some reason or other?"

The boy's eyes narrowed. "Because it was necessary. There was no crime there."

"Of course – of course it was necessary," rejoined Flannery heartily. "We wouldn't do anything to the Colonel because of that. We have no authority over things that happen outside of San Francisco. We're just curious, that's all. Do you remember what trip it was during which the Colonel shot this man?"

"Sure. It was the journey from Peshawar through Khyber Pass over Afghanistan."

"It happened in Afghanistan?"

"Yes. A very bad man. Muhamed Ashref Khan, keeper of the camels. He was trying to steal—"

"To steal what?"

"A pearl necklace. Colonel Beetham saw him go into the tent – the tent which no man must enter at cost of his life—"

"What tent was that?"

"The woman's tent."

There was a moment's tense silence. "The woman's tent?" Flannery repeated. "What woman?"

"The woman who was traveling with them to Teheran. The woman from Peshawar."

"Did your cousin describe her?"

"She was beautiful, with golden hair, and eyes like the blue sky. Very beautiful, my cousin said."

"And she was traveling with them from Peshawar to Teheran?"

"Yes. Only Li Gung and the Colonel knew it when they went through the pass, for she was hidden in a cart. Then she came out, and she had her own tent, which Colonel Beetham said no man must enter or he would kill him."

"But this camel man – he disobeyed? And he was shot?"

"Justly so," observed Willie Li.

"Of course," agreed Flannery. "Well, son – that's all. I'm very much obliged to you. Now run along. If I had anything to say in the scouts, you'd get a merit badge for this."

"I have twenty-two already," grinned Willie Li. "I am Eagle Scout." He and Manley went out.

Flannery got up and paced the floor. "Well, what do you know?" he cried. "This is too good to be true. Eve Durand disappears in the night – her poor husband is frantic with grief – the whole of India is turned upside down in the search for her. And all the time she's moving on through Afghanistan in the caravan of Colonel John Beetham – the great explorer everyone is crazy about, the brave, fine man no one would dream of suspecting." Flannery turned to Chan. "I see now what you meant. Romance, you called it. Well, I've got a different name for it. I call it running away with another man's wife. A pretty scandal in the Colonel's past – a lovely blot on his record – by heaven – wonderful! Do you see what it means?"

Chan shrugged. "I see you are flying high tonight."

"I certainly am – high, wide, and handsome. I've got my man, and I've got the motive, too. Sir Frederic comes to San Francisco hunting Eve Durand. And here is Colonel John Beetham, honored and respected by all – riding the top of the wave. Beetham learns why Sir Frederic has come – and he wonders. He hears the detective has been in India – has he found out how Eve Durand left that country? If he has, and springs it, the career of John Beetham is smashed. He'll be done for – finished – he won't collect any more money for his big expeditions. Is he the sort to stand by and watch that happen? He is not. What does he do?"

"The question is for mere effect," suggested Chan.

"First of all, he wants to learn how much Sir Frederic really knows. At dinner he hears that about the safe being open. He's crazy to get down there and look around. At the first opportunity he creeps downstairs, enters Mr Kirk's office—"

"Through a locked door?" inquired Chan.

"The elevator girl could get him a key. She's Eve Durand – don't forget that. Or else there's Li Gung – he's on the scene – maybe that's just by accident. But he could be used – the fire-escape—Anyhow, Beetham gets into the office. He hunts like mad, gets hold of the records, sees at a glance that Sir Frederic has discovered everything. At that moment Sir Frederic comes in. The one man in the world who knows how Eve Durand got out of India – and will tell. The man who can wreck Beetham for ever. Beetham sees red. He pulls a gun. It's a simple matter for him – he's done it before. Sir Frederic lies dead on the floor, Beetham escapes with the records – the secret of that old scandal is safe. By the Lord Harry – who'd want a better motive than that!"

"Not to mention," said Chan gently, "the velvet slippers. The slippers of Hilary Galt."

"Oh, hell," cried Flannery. "Be reasonable, man! One thing at a time."

XVIII

FLANNERY'S BIG SCENE

Greatly pleased with himself, Captain Flannery sat down behind his desk. His summing up of the case against Beetham seemed, to his way of thinking, without a flaw. He beamed at the assembled company.

"Everything is going to work out fine," he continued. "Tomorrow evening in this room I stage my big scene, and if we don't get something out of it, then I'm no judge of human nature. First, I bring in Major Durand. I tell him Eve Durand has been found and is on her way here, and while we're waiting I go back to the question of how she got out of India. I plant in his mind a suspicion of Beetham. Then I bring the woman into the room – after fifteen years' suffering and anxiety, he sees his wife at last. What's he going to think? What'll he ask himself – and her? Where's she been? Why did she leave? How did she escape from India? At that moment I produce Colonel Beetham, confront him with the husband he wronged, the woman he carried off in his caravan. I tell Durand I have certain knowledge that his wife left with Beetham. Then I sit back and watch the fireworks. How does that strike you, Sergeant Chan?"

"You would chop down the tree to catch the blackbird," Chan said.

"Well, sometimes we have to do that. It's round-about, but it ought to work. What do you think, Inspector?"

"Sounds rather good, as drama," Duff drawled. "But do you really think it will reveal the murderer of Sir Frederic?"

"It may. Somebody – the woman, or Beetham – will break. Make a damaging admission. They always do. I'll gamble on it, this time. Yes, sir – we're going to take a big stride forward tomorrow night."

Leaving Captain Flannery to an enthusiastic contemplation of his own cleverness, they departed. At the door Chan went off with Inspector Duff. Kirk and the girl strolled up the hill together.

"Want a taxi?" Kirk asked.

"Thanks. I'd rather walk – and think."

"We have something to think of, haven't we? How does it strike you? Beetham?"

She shrugged her shoulders. "Nonsense. I'll never believe it. Not if he makes a full confession himself."

"Oh, I know. He's the hero of your dreams. But just the same, my lady, he's not incapable of it. If Sir Frederic was in his way – threatening his plans – and it begins to look as though he was. Unless you don't believe that Eve Durand was in the caravan?"

"I believe that," she replied.

"Because you want to," he smiled. "It's too romantic for words, isn't it? By George, the very thought of it makes me feel young and giddy. The gay picnic party in the hills – the game of hide-and-seek – one breathless moment of meeting behind the tamarisks. 'I'm yours – take me with you when you go.' Everything forgotten – the world well lost for love. The wagon jolting out through the pass, with all that beauty hidden beneath a worn bit of canvas. Then – the old caravan road – the golden road to Samarkand – the merchants from the north crowding by – camels and swarthy men – and mingled with the dust of the trail the iron nails lost from thousands of shoes that have passed that way since time began."

"I didn't know you were so romantic."

"Ah – you've never given me a chance. You and your law books. Eight months along that famous road – nights with the white stars close overhead, dawns hazy with desert mist. Hot sun at times, and then snow, flurries of snow. The man and the woman together—"

"And the poor husband searching frantically throughout India."

"Yes, they rather forgot Durand, didn't they? But they were in love. You know, it looks to me as though we had stumbled on to a great love story. Do you think—"

"I wonder."

"You wonder what?"

"I wonder if it's all true – and if it is, does it bring us any closer to a solution of the puzzle? After all, the question remains – who killed Sir Frederic? Captain Flannery hadn't an iota of proof for any of his wild surmises involving Beetham."

"Oh, forget your worries. Let's pretend. This deserted street is the camel road to Teheran – the old silk road from China to Persia. You and I—"

"You and I have no time for silk roads now. We must find the road that leads to a solution of our mystery."

Kirk sighed. "All right. To make a headline of it, Attorney Morrow Slams Door on Romance Probe. But some day I'll catch you off your guard, and then – look out!"

"I'm never off my guard," she laughed.

On Friday morning, after breakfast, Chan hesitated a moment, and then followed Barry Kirk into his bedroom. "If you will pardon the imposition, I have bold request to make."

"Certainly, Charlie. What is it?"

"I wish you to take me to Cosmopolitan Club, and introduce me past eagle-eyed door man. After that, I have unlimited yearning to meet old employee of club."

"An old employee? Well, there's Peter Lee. He's been in charge of the check-room for thirty years. Would he do?"

"An excellent choice. I would have you suggest to this Lee that he show me about club-house, roof to cellar. Is that possible?"

"Of course." Kirk looked at him keenly. "You're still thinking about that club year-book we found beside Sir Frederic?"

"I have never ceased to think of it," Chan returned. "Whenever you are ready, please."

Deeply mystified, Kirk took him to the Cosmopolitan and turned him over to Peter Lee.

"It is not necessary that you loiter on the scene," Chan remarked, grinning with pleasure. "I will do some investigating and return to the bungalow later."

"All right," Kirk replied. "Just as you wish."

It was close to the luncheon hour when Chan showed up, his little eyes gleaming.

"What luck?" Kirk inquired.

"Time will reveal," said Chan. "I find this mainland climate bracing to an extremity. Very much fear I shall depopulate your kitchen at lunch."

"Well, don't drink too heartily of the hydrocyanic acid," Kirk smiled. "Something tells me it would be a real calamity if we lost you just at present."

After luncheon Miss Morrow telephoned to say that Grace Lane, accompanied by the two policemen, would reach Flannery's office at four o'clock. She added that they were both invited – on her own initiative.

"Let us go," Chan remarked. "Captain Flannery's big scene should have crowded house."

"What do you think will come of it?" Kirk asked.

"I am curious to learn. If it has big success, then my work here is finished. If not—"

"Yes? Then what?"

"Then I may suddenly act like pompous stager of shows myself," Chan shrugged.

Flannery, Duff and Miss Morrow were in the Captain's office when Chan and Barry Kirk walked in. "Hello," said the Captain. "Want to be in at the finish, eh?"

"Pleasure would be impossible to deny ourselves," Chan told him.

"Well, I'm all set," Flannery went on. "All my plans made."

Chan nodded. "The wise man digs his well before he is thirsty," he remarked.

"You haven't been doing any too much digging," Flannery chided. "I got to admit, Sergeant, you've kept your word. You've let me solve this case without offering very much help. However, I've been equal to it. I haven't needed you, as it turned out. You might as well have been on that boat ten days ago."

"A sad reflection for me," said Chan. "But I am not of mean nature. My hearty congratulations will be ready when desired."

Colonel Beetham was ushered into the room. His manner was nonchalant, and, as always, rather condescending.

"Ah, Captain," he remarked, "I'm here again. According to instructions—"

"I'm very glad to see you," Flannery broke in.

"And just what can I do for you today?" inquired Beetham, dropping into a chair.

"I'm anxious to have you meet – a certain lady."

The Colonel opened a cigarette case, took out a cigarette, and tapped it on the silver side of the case. "Ah, yes. I'm not precisely a lady's man, but—"

"I think you'll be interested to meet this one," Flannery told him.

"Really?" He lighted a match.

"You see," Flannery went on, "it happens to be a lady who once took a very long journey in your company."

Beetham's brown, lean hand paused with the lighted match. The flame held steady. "I do not understand you," he said.

"An eight months' journey, I believe," the Captain persisted. "Through Khyber Pass and across Afghanistan and eastern Persia to the neighborhood of Teheran."

Beetham lighted his cigarette and tossed away the match. "My dear fellow – what are you talking about?"

"You know what I'm talking about. Eve Durand – the lady you helped out of India fifteen years ago. No one suspected you, did they, Colonel? Too big a man – above suspicion – all those medals on your chest. However, I know you did it – I know you ran away with Durand's wife – and I'll prove it, too. But perhaps I needn't prove it – perhaps you'll admit it—" He stopped.

Beetham unconcernedly blew a ring of smoke toward the ceiling, and for a moment watched it dissolve. "All that," he remarked, "is so absolutely silly I refuse to answer."

"Suit yourself," replied Flannery. "At any rate, Eve Durand will be here in a few minutes, and I want you to see her again. The sight may refresh your memory. I want you to see her – standing at her husband's side."

Beetham nodded. "I shall be most happy. I knew them both, long ago. Yes, I shall be a very pleased witness of the touching reunion you picture."

A policeman appeared at the door. "Major Durand is outside," he announced.

"Good," said Flannery. "Pat – this is Colonel Beetham. I want you to take him into the back room – the second one – and stay with him until I send for the both of you."

Beetham rose. "I say, am I under arrest?" he inquired.

"You're not under arrest," returned Flannery. "But you're going with Pat. Is that clear?"

"Absolutely. Pat – I am at your service." The two disappeared. Flannery rose and going to the door leading into the anteroom, admitted Major Durand.

The Major entered and stood there, somewhat at a loss. Flannery proffered a chair. "Sit down, sir. You know everybody here. I've great news for you. We've located the woman we think is your wife, and she'll be along in a few minutes."

Durand stared at him. "You've found – Eve? Can that possibly be true?"

"We'll know in a minute," Flannery said. "I may tell you I'm certain of it – but we'll let you see for yourself. Before she comes – one or two things I want to ask you about. Among the members of that picnic party was Colonel John Beetham, the explorer?"

"Yes, of course."

"He left the next morning on a long journey through the Khyber Pass?"

"Yes. I didn't see him go, but they told me he had gone."

"Has anyone ever suggested that he may have taken your wife with him when he left?"

The question struck Durand with the force of a bullet. He paled. "No one had ever made that suggestion," he replied, almost inaudibly.

"All the same, I'm here to tell you that is exactly what happened."

Durand got up and began to pace the floor. "Beetham," he muttered. "Beetham. No, no – he wouldn't have done it. A fine chap, Beetham – one of the best. A gentleman. He wouldn't have done that to me."

"He was just in here, and I accused him of it."

"But he denied it, of course?"

"Yes – he did. But my evidence—"

"Damn your evidence," cried Durand. "He's not that kind of man, I tell you. Not Beetham. And my wife – Eve – why, what you are saying is an insult to her. She loved me. I'm sure of it – she loved me. I won't believe – I can't—"

"Ask her when she comes," suggested Flannery. Durand sank back into the chair and buried his face in his hands.

For a long moment they waited in silence. Miss Morrow's cheeks were flushed with excitement; Duff was puffing quietly on his inevitable pipe; Charlie Chan sat immobile as an idol of stone. Kirk nervously took out a cigarette, and then put it back in the case.

The man named Petersen appeared in the door. He was dusty and travel-stained.

"Hello, Jim," Flannery cried. "Have you got her?"

"I've got her this time," Petersen answered, and stood aside. The woman of so many names entered the room and halted, her eyes anxious and tired. Another long silence.

"Major Durand," said Flannery. "Unless I am much mistaken—"

Durand got slowly to his feet, and took a step forward. He studied the woman intently for a moment, and then he made a little gesture of despair.

"It's the old story," he said brokenly. "The old story over again. Captain Flannery, you *are* mistaken. This woman is not my wife."

XIX

A VIGIL IN THE DARK

For a moment no one spoke. Captain Flannery was gradually deflating like a bright red balloon that had received a fatal puncture. Suddenly his eyes blazed with anger. He turned hotly on Charlie Chan.

"You!" he shouted. "You got me into this! You and your small-time hunch. The lady is Jennie Jerome. She is also Marie Lantelme. What does that mean? It means she is Eve Durand. A guess – a fat-headed guess – and I listened to you. I believed you. Good lord, what a fool I've been!"

Profound contrition shone in Charlie's eyes. "I am so sorry. I have made stupid error. Captain – is it possible you will ever forgive me?"

Flannery snorted. "Will I ever forgive myself? Listening to a Chinaman – me, Tom Flannery. With my experience – my record – bah! I've been crazy – plumb crazy – but that's all over now." He rose. "Major Durand, a thousand apologies. I wouldn't have disappointed you again for worlds."

Durand shrugged his shoulders wearily. "Why, that doesn't matter. You meant it kindly, I know. For a moment, in spite of all that has happened, I did allow myself to hope – I did think that it might really be Eve. Silly of me – I should have learned my lesson long ago. Well, there is nothing more to be said." He moved toward the door. "If that is all, Captain—"

"Yes, that's all. I'm sorry, Major."

Durand bowed. "I'm sorry, too. No doubt I shall see you again. Good-by."

Near the door, as he went out, he passed the girl who called herself Grace Lane. She had been standing there drooping with fatigue; now she took a step nearer the desk. Her face was pale, her eyes dull with the strain of a long, hard day. "What are you going to do with me?" she asked.

"Wait a minute," growled Flannery.

Miss Morrow rose, and placed a chair for the other woman. She was rewarded by a grateful look.

"I just remembered Beetham," said Flannery. Again he scowled at Chan. "I've tipped off my hand to him – for nothing. I can thank you for that, too."

"My guilty feeling grows by jumps and bounds," sighed Charlie.

"It ought to," the Captain replied. He went to the inner door and called loudly: "Pat!" Pat appeared at once, followed by the Colonel. For an instant Beetham stood staring curiously about the room.

"But where," he remarked, "is the touching reunion? I don't see Durand. No more do I see his wife."

Flannery's face grew even redder than usual. "There's been a mistake," he admitted.

"There have been a number of mistakes, I fancy," said Beetham carelessly. "A dangerous habit, that of making mistakes, Captain. You should seek to overcome it."

"When I want your advice, I'll ask for it," responded the harassed Flannery. "You can go along. But I still regard you as an important witness in this case, and I warn you not to strike out for any more deserts until I give you the word."

"I shall remember what you say," Beetham nodded, and went out.

"What are you going to do with me?" Grace Lane persisted.

"Well, I guess you've had a pretty rough deal," Flannery said. "I apologize to you. You see, I got foolish and listened to a Chinaman, and that's how I came to make a mistake about your identity. I brought you back on a charge of stealing a uniform, but probably Mr Kirk won't want to go ahead with that."

"I should say not," cried Barry Kirk. He turned to the woman. "I hope you won't think it was my idea. You can have a bale of my uniforms, if you like."

"You're very kind," she answered.

"Not at all. What is more, your old position is yours if you want it. You know, I'm eager to beautify the Kirk Building, and I lost ground when you left."

She smiled, without replying. "I may go then?" she said, rising.

"Sure," agreed Flannery. "Run along."

Miss Morrow looked at her keenly. "Where are you going?"

"I don't know. I—"

"I do," said the deputy district attorney. "You're going home with me. I've got an apartment – there's loads of room. You shall stay with me for this one night, at least."

"You – you are really too good to me," replied Grace Lane, and her voice broke slightly.

"Nonsense. We've all been far too unkind to you. Come along."

The two women went out. Flannery sank down behind his desk. "Now I'm going at this thing in my own way for a change," he announced. "This has been an awful upset, but I had it coming to me. Listening to a Chinaman! If Grace Lane isn't Eve Durand, who is? What do you say, Inspector Duff?"

"I might also warn you," smiled Duff, "against the dangers of listening to an Englishman."

"Oh, but you're from Scotland Yard. I got respect for your opinion. Let's see – Eve Durand is about somewhere – I'm sure of that. Sir Frederic was the kind of man who knows what he's talking about. There's that Lila Barr. She fits the description pretty well. There's Gloria Garland. An assumed name – Australia – might be. There's Eileen Enderby. Rust stains on her dress that night. But I didn't see them. May have been there – probably not. Another guess on Sergeant Chan's part, perhaps."

"There is also," added Charlie, "Mrs Tupper-Brock. I offer the hint with reluctance."

"And well you may," sneered Flannery. "No – if you fancy Mrs Tupper-Brock, then right there she's out with me. Which of these women – I'll have to start all over again."

"I feel humble and contrite," said Chan. "In spite of which, suggestions keep crowding to my tongue. Have you heard old Chinese saying, Captain – 'It is always darkest underneath the lamp'?"

"I'm fed up on Chinese sayings," replied the Captain.

"The one I have named means what? That just above our heads the light is blazing. Such is the fact, Captain Flannery. Take my advice, and worry no more about Eve Durand."

"Why not?" asked Flannery, in spite of himself.

"Because you are poised on extreme verge of the great triumph of your life. In a few hours at the most your head will be ringing with your own praises."

"How's that?"

"In a few hours you will arrest the murderer of Sir Frederic Bruce," Chan told him calmly.

"Say – how do you get that way?" queried Flannery.

"There is one condition. It may be hard one for you," Chan continued. "For your own sake, I beseech you to comply with same."

"One condition? What's that?"

"You must listen once more – and for the last time – to what you call a Chinaman."

Flannery stirred uneasily. A hot denial rose to his lips, but something in the little man's confident manner disturbed him.

"Listen to you again, eh? As though I'd do that."

Inspector Duff stood up, and relighted his pipe. "If it is true that you respect my opinion, Captain – then, quoting our friend, I would make humble suggestion. Do as he asks."

Flannery did not reply for a moment. "Well," he said finally, "what have you got up your sleeve now? Another hunch?"

Chan shook his head. "A certainty. I am stupid man from small island, and I am often wrong. This time I am quite correct. Follow me – and I prove it."

"I wish I knew what you're talking about," Flannery said.

"An arrest – in a few hours – if you will stoop so far as to do what I require," Chan told him. "In Scotland Yard, which Inspector Duff honors by his association, there is in every case of murder what they call essential clue. There was essential clue in this case."

"The slippers?" asked Flannery.

"No," Charlie replied. "The slippers were valuable, but not essential. The essential clue was placed on scene by hand now dead. Hand of a man clever far beyond his fellows – how sad that such a man has passed. When Sir Frederic saw death looking him boldly in the face, he reached to a bookcase and took down – what? The essential clue, which fell from his dying hand to lie at his side on the dusty floor. The year-book of the Cosmopolitan Club."

A moment of silence followed. There was a ring of conviction in the detective's voice.

"Well – what do you want?" inquired Flannery.

"I want that you must come to the Cosmopolitan Club in one-half hour. Inspector Duff will of course accompany. You must then display unaccustomed patience and wait like man of stone. Exactly how long I cannot predict now. But in due time I will point out to you the killer of Sir Frederic – and I will produce proof of what I say."

Flannery rose. "Well, it's your last chance. You make a monkey of me again and I'll deport you as an undesirable alien. At the Cosmopolitan Club in half an hour. We'll be there."

"Undesirable alien will greet you at the door," smiled Charlie, "hoping to become desirable at any moment. Mr Kirk – will you be so good as to join my company?" He and Barry Kirk went out.

"Well, Charlie, you're certainly in bad with the Captain," said Kirk, as they stood in the street waiting for a taxi.

Chan nodded. "Will be in even worse presently," he replied.

Kirk stared at him. "How's that?"

"I shall point him the way to success. He will claim all credit, but sight of me will make him uncomfortable. No man loves the person who has guided his faltering footsteps to high-up rung of the ladder."

They entered a taxi. "The Cosmopolitan Club," Chan ordered. He turned to Kirk. "And now I must bow low in dust with many humble apologies to you. I have grieviously betrayed a trust."

"How so?" asked Kirk, surprised.

Chan took a letter from his pocket. It was somewhat worn and the handwriting on the envelope was a trifle blurred. "The other morning you wrote letters in office, giving same to me to mail. I made gesture toward mail chute, but I extracted this missive."

"Great Scott!" cried Kirk. "Hasn't that been mailed?"

"It has not. What could be more disgusting? My gracious host, at whose hands I have received every kindness. I have besmirched his confidence."

"But you had a reason?" suggested Kirk.

"A very good reason, which time will uncurtain. Am I stepping over the bounds when I seek to dig up your forgiveness?"

"Not at all," Kirk smiled.

"You are most affable man it has yet been my fate to encounter." The taxi had reached Union Square. Chan called to the driver to halt. "I alight here to correct my crime," he explained. "The long-delayed letter now goes to its destination by special, fleet-footed messenger."

"I say – you don't mean—" Kirk cried in amazement.

"What I mean comes gradually into the light," Chan told him. He got out of the taxi. "Be so kind as to await my coming at the club door. The guardian angel beyond the threshold is jealous as to who has honor of entering Cosmopolitan Club. It has been just as well for my purpose, but please make sure that I am not left rejected outside the portal."

"I'll watch for you," Kirk promised.

He rode on to the club, his head whirling with new speculations and questions. No – no – this couldn't be. But Charlie had an air—

Shortly after he had reached the building Charlie appeared, and Kirk steered him past the gold-laced door man. Presently Flannery and Duff arrived. The Captain's manner suggested that he was acting against his better judgment.

"I suppose this is another wild-goose chase," he fretted.

"One during which the goose is apprehended, I think," Chan assured him. "But there will be need of Oriental calm. Have you good supply? We may loiter here until midnight hour."

"That's pleasant," Flannery replied. "Well, I'll wait a while. But this is your last chance – remember."

"Also your great chance," Chan shrugged. "You must likewise remember. We do wrong to hang here in spotlight of publicity. Mr Kirk, I have made selection of nook where we may crouch unobserved, but always observing. I refer to little room behind office, opening at the side on check-room."

"All right – I know where you mean," Kirk told him. He spoke to the manager, and the four of them were ushered into a little back room, unused at the moment and in semi-darkness. Chairs were brought, and all save Charlie sat down. The little detective bustled about. He arranged that his three companions should have an unobstructed view of the check-room, where his friend of the morning, old Peter Lee, sat behind his barrier engrossed in a bright pink newspaper.

"Only one moment," said Chan. He went out through the door which led behind the counter of the check-room. For a brief time he talked in low tones with Lee. Then the three men sitting in the dusk saw him give a quick look toward the club lobby, and dodge abruptly into his hiding-place beside them.

Colonel John Beetham, debonair as usual, appeared at the counter and checked his hat and coat. Kirk, Flannery and Duff leaned forward eagerly and watched him as he accepted the brass check and turned away. But Chan made no move.

Time passed. Other members came into the club for dinner and checked their belongings, unconscious of the prying eyes in the little room. Flannery began to stir restlessly on his uncomfortable chair.

"What the devil is all this?" he demanded.

"Patience," Charlie admonished. "As the Chinese say, 'In time the grass becomes milk.'"

"Yeah – but I'd rather hunt up a cow," Flannery growled.

"Patient waiting," Chan went on, "is first requisite of good detective. Is that not correct, Inspector Duff?"

"Sometimes it seems the only requisite," Duff agreed. "I fancy I may smoke here?"

"Oh, of course," Kirk told him. He sighed with relief and took out his pipe.

The minutes dragged on. They heard the shuffle of feet on the tiled floor of the lobby, the voices of members calling greetings, making dinner dates. Flannery was like a fly on a hot griddle.

"If you're making a fool of me again—" he began.

His recent humiliation had been recalled to his mind by the sight of Major Eric Durand, checking his Burberry and his felt hat with Peter Lee. The Major's manner was one of deep depression.

"Poor devil," said Flannery softly. "We handed him a hard jolt today. It wasn't necessary, either—" His accusing eyes sought Chan. The detective was huddled up on his chair like some fat, oblivious Buddha.

A half-hour passed. Flannery was in constant touch with the figures on the face of his watch. "Missing my dinner," he complained. "And this chair – it's like a barrel top."

"There was no time to procure a velvet couch," Chan suggested gently. "Compose yourself, I beg. The happy man is the calm man. We have only begun to vigil."

At the end of another half-hour, Flannery was fuming. "Give us a tip," he demanded. "What are we waiting for? I'll know, or by heaven, I'll get out of here so quick—"

"Please," whispered Charlie. "We are waiting for the murderer of Sir Frederic Bruce. Is that not enough?"

"No, it isn't," the Captain snapped. "I'm sick of you and your confounded mystery. Put your cards on the table like a white man. This chair is killing me, I tell you—"

"Hush!" said Chan. He was leaning forward now, staring through the door into the check-room. The others followed his gaze.

Major Eric Durand stood before the counter. He threw down the brass check for his coat and hat, it rang metallically in the silence. Peter Lee brought them for him. He leaned across the barrier and helped Durand on with his coat. The Major was fumbling in his pockets. He produced a small bit of cardboard, which he gave to Peter Lee. The old man studied his treasures for a moment, and then handed over a black leather briefcase.

Chan had seized Flannery's arm, and was dragging the astonished Captain toward the club lobby. Kirk and Duff followed. They lined up before the huge front door. Durand appeared, walking briskly. He stopped as he saw the group barring his way.

"Ah, we meet again," he said. "Mr Kirk, it was thoughtful of you to send me that guest card to your club. I deeply appreciate it. It arrived only a short time ago. I shall enjoy dropping in here frequently—"

Charlie Chan came of a race that likes its drama, and his fat face was shining with joy. He raised his arm with the gesture of a Booth or a Salvini.

"Captain Flannery," he cried. "Arrest this man."

"Why – I – er – I don't—" sputtered Flannery.

"Arrest this man Durand," Chan went on. "Arrest him at same moment while he holds beneath his arm a briefcase containing much useful information. The briefcase Sir Frederic Bruce checked in this club on the afternoon of the day he died."

XX

THE TRUTH ARRIVES

All color had drained from Durand's face, it was gray as fog as he stood there confronted by the triumphant little Chinese. Flannery reached out and seized the leather case. The Major made no move to resist.

"Sir Frederic's briefcase," Flannery cried. His air of uncertainty had vanished; he was alert and confident. "By heaven, if that's true, then our man hunt is over." He sought to open the case. "The thing's locked," he added. "I don't like to break it open. It will be a mighty important piece of evidence."

"Mr Kirk still holds in possession Sir Frederic's keys," suggested Charlie. "I would have brought them with me but I did not know where they reposed."

"They are in my desk," Kirk told him.

A curious group was gathering about them. Chan turned to Flannery. "Our standing here has only one result. We offer ourselves as nucleus for a crowd. Humbly state we should go at once to bungalow. There the matter may be threshed out like winter wheat."

"Good idea," replied Flannery.

"I also ask that Mr Kirk visit telephone booth and request Miss Morrow to speed to bungalow with all haste. It would be amazing unkindness to drop her out of events at this junction."

"Sure," agreed Flannery. "Do that, Mr Kirk."

"Likewise," added Charlie, laying a hand on Kirk's arm, "advise her to bring with her the elevator operator, Grace Lane."

"What for?" demanded Flannery.

"Time will reveal," Chan shrugged. As Kirk sped away, Colonel John Beetham came up. For a moment the explorer stood, taking in the scene before him. His inscrutable expression did not change.

"Colonel Beetham," Charlie explained, "we have here the man who killed Sir Frederic Bruce."

"Really?" returned Beetham calmly.

"Undubitably. It is a matter that concerns you, I think. Will you be so good as to join our little party?"

"Of course," Beetham replied. He went for his hat and coat. Chan followed him, and retrieved from Peter Lee the pasteboard check on receipt of which the old man had relinquished Sir Frederic's property.

Kirk, Beetham and Chan returned to the group by the door. "All set," announced Flannery. "Come along, Major Durand."

Durand hesitated. "I am not familiar with your law. But shouldn't there be some sort of warrant—"

"You needn't worry about that. I'm taking you on suspicion. I can get a warrant when I want it. Don't be a fool – come on."

Outside a gentle rain had begun to fall, and the town was wrapped in mist. Duff, Flannery and Durand got into one taxi, and Chan followed with Kirk and the explorer in another. As Charlie was stepping into the car, a breathless figure shot out of the dark.

"Who was that with Flannery?" panted Bill Rankin.

"It has happened as I telephoned from the hotel," Charlie answered. "We have our man."

"Major Durand?"

"The same."

"Good enough. I'll have a flash on the street in twenty minutes. You certainly kept your promise."

"Old habit with me," Chan told him.

"And how about Beetham?"

Chan glanced into the dark cab. "Nothing to do with the matter. We were on wrong trail there."

"Too bad," Rankin said. "Well, I'm off. I'll be back later for details. Thanks a thousand times."

Chan inserted his broad bulk into the taxi, and they started for the Kirk Building.

"May I express humble hope," remarked the little detective to Kirk, "that I am forgiven for my crime. I refer to my delay in mailing to Major Durand your letter containing guest card for Cosmopolitan Club."

"Oh, surely," Kirk told him.

"It chanced I was not yet ready he should walk inside the club," Chan added.

"Well, I'm knocked cold," Kirk said. "You must have had your eye on him for some time."

"I will explain with all my eloquence later. Just now I content myself with admitting this – Major Durand was one person in all the world who did not want Eve Durand discovered."

"But in heaven's name – why not?" Kirk asked.

"Alas, I am no miracle man. It is a matter I hope will be apparent later. Perhaps Colonel Beetham can enlighten us."

The Colonel's voice was cool and even in the darkness. "I'm a bit weary of lying," he remarked. "I could enlighten you. But I won't. You see, I have made a promise. And like yourself, Sergeant, I prefer to keep my promises."

"We have many commendable points in common."

Beetham laughed. "By the way – that was extremely decent of you – telling the reporter I wasn't concerned in this affair."

"Only hope," responded Chan, "that events will justify my very magnanimous act."

They alighted before the Kirk Building and rode up to the bungalow. Paradise had admitted Flannery and Duff with their prisoner.

"Here you are," said Flannery briskly. "Now, Mr Kirk – let's have that key."

Kirk stepped to his desk and produced Sir Frederic's keys. The Captain, with Duff close at his side hastened to open the case. Charlie dropped down on the edge of a chair, his intent little eyes on Major Durand. The Major was seated in a corner of the room, his head bowed, his gaze fixed on the rug.

"By George," cried Duff. "It's Sir Frederic's case, right enough. And here – yes – here is what we have been looking for." He took out a typewritten sheaf of paper. "Here are his records in the matter of Eve Durand."

The Inspector began to read eagerly. Flannery turned to Durand.

"Well, Major – this settles your hash. Where did you get the check for this briefcase?"

Durand made no reply. "I will answer for him," Charlie said. "He extracted same from the purse of Sir Frederic the night he killed that splendid gentleman."

"Then you visited San Francisco once before, Major?" Flannery persisted.

Still Durand did not so much as raise his eyes.

"Naturally he did," Chan grinned. "Captain Flannery, at any moment reporters will burst upon you desiring to learn how you captured this dangerous man. Would it not be better if I told you so you will be able to make intelligent reply?" Flannery glared at him. "The matter will demand your close attention. I search about, wondering where to begin."

Duff looked up. "I suggest you start with the moment when you first suspected Durand," he said, and returned to his perusal of the records.

Chan nodded. "It was here in this room, same night when Durand arrived. Have you ever heard, Captain, – do not fear, it is not old saying this time. Have you ever heard Chinese are psychic people? It is true. A look, a gesture, a tone of voice – something goes click inside. I hear Mr Kirk say to the Major he will send guest card for club or two. And from the sudden warmth of the Major's reply, I obtain my psychic spasm of warning. At once I ask myself, has the Major special interest in San Francisco clubs? It would seem so. Is he, then, the man we seek? No, he cannot be. Not if he came entire distance from New York with good Inspector Duff.

"But – I advise myself – pause here and ponder, What has Inspector Duff said on this point? He has said that when he got off Twentieth Century in Chicago, he discovered Major had been on same train. I put an inquiry to myself. Has this clever man, Duff, for once in his life been hoodwinked? Inspector does me high honor to invite to dinner. During the feast, I probe about. I politely inquire, did he with his own eyes see Major Durand on board Twentieth Century while train was yet speeding between New York and Chicago? No, he did not. He saw him first in Chicago station. Durand assures him he was on identical train Inspector has just left. He announces he, too, is on way to San Francisco. They take, that same night, train bound for coast.

"The matter, then, is possible. Men have been known to double back on own tracks. Study of time elapsed since murder reveals Major may have been doing this very thing. I begin to think deep about Durand. I recall that at luncheon when Sir Frederic tells us of Eve Durand case, he makes curious omission which I noted at the time. He says that when he is planning to go to Peshawar to look into Eve Durand matter, he calls on Sir George Mannering, the woman's uncle. Yet husband is living in England, and he would know much more about the affair than uncle would. Why, then, did not Sir Frederic interrogate the husband? I find there food for thought.

"All time I am wondering about Cosmopolitan Club year-book, which hand of Sir Frederic drops on floor at dying moment. Mr Kirk kindly takes me to lunch at club, and checks a briefcase. I note check for coat is of metal, but briefcase check is of cardboard, with name of article deposited written on surface by trembling hand of Peter Lee. A bright light flashes in my mind. I will suppose that Sir Frederic checked a briefcase containing records we so hotly seek, and check for same was in pocket when he died. This the killer extracts; he is clever man and knows at last he has located papers he wants so fiercely. But alas for him, club-house door is guarded, only members and guests may enter. In despair, he flees, but that check he carries with him spells his doom unless he can return and obtain object it represents. He longs to do so, but danger is great.

"Then fine evidence arrives. The velvet slippers come back to us on tide of events, wrapped in newspaper. On margin of paper, partially torn, are figures – a money addition – $79 plus $23 equals $103. This refers to dollars only. Cents have been torn off. I visit railroad office. I decide what must have been on that paper before its tearing. Simply this, $79.84 plus $23.63 equals $103.47. What is that? The cost of railroad fare to Chicago with lower berth. Then the person who discarded those slippers was on Oakland ferry Wednesday morning after murder, bound to take train from Oakland terminal to Chicago. Who of all my suspects might have done that? No one but Major Durand.

"I think deep, I cogitate, I weave in and out through my not very brilliant mind. I study time-tables. Presume Major Durand was on that train out of Oakland Wednesday noon. He arrives in Chicago Saturday morning at nine. He is still distressed about check for briefcase, but his best plan seems to be to proceed eastward, and he hastens to LaSalle Street station to obtain train for New York. He arrives in time to see Inspector Duff, whom he met once in Paris, disembarking from Twentieth Century. He is smart man, a big idea assails him. First he will give impression he is alighting from same train, and then he will return to California in company of Scotland Yard Inspector. Who would suspect him then? So the innocent Inspector Duff himself escorts the killer back to the scene of the crime.

"All this seems to possess good logic. But it hangs on one thing – has briefcase been checked by Sir Frederic? This morning I visit with Peter Lee, keeper of Cosmopolitan Club check-room. I can scarce restrain my joy to learn Sir Frederic did indeed leave such an object the day he died. His dying gesture then, was to call our attention to the fact. He sought to present us with essential clue – what a man he was! I fondle the case lovingly, observing dust. Inside is no doubt very important information. But I do not desire to open it yet. I desire to set a trap. I have unlimited yearning to show Captain Flannery the man we have sought, standing by the check-room counter with this briefcase under his arm. Such evidence will be unanswerable.

"So I leave club, very happy. The affair has now pretty well unveiled itself. I have not yet discovered motives, but I am certain it was Major Durand who objected so murderously to the finding of his lost wife. He has not come to this country in answer to a cable from Sir Frederic. That is a lie. Sir Frederic did not want him. But he has learned, probably from the woman's uncle, that Sir Frederic is on point of revealing wife. For a reason still clouded in dark, he determines this must not happen. He arrives in San Francisco same time as Sir Frederic. He locates great detective, learns of the office, watches his chance. To prevent detective from revealing wife, two things are necessary. He must destroy the records, and he must kill Sir Frederic. He decides to begin with records, and so on night of dinner party he forces his way into office, unseen by anybody. He is searching when Sir Frederic creeps in on the velvet slippers and surprises him. His opportunity has come, Sir Frederic is unarmed, he shoots him dead. But his task is only half completed, he hunts frantically for records. He does not find them. But he finds the check for the briefcase. He abstracts same, casts longing thought toward club, but does not dare. On the next train out he flees, the check burning in his pocket. If only he could return. In Chicago his great chance arrives.

"Building on all this, I set tonight my trap. And into it walks the man who killed Sir Frederic Bruce."

Inspector Duff looked up. He appeared to have been reading and listening at the same time. "Intelligence, hard work and luck," he remarked. "These three things contribute to the solution of a criminal case. And I may add that in my opinion, in this instance, the greatest of the trinity was intelligence."

Chan bowed. "A remark I shall treasure with jealous pride all my life."

"Yes, it's pretty good," admitted Flannery grudgingly. "Very good. But it ain't complete. What about the velvet slippers? What about Hilary Galt? How is Galt's murder mixed up in all this?"

Chan grinned. "I am not so hoggish. I leave a few points for Captain Flannery's keen mind."

Flannery turned to Duff. "Maybe it's in those records?"

"I've got only about half-way through," Duff answered. "There has been one mention of Hilary Galt. It says here that among the people who called at Galt's office on the day the solicitor was murdered was Eric Durand. Captain Eric Durand – that was his rank at the time. To discover the meaning of that, I shall have to read further."

"Have you learned," Chan inquired, "this thing? Did Sir Frederic know which of the ladies we have suspicioned was Eve Durand?"

"Evidently he didn't. All he knew was that she was in the Kirk Building. He seemed to favor Miss Lila Barr."

"Ah, yes. Was he aware how Eve Durand escaped from India?"

"He was, beyond question."

"He knew she went by the caravan?"

"By the caravan, through Khyber Pass. In the company of Colonel John Beetham," Duff nodded.

They all looked toward the Colonel, sitting silent and aloof in the background. "Is that true, Colonel Beetham?" Flannery asked.

The explorer bowed. "I will not deny it longer. It is true."

"Perhaps you know—"

"Whatever I know, I am not at liberty to tell."

"If I make you—" Flannery exploded.

"You can, of course, try. You will not succeed."

The door opened, and Miss Morrow came quickly through the hall. With her came the elevator girl. Jennie Jerome? Marie Lantelme? Grace Lane? Whatever her name, she entered, and stood staring at Eric Durand.

"Eric!" she cried. "What have you done? Oh – how could you—"

Durand raised his head and looked at her with bloodshot eyes. "Go away from me," he said dully. "Go away. You've brought me nothing but trouble – always. Go away. I hate you."

The woman backed off, frightened by the venom in his tone. Chan approached her.

"Pardon," he said gently. "Perhaps the news has already reached you? It was this man Durand who killed Sir Frederic. Your husband – is that not true, Madam?"

She dropped into a chair and covered her face. "Yes," she sobbed. "My husband."

"You are indeed Eve Durand?"

"Y – yes."

Charlie looked grimly at Flannery. "Now the truth arrives," he said. "That you once listened to a Chinaman is, after all, no lasting disgrace."

XXI

WHAT HAPPENED TO EVE DURAND

Flannery turned fiercely on Eve Durand. "Then you've known all along?" he cried. "You knew the Major had been here before – you saw him that night he did for Sir Frederic—"

"No, no," she protested. "I didn't see him – I never dreamed of such a thing. And if he knew I was in the building that night, he took good care to keep out of my way. For if I had seen him – if I had known – it would have been the final straw. I'd have told. I'd have told the whole story at once."

Flannery grew calmer. "Well, let's go back. You're Eve Durand – you admit it at last. Fifteen years ago you ran away from your husband in Peshawar. You went with the caravan of Colonel Beetham here—"

The woman looked up, startled, and for the first time saw the explorer. "That's all true," she said softly, "I went with Colonel Beetham."

"Ran away with another man – deserted your husband? Why? In love with the Colonel—"

"No!" Her eyes flashed. "You mustn't think that. Colonel Beetham did a very kind act – an indiscreet act – and he shall not suffer for it. Long ago, I made up my mind to that."

"Please, Eve," said the Colonel. "I shan't suffer. Don't tell your story on my account."

"That's like you," she answered. "But I insist. I said if I was ever found, I'd tell everything. And after what Eric has done now – it doesn't matter any longer. Oh, I shall be so relieved to tell the whole terrible thing at last."

She turned to Flannery. "I shall have to go back. I was brought up in Devonshire by my uncle and aunt – my parents had died. I wasn't very happy. My uncle had old-fashioned ideas. He meant well, he was kind, but somehow we just didn't get along. Then I met Eric – he was a romantic figure – I adored him. I was only seventeen. On my eighteenth birthday we were married. He was assigned to a regiment stationed in Peshawar, and I went with him.

"Even before we reached India, I began to regret what I had done. I was sorry I hadn't listened to my uncle – he never approved of the match. Under his dashing manner I found that Eric was mean and cheap. He was a gambler, he drank too much. His real character appalled me – he was coarse and brutal, and a cheat.

"Soon after our arrival at Peshawar, letters began to come from London – letters in dirty envelopes, the address written in an uncultivated hand. They seemed to enrage my husband; he wasn't fit to associate with after their appearance. I was puzzled and alarmed. On a certain day – the day of the picnic, it was – one of those letters was put in my hand during Eric's absence. By that time I was desperate. I knew only too well the outburst that would come when he saw it. I hesitated for a while. Finally I tore it open and read it.

"What I read wrecked my life for ever. It was from a porter in an office building in London. It said he must have more money – at once. It didn't hint – it spoke openly. Everything was all too plain. Eric – my husband – was being blackmailed by the porter. He was paying money to keep the man quiet. If he didn't, the porter threatened to reveal the fact that he had seen Eric leaving a London office one night a year previously.

Leaving an office on the floor of which lay Hilary Galt, the solicitor, with a bullet in his head."

Eve Durand paused, and continued with an effort. "My husband, then, was being blackmailed for the murder of Hilary Galt. He came home presently, in rather a genial mood – for him. I said: 'I am leaving you at once.' He wanted to know why, and I gave him the opened letter.

"His face went gray, and he collapsed. Presently he was on his knees, groveling at my feet, pleading with me. Without my asking for it, he gave me the whole terrible story. Hilary Galt and my uncle, Sir George Mannering, were old friends. On the morning of that awful day, the solicitor had sent for Eric and told him that if he persisted in his intention of marrying me, he – Mr Galt, I mean – would go to my uncle with the story of certain unsavory happenings in Eric's past. Eric had listened, and left the office. That night he had gone back and killed Hilary Galt, and the porter had seen him coming away.

"He did it for love of me, he said. Because he must have me – because he was determined nothing should stand in his way. I must forgive him—"

"Pardon," put in Chan. "Did he, in that unhappy moment, mention a pair of velvet slippers?"

"He did. After – after he had killed Mr Galt, he saw the slippers lying on a chair. He knew that Scotland Yard always looks for an essential clue, and he resolved to furnish one. One that meant nothing, one that would point away from him. So he tore off Hilary Galt's shoes and substituted the slippers. He was rather proud of it, I think. Oh, he was always clever, in that mean way of his. He boasted of what he had done, of how he had thrown Scotland Yard off the scent. Then he was pleading again – he had done it for me – I must not tell. I couldn't tell. I was his wife – no one could make me tell. Heaven knows, I had no desire to tell, all I wanted was to get away from him.

I said again that I was going. 'I'll kill you first,' he answered, and he meant it.

"So I went on that picnic, with my life all in pieces, frantic, insane with grief and fear. Colonel Beetham was there – I had met him once before – a fine man, a gentleman, all that Eric was not. He was leaving in the morning – it came to me in a flash. He must take me with him. I suggested the game of hide-and-seek – I had already asked the Colonel to meet me in a certain spot. He came – I made him promise never to tell – and I explained to him the horrible position I was in. If I tried to leave openly I was afraid – I was sure – Eric would carry out his threat. Colonel Beetham was wonderful. He arranged everything. I hid in the hills all night. He came with Li Gung in the wagon at dawn – he had added it to his caravan, intending to abandon it when we got through the pass. I rode out hidden in that, and beyond the Khyber there began for me the most wonderful adventure a woman ever had. Eight months through that wild country on a camel – the stars at night, the dust storms, the desert stretching empty but mysterious as far as the eye could see. Outside Teheran I left the caravan and got to Baku alone. From there I went to Italy. Eight months had passed, as I say, and the hue and cry had died down.

"But now I realized what I had done. Colonel Beetham was a hero, he was honored everywhere. What if it became known how I had left India? No journey could ever have been more innocent, but this is a cynical world. Doing a kind act, a gallant act, Colonel Beetham had put himself in the position, in the world's eyes, of running away with another man's wife. If it became known, the Colonel's splendid career would be wrecked. It must never become known. I made up my mind I would see to that."

"And you have," remarked Beetham softly. "Gentleman, you have just heard what I did referred to as a gallant act. But it was as nothing compared with Eve Durand's gallantry ever since."

"First of all," the woman went on, "I wrote a letter to Eric. I told him he must never try to find me – for his own sake. I said that if I was found, if the story came out of how I had left India, I would not hesitate a moment. I would clear Colonel Beetham's name at once by a clear account of why I had gone. I would say I left because I discovered my husband was a murderer. Eric didn't answer, but he must have received the letter. He never tried to find me after that. He did not want anyone else to find me – as he has recently proved to you."

She paused. "That is about all. I – I have had rather a hard struggle of it. I sold my jewelry and lived on the proceeds for a time. Then I went to Nice, and under the name of Marie Lantelme, I got a place in the opera company. There, for the first time, I realized that another man was on my trail – a man who would never give up. Sir Frederic Bruce of Scotland Yard, in charge of the Hilary Galt case. He knew that Eric had visited Galt's office the day of the murder, and when he read of my disappearance in India, he must have sensed a connection. One night when I came from the theater in Nice, an Inspector from Scotland Yard stopped me on the Promenade des Anglais. 'You are Eve Durand,' he said. I denied it, got away from him, managed to reach Marseilles. From there I went to New York. I changed my appearance as much as I could – the color of my hair – and under the name of Jennie Jerome, secured a position as a model. Again Scotland Yard was on my track. I had to disappear in the night. Eventually I arrived in San Francisco, desperate, penniless. On a ferry I met Helen Tupper-Brock, who had lived near us in Devonshire. She has been so kind – she got me my position here. I was happy again, until Sir Frederic Bruce came, still following that old trail."

Durand got slowly to his feet. "I hope you're satisfied," he said thickly.

"Oh, Eric—"

"You've done for me. You ought to be satisfied now." His eyes flamed red. "You've saved the spotless reputation of your damned Sir Galahad—"

"You're going to confess?" cried Flannery.

Durand shrugged his shoulders hopelessly. "Why not? What else is left?" He turned his blazing eyes on Charlie Chan. "Everything this devil said was true. I admire him for it. I thought I was clever. But he's beat me—" His voice rose hysterically. "I killed Sir Frederic. Why shouldn't I? It was the only way. He stood there grinning at me. My God – what a man! He wouldn't give up. He wouldn't call quits. Sixteen years, and he was still at my heels. Sixteen years, and he wouldn't forget. Yes, I killed him—"

"And the velvet slippers?" Chan inquired softly.

"On his feet. The same old velvet slippers I'd left in that office, long ago. I saw them just after I fired, and then my nerve went. It was like a judgment – my trade-mark – on the feet of Sir Frederic – pointing to me. I snatched them off – took them with me. I – I didn't know what to do with them. My nerve was gone – but I'd killed him first. Yes – I killed him. And I'm ready to pay. But not in the way you think."

Suddenly he wheeled about and crashed through the French window into the garden of the bungalow.

"The fire-escape," Flannery shouted. "Head him off—"

The Captain, Duff and Chan were close behind. Charlie ran to the fire-escape at the left. But it was not that for which Eric Durand was headed tonight. He leaped to the rail that enclosed the garden; for an instant his big figure poised, a dark silhouette against the misty sky. Then silently it disappeared.

They ran to the rail and looked down. Far below, in the dim light of a street lamp, they saw a black, huddled heap. A crowd was gathering around it.

XXII

HAWAII BOUND

Their pursuit so tragically ended, the three men came slowly back into the living-room of the bungalow.

"Well," said Flannery, "that's the end of him."

"Escaped?" Miss Morrow cried.

"From this world," nodded the Captain. Eve Durand gave a little cry. Miss Morrow put an arm about her. "There's work for me below," added Flannery, and went quickly out.

"We'd better go home, my dear," said Miss Morrow gently. She and Eve Durand went to the hall. Kirk followed and opened the door for them. There was much he wanted to say, but under the circumstances silence seemed the only possible course.

"I can get my car," he suggested.

"No, thanks," answered Miss Morrow. "We'll find a taxi."

"Good night," he said gravely. "I shall hope to see you soon."

When he returned to the living-room, Colonel Beetham was speaking. "Nothing in his life became him like the leaving it. What a washout that life was! Poor Major."

Duff was calmly filling his pipe, unperturbed as a Chinese. "By the way," he drawled, "I had a cable about him this morning. He was dishonorably discharged from the British

Army ten years ago. So his right to the title may be questioned. But no doubt you knew that, Colonel Beetham?"

"I did," Beetham replied.

"You knew so much," Duff continued. "So much you weren't telling. What were you doing on the floor below that Tuesday night?"

"Precisely what I told Flannery I was doing. I ran down to inform Li Gung that he needn't wait."

"I didn't know but what you'd gone down for a chat with Eve Durand?"

The Colonel shook his head. "No – I'd had my chat with Eve. You see, I'd located her several days before the dinner party. After losing track of her for ten years, I came to San Francisco on a rumor she was here. My errand on the floor below was with Li Gung, as I said it was."

"And the next day you shipped him off to Honolulu?"

"I did, yes. At Eve's request. I'd arranged that two days before. She heard Sir Frederic was interested in him, and she was afraid something might happen to wreck my next expedition. The thing was unnecessary, Li Gung would never have told, but to set her mind at rest, I did as she asked."

Duff looked at him with open disapproval. "You knew that Durand had committed one murder. Yet you said nothing to the police. Was that playing the game, Colonel Beetham?"

Beetham shrugged. "Yes, I think it was. I'm sure of it. I did not dream that Durand had been in San Francisco the night of Sir Frederic's murder. Even if I had known he was here – well – you see—"

"I'm afraid I don't," snapped Duff.

"There is really no reason why I need explain to you," Beetham went on. "However, I will. Something happened on that long trek across Afghanistan and the Kevir Desert. Eve was so brave, so uncomplaining. I – I fell in love. For the first and last time. What she has done since – for me – damn it, man, I worship her. But I have never told her so – I do not know whether she cares for me or not. While Durand lived, he was my rival, in a way. If I had given him up – what would my motive have been? I couldn't have been quite sure myself. I did suggest that Eve tell her story, but I didn't press the point. I couldn't, you see. I had to leave the decision to her. When she escaped that night from Flannery's men, I helped her. If that was what she wanted, I was forced to agree. Yes, Inspector – I was playing the game, according to my lights."

Duff shrugged. "A nice sense of honor," he remarked. "However, I will go so far as to wish you luck."

"Thanks," returned Beetham. He took up his coat. "I may say that, no doubt from selfish motives, I was keen to have you get him. And Sergeant Chan here saw to it that I was not disappointed. Sergeant, my hearty congratulations. But I know your people – and I am not surprised."

Chan bowed. "For ever with me your words will remain, lasting and beautiful as flowers of jade."

"I will go along," said Beetham, and departed.

Duff took up Sir Frederic's briefcase. "Perhaps you would like to look at these records, Sergeant," he remarked.

Chan came to with a start. "Pardon my stupidity."

"I said – maybe you want to glance at Sir Frederic's records?"

Charlie shook his head. "Curiosity is all quenched, like fire in pouring rain. We have looked at last behind that curtain Sir Frederic pictured, and I am content. At the moment I was indulging in bitter thought. There is no boat to Honolulu until next Wednesday. Five terrible days."

Duff laughed. "Well, I've been through the records hastily," he went on. "Sir Frederic had talked with certain friends of that porter in London. But the man himself had died before the Yard heard about him, and the evidence of his associates was hazy – hardly the sort to stand up in the courts. It needed the corroboration of Eve Durand, and that was what Sir Frederic was determined to get at any cost."

"How did Sir Frederic know that Eve Durand was in San Francisco?" Barry Kirk inquired.

"He got that information from a letter written by Mrs Tupper-Brock to an aunt in Shanghai. There is a copy of the letter here. In it Mrs Tupper-Brock mentioned that Eve Durand was in this city, employed in the Kirk Building. All of which explains his eagerness to make his headquarters with you, Mr Kirk. But he hadn't located her – he died without that satisfaction, poor chap. His choice was Miss Lila Barr. He didn't dare say anything to Mrs Tupper-Brock, for fear Eve Durand would slip through his fingers again. On the night of the dinner he was setting a trap – the desk unlocked, the safe open. He rather hoped someone would creep in for a look around. That and the chance of identifying Jennie Jerome, or Marie Lantelme – on these things he placed his reliance."

"He would have won, if he had lived," Chan remarked.

"No doubt of it. In Peshawar he established to his own satisfaction the manner in which Eve had left India. When he found her he would have told her what he knew, and she would have related her story, just as she did here tonight. His long search for the murderer of Hilary Galt would have ended then and there. Poor Sir Frederic." Duff picked up his coat, and Kirk helped him. "I'll take the briefcase," the Inspector continued. "It will be useful at the Yard." He held out his hand. "Sergeant Chan, meeting you would alone have repaid me for my long journey. Come to London some day. I'll show you how we work over there."

Chan smiled. "You are too kind. But the postman on his holiday has walked until feet are aching. Free to remark that if he ever takes another vacation, same will be forced on him at point of plenty big gun."

"I don't wonder," replied Duff. "Mr Kirk – a pleasure to know you, too. Goodby and good luck to you both."

Kirk let him out. When he returned, Charlie was standing at the window, staring down on the roofs of the city. He swung about. "Now I go and pack."

"But you've five days for that," Kirk protested.

Charlie shook his head. "The guest who lingers too long deteriorates like unused fish. You have been so good – more would make me uncomfortable. I remove my presence at once."

"Oh, no," Kirk cried. "Good old Paradise will serve dinner in a few minutes."

"Please," Chan said, "permit me the luxury of at last beginning to mean what I say."

He went into his bedroom and in a surprisingly brief time returned. "Luggage was pretty much ready," he explained. He glanced toward the window. "Bright moon shines tonight in Honolulu. I am thinking of those home nights – long ones with long talks, long sipping of tea, long sleep and long peaceful dreams." He went to the hall, where he had left his coat and hat. "I am wondering how to make words of the deep thanks I feel," he said, returning. "Faced with kindness such as yours—"

The door-bell rang, a sharp, insistent peal. Charlie stepped into the bedroom. Kirk opened the door, and Bill Rankin, the reporter, rushed in.

"Where's Charlie Chan?" he demanded breathlessly.

"He's gone into his room," Kirk answered. "He'll be out in a minute."

"I want to thank him," Rankin continued loudly. "He sure treated me like a prince. I beat the town. And I've news for him – a woman has just been murdered over in Oakland under the most peculiar circumstances. There are all sorts of bully clues – and since he can't leave until next week—"

Kirk laughed. "You tell him," he suggested.

They waited a moment, then Kirk went into the bedroom. He cried out in surprise. The room was empty. A door leading to the passageway stood open. He stepped through it, and discovered that the door at the top of the stairs leading to the offices was also ajar.

"Rankin," he called. "Come here, please."

Rankin came. "Why – where is he—"

Kirk preceded the reporter downstairs. The offices were in darkness. In the middle room, Kirk switched on the light. After a hurried glance around, he pointed to the window that opened on to the fire-escape. It had been pushed up as far as it would go.

"The postman," Kirk remarked, "absolutely refuses to take another walk."

"Done an Eve Durand on us!" Rankin cried. "Well, I'll be dog-goned."

Kirk laughed. "It's all right," he said. "I'll know where to find him – next Wednesday noon."

Intent on verifying this prediction, Barry Kirk appeared in Miss Morrow's dusty office the following Wednesday morning at eleven. He had stopped at a florist's and bought an extravagant cluster of orchids. These he handed to the deputy district attorney.

"What's the idea?" she asked.

"Come on," he said. "The morning's as bright as a new gold piece, and down at the docks there's a ship about to set out for the loveliest fleet of islands in any ocean. The flowers are my *bon voyage* offering to you."

"But I'm not sailing," she protested.

"We'll pretend you are. You're going as far as the pier, anyhow. Get your hat."

"Of course." She got it, and they went down the dark stairs.

"Have you heard anything from Charlie Chan?" she asked.

"Not a word," Kirk told her. "Charlie isn't taking any chances. But we'll find him aboard the boat. I'd gamble all I've got on that."

They entered his car, and Kirk stepped on the gas. "What a morning," he remarked. "Cooped up in that dark office of yours, you've no idea the things that are going on outside. Lady – spring is here!"

"So it seems. By the way – you know that Colonel Beetham sailed last night for China?"

"Yes. What about Eve Durand?"

"She's starting tomorrow for England. Her uncle has cabled her to come and stop with him. The Colonel is to be in the Gobi Desert for a year, and then he's going to England too. It will be spring in Devonshire when he arrives. A very lovely spring, they seem to think."

Kirk nodded. "But a year away. Too bad – so long to wait. Enjoy the spring you've got. That would be my advice."

He steered his car on to the pier. Another sailing day – excitement and farewells. Tourists and traveling salesmen, bored stewards waiting patiently in line.

Miss Morrow and Kirk ran up the gangplank on to the deck of the big white ship. "Just stand here by the rail, please," said Kirk. "With the orchids— "

"What in the world for?"

"I want to see how you'll look in the rôle. Back in a minute."

When he returned, Charlie Chan was walking lightly at his side. The detective's face was beaming with a satisfaction he could not conceal.

"Overwhelmed by your attention," he said to the girl.

"Where have you been?" she cried. "We've missed you terribly."

He grinned. "Hiding from temptation," he explained.

"But Captain Flannery has taken all the credit for your wonderful success. It isn't fair."

Chan shrugged. "From the first, I knew my work on this case was like bowing in the dark. Why should I care? May I add that you present charming picture of loveliness this morning?"

"What does she look like to you, Charlie?" Kirk inquired. "Standing there by the rail with those flowers?"

"A bride," answered Chan promptly, as one who had been coached. "A bride who sails for honeymoon in pleasant company of newly-captured husband."

"Precisely," Kirk agreed. "She's rehearsing the part, you know."

"The first I've heard of it," objected Miss Morrow.

"Wise man has said, 'The beautiful bird gets caged,'" Chan told her. "You could not hope to escape."

The girl handed him a little package. "This is for – the other Barry – with my love."

"My warmest thanks. He will be proud boy. But you will not give him all your love. You will not overlook original of same name. Chinese are psychic people, and I have sensed it. Am I right? My precious reputation hangs shaking on your answer."

Miss Morrow smiled. "I'm very much afraid – you're always right."

"Now this is truly my happiest day," Chan told her.

"Mine too," cried Kirk. He took an envelope from his pocket. "That being arranged, I also have something for little Barry. Give it to him with my warm regards."

Chan accepted the envelope, heavy with gold pieces. "My heart flows over," he said. "Small son will express thanks in person when you arrive in Honolulu thrilled with the high delight of honeymoon."

"Then he'll have to learn to talk mighty soon," Kirk answered. "But with a father like you—"

The final call of "visitors ashore" was sounding. They shook hands with Charlie and ran. At the top of the gangplank they were engulfed in a very frenzy of farewell. Mad embraces, hasty kisses, final promises and admonitions. Kirk leaned quickly over and kissed Miss Morrow.

"Oh – how could you!" she cried.

"Pardon me. I was still pretending you were going too."

"But I'm not. Neither are you."

"No one will notice in this mêlée. Come on."

They descended to the pier, and ran along it until they stood opposite Charlie Chan. The detective had procured a roll of bright pink paper, and holding fast to one end, he tossed it to the girl.

Kirk smiled happily. "If anyone had told me two weeks ago I was going to kiss a lawyer – and like it—" He was interrupted by the hoarse cry of the ship's siren.

Slowly the vessel drew away from the pier. The pink streamer broke, its ends trailing in the water. Charlie leaned far over the rail.

"Aloha," he called. "Until we meet again." His fat face shone with joy. The big ship paused, trembled, and set out for Hawaii.